There were five of them with appointments to see the most prestigious divorce lawyer in all of San Francisco, five women, five complex stories, five isolated lives tied by a common bond....

Street-smart and poor, *Morning Glory Browne* was married to an ex-baseball player and wife-beater—and she wanted out before he could hurt her again.... Classy *Chanel Devereau* wanted a divorce from husband number two to find a man who could finance her way into high society.... *Stephanie Cornwall* was a nice, content suburban housewife and mother—until she discovered her lawyer husband in bed with someone else.... *Ariel di Russy* was old money, but her psychiatrist husband kept her in emotional bondage—until *he* wanted a divorce....

Only *Janice Morehouse* was happily married—she was merely paying the lawyer a social call. It was Janice who came up with the idea of a divorce club, a support group, to study the four other women and collect material for a paper. She had no idea that once they all began to meet, one day a month, her own marriage would be exposed—and that each woman, though vastly different, would influence the way the others think, dress, dream, and even love.

BOOK WORLD
THOUSANDS OF USED PAPERBACKS
TRADE 2 FOR 1 SAME PRICE AND TYPE
3111 N. HANCOCK ST.
COLORADO SPRINGS, CO 80907

Also by Ruth Walker:

OTHER PASSIONS, OTHER LOVES
SURRENDER*
SONATA FOR MY LOVE
CUSTODY*
COUNTRY LOVE SONGS, CITY LIES*
THROUGH NIGHT AND DAY
SPANGLES
GAMES
MASKS
AIR FORCE WIVES*
ENDURING PASSION

Young Adult Science Fiction

PORTAL TO E'WHERE
INHERIT THE EARTH

*Published by Ballantine Books

THE CLUB

Ruth Walker

BALLANTINE BOOKS • NEW YORK

Copyright © 1988 by Irma Walker

All rights reserved under International and Pan-American Copyright Conventions. Published in the United States of America by Ballantine Books, a division of Random House, Inc., New York, and simultaneously in Canada by Random House of Canada Limited, Toronto.

Library of Congress Catalog Card Number: 87-91892

ISBN 0-345-34316-6

Manufactured in the United States of America

First Edition: July 1988

To my dear friend, Marge Inglin

PROLOGUE

IT WAS ARNOLD WATERFORD'S HABIT, WHEN WEATHER PERMITted, to have his chauffeur/houseman drop him off in Union Square so he could walk the rest of the way, four city blocks, to his law offices on Leavenworth. Not only did he need the exercise—he loathed jogging and other such atrocities—but he loved San Francisco when the sun hadn't yet dissipated the night mists and the foghorn on Alcatraz was still giving out its three-toned warning, sounding like the mating calls of the sea lions on the rocks near Sea Cliff.

Arnold Waterford's love affair with San Francisco had started in the mid-fifties when he had first come to California, a callow young man fresh out of a Kansas City law school. Since those days, he had become familiar with the city's numerous warts, but his passion for her had never faltered. Although he loved the city in all her moods as a man loves a beautiful but capricious woman, he loved her best in the fall when, golden and glowing and seductive, she preened herself for the natives as if gratified that the tourists had gone home until next spring.

Because this was a particularly fine September morning, Arnold decided to take the long way to his offices. As he strolled across Union Square, then along Geary Street, past the faded elegance of the aging Curran Theatre, he mentally reviewed the four clients he would be seeing that morning.

Arnold Waterford was a divorce lawyer. Oh, he knew what other lawyers called him behind his back. "Shyster" was the mildest of the epithets they used. What they didn't understand was that he was genuinely sympathetic to his women clients. He liked women—and in his opinion, more often than not they got the short end of the stick in a no-fault, community property state when it came to divorce settlements, especially the older women.

The husband of his very first client had been a wife-beater. Because Arnold had been young and inexperienced, his middle-

1

aged client had taken a beating in court as well as in her bedroom. Well, he'd learned from that experience, which was why he was probably the most famous—or infamous, depending on who was talking—divorce lawyer in northern California.

He gave a passing acquaintance a genial nod, but he didn't stop to talk. He was already running late, and besides he was eager to get through his morning appointments quickly today because, like icing on a cake, he was having lunch with Janice Morehouse at one o'clock. Not only was Janice his goddaughter, but she was one of his most favorite people in all the world.

Arnold eyed with appreciation a youngish woman with an exceptionally fine pair of legs as he paused at the corner of Geary and Taylor, waiting for the light to change. He started across the street, had almost reached the opposite curb when the squealing of brakes warned him of danger even before he saw a small sports car careening around the corner toward him.

With surprising agility for a man who was four years past his fiftieth birthday, he dived to one side, only to come up a cropper against the side of a parked car.

His last thought, during those seconds between shock and the loss of consciousness, was the regret that not only would he miss his morning appointments but also his lunch date with Janice.

CHAPTER ONE

WHEN CHANEL DEVEREAU INFORMED HER HUSBAND THAT SHE was filing for a divorce, he hadn't tried to change her mind. In fact, their separation had been very amicable, which wasn't so surprising since they hadn't slept together for almost ten years.

She did regret moving out of the Devereau mansion, which had been one of the reasons why she'd married Jacques, but she couldn't very well ask *him* to leave, could she? After all, three generations of the Devereau family had occupied the big Italian Renaissance house in Pacific Heights—or had it been four?

As Chanel sat at her dressing table, expertly swirling her thick silver-blond hair into its usual sleek arrangement, she reflected that her life-style hadn't changed all that drastically since she'd left Jacques. The rent for her posh new apartment was outrageous, even for Pacific Heights, but since she was having all her bills sent to Jacques, she'd signed a year's lease for the six-room apartment, then contracted for the best interior decorator she could find, ending up with custom-made furnishings throughout.

So far, Jacques, who had a stingy streak, had been surprisingly quiet about her bills, which convinced her that his complaints these past few years about being short on "liquid assets"—he never called it anything as vulgar as money—had been a lie. Maybe he'd decided to be generous for the simple reason that she'd disrupted his life so much this past year, he was afraid she'd move back in with him.

Chanel gave her mirrored image a small, satisfied smile. She'd kept things stirred up on purpose, of course, because she'd known that Jacques would be content to let their marriage drift forever if she didn't shake him out of his comfortable routine. These days, he seldom left the house; most of the time he shut himself up in the climate-controlled room where he kept his first editions and his wretched stamp and coin collections, coming out only to eat his meals and to go to bed.

And just wait until he found out she had designs on those collections. That would really shake him up. He would either have to sell some of his treasures or raise the money elsewhere to pay her the settlement she was demanding. He'd acquired a good portion of his collections during their fifteen-year-marriage—and that meant he'd have to cough up half their value to pay her off.

What's more, she had taken the precaution of photographing his rarest stamps and coins and first editions last year when he'd gone into the hospital for that hernia operation. There'd be no salting the rare ones away in order to cheat her out of her share.

Unexpectedly, Chanel felt a rare twinge—not of guilt exactly, but something close to it. Regret, perhaps. In some ways Jacques wasn't so bad. A hermit, yes. More than tight with his money— that, too. But they'd had a few laughs together. Jacques could be amusing if you went in for dry wit—but not enough to outweigh his faults. How many invitations had she been forced to turn down because she didn't have an escort? As for entertaining at home, that had become totally out of the question lately because Jacques not only refused to attend his own parties but also to pay for them.

Well, all that was behind her. From now on, things were going to be different. Two marital mistakes were enough. When she married again, she was going for the gold. What's more, she'd already chosen her next husband—and Laird Fairmount was solid gold all the way through, not gold-plated brass as Jacques had turned out to be.

Chanel laid down her brush and stood, but before she turned away from the dressing table to finish dressing, she examined herself carefully in the mirror, making sure that every gleaming hair was in place, that her makeup was impeccable. Even though her only appointment today was with her lawyer, Arnold Waterford, she chose a Diane Dickinson original, a fur-trimmed walking suit, from her huge walk-in closet, just as if she were going out to lunch at an elegant restaurant like Compton Place.

It had been Chanel's observation that life had a way of tossing opportunities in your path when you least expected them, so it didn't do to get careless and let down, even a little. Who knows, she thought as she adjusted the fur hat that complemented her suit, maybe something really exciting, like running into Laird Fairmount, would happen today. If so, Chanel O'Hara Devereau was prepared to take advantage of it—as always.

CHAPTER TWO

GLORY BROWN HAD JUST TURNED SEVENTEEN WHEN SHE'D MAR-ried Buddy Prichett, but even at that young age, she'd had no starry-eyed illusions about marriage or forever afters. Ironically, it had been her mother who had put her own secret doubts into words.

"From now on, you're on your own—and good riddance," Flora Brown had said, waving the can of beer in her hand for emphasis. "You've been nothing but trouble since the day you was born. You think marriage to that hotshot baseball player is gonna change things, but it won't. You'll be back living in the projects as soon as he gets tired of balling you and kicks you out.

Well, don't you come whining to me when it happens 'cause I'm washing my hands of you, once and for all.''

Glory hadn't argued with her. She hadn't pointed out that as far as her mother was concerned, she'd been on her own as soon as she was old enough to fend for herself in the streets. She went on folding her wardrobe of jeans and T-shirts and cheap cotton underwear, packing it into shopping bags because she didn't have any luggage, hiding her hurt behind silence, knowing that nothing she could say would ever make her acceptable to her mother.

Later, she wasn't surprised that her mother and sisters didn't show up for her wedding brunch. Oh, they'd all had excuses, but it was more of the same old shit. They resented her because she wanted to better herself, to get out of public housing and off the welfare rolls. Most of all, they resented it because she was the first one in her family in two generations to have a bona fide marriage.

Yes, it had been some kind of celebration, that wedding brunch. Buddy's people had been there, their noses in the air because she could only scrape together enough money for a simple spread at a crummy North Beach café. But she had put up a good front, pretending not to notice the sly remarks, the insults that passed for jokes. After all, she had her pride, the same pride that had kept her hanging in there all through her freshman year at Lowell High when the other kids had laughed at her St. Vincent De Paul thrift shop clothes, her public housing address—and her ridiculous name.

Morning Glory Brown . . .

How had her mother come up with that one? True, her older sisters were named after flowers, too—Rose and Lily and Violet— but *Morning Glory*? The teasing she'd taken from other kids had been murder. Every time her family had moved, which was whenever Ma fell too far behind on the rent, and she'd had to start in at a new school, she'd prayed that this time no one would find out her full name. But they always did, and usually it was her sisters who gave away her secret.

Why did the three of them hate her when she'd never wished any of them harm? Okay, she didn't look like them. They were all short and dark-haired, with big asses like Ma, while she was red-haired, fair-skinned, and blue-eyed like the father she'd never seen. Since none of them had the same father, why did her sisters hold it against her because she was different? Sure, she had a good build. So what? What had it ever done for her except get her into trouble? If she hadn't been stacked, Buddy would never have given her a second look—and wouldn't *that* have been a blessing?

Glory blinked her eyes hard, determined not to cry. Right now she had more important things to think about than the past. For more than an hour, she'd been huddled on the bed next to Buddy, watching him through eyelids that stung like fire from her crying after the beating he'd given her earlier.

Buddy's big, loose-limbed body was sprawled out across the mattress, taking up most of the space and crowding her into one corner. He had stripped off his clothes before he'd flung her on the bed, and the sight of his naked body, still showing evidence of intercourse, made her stomach churn. Although it didn't lessen her outrage, she knew she was lucky that he'd only used his open palm to slap her around when he could have done a lot more damage with his fists. He was a powerfully built man, a professional baseball player, who would probably be burly when he got a few more years—and a thousand more cans of beer—in him.

Like his pig of a father, Glory thought scornfully.

She took a deep breath—and then almost gagged as she inhaled the raw fumes of whiskey. Buddy had finished off most of the fifth of Jim Beam he'd brought home—was he asleep or had he passed out? Or was he lying there awake, brooding over his grievances with the minor league baseball team that had dumped him five months ago, with her and everybody who didn't appreciate Buddy Prichett, the world's greatest baseball pitcher?

And what exactly had set him off tonight? Surely, it hadn't been because she'd commiserated with him about not getting that job today? Maybe it was because she'd refused to drink with him. He knew she never touched alcohol, not even beer. God knew she'd had a bellyful of it as a kid with an alcoholic mother who drank like a fish.

But when she'd seen what a foul mood Buddy was in, maybe she should've had a glass of beer with him to keep the peace. Well, if it hadn't been that, it would have been something else. From the way he looked at her sometimes, as if he hated her, he'd been spoiling for a fight for a long time. Which was why she'd been so careful not to disagree with him, ever since he'd come back from spring training.

It wasn't that she'd been physically afraid of him—not until tonight. But she hadn't wanted to put him into one of those moods where he sprawled on the living room sofa, silent and glowering, staring at the TV set and consuming six-packs of Berg's, the price of which they could ill afford.

When he'd come back from spring training early to tell her that he'd been dumped by his team, the San Jose Bees, replaced by a rookie still wet behind the ears, she'd tried to comfort him, but he'd wanted no part of her sympathy. So she'd waited out his moods, his brooding, the anger that could erupt so swiftly, and she'd tried to make him believe that she didn't feel any less respect for him just because he hadn't made it with a minor league baseball team.

"So what?" she'd said rashly, not understanding that in Buddy's mind, she was to blame for his failure. "You can always do something else. Who needs baseball?"

That's when he'd exploded. But even then he hadn't hit her, although his blistering accusations, that if she hadn't got pregnant and pressured him into marriage, he would have kept his mind on his job, had stung. Maybe she should have seen what was coming and left him then, only where would she have gone? Not to her mother, who'd made it plain she wasn't welcome, nor to her sisters, who hadn't tried to hide their satisfaction when Buddy bombed out as a professional baseball player.

Well, no use dwelling on the past. She was completely on her own now because she sure wasn't going to stay around and become a battered wife. A man who beat his wife once would do it again—that was one thing she'd learned, growing up in the Tenderloin and in the projects.

The man on the bed muttered a curse and flung his hands over his head. Glory stiffened, sure he would awaken, but instead he began to snore. So now was her chance to pack up and split—only what if Buddy woke up before she was gone? There was no telling what he would do to her—and she wasn't about to be raped again, not even by her own husband.

Or *was* it rape just because she hadn't wanted it? Okay, she hadn't resisted. She'd been too afraid of Buddy's big fists. But that didn't mean she was going to hang around and let him use her as a punching bag. And he would. He'd liked it—it had really turned him on, knocking her around and then having sex.

Glory slid off the bed, wincing at the protest from her bruised body. For a moment she stood there, staring at the naked man on the bed, and unexpectedly, her eyes filled with tears. When had it all gone away—the excitement and the dreams, the nights she couldn't sleep for thinking about Buddy, the way she'd felt when he kissed her, touched her, made out with her?

Glory picked up her robe, but when she slipped it on, she discovered the belt was missing. She spotted it, looking like a red plush snake on the rug where Buddy had flung it when he'd torn off her robe. As she bent to retrieve it, an idea came to her. If Buddy was tied up, what difference would his big muscles make? So what if he came to and caught her packing? If he was in no position to stop her, then she could take her time and make sure she didn't leave anything that belonged to her behind.

Moving carefully, she picked up the belt, then opened the chest drawer where Buddy kept his ties. They were all expensive ones— thirty dollars or more a pop. Nothing but the best for Buddy Prichett—Buddy the Prick!—who spent his money as if it were water.

That had been another bone of contention—that she was the prudent one who wanted to put something aside for a rainy day. When the rainy day had come, she'd held her tongue and hadn't reminded Buddy that she'd wanted to save for just such an emergency, nor had she complained that he was drinking up his severance pay. In the end, it hadn't made any difference. He still blamed her for the whole thing, for getting pregnant, for their quick marriage, for losing the baby. . . .

The old grief, still raw and close to the surface even after two years, welled up inside her, but she blinked furiously, pushing back both the tears and the memory. Trying to breathe shallowly, she bent over Buddy and gingerly twisted the robe belt around his right wrist three times, then fastened it to the wooden bedpost in a tight double knot. As she circled the bed, her heart beat so hard she was sure he'd hear it, and she paused briefly to get her breathing under control, afraid she might hyperventilate and pass out. Only when his left hand and both ankles were secured by his own ties, did she allow herself a small sigh of relief.

Briefly, she wondered if she hadn't tied him up too tightly, but then she shrugged. Once she was safe, she would call the police— he could make up some lie to save face, or he could tell the truth. It didn't matter to her.

The hell with Buddy.

From the top shelf of the bedroom closet, she got down the fancy set of suitcases that Buddy's parents had given him when he'd first signed up with the San Jose Bees. Moving swiftly, she began to pack, emptying out drawers, folding clothes, and packing them away. Still in her robe, she went into the kitchen to fill two cardboard cartons with half the utensils, dishes and silver, linen and towels they'd accumulated during their brief marriage, leaving the rest for Buddy.

She hesitated over their portable TV, but in the end, she took only the small radio that she'd paid for herself with baby-sitting money before her marriage. She seldom watched TV—and Buddy stayed glued to it most of the time he was home. Besides, it would be hard to store something as big as a TV set while she was looking for a place to live.

The last thing she did was empty out Buddy's wallet. She left him a twenty-dollar bill, enough for taxi fare to his parents' house in Daly City with enough left over for a six-pack of Berg's.

She took a shower then, scrubbing herself until her skin stung under the needle-fine spray, washing away all evidence of intercourse. As she dried herself, she reflected that she'd miss the apartment. It was pretty small for two people, but it had seemed like a palace when Buddy had first brought her here. The bathroom, with its shiny fixtures and gleaming tile, had delighted her because she'd never taken a shower in a tiled stall before—unless you counted those doorless wonders at school.

And the kitchen—the sight of a range that wasn't rusty and covered with grease had made her clap her hands and laugh out loud. Buddy had been embarrassed because the apartment house manager had been showing them the place, but she hadn't cared. She'd been too happy about furniture that matched and wasn't worn to the nub, with rugs instead of bare linoleum floors, with window sills that weren't crusted over with layers of old paint.

It was unlikely that she'd be able to afford anything half as nice for a long time even if she got a job right away. Not that she intended to move back to the projects. She'd rather live in the streets than share a crummy flat with Ma and her latest sleep-in boyfriend, even if Ma offered to take her in—which she wouldn't.

Buddy had stopped snoring when she returned to the bedroom. She kept her back turned to the bed while she dressed and didn't realize he was awake until he spoke.

"What the fuck's going down here? Is this some kind of sick joke?"

She turned to look at him, and the sight of his bloodshot eyes and puffy face made her stomach roll again. She didn't answer him as she folded her robe and tucked it away in one of the suitcases.

"Untie me, like right now, or so help me I'm going to beat your ass until it looks like a piece of hamburger," Buddy said, his voice ominously even.

"Like hell you will," she retorted, and then was sorry she'd spoken when Buddy began to struggle with his bonds, his voice grating on her nerves as he described in detail what he was going to do when he got his hands on her again.

Her lips tight, she opened a chest drawer and snatched out several of his handkerchiefs. As she approached the bed, Buddy's eyes bulged, and she knew he'd just realized how helpless he was. His tone conciliatory now, he told her that hell, he'd just been kidding, that he was sorry about working her over.

"I lost my head—look, honey, I promise I won't lay a hand on you again. It was just that I've had a rotten day, taking shit off that lousy personnel guy just to get a two-bit sales job."

"You didn't have to take it out on me," Glory said. "I'm in your corner—remember? Or I was until now. But when you slapped me that time, I told you what would happen if you ever hit me again. So I'm getting out—and don't bother to come looking for me because I'm leaving town."

Buddy's face seemed to swell before her eyes. "And how you going to support yourself? Flipping hamburgers at McDonald's for three bucks an hour? Of course, you could go on the streets. You'd make a good hooker, the way you like sex. Maybe you can get a job showing your tits in one of those topless joints in North Beach—or you can always go on welfare like your sisters and old lady."

"Keep on talking," she said. "Just keep it up, and so help me I'll gag you."

"Yeah? Well, I'll get loose eventually and then you'll wish you'd never been born, you cunt—"

Glory felt a rush of heat to her head; her face must have changed color because all of a sudden, Buddy's tone changed.

"Hey, I was just letting off steam again." He tried out a smile, and she winced, remembering how that same slow grin had once made her bones melt. "You can't blame me for getting sore after all I've been through lately—and it doesn't help, the way you're still moping around about losing the kid when what you should've done was have that abortion like I wanted."

Glory realized that she'd had enough. She stalked over to the bed and forced the wad of handkerchiefs between Buddy's teeth. As he frantically tried to spit them out, his helplessness touched her, and she almost changed her mind about gagging him—until she saw the hatred in his eyes. Again, his fury sparked off her own anger, and this time, it went completely out of control.

Snatching Buddy's trousers off the floor, she jerked the belt out of the loops, then raised the belt and brought it down across his chest. "That's for giving me a black eye," she said. The belt cracked like a whip as she hit him again, this time across his genitals. "And that one's for raping me. I hope you remember this the next time you decide to beat up on a woman."

Buddy writhed against his bonds, his eyes like burnt coals in his gray face, and suddenly Glory's anger left her. She threw the belt down and turned away, and the tears she'd been able to hold back when their roles had been reversed slid down her cheeks.

Buddy was still now—ominously still. The skin on the back of her neck prickled suddenly, and she whirled, sure that he'd escaped his bonds and was standing behind her. But no, he was still lying on the bed, his ankles and wrists still tied to the posts; two angry red welts stood out plainly against his pale skin. He was staring straight at her, and there was no expression at all on his face now.

Picking up a piece of luggage, she told him, "I'll call the cops from the airport. They can untie you. I'm taking your luggage, and I cleaned out your wallet—I figure I've got something coming for that beating. You can get a loan from your old man. He'll be so glad to get rid of me he should be willing to support you until you get a job. As soon as I get settled, I'm filing for a divorce. Or you can do it. You can always charge me with desertion—or with cruelty to animals."

It took Glory three trips to carry the luggage and the cartons of household goods downstairs. After she'd called a cab and before she left the apartment with the final load, she hesitated, not sure whether or not to lock the hall door. In the end, she left it unlocked so the police could get in without breaking it down.

Half an hour later, she dialed 911 from a phone booth at the Greyhound Bus Depot on Mission Street. After she gave the address of the apartment in the Avenues, she said she'd been passing the door of Apartment 4B when she'd heard a strange noise. No, it wasn't a fight. More like someone trying to call for help with a gag in their mouth. Refusing to give her name, she hung up.

She had already stored her belongings in three large lockers at the bus terminal and now, unencumbered with luggage, she went looking for a place to stay.

She'd never had any intention of leaving San Francisco. After all, it was a big city. The chances were good that she could avoid running into Buddy—and besides this was her hometown. She knew which muni-bus serviced any neighborhood in the city, which streets to avoid after dark, the location of restaurants that sold good, cheap Mexican or Chinese or Thai food. Also, her chances of getting a job quickly were much better here where she had a few local references.

And her mother and sisters were here, too. In case of a real emergency—and it had better be something like terminal illness—she had someone to contact. Besides, she wasn't about to let Buddy drive her out.

The hell with Buddy.

That afternoon, Glory rented a hotel room on Post Street where the sagging bed and scarred bureau reminded her of the evil-smelling bedrooms she'd once shared with her older sisters. The next day, she got a job as a cocktail waitress in a North Beach nightclub, and a week later, after a diligent search, she found a two-room apartment on Russian Hill.

The apartment was small and unfurnished except for a tiny refrigerator and range; it was tucked behind the landlord's street-floor garage, San Francisco style, but the rent was affordable, and the windows faced east and caught the early morning sun.

Her landlord, a large elderly Italian man, was planting bulbs in the backyard the day she answered the ad, and the prospect of looking out her windows at blooming daffodils and tulips appealed to her, even though she'd have to wait until spring. It certainly was a few steps up from the projects or the Tenderloin, even if the cleaning deposit and the first and last month's rent had almost depleted the money she'd taken from Buddy's wallet.

After she'd moved her belongings in, she borrowed her landlady's phone and started calling lawyers whose name she found in the yellow pages of the phone book. But none of them would take her on as a client—or even give her an appointment. They all asked for personal and banking references, and when she couldn't come up with any, she was advised to go to another lawyer—or to Legal Aid.

Later she was glancing through a day-old copy of the *San Francisco Chronicle* when she came across the photograph of a white-haired man with a smile so benevolent, it could only be described as saintly.

He was standing beside a middle-aged woman, and the caption

under the photograph read: "Divorce lawyer Arnold Waterford and his client, society matron Patricia Longworth, leaving the courthouse after a divorce settlement, reportedly in the millions, was reached with Mrs. Longworth's husband, industrialist Philip Longworth."

Glory studied Arnold Waterford's picture a long time before she put the paper aside and went upstairs to borrow her landlady's phone again. She got Arnold Waterford's office number from the phone book, and a minute later, a woman's voice, crisp and businesslike, came on the line. "Arnold Waterford, attorney at law. May I help you?"

"I'd like to make an appointment with Mr. Waterford."

"Have you consulted him before?"

"No, this is the first time."

"May I ask who referred Mr. Waterford to you?"

"I don't understand—"

"Where did you get Mr. Waterford's name?" Although the woman was still pleasant, there was a tinge of impatience in her voice now.

"Oh . . . Patricia Longworth—she recommended Mr. Waterford to me."

"Mrs. Longworth is a friend of yours?" Already, the voice had warmed up several degrees.

"A *personal* friend," Glory said firmly.

"And your name is—?"

"Glory—M. Glory Prichett—no, make that Brown. I'm using my maiden name again."

"Is that Em—as in Emily?"

"No, it's an initial. The *M* stands for Morning."

There was a brief silence. "Your name is Morning Glory Brown?"

"Yes."

"Do you spell Brown with an *e*?"

Gloria thought a moment. Browne sounded sort of classy—and she was beginning a brand-new life, wasn't she? Why not start with a new version of her old name?

"Yes, with an *e*," she said.

"Very well, Mrs. Browne. I'll put you down for—how does ten-thirty next Friday morning suit your calendar?"

"Can't you make it sooner?"

"I'm sorry. In fact, if it hadn't been for a canceled appointment, I couldn't schedule you this week at all."

"Okay—Friday morning at ten-thirty it is," Glory said.

It was after she'd hung up and was back in her own apartment that Glory realized she should have asked the woman two very important questions: How much did Mr. Waterford charge for getting a divorce for a client—and did he extend credit?

CHAPTER THREE

STEPHANIE CORNWALL PULLED INTO THE DRIVEWAY OF HER condo and killed the motor of her station wagon, but she didn't get out right away. For one thing, she was bone tired because she'd been on the run most of the afternoon, doing errands and shopping for groceries for the coming weekend. For another, she enjoyed looking at the place where she'd been living with her husband and twin sons for the past six months.

David and she had searched for a long time before they'd decided to settle in Mill Valley. Since neither of them enjoyed yard work—and because the twins would be off at college in four more years—it made sense to buy a condo. Not that this place qualified for stereotypical condo living. The big, sprawling eight-unit complex, with its shake sidings and roofs, its arched windows and skylights, with each unit adroitly situated so as to assure total privacy, rambled through a redwood grove that the developer had been canny enough to leave untouched, giving the illusion that the whole structure had sprouted from the ground spontaneously.

The real estate dealer had glibly compared its architect with Frank Lloyd Wright when he'd showed them through the unit they'd eventually bought. "The best of both worlds," he'd enthused, adding the observation that despite its air of isolation, it was just a block away from the business center of Mill Valley, that most snug of Marin County villages, and yet it was an easy half-hour commute to the heart of San Francisco's financial district, where David had his law offices.

Stephanie gave a rueful smile as she slid out of the station wagon. It had also been horribly expensive, but then, David's

practice had increased so much these past few years that he'd taken
in two younger lawyers to help with the overload. Who would
have thought when she'd married a struggling young lawyer fifteen
years ago that he would become such a success? Those first years
he'd been happy when he made enough to feed them, pay the rent
on a tiny row house in the Richmond district of the city, and meet
the payments on his college loan. Now they lived in a luxury
condo in the most desirable section of Mill Valley.

"Who would've thunk it," Stephanie said aloud, using one of
her twins' pet phrases.

As she went up the steps of their unit, carrying a bag of groceries, she heard her sons' voices, and because they were yelling
at each other, she made a face. She wasn't in the mood to be the
arbitrator of two warring factions—and besides, David and she did
have a houseguest who was taking an afternoon nap. If the boys
awakened Ted, so help her, she'd take away their allowance for a
month. . . .

She shifted the bag of groceries to her hip and groped in her
jacket pocket for her key ring, but before she found it, the door
flew open and one of her fourteen-year-old twins came barreling
through. When he saw Stephanie, he skidded to a stop, looking
abashed.

"Oh—hi, Mom," Chuck said. "I didn't hear the doorbell."

"I didn't ring it. I figured you two were so busy yelling at each
other you wouldn't hear it."

"Yeah, well, Ronnie started it. He's been pawing through my
stuff again. I told him to lay off, and then he began making cracks
about sleazeballs so I—"

"Please. Spare me the gruesome details," Stephanie said.
"And I could use some help bringing in the groceries."

"Sure, Mom. I've got soccer practice in half an hour, but I
guess I can spare the time."

"Thanks a bunch," Stephanie said dryly. "And be careful with
the eggs."

"So if I drop them, we'll have an omelet for supper, right?"
Chuck grinned at her, and as always, she couldn't help smiling
back. He was such a handsome boy—was it wrong to be proud
of him because he looked so much like David? Probably—but the
devil with that. Whenever she looked at her sons or her husband,
she almost OD'd on pride. And anyway, what was wrong with a
little partisanship?

"Uncle Ted says we eat too many eggs," Chuck informed her. "Too much cholesterol."

"I know, I know," she said.

"He's really into health food. All that special food must be a drag for you to fix. Did you hear him yesterday, going on about seaweed?" Chuck snickered. "I'll bet if you picked some ragweed, put it in a salad bowl, and poured salad dressing over it, he wouldn't know the difference."

"I'll wash your mouth out with soap if you don't lower your voice," Stephanie threatened, although she wanted to laugh, too.

Ted Towne was a childhood friend who had just come back into David's life. He was an actor—his real name was Timothy O'Clarke—and he'd been their houseguest while he appeared as the romantic lead in a new play that was trying out at a small Berkeley theater. If the play continued to get critical approval, his company would tackle the New York Off-Broadway audience next.

Although, in Stephanie's private opinion, he wasn't nearly as handsome as David, Ted had a certain boyish charm and a line of flattery that could either be attractive or annoying, depending upon whether one was hosting him for an evening or for a week.

Because Stephanie had been picking up after Ted and planning her meals around his health food diet for the past two weeks, his charm had worn thin, an opinion she was careful to keep from David. Her husband, always so reserved and within himself, had few close friends. The last thing she wanted was to make Ted feel unwelcome. One bright spot—the reviews had been universally good and in three days Ted and his company would be leaving for New York.

And good riddance, she thought.

"Thank you for being such a good sport about—about everything," she told Chuck. "I know it hasn't been easy, sharing your room with your brother so Ted could have Ronnie's bed."

"Aw, Uncle Ted is okay, I guess. But it does get old when he keeps getting Ronnie and me mixed up. After all, we don't even look alike. At least, he hasn't asked us how it feels to be twins— but I'm expecting it any minute now. And those stories about all the important people he knows—he's a real ham, which is kind of weird, him being a vegetarian and all."

He snickered again. "Can you believe that stuff about Dad and some other guys painting Uncle Ted's balls blue when he was drunk? Man, he must really have been zonked out."

"Boys who listen to other people's private conversations get their allowances cut," she warned.

"Hey, Mom, we couldn't help hearing it. We were in the kitchen, getting Cokes, and Uncle Ted was talking pretty loud—"

"Well, watch it in the future," she said hastily and moved past him into the house.

A few minutes later, she had finished putting away her groceries and was chopping vegetables for a salad when she heard footsteps coming down the stairs. She knew it was Ronnie because he moved like a cat, unlike Chuck's clatter, clatter, bump, bump.

How different her two boys were. Chuck, to use an old phrase, never met a stranger—a true Aries, if you believed in such things. He was at ease with strangers, be they female or male, old or very young, while Ronnie stood back, slow to make up his mind about people, just like his father. As different as night and day. As different, in fact, as their father and mother. Strange bedfellows, the Cornwalls. . . .

"What's the joke, Mom?" Ronnie said from the doorway.

Stephanie looked at her younger son—by half an hour—and her smile widened. He still hadn't adjusted to his latest spurt of growth, and he looked very young, very vulnerable, as he leaned against the doorjamb. Although he didn't have his brother's husky build and good looks, he was already getting his share of calls from girls—which rather surprised her. True, he did have his father's rare smile, which was the thing that she'd first fallen in love with.

And when he bent his head over his schoolbooks, the back of his neck, still so thin and undeveloped-looking, always made Stephanie want to cry. Life was going to be more difficult for Ronnie than for Chuck—but maybe it would have more lasting rewards, too.

"So why the big grin, Mom?" he persisted.

"A private joke," she said. "Not suitable for your adolescent ears."

"Something about you and Dad making out, right?"

Stephanie found herself blushing; she decided she could do without her son's knowing grin. "Have you seen Ted yet today?" she said. "I wonder how the play went last night—"

"Well, you can ask him yourself. He's up. I heard the john flush just now."

"I hope you boys didn't disturb him. I could hear you bellowing at each other all the way down the walk."

Ronnie's face lengthened. "Chuck started it. He was bugging me about messing around with his things. All I did was move some of the junk off his desk so I could do my homework. Boy, I'll sure be glad when I'm back in my own room."

"Well, it won't be long now. Ted will be leaving in three days."

"Yeah. I keep telling myself that."

"Watch it, boy—it hasn't been too bad, has it?"

Ronnie hesitated; it seemed to her that he was avoiding her eyes. "Naw. It's been okay. But I'll be glad when we have the house to ourselves again." He rooted around in the refrigerator and came up with two apples.

"Don't ruin your dinner, Ronnie," she warned. "How about just one?"

"Okay—but you're always telling me I should put on some weight." He put one apple back into the refrigerator. "Besides, that rabbit food we've been eating lately doesn't stick to the ribs very long."

"Speaking of ribs—how about a barbecue the night after Ted leaves?"

"With your special barbecue sauce?"

"Right. And gobs of greasy, indigestible ribs."

"Okay. I'll buy that. You're a pretty okay mom, you know that?" He bestowed an apple-flavored kiss on her cheek and went swinging out the door.

They had dinner at six because of Ted's eight o'clock curtain call, and although she didn't let it show, Stephanie relaxed only after he'd left for the theater. It wasn't that he was a bad house-guest, she thought, trying to be fair, as she gave the tub in his bathroom a quick scrub, made his bed, and picked up the clothes he'd strewn around the room. It was just that their house, although roomy enough for the four of them, wasn't expandable, not enough to include Ted, who for some reason seemed to take up so much space.

The four of them watched TV for a while after dinner and then went to bed early, David declaring that he'd had a hard day and needed some rest. Stephanie had taken this as a signal that he wanted to make love, but after he kissed her good night, he rolled over on his side even before she pulled the sheet up over her shoulders. Feeling both relieved and also a little hurt—it had been three weeks since they'd had sex—she read for a few minutes before she turned off the light and went to sleep, too.

The next day, a Saturday, was the annual luncheon meeting of her Gray Lady chapter. Dressed in a dark blue fall suit, she left David and Ted swapping reminiscences over martinis and drove into the city. But when she arrived at the Cliff Hotel, the designated meeting place, she discovered that the luncheon had been canceled due to the sudden illness of the guest of honor, a state Congresswoman. Feeling put out because she hadn't been notified, she decided she wasn't in the mood for shopping.

Well, nothing to it but to return home. Lord knew there was plenty to do there. Not that she minded household chores, especially because she had day help twice a week to do the heavy work. She'd never been sorry that she hadn't gone out to work after her marriage. Even though they'd needed money badly at the time, David had been adamant that she stay home. He liked to think of her there, he'd told her, holding down the fort, while he made a living for them. He'd been raised in a one-parent family by a working mother, a lawyer like himself, which was why he'd been sent off to boarding school so young. His mother hadn't remarried after being widowed—which was another story, Stephanie thought, unconsciously making a face.

As she drove beneath the orange-red towers of the Golden Gate Bridge and then through misty, verdant Waldo Pass, she reflected that the only time she ever wished she had an exciting job was when someone asked what she was into—a phrase she hated. But she never tried to justify her decision, to point out that her life was serene and pleasant and satisfying. And never boring, not with two precocious sons, with David as attentive as ever and still her lover.

True, she sometimes wondered lately if she and David hadn't fallen into a rut. Maybe it was time they took that trip to Europe they were always talking about. Once their houseguest was gone, she'd feel David out. He did seem restless, especially since Ted had descended upon them. Was he getting a little bored with childhood reminiscences, with Ted's constant name-dropping and the lengthy recitals of his successes? Or did he simply need some time away from work, a long revitalizing trip?

She took the Mill Valley turnoff off Interstate 101, and a few minutes later was letting herself into the condo with her key. She paused briefly, listening for men's voices, but it was so quiet that she suspected David and Ted had gone out—probably to have lunch at the Irish bar-and-grill down the street.

That meant she had the house to herself, because the boys were at Saturday soccer practice. Maybe she should take advantage of the peace and quiet to take a nap—and a long bubble bath instead of a hurried shower would be pure bliss.

She shrugged out of her suit jacket and, holding it over her arm, went upstairs. She had almost reached the master bedroom when she heard a strange sound—like someone moaning. Was it the wind in the blinds? David was a fresh air fiend and insisted on sleeping with the windows open. He'd still been asleep when she'd dressed and gone downstairs this morning—had he forgotten to close the windows after he got up?

Feeling irritated—with three floors to heat, their heat bills were phenomenal—she opened the bedroom door and then stood there, frozen with shock.

David and Ted hadn't gone out for lunch, after all. They were lying on the bed, and both of them were naked. They were so absorbed in each other that they hadn't noticed the door opening, even though it created a draft that rattled the vertical window blinds. As for what they were doing—oh, God, they were having sex with each other in a crazy perversion of the missionary position—

Stephanie felt a piercing pain, as if a knife were twisting in her guts. She knew she was going to be sick—but she wanted to die instead. This was her husband, and Ted was doing things to him that were an abomination, doing them on the same bed David had shared with her for the last fifteen years. David's eyes were closed; his face held a blind, rapt expression as Ted's hands moved over the brown, husky body that she knew so well, as he nuzzled David intimately with his lips, making him groan like a man in pain. . . .

Although she still hadn't made a sound, David opened his eyes and looked straight into Stephanie's frozen face. His face turned an ugly gray, as if the blood had suddenly drained out of his body, and his eyes were sick, stricken.

"Oh, God," he groaned. "Get off me, Ted!"

Ted turned his head. He saw Stephanie standing in the doorway, and briefly something furtive and triumphant flared in his deep-set eyes. But he rolled away from David immediately and sat up. He even managed a weak smile.

"Look, I'm sorry about this. We had too much to drink and

we got to wrestling around and the first thing you know—this doesn't mean a damned thing, Stephie.''

"You bastard," she said. "You filthy bastards!"

Ted groped for his clothes and hurriedly pulled on his jeans and sweatshirt. This time he sounded sincere as he told her, "Don't blame David—it's all my fault, Steph. It started out as a joke. I told you about that time he and these other guys got me drunk, painted my balls blue, and then told me I had a new venereal disease that was going around? Well, I decided to pull the same gag on David. I got him drinking—you know he can't hold his liquor worth a damn—and when he went upstairs to sleep it off, I got some blue ink from your desk and followed him. Only he wasn't as drunk as I thought, and we started wrestling and—well, one thing led to another. Look, I'm sorry as hell. I hope you won't go off half-crocked and do something stupid—"

Stephanie didn't stay to hear the rest although Ted was still talking when she left the room. If she remained there one more second, she knew, she would snatch up something and brain both of them.

As the door slammed behind her, the sickness came rolling back. She made it to Chuck's bathroom in time—but just barely.

A while later, she was sitting on the edge of Chuck's bed, still holding a wet towel to her burning face, when the door opened. She looked up—into David's eyes; she began to shake inside.

"I want you out of here before the boys get home," she said, her voice shrill. "And don't worry. When I file for divorce, I'll give incompatibility as the reason—God knows that's the truth. But if you try to get custody of the boys, I'm going to stand up in the courtroom and tell everybody that my husband is a flaming gay."

David's face looked haggard, old; he rubbed his eyes with the heel of his hand as if they smarted. "Don't make any decisions yet, Stephie. You don't really mean that about keeping me from the boys—"

"Oh, I mean it. Don't fight me on this, David. How do you think your clients would feel about having a gay lawyer handling their corporate affairs? The Bay Area may be liberal, but *your* clients are all superconservative. Then there's your mother. She's quite a joiner, but I don't think she'd like belonging to the Parents of Gays group. And of course there's your—your buddy. If it got out that Ted was gay, that would be the end of those romantic roles he specializes in. Of course, he could always get a part in *La Cage aux Folles*. He'd be a natural for that one, wouldn't he?''

"Stop it, Stephie!" David groaned. "You're talking nonsense. Ted isn't gay—"

"Oh? Then what was that I saw a few minutes ago? A new kind of wrestling?"

"Look, it only happened this once. And it will never happen again. Okay, it was stupid, crazy—we'd been drinking, celebrating the good reviews of Ted's play. I went upstairs to take a nap, and he tried to play that fool trick on me and then—"

"And then one thing led to another, right?"

"That's how it happened, Steph. Hell, he's been living with a woman for the past three years. They're talking about getting married—"

"She must be very understanding. Or maybe she's a little kinky, too."

"This isn't you, talking like this—"

"Maybe you don't know the real me. I certainly didn't know the real you, did I?" Stephanie stood and smoothed down her skirt. Her hands were shaking, but she couldn't help that. "I hope you told Ted to pack up his things and get out. I don't want him around my boys."

"*Our* boys, Stephie."

"Oh, no. You forfeited the right to be their father. As for that pervert friend of yours—" She stopped, her eyes widening. "Oh, my God! They already know. That's why they've been so uncomfortable around Ted. They know he's queer."

"You're wrong—he isn't a homosexual. He wouldn't make a pass at my kids. It would never enter his mind."

"If you believe that, you're a fool. And I'm leaving before I throw up again. I'll be in the kitchen—but don't bother to say good-bye. Pack your things and—just go. You'll be hearing from my lawyer as soon as I can arrange things."

She took a wide detour around David and left the room, not looking back, and went downstairs to drink cupful after cupful of scalding hot coffee, her every sense attuned to the mutter of voices upstairs, the sounds that told her they both were packing. A dozen questions scurried through her mind, questions she couldn't answer.

Had their marriage been a sham from the start? Had David preferred men all along? Their lovemaking—it had always been disappointing to her. Had it been something he did only because it was expected of him? Was David gay—or bisexual? And why had he married her? To have kids, a home—or a front to hide his homosexuality behind?

She heard footsteps coming down the stairs, and she braced herself, preparing for a new assault upon her nerves.

"Stephie—"

"Go away," she said without turning her head. "If you've left anything behind, you can pick it up while the boys are in school. Anything of yours I find, I'll put out in the garage so you won't have to come inside the house again."

"We have to talk. We have to make some decisions."

"I've already made mine. I'm divorcing you as soon as I can get to a lawyer."

"I can't leave you in this mood—"

"Get out, David, before I start screaming and throwing things."

"You're too upset to think straight right now, and I'm still feeling those martinis. I'll be at my mother's place—I'll give you a call tomorrow after we've both had time to—to calm down. God knows, I'm sick about this. You've got to believe that. It was a stupid mistake—I can only repeat that it wasn't planned—"

"Please go," she said wearily. She slumped against the table and buried her face in her folded arms, waiting for him to leave. She thought she felt something touch her hair, but if so David was gone when she lifted her head. Until this moment, anger had been sustaining her, but now she cried, overwhelmed by grief and a deep sense of loss.

But the storm didn't last long. There was too much to do before the boys came home. She went upstairs and gathered up the things David had left behind—his sports equipment, his college mementos, his out-of-season clothing, his books—and put them into cardboard cartons left over from their move from the city. One by one, she carried the boxes downstairs and stored them in the back of the garage.

When she returned to the master bedroom, she stripped the bed down to the mattress, threw all the bed linen into the trash cans in the service area behind the condo—including the goose down pillows and comforter/spread that she'd bought when they'd first moved into the condo.

Using a solution of Lysol so strong that its fumes burned the membranes of her nose, she sterilized the bed frame and sprayed the room with disinfectant, then did the same to the bed in Ronnie's room where Ted had been sleeping. When she was finished, both bedrooms stank of disinfectant, but she fancied she could still detect Ted's cologne, the lemony after-shave that David favored—and the musky odor of sex.

It was almost five now, and the boys would soon be home, but before she told them that she and their father had decided to live apart, that it had nothing to do with them, she had one more thing to do.

She called information and got the phone number of the lawyer who had arranged for a friend's divorce. She punched out the number, and because it was a Saturday, she was a little surprised when someone answered.

"Arnold Waterford, attorney at law," a woman's voice said.

"I'd like to make an appointment to see Mr. Waterford as soon as possible," Stephanie said.

After she'd given several references and answered a few questions, the woman told her that the next available opening was the following Friday at eleven-thirty; would that be satisfactory?

"I'd prefer an earlier date but—Friday will have to do, won't it? And yes, eleven-thirty will be fine."

CHAPTER FOUR

A STRANGE THING HAPPENED TO JANICE JORDAN THE FIRST TIME she met Jake Morehouse. She fell in love at first sight, something so alien to her practical nature that she didn't recognize it for what it was until much later.

It was in the late sixties, and she was eighteen years old, a freshman at Berkeley. That afternoon, she was walking across the campus with her friend and roommate, Casey, when she looked up and saw a wiry, dark-haired man, wearing a "Hell, No!" sweatshirt, in the center of a gesturing, arguing group of students. Fascinated by the quick, staccato movements of his hands, by the mercurial smile that flashed when one of the women students told him shrilly that he was full of shit, to knock it off, she stopped abruptly to stare.

Casey nudged her. "Okay, you've had a look at the infamous Jake the Make, so how about moving your tail? We've got a math class in ten minutes and besides, it won't do you any good to ogle him. He goes for bunnies with big boobs, which doesn't describe you, freshie."

Janice started to tell Casey she had no interest in anyone called Jake the Make when the dark-haired man turned his head and looked directly at her. And that's when it happened. Suddenly, there was a hollowness behind her ribs, a keening sound in her ears, a dryness in her mouth, all very uncomfortable and not a bit pleasant.

Then he was walking toward them, leaving the fermenting group of students behind, the rays of the fall sun falling upon his face and turning to amber eyes she would later find out were dark brown, his smile honed in on her.

"Hi, Casey," he said, but he was looking at Janice. "Back for another year of culture and ulcerated life-styles, huh?"

Casey rolled her eyes. "Okay. Let's get it over with. Her name is Janice Jordan, and she's fresh out of the valley—Fresno, no less—and she's much too nice for you. So give her a break and leave her quietly."

Jake shook his head. "Don't believe anything she says," he told Janice. "Casey's got a yen for my body."

Involuntarily, Janice glanced at Casey; briefly, so briefly that she almost missed it, she caught a flash of discomfiture in her roommate's eyes. "And you've got to be the most conceited man I've ever met, Jake Asshole," Casey said. "I'd rather go to bed with a toad than you!"

Unexpectedly, Jake's smile wavered. Why, he's really hurt! Janice thought, frowning at Casey.

Her friend gave an exaggerated sigh. "I see the old black magic's already working," she said, sounding more resigned than angry. "Well, don't say I didn't warn you, Janice—and not to worry. I'll never say 'I told you so.' "

She ambled off, her hands thrust deep into the pockets of her sweater jacket, leaving Janice tongue-tied with embarrassment. She started to follow her friend, but Jake's hand on her arm stopped her.

"Look, Casey's all wrong about me. My reputation for being a make-out artist is highly overrated. Do you believe me?"

She eased away from his hand. "What difference does it make if I believe you or not?"

"Come on. You can't be that naive. You felt it, too."

"Felt what?"

"The chemistry, the instant vibes. Something happened when we looked at each other. Why do you think I left a perfectly good argument—one I was winning, incidentally—to talk to you? You did feel it, too, didn't you?"

Janice had—but she wasn't going to admit it. Casey's warning could stem from a lot of things—personal dislike, or a thwarted sex interest in Jake Morehouse—but one thing she knew for sure. It had been sincere. So she was going to be careful. No heartaches for this freshman.

Her resolution lasted about an hour into their first date. Jake had held her there by the force of his arguments, his intensity. He didn't seem to hear her excuses, and in the end, she weakened and agreed to meet him the next evening for hamburgers and fries at the Burger Hut, prudently adding that she'd have to go home soon afterward because she had an early class the next day.

But after they ate, Jake talked her into walking across the campus to read the notices pasted on the kiosk in front of the admin building. He told her cheerfully that he'd like to take her someplace to boogie, but his wallet was almost bare, a chronic problem with him. Eventually, not really sure how it happened, she found herself in the off-campus apartment he shared with two other postgrads.

By then, she knew that he was an orphan, the only child of a widowed mother—"Make that 'doting' mother," he said—that he'd been raised in Oakland in a blue-collar neighborhood; that he was a sociology major, now going for his masters; that he was putting himself through Berkeley on scholarships, part-time jobs, and spit; that he loved cats, hated birds; that his favorite author was Loren Eiseley, the naturalist.

Later Janice looked up Loren Eiseley at the library so she could discuss him with Jake, a discussion that never came off because when she quoted Eiseley's most famous lines about frost and minor gods, Jake looked blank and then changed the subject.

But that first night, she only knew that Jake was like quicksilver, like the changing of the seasons, like the tides, never settling long enough to be labeled, always a moving target.

That he was also one to look ahead and lay plans, she didn't realize until later when she mentally reviewed their first evening together. What else but careful planning could explain why it was that both his roommates were gone on a weekday night? That the apartment she would see in such incredible disarray later was neat and reasonably clean that first night? That there was a jug of mountain red, a selection of cheeses and crackers in a larder that she would soon learn was customarily empty?

Jake didn't make his pass right away. He wined and fed her, made her laugh, then turned very serious and told her about a boyhood tragedy concerning a pet dog and a city garbage truck that made her cry. When he put his arms around her, she forgot all about Casey's warning because the feeling was back—the drop in the stomach, the pain/pleasure that was new to her.

She was a virgin, a secret she'd kept to herself. Her virginity didn't stem from morality or from fear of pregnancy or because she hadn't been asked. She was still a virgin because she'd never yet met a man who could get past her natural defenses. In fact, she'd often wondered if she wasn't frigid—or a sexual cretin.

Jake didn't suspect it was her first time, and she didn't tell him. His lips were surprisingly soft, surprisingly mobile, as he kissed her; his tongue quivered against hers, setting up a responding quiver deep inside her. He kissed her for a long time, taking his time, moving in on her by degrees.

When she was naked, having been expertly divested of her clothes, he looked at her with such admiration that she didn't feel shy, not even when he stripped in front of her. Clothed, he seemed a little too thin, his body too slight. Naked, he looked much larger because his smooth, well-developed muscles hugged his bones so tightly. His flesh had a hard, unyielding look, but when he turned to face her, she saw that the thick dark hair that covered his chest and genitals was silky and fine, a few shades darker than the hair on his head.

She also understood now why he had a reputation as a swordsman, and she was suddenly afraid—until he took her hand and pressed it against his hard shaft.

"You have met the enemy, and he is yours," he said solemnly, and she knew he'd caught her fear. "I promise I'll make it good for you. Trust me, Janice."

And she did. She let him lead her, show her what made him feel good, let him initiate her into a world of sensuality that she'd only heard about secondhand. All the reading she'd done about sex had either been dry and clinical or pure romantic fantasy. None had described the way Jake made her feel about herself. She hadn't guessed that her whole body, even the soles of her feet and the tiny triangle of flesh at the base of her spine, were erogenous zones. She hadn't known that it was possible for a virgin to come to climax more than once during her first sexual experience.

"My God—you're a natural, Janice girl," Jake murmured as they lay exhausted in each other's arms. "But why the hell didn't you tell me you were new at this? I would have made it better for you."

"Better than *that*?" she said in wonder, and was surprised when he laughed.

A month later she moved in with him, his roommates having been evicted. She was wildly in love, her senses so acute that she seemed to be living on a perpetual high. Even the discovery that Jake seldom hung up an article of clothing or replaced anything that he took out of a drawer, that he could turn the kitchen into a disaster zone just by making himself a cup of instant coffee, couldn't dampen her obsession.

Casey, who still had doubts, shook her head when Janice told her she was moving in with Jake. "So maybe I was wrong. I hear Jake has even given up his groupies. I wouldn't be surprised if you didn't do something as uncool as get married."

The following spring, when Jake received his masters, Janice expected that he would get a teaching job, but Jake decided to go for his doctorate instead, and she had to admit that his reasoning made sense.

"Look, you know I want to teach," he told her. "That's what I've been aiming for all my life. But it doesn't make sense to settle for silver when I can go for the gold. If I don't get my doctorate, I'll end up teaching high school kids. You know how I am—I have to have mental stimulation. And that means teaching at college level. Sure, I could go for my doctorate while holding down a teaching job, but it's taken me three years to get my masters. I'm sick to death of doing it piecemeal, doing a little research here, a little more there, taking a few classes while I hold down a job—"

"So why don't I get a job while you work on your dissertation?" Janice said, sensible as always. She had already learned that the practicality and financial management part of their relationship must come from her. "When you get your doctorate, then it will be my turn."

"Hell, no, honey, I can't do that. That wouldn't be fair to you."

"I have the income from that trust fund my mother left me," she went on as if he hadn't spoken. "And I can work for a year.

Luckily, my stepparents insisted I take some bus ed courses in high school.''

''It would have to be a loan. I insist on it.'' Jake grabbed her by the waist and whirled her around. ''God, I love you—and I think it's time to make you an honest woman. How about getting married, Janice?''

And it had worked out just fine because now Jake could devote himself to his doctorate program without pressure, and for the first time since her mother's death, Janice had been admitted to the inner sanctum of someone else's life instead of standing outside, looking on.

Janice's mother had died when she was five, and then her father had remarried a woman who already had three small children. Three years later, after he was killed in a street accident, her stepmother married again, another widower with two toddlers, giving Janice a stepfather as well as a stepmother. In the next two years, they produced two more offspring, both boys, and now Janice had three sets of stepsiblings. It was clear to her, even at that young age, that if she expected to remain a member of her stepparents' family, she had jolly well better make herself indispensable. So she'd bought acceptance, if not affection, by becoming Little Miss Reliable—baby-sitter, cook, and all-round household drudge.

When she was eighteen she came into the income from a small inheritance that her mother had left her. She'd already been accepted at Berkeley, so when she packed her things, she knew it was for good, that she would never return to Fresno to live, and she was all primed to go it alone. Instead she'd met Casey, and then Jake—and a whole new life had opened up for her.

Although she was aware that her new circle of friends were the fallout from Jake's personal popularity, she didn't think of this as crumbs because she was sure they genuinely approved of her. Jake never tried to hide their financial arrangement. He always included her when congratulated for some laurel with a generous, ''Hell, half of this award (or honor or high grade) should go to Janice.'' And then his smile would flash and he'd add, ''Not only does she support me but she types up my research notes so they make sense.''

Janice blossomed under the umbrella of his praise. If she had moments when she secretly wished they had more time alone together, it was a small price to pay for finally being on the inside where it was warm and safe.

There was a celebration when Jake received his doctorate degree. Janice worked three days, getting everything ready.

"Let's make it a real wingding," Jake said, and although she had a few uneasy thoughts about the balance in their checking account, Janice agreed. After all, it was her celebration, too. Jake had already accepted an assistant professor's position in the sociology department at Stanford when school started in the fall.

Meanwhile, she would work for another year to give them a nest egg, and then she would enroll at Stanford, something they could afford on his pay only because she was entitled to reduced tuition as a faculty wife.

But it didn't work out that way. By the following fall, Janice knew she'd have to work awhile longer, after all. Not only did they need a newer car to replace their old VW, which was on its last legs, but they now had social obligations. As Jake put it, even a lowly assistant professor couldn't be a hermit.

No longer a secretary, Janice was now office manager for a group of engineers, pulling down wages that kept their heads above financial high water. It didn't make sense to give up such a good job in order to return to college full-time, so she signed up for night courses instead.

The year before, when Jake started his teaching job at Stanford, they had used her trust find, which had matured when she turned twenty-one, for the down payment on a fine old Queen Anne in Professorville, a turn-of-the-century neighborhood that had once housed most of Stanford's faculty.

Jake had been the one who first saw the possibilities of the house. "We can fix it up while we live in it," he argued. "Okay, it looks pretty beat now, but look at all that space and those high ceilings and that fruitwood wainscoting. Once it's been restored, it'll be a showcase. Hell, honey, let's go for it."

He gave her the smile that she couldn't resist even when she disagreed with him. "I've always wanted a house like this. The street where Mom and I lived in Oakland was a garbage heap— drunks puking on the sidewalk and drug dealers making their pitch at the corner and johns picking up working girls right in front of our front door. I used to dream about moving Mom into a classy place like this."

"I'm sorry I never got to meet your—"

"There's something else, too. It's important, in my position, to put up a good front."

"But you're already one of the most popular professors in your department."

"Which doesn't cut any ice with the old fogies who run things at Stanford."

"Maybe not, but how many people get excerpts from their doctorate dissertation published in an anthology? As for publish or perish—you've had those articles published in *Sociology Today*, which isn't some obscure magazine nobody ever heard of. That has to be more important than where you live. The thing is—the payments on the house would be so steep I'd have to keep working—"

Jake slapped his forehead with the flat of his hand. "Hell, you're right. What was I thinking of? I'm a selfish bastard, honey. I don't know why you put up with me."

She had ended up assuring him that he wasn't selfish, that she really didn't mind working a couple more years. She pointed out that she could keep on taking night courses, building up credits toward her BA. When Jake got promoted to associate professor, she could go back to school full-time. Which wouldn't be all that long. Everybody said he was on his way up the academic ladder.

And it *had* worked out that way—eventually. The year they celebrated their seventeenth anniversary, Jake got his tenure as a full professor. Of course, it had taken longer than expected. There'd been some problems with his department head, an elderly man who, until he'd finally retired, had given Jake very lukewarm recommendations.

By now, Janice had her masters. She'd earned both her degrees piecemeal, a few credits here, a few there. She hadn't planned on getting her doctorate the same way, but she was forced to continue working for another year in order to pay for some unexpected repairs on the house. She'd never told Jake, but she wasn't all that fond of the old Queen Anne. It was drafty and cold in winter— and it absorbed money like a sponge soaking up spilled milk. The repairs, the heating, and other utility bills were out of sight—and she was sick to death of ancient plumbing that rattled and knocked, of the lack of water pressure, of other deficiencies.

But there was no question about selling it and getting a smaller, more modern place. Jake was a social person, and the house was perfect for entertaining. He was never happier than when a group of students were hanging on his every word during the impromptu evenings, two or three times a week, when he brought a gang home for one of Janice's home-cooked meals, followed by vino and cheese in front of the fireplace in his den.

Although their food bills were astronomical, Janice didn't have the heart to complain. Besides, she enjoyed the evenings, too, even if she sometimes felt as if she were the maid, keeping the wine flowing and passing around an endless supply of snacks.

"Honey, this is Sheri and Mark—and you remember Nancy, don't you? How about throwing a few more potatoes in the stew? We're all starving," Jake would say. And then later, in the kitchen, there were his confidences, the assumption that she would do her mother hen thing and provide a sympathetic ear to yet another troubled soul.

"Sheri's had a rough time of it lately—a relationship went sour on her." Or Karen had just had an abortion. Or Jason had totaled his car. "She needs a little tea and sympathy. You don't mind, do you?"

And of course she always shook her head. After all, the rewards were so good—Jake's praise and appreciation. That they still had such an active sex life after all these years seemed like a miracle.

"My own private swordsman," she called him.

After dinner one evening, Casey asked, "You two still have the old sex thing going, don't you?"

Janice's friend and ex-roommate had married Merv Scranton, an assistant professor at Berkeley, after she'd graduated. Five years later, when Merv had switched to Stanford, they had moved to Palo Alto and were living with their two kids in a comfortable tract house several miles away from campus. Although they existed from payday to payday, Casey took it in stride. Sometimes, as Janice listened to Casey's blow-by-blow description of her turbulent marriage, she felt embarrassed at her own peaceful life.

"I don't know how you two manage to keep that honeymoon glow. I'd hate to tell you what I thought of your chances of making it with Jake." Casey was perched on a kitchen stool, watching Janice tidy up the kitchen. "Jake hasn't lost his golden touch, I see—and I'm not just talking about the way he's climbing the promotion ladder."

"So eat your heart out," Janice said, laughing.

"Academia runs on politics," Casey said. "And I thought when I married a professor I was going to lead a stress-free life. Hell, there's more intrigue at Stanford than there is in Washington."

Although Janice nodded agreement, she felt a little uncomfortable. Casey was right about politics in the hallowed halls of Stanford—and about Jake knowing how to work the system. He'd once told her that the trick was never to show how hungry you were. Jake was the master of the art of being cool—was that why, when promotions or other plums came around, he always seemed to get more than his share?

"You're right about campus intrigue," she said, realizing Casey had fallen silent. "But all the organizations have it, don't they? Look at our own Faculty Wives Club—you'd think it was the end of the world, electing a new board. And that PTA business you were telling me about. Didn't you say that half the members resigned over some trifle?"

"Yeah. Not to change the subject or anything but what's happening with your dissertation prospectus? You think Professor Yolanski will give you his okay this time so you can present it to the Graduate Committee?"

"God, I hope so. I've already done so much work on it. You know how intimidating that whole process is—but, as Jake says, that's the system. I'll find out Monday morning, one way or another, when I have my appointment with Yolanski."

That weekend, she didn't sleep well. She hadn't been this nervous since she'd taken her Prelims and later, her seminar orals. Having had her first dissertation prospectus rejected by her adviser, Professor Yolanski, she was especially worried. Jake had scoffed at her when she told him that Professor Yolanski seemed to have some special grudge against her. He pointed out that when Yolanski had been his adviser, he'd been more than fair.

"The old guy is tough—but that's what getting a doctorate degree is all about. If it were easy, the degree wouldn't have any value," Jake added.

Monday morning, as Janice tossed a load of towels into the washer in the service room, she discovered that her mouth was dry, her hands sweating—all the symptoms of stress. This time, it *had* to work. She'd already told her company that she'd be quitting her job in a couple of months so she'd have time for the extensive research her dissertation would need.

For some reason obscure to her, she hadn't told Jake when she'd first started working on the second prospectus. When she finally did, he'd taken her notes into his den to read, and it was a long time before he came out. She'd thought for a few dark moments that he was going to tell her it was a piece of garbage—until he'd smiled and told her to go for it. And then he'd warned her to stay cool, to not get her expectations up, which had dampened her spirits again.

She knew why he'd cautioned her, of course, but what she'd really needed at the time was his total approval. When he'd been in the same spot, he had literally walked the floors, and she'd knocked herself out, encouraging him. But of course it was different with Jake. He'd had such a reputation for brilliance at Berkeley that everybody expected so much from him. If she failed again, it wouldn't cause a ripple among their friends. Most of them already thought she was silly to go for a doctorate in sociology when she already had such a good job.

Well, Jake didn't have the market cornered on optimism. If—no, *when* she got the go-ahead, she would start to work immediately, expanding the prospectus that listed her proposed dissertation topic, the research methodology, and, most important, the importance of the study. If it won the approval of the Graduate Committee, then she would finish the dissertation—and she was really looking forward to that final phase. There was something that appealed to her logical mind about working her way through a progression of facts and hypotheses, ending with a reasonable and studied conclusion.

She particularly liked research. In fact, she did most of the research for Jake's articles, just as she'd once researched most of his doctorate dissertation material. Since Jake hated research, it only made sense, just as it had made sense for her to edit his dissertation, a job that bored Jake. In fact, he'd given her carte blanche to make any changes needed when she typed up his material, and she seldom bothered him about minor corrections—and even some not so minor.

But this time she'd be writing and editing her own paper, the product of her own research. It wasn't that she expected to even come close to Jake's scholarship. She would be satisfied just to squeak past the Doctorate Committee.

And then what? Try for a job at a junior college in the area for less money than she was making as an office manager? Go for a career with one of the research institutes connected with Stanford or Berkeley? Well, it was too early to even think about that. . . .

"Where are you, Jan?" Jake called from the kitchen.

"I'm putting a load of towels in the washer before I leave for my appointment with Professor Yolanski. How come you're home?"

"I—look, come in here. I have something to tell you."

Alerted by the flatness in his voice, Janice hurried into the kitchen. Jake was standing at the sink, filling the electric kettle with water.

"What is it?"

"Wait until I plug in the kettle," he said. "I'm fixing you some coffee."

By the time he turned around, she was already prepared for bad news. Why else would Jake, who hated doing anything in the kitchen, fix her a cup of coffee unless he thought she'd need it?

"Okay, let's have it, Jake. You're scaring me to death—"

"I'm sorry. It isn't the end of the world—remember that, will you? But it isn't fair to let you—look, let's sit down, okay?"

Janice perched on the edge of a kitchen chair. "What is it?" she said again.

"Yolanski called me in for a little talk this morning—"

"What *is* it, Jake?"

"It's about your prospectus. He wanted me to tell you so you wouldn't go over to see him all filled with—with optimism."

"He doesn't like it, does he?"

"I'm sorry as hell. He decided it simply doesn't have enough possibility for original research. The subject's been done too many times before and the chances that you would come up with something new—well, he rejected it. What more can I say?"

"And you agree?"

He looked miserable. "Hell, honey, how can I be objective? That's an unfair question."

"In other words, you do agree. So why didn't you say something before I put so much work into it?"

"Because I could have been wrong. I couldn't take that chance. And why don't you put it out of your mind? You don't need this kind of aggravation. You've got your masters. If you want to teach, you can start out as a substitute at the local high school and work your way into a permanent slot."

"But I want to teach at college level—"

"Honey, be realistic. There's no chance you could get a teaching job at Stanford, even with a doctorate. I doubt if you could get on at any other college in this area, the competition being what it is."

"You did," she said, then bit her lip because it was like comparing apples with nuts. Jake's magnetism, his superior dissertation, which had been excerpted for an anthology by the University of Chicago Press, was the reason he'd been chosen over a hundred other applicants for a teaching slot at Stanford. But it hurt that Jake didn't even consider the possibility of her being accepted at a local junior college.

"What did you say to Professor Yolanski when he gave you the news?" she asked.

"I told him he had rocks in his head, but of course I'm a bit prejudiced." He grinned at her. "Look, why don't you shelve it until after the holidays—or wait until spring? Maybe by then you can come up with something new and fresh."

Janice was silent. She had been so patient during all the delays—didn't Jake realize how important this was to her? Or was he trying to ease her disappointment the only way he could—by treating it lightly?

Jake put his arm around her shoulder and kissed her. When she began to cry, he took her by the hand, led her upstairs to their bedroom, and made love to her. It didn't cure her disappointment, but it eased the pain.

"My own special swordsman," she murmured as he lay with his face buried in her breast, his breathing still turbulent. She hadn't reached the ultimate peak this time, but it didn't matter. It was comforting, just being close to Jake—as he'd known it would be.

The next morning, Janice got a call from an old friend, Arnold Waterford. His voice, a rich baritone, was an echo from her childhood that made her smile. "Is this my favorite goddaughter?" he asked.

"It is. As far as I know, I'm your *only* goddaughter."

"Always the pragmatist, aren't you? It just occurred to me that it's been a long time since we had one of our tête-à-têtes over lunch. Remember how you used to talk my ear off when you were a kid?"

"You were the most important male in my life," she said. "My stepfather had a hard time remembering my name from day to day."

"That man has the personality of a wet fish—and your stepmother should've been an old maid. If I hadn't kept reminding her that I was your legal guardian as well as your godfather, I don't think she would've let me in her house."

"She doesn't have a very high opinion of lawyers, especially ones who specialize in divorce."

"But think of all the injustice I prevent," Arnold said. "How many poor women get scuttled in the divorce courts just because they aren't adequately represented?"

"Uh-huh. And how many *poor* women do you represent?"

"As a matter of a fact, for some worthy cases, I only charge costs. It's good for my soul," he said, sounding very virtuous.

"You're an old scoundrel. Why do I put up with you?"

"Because you adore me. All women, young and old, adore me. That's why I've been married—and divorced—four times."

"Oh, no—not again! What happened to Ilka?"

"She decided that she could do better for herself than a broken-down divorce lawyer. She's in Tinsel Town, I understand, living with a producer. The divorce was final last week."

Because he sounded remarkably cheerful, Janice didn't commiserate with him except to say with certainty, "You'll meet someone else."

"Probably. But in the meantime, I'm lonely. So how about having lunch with a pathetically lonesome old man tomorrow?"

"You'll never grow old. And the answer is yes. You can cheer me up, too," she said.

"What's wrong?"

"I'll tell you about it tomorrow," she said. "What time should I meet you?"

"Why don't you come to my office at—say, just before twelve? I'll have Martha make reservations for us at the University Club for twelve-thirty, and we can have a drink in the bar first. You can tell me your sad story—and I'll tell you how much it cost me to get rid of that rapacious little bitch, Ilka."

Janice was smiling as she hung up. Already her mood had changed for the better. Not that she believed Arnold's comment about his ex-wife getting the best of him. If anyone got taken in the divorce courts, it wouldn't be Arnold Waterford, the man the newspapers called the Santa Claus of the divorcé set.

Some of what they said about him was true, that he was shrewd and out for the buck, but he'd been her good friend all her life. No matter what else he was, he was still the one person who would understand her disappointment—and her determination to try again, to keep on trying until she got it right.

CHAPTER FIVE

ALL HER LIFE, ARIEL DI RUSSY HAD BEEN LATE FOR MEALS, FOR doctor and dentist appointments, even for her own wedding, so it was entirely in character that she'd be late for her appointment with the divorce lawyer, Arnold Waterford.

Until she'd married Alex, it hadn't mattered all that much because her parents had become resigned to her chronic tardiness. But not Alex. He never forgave—or forgot—anything she did wrong. And of course, she'd done everything wrong since their wedding day when she'd arrived at the church half an hour late.

Well, today she was finally doing something that should please him. Wasn't she sitting here in Arnold Waterford's office reception room, with its American Empire furniture, red-flocked wallpaper, and walls of leather-bound books, waiting to sign papers to initiate a divorce, just the way Alex wanted?

God knew *she* didn't want a divorce. She'd pleaded with Alex, promising to change her ways, to be a better wife, to be on time, to be charming and sociable when they entertained his colleagues instead of hiding in a corner. She'd even promised to please him in bed, something that was increasingly difficult to do.

But all her promises hadn't changed Alex's mind, and she'd cried so much the past week that her eyelids had a bruised, swollen look. Marriage to Alex wasn't perfect—most of the time, it was barely endurable—but she needed him to keep the demons away. When the nightmares came in the middle of the night, she could banish them only by reaching out and touching his warm body, even though she had to be careful not to disturb his sleep.

Alex didn't like being awakened at night. He'd once told her that this was the reason why he'd become a psychiatrist instead of a medical doctor who got called out in the middle of the night to deliver a baby or sew up some crash victim.

In fact, he didn't care for changes of any kind. His life was divided into neat little compartments—so many hours of sleep

38

every night, meals at regular times, an exercise routine that never varied by more than a few seconds. Everything in Alex's life was regimented, including sex three times a week on Mondays, Wednesdays, and Saturdays. No wonder she, with her haphazard ways, drove him crazy.

So here she was, waiting to talk to a lawyer about getting a divorce, and feeling miserable and very shaky inside. How she envied the dark-haired woman who was sharing a love seat with her and wished she had that kind of poise. Alex claimed that her whole personality had been distorted by having elderly parents, and because he was a psychiatrist, he was probably right—but then they'd done their best to raise her right, hadn't they? It wasn't their fault that she was full of irrational fears and a complete zero when it came to dealing with other people. . . .

The strange thing was that, until Alex had pointed it out, she hadn't realized that being taught at home by her own parents and not having friends her own age had made her neurotic. It was because of that bout of rheumatoid arthritis when she was five, of course. No excitement, no rough play, the doctors had warned. Her father, who'd been ''in stocks and bonds,'' had once wondered out loud where Ariel had inherited her weak constitution because both he and her mother came from such good sturdy stock.

''Old San Francisco stock,'' he'd added, because he was proud of being the descendant of pioneers.

Which made it so ironic that her mother, at the age of fifty-five, had been killed in a fall in her bathroom, and that her father had died from an infected tooth on his sixty-fifth birthday, leaving Ariel an orphan at eighteen.

She'd been in a state of panic when she first met Alex. Because of the heart flutters and sweating spells that her doctor had diagnosed as being psychosomatic, she'd gone to see the psychiatrist he'd recommended. She'd taken one look at Alex and had almost fainted because he looked so much like her father—the same full beard, the same stocky build and piercing blue eyes.

When he'd turned those pale eyes upon her, she'd felt a deep relief, sure that this was a man to whom she could safely turn over her secrets, her doubts and fears, her whole life.

She'd also been—still was—more than a little afraid of him. Which was why she always took such care not to cross him. And wasn't it strange that during his tirade—if you could call such a measured monologue a tirade—when he'd asked for a divorce, he'd said that she was smothering him with her clinging vine ways?

Which just wasn't fair. The few times during their three years of marriage when she'd tried to stand up to Alex, he'd been furious and had said some cruel things about ball-busting women. It always surprised her that he used such vulgar language when they were alone. With other people, especially women, he was so—so genteel. What would his patients think if they heard the words he used during sex? How would they feel about going to a psychiatrist who liked to watch porno on the VCR before he took his wife to bed?

As for telling her that he wanted a divorce—that had come out of the blue.

Of course, Alex had been in a strange mood the day he'd returned from his monthly trip to Washington, DC, to treat a longtime patient, a congresswoman who was still in therapy. After dinner, he hadn't disappeared into his den as usual. Instead, he told Ariel he wanted to talk to her. After she'd followed him to his den, he stared at her, saying nothing, for a long time, and she'd thought she knew what was coming, even though it wasn't Monday. But instead of instigating sex, he informed her, as matter-of-factly as if he were talking about the fall weather, that he wanted a divorce.

"You're a weak vessel, Ariel," he said. "I should've had more sense than to marry you. I need a real woman, not a neurotic, someone who can grab hold and run with the ball."

Ariel could only stare at him, although it did occur to her how strange it was that Alex, who abhorred spectator sports, so often used sports terms in his conversation.

"You'll need a lawyer. I've already talked to James Cravett," he went on. "He'll see that your interests are protected."

He hesitated briefly, his pale eyes watching her. "You do understand that this is a community property state, don't you? Half of my assets are yours—and vice versa, of course. I'm quite willing to buy your half of this house at an equitable price. Because I have my office here, it would be inconvenient to move—and besides, you'd just rattle around here alone. An apartment would be ideal for you—those town houses going up near the Embarcadero Plaza should be more than adequate for your needs."

Ariel had found her voice then and had tried to make him change his mind, but it had been useless. In the end, as always, Alex had gotten his own way.

In retrospect, she realized that her one act of rebellion later had been a little childish. Following the advice of Laird Fairmount, her second cousin and only living relative, she'd made an appointment with Arnold Waterford. The idea of discussing the intimate details of her marriage with James Cravett, who played handball with Alex on Wednesday afternoons, was too humiliating. Of course, she hadn't had the nerve to tell Alex yet. He had no idea that she was here this morning, waiting to talk to a strange lawyer. Not that it mattered. Nothing mattered now that her life was in shambles.

A tiny sob escaped her throat. The brown-haired woman sitting beside her glanced up from her magazine, and Ariel ducked her head and pretended to be absorbed in the year-old copy of *The New Yorker* that was lying open in her own lap. She wondered if it was possible that she'd met the woman someplace. She never remembered faces—or names. Another bone of contention with Alex who never forgot anything, especially a grievance.

She started nervously when the waiting room door flew open, banging against the doorstop. The receptionist, a middle-aged woman with sharp features, untidy salt-and-pepper hair, and a harassed manner, looked up with obvious annoyance. She must have recognized the newcomer because suddenly she was all smiles.

"Mrs. Devereau—I'm afraid you'll have a wait for your appointment today," she said. "Mr. Waterford has been delayed, but I expect him any minute now."

The woman she'd called Mrs. Devereau looked annoyed. Her eyes moved restlessly around the room, lighting first on Ariel and then on the woman sitting beside her; she dismissed them both with obvious disinterest. "Great. If there's anything I hate, it's waiting."

"I did try to reach you at home, but no one answered."

"I left early to do a bit of shopping—and this is my housekeeper's day off."

Her voice was quick, impatient. She was wearing a dark gray suit, the jacket trimmed with mink, and a matching fur hat that looked vaguely Russian to Ariel, who knew very little about current fashions. Although Mrs. Devereau wasn't, strictly speaking, classically beautiful, Ariel was sure that most people would describe her that way, especially Alex, who liked elegant women.

Unconsciously, she sighed, and the woman sitting beside her, who had been watching the newcomer settle herself in a high-backed chair nearby, gave her a sympathetic look. "Waiting is the pits, isn't it?" she said.

Ariel eyed her uncertainly. The woman looked very tweedy in her tartar plaid skirt, wool jacket, and heather-mauve beret. For herself, Ariel preferred soft materials and loose-fitting styles, and seldom wore anything that felt heavy or bulky against her skin. Since her marriage, she'd tried very hard to dress appropriately for the occasion, to reserve the clothes she really liked—most of them retrieved from trunks in the attic—for home wear. Today was an exception because she hadn't been able to decide what *was* appropriate for consulting a divorce lawyer—unless it was sack-cloth and ashes.

She had spent almost an hour this morning looking through the racks of clothing in her big walk-in closet. In the end, because she hoped it would raise her spirits, she had chosen one of her favorite outfits, a misty-green voile with a dropped waistline that could have come right off the cover of a 1924 copy of *Vogue*.

How often she'd wished she'd been born six decades earlier. Her pencil-thin body and long, slender neck would suit the art deco era—and because she would fit in, maybe so much wouldn't be expected of her. The eighties might be a better era for most women—but what about the ones who didn't know how to be independent? How were they supposed to fit in?

"What time's your appointment?" her seatmate asked.

Ariel gave her a shy smile. "Ten o'clock. I was half an hour late, but I guess I didn't miss my appointment, after all."

"I wonder why Arnold—why Mr. Waterford has been delayed?"

"I don't know. What time are you seeing him?"

"Actually, I wasn't supposed to be here until twelve, but I finished my shopping early." She gave Ariel a friendly smile. "I'm Janice Morehouse."

"Ariel Fair—I mean, Ariel di Russy," Ariel said. She decided that she liked the woman's voice—strong and full-bodied. It occurred to her that Janice Morehouse was probably older than her own twenty-two by fifteen years or even more, then wondered why she was so sure when there was no gray in the woman's chestnut-brown hair and only a few laugh lines beside her generous mouth. As for makeup—she wore very little, if any. Not that she needed it. She radiated health and energy, and Ariel felt like a wraith beside all that vitality.

She was trying to think of something else to say when the hall door opened again, admitting another woman.

The receptionist looked up; her mouth fell open. The newcomer was obviously young, so young that her eyelids still had the uncreased look of a baby. Although she was slender, the bright orange sweater she was wearing clung to her body, and her full, well-developed breasts seemed intrusive and vaguely threatening. But it was her hair that made Ariel forget her manners enough to stare. It was red—not ginger or carrot-colored or auburn, but flaming red—and it stood out around her head like a halo gone wild.

"God, look at that!" Janice Morehouse said in a low voice. "She looks like an Irish Zulu."

Ariel wasn't sure what a Zulu was, but she nodded agreement. "Her hair is really red, isn't it?" she ventured.

"It has to be natural," the blond woman the receptionist had called Mrs. Devereau said, looking amused. "Who'd dye her hair that color?"

Janice Morehouse leaned forward to place the copy of *Town and Country* she'd been reading on a nearby marble-topped table. There was a strange look on her face, as if she'd just been struck by lightning—or by an idea, Ariel thought with a perception that was rare to her.

"How about that?" Janice Morehouse breathed.

"I beg your pardon?" Ariel said politely.

"I just had a brainstorm—"

The receptionist's voice, slightly raised and definitely sharp, interrupted her. "Do you have an appointment, miss?"

"It's still Mrs. That's why I'm here. And I do have an appointment. I called last Monday and you said you could fit me in."

"Oh, yes. Morning Glory Browne, wasn't it?"

"With an *e*." The newcomer smiled suddenly. "And I answer to Glory, not Morning Glory."

Ariel stared at her with mesmerized eyes. Strange how that smile changed her whole appearance. With those flashy clothes and all that makeup, she looked sort of—well, cheap until she smiled. Why did she wear so much makeup, anyway, with a perfect complexion like that? Was it to hide the bruise, faded but still perceptible, that circled one eye?

The smile seemed to disarm the receptionist, too. She was soon explaining the delay, telling Morning Glory Browne more than she'd told the others.

"I'm beginning to get worried about Mr. Waterford," she confided. "He usually calls even if he's only going to be a few minutes late. You can wait if you like, of course, but all these other ladies are ahead of you."

"I'll wait," Glory said. "I don't have to be at work until six. Besides, my feet are killing me."

Automatically, Ariel looked down at Glory Browne's feet. She herself favored sandals—handcrafted and custom-fitted to her narrow feet. But the heels Glory Browne was wearing were at least four inches high and the expanse of hose her short leather skirt revealed was black, very sheer. When had clocked hose come back in style? Ariel wondered.

"It takes all kinds," the blond woman murmured. She caught Ariel's glance and added, "It looks like we're all in the same boat, doesn't it?"

Ariel wasn't sure if Mrs. Devereau meant they were all having to wait—or all getting a divorce, so she only nodded.

Janice Morehouse, who had been staring into space, stirred. "What do you mean about all of us being in the same boat, Mrs. Devereau?"

"Chanel—and isn't it obvious? Arnold only handles divorce cases. Why else would we be here if it wasn't for a divorce?"

"Why else indeed," Janice murmured.

Ariel wondered idly if she was one of those women intellectuals. She met Janice's eyes and was surprised by the warmth and lively interest there. She looked as if—well, as if she were enjoying herself, which was strange considering where they were—and what they were here for.

"I'm giving Waterford a few more minutes and then I'm leaving," Chanel Devereau said. "I hate waiting."

Ariel nodded although she really didn't mind waiting. She flushed when Chanel Devereau pinned her with a hard stare.

"You look so familiar—have we met somewhere?"

Ariel shrank back against the love seat. "I'm sure I'd remember you if we had," she said faintly.

She was relieved when the red-haired woman finished her conversation with the receptionist, crossed the room, and dropped into a chair next to Chanel. "Is it okay if I sit here?" she said.

"Join the club," Chanel said, and it seemed to Ariel that the blond woman's smile held a tinge of malice now.

CHAPTER SIX

ONE OF THE LUXURIES THAT WAS ESSENTIAL TO CHANEL DEV-
ereau's well-being was to be elegantly dressed, no matter what
the occasion. Not to be *fashionably* dressed, which was a different
thing, but to dress with impeccable taste. To this end, she had
made a lifelong study of fashion, and was so knowledgeable that
she could identify the work of the better-known designers by a
glance. She also loved to shop. Often she spent a whole day just
going from Neiman-Marcus to I. Magnin to a hole-in-the-wall
boutique near Mission Dolores that she'd discovered by accident,
all this just to find some minor accessory—a belt, hose, even a
single button—to complement a new outfit.

In fact, she often shopped all day and never bought anything
because the shopping itself was enough to keep her happily occupied. One reason she was divorcing Jacques Devereau was because he'd cut off her clothes allowance, declaring that she was
bankrupting him with her extravagance. Which was absurd. The
truth was that she shopped wisely, found bargains that would have
been the envy of her friends were she dumb enough to tell them
that she wasn't above shopping discount houses and factory outlet
stores.

She could go through a sales rack, pull out the one blouse or
gown or skirt, with or without a designer's label, that was a true
bargain. And she wasn't averse to patronizing second-time-around
shops, either. But what she bought had to be top quality—and
totally useful. As she told her daughter, Fern, this was something
Jacques didn't understand.

"I'm not extravagant at all. I'm sure Jacques's mother spends
four times what I do for clothes."

"But it's her own money," Fern had murmured, earning a
sharp—and not very motherly—look from Chanel.

Fern, now seventeen, was the product of Chanel's first marriage, and as such a constant reminder of that old mistake.

Chanel had been sixteen when she'd eloped with the riding instructor at Burlingame Academy, the prep school she had attended. Abdul had been tall and slender; his brown eyes pools of darkness, and he looked, in his close-fitting riding jacket and leather boots, like the Arabian sheikh's son that he claimed to be. They held their nightly trysts in the stable tack room, and his lovemaking had been fervent, his words of undying passion so convincing that she finally had run off with him to Reno to get married.

The problem was that both of them had lied.

He'd believed—because she'd told him so—that she was wealthy in her own right, while Chanel believed that Abdul was descended from a royal Arabian family that Had fallen upon hard times. She also believed he would continue to be great in bed. Both beliefs were wrong. In fact, she quickly found out that he wasn't Arabian at all, that he'd been born plain Alberto Rossillini, the son of a city trash collector in Yonkers, New York.

She might have forgiven him for this, at least for a while, if he hadn't bombed out as a lover. By the time she had realized that her widowed father, until now always so indulgent toward her, wasn't about to support a nobody son-in-law, the honeymoon was over. Not only had the riding instructor lied to her, he'd also run out of steam because the sexual demands of his lusty young bride were too much for him.

So Chanel left Al Rossillini, alias Abdul Hassan, and returned home with indecent haste. She would have put the whole fiasco out of her mind if she hadn't discovered that there was going to be a living souvenir of her escapade. Her father wouldn't hear of an abortion, and Fern was born several months later.

She'd been a thorn in Chanel's side ever since.

To add to Chanel's troubles, shortly after Fern was born, her father had got involved in a shaky bond deal and had lost almost everything he had in a vain attempt to recoup his loss. So Chanel, who may not have come from blue blood but who certainly had every reason to expect to be rich all her life, became relatively poor and a reluctant mother at one and the same time.

When the baby was two months old, Chanel went back to school, leaving Fern with her father. She would have been expelled for her elopement except that her father held the school accountable and threatened a lawsuit. As he pointed out, it was their duty to screen their personnel more carefully. When he added that he'd already consulted his lawyer, they had a change of heart and allowed Chanel to return to school, even waiving tuition for her final two years.

That she didn't become a pariah at school was because her tongue was too sharp and her knack for getting her own back too formidable, but there were a lot of snickers and veiled insults behind her back. The knowledge that her so-called girlfriends were deriving so much pleasure from her downfall rankled unbearably, but she stuck it out, pretending an indifference she didn't feel. Two years later, she left Burlingame Academy with a diploma and the determination to make her tormentors pay for their insults if it took her the rest of her life.

And right now, it looked as if that was exactly how long it would take. She'd married Jacques Devereau when she was twenty-one, shortly after her father had died from a heart attack, under the mistaken belief that Jacques's wealth matched the distinction of his family name. The impressive old Italian Renaissance mansion in Pacific Heights that had been in his family even before the '06 earthquake and conflagration, plus the social circles in which he and his mother traveled—all this conspired to fool her.

So she set her cap for him, let him bed her after a long, hard chase, and married him two months later in a society wedding at Old St. Mary's Church with a reception at the Francisca Club that drew newspaper coverage and an impressive guest list.

It didn't take Chanel long to realize that she'd made another mistake. Not only was Jacques not rich, certainly not to the extent she'd assumed, but he was also stingy to a fault. To pry money out of him became her full-time occupation. Only the fact that being married to a Devereau gave her automatic entrée into San Francisco society had kept her from divorcing him years earlier.

But now he'd gone too far. He'd become increasingly difficult the past year and just recently had declared that not only was he cutting her allowance and putting her on a stringent budget, but that they were dropping out of the social whirl.

Chanel didn't argue with him. How could you quarrel with a zero, a zilch, who had the obstinance of a mule? Instead, she turned on her heel and went to the phone to call Arnold Waterford, the same lawyer who'd arranged for her first divorce.

So here she was, at thirty-four, sitting in Arnold Waterford's waiting room for the second time in her life, armed with a long list of grievances against Jacques Devereau. What had her daughter called her when she'd heard about the divorce? A two-time loser? Well, Fern would thank her when she'd acquired a new stepfather, one who was not only loaded but who had impeccable social connections. . . .

Chanel moved restlessly and glanced down at the thin gold watch on her wrist. It was almost twelve—where *was* that man? She'd already told his receptionist that she had another appointment at one—not true—and that she was tired of waiting, which was true. The woman, a dried-up excuse for a female, had been so vague.

"I'm sure Mr. Waterford will be here shortly," she'd said primly when Chanel had gone up to complain for the second time. "Something important must have delayed him. He's very conscientious about appointments."

Thoroughly bored with the old issue of *Architectural Review* she'd been reading, Chanel let the heavy magazine drop to her lap and turned her attention to the other women in the waiting room. The redhead with the wild hair she dismissed out of hand. Cheap and common was her verdict. The other two women had been here when she came in and by now, they must be bored out of their skulls. If the one on the left wasn't so young, she could've been a straggler from the old flower children/Haight-Ashbury days—all that pale, flowing hair and those period clothes. Expensive clothes, to be true, but obviously out of someone's old trunk— or a costume store. Still, the woman did have an air of—well breeding about her. She also looked familiar, too—but from where?

The second woman was a sharp contrast in her Brooks Brothers jacket, plaid skirt, and boots. Attractive in a preppy way. About ten pounds overweight, but she had great teeth and that thick, shiny hair was a plus. She'd be really good-looking if she'd do something to lighten her appearance.

Not my cup of tea, Chanel thought, and turned her attention to a newcomer, who was just seating herself nearby. Now *this* one was pure suburbia. She'd probably shopped at Macy's for those sensible pumps that fairly shrieked "suitable for town" and that fake-cashmere coat. Her leather handbag, on the other hand, had cost more than the rest of her outfit put together. A gift, Chanel decided. The sort of Christmas present a man bought for his wife when he fell into the hands of a savvy salesclerk.

She realized that her scrutiny was being returned, and automatically gave the woman a social smile. Although the woman responded, her smile didn't reach her eyes. Hurting—the lady is really hurting, Chanel thought, and a rare sympathy made her lean forward and say pleasantly, "What time is your appointment?"

"Eleven-thirty—the receptionist says the rest of you are ahead of me."

"If he doesn't come soon, I'll have to leave," Chanel said, shrugging.

"Are you—" The woman broke off, looking embarrassed. "Sorry, it isn't any of my business."

"We're all here for the same reason," Chanel said. "No need to be coy about it. This your first?"

The woman's face tightened. "And last," she said.

"Well, this is my second divorce, but that's not going to stop me from looking around. In fact, I already have—" Chanel broke off; her eyes shifted to the woman she'd mentally labeled the Flower Child. Of course! *That's* why she looked so familiar. Her name was—uh, Ariel Something-or-Other, and they'd met once at a charity luncheon. The woman had been in the company of Laird Fairmount. In fact, he'd introduced her as—wasn't she his cousin? Married to a psychiatrist—and about to be divorced if all the signs were right. No wonder she was dressed so oddly. When you had the kind of money the Fairmounts had, you could wear gunnysacks and nobody was going to complain.

"You already have—?" the woman prompted.

"Never mind that." Chanel smiled politely. "I guess I should introduce myself. I'm Chanel Devereau."

"Stephanie Cornwall—you have a lovely name."

Her words sounded forced, and Chanel felt a sudden irritation with her. "Come on, lighten up," she said briskly. "You have to take divorce, like any other natural phenomenon, in stride."

"I'm afraid I can't do that. It's probably the worst thing that's ever happened to me."

"Well, think positive. Consider this: You have a chance to start all over. Who knows what will happen?"

"You're right. Who knows what will happen." But Stephanie's words had a hollow sound.

Chanel realized the women on the love seat had stopped talking and were listening. She grabbed the chance to bring Laird's cousin into the conversation. "Oh, say—I think I know you," she said, her voice at its most ingratiating. "You're Laird Fairmount's cousin, aren't you?"

The woman nodded. "Do we—oh, I met you once at that awful—" She stopped, flushing.

"I agree. The Morrisons' bash was pretty terrible. All that ghastly food—and those interminable speeches. If it hadn't been for charity, I would have skipped the whole thing. I do remember thinking at the time that I'd like to know you better. But of course you can't really talk at one of those crushes, can you?"

"No—no, you can't. I hate crowds. Alex says—" Ariel broke off, her eyes suddenly watery.

"Is Alex your husband?" the dark-haired woman asked.

"Yes. He says you have to keep circulating, but I always end up alone in a corner somewhere, wishing it were time to go home. Alex is so good socially. He knows how to say a lot in a few words without shouting to be heard—"

"Well, I'm with you. I don't enjoy cocktail parties," Stephanie Cornwall said, sighing.

"And faculty teas," the woman sitting next to Ariel said. She included Stephanie in her smile. "My husband's at Stanford—sociology prof. Sometimes I think if I ever have to attend another faculty wives function, I'll die."

"But you won't have to now, will you?" Chanel said smoothly, resenting the intrusion into what she had hoped to be a cozy little tête-à-tête with Laird's cousin.

"I don't under—" Janice broke off, her eyelids flickering. "Oh, I see what you mean. Actually, I'm not—"

The receptionist's voice interrupted her. "I'm really sorry, ladies." Strands of mousy brown hair had escaped her chignon, and she looked flustered as she tried to poke them back in place. "That was Mr. Waterford on the phone. He's had an accident."

At Janice Morehouse's gasp, she added quickly, "Nothing serious, Mrs. Morehouse. But the hospital insists on keeping him overnight to make sure he doesn't have a concussion. He suggests that I reschedule all of you for another day—if possible on a Saturday, as he does have such a full load right now."

She bustled away without waiting for an answer, leaving silence in her wake. Chanel was trying to think of an excuse to continue her conversation with Ariel when the professor's wife spoke.

"I have a great idea," she said with an enthusiasm that seemed out of place to Chanel, considering the circumstances. "Since none of us has eaten, why don't we continue this conversation over lunch? As it happens, I made a reservation at the University Club for twelve-thirty o'clock. I'd be delighted if you'd join me. As my guests, of course."

CHAPTER SEVEN

FROM THE MOMENT SHE'D WALKED INTO ARNOLD WATERFORD'S fancy waiting room, Glory had felt out of place. Although none of the women already there stared at her openly, not after the first couple of minutes, she was sure they were laughing at her, thinking she had a nerve, consulting a classy lawyer like Arnold Waterford. Which is why she had a hard time concealing her surprise when she was included in Janice's lunch invitation.

It had been her surprise—and her overdeveloped curiosity—that had trapped her into nodding, thereby accepting the invitation. But by the time they had reached their destination, a shabby marble-and-granite building two blocks from Waterford's office, she was wondering what she'd let herself in for. Even at that late date, she probably would have made some excuse to leave except for her stubborn streak.

"Stubborn as a cross-eyed mule," her grandmother, who had come to California from Arkansas during the Depression, had called it.

"Just plain pigheaded" was her mother's opinion, and if Glory was careless enough to be in reach, she usually added a slap for emphasis.

It was stubbornness that had gotten Glory into prestigious, college-oriented Lowell High School against all odds, and she was secretly proud of it. If she was like her sisters, who had about as much gumption as a lump of clay, she'd still be taking Buddy's shit, wouldn't she? On the other hand, it had been the streak of mule in her that had kept her hammering away at Buddy to get married when she'd found out she was pregnant.

Not that he hadn't been hot for her even after she told him she was expecting. He'd jumped her bones every time he got the chance. But he'd also wanted her to get an abortion, and when she told him that no way was she going to murder her own baby, he'd tried to talk her into signing up with one of those places that

51

pay your hospital bills and then arrange for an adoption after the baby's born.

He also made a lot of hurtful remarks about how dumb she was for not being on the pill, and when she reminded him that it took two to make a baby and he could've put on a rubber, he shrugged and said it was up to the girl to take care of things like that. She really blew up then and threatened to file a paternity suit and make a lot of trouble for him. His contract with the farm team he'd signed up with had a morality clause, so he'd finally caved in and married her.

Putting it like that, the whole rotten mess was as much her fault as it was Buddy's. But that was all water under the bridge. The baby had been stillborn, and she'd learned a lesson. The next time she was tempted to get into anything heavy with a man, she would listen to her head, not her fucking glands.

Meanwhile, she wasn't going to let a bunch of frozen-faced, middle-class women psych her out. With satisfaction, she remembered how quickly she'd jollied the receptionist into acting human. Yeah, she was good at that. Charm, one of her teachers had once called it. Two-faced, was her family's opinion, maybe because she'd given up trying to please *them* a long time ago.

But she could bring most other people around—when she wanted to. She'd proved that at Lowell High when the other kids had elected her Most Popular Sophomore Girl. The same kids had made life miserable for her during her freshman year, and it had taken real guts to win them over by clowning around and pretending not to understand their cracks about her clothes and her red hair and the way she talked.

And because she'd already accepted this lunch invitation, she'd go through with it, too. Hell, she might even learn something.

She followed the other women through brass-trimmed doors that bore a discreet brass sign—UNIVERSITY CLUB—and were so old that the varnish on the wood was feathered with tiny hairline cracks. As she paused to look around an immense underlighted lobby, she almost changed her mind again.

From the outside, the University Club had looked like a thousand other pre-earthquake buildings—a lot of stone and marble, not in the best of condition. But inside—well, the place had class. Yes, that was the word for it.

Although she knew she didn't have it herself, Glory recognized class when she saw it. There might be tarnish on the brass statuary and cracks in the brown leather sofas and chairs, but the faded rugs scattered around the lobby were genuine Oriental, and the oil paintings on the walls were very old, like the ones in the de Young Museum.

And when they went into the restaurant just off the lobby, the tablecloths were snowy white, real linen, and the ornate silver, the fresh flowers in crystal vases on each table, even the elderly waiters in their rusty black jackets, all had the look of something Glory lumped under the category of Class. With a big *C*.

Someday she intended to have it herself—which was why she'd been studying the other women so carefully. Ariel, the one with the long, floaty hair and the rumpled, too-loose dress and coat, she dismissed out of hand. Tacky, tacky. But the blond, Chanel Something-or-Other—Lord Almighty, what she wouldn't give to look like that!

She wasn't quite so impressed with the other two—one was named Janice and the other Stephanie. During the trip over here, they'd walked together, talking about some concert they'd both attended, not exactly cutting the others out, but still—not including anyone else in the conversation, either.

In a different way from Chanel, Janice, the professor's wife, had an upper crust look—and yet, how much could a plaid skirt and a nubby-looking beret cost? Stephanie, now—she was probably the prettiest one of the other women, but that hairdo was right out of a 1970 high school yearbook and her clothes—well, they looked matronly. Yes, that was the right word. Matronly.

The strange thing was that Chanel was so friendly to Ariel. As they were ushered to a table, it was obvious she was trying to draw Ariel out—and having a hard time of it. Glory could have told her it was useless to try to get that one to talk. Couldn't she see that the poor girl was either in a trance or on something—like maybe tranquilizers?

A waiter, who looked every bit as old as the building, came to take their orders. Glory would have preferred a taco or pasta, but neither one was on the menu, so she followed Chanel's lead and chose a luncheon salad. Unlike Chanel, she didn't tell the old guy to hold the dressing. A luncheon salad might be genteel and all that, but without mayo or some kind of dressing, it would taste like shit.

She jumped a little when Chanel, evidently deciding that trying to draw Ariel out was a lost cause, turned to her. "As you can see, I'm counting calories," she said.

"I don't know why," Glory said, looking her over. "You look

pretty skinny to me. Now me—everything I put in my mouth goes right to my hips. I'll probably look like a blimp by the time I'm forty.''

Janice, the professor's wife, leaned forward. "Why don't you join an exercise program? I can't resist desserts, so I take a class three times a week. I've figured it out—if I burn off five hundred calories, I can have dessert that night.''

Glory wasn't sure if she was supposed to laugh or not, so she settled for a smile.

"I love your name—it's really different," the woman went on. "I've never thought my name suited me. A Janice should be all ruffles and bows, and I detest ruffles—'' She broke off as the waiter came up with the carafe of Chablis she had ordered.

Glory gave her a hard look. What the fuck was wrong with the woman? That remark about ruffles was way off base. Ariel had more ruffles around her neck and wrists than a toad-frog had warts. Right now, the poor thing looked like she wanted to sink under the table.

"Well, I don't like my name at all," Glory said briskly. "Morning Glory Browne—that's pretty yucky, right? My old lady must've really been tilting the bottle the day she came up with that one.''

"I rather like my name," Chanel said. "My mother was a Chanel junkie.'' At Glory's blank look, she explained, "You know, Coco Chanel, the fashion designer. I think the name has a certain élan.''

"I was named after an aunt," Stephanie said. "She'd married well, and my folks thought she might leave her money to a name-sake—'' She stopped and shook her head. "Now, why did I say that? I don't think I've told anyone that before, not even David.''

To Glory's surprise, because her voice had been so cool, Stephanie's eyes took on a shine. She dabbed at them furiously, but the tears kept coming. "I'm sorry," she said thickly. "I'm making a fool out of myself.''

"So what does it matter?" Chanel said briskly. "We're all strangers—you know, the strangers-on-a-train syndrome. A lot better than letting down your hair to friends with long memories.''

"That's very perceptive of you," Janice said, nodding. "We all need someone to confide in who's safe. That's why support groups are so popular, of course.''

She waited, as if expecting a comment. When nobody spoke,

she went on, "You know—an idea just came to me. We're all in the same boat, right? We've got a lot of anger and pain to get out of our systems. What would you think if—no, it's too bizarre!"

"You were about to suggest that the five of us form a support group, weren't you?" Chanel's gaze drifted to Ariel's pale face. "It *is* pretty far-out. They're usually headed by a psychologist or a trained counselor, aren't they? On the other hand"—again, her eyes sought out Ariel—"we could have lunch together once in a while. What do we have to lose?"

"You mean—talk about why our marriages failed?" Stephanie said; a frown puckered her forehead. "I couldn't do that. It would be too painful."

A shudder shook her body; she rubbed her upper arms as if she were cold. Glory, watching her, wondered what her problem was. Something pretty bad, because it shook her up just thinking about airing it.

And what about her own problems? Did she really want to tell these women that Buddy was a wife-beater? Now, that would probably ruffle their refined feathers no end. On the other hand, this was probably as close as she'd ever get to someone like Chanel. If she wanted a model to study at close hand—yeah, this might be her only chance.

"What exactly do you have in mind?" Chanel asked Janice.

"Well, we could meet here—say, once a month?" There was an eagerness in Janice's voice that made Glory wary again. "I'm sure I can arrange for us to use the solarium on a regular basis. It's a lovely room—and we'd have complete privacy."

"I suppose I could make it once a month," Stephanie said. "Of course, I'll be job hunting soon. I don't know what days I'll be working—or what kind of hours."

Chanel gave her a long assessing look. "This *is* a community property state, you know. Didn't I hear you telling Janice that your husband's a corporate lawyer? You aren't going to let him cheat you out of what's coming to you, are you?"

"I don't want anything from David except child support," Stephanie said tightly.

Chanel looked displeased, as if Stephanie's words were a personal affront. Before she could speak, Ariel asked, "How many children do you have, Stephanie?"

"Two boys. Fourteen-year-old twins. We're—I'm very proud of them."

Ariel gave her a shy smile. "You're really lucky."

"In that way, yes." There were shadows in Stephanie's eyes, and Glory's curiosity stirred again. Something was really eating away at her, for sure. Was it possible that for all her lawyer husband, Stephanie was a battered wife, too?

In an effort to turn attention away from Stephanie, who looked as if she might go to pieces at any moment, she turned to Chanel. "I heard you say that you'd been divorced once before. You must know a lot about the—y'know, the legal stuff and all."

"I know enough not to let my husband off the hook so easily," Chanel said, her eyes still on Stephanie. "It cost my father a small fortune to get rid of my first husband. This time, it's going to be different. I'm not going to be left holding the bag again." She gave Ariel a bright smile. "You must feel the same way since Arnold Waterford is your lawyer."

Ariel didn't respond to her smile. She looked down at the half-empty wine glass in her hand. "I don't know much about Mr. Waterford—we just talked a couple of times on the phone. My cousin recommended him. And Alex is the one who wants the divorce."

"I *am* sorry." Chanel's concern seemed genuine. She reached across the table and patted Ariel's arm, a gesture that seemed totally out of character. What *was* the woman up to, Glory wondered. Why was she coming on so strong to Ariel?

"It was all so sudden." Ariel's voice was almost inaudible. "I've been trying so hard. That's why I was so surprised when he asked for the divorce."

"Didn't he give you a reason?" Janice said.

"Just that he was tired of me. He said—well, he did say I've been drinking too much, but that isn't true. I have a glass of wine with meals, but I'm not an alcoholic."

"Look, Ariel, don't fight it," Chanel said. "If he wants a divorce, give it to him. But take him for all you can—the house and furniture—"

"The house and furniture are mine." Ariel dabbed at her eyes with a handkerchief—a real one, very dainty and lacy, Glory noted. It was obvious Ariel didn't do her own laundry. Was she more prosperous than she looked in that tacky dress? She evaluated the tiny watch on Ariel's wrist, the cameo at her neck, and the ring that she kept twisting around her finger. Prime stuff—that watch was solid gold, and if that diamond wasn't at least two carats, she'd eat it. So what was it with Ariel—why the weird clothes?

"You live on Marina in that large Tudor with the topiaries in the front, don't you?" Chanel asked. "Doesn't Laird live on the same block?"

"Just down the street," Ariel said. "But I only see him once in a while when I'm taking a walk and he's out with his dog. I'd like to invite him to the house but Alex—" She broke off.

"But your husband doesn't like him?"

"Laird said something once that offended Alex, and he never forgets that sort of thing."

"Well, after you're divorced, you can renew your old friendship with your cousin."

"We never were that close—he's quite a bit older than I am, you know. That time he introduced us at the luncheon, I had come with Alex. It was just a coincidence that Laird happened to be there, too."

"I see." Chanel tapped her fingertip on the table. Glory would have sworn Ariel's words displeased her.

Their food came, and Glory, who had skipped breakfast, dug into her salad and finished it off quickly, wishing there were more. It wasn't until she was buttering her second roll that she realized the others were only half-finished. To hide her embarrassment, she began hunting through her purse for a tissue.

"Would you like a Tums?" Janice asked her.

"No, I need a Kleenex. The hot coffee made my nose run."

Janice handed her a small package of tissues. "You've been very quiet. I guess this divorce business is upsetting all of us."

"You seem to be holding up real good. What's your problem, anyway?"

"Problem?"

"With your husband. I'll bet it's groupies. You know, the kind that hang around men teachers and sports figures and rock stars? It always bugged me, the way they kept coming on to Buddy when he was playing with the Bees. You wouldn't believe the things they did to get his attention—but I don't have to tell you. You must know all about it."

"Oh, no, Jake doesn't—" Janice paused briefly, then went on, "Jake never encourages that sort of thing with his female students. In fact, he makes—made a point of bringing them home to meet me."

"Maybe he was just being clever," Chanel said, her smile thin. Glory wasn't surprised that Janice's answer was defensive.

"Jake isn't a womanizer. He—well, he just likes people. That isn't our problem."

"So what is?" Glory asked, a little bored with the whole subject.

"I haven't come to terms with it yet." Janice's voice held strain. "Next time we meet, I should have my head together enough to—to discuss it."

"Right. Next time," Glory said.

"Why don't we all agree to meet here—say, the first Saturday each month?" Janice said brightly. She took a small pocket calendar out of her purse and studied it briefly. "The next meeting would be October third. If Stephanie is working by then and can't make it on a Saturday, we can always change the day." Janice gave Stephanie a quick smile. "What kind of job are you looking for, Stephanie?"

"Oh—anything I can get. Office work of some kind, I guess."

"In that case, you probably won't be working Saturdays. I'll arrange for a private room so we can talk as freely as we like—is it a deal? How about you, Glory?"

Glory hesitated. Why was Janice pushing this support group thing when she'd been so evasive about her own marital problems? Well, this whole business might turn out to be a bore, but it was a good chance to mingle with the upper crust. If she wanted to change her image—and God knew, she wanted that!—this was the place to start.

"Okay, count me in," she said, making up her mind.

Chanel nodded. "I'll give it a try." She turned a smile upon Ariel. "You *can* make it, can't you?"

Ariel hesitated so long that Glory was surprised when she finally said, "Yes, I'll be here."

"And what about you, Stephanie?" Janice persisted.

"I don't know—oh, it isn't that I don't appreciate your offer, but I wonder if it really helps to air one's problems? It might exacerbate them."

Glory frowned at her. "What does that mean—exacerbate?"

"It means—well, to make things worse."

"What do you have to lose?" Janice said. "We don't have to talk about anything we don't want to. Just being with other women who are going through the same experience should help, I'd think."

In the end, Stephanie agreed to join the group, but Glory wondered if she would turn up the next time. Well, that was her

business. It was Chanel and Janice she wanted to study at close
hand. For one thing, she meant to ask Janice where she'd bought
that plaid skirt. It was very plain, but the colors were really neat,
the way they sort of blended in together. And how did she keep
herself so—so altogether? Not a hair out of place or a chip on her
rose-colored nails or a smudge on her highly polished calf-high
boots.

An image slipped into Glory's mind—of her mother in one of
the billowing tent dresses she wore everywhere, with her hair
bleached blond because she thought it made her look younger
when all it really did was make her look like a blowsy old
tart. . . .

"Just look at that," Chanel's amused voice said.

Glory followed Chanel's look to a young couple who were sitting close together at a corner table. They were holding hands,
and the girl's eyes were very bright, very expectant.

"Maybe I should tell her 'You'll be sorry,' " Chanel murmured.

The other women exchanged glances. Then they were all laughing, even Ariel and Stephanie, and Glory was suddenly sure that
the lunches wouldn't be too dreary, after all. It wasn't that she
needed a support group, but it did look as if she might get a few
perks from those meetings.

Besides, she did want to acquire a little polish, didn't she? So
what better way to start than to use Chanel—and possibly Janice—
as her models?

CHAPTER EIGHT

IT WAS ALMOST SIX O'CLOCK WHEN JANICE PARKED IN FRONT OF
the tall Queen Anne house in Professorville. Because she wouldn't
be going out again that evening, she ordinarily would have put
her vintage compact into the two-car garage, but Jake's sports car
was parked in the middle of the drive, blocking the way. As she
got out, she regarded the house with rare equilibrium—and with-

out the usual mental list of all the repairs and renovations that still remained to be done.

In the mood she was in right now, anything as trivial as termites in the cellar, dry rot on the back stairs, or bats in the attic she could take in stride. Finding the right subject for her doctoral dissertation had been a hard struggle—and, of course, it still wasn't cut-and-dried. She had a lot of work to do just getting the prospectus ready for Professor Yolanski's preliminary appraisal, but this time she had a gut feeling that she was on the right track. . . .

Dr. Janice Morehouse has a nice ring, she thought.

Automatically, she checked the mailbox, found it crammed full of bills and notices and junk mail. A brief irritation made her frown. If it were up to Jake, the mailbox would be overflowing all the time. It never seemed to occur to him to lift the lid, take out the mail, and carry it into the house, much less go through it. Once, when she'd gone to Carmel for a three-day computer seminar, she'd returned home to find the mail stacked under the box with a note from the mailman that he couldn't get any more in.

Jake had shrugged it off, saying that since phones had been invented nothing really important ever came by mail, which sounded quite profound and which was actually absurd because past-due bills and draft notices and paychecks came by mail, didn't they?

Janice smiled, remembering that when she'd pointed this out, he had conceded the argument, a rare occurrence because Jake, whose mind was so facile and quick, usually won hands down when it came to their rare differences of opinion.

She let herself into the musty-smelling entry hall, dropped the mail on a marble-topped library table, and hurried toward the back of the house. Even before she reached the kitchen, a woman's voice alerted her that they had company. Dammit—that meant she'd have to postpone sharing her news with Jake.

When she went into the kitchen, she didn't see Jake, but the girl standing at the sink, breaking eggs into a mixing bowl, was familiar. She was one of Jake's sophomore students, a tall, bone-slender girl with a mass of brown hair, a tan more characteristic of southern California than San Francisco, and coltish legs that seemed to go on forever.

"Hey, honey, what do you say to some canned mushrooms for that omelet you're concocting?" Jake's voice came from the depths of the big walk-in pantry that was one of the reasons he was so enamored with the house. "And how about something to go with it? Jan keeps canned ham in her emergency cache. Always prepared, that's her motto. When the big one hits, we'll be able to cope just dandy. Even an earthquake can't faze my practical wife—"

He broke off as he came out of the pantry and saw Janice standing in the doorway. For a moment, his lean, clever face looked disconcerted, but then he was smiling at her, the three-cornered smile that always made her think of Peter Pan.

"Hi, honey. I brought Teri home for one of your home-cooked meals. Then I saw your note and—"

"Note?"

"Yeah—the one you left on the bulletin board saying you were going out, to fix myself something to eat."

"Lunch, Jake. I was supposed to have lunch with Arnold Waterford at—"

"Well, it didn't say lunch. Besides, you knew I was eating lunch with MacEntyre at the Faculty Club today."

"No, I didn't know. You must have forgotten to tell me."

"But I'm sure—well, no matter. Teri took pity on me and offered to whip up an omelet. I told her I was all thumbs when it came to cooking."

"I can add a couple of eggs to the omelet, Mrs. Morehouse," Teri said hesitantly.

"Why don't you call me Janice? And I'll take over here. You two go into Jake's den and talk shop. I'll call you when dinner's ready," Janice said pleasantly.

Teri stared at Jake expectantly, her soft, childish mouth slightly open. Either the poor thing has adenoids or she has a terminal case of hero worship, Janice thought in exasperation—and if she eats more than a few bites of omelet, those jeans are going to bust wide open and show her tender little arse. . . .

When she was alone, Janice made a salad and got out a can of refrigerated biscuit dough. She arranged the biscuits on a baking sheet and put them in the oven to brown while she popped bacon strips wrapped in a paper towel into the microwave, then added two eggs and a dash of cream to the eggs Teri had been beating, poured the mixture into an iron skillet she used only for omelets. When the eggs were lightly browned but not quite set in the middle, she added cheese and canned mushrooms, and when the cheese had melted, she expertly flipped the omelet onto a heated plate. While the biscuits finished browning, she set out plates and silver on the round yellow-oak kitchen table. If they ate in the dining room, Jake would linger over the meal for ages, laughing and talking and holding court—and this was one evening she wanted him to herself.

Her impatience must have shown because Teri left early. When Jake came back from driving her to students' housing on campus, he was frowning.

"Weren't you a little cool to Teri?" he said. "She thinks you don't like her."

"What's not to like? Sugar and spice and everything nice, that's what little Teri is made of. And I have something to tell—"

"Look, you should be careful how you treat the undergrads. They're pretty damned vulnerable at that age."

The sharpness in his voice startled her. "I was friendly—as I always am with your strays. And since I put myself out several nights a month to entertain and cook for them, I don't think that remark was called for."

"You could show a little more sensitivity," he countered.

"Sensitivity? What do you want from me? I feed them, listen to their troubles—are you asking me to be their surrogate mother, too?"

"It wouldn't hurt. God knows you're always moaning about how you wish you could have a kid."

His words seemed to echo in the empty recesses of Janice's heart. She turned her back on him and began scouring out the sink. "I'll try to be more cooperative in the future," she said tightly. "I'd forgotten that *you* have the monopoly on sensitivity in this family."

"Hey, I'm sorry." Jake came up behind her and turned her around to face him. "Look, this conversation is going nowhere. Let's go back to square one and start all over. You said you have something to tell me, right? So what is it? Something to do with having lunch with your stuffy old lawyer friend?"

"Arnold isn't stuffy—and he's only in his fifties. Besides, I didn't have lunch with him, after all. He had a minor traffic accident—nothing serious, but he had to cancel his appointments, including our luncheon date. As it happened, I had lunch with four of his clients."

"Four divorcées? God, that sounds ghastly. What did they talk about—their ex-husbands?"

"As a matter of fact, we talked about—well, what women usually talk about over lunch. There were all sorts of undercurrents, of course—they're all hurting, more or less.''

''You mean there wasn't at least one barracuda, out to take her ex for all he's worth?''

''One of them—Chanel Devereau—might fit into that category, but I could be wrong.''

''Devereau? Is she related to Jacques Devereau?''

''His wife.''

He whistled softly. ''Old money. Devereau's great-grandfather endowed several buildings and scholarship funds at Stanford. What's his wife like?''

''Elegant—and probably hard as nails under the charm and the designer clothes. But interesting, too. In fact, she was very kind to one of the other women and tried to draw her out.''

''Only tried? Didn't succeed?''

''Well, the woman seemed to be in a fog or something. She told us her husband was the one who wanted the divorce.''

''Sounds like you had some kind of day. How did you get trapped into it, anyway?''

''You've got it wrong. I instigated the whole thing,'' she said smugly.

''Why would you do that?''

''We got to talking while we were waiting for Arnold, and all at once, I got this great idea. I'm looking for a subject for my dissertation, something timely and also conducive to original research, right? What could be more timely than a paper about the effect of divorce on women, limiting it to the year following their divorces? You know—how they cope with going back to work, with being single parents and reentering the dating process, that sort of thing.''

She paused expectantly, but Jake was a long time answering her.

''Honey—look, I don't like being a pessimist, but I think you're going to have to come up with something better than this. For one thing, wouldn't your study be too narrow and limited—with only four women, I mean? And the whole subject of divorce has been done so often. Besides, what kind of theorem can you prove by talking to these women for an afternoon? How do you intend to follow it up? As soon as they learn what you're up to, they'll either dry up or start trying to justify themselves, and then the whole picture will be distorted.''

''But I've solved that. We've formed a support group that will meet once a month—twice a month if I can talk them into it. And the difference would be that it's an ongoing thing, not just four women talking about their divorces, past tense. I'll be living their divorces, as well as the aftermath, with them and—''

Jake stopped her with a wave of his hand; it occurred to her how seldom she got to finish a sentence when she was talking to him. ''I don't like to discourage you, hon, but I think you're wasting your time. The whole subject is just too trivial.''

''One out of every two marriages in this country ends up in divorce these days,'' she said, trying to hold on to her temper.

''Maybe so, but I'm afraid you're just setting yourself up for another disappointment. I don't understand why you want to rush into this, Janice. What do you expect to get out of it except a title?''

''A teaching job at college level. Personal satisfaction. The knowledge that I didn't cop out just because I've had a couple of disappointments. Maybe even to prove to myself that I can do it,'' she said through stiff lips.

''Well, if you're sure it's what you want . . . but I don't have to remind you that you have to get it past Yolanski. This is your third try—I'd do some very serious thinking before I went to him with this.''

''But I already have.''

Jake's eyes sharpened. ''You talked to Yolanski?''

''This afternoon. That's why I was so late getting home. He was very encouraging and told me to go ahead with it. It's unofficial, of course, but he asked me a lot of questions, gave me some good advice. Maybe, now that he's semiretired, he's mellowing out or—''

''You did this without thinking it over for a while?''

''I was all keyed up and I just couldn't wait. As it happens, it was the right thing to do. He seemed flattered that I'd want his opinion this early in the planning stage.''

''Yeah, well, I'd take that with a grain of salt. Besides, it could get sticky, becoming involved with those women.''

''What does *that* mean?''

''Just to go slow. Remember how enthusiastic you were about the last one?''

''I'm going through with it, Jake,'' Janice said stubbornly. ''Besides, the research should be fascinating.''

''How can you be sure the answers you get aren't aimed toward self-justification? People tend to tell an interviewer whatever makes themselves look good.''

''I'm not going to tell them I'm writing a dissertation. To them, I'm just another divorcée.''

''Hold on—you've got an ethics problem here. What if they tell you something that would put them or their ex-husbands in a bad light, such as—well, income tax evasion? What do you do then?''

''I won't invite that kind of confidence. And before I turn in my paper, I'll explain what I've been up to and ask their permission. When they realize I'll be using coded names, that their anonymity will be protected, I'm sure they'll give it. After all, it's unlikely that anyone except Dr. Yolanski and the Graduate Committee will ever read the finished paper—I'm not going to try for publication.''

''And if they don't give their permission?''

''Then I'll shelve the whole thing—but I don't anticipate any problems along those lines,'' she said, hiding her own doubts. ''As for not having enough depth in the study—I intend to do a survey of other divorcées, too. Maybe Arnold can help me there. But these four will be the pivotal ones, done in detail.''

''I hope this doesn't blow up in your face, Janice.''

Janice gave him a searching look. ''Why are you so negative about this? I thought you'd be pleased that I haven't let two strikes get me down.''

''Maybe I don't like the idea of you getting chummy with a group of embittered women, Janice. First thing you know, they'll be putting ideas in your head about how rotten husbands are. Incidentally, how do you plan to blend in with that bunch? Tell them lies about your own marriage?''

''Something like that,'' she admitted. ''I thought I'd make up a few marital problems, using the experience of some of our friends. God knows I've heard enough of that sort of thing to fill a book.''

''It's a snakepit on Faculty Row,'' he said, grinning for the first time.

She smiled back. ''I do hold a masters in sociology, Jake. Maybe I can help them this next year. One of them mentioned her husband's unfaithfulness—she had bruises on her face and the remnants of a black eye. It's my guess that she was a battered wife.''

''Well, good luck. I have a hunch you'll need it. And what say we toddle off to bed? I've got a lot to do tomorrow.''

"Including some yard work?" she said hopefully.

"Honey, I've got two counseling sessions in the morning—and don't forget that my 28-C class is coming for barbecue tomorrow evening. And don't we have something on with Ed and Georgette?"

"That Bach concert—Sunday evening. But you do have Sunday morning free—"

He shook his head. "Don't you remember? I invited several postgrads over for brunch and a rap session Sunday morning. Look, why don't you go ahead and hire someone to do the yard work?"

"Better still, why don't we move to a condo?"

"I know you're kidding but—"

"Who's kidding? No yard work, no repairs, no crumbling walls or peeling paint or—"

"And neighbors crowding you from both sides. Thin walls and no privacy."

"Not if you buy wisely. One of the women I had lunch with moved into a condo last year and she's crazy about it."

"I'm sure she is. But I wouldn't be—and neither would you. After all the work we've done on this place, it would be stupid to sell. We'd never get back all the money we've poured into it."

Janice had to bite her tongue to keep from reminding Jake that she'd said the very same thing when he'd first fallen in love with the old Victorian. She changed the subject instead.

When they went to bed, Jake made love to her, and while she enjoyed the intimacy, she felt oddly aloof, as if she were a witness instead of a participant. Even though Jake didn't hurry, his caresses and kisses, the single-minded devotion that he always brought to lovemaking, left her untouched, and she was still unaroused by the time Jake gave a shuddering cry of climax. He kissed her lightly, told her she was one sexy lady, then rolled over on his side, murmuring something about it having been a long day.

Janice found it difficult to fall asleep. It wasn't that she felt sexually frustrated; she hadn't been aroused enough for that. No, it was just that she felt—let down. Deflated. Jake's judgment on academic matters was impeccable. He'd proved that by his own success. So maybe he was right about her dissertation premise being too general, not original enough.

On the other hand, Dr. Yolanski had been enthusiastic, had told her to go ahead and do a preliminary prospectus, to consult him again when she had something down on paper. . . .

She rolled over, her back to Jake, and because she still wasn't sleepy, she began the ritual she always used when she couldn't sleep, tensing her muscles and then consciously letting the muscles relax, one by one. Even so, she was still awake a few minutes later when Ariel's phone call came.

CHAPTER NINE

FOUR GENERATIONS OF ARIEL'S FAMILY HAD OCCUPIED THE BIG graystone house on Marina Boulevard. In a favored corner location, the house faced the Marina Green, that famous strip of meadow that separates the bay's oldest marina from the city. Flanking the old graystone on both sides was a spacious Italian garden, a rarity on a street where most lots were so narrow that the houses hugged one another like lovers.

Ariel's great-grandfather, who had built the house, had been a lumber baron, not only rapacious in nature but shrewd enough to tie up his money so future generations of Fairmounts couldn't deplete it. His wife had borne him two sons before she died of fever, brought on by bad water in the aftermath of the '06 earthquake; the youngest had been Ariel's grandfather, who had married a Crocker, thereby enlarging his already awesome inheritance.

Ariel had never known her grandparents, all four of them having died by the time she was born. Her parents, who were middle-aged when she arrived, seemed perpetually bewildered by the sickly stranger in their midst and finally solved the predicament by going on with their lives, leaving her to the care of nurses, then governesses and tutors.

It would have been unthinkable to break the genteel serenity of the Fairmount home with anything as gauche as noise, and Ariel grew up a quiet child in silent rooms and empty halls. Sometimes, as she drifted up the gracefully curved staircase or sat with her parents at the dinner table, she felt invisible, a ghost who'd come back to haunt the old house. Because of a family feud, she'd had no contact with her other two living relatives, one of them being a widowed great-aunt, now dead. But because her great-aunt lived just a few doors down the street, she did have a slight acquaintance with Laird Fairmount, her second cousin, enough to build a few childhood fantasies around.

Although they weren't really close, they exchanged words when they met on the Green, and she had overcome her natural shyness enough to tell Laird she was getting a divorce. It was his advice and recommendation that had led her to Arnold Waterford.

Even before her parents' deaths, Ariel had achieved a life of her own, built around music and art and literature. That her taste was untrained and therefore suspect, she was well aware, and she seldom mentioned her preference for the brief art nouveau period at the turn of the century or for the art, poetry, music, and even the black-and-white movies of the twenties and thirties.

Once, early in her relationship with Alex, she had mistaken his silence for interest, and had expressed an admiration for Alphonse Maria Mucha, an artist popular in the twenties. He had informed her coldly that not only was she culturally naive but afflicted with rotten taste. Since then she had kept her opinions to herself.

Alex had been her psychiatrist first, then her lover, and finally her husband. Her life revolved around him, and ever since he'd asked for the divorce, she had lived in terror of the day when he'd ask her to move out of the only home she'd ever known. True, the house did belong to her, but he'd explained that since his office was there, it was ridiculous for *him* to leave. And when she'd asked how soon he wanted her to find another place, he'd shrugged and told her there was no hurry, that James Cravett would make all the arrangements for the divorce and take care of the legal aspects, while also seeing that both their interests were protected.

So the only real change came when Alex asked her to move into one of the guest rooms. Knowing that she'd no longer have an anchor when the nightmares came, she'd wanted to beg him to let her sleep in his room on a cot if not in his bed, but she was afraid of arousing his temper. It wasn't sex she'd miss. Most of the time when they had sex, she retreated into a protective shell until it was over, his lovemaking being the price she paid for not being alone when the nightmares wracked her sleep. Sometimes, when he lay beside her after they'd had sex, his solid presence a bulwark against the night terrors, he would talk to her, describing a difficult case, repeating a compliment from a colleague, using her as a sounding board for some problem that had come up during the day, and for a while she would feel warm and protected and safe.

But she hadn't had even this much for the past two weeks. Mainly, Alex ignored her, and once, when she'd tried to draw him into conversation, he told her that there was nothing more to say, that divorce was the only solution.

Solution to what? she had wanted to ask. Is there another woman? Have you already chosen your next wife?

But she didn't ask him these questions. She kept out of his way, spending most of her time in her room, coming down only for meals. Since Maria, the Mexican woman who was both their cook and housekeeper, and José, their part-time gardener, had always gone to Alex for their instructions, she doubted if they realized she had taken on the status of unwanted guest.

And when the divorce papers were signed and she was forced to move out, where would she go? To a hotel? She knew nothing about hotels or apartments or, for that matter, how to take care of herself. She couldn't cook, didn't know how to buy groceries or clean a house or do her own laundry. There had always been servants to do those things. On their wedding day, Alex had fired the cook, the housekeeper, and the gardener who had worked for the Fairmounts for years, saying they were an extravagance, that using illegal aliens would save money. That's when he'd hired Maria and José, both of whom he paid in cash.

Maybe she could hire a housekeeper after she found an apartment—would there be enough money for that? There was the money her father had left her, of course, but it was all tied up in a trust. Hadn't Alex once told her that it took all of the income from her trust fund just to pay the expenses on the house? If she moved out—surely, that income would come to her instead of going into Alex's checking account as it did now.

Anything to do with money or finances gave her a headache, but even so, she'd intended to ask Mr. Waterford these questions today. She'd been tempted to ask the advice of the women with whom she'd had lunch, but she'd been ashamed to admit how ignorant she was about finances. They were all so self-confident, so sure of themselves. In fact, it surprised her that they even needed a support group.

Chanel Devereau—she was almost as overwhelming as Alex. All sharp edges and that odd half smile, as if she found all of them amusing. Chanel made her uncomfortable, even though she'd acted as if they were old friends. Which they weren't, of course. Maybe Chanel had been so friendly because Laird was her cousin. She had talked about him a lot, as if she knew him quite well.

And the one with the spiky hair and the strange name, Morning Glory Browne—she looked so angry, as if she wanted to tear into someone and tell them off. When that nice old waiter had asked if they needed anything more, she'd stuck out her chin and told him that yes, he could keep her water glass filled like he did the others'. True, he had seemed to—well, not ignore Glory so much as to be a little wary of her.

Of course, Stephanie, the one who had twin boys and lived in Mill Valley, had been pleasant enough even though she'd obviously had a lot on her mind. She was kind of—well, motherly, which was strange because she was so pretty and not all that old. In fact, with that pink-and-white complexion and those sort of melting eyes, she looked like the woman in the Monet painting that hung in one of the guest rooms. Hard to believe she had fourteen-year-old boys.

Which left the professor's wife, Janice. She'd kept things going, had made sure everybody was included in the conversation. She'd been really competent, having them all exchange names and addresses and phone numbers. Well, she was probably one of those club women types, used to organizing things. . . .

The taxi pulled up in front of Ariel's house and she paid the man, adding a tip that she suspected was too generous because he thanked her so effusively. She always got so flustered when it came to figuring out tips. It had been so much easier when it was ten percent instead of fifteen.

As she let herself in the front door, she sighed with relief, glad to be home. The house had its own special odor—a little acrid, like marble dust, with traces of old leather, old paper, old wood, old dreams. No amount of cleaning or dusting or waxing obliterated the odor for long. Not that she minded—it was Alex who complained.

As she started up the staircase, she heard men's voices in the large room off the hall that had once been the library and that was now Alex's office. The walls were still lined with her father's and grandfather's books—not that Alex ever read them, not being interested in philosophy and archaeology and history.

"No," he'd told her once when she'd asked him if he didn't

want to replace them with books more to his own taste. "Leather-bound books are always impressive, and good for one's image."

When she'd first consulted Alex professionally, three years ago, his offices had been downtown in a new high-rise building. At first, she'd been alarmed by the aggressively modern decor, by his sharp-eyed receptionist, and then by Alex himself. His hair, straight and thick and tinged with gray, rose above his forehead like a rooster's crest, and his strong features, his flaring eyebrows, so like her father's, had given her a feeling of security at the same time they intimidated her. But his voice was all his own. Hypnotic and smooth, she'd soon learned that it could purr like a cat's or sting like a whip—and she found it impossible to look away when he fixed his electric blue eyes on her.

When exactly had she fallen in love with him? It must have been almost immediately, because she'd found herself looking forward to her appointments, almost sick with impatience. She would plan what to say ahead of time, embroidering on what she knew in her heart to be pretty dull stuff. At first, he had treated her in a dispassionate, professional manner. In fact, she'd been so sure that he was bored by their sessions that she'd made up a few exotic dreams, just to hold his attention.

Then things had changed. At first, it was just casual touching—a pat on her knee, a friendly arm around her shoulders as he walked her to the door, holding her hand while she described one of her real nightmares. The first time he'd kissed her, it had been so casual that it had hardly registered. Then the kisses became more frequent, and because she had already come to depend upon him, she had stood there docilely the first time he thrust his tongue into her mouth. Afraid that he would get angry, she hadn't pulled away even when he fondled her breast.

At her next appointment, he dropped down beside her on the leather couch where she was lying, and without saying a word, he kissed her deeply, drawing her tongue into his own mouth. His hands moved over her body, pushing up her skirt and when she felt the chilly office air against her bare thighs, a strange lassitude, like a rabbit fascinated by the stare of a predator, crept over her.

Then he murmured that she must trust him, that she needed release from that cast-in-amber world of hers. He would be her teacher, and she would learn how to relax, how to enjoy the nat-ural desires of a woman. He would take care of her—she didn't need to worry about consequences. All she had to do was lie back and relax. He would do the rest, give her more pleasure than she could possibly give herself. . . .

He fondled her gently, expertly, and while she didn't feel anything in particular, she wasn't afraid. In fact, she felt safe—very safe. For a long time, he stroked her between the thighs, his kisses deeper, more intense. In her ignorance, she'd been alarmed when his breathing became strident, when his eyes took on a glaze, because she'd thought something was wrong with him.

His touch became more intimate, more probing, and then he lowered his face and nuzzled her thighs wide open.

"Are you still a virgin?" he muttered, raising his head, his voice so thick she could hardly understand him.

She wet her lips, so embarrassed that it was hard to speak. "Yes," she managed.

His eyes glittered like bits of blue glass. "Good—we'll keep it that way," he said, and pulled her panties down over her knees.

She felt excited suddenly, as something soft and wet quivered against flesh that she hadn't realized was so sensitive. When she realized it was his tongue, her shocked mind screamed for him to stop, but nothing came out of her mouth because suddenly something strange was happening to her—a pleasant tingling that grew more intense, followed by a rush of sensation that bewildered her even as she writhed with pleasure, and then an explosion, deep and pulsing and so devastating that she lost her breath. As she lay there, trembling and bewildered, Alex gave a grunt and raised his head. He kissed her, and she shuddered, repelled by the scent of her own body on his breath.

"Next time it will be better," he said against her ear. "There are other things you'll enjoy—but now it's my turn."

He didn't wait for an answer. He took her limp hand and pressed it against the hard shaft that protruded from his unzipped fly. "Touch it," he said roughly. "I want you to touch it."

When she tried to pull away, he squeezed her hand so hard it hurt. "You want to please me, don't you?" he said. He unfolded her rigid fingers and positioned them carefully. "Do this"—he showed her what he wanted—"and this and this. Don't be afraid. Sex is a natural part of life. And you don't have to worry about getting pregnant if we do it this way."

His eyes were hot, his face a deep red as he moved convulsively under her uncertain touch. "No, do it faster—harder. Pretend you're stroking a cat. . . . That's it—don't stop . . . don't stop. . . . Oh, you're killing me, killing me—"

His body jerked convulsively, and he gave a long groan. Ariel jerked her hand away, staring in horror at the pink thing, so shriveled and wet and depleted-looking that dangled against his thigh now. How ugly, how repulsive—oh, God, was she going to be sick?

She was glad when Alex turned away to zip up his trousers. When he turned back, he was smiling, looking so benign that it was hard to believe what had just happened.

Solicitously, he pulled up her panties, then straightened her skirt. His rich voice spilled over her, calming and relaxing, as he pushed a wayward strand of hair away from her face. "You're like a just-opened flower, Ariel, and I'm the gardener who will keep you from withering on the vine. You're an emotionally frustrated woman, denied a normal sexual outlet. I'll give you what you need, be your mentor, your guide. All you have to do is trust me. You do trust me, don't you?"

And, mesmerized by his touch, his voice, and maybe by her own newly awakened sexual needs, she had nodded.

Two evenings later, Alex came to her house to see her. As if he were a real estate salesman, he inspected the house from top to bottom, poking into every corner, including her father's extensive wine cellar in the basement.

Silently, he surveyed the ornamental chests and settees and chairs from the art nouveau period, the black marble-and-gold fireplace in the library and the black lacquered piano in the drawing room. He lingered a long time in front of the Degas painting of a ballerina that hung over the library fireplace, even longer over several paintings that Picasso had painted in the early twenties, which hung in the dining room, and several Monet paintings, a riot of glowing pastel on the drawing room walls, but he dismissed the collection of perfectly preserved posters by Alphonse Maria Mucha in the music room after one cursory glance.

"Art nouveau and art deco—art decadent, if you ask me," he said as he inspected the statuary of nymphs and flute-playing, sly-eyed pans; a porcelain flapper with bobbed hair, created by Icart, and several black lacquer lamps by von Frankenberg. "Some of those paintings must be worth a fortune. The rest of this stuff is junk."

He smiled at Ariel then. "Well, Ariel, why don't we go upstairs to your bedroom? Since I'm already here, we may as well have our sessions now. It'll save you coming to the office tomorrow."

This time he didn't bother with the casual conversation that usually initiated their fifty-minute appointments. He undressed Ariel quickly, then pushed her down on the bed. He spread-eagled her legs and placed her hands upon her own genitals.

"It's time we started your therapy, Ariel. The scenarios we act out will eventually expel the fears that have been causing your nightmares. In this one, you're a schoolgirl, just come home from school. Mommy is out—and I'm your daddy, and I've come into your room and caught you lying on the bed, playing with yourself. I have to punish you, of course—you do understand that you have to be punished, don't you?"

Ariel didn't like this kind of therapy. Not only was it humiliating to lie there exposed to Alex's gaze, but it struck too close to home. There had been those years, after her mother died, when her father had come to her room, night after night. She would lie there in the dark, the distinctive cologne he wore in her nostrils, listening to his hard, fast breathing and the strange rustling sounds, like dry skin rubbing against cloth, that frightened her even though she had no idea what they were. After a while, he would go away, leaving her bewildered and yet excited, and also filled with shame, as if she'd done something wrong.

Now, finally, she knew what he'd been doing there in the dark, and she wanted to cry because she'd loved her father even though he'd always seemed so old, so remote. During her sessions with Alex, she'd told Alex about those nights when she'd lain there in the dark, hardly daring to breathe, while her father stood beside her bed. Would acting out her fears really help her get rid of the nightmares?

As Alex came toward her, naked now, some part of her, something vulnerable and afraid, retreated from the bed, from reality. A spectator, she crawled far back inside herself, and because it wasn't really she doing these things, she followed Alex's instructions, even though they shamed her and made her gag with repulsion.

Afterward, he held her on his lap as if she really were a child and he her father. "It won't be long before those nightmares about your father will stop," he crooned. "By exposing your fears and acting out your fantasies—yes, I know you have them even if you won't admit it—I'll release you from the devils in your mind. We'll do this again and again until all the old poison has been rooted out. And I'll make it as pleasant for you as I can, of course."

And because there *had* been a shameful pleasure, a dark pleasure in surrendering her will to someone stronger, older, more experienced than herself, she had gone back to him again—and again.

Even after their marriage, she remained a virgin. Although some of the things he did to her were painful, he never took her maidenhead. That her virginity added to his pleasure and had something to do with his own sexual fantasies, she came to realize as she became addicted to the sexual release he permitted her during their love-play. She learned not to protest about his "scenarios," not even the times when they were painful. By now, she had learned to fear Alex's displeasure, his violent rages. Sometimes she wondered why a man who had been trained to unravel other people's psychoses didn't consult a psychiatrist about his own sexual preferences and violent temper. But she kept this question to herself. By now, Alex had become necessary to her, a buffer between her and the nightmares and a world that was so bewildering. Perhaps it was a form of love—to Ariel, it was still preferable to being alone.

And now, although she'd done everything to please Alex, he wanted a divorce. Had he fallen in love with another woman, someone smarter, more mature, and sophisticated than she, someone who was always on time, who wasn't afraid to leave the house, to be in crowds? Someone who could satisfy him sexually in a way she couldn't?

Ariel put her coat away in the hall closet and was halfway up the stairs when Alex came to his office door.

"I was beginning to worry about you, Ariel." The rebuke in his voice was subtle, and she knew this was because he had company. "You so rarely go out these days, you know."

"I—I had an appointment, but it was canceled," she said.

"Well, come have a drink with me. James Cravett is here. He has some papers for you to sign."

Ariel couldn't help a guilty start. Feeling like a sneak thief who'd just been caught with her hands in someone's pocket, she followed Alex into the library.

James Cravett was standing in front of the black marble-and-gold fireplace, warming a brandy snifter between his plump hands. He was a heavyset man; his prominent belly showed the results of a hearty appetite and an indolent nature. Although he was shorter than Alex by some four inches, he was still almost six feet tall, and he'd always made Ariel nervous, maybe because he never

looked directly at her. Tonight he seemed very conscious of her—
at least, he was directing a genial smile in her direction.

Although she took the brandy glass Alex offered, she only pretended to sip it. Alcohol made her sleepy, a condition to be courted
most of the time, but not when Alex was watching her like a cat
getting ready to pounce.

"Well, young lady, it's good to see you again," James Cravett's
too-hearty voice boomed out into the room. "I thought I was
going to have to leave before you got home."

She sank down on a cane-backed settee. Miserably, she stared
into the ruddy liquor in her glass, wishing she'd managed to reach
her room without being caught.

"It won't take but a few minutes. Just a few papers for you to
sign."

"I—I don't think I'm supposed to sign anything until"—she
took a shaky breath—"my lawyer sees it first."

Alex's eyes sharpened. "Lawyer? What lawyer? James is your
lawyer."

"I understand it isn't proper to share one with you."

"What kind of nonsense is this?" Alex demanded. "Who've
you been talking to?"

"My cousin Laird," she said. "When I told him you wanted
a divorce, he asked who my lawyer was. I told him Mr. Cravett
was handling things for both of us, and he insisted that I consult
Arnold Waterford." She hesitated, staring at the dark red splotches
on her husband's face. "Mr. Waterford is—well, he sounded very
nice the times I talked to him on the phone."

"Nice? The man's a shark." James Cravett gave Alex an annoyed look. "I think we'd better reconsider—think some things
through before we go on with this."

"I agree. Maybe you'd better go."

The lawyer rose, gave Ariel a stiff nod, and headed for the door.
Alex followed him out into the hall, and as Ariel listened to their
low voices, she knew that Alex was furious with her. She took a
long drink from her brandy snifter, draining the glass, although
she didn't particularly like the smoky taste of the brandy. Wine,
which had been her father's drink, was what she preferred; since
her marriage, it had become her escape when the world became
too much for her.

But the brandy warmed her belly, and suddenly she wasn't quite
so apprehensive. After all, the worst had already happened; Alex
wanted a divorce. What could top that? On the theory that if one

brandy did so much for her courage, another would do more, she got up and went to the small antique sideboard where Alex kept his liquor. She poured herself another brandy, drank it down, and then refilled the bulbous glass for the third time.

When Alex returned to the room, she was back on the settee, sipping from the brandy snifter.

"Okay, what's this all about? Why did you tell that bastard Laird our private business?"

To her surprise, his voice was controlled; she wouldn't have known how angry he was if it hadn't been for the telltale splotches on his face. She took a long drink from her glass, waited until the warmth hit her stomach before she answered.

"He asked if I was okay. I guess I looked a little pale—"

"When did all this happen?"

"About two weeks ago. I was taking a walk on the Green, looking at the boats, when he came along with his dog. He stopped to talk and—well, it just came out. It isn't a secret that we're getting a divorce, is it?"

When he didn't answer, she went on, her voice stronger. "Laird has always been very kind to me. He used to help me fly my kites when I was growing up, and when Daddy died, he took care of all the arrangements. In fact, he invested the—uh, liquid assets Daddy left me in long-term government bonds. Mr. Waterford was interested in the bonds and in the trust fund, but I couldn't tell him much about it, so he sent me some papers to sign—"

"Bonds? You never mentioned any bonds to me—and what's this about signing some papers?"

"It has something to do with giving him permission to find out more about the trust fund. All I could remember was that Daddy left the house and its contents to me, but only for as long as I live. Then it goes to the de Young Museum—and whatever's still left in the trust fund, too, to pay the expense of turning the house into a museum. I'm not sure I got it all straight, but that's how I remember it."

Ariel felt a little dizzy now; Alex's face had a distorted look, as if it were melting. Very carefully, she set the brandy glass down on the lamp table beside her chair.

"He—Mr. Waterford, I mean—said he needed to know how things stood so he could protect my interests—you know, the way you wanted?" she went on. "Why don't you ask Mr. Waterford about it? Only you'll have to wait until tomorrow because he was in an accident today and he's spending the night in the hospital. I

hope you aren't mad at me. I did follow your advice. The only
thing different is I went to another lawyer. The truth is—well, I
don't like Mr. Cravett very much.''

The splotches on Alex's face seemed to be growing. He turned
abruptly and started for the door. ''I'll be back shortly,'' he said
over his shoulder. ''Why don't you have another brandy?''

She heard men's voices again, which was strange because she'd
thought Mr. Cravett had left the house. By the time Alex returned,
a few minutes later, Ariel had finished her fourth brandy. She had
also made a discovery—she liked brandy even better than wine
because it put a pink glow over everything in the room—including
Alex. She giggled when he took the snifter out of her hand and
pulled her to her feet.

''I've missed you, Ariel. You don't know how hard it's been,
keeping my hands off you lately.''

He kissed her, and when he finally pulled away, his eyes burned
into hers, making her blink. ''Let's go upstairs—it's been a long
time since you've had a therapy session.''

She wanted to tell him that what she needed was a long nap,
but she let him lead her upstairs without protest. When they got
to the bedroom they'd shared until two weeks ago, he closed all
the shades and then switched on a bedside lamp. It cast a soft
glow over the mellow old furniture, and there was a mist in the
corners of the room as if it had been invaded by a summer fog.

''You're a little girl,'' Alex said, his eyes so shiny they looked
as if they'd just been polished. ''And I'm your daddy. I just caught
you in the gardener's shed with a boy. And now I have to punish
you. So take off your clothes—but leave your panties on.''

Ariel wanted to refuse to play his game, but she was afraid of
making him angry. Reluctantly, she began to undress, letting her clothes drop to the floor because she was too dizzy to
pick them up. When she turned to face Alex, she saw that he had
already undressed and was sitting on the edge of the bed, watching her.

''You've been a wicked girl, and it's time to take your punishment.'' There was a singsong quality in Alex's voice that made
her feel dizzy again. ''Come over here, little girl.''

She went toward him slowly. The room seemed a little tilted,
as if it were listing to one side. Alex bent her, facedown, across
his knees, and his hard shaft pressed painfully into her soft belly
as he pulled her panties down. Although she had been expecting

it, the first slap of his hand against her buttocks surprised her, and she gave an involuntary cry.

"That hurt, didn't it? It should. You've been naughty, and Daddy has to make it hurt so you won't do it again. Showing your cunt to that boy was wicked—the only way to make you behave is to punish you"—he slapped his open palm on her buttocks again—"and punish you"—*slap*!—"and punish you." *Slap. Slap.*

The slaps increased in intensity; frantic to stop the stinging pain, Ariel tried to protect herself by putting both hands over her buttocks, only to have him push them away.

"No, no—you're only making it worse," he said.

A sob escaped Ariel's throat as his hand descended once more. They had done this scenario before, but he had always stopped after a couple of slaps and gone on to exact the rest of her "punishment" in other ways. As the rise and fall of his open palm continued, the fog came back, obscuring her vision. Beneath her belly, his hard shaft pressed into her belly, and she knew she would show a bruise there the next day. Will it be in the shape of a penis? she wondered dimly.

The question faded from her mind. Something odd was happening to her now. She was aware of heat—a hotness that seemed to come from within as well as from without. The heat spread over her belly and between her thighs, penetrating deep into her private parts. The pain was still there, but now it was pleasant, desirable, nothing to be feared. A languor invaded her limbs, and moisture formed between her thighs while conversely, her mouth was suddenly very dry. Her tongue seemed too large for her mouth, as if it were growing, and suddenly she didn't want Alex to stop spanking her—

A cry tore through her throat as the pleasure/pain reached a peak. Helpless under the rush of orgasm, she writhed and twisted on Alex's lap, her body moving convulsively.

It was over quickly, leaving her limp and ashamed. Alex was very still, as if listening to some voice she couldn't hear. When he spoke, his voice seemed to come from a long way off.

"So punishment turns you on, does it?" he said. "Well, it turns me on, too. I'm horny as a toad—"

It was later, after she'd satisfied him, and they were lying on the bed together, that he told her he'd changed his mind about a divorce.

"I think we should give it another try. And we'd better continue your therapy sessions, too. You still don't have all the kinks worked out of your mind. Tomorrow, I want you to get that bastard—get Waterford on the phone and tell him you won't be needing his services, after all.''

Ariel didn't answer him. Her mouth was sore, swollen by the excesses of his demands; her buttocks stung so badly that it hurt when she rolled over to her back. She wanted Alex's approval, of course, but the things they'd done—she felt sick, as if she were going to vomit. Or maybe it was all the brandy she'd drunk. That must be it. After all, Alex was so sure the therapy sessions were good for her. Catharsis, he called them.

Later, they ate cold roast and salad and sourdough rolls, their usual dinner on the three times a week that Maria took off early in lieu of a full day off. Afterward, Alex told her that while he wanted her to remain in the guest room because he slept so much better alone, he would be resuming his conjugal visits.

After they'd gone to their separate rooms, Ariel waited until the lights went off in Alex's room before she rose quietly, put a robe on over her nightgown, and went downstairs to retrieve the slip of paper on which Janice had written her phone number from her coat pocket.

She dialed Janice's number, not thinking about the time until Janice's sleepy voice answered. After she'd apologized for the lateness of the call, she told Janice that she wouldn't be joining the support group after all because her husband had changed his mind and didn't want a divorce.

CHAPTER TEN

THE DAY AFTER CHANEL DEVEREAU HAD LUNCH AT THE UNIversity Club—a place she privately thought dreary, stuffy, and hopelessly outdated—she went shopping for a purse to complement a dress she'd bought at a small shop featuring odd-lot merchandise from New York fashion houses. But nothing she saw satisfied her, and she finally gave it up as a waste of time and caught a taxi home. Shopping took dedication, stamina, and concentration; today her mind was elsewhere—in fact, on Ariel di Russy.

There must be a way to use Ariel in her plans to snare Laird Fairmount, but just how to go about it she hadn't yet figured out. The woman was a social cretin, which made her difficult to manipulate. When Chanel had suggested, oh, so casually, that they get together for lunch soon, Ariel had blinked, then looked away and mumbled something about seldom going out.

What exactly was wrong with the woman? At lunch, she'd seemed to be in a trance most of the time. Some kind of debilitating illness might explain it—or alcohol, although there'd been no telltale odor on her breath. She'd had a glass of the Chablis Janice Morehouse had ordered with their meal, but so had everybody else except Glory, who had ordered, of all things, a bottle of "orange pop." So help her, that's what she'd called it. Orange pop. One thing was for sure: Whatever Ariel's problems, whether mental or physical illness, alcohol, or drugs, she hadn't registered half of what was going on.

Not that there'd been much going on except polite chitchat. Which was why Chanel had always found the company of other women dull. If it wasn't for Ariel, she would have opted out of the lunch. No pain without gain was her philosophy. And being bored was real pain.

However, because she did have something to gain, she was going to turn up at the next meeting. Which explained *her*. But what about the rest of them? Why had they all agreed to another luncheon when it was obvious none of them had anything to gain?

Or *was* that true? Hadn't there been something too eager, too accommodating about Janice, the one who was married to a Stanford professor? She'd practically forced the rest of them to agree to at least one more meeting. Come to think of it, it had been her idea for them to have lunch together, and later, she'd been the one who'd suggested forming a support group. Which was rubbish. Who needed the support of other women, especially the types represented by those four?

True, the one from Mill Valley, Mrs. Suburbia, obviously needed support of some kind. So it made sense that she'd agree to a second meeting, especially after she and Janice had hit it off so well. But what about the redhead with the weird hairdo? God, what a hoot she was in those four-inch heels and punk clothes and all that eye makeup. Someone should take her aside and tell her she looked like a Tenderloin hooker. Which, come to think of it, she might very well be. She'd obviously been uncomfortable, for all her brashness and those throwaway quips, so why had she agreed to come again?

And Ariel—she had said that yes, she'd be there the next time, but Chanel wondered if she'd really show up. . . .

The taxi swung to the curb in front of a tall apartment building that was so starkly modern, it clashed with the large turn-of-the-century houses on the rest of the tree-lined street. As Chanel got out of the taxi, a breeze, fresh off the bay, ruffled her blond hair. She gave the driver a ten percent tip, which earned her a less-than-enthusiastic "Thanks a bunch, lady," and hurried into the building.

The elegant, well-appointed lobby was empty, as was the elevator that Chanel entered; as she punched the button for the third floor, she wondered idly what the women she'd met that day would think if they realized how tentative her place in local society really was.

Oh, she had a small foothold at a certain level of San Francisco society. The Devereau name assured her of this. She was on the B list for the larger parties, the charity affairs, the big holiday gatherings, but she hadn't made any really important friends, not the kind who could sponsor her socially and see that she got invited to those affairs that really mattered.

And the girls—no, women now—with whom she'd gone to school? The ones with impeccable social credentials who by all rights should have backed her all the way and been *her* support group? Those bitches had closed ranks against her, had never let her in, not even after she'd married Jacques. . . .

She closed her eyes, repudiating the pain of that old rejection. Her stomach churned, as if she'd swallowed something bitter, but she gritted her teeth and blamed it on the salad she'd had for lunch. What she needed was a bromide—when would she learn not to eat cucumbers?

When she let herself in with her key, the apartment was very quiet. Which was as it should be since her part-time housekeeper only came twice a week now, and her daughter was away at school. She dropped her purse on a hall chair, kicked off her shoes, and turned into the living room, only to stop short in the doorway because it was already occupied.

"Hello, Mother," Fern said.

Fern was seventeen, nubile and petite, with her father's dark eyes and hair, and a small, round-cheeked face that always reminded Chanel of the French dolls she'd collected as a child. Right now, Fern was curled up in a large white lounge chair, a book lying open in her lap, looking like a sleepy kitten as she gave Chanel a lazy smile. As usual, she wore jeans and a rumpled sweatshirt, the uniform of her age group, and was a sharp contrast to the elegance of the room.

It was a few seconds before Chanel echoed her greeting. She always had to make a small adjustment in her mind when it came to having a daughter. She had carried Fern for nine miserable months, had given birth to her after a difficult delivery, had even, at her father's insistence, nursed her for a short time until her milk dried up, but Fern had always seemed unreal, like someone she'd dreamed up in a nightmare.

"So you decided to come home for the weekend," she said. "This is quite a surprise."

"One of those spur-of-the-moment things. I thought we could have lunch together, but you weren't home." There was a faint accusation in Fern's voice that set Chanel's teeth on edge.

"Are you in some kind of trouble?" she asked bluntly, because it was so rare for Fern to seek out her company. They had led separate lives for so long, they seldom had anything to say to each other.

Fern's eyes widened, a trick of expression that irritated Chanel because she recognized it as one of her own. Was Fern mocking her—or had she picked it up unconsciously?

"Why would you say that?" Fern asked.

"It's a natural question. You don't usually make any effort to spend your weekends with me."

"Or you with me, Mother."

"Do call me Chanel. You always have until just lately. Is this some kind of phase you're going through?"

"You *are* my mother—although sometimes you seem to forget it."

Chanel gave an exasperated sigh. "I've done my best. I was only sixteen when you were born—a year younger than you are now. If you had a year-old child to worry about right now, what would you do? Jump with joy?"

"It's a moot question because I'd be on the pill. But if I slipped up and got caught anyway, I'd have an abortion," Fern said.

"What a terrible thing to say!"

"Why terrible? It's the truth." Fern reached out and plucked a grape from a saucer on the table near her chair. Her teeth, as even and white as expensive orthodontics could make them, glistened as she bit into the grape. "And if my rich daddy threatened to cut off my allowance if I didn't have the baby, I'd do just what you did. As soon as it was born, I'd wash my hands of motherhood and go back to school. On the other hand, I wouldn't expect any gratitude from my offspring when she was seventeen, either."

"Enough yet. You haven't been neglected, not by any means. You've gone to the best schools. You have your own car and a generous allowance, and you've never been abused—"

"How would you know, Mother?"

"Are you saying that you *have* been abused?" Chanel demanded.

Fern's eyes shifted. "No. Not physically, but some of the women you hired to take care of me were real horrors. One of them smelled like she brushed her teeth with a clove of garlic. How'd you like someone with garlic breath to put you to bed every night?"

"If I'd dumped you on your father's people, it would've been a lot worse," Chanel retorted. "His parents were really into garlic. I used to think they put it in their coffee, for God's sake."

"But maybe they were warm and loving people, too," Fern said.

Chanel snorted. "Warm and loving? Your grandmother tried to push me down a flight of stairs when your father took me to Yonkers to meet them. This was after I'd found out he was Italian and not an Arabian sheikh. It was a ghastly experience. She claimed I was a witch who had put a spell on her son, and she used to give me the sign"—she extended her index and little fingers—"every time she saw me. It didn't matter that he'd lied his tongue off about his background, that he was twenty-eight to my sixteen."

"I'm really loaded with great genes, aren't I?" Fern drawled. "A liar and a superstitious old bitch on one side—and an embezzler on the other—"

Chanel reached her in three long strides. She seized Fern's slender shoulders and gave her a hard shake. "Don't you ever—*ever*—say that about your grandfather again. He was a wonderful man—it was his filthy partners who altered those books and put all the blame on him. If he hadn't had that heart attack, he would've proved it eventually, too."

Fern struggled to get away, and Chanel let her go, feeling a little ashamed now.

"Let's drop the whole subject. Since you are home, why don't we go out to dinner?" she said in repentance, although the prospect of a whole evening in Fern's company made her groan inwardly. "As it happens, I have a free evening."

"You have a lot of free evenings since you and Jacques split, don't you?" Fern's expression was bland. "Have you lost interest in the—uh, social whirl?"

Chanel bit her lip to keep from screaming at her. Irritating child—no, not really a child anymore. It was surprising how mature Fern looked these days. . . .

She forgot her pique as she studied her daughter, trying to be objective. Not a raving beauty, but she did have a certain—well, air. Certainly, the boys seemed to go for her. Which was all very strange because Fern didn't look sexy, not with those too-narrow hips and those too-small breasts. In fact, she looked more like a boy than a woman.

On the other hand, she did have that marvelous hair—thick and manageable and black as midnight—and those outsize eyes that gave her a deceptively innocent look. Fey, Jacques had called her, and then had gone on to say Fern always looked as if she'd just been dancing with the fairies on the lawn. Funny how only she, her mother, seemed to notice that under that wide-eyed innocence, Fern was just like her. Practical, self-serving, and hard as rocks.

Maybe—yes, maybe it was time to think about marrying her off. Not to some callow kid who couldn't support her. To someone older, someone substantial.

Fern's school grades were too average for a scholarship—and tuition for a good school like Smith or Radcliffe was outrageously high. Nor did she have any special talent that might get her an acceptable job—say, in publishing or interior decorating or fashion. She, personally, had no intention of supporting an adult daughter. It made good sense to see that Fern married someone comfortably off and socially acceptable, especially because Fern had never expressed any interest in having a career.

In fact, her daughter's only passion was horses, a very expensive passion, what with boarding fees, vet bills, and the price of oats. Until now, Jacques, in a rare quirk of generosity, had been paying the bills for that hayburner Fern was so crazy about, but this would end once he realized that the divorce was going to cost him everything she could get her hands on. . . .

"What are your plans once you graduate next spring?" Chanel

asked. "Your grades probably won't qualify you for a really good college, you know, even if I could afford to send you there."

"Oh, I'll think of something," Fern said. "I might even get married."

"Married? Are you serious about some boy?"

"Not yet. But when it's the right time—who knows?" She gave Chanel a sidelong look. "I can't see myself working at some grubby job. Which leaves marriage. I'm sure you don't want me on your hands for the rest of your life, right?"

Chanel frowned at her. It was uncanny the way Fern sometimes seemed to pick her thoughts out of the air. . . . "Well, be careful. Make sure the man can support you the way you're accustomed to. You have some very expensive tastes. I made a couple of mistakes along those lines, you know."

"I'm sure number three will be really loaded," Fern said.

There was a tinge of malice in her smile as she rose, stretching like an indolent kitten. "I'd better get dressed—how about trying out that new French restaurant on Polk? A friend told me it was really super."

Chanel winced. Superexpensive was what Le Petit Lapin was. And she never enjoyed spending her own money on anything as transitory as food.

"I've got a better idea." Chanel pumped enthusiasm into her voice. "Why don't I fix an omelet and a salad, and we can eat in front of the fireplace? We can watch TV later—or just talk."

"But it would be so neat, dressing up and having dinner at that French restaurant, just the two of us."

Chanel eyed her suspiciously. "What are you up to, anyway?"

Fern wasn't quick enough. Before her eyelids dropped, her eyes revealed what could be discomfiture. "I don't know what you're talking about, Mother."

"You're a junk food addict—you don't give a damn about French food. So what's going on here?"

"As it happens, I *am* interested in French cooking. But the real reason I want to go out to dinner with you is because—well, the kids at school are always bragging about the great places their parents take them, and I never can—not without lying."

"I see," Chanel said. "Very well. We'll go to Le Petit Lapin. I'll phone for reservations—if it isn't too late."

"I already have, Mother. I figured we could cancel them if you couldn't—y' know, make it." She gave Chanel another wide-eyed look. "I'm glad it's just the two of us."

Feeling a little flattered although still suspicious—when had Fern ever been thrilled at the prospect of spending an evening alone with her?—Chanel went to get dressed. As she looked over her wardrobe, she tried to remember the last time she'd had dinner out with her daughter. How quickly Fern had changed from a child to an adult, as if she'd had a sudden spurt of growth hormones. If people started counting up years, they would realize that Fern's mother had to be at least thirty-four instead of the thirty-one she claimed. Well, she wasn't likely to run into anyone she knew tonight. Le Petit Lapin, for all its fancy decor and exorbitant prices, had yet to be taken up by the people who counted.

But later that evening, when they reached the restaurant, Chanel discovered that she'd been wrong about that—very wrong.

Laird Fairmount, she thought. Of all people . . .

They were being seated when she glanced up and found herself staring straight at Laird Fairmount's face. It was a very attractive face. That had been one of the things she'd taken into account when she'd decided to make him her third husband. No more bedding down with a gnome like Jacques. She'd thought it wouldn't matter that she found Jacques sexually unattractive, but it had—at least at first when he'd still been fumbling around, glorying in the manhood thing.

Later, when she'd moved to a separate bedroom, it hadn't been a problem. She'd taken care of that by using a combination of excuses and pretended illnesses and even a vague "female complaint." Jacques had been old-fashioned enough to believe her— or if he hadn't, at least he'd never complained.

But this time she wanted a husband who could perform well in bed, someone to whom she didn't have to invent excuses. The truth was, she liked sex—and it was such a bore, finding trustworthy bed partners all the time. In fact, with things like herpes and AIDS a problem, it was foolish to sleep around indiscriminately.

So wasn't it lucky that Laird was so attractive? Oh, not in a conventional way. His features were irregular, a bit too lean, his nose too aquiline. His shoulders were a touch narrow, and for all his popularity, he was reserved, maybe even a little shy, which seemed ridiculous in a man who had more millions than he could count. But his eyes were very handsome indeed, and he had a first-rate smile. . . .

She realized that while she'd been staring, Laird had left his table and was coming toward her. It was the first time he'd shown more than a polite interest in her, and she had to hide her surprise when he stopped to smile down at her.

"Good evening, Mrs. Devereau," he said pleasantly.

"Surely we're Chanel and Laird by now," she countered.

"Chanel, then. I ran into Ariel this evening as I was leaving the house. She told me she'd had lunch with you last Saturday, that you were very kind. I really appreciate that—she's a very lonely and confused young woman these days, I'm afraid."

Only *these* days? Chanel wanted to say as she gave Laird her best smile. "Ariel is very charming. I hope we can become friends. She'll need friends, what with the divorce and all."

"As it happens, the divorce is off." The crease between his eyebrows deepened. "I can't help being sorry about that. Alex isn't good for her."

"Then, she needs friends even more. I'll give her a ring and see if we can't get together for lunch. Maybe you'd like to . . ." She let her voice trail off.

"Like to join you? Why don't I call you next week, and we'll set a date we can all agree on."

Fern bent forward to pick up her glass of mineral water, attracting Laird's attention; her eyes guileless, she smiled up at him, and Chanel realized she had no choice but to introduce them.

"This is Fern," she said sweetly. "She's visiting me for the weekend. She goes to Burlingame Academy, my old school."

"Nice meeting you, Fern," Laird said. "Dinner out must be a treat for you after school food."

"It really is—and so is having Mother all to myself for an evening," Fern said.

Laird's eyelids flickered; Chanel could almost see him adding up the years. "So you're Chanel's daughter," he said. "I can see the resemblance now."

"Fern looks more like her father," Chanel said. "It was one of those childhood infatuations. I was fifteen, just a child really— and very romantic. Abdul was terribly handsome, related to Arabian royalty, and a wonderful horseman, too, so I was quite literally swept off my feet." Her laugh tinkled out in the room.

Laird smiled, his eyes still on Fern. "That happens. I remember my first crush—on an actress I saw in some stage show. She must have been my mother's age, but that only made her more attractive."

A waiter came with their menus, and Laird excused himself,

saying he had to return to his own party. When the waiter had taken their orders and was out of earshot, Fern turned to her mother. "Why did you tell Mr. Fairmount that junk about my father being Arabian royalty?"

"Would you want him to know that your father was a glorified stable boy, one generation out of a Florence, Italy, slum? That your grandfather was a garbage collector? You should know by now that people take you at face value. If you're smart, you present the best image you can. And don't look so superior. What do *you* tell your friends about your father?"

"I tell them the truth—that I don't remember him, that he was really into horses, that the two of you had a whirlwind romance—and that you were widowed very young," Fern said, deadpan.

Chanel was surprised into a laugh. "You're learning fast, Fern."

Fern was quiet a moment, her eyes pensive now. "It's really strange, isn't it? You can do just about anything you want. What really matters is not getting caught."

"It's tough out here in the real world," Chanel said.

The waiter arrived with their orders. Fern ate her coq au vin with a healthy appetite, and finished the meal off, to Chanel's disapproval, with an éclair. Half of Chanel's sole meunire was still on her plate by the time Fern had finished her dessert.

"Are you going to eat that fish, Mother?" she asked, eyeing Chanel's plate.

"No—and neither are you. It's time you started watching your calories. You can't be too thin—"

"Or too rich. So I've heard. But I'm still hungry."

"You won't be in fifteen minutes."

Fern looked sulky, but she dropped the subject. "What was that all about—what Mr. Fairmount said about you being kind to his cousin? I didn't know you made a habit of having lunch with other women."

"I don't make it a habit. I had an appointment with my divorce lawyer, and at the last minute, he was detained, so I had lunch with the other women who were waiting in his office. Laird—Mr. Fairmount's cousin was one of them."

"It was kind of you to be so kind to her." Fern's voice was smooth, but Chanel gave her a sharp look. "What did you talk about—all of you being strangers, I mean?"

"Actually it was rather interesting . . ." Chanel told her about Ariel, about Morning Glory Browne, which Fern thought was a

really neat name. As she enlarged on the experience, making a
good story out of it, Fern listened intently, smiling several times.

How like her father she is, Chanel thought involuntarily. She
has his smile. What else has she inherited from him—and from
me?

She was ordering coffee when she noticed how often Fern
glanced around the room, obviously looking for someone. Fern
must have found the object of her search because suddenly she
smiled—a thin-edged smile that held both satisfaction and something less pleasant.

A few minutes later, when a tall, rangy busboy came to clear
their table, Fern was staring off into space as if she weren't aware
of his existence. But it was obvious that the young man was aware
of her. His eyes averted, he quickly stacked their dishes on his
tray, and started to turn away. It was then that Fern gave a theatrical start.

"What are *you* doing here, Stephen?" she asked.

"I work here sometimes," he mumbled.

"Imagine that." Fern widened her eyes at him. "What's the
big secret? There's nothing wrong with honest labor—especially
if you need the bread. What's uncool is telling the kids at school
that you're going to spend the weekend on your uncle's yacht."

The boy's face was dark red now. "I have to get back to
work—"

"You do that. Oh, but first, how about filling our water gob-
lets—or are you allowed to serve the customers?"

"I'll get your waiter. Is there anything else?"

"Not a thing," she said sweetly.

"Well—see you at school," he said awkwardly, and hurried off
with his loaded tray.

Chanel stared at her daughter. "Why were you needling that
boy?"

"Whatever do you mean?"

"You deliberately chose this restaurant because he works here.
And don't waste that wounded-doe look on me. I'm on to your
tricks."

"I hardly know Stephen—he goes to Burlingame Academy, but
he doesn't belong to my crowd. In fact, he's not my type at all."

"What happened? Did he stand you up?"

Fern flushed. "I hardly know him," she said again.

"Indeed. Let's see if we can't get to the bottom of this since
it's already cost me the price of two very expensive meals. This

Stephen did something to you he needed to be punished for. What was it?''

''Well, if you must know . . . he told one of my friends I was a snob, that he wouldn't go out with me if I paid him to. As if I'd go out with a dork like that. The only reason he's at Burlingame Academy is because he got a basketball scholarship—''

''So how did you find out he worked here weekends?''

Fern's eyes slid away. ''I have my ways.''

''Uh-huh. Translated, that means you did some snooping, probably through the office files at school, and for some puerile revenge, you let me shell out almost eighty dollars for a wretched meal that tastes like sawdust! Well, it's coming out of your allowance—do you understand? Out of *your* allowance, young lady!''

Fern gave her a sulky look. ''I couldn't let him get away with it.''

''It was stupid. You're going to get maligned many times in your life. Make up your mind to it. This boy—he's a nobody. All he did was bend your pride a little. Do you understand what I'm saying?''

''Oh, I understand all right.''

''Good. Then, let's drop it. And maybe I'll forget about taking the dinner out of your allowance, after all.''

Chanel was inclined to be generous because it had just occurred to her that Fern's little plot had worked to her advantage. Despite the encouragement she'd given Laird, he had never made any effort to seek out her company before. He must be very fond of his cousin to make such a point of thanking her for being kind to Ariel. But if she hadn't run into him tonight, would he have bothered to call her up to tell her so? Somehow she doubted it. So she had Fern to thank for her luncheon date with Laird—if you could call a threesome a real date.

One thing was for sure—if Ariel wasn't getting a divorce, she would have no real reason to come to that luncheon next month—except maybe curiosity.

Fern had just turned eleven when it first occurred to her that what she felt for Chanel held no resemblance to what her friends felt for their mothers. She'd wanted to be important to Chanel, to win her approval, but at the same time she'd wanted to punish her, too.

She also wanted to be better-looking than Chanel, something she was well aware was never going to happen. Where Chanel was all flawless complexion, silver-blond hair that needed only a little cosmetic help, and incredible dark green eyes, with a slender figure that never seemed to gain one ounce, Fern was dark-haired, her body too narrow, her legs too long, her breasts too small. True, people were always complimenting her on her eyes and smile, but while she was growing up, all she'd seen in her mirror was someone who looked more like a boy than a girl.

Then, when she was thirteen, she made an important discovery. Just by turning up the voltage of her smile, by looking demure and widening her eyes as Chanel did, she could get the attention of just about any boy she wanted. That the sultry look was deceptive, because making out with boys left her cold, didn't seem to matter. Something about her, some trick of expression or deceptive air of coolness, turned on boys, and a girl who is popular with boys has all the girlfriends she wants as long as she doesn't get greedy and try to hog them all for herself.

When she was a child, she'd tried to gain Chanel's attention by naughtiness—tantrums and tricks such as locking Jacques's cat in Chanel's closet overnight. All she'd achieved for that last escapade was to be banished to a highly disciplined boarding school, one far enough away that Chanel wasn't obligated to visit too often.

Because Fern was a listener at doors, she'd heard her mother and stepfather talking about her the week before she'd been sent away.

"A kid that age should be with her parents," Jacques had protested.

"Fern's unmanageable," Chanel said. "Maybe some discipline will teach her to appreciate her home."

Jacques had changed the subject then, something for which Fern had never forgiven him. But being banished to boarding school had done one thing for her: It had made her finally realize how hopeless it was to try to win her mother's love or even her attention. So she'd turned her energies to other things, such as winning the praise she craved from her teachers. By being accepted by the "in" clique at school. By getting elected class president in her junior year at Burlingame Academy and winning the female lead in the class play two years running.

One thing hadn't changed: She still wanted to pay Chanel back in the worst way.

When Chanel called to say that she had left Jacques, Fern wasn't sure whether to be sorry or not. After she'd enrolled at Burlingame Academy, with its elitism and snobbishness, she'd quickly become aware that being Jacques's stepdaughter had a certain snob appeal to the girls—and teachers—who counted. After all, Devereaus had been attending the Academy since the turn of the century. So Jacques had his uses even if she did find his hot eyes and his dry hands distasteful. The way he looked at her sometimes made her want to barf—and besides, he was so damned stingy with his money.

The only reason he'd bought her a horse was because she'd let him have a few surreptitious feels—and then promised not to tell Chanel.

She had cut school for one purpose today. She was itching to get back at Stephen Korel. Originally, she'd gone all out to date him because everybody knew he was a shoo-in for Harvest Dance King—and therefore the girl he escorted to the dance would be Queen. But after she'd tried all her tricks on him, she'd been painfully surprised when he'd asked Charlene Lacey to the Harvest Dance instead of her. That alone would have been enough to enrage her. The remark he'd made about her, repeated so gleefully by a so-called friend, had been the last straw.

So she'd gotten into the school's office files one night, had learned from the work permit in Stephen's records that he'd been lying about where he spent his weekends. That's when she'd cooked up a plan to get her revenge. He'd been a fool to lie. The thing he hadn't understood, maybe because, for all his popularity, he wasn't really one of them, was that no one at school cared about his grubby job. A lot of the seniors took weekend jobs as a kick. It was the fact that he'd *lied* about it that could ruin things for Mr. Cool.

Strangely, now that she'd given Stephen a hard time, she really didn't want his stupid little secret to get out. It was enough that *he* knew she could expose him anytime she wanted to. Well, she'd play it by ear. Meanwhile she had something else to think about— the diary she'd found locked away in Chanel's desk drawer.

She'd been alone for several hours today, waiting for Chanel to turn up, which had given her plenty of time to hunt—and find— the key to the drawer in Chanel's elegant little Queen Anne desk that she always kept locked. Mainly, the small leather diary she found there was an account of Chanel's social engagements, remarks about the people she'd met, what she'd worn, bits of scandal she'd heard. There were long gaps in the entries, as if she'd lost interest from time to time, but here and there, Chanel had really let down her hair, such as an account of her successful campaign to marry Jacques. Most intriguing of all, the later pages of the diary gave an item-by-item description of her attempt to hook someone she called "L."

And now Fern knew who this mysterious "L" was—that absolutely awesome Laird Fairmount. He looked so—well, sensitive. And very sexy. Of course, he was pretty old, but his smile really turned her on. All those white teeth and that tanned skin and his devastatingly short upper lip—she got shivers down her spine just thinking about his mouth.

God, he must be great in bed. Those sensitive types usually were—or so she'd heard. And Chanel would land him, of course. What man could resist her mother when she really turned on the charm, even though she *was* getting up there, thirty-four now. The thing was, Chanel wouldn't be chasing him so hard if he weren't really loaded.

Well, Fern had no quarrel with that. Money was something she meant to have someday. Tons and tons and tons of it. So much money that she could do anything she wanted, have a whole closetful of designer clothes like Chanel, live in a big, big house, and have a whole stableful of horses.

So she intended to be rich someday. She hadn't been kidding when she'd told Chanel that she might marry young. And it wouldn't be to a loser like her father—or her stepfather. No, it would be someone like Laird Fairmount. He might be old, probably in his mid-thirties, but he was really sexy.

What a shame that Chanel had seen him first.

As for Chanel's diary, that stuff about scheming to get invited to the same parties, all that jazz—it was clear it hadn't worked. From what she'd seen tonight, Laird was still pretty indifferent to her mother. Which was strange, because Chanel's plan to land him should have worked. There were all those "accidental" meetings with Laird—once Chanel had even staked out a bench in the plaza near his brokerage firm, had waited there around noon for three days running until he finally passed on his way to lunch. She obviously hadn't been asked to join him because she'd written a big black *DAMMIT!* in the margin of her diary.

Then she'd managed to get invited to several parties where he'd be—once she must have done some arm-twisting because she'd written that she was on "Shanna's list" now and it hadn't been worth it because Laird hadn't even asked her to dance.

Well, Chanel might not have such an easy time snagging him, after all. Sure, she was an expert on men, but didn't she realize that a man Laird's age was probably looking for someone younger? If he was rich, he could pick and choose—it would take a really clever woman to get a proposal out of someone like that.

On the other hand, Chanel's tactics had certainly worked tonight. Laird had been taken in by her pretense of interest in his cousin. And it was all an act, because Fern knew her mother was indifferent to most women—including her own daughter.

So she might end up with a brand-new stepfather, one who was not only rich but also some kind of fox. It would be interesting to see if the same tactics would work for her. Until now, she'd just let nature take its course. But making it with boys, no matter how big on campus they were, was far different from making it with someone older and more sophisticated.

Maybe she'd give it a try with an older man, just for the hell of it. It was one way to prove that she was just as smart as her mother. In fact, she didn't really need Chanel to show her how to get what she wanted out of life—including a rich husband of her own.

CHAPTER ELEVEN

STEPHANIE WAS FRYING BACON IN THE BIG, SUNNY KITCHEN she'd decorated so lovingly just six months earlier and for which, at present, she didn't give a damn. Since David had left, it was surprising how little she cared about things that once seemed so important—like finding the just-right vase to complement the Gloria Vandenberg wallpaper in the reception hall or calling around to locate the framed French cartoons she'd seen in a *House and Garden* linoleum ad that would be perfect for the downstairs powder room.

Was her preoccupation with decorating these past months the reason why David had been so susceptible to Ted Towne's sexual overtures? Had she neglected him for the new place she'd been so proud of? "House proud," he'd called her once. At the time she'd thought he was teasing her, but hadn't there been a sting in that remark?

The bacon in the frying pan made a popping sound, and hot fat splattered on her hand before she could jump back. She expelled an explosive "Damn!" and popped her stinging fingers in her mouth. No, she was *not* going to blame herself for David's aberration. Even now, when she should be getting used to it, she felt a little nauseated every time *that* image crept back into her mind—Ted's slight, city-white body pressed against David's huskier, darker one . . . their obscene position . . . David's moans . . . the shock on his face when he'd opened his eyes and seen her standing in the doorway. . . .

And then, like acid searing proud flesh, an older image edged out the first, and in her mind's eye, she saw them again, as clearly as the day it had happened—Jeff, her older brother, the person she'd always gone to for comfort when her friends or her teachers or her parents let her down, and Claude, his best friend.

People in their small Oregon farm community had laughed at Claude because of his strange ways. Everybody wondered how Jeff, so popular and good-looking, could be friends with such a misfit.

"That Evans boy's got a soft heart," they'd said. "Always bringing home strays."

It had happened in the weathered old barn behind her family's farmhouse. The barn had been abandoned, replaced by a larger, more modern one, and it was a good place to hide out because nobody else ever went there those days. She'd gone to be alone, as she often did, climbing up into the loft, which still smelled of hay and the sweet-sour odor of salvage.

She stretched out on her stomach to look at a magazine she'd found under her brother's mattress. The magazine puzzled her. All those pictures of men—why would Jeff want to look at pictures of men, she'd wondered, both fascinated and repelled by so much naked masculinity.

Although usually tolerant of his younger sister, Jeff had a temper that could erupt unexpectedly at some small offense, such as when Stephanie went into his room uninvited. He was also possessive about his belongings, so when Stephanie heard his voice, she hunkered down behind an old footlocker to hide.

That's why, a few minutes later, she witnessed what was so inexplicable to a nine-year-old. As she stared through a crack between the loft's warped floorboards, she saw a strange tableau below. Her brother's friend Claude was kneeling in front of Jeff—as if he were saying his prayers, she thought—his arms loosely embracing Jeff's hips, his face buried in Jeff's belly. Jeff, his jeans around his ankles, stood with his eyes closed, his head thrust back, his face twisted with what seemed to Stephanie's young eyes to be pain. Although she didn't understand what Claude was doing to her brother, she knew it was wrong, something so evil and disgusting that she suddenly felt sick.

It was the retching sound she made that betrayed her. A minute later, Jeff was hauling her down from the loft. His face red with anger, his eyes blazing, he threatened to twist off her arm if she told on them—Jeff who had always been so kind to her! It was the worst thing that had ever happened to Stephanie, even worse than having her tonsils out when she was six or the time she'd lied to her father and he'd washed her mouth out with laundry soap.

Claude didn't join in. He stood looking at her with his oddly shaped eyes, and his silence frightened her far more than Jeff's threats did. She knew, instinct told her, that he was capable of doing worse things to her than twist off her arm.

Sobbing and hiccupping, she promised not to tell, and after a while, they let her go, but she lived in terror after that, afraid to be alone, afraid to leave the house, even to walk along the farm road to the highway where she caught the school bus, and she avoided Jeff as much as possible, although she grieved for the loss of their old friendship.

That her fear was justified she had no doubt. They—Jeff or Claude or both of them together—made sure of that. Things happened. Her schoolbooks disappeared off the porch where she'd left them and turned up later under a bush, wet and dirty, earning her a whipping from her father. Her beloved bike that she was so proud of was stolen, never found, and then there was that terrible thing that happened to her kitten. . . .

A shudder ran through Stephanie's body, even though the kitchen was steamy-warm. It had been months since she'd thought about the reign of terror she'd lived through before Jeff and his friend went off to college that fall. She'd been glad, deliriously glad that Jeff was gone. It was as if she'd been in prison and had suddenly been given a pardon.

She'd never made up with Jeff, even though he'd tried to explain, years later, that all boys go through an experimental stage, that what she'd seen had been part of growing up. He also denied that he'd had any part in the series of mishaps that befell her. She

hadn't believed him, and when he graduated from college, she'd
developed a high fever and was unable to go to his graduation.
Since then, she'd seen him only a few times at Christmas and
family reunions, but she never could make herself touch him, not
even to give him a sisterly hug.

And now, like a recurring nightmare, the same thing had happened again. God, how could she bear it? How could she possibly
deal with seeing, talking to, David in the future—as she must?

The boys had taken his absence hard. Sometimes she caught
them looking at her, and she knew they blamed her for depriving
them of their father. What had David told them the day he'd come
to the house to see them while she was in the city looking for a
job? She hadn't questioned the boys about his visit. In fact, she
seldom spoke David's name to them because she was afraid some
of her revulsion might show through.

But the night after he'd talked to the boys, she'd called David
at the phone number he'd left for her. She told him that if he ever
came near Chuck and Ronnie again, she would tell them what
she'd seen—and she wouldn't try to soften its ugliness. They knew
about gays, of course. Anyone living in the Bay Area couldn't
help but know about this particular "alternate life-style"—as people called it. She'd heard the twins making jokes about homosex-
uals, and God help her, she'd actually rebuked them, had brought
out the old platitudes about live and let live and walking in another
person's moccasins, telling them they should be tolerant of other
people's life-styles. But maybe what she *should* have done was
talk about mortal sin and disgusting sexual practices, the way her
own parents had when she was a youngster.

One thing was for sure—she would never let David have custody of them. Never!

The phone rang as she was putting plates into the oven to warm.
She made a face and pulled the sizzling skillet off the burner
before she went to the kitchen wall phone.

"Hello?" she said, and because her finger was still smarting
from the hot grease, her voice was a little sharp.

There was a brief silence. "Hello, Stephie."

Her hand tightened around the phone. "What do you want,
David? I told you—"

"Yes, I know what you told me. But Chuck called and asked
if I would come to see their soccer game this Saturday, and I
thought I'd better clear it with you before—"

"The answer is no. Absolutely and positively no."

"I think you should reconsider, Stephie. The boys need a father—"

"Not a lousy homosexual father," she said.

"That isn't true. I'm not a homosexual. It was a—a momentary lapse in judgment because I'd been drinking. What more can I say except that I'm sick about it?"

"How can I ever trust you again, David? It isn't as if you didn't know how I feel about—about gays. Before we were married, I told you about Jeff and what I went through as a kid. Why did you marry me, knowing that I was bound to find out about you someday?"

"There was nothing to find out, Stephie. I made a mistake. Why don't you try to understand how it could happen?"

"I'm trying hard not to judge you, but I have to protect Chuck and Ronnie. Do you understand? I won't have you setting a bad example for them. From now on, just forget we exist—"

She replaced the phone in its cradle and discovered her hands were trembling, that her mouth was distorted into a rictus grin. She put her face down on her arm, breathing hard, trying not to cry. How like a harpy she'd sounded—she'd never talked to anyone like that in her whole life. She hadn't known there was so much bitterness stored up inside her, waiting to boil out. If only there was someone she could confide in, ask for advice. She had hoped the lawyer, Arnold Waterford, would serve that purpose, but now she wouldn't be seeing him until next week. Besides, he was a stranger, only interested in the legal aspects of the case— and he was also a man.

And wasn't it strange how few friends she had these days? She'd only heard from one friend since David and she had split up, and even then she'd had the impression it was curiosity that prompted the call. She'd always been too reserved for easy relationships, but she'd had a few good friends in college, had dated several boys, even had a couple of lovers.

Then she'd met David, and he'd filled her life so completely that she hadn't had time for anyone else, and her friends had dropped away, one by one. She hadn't missed them because David and the boys had been enough. Good friendships needed regular nurturing, and she'd been too busy maintaining the kind of home David wanted and deserved—no, the kind she'd *thought* he deserved—for any outside interests except her volunteer work.

So now when she desperately needed a confidante, there was no one she could turn to. Certainly, she couldn't go to her family.

A year ago, her father had leased out his fields, bought a motor home, and now he and Mom seemed always to be away somewhere, trekking around the country.

"We're seeing all those places we only saw on maps and postmarks before," he'd said the last time they'd talked on the phone. Even if they were available, they wouldn't understand. Both of them thought homosexuality was a mortal sin. How could she tell them that the son-in-law they thought so great, the father of their grandsons, was gay?

She glanced at the clock above the sink. Usually she didn't have to call the boys—they were never late for meals. But for the past few days, they hadn't seemed hungry. Were they grieving for David?

The thought was so distasteful that she realized she was jealous. Which was stupid. Despite the good relationship she had with Chuck and Ronnie, they were normal boys, sports-minded and physically active. It was only natural they'd be close to their father, the one who shared their interests.

"Hi, Mom—what's for breakfast?"

It was Chuck, as always the first one down in the morning. He was staring at the half-cooked bacon, congealing in grease in the big iron skillet, his usually cheerful face glum.

"Sorry—I got a phone call," Stephanie apologized. "Sit down and start on your cereal and juice. I'll have bacon and eggs and English muffins ready in a few minutes. Where's your brother?"

"He's on his way down. He broke a shoestring and had to put in a new one." He upturned the milk carton above his bowl of cereal, and some of it splashed out on the tablecloth. Ordinarily, she would have told him to watch it, but today she turned the burner back on under the bacon, pretending not to see his sidelong glance.

"Sorry, Mom," he said. "Old fumble-fingered me, huh?"

"It's okay. How many muffins do you want?"

"Just one—and no eggs. I'm watching my diet," he said.

"You're what? Chuck, the human garbage disposal, is watching his diet? Watching it do what?" she said, trying for a joke.

"Very funny, Mom," he said. He began shoveling cereal into his mouth.

Five minutes later, Stephanie was having a hard time keeping peace between the boys—and controlling her own temper. Ronnie, in a bad mood, had grumbled about the bacon, which he said—truthfully—was too greasy. He'd also managed to upset his orange juice, which joined the milk stains on the freshly laundered cloth, and then he'd picked a quarrel with Chuck, who seemed to have misplaced his sunny nature somewhere.

"Okay, that's it!" Stephanie said, slamming down her fork. "You're both under restriction—no TV tonight or tomorrow. And I want you home right after school, too. No loitering along the way. I'll be in the city job-hunting, but I'm going to call home about three—and you'd both better be here."

"Aw, Mom—I promised Larry I'd go over to his house after school to shoot some baskets with him."

"Yeah, and I have to go to the library," Ronnie protested. "I've gotta look up some stuff for a history report."

"No exceptions. Ronnie, you can go to the library after dinner. And remember—you're both on restriction. No TV."

Chuck sniggered. "How will you know if we do or don't?"

"Oh, I'll know. And you'd better stop smarting off at me if you don't want another restriction."

"Is that why Pop left?" Ronnie blurted out. His face was very pale, his eyes too bright. "Did he get pissed off because you were always telling him what to do?"

The cruelty—and unfairness—of his remark silenced Stephanie for a moment. She felt the smart of tears under her eyelids, but she gave him back stare for stare. "What goes on between your father and me is none of your busines—and you'd better clean up your language if you don't want me to ground you an extra day. Now I want you two to buck up—"

To her horror, although she'd thought she was holding up just fine, her voice suddenly took on a wobble. As she jumped up from the table and hurried from the room, she heard Chuck say, "Now you've done it, asshole. You made Mom cry."

"I don't care," Ronnie said, his voice rising. "She's been acting real bitchy—and you know it."

Upstairs in her bedroom, Stephanie threw herself down on the bed, but she'd already stopped crying. Ronnie was right. She'd been acting like a shrew lately. Just when she needed to keep things normal for the sake of the boys, too. Had they sensed her depression, her desperation? Were they testing her to find out how far they could go? Or did they blame her for the breakup of their family? It was so unfair! David was at fault, but there was no way she could tell them the truth.

Well, she had to do something—and soon. She didn't have a minister to turn to because she'd dropped away from her church after she'd left home. Maybe she should enroll in one of those group therapy things. But didn't they insist on total honesty? How could she possibly tell a bunch of strangers that her husband was gay? Their advice would probably be to accept his aberration and be tolerant. She might even be censored as a bigot, which wouldn't surprise her, this being liberal Marin County.

So she'd have to work this out alone. God, she did miss having someone to talk to! David had always been there for her—it was so hard, knowing that she had to depend upon herself now. *Out there on my own again . . . Wasn't that the name of a song or a book? If not, it should be.*

But at least she had learned something from the past few days. Never again would she blindly, stupidly, trust a man—and what was she going to do about sex? Become celibate? Of course, it had never been a really important part of her life. It was David who was the passionate one—or had been. When they were first married, if he'd had his way, they would have spent most of their time in bed, making love. . . .

Strange that she hadn't been concerned about the slow decline of their sex life. Like some strange reversal of roles, there had been times when she'd needed the closeness, the cuddling of love-making, but David had complained of headaches and she—stupid, stupid!—had felt guilty because she hadn't noticed how over-worked he was. And all the time he must have been—

No, she wasn't going to think about that possibility. It opened the door to another kind of fear. It was the future that concerned her now—and the boys came first. Somehow she must take up the slack that David's absence had left in their lives. And just how was she going to do that? She was the nonathletic one in the family. They always teased her about that—how could she possibly take David's place?

Well, for starters she could start attending their soccer games. Okay, she didn't know a thing about soccer, but it was about time she showed some interest. She couldn't talk for hours about the Forty-Niners and the Giants, like David could, but she could listen, ask questions, take an interest, couldn't she?

And at the same time, she had to take stock of her own needs. She'd been pinching pennies, trying to make the money in their checking account stretch. But she needed a perm, a haircut, and styling—maybe she'd treat herself to a professional manicure, too. She couldn't help noticing at lunch today how beautifully turned out Chanel and Janice had been. Her own nails—well, she kept them filed and all, but it was obvious that she never had them done by a manicurist.

Maybe better grooming would help her with job interviews, too. It certainly would improve her confidence. Not that it would do anything for her nonexistent job skills. She knew now that she should have taken something marketable in college along with her art and music classes, but she hadn't looked beyond her own personal interests.

One of the job interviewers she'd talked to this week, a pleasant middle-aged man, had suggested that she enroll in the reentry programs at Marin JC.

"They're for women who want to reenter the job market," he'd said. "They're great for giving you direction—you know, to help you decide what you're qualified for."

Well, she didn't have time to waste on college programs. Luckily, money wasn't an immediate problem yet. David had added a couple of thousand to her checking account last week so the bills were all paid for the month. Although she was postponing any expense not absolutely necessary, there was nothing she could do about food and utilities and gasoline and mortgage payments.

She would let Mr. Waterford handle the business of getting the going rate for child support—whatever it happened to be. She knew David's income was above average, even for a lawyer, although he'd always been a little secretive about such things. In fact, it was surprising how little she knew about their financial situation. Her mother-in-law was like David, closemouthed when it came to talking about her financial affairs—and what the devil was she going to do about her mother-in-law?

Mrs. Cornwall doted on the twins, which hadn't stopped her from giving a lot of unsolicited advice and criticism to their mother. Right now, she was probably on David's back, demanding that he ask for visitation rights or even for full custody. Mrs. Cornwall—she'd never been able to call David's mother by her first name, Stella—was a bona fide, card-carrying bitch—and David was her only son, the main recipient of her complaints and self-pity and tirades.

Maybe this had influenced his sexual preferences. What other secrets were hidden beneath that wall of reserve he wore like armor? And why hadn't that reserve bothered her more? Most women complained when their husbands failed to communicate with them. Was it because she was comfortable inside her own armor? Had she wanted it that way, been content not to get too close to David?

If there was only someone she could discuss these things with, a close friend. Or maybe a disinterested stranger would be better—like the women she'd had lunch with last week. Not that she had much confidence in the advice of strangers. Even though they were all in the process of getting divorces, their situations weren't the same. If she let down her guard—to say, Chanel, and told her why she was getting a divorce, Chanel would look at her with those cool eyes, and make some remark that would sting even while it seemed artless and even funny.

The only one that she'd felt halfway comfortable with was Janice. Glory was—well, she was pretty common and she used terrible language, while Ariel seemed to be off in some world of her own. But Janice and she had things in common, such as both belonging to the same sorority. And Janice was a good listener. She hadn't said much about herself, but she'd done a good job of drawing the rest of them out. How had Chanel put it? The strangers-on-a-train syndrome?

So maybe she'd go to that luncheon next week, after all. If she got the chance, she would take Janice aside and ask if she'd like to go out to lunch someday soon, just the two of them. They could meet at some nice restaurant—maybe that English pub on Post that had such good prime rib sandwiches, and while they were having lunch, she could bring the conversation around to gays.

She didn't have to say that it was her own problem if she didn't want to. She could always claim she had this friend who'd just found out her husband was a homosexual and didn't know what to do about keeping him away from their kids . . .

CHAPTER TWELVE

GLORY SAT IN THE MIDDLE OF A MATTRESS THAT RESTED DIrectly on the floor, surrounded by a welter of newspapers, a stack of paperback mystery novels, a couple of well-worn stuffed dogs, and the remains of her lunch. She was wearing a bedraggled pink teddy and nothing else. Most of the time she was home, she spent on the mattress for the simple reason that it was the only place on which to sit in her apartment except for a rusty folding chair that she'd retrieved from her landlady's trash.

Although she hadn't yet bought a matching box spring for her mattress, the pillows against her back were down, and the sheets and pillowcases were top quality, all of which, in Glory's opinion, had cost her an arm and a leg.

Or more like a breast, since it was the generous display of that part of her anatomy that earned her respectable tips at the Oral Cookie. She could have bought a cheaper mattress and had enough for the springs, too, but her bed was to be the nucleus of the home she hoped to have someday, so she'd wanted everything to be the best. And new. It had to be brand spanking new.

The night she'd left Buddy, she'd made the decision to go first-class from then on. A fresh start meant just that—no compromises. She was already studying to pass the GED test so she could get a high school diploma, and when she could sandwich them in, she planned to sign up for some classes at San Francisco State. She hadn't decided just what to study because it was still unclear to her what to do with the rest of her life.

Making money came first, of course. Without money, you had no power, no safety, no slack. The least little thing—sickness, a spell of bad luck like someone ripping you off, or the loss of your job—and you were living on the streets. Her present job, to put it mildly, was a dead end. Good tips, but still—once your body started to sag, the tips started dropping and eventually you were out on your ass.

And besides, she hated working as a cocktail waitress, hated the losers who patronized the Oral Cookie, hated the lewd remarks and the passes and the assumption that just because she worked in a nightclub, she was for sale. If she wanted to be a hooker, she'd set herself up in a fancy apartment somewhere as a call girl, thank you, not run her feet off in a North Beach garbage dump. As far as she was concerned, the job was temporary, a stopgap. As soon as she decided which direction to go, she intended to quit.

But first, she meant to work on changing her image.

She stared down at the art pad in front of her. It had taken her a while to get the four women of the support group down so they were recognizable. Luckily, one of the things she'd been good at in school was art.

"You've got a lot of natural talent," her eighth-grade art teacher had said. And then she'd gone on to complain about how hard it was to make a decent living as an artist. So Glory had dumped the idea of becoming an artist fast. Even so, her talent came in useful sometimes. And she did have that trick memory. She could recall just about anything she saw and put it down on paper later.

Maybe she should apply for a job as a police artist. Wouldn't *that* shake her old lady up! Ma had a lifelong hatred for the law in any form—she'd wet her pants if one of her girls got a job with the police department. Funny about that because Ma hadn't turned a hair when Violet went to work in that North Beach massage parlor. In fact, she'd bragged about Violet's big tips.

Pensively, Glory thought of her most recent encounter with her mother. Why she'd weakened and gone to see Ma she still couldn't figure out. Sometimes, almost as if she'd gone bonkers, she did go back to the Pink Palace—what the tenants called the Western Edition housing project where Ma lived—and it was always the same.

Ma had started in on her even before she got her foot inside the door. "You ain't getting no money from me!" she said. "I'm stone cold broke—I won't have a dime until my next welfare check."

"I didn't come here for money," Glory said.

The expression on her mother's face hadn't changed, but she'd opened the door wide enough for Glory to squeeze past. She was a short, swarthy-skinned woman, blowsy and untidy, with swollen ankles and an enormous stomach that joggled when she walked. Which was as seldom as possible.

"Okay, you can come in for a while. But Joey'll be back soon, and you know he don't much like you. Says you're stuck on yourself." She gave Gloria a sly look. "Can't see what reason you'd have for that. You oughta get yourself a haircut or something. It looks like shit, sticking up like that."

"I've only got a few minutes, so I'll be gone before Joey gets back," Glory said, ignoring the comment.

Joey was Ma's latest sleep-in. He was big and loud and he couldn't leave the horses alone, but Ma doted on him. When hadn't she doted on some man—and all of them losers?

"Where you living now Buddy kicked you out?" Ma said, the question so casual that Glory knew she was being pumped. She felt a flash of anger, then hurt. Didn't Ma know why she'd left Buddy—or had he lied about that?

"As it happens, I'm in the process of moving," she said. "That's why I came by. I wanted to say good-bye before I leave town."

"Leave town? Where you going?"

"To Seattle. I've got a job waiting for me there. I don't know where I'll be staying, but I'll send you my address as soon as I get settled."

But don't hold your breath, Ma, because you'll smother if you do.

"What kind of job? Some guy setting you up as a hooker?"

It took Glory a while to answer. What hurt so much was the knowledge that Ma wasn't being deliberately insulting. She really thought hooking was in the cards for her youngest daughter. "I'll be working in a bank," she said finally.

Ma snorted. "Yeah? Doing what? You're lying—I always can tell. Your trouble is that you think you're better'n the rest of us. Just like your old man—if he really was your old man. He thought he was a cut above everybody else, which is why he never lasted long on a job. Soon as he heard I was knocked up, he split on me. Well, let me tell you a few things—"

It ended as it always did, with the two of them yelling at each other. But this time there was a difference. At some point during the quarrel, when her mother was heaping abuse upon her head, something snapped inside Glory, a pulling back, a giving up, and she knew with cold certainty that this was the last time she would ever visit her mother. From now on, she was an orphan—and that went for cutting off all contact with her sisters, too.

There was pain in the decision, but also relief. Now she could do what she wanted without ever having to explain herself again. And what she wanted was to be somebody. To matter. To register.

The trouble is, she thought now, how did you go about becoming somebody who mattered, who registered? Did you start with your appearance?

She ripped the sketches out of her pad and lined them up before her on the mattress. The four women she'd met in Mr. Waterford's waiting room were depicted accurately on the pad although she'd taken a few liberties with their facial features. Chanel's chin had been elongated, giving her a witchy look, and Ariel's hair floated above her head, defying gravity, much fuller and looser than it really was. Stephanie, who had a rather buxom figure, was now undeniably fat, while Janice's square jaw had an aggressive jut that made her look like a man in drag.

But they were all identifiable, and their clothes had been depicted, line for line, with accuracy.

For a long time, she studied the sketches. Chanel, of course, was the one she wanted to be like. Janice had a preppy look that was just right for *her*, but not for a redhead with wiry hair. Ariel she dismissed out of hand. Dimly she realized that Ariel had an elusive air of quality, but again, it wasn't for her. And Stephanie? Well, she dressed okay for a suburban housewife, but those quiet, everything-matching outfits just weren't for her. But Chanel—oh, yes, she could just see herself in that spiffy fur-trimmed suit Chanel had been wearing.

A size or two larger, of course.

So what to do about it? No way could she afford designer suits and elk handbags and shoes. Maybe she could alter something she already had to look more like what Chanel had been wearing? After all, she had taken Home Ec for two years at Lowell High.

Uncurling her legs, she rose and went to her closet. It was full of clothes, most of them old because she never threw away anything if she could help it. Pack rat, Buddy had called her once, back when they were still getting along.

Briefly, her throat thickened, but she gave her head a shake, repudiating the weakness. Never again was she going to get soft over some man, certainly not Buddy—and why had he contacted Ma to find out where she was living? What did he want with her? To give her another bashing? She winced, remembering the fury in Buddy's eyes, the welt she'd put on his genitals with his own belt.

Well, if he contacted Ma again, maybe he'd believe that she had really left town. Of course, the divorce papers, when he got them, would tell him differently, but that was off in the future. With luck, she could avoid running into him—and even if she did, so what? It was a free country. If he even looked at her cross-eyed, she would start yelling for the cops.

Glory shrugged off her unpalatable thoughts and began examining the clothes hanging in her closet. Seeing them through Chanel's eyes, she knew they were all cheaply made and much too busy with all those tucks and gathers and decorations. Why was it that the less you paid for a dress, the more junk was tacked onto it? The jacket of Chanel's suit had been all straight lines that fell from the shoulder to the hem, touching her lightly where it mattered. And there hadn't been a wrinkle in her skirt or jacket, even though she'd been sitting for a couple of hours. Which proved that quality did count. The trouble was—quality cost more money than she could spare.

Well, there *was* that wool dress she'd bought on sale at I. Magnin that time. Buddy had yelled about the price and she'd promised to return it, but she never had. She found it almost impossible to give up anything once it was hers. She felt secure, having lots of clothes, even if most of them were out-of-date. It was the same way with food. The first thing she'd done after she'd rented this apartment was to stock up on canned goods. Just in case.

So she still had the I. Magnin dress although she hadn't dared wear it around Buddy. It was plain and not quite—well, right for her figure. In fact, it pulled across her breasts and was too snug in the hips. Still—it was a step in the right direction. Yeah, she would wear it to the luncheon next Saturday—and she'd do something with her hair, too. Of course, she couldn't afford a fancy hairdresser. Maybe she could set it in big rollers with lots of mousse to get some of the crinkles out of it. And she would use less makeup, too, although she'd swear that Chanel'd had on as much as she did, only it just didn't show.

Maybe she should buy some new clothes and let her other plans go for a while. Not that changing her appearance was going to help if she didn't change her life in other ways. A different job— that had to be one of her first priorities. But could she make it on a sales clerk's or a receptionist's pay? Well, nothing was easy. Nothing worth going after.

And she did have that big itch to be respectable, to have—well, call it class. Which was why she intended to show up at the luncheon next Saturday, even though she didn't really fit in with that bunch. After all, she wasn't committing herself to anything permanent. Hell, she could stop anytime she wanted, like when she had something more important to do. . . .

CHAPTER THIRTEEN

JANICE WAS THE FIRST ONE TO ARRIVE AT THE UNIVERSITY Club—and not by accident. She wanted to confer with Maurice, the club's manager. As one of her good works, obligatory for the wife of an ambitious Stanford professor, she had taken over the thankless job of cochairing a drive to raise money to bring the aging University Club building up to the new California earthquake code. Without those very expensive repairs the building would have been condemned. Since there was no building fund, the eighty-five-year-old club would have ceased to exist— and there were few jobs open for waiters and cooks and club managers in their sixties, and, in some cases, in their seventies.

So when Janice asked a favor of Maurice, it was instantly granted. She seldom used her influence with him, so she didn't feel guilty. In fact, this favor was quite small—the use of one of the club's private dining rooms once a month without charge, a special rate for the luncheons—with a liter of house wine thrown in, courtesy of the club.

Maurice told her now that he'd arranged for the Solarium Room to be reserved for her group on a regular basis, and later, as she waited for the other women to arrive, she examined with approval the long, narrow room's profusion of hanging vines, potted nasturtiums and geraniums, the comfortable wicker furniture. The tall, multipaned windows, with their fan-shaped cornices, fronted on busy Sutter Street, but the roar of traffic was muted by the building's thick walls. Through the tinted glass of a skylight, the October sky was a pearly blue—a good omen for this new venture, Janice thought.

She studied the table, which was set with mellow old silver, a threadbare but undoubtedly pure linen cloth, and crystal that glowed rather than sparkled because of years of use. Although there had been no money to replace the accoutrements of its more gracious past, the club still knew how to do it right—which was also the motto of the city of San Francisco.

So why, when all the signs were good, didn't she feel more optimistic? Why did she have this uncomfortable feeling, almost of guilt? Was her conscience acting up—as Jake had implied it would? And why had he been so negative about the project? Of course, Jake did love to play the devil's advocate. . . .

As for guilt—that was ridiculous. How could anyone possibly get hurt? She intended to get their permission before she turned in her dissertation, didn't she? And also, she would shield their identification, using code names and erroneous physical descriptions. It would be almost impossible to identify them even if she didn't take these precautions. After all, they were perfectly ordinary women—well, maybe not really ordinary. Not average, for sure. In fact, she couldn't have chosen a more diverse group if she'd deliberately gone out and selected them.

Glory Browne was the outstanding example of being atypical of the others—which brought up an interesting question. Could she possibly be one of Arnold's "worthy" cases? Obviously, she couldn't afford his high fees. Whatever the answer, she was a lucky addition to the group.

Janice heard a sound at the door and turned to meet Stephanie's tentative smile. Since she'd classified Stephanie as being pretty but without much animation at their first meeting, she was surprised how different she looked today. Was it the October wind that made her eyes glow, or was she simply wearing more make-up? Or was it the prospect of having lunch with women who shared her own problems? It would be interesting to find out. . . .

"It looks as if we're the first to arrive," Janice said.

"Yes—but I'm glad you're here. I wanted to ask if you—" Stephanie broke off as the door opened again. Chanel, looking cool and composed, her hair in perfect order, came into the room. She gave the table an appraising look, then turned the same look upon Janice and Stephanie.

Either she'd stopped at the rest room to smooth down her hair or she had it trained to stay in place, even in the San Francisco breezes, Janice thought, suddenly amused. She was betting on the latter.

"Are we the only ones who turned up?" Chanel asked as she removed her coat, revealing a silk-and-wool dress so beautifully cut that it must have been custom-tailored to her petite figure.

A size five at the most, Janice thought with a twinge of envy.

"We're still a few minutes early," she said. "Ariel called to say she didn't see any point in coming since her husband and she are back together." She realized she sounded disgruntled and added quickly, "I'm delighted, of course. She obviously didn't want the divorce. But, as I pointed out to her, she could still get something out of a support group. She said she'd think about it. I hope she turns up."

"So do I," Chanel said.

Again the door opened and this time it was Ariel and Glory—a strangely transformed Glory.

Janice stared in amazement at Glory's slicked down hair, which had an oily look, as if she'd slathered it with lotion. She was carrying her coat, and the dress she wore would have been attractive if it hadn't been so tight across her high, pointed breasts. And her shoes—the heels were so high, they forced Glory's in-step into an unlikely curve that made Janice wince.

"Are we late?" Glory's eyes lingered on Chanel. "Ariel and I met out front. She decided to come even though she's not getting a divorce, after all."

"Since we're all here, why don't we order and then we can talk?" Janice said, eager to get things started.

She waited until they were seated in high-backed wicker chairs around a rattan-and-teakwood table and had given their orders to the same elderly waiter who had served them the first time. When the waiter left the room she said brightly, "Well, why don't we get started?"

Chanel fingered the rosy pearls knotted at her throat. "Don't these support groups usually have a professional leader—like a marriage counselor or a psychologist?"

"You're right. But since this is so informal, I'm sure we can make do without," Janice said.

"But we do need a—a coordinator. Someone we can phone when we can't make it." Chanel smiled at Ariel. "What do you think, Ariel?"

Ariel's eyes went blank for a moment. "Yes—a coordinator would help," she said finally.

"Does everybody agree?" Janice said. Not to her surprise, everybody nodded.

"Since this was your idea, Janice, I think you should be the leader." Glory took a sip of water from her glass, then made a face. "Ugh. It tastes funny—sort of flat," she said.

"It's bottled water," Janice said. "And of course I'd be glad to act as—well, let's call it a secretary. That's really what I'd be doing—or maybe someone else would like the job?"

When no one spoke, she went on, "What should we do first? I'm open to ideas."

"Maybe we should decide on our goals, our direction, what we want to accomplish." Stephanie's voice was hesitant.

"I agree," Chanel said. "And I think we should start by agreeing to respect one another's confidences. No carrying tales out of school."

Janice forced herself to nod. *I do not like thee, Mrs. Fell—the reason why I certainly can tell. . . .* "That's fine with me," she said aloud. "We're here to help one another, to provide a—a sounding board. Since we're strangers to one another, I think it would be a good idea if it stayed that way outside our meetings, don't you?"

Chanel gave her a hard look. "Why don't we make it a rule not to make rules and just do what comes naturally?"

Janice fought to hide her annoyance. This wasn't going to be easy—but then, when had anything ever been easy for her except falling in love with Jake?

"You're probably right," she said, although the words threatened to choke her. "Should we give ourselves a name?"

"Such as?" Glory asked.

"Oh—how about simply calling ourselves the Support Group?"

"That's appropriate enough—especially if we all draw alimony," Chanel drawled, and everybody except Janice laughed.

"How about calling ourselves the 'Out There on Our Own Again Girls?'" Stephanie said, her smile painful.

"But Ariel isn't really out there on her own," Glory pointed out.

"How about 'The Walking Wounded Club'—or maybe 'Saturday's Children.' How does that old rhyme go? Saturday's child has to work for a living?" Chanel said, and they all laughed again.

"Why don't we call ourselves 'The Club' until we come up with a better name?" Janice said, wishing she'd never brought up the subject.

"That's okay with me." Chanel sounded bored. "Does anyone mind if I smoke?"

"I'm afraid I do," Ariel said apologetically. "It's this respiratory problem I have."

A little to Janice's surprise Chanel nodded agreeably. "Then

I'll sneak out to the lobby later. Any other sinner here? You're welcome to join me.''

"I quit a while back, but I may take it up again," Glory said. "This place where I work is always so full of smoke, I figure my lungs are taking a beating anyway."

"Where do you work?" Janice asked.

"At a bar in North Beach. It's sort of a nightclub, really, since we have nightly entertainment."

"That must be interesting," Stephanie said.

"Interesting, shit. It's a dump is what it is," Glory said. "I'm going to look for another job as soon as I get on my feet financially."

"How can you afford to—" Stephanie broke off, looking uncomfortable.

"How can I afford Arnold Waterford? He's waiving his fees and just charging me expenses. He told me he did that sometimes for worthy clients—and he thinks my case is very worthy, especially after I showed him my bruises. I figure he's looking for a freebie, but so far he hasn't made his move."

"I'm sure you're mistaken," Janice said stiffly. "I've known Arnold—Mr. Waterford all my life, and he isn't a—a—" She stumbled over the word.

"A lech? Honey, all men are leches. It just takes the right button to set them off." Glory sounded more resigned than angry. "On the other hand, their glands can be their downfall. That's how they become husbands." She was silent for a moment, her expression thoughtful. "A lot of smart girls have set themselves up for life by marrying a rich man who's got the hots for them."

"If you're going that route, you'd better make sure of your target. You could get burned," Chanel said.

"Well, I'm not anxious to remarry. Not that I intend to do without sex."

Stephanie looked away, and Janice knew she was embarrassed by Glory's frankness. "So we all agree that the purpose of the group is to help one another?" she said.

"Yeah—and no fang and claw stuff," Glory said. "I get enough of that on my job."

Janice glanced down at her watch. "Then, why don't we start? Service here is always a little slow. Should we take turns talking? How about you, Glory? Do you want to go first?"

"Talking about what?"

"Telling us how you feel about—well, marriage."

"Oh, it was a blast, especially when I got the stuffing knocked out of me by Mr. Macho because I made the mistake of saying I was sorry he'd had a rotten day." Her eyes were brooding as she stared down at her long pearl-white nails. "But I fixed him. When he passed out, I tied him to the bedposts so I could pack my things and clear out. When he woke up and started cursing me, I gave him a couple of whacks with his belt, one in the place where the sun don't shine. I'll bet he had a hard time peeing for the rest of the week."

"You mean you hit him in the—" Stephanie broke off, flushing.

"Right in the family jewels," Glory said.

Chanel laughed. "Well, you did say we should be honest with one another," she told Janice.

Glory gave her a considering stare. "What about you, Chanel? What busted up your marriage?"

"Boredom. Pure and unadulterated. Jacques never wants to go anyplace, do anything—and besides, he's impotent as a eunuch. I could have been living with a monk. I decided to get out from under while I was still young enough to catch another fish."

She paused, obviously amused by their reaction. Chanel knew, a few minutes into the luncheon, that no one there had any intention of telling the whole truth about her divorce. Which was why, for some perverse reason, she decided to be frank—up to a point. Jacques *was* impotent, had been for a long time, but that had been a plus. The real reason she was divorcing him was his stinginess.

Of course, the signs of his penny-pinching had been there even before she'd married him. While they were dating, his idea of a hot time on the town was to go to some hole in the wall that served good pasta. She should have caught on then, but she'd been misled by the knowledge that so many rich people were stingy. Look at old Henry Ford with his shiny dimes—or was that Rockefeller?

But maybe she'd made a mistake, telling the group that she was divorcing Jacques before she got too old to land a richer man. Was it the wrong thing to say with Ariel sitting there, taking it all in? What if she repeated this conversation to Laird?

There was something else that she noticed. While Janice was quick to get things organized, she had very little to say about her own problems. Time to throw Janice a curve.

"I have to admit it's a relief to let my hair down." Her gaze shifted to Janice. "And since we're taking turns being honest with one another, how about you, Janice? What's the reason for *your* divorce?''

After a brief, uncomfortable silence. Chanel prodded, ''Well? Don't tell me you're going to hold out on us.''

''It was just that your question caught me by surprise,'' Janice said. ''And the answer is simple. We—Jake and I are totally incompatible.''

''What do you mean by incompatible?'' Glory asked.

''We don't have the same interests. What's important to me isn't important to Jake. And vice versa. We've been going our own ways a long time now,'' Janice said, so glibly that Chanel didn't believe a word of it.

''Is that all?'' Glory sounded disappointed. ''With me, it started out with Buddy and other women. You wouldn't believe the groupies that hang around professional ball players—and Buddy was never one to overlook a free bang. Then there was his heavy hand. If that kind of thing is being incompatible, I guess you could say that's why we broke up, too.'' She gave Stephanie a curious look. ''How about you, Stephanie?''

'I guess David and I were lucky that way. We have—had the same life goals, the same likes and dislikes, and of course we're both crazy about our boys.''

''So why get a divorce?''

Stephanie hesitated; her face was pale, and there was a thin beading of sweat on her upper lip. ''David—well, he decided he wanted someone else,'' she finally said.

''Those things happen. Men will be men. Why didn't you just let it burn out—provided you still want the guy?'' Chanel said.

''I don't want him!'' Stephanie's voice rose. ''I hate him—I never want to see him again!''

There was a brief silence. Glory broke it first. ''I hear you talking. I feel the same way about Buddy.''

''But it's not the same, is it?'' Ariel said unexpectedly. ''Stephanie has two children. It must have been hard, deciding to divorce their father.''

''Hard? Oh, yes, it was hard,'' Stephanie said dully.

Janice leaned toward her. ''You said something about getting a job—isn't he willing to support you?''

''We haven't discussed it—Mr. Waterford is handling the financial arrangements.''

''Well, make sure your rights are protected,'' Chanel advised. ''Didn't you say your husband is a lawyer? It's a good thing you have decent representation. He's probably busy hiding his assets right now."

Stephanie's cheeks flushed. "Oh, David wouldn't do that! He isn't that kind of person."

Chanel gave her a pitying look. "Come on—you aren't going to let him get away with anything, are you? Being a lawyer, he knows all the tricks."

"Most lawyers are honest—"

"I think we're getting a little far afield," Janice interrupted. She started to say something more when the door opened and their waiter appeared, pushing a serving cart. Like the old waiter himself, the silver-plated serving dishes had seen better days, but the food was surprisingly good and, Chanel thought later when the bill came, surprisingly reasonable.

When the bill was presented, there was the usual flurry over which woman had ordered what. Chanel noticed how efficiently Janice managed the settling-up process. Not only was she quick to take over, but she obviously was experienced at handling what could have been an awkward situation. Just as obviously, she didn't need any moral support from anyone, not this cool lady. So why the hell had she organized a support group? What was she getting out of it?

Chanel discovered that she needed a cigarette in the worst way. It looked like these monthly luncheons were going to be something of a trial, thanks to Ariel. If—no, *when* she married Laird, she intended to make very sure that invitations to Ariel, with her respiratory problem, were few and far between.

CHAPTER FOURTEEN

LATER, CHANEL WASN'T SURE WHY SHE INVITED GLORY TO HAVE lunch with her. They were having cigarettes together in the musty lobby of the University Club after the other women had left, and something about Glory's obvious admiration got through to Chanel. When, with a rare impulsiveness she immediately regretted, she suggested that they get together for lunch soon, Glory promptly pinned her down to a date.

Because she was stuck, she chose the Mayflower Tearoom for their meeting place, and on the day of their luncheon, she made sure she arrived first because she wanted to witness Glory's entrance.

The restaurant, tucked into a cul-de-sac off Maiden Lane, was patronized almost totally by women, most of them middle-aged or older. The only male in the room, who obviously had been coerced into coming there, looked sheepish, as if he were a voyeur who'd just been caught peeking through an old maid's bedroom window. The restaurant's menu featured ribbon sandwiches, luncheon salads, rich desserts, and made a fetish of serving English teas, leaning heavily toward Twining's Earl Grey, properly brewed in heated pots. It was also the domain of a bevy of blue-haired waitresses who could have been charter members of the Colonial Dames.

In this atmosphere, Glory was like an exotic bird among sparrows. In a kelly-green jumpsuit that hugged her breasts and hips, with her flaming red hair looking as if it had just left perm rollers and hadn't yet been combed out, she was the focus of all eyes as she threaded her way through the tables toward Chanel. Glory's outward insouciance was so deceiving that Chanel would have sworn she was unaware of the attention she was getting if her small pointed chin hadn't been elevated a shade too high.

"What a weird place," she commented as she plopped herself down in the chair opposite Chanel. "Looks like an old ladies' home."

Her manner radiated aplomb, but Chanel wasn't fooled. "Doesn't it, though," she purred. "But it's a great place for girl talk. No men around to distract you—and you can sit here as long as you like over your tea."

Glory made a face. "I can't stand tea. Can I order coffee?"

"You can order almost anything as long as it doesn't contain alcohol."

"Well, that's no problem. I don't drink."

"Not even wine?"

"Not even wine. Alcohol just fucks up your life."

"Well, I'm not sure I agree. Wine is the oil of social life."

Glory's eyes focused on her. "Why?"

"Because it's so civilized, I suppose."

"Yeah. I'll remember that the next time some smelly old wino hits me up for a dollar to buy a bottle of muscatel. 'How civilized, old fellow,' I'll say.''

Chanel was startled into a laugh. Glory's voice had been a remarkably good imitation of an upper-class British accent.

A waitress, blue-white hair glistening, came to take their order. Glory, seemingly absorbed in the menu, let Chanel order first. When she chose the same luncheon salad, Chanel smiled to herself. A quick study, this Morning Glory Browne. It might be a kick to do the Pygmalion thing—as long as it didn't require an outlay of cash.

"So what are your plans now that you're on your own again?" she asked.

"First, to get well financially," Glory said promptly. "Then look for a better job. God, you wouldn't believe the jerk-offs I have to put up with at work. This guy put his hand up my skirt last night, and when I slapped it away, he threatened to have me arrested for assault. Can you believe it? For assault!"

"So what happened then?" Chanel said, fascinated.

"Jimbo—he's head night bartender—tossed him out. Jimbo's got a thing for me."

"It's good to have influential friends in high places," Chanel said. "Why do you stay on there?"

"For the tips." Glory looked around the quiet dining room with its hanging ferns and creeping Charlie vines, its bentwood chairs and glass-topped tables and wall murals depicting Colonial country scenes. "You take a place like this—a waitress might pull down twenty, twenty-five dollars a day in tips—tops. But I make twice that. Of course, I hafta put up with a lot of shit, too."

"Couldn't you live on a little less?"

"Maybe—but there's a lot of things I wanta do, and they all cost money. I rent unfurnished, and all I've got in my flat is a mattress, a card table, and a tacky old chair. And I need some new clothes, too, before I start looking for a decent job."

"If you ask me, you're going about it the wrong way."

"What does that mean?"

"If you want security—and that's what you're talking about, isn't it?—the fastest way is to marry a rich man."

"Is that what you're gonna do?"

Chanel hesitated. She'd already said too much. For a moment, she'd forgotten that Glory, who was no dummy, just might figure out why she'd been cultivating Ariel.

"I hope to get married again—provided I meet someone compatible," she said cautiously. "Don't you?"

Glory sighed. "No way. Marriage was a real bust."

"How did you happen to marry so young?"

"I met Buddy when he came back to Lowell High to see his old coach. He'd just been signed up by the Bees, and I guess he wanted to show off or something. He saw me in the halls, and when I got out of school that afternoon, he was waiting for me. We started seeing each other and then I got pregnant and we got married."

"You have a child?" Chanel said, startled.

Glory's face stiffened; for a moment, Chanel thought she wasn't going to answer. "I lost the baby. Stillborn. Even so, everything was okay between Buddy and me that first year. Not great, but okay. He was really disappointed when he wasn't tapped for the majors, but he wasn't too worried because he'd had a—uh, personality clash with the team manager and he figured it was a grudge thing. Then he got hit by a bunted ball and cracked a wrist bone. He was on the bench for a couple months while it healed and when he started pitching again, he'd lost his curve. Everything went downhill after that. He never got his stuff back and after the team dropped him, things really fell apart. He kept saying it was my fault, that being married distracted him when he was out on the mound. Which was a lie, because he never let me come to see him play. I figure he was ashamed of me or something. Then he came home loaded one night and started knocking me around. I was really hurting, but he still wanted sex. After he went to sleep, that's when I tied him to the bedposts so I could pack my things and split. I knew he'd never let me just walk out on him."

"So you actually did tie him to the bedposts," Chanel said. "Weren't you afraid of what he'd do after he got loose?"

"You better believe it. I didn't leave no forwarding address behind. Not even my mom knows where I live." Glory paused, her eyes retrospective. "I wouldn't've whacked him with his belt before I left if he hadn't woke up and called me a cunt."

A strangled sound came from Chanel's throat.

"I guess it *is* kinda funny at that," Glory said. "You shoulda seen the look on his face. Well, I'm not sorry. He had it coming. I ached all over for a week, and I was covered with bruises. I hope I gave him a few, too, only I don't think men bruise down there. But I'll bet old Buddy the Prick had to wear his jockstrap loose for a while."

Chanel gave a whooping laugh. Glory grinned at her, looking so young that when Chanel could speak again, she asked, "How old are you, anyway?"

"Eighteen, but they think I'm twenty-one at work."

Chanel got a tissue from her purse and dabbed her eyes, careful not to smudge her mascara. "I like you, Morning Glory Browne. I haven't laughed like that for ages."

"Well, I can laugh about it now, too, but I was pretty scared at the time. I still keep an eye out for that jerk. I just hope he doesn't show up at the divorce hearing. One thing bad about getting the divorce. I told Buddy and my mom that I was moving to Seattle. Now he's gonna know for sure that I'm still here in the city."

"Your mother isn't supportive?"

"She lives on welfare. She can't afford to help me out."

"No, no. What I meant was—doesn't she back you up on your divorce?"

"Ma? No way." Glory's tone was matter-of-fact, as if this information was so self-evident that it didn't need any embellishment. "I went to see her after I left Buddy. Sure enough, Buddy'd been around, asking questions. He's got this weird streak of—y'know, being real possessive. It would've been okay if he'd left *me*, you understand, but not the other way around."

"Did you go to the police?"

Glory looked surprised. "What for?"

"For protection. To report his assault."

"Hey, I don't want to get mixed up with no cops. What good would that do?"

"Well, I hope you're careful. Your husband sounds dangerous."

"Yeah. Buddy thinks the only way to settle things is with his fists. One reason they dropped him from the Bees was because he was always getting into fights with the other guys."

The waitress came with their orders, and both women devoted themselves to their food. Chanel kept her eyes averted from her companion to discourage further conversation because she liked to concentrate on her food when she was eating. The salad was surprisingly good, a plus for eating here. Another plus was the fact that no one she knew would be caught dead in this place. Also, the restaurant was only a short walk from Arnold Waterford's office. Her final consultation with him before the divorce hearing was at three. Today, she would find out just how many concessions he'd managed to pry out of Jacques's lawyer—and how large the divorce settlement would be.

She realized that Glory had spoken, that she'd missed it. "I'm sorry—what did you say?"

"I said I like your hat—and the rest of your outfit, too."

"Thank you," Chanel said, and then because she was feeling mellow, she added, "I got it at cost from James Fray designs—he's a local designer and damned good. I tried it on at his shop but decided it was too expensive. Then I steered a friend to his shop and she bought a full-length ranch mink. Fray called and offered to sell me the suit at cost. Since there's a four hundred percent markup on his originals, it was an offer I couldn't refuse. This was three years ago. I expect I'll still be wearing it ten years from now. Good style is good style—but fashions change every time someone sneezes."

Glory absorbed this for a moment. "Even at cost, it'd be more than I can afford," she said. "And even if I had a lot of money to spend on clothes, I wouldn't know what to buy." She hesitated, then added, "I was wondering if maybe you'd give me some tips—like what colors I'd look best in."

Despite herself Chanel was flattered. At least enough to volunteer an opinion. "If you want to change your look, you should start with your hair. That crinkled look is out—it never was really in with people who count. You should think about soft curls or waves to show off the—uh, remarkable color of your hair. That *is* its natural color, isn't it?"

"Yeah—and so are the crinkles. I was born with them."

"Sorry—those heavy bangs overwhelm your face, you know. A softer style would be best. You have a true redhead's complexion, too. You really shouldn't use much makeup—just a bit of blush to tone down the paleness." Chanel discovered she was enjoying herself—maybe too much. Well, she was a Leo—and Leos did love to give advice. "You could afford to lose some weight—ten pounds or even more," she went on. "Since you're small-boned, I'd say the highest acceptable weight for you is a hundred and twenty."

"How did you do that? How did you know I weigh a hundred and thirty pounds?"

"One of my many talents," Chanel said complacently. "I could make my living guessing weights at a carnival."

"Way to fucking go," Glory said, obviously impressed.

Chanel shook her head. "You should clean up your language,

Glory. You can get away with a four-letter word on occasion, but never use them gratuitously.''

She waited for Glory to ask what gratuitous meant, but Glory fooled her.

"Like when the occasion demands it and only then?" Glory said.

"Exactly.''

"And after I get a new hairdo and lose ten pounds, what next? What kind of clothes should I buy?''

"How much can you spend?''

Glory considered her thoughtfully. "About three hundred if I don't dip into my reserve—that's what I'm saving for an emergency, like if I get sick and can't work. I've been saving for a box spring, too, but I can let that ride.''

"Well, enroll in an aerobics class. When you're down to a size ten, we can talk about a new wardrobe.''

"Three hundred won't buy much, will it?''

"You'd be surprised what it'll buy in a good thrift shop or factory outlet.''

Glory shook her head. "I want to go first-class—and that don't mean wearing someone else's old clothes. I never had a stitch that wasn't passed down until I was old enough to baby-sit and earn some money of my own.''

"That's false pride. I shop the secondhand clothes stores all the time." Chanel broke off a piece of roll and ate it without butter.

"*You* wear secondhand clothes?''

"Indeed I do. Not that I advertise it, you understand. The trick is to shop at the right places. There are several stores in town that sell secondhand designer clothes and factory odd lots.''

"But I wouldn't know designer's clothes from a Sears special.''

Chanel hesitated. Did she really want to go on with this? Getting involved with people who couldn't further her ambitions was a waste of time. On the other hand, she liked Glory, if for no other reason than this little street waif made her laugh. So it might be interesting to give her advice—and how often did she get a chance to show off her shopping acumen to someone else?

"I'll make a bargain with you," she said. "You lose ten pounds and I'll take you shopping and steer you to the places that give full value for your money.''

Although Glory played it cool, her thank-you made Chanel feel magnanimous—and a bit sad. Why couldn't she and Fern have this kind of relationship? After all, Glory was only a year older than Fern—she could be her own daughter.

Bite your tongue, Chanel, she thought, but she discovered she was smiling again.

Later, after they had parted in front of the tearoom and she was walking along Maiden Lane heading for Arnold Waterford's office to keep her appointment, she had a few second thoughts about her offer. It was Ariel she should be cultivating, not a nobody like Glory. Besides, shopping took time—her kind of shopping did— and if everything went well, she'd soon be deeply involved with Laird.

On the other hand, it might be a kick, playing Pygmalion to Glory's Eliza, and anyway, how much time could it take to steer the poor girl in the right direction?

Arnold Waterford was something of a house snob who prided himself on the authenticity of the antique furniture and Americana that graced not only his spacious apartment on Nob Hill, but his offices on Polk Street.

His second wife had given him the American Empire desk that had sparked his interest in antiques and near-antiques, and the rest he'd acquired via judicious shopping and a respectable outlay of money. That particular wife had gone out of his life years ago, but he'd heard a rumor that she had married a CPA and was living in, of all places, Modesto. He wished her well, since their divorce had been amicable.

The truth was that he'd genuinely loved all his wives, each in a different way. Annette for her fresh young body, her naïveté; Susan for her sexual prowess and her feline smile; Dorothy for her cool sophistication and her spectacular legs. Even Ilka had had her good points, even if she had turned out to be a gold-digging bitch who would've walked off with half of everything he owned if he hadn't outsmarted her via some very clever bookkeeping and by burying most of his considerable assets in a Swiss bank account.

But his last encounter with matrimony had left him more than a little gun-shy—at least to the extent of not wanting to marry again. Of course, he'd said that after each of his divorces, but this time he meant it. Still—he did like domestic life. If it hadn't been for his weakness for other women—or if Annette, his first wife, had been more tolerant—he'd probably still be married to her.

But he did love women. Plural. He loved the way they looked, moved, talked, felt. He loved their irrational, illogical, and totally incomprehensible thought processes. He was enamored of their mystery and their mystique, by their soft, warm skin, was stirred by the natural scent of feminine flesh, by the lower range of feminine voices. He even had a secret admiration for the bitchy ones, such as the cool, sleek blonde sitting across the desk from him, her slender ankles demurely crossed, her eyes hidden in the shadow of a delightfully whimsical hat.

Chanel Devereau—the name suited her. Her bones were small, her body exquisitely slender. The way she looked at him from under her eyelashes was provocative, consciously or unconsciously, and to top it off, she had brains. Of course, she also had the instincts of a barracuda. And her class, which she had in abundance, was not inherited. Arnold knew his old San Francisco families, knew their pedigrees back several generations, knew who counted and who didn't. An irrepressible snob himself, he could name off the antecedents of everybody of importance in the city—and its environs.

And Chanel was the daughter of Murray "Tincan" O'Hara, an opportunist and entrepreneur who had parlayed a knack for sniffing out oil into a vast fortune, only to lose it to two even more rapacious rascals with blue blood in their veins. As for Chanel's mother—although she hadn't been around long, he happened to know that she'd been an unsuccessful Hollywood starlet who had caught Tincan's eye while he was still accumulating his fortune.

So how to account for Chanel's air of breeding? Of course, she *had* gone to Burlingame Academy, one of the better West Coast prep schools. Maybe she'd picked it up there. Whatever the truth, she was always turned out beautifully. Never too obviously so. Only the nouvelles riches wore everything new, everything fashionable. That Chanel's cool manner was deliberate, he was sure. He'd always had a special weakness for sexy women who kept their emotions under control. Which was why he was practically gibbering with curiosity to find out how she was going to take the news.

Would Chanel Devereau finally lose her cool today?

When Chanel had first arrived, he'd edged into his revelations carefully. First he concentrated on the dry legalese of the appraiser's report concerning Jacques Devereau's assets. From her creased brow, he knew Chanel was struggling to understand the meaning of what he was saying.

"Forget the details," she said finally. "What do those figures mean? Are you questioning the value of Jacques's collections? If his lawyer is trying to pull something—what about the photocopies of Jacques's records, as well as the snapshots of the most valuable stamps and coins and first editions in his collections that I turned over to you?''

"I'm afraid your husband has gradually, over the past few years, sold off the best of his collections. Some items, especially stamps, he replaced with valueless reproductions.'' Arnold paused for a dry cough, a little unnerved by the frozen expression on Chanel's face. "There's some mystery about where he got the replacements, but they are definitely not the genuine articles. The photos and records you copied were all true as far as they go. But he keeps an additional set of records itemizing his sales. He's been meticulously honest to the IRS about his capital gains from those sales, too. So what I have here is the evaluation of what remains, done by our own appraiser.''

"I don't believe any of this. He's got them stashed away someplace—''

"The sales were genuine. His lawyer turned over the affidavits and insurance records to prove it. He sold them all right, but it was done under the counter. I suspect secrecy was part of the deals he made, probably so he could get better prices on subsequent sales. Once a rumor of a distress sale gets started, the prices plummet. Or maybe he had another reason for not wanting anyone to know he was dissolving his collection.''

Chanel's nostrils flared; it was the only sign of what Mr. Waterford knew must be intense disappointment. "So what happened to the money? Did he stash it away in a Swiss bank account?''

"It's gone. Spent. A large portion went into oil futures, unfortunately at the wrong time, and the rest was spent to keep up the house, for living expenses, entertaining, your daughter's tuition at Burlingame Academy, your own very generous allowance.'' He sat back to watch her reaction.

To give her credit, Chanel absorbed the news, then moved on. "Then, he'll have to sell the house to settle with me,'' she said. "Too bad. I was hoping this wouldn't be necessary. It's been in his family for ages, you know.''

Arnold shook his head. "You don't understand. The house doesn't belong to Jacques. It belongs to his mother. When she dies, I presume he'll inherit it, but in any case, it's untouchable as far as you're concerned.''

Chanel stared at him fixedly. A flush covered her face. "He screwed me," she whispered. "The bastard screwed me."

"It could be worse. He does have a few assets left. The remainder of his collections, that part he acquired while married to you, should bring in enough to keep you going for a while—if you're very careful. You're still a young woman. Surely, you'll marry again."

Chanel didn't seem to hear him. She rose, gave herself a little shake as if ridding herself of a pesky fly. The steely look in her eyes made Arnold wince even though he knew her fury wasn't directed at him. "I'll fix that son of a bitch. I don't know how, but I'll find a way."

Arnold cleared his throat again. "He's provided quite well for you—and your daughter—for a number of years," he protested mildly.

She raked him with a hostile look. "You can tell his lawyer to put up the remainder of the collections for sale right away. And I want a search made for any assets he might have hidden. Moreover, I want a settlement as soon as possible."

She stalked out of the office—without, Arnold thought disapprovingly, a word of farewell, a thank-you-very-much, or by your leave. It wasn't until the door had closed behind her that he remembered he'd intended to ask Chanel out for dinner at The Blue Fox tonight. In retrospect, he was glad now that he hadn't gotten around to it.

CHAPTER FIFTEEN

SINCE LAIRD HADN'T PHONED CHANEL, AS PROMISED, THE WEEK following her dinner out with Fern, she decided to call him with the excuse that she was concerned about his cousin's state of mind, gradually leading into the subject of his casually offered luncheon "date." But to her gratification, as soon as she identified herself, Laird told her he'd been planning to call her to set a date for lunch.

"I've had trouble contacting Ariel. She used to take a walk on the Marina Green almost every evening, but I haven't seen her for the past week. When I called her house, I got her husband's answering service. I left a message, but she hasn't called back."

"Well, I'm sure I can reach her. Is Thursday okay? I'd like to be able to give her specifics."

"Thursday is fine. I'll have my secretary make a reservation at—how about one o'clock?"

"Great. Maybe we should arrange to meet Ariel at the restaurant. No use causing her any problems with—what's his name? Eric?"

"Alex."

"Why does he object to you seeing Ariel? You *are* her only relative, aren't you?"

"As far as I know. I'm very fond of Ariel even though there's a thirteen-year gap in our ages. She's always lived in some kind of never-never land. Old parents, a childhood illness that kept her out of school, that sort of thing. Have you seen that house? Art deco wedded to art nouveau—and Ariel fits right in. I've always thought how much she looks like one of those porcelain figurines so popular in the twenties. Persephone rising from her bath—you know the ones I mean?"

"Indeed I do."

"She's so cut off from the real world, something Alex should discourage. He is, after all, a psychiatrist."

"Maybe it suits him to have her completely dependent upon him," Chanel said, a little bored with the whole subject. "I think it's wonderful that you're so concerned. Most men—well, they really aren't all that sensitive."

"I'm very fond of Ariel," Laird said again. "Let's decide on a restaurant. Since Ariel's a vegetarian, it should be a place that specialized in salads and the like."

"There's that vegetarian place at Fort Mason—I think it's called Greens. But what about you? Wouldn't you prefer a more substantial meal?"

"I'm something of a vegetarian myself. Greens will be fine," he said.

When Chanel hung up, she was well pleased with the conversation. Nothing personal had been said—they might have been two men arranging a business lunch—but it was a start. She'd have her chance to make an impression on Laird during lunch. Luckily, Ariel wasn't one to dominate a conversation.

When she dialed Ariel's number, she got right through to Ariel;

a little to her surprise her lunch invitation was accepted without hesitation this time.

The following Thursday, when Chanel arrived at Greens, she was well primed to make a good impression on Laird. She had made a study of the women she'd seen him escorting, and she was pretty sure he had a weakness for a certain type, at least as far as outward appearance went. San Francisco chic was her own private name for it. Not the lacquered chic of New York, or the theatrical, faintly absurd chic of Beverly Hills or yet Parisian chic, starkly sophisticated and a little decadent, that she always thought of as the "Fifi look." No matter how much the price tag, true San Francisco style had an offbeat casualness, a bit of whimsy that said, "Hey, look—I know what the latest fashions are. I just don't choose to follow them rigidly."

So she wore a simple shift of coral silk with a matching jacket from one of the young local designers. She'd bought it on sale—but no one would guess it. And for the requisite touch of whimsy, she wore a chunky mother-of-pearl necklace that she'd bought at Cost Plus, and that would have looked tacky except the color was a perfect match for her silver-blond hair.

The restaurant, run by a Zen group, featured such exotica as basil pasta and mayorquina soup, with a predominance of cheese dishes, focaccia bread, and also fresh fruit crisp, which was pure midwestern. There was nothing cozy about the warehouse-sized restaurant, despite its pink napery and lowered lights, but it had a beautiful view of the bay and the service was swift, the staff solicitous, the food superlative.

From the beginning, things went well. Laird was amusing, in a good mood—or pretending to be for Ariel's sake. He was gallant to both women, treating them equally. Ariel lost her original shyness somewhere in the middle of her leek soup. She asked her cousin about his dog, which had been ailing, and about a trip to New York he had told her he was planning to take during the coming holidays, and she was friendly if a bit reserved toward Chanel.

"Does your husband know you're having lunch with us today?" Chanel said casually.

"Actually, Alex isn't home. He's in Washington. He has a client in—well, government. Once a month, he flies to Washington to give a therapy session. He'll be home tomorrow."

"You must miss him when he's gone," Chanel said, because it seemed the thing to say.

Ariel hesitated briefly. "The house seems very empty," she said.

Which was an evasive answer if ever she'd heard one, Chanel thought.

"I was surprised to learn that you two had reconciled," Laird commented. "What happened? Did the great—did Alex have second thoughts?"

"Alex says he never really wanted the divorce," Ariel said in her whispery voice. "He was overtired and wasn't thinking straight. Everything's fine between us now. It really is."

At this obvious lie, Chanel held her tongue. A little to her surprise, so did Laird. "Well, if you ever need a friend, don't forget that I'm right down the street," was all he said.

Ariel nodded, and Chanel wondered what was going on behind that shuttered expression. Not that she wanted to become Ariel's confidante. Getting involved in other people's lives entailed responsibility and unwanted demands upon your time. And she had enough troubles of her own to last her for the rest of her life.

For a moment, bitterness toward Jacques stirred. Jacques would go on being accepted by local society because he was one of them, no matter that he was no longer rich. But not Chanel. Oh, no, the divorce would make her persona non grata—unless she married someone richer, someone like Laird. . . .

"Are you okay?" Laird said, and Chanel realized she'd been clutching her hands so tightly around her fork that her knuckles were white.

"Oh, yes. I was thinking how devastating a bad marriage can be. When I married Jacques, I had such high hopes—but he was so much older than me, you see, so set in his ways. But I haven't given up on marriage—or at least on a good relationship. I guess I'm a hopeless romantic." She smiled ruefully.

Laird was watching her closely, his interest obvious, as she went on, carefully choosing her words. "The problem with being a divorcée is that suddenly you don't have an escort. Like this weekend. I had to turn down an invitation to the Andersons' dinner party because I didn't want to be a fifth wheel."

"Is that the Lars Andersons?"

"Yes. Nancy and I were schoolmates at Burlingame Academy."

"As it happens, I was invited to their dinner party, too, and asked to bring my own date. I had intended to—actually, I hadn't decided whether to go or not. Would you consider going with me?"

Chanel had a hard time concealing her elation. To turn up at Nancy's party on Laird's arm—what a coup! And there was little chance that Laird would learn the truth, that she hadn't been, never would be, invited to have dinner with the Lars Andersons. But as Laird's date, Nancy would have no choice but to be polite because he was several steps higher up the social scale. For one thing, he had something Lars lacked and that was an old, respected San Francisco family name. . . .

She smiled at Laird. "It sounds like fun. Are you sure you intended to go? You aren't just doing this to please me?"

Laird's eyelids flickered, and Chanel knew she'd guessed right. "The reason I hadn't accepted yet was because I thought it might conflict with another engagement. However, I was wrong. Shall I pick you up at seven? It's an hour's drive to Hillsborough."

As they made arrangements, Chanel was already planning what to wear. Something that would knock Nancy's eyes out. Nancy had let herself go—her dress size was at least a fourteen these days, and she favored cover-ups that looked a little dowdy, no matter what she paid for them. Later, when Laird took her home, she would invite him in for a nightcap. What happened after that she would play by ear.

During the rest of lunch she set out to make herself amusing. That Laird was enjoying her company she knew from the frequency of his laughs. Even Ariel responded to her gentle teasing with a smile. It was when Laird had excused himself and left the table that Ariel asked her diffidently, "Is it possible to talk to you in private soon? I—I need some advice."

Although Chanel was instantly wary, she had no choice but to nod. "Of course. What are friends for? Can you give me a hint what it's about?"

"It's—well, I have a personal problem that is rather embarrassing. Maybe I shouldn't trouble you with it—"

Was the poor wimp talking about sex? "Maybe you should," Chanel said, her curiosity aroused. "After all, we're both adults. If I can help . . ." She let her voice trail off.

"It's—it's something of a sensitive nature. I don't know if it's normal or not." She flushed bright red.

So that *was* it. Little Miss Goody Two Shoes was having sexual problems. What did her husband want her to do—have oral sex with him?

"You wouldn't be talking about sex, would you?" she asked, trying to look sympathetic.

"Well, that's part of it. Alex—oh, I can't talk about it, after all."

Chanel knew it would do no good to push it. She was really curious now—who wasn't curious about other people's sex lives?—but she was also relieved. The less she got involved with Ariel, the better. After all, she didn't want her hanging around after she was married to Laird.

She was still thinking about her conversation with Ariel when she reached home. As she hung up the clothes she'd worn to lunch, something about her walk-in closet bothered her. She kept her clothing in perfect order, each satin-padded hanger turned the same way, the colors together so she could find what she wanted quickly. And now they were out of order. A brown dress was hanging among the blues—and several of the hangers were turned the wrong way.

It didn't take her long to find out what was missing. A blue cocktail dress with a saucy, too-flirty look that she'd never worn because she'd realized when she got it home that it was too young for her. It had been one of her rare mistakes because she'd bought it "as is" and couldn't return it. In fact, she still kept it hanging in her closet as a reminder that when she was hurried or too tired, her taste was not infallible.

Breathing fire, she searched the chests and the armoire where she kept her sweaters and skirts only to discover that two of her cashmeres and a newly purchased skirt of Icelandic wool were gone, too.

She had no doubt what had happened to them. While she'd been out today, Fern had raided her closet. Did the little bitch think they wouldn't be missed? Or was she finally coming out into the open with her hostility instead of hiding it behind those smarmy remarks and sly smiles? Whatever the answer, Fern wasn't going to get away with it. It would set a precedent if she did. The next time it could be something that really mattered—and besides, the idea of someone else, even her own daughter, pawing through her clothes made her furious.

Chanel called Fern at school, but was told by the young voice that answered the dorm phone that Fern wasn't in her room. She left a message for Fern to call her mother about her allowance and then hung up. Fern would call fast enough when she realized her allowance was at stake. In fact, Chanel wasn't too unhappy that she had a good excuse to cut back on it. Once she'd paid all those horrendous bills that she'd accrued in anticipation of a large settlement from Jacques, she'd be living on a very strict budget. She needed every cent she had to maintain a front for Laird—provided he asked her out again. The question was—could she make her money stretch until she got a proposal out of him?

CHAPTER SIXTEEN

CHANEL FELT VERY SATISFIED WITH HERSELF AS SHE AND LAIRD stepped out of the elevator into the lobby of her apartment building. She hadn't really needed Laird's compliments or the admiration in his eyes to know that she had never looked better. At a cost she could ill afford, she'd spent the day at Adolfo's Salon on Maiden Lane, being packed in clay and massaged and manicured, having her toenails done and her legs waxed and her hair enhanced with subtle silver lights. And the gown she was wearing under her mink was one of her favorites, a misty rose velvet that enhanced her coloring without being too obvious.

One thing she could have done without was the unexpected appearance this afternoon of Fern, who had turned up with some tale about wanting to spend some time at home because she was bored, bored, bored with dorm gossip and lumpy dorm beds. When Chanel ticked her off for borrowing her clothes without permission, she looked so contrite and apologized with what seemed such genuine sincerity that Chanel had decided not to cut back her allowance. Time for that if things got tighter—or if her relationship with Laird didn't work out.

Fern had been snuggled up with a book on one of the living room sofas when Laird arrived. She jumped up to greet him, glowing and smiling and looking about sixteen. To her credit, she hadn't dropped any of those sly remarks that always made Chanel want to slap her. In fact, she chatted with Laird as if they were old friends, and when they left, she kissed Chanel's cheek, said

she looked simply awesome, and then added, ''Do have a marvelous time, Mummy.''

She'd even managed to look wistful, as if she wished she'd been
invited to go along.

Chanel wondered what Fern was up to—and then forgot her as
Laird helped her into his car, a navy blue Mercedes-Benz that she
privately thought much too conservative for someone who could
afford the very best. Of course, Laird also had a gray Rolls limo—
she'd seen him in it twice. Evidently he only used it when it was
expedient to be chauffeured somewhere. Too bad he was driving
tonight. She would have loved to have arrived at Nancy's house
in a Rolls limo.

During the long drive to Hillsborough, she concentrated on
charming Laird. He seemed both amused and bemused by her
bits of innocuous gossip, the throwaway humor she was so adept
at. Adroitly, she slipped the names of people they both knew into
the conversation, pretending friendships when acquaintance was
the truer situation, eventually shifting the conversation to Ariel.

"I'm worried about your cousin," she said. "She's so vulnerable."

"I'm glad Ariel has you for a friend," Laird told her, looking
very sober.

The dinner party, as Chanel expected, was not all pure pleasure. Oh, Nancy Anderson was subtle. The put-downs were so
adroitly administered that Chanel was sure no one else suspected
that her ex-schoolmate's solicitous inquiry about the health of
"your poor Daddy" was intended purely to make her squirm.
This satisfaction she denied Nancy by looking very sad, then reminding her in an obviously diplomatic voice that "Daddy" had
passed away years ago.

"The flowers you sent were lovely," she added sweetly. There
had been, of course, no flowers for Tincan O'Hara from Nancy
or from any of her former classmates. "But then I'd hardly expect
you to remember. You were going through some kind of crisis
around that time—a divorce, wasn't it?"

"You're mistaken," Nancy said, her voice frosty. "Lars is my
first husband—and I hope the last."

"Oh? Now, how could I have made such a mistake? It must
have been someone else," Chanel said, looking so embarrassed
that she knew everybody within earshot believed Nancy was lying.

So she had parried Nancy's barbs effectively, but it wasn't really the kind of triumph she wanted. It was her ex-schoolmate's acceptance—or at least her deference—that she was after. Being Laird's date might protect her from out-and-out hostility but it still didn't make her socially acceptable in her own right.

There were sixteen around the Anderson dinner table. The dining room was furnished in Chippendale, with silver birds, circled with low vases of tiny white orchids as a centerpiece. There was Indian crewelwork on the walls, a magnificent antique eight-paneled coromandel screen in one corner, and a collection of ivory and jade figurines in a glass-fronted cabinet. That explained the Indian sari Nancy was wearing, which Chanel thought an unfortunate choice for a figure that was borderline stout.

Chanel was sandwiched between a well-known New York art dealer, who talked intelligently about the latest art scandal, and a rather effete but charming man-about-town who wore too much cologne and whose gossip had a bitchy tinge.

Across the table, Laird was the recipient of avid feminine attention from the women on each side. One, the attractive young wife of San Francisco's French ambassador, seemed enchanted with him—or at least she talked to him exclusively, giving only perfunctory attention to her host, who was on her left. The other woman, Nancy's eighteen-year-old stepdaughter, whom Nancy had already let Chanel know would be debuting at the Christmas Cotillion in a few weeks, was no match for the ambassador's wife. She finally gave up and sat picking at her food, her mouth sulky.

As Chanel chatted amicably, dividing her attention equally between the men on each side, she couldn't help feeling smug. Of all the men there, Laird was tops in the looks and personality departments. That he was also probably the richest was icing on the cake.

After they left the party, Laird suggested they stop at the Venetian Room at the Fairmont Hotel to take in the new show, a well-known female singer who was on the comeback trail. Chanel agreed it might be fun—but not so eagerly that Laird would guess how much she'd been hoping for this.

When they reached the Venetian Room, even though they had no reservations, they were immediately shown to one of the better tables. In the wake of the maître d', they passed several couples Chanel recognized, and she knew the fact that Laird and she were dating would be making the gossip rounds the next day. During the rest of the evening, she chatted away vivaciously, as if unaware that her leg was lightly touching Laird's under the table.

The only thing that marred her enjoyment of the evening was the realization that Fern would probably still be up when Laird brought her home, so when he asked if she'd like to stop for a nightcap before they called it a night, she murmured, "At your place?"

He hesitated briefly, then said, "If you like."

"I'm just dying to see your house," she confided. "I've heard so much about it from Ariel."

"Oh? I didn't realize she'd ever been there. Our families didn't associate with each other, you know."

Chanel bit her lip, vexed with herself. "Actually, Ariel said that it was a marvelous old place. I assumed she was speaking from personal observation."

Laird nodded, and the subject was dropped. Fifteen minutes later, they were turning into the driveway of an impressively large house that faced the Marina Green. Its style was Tudor rather than art deco—"Moderne," Laird called them—as most of the houses along the street were, but the furnishings, she soon discovered, were pure turn-of-the-century.

"Too old to be fashionable and too new to be antique," Laird said of a matching pair of red plush Victorian sofas. "I keep thinking I should do something about refurnishing, but I never seem to get around to it."

"I wouldn't touch a thing if I were you. It's really charming," she said, although she privately thought it was pretty grim. "The Victorians and Edwardians knew how to be comfortable, didn't they?"

"It was a good life—if you were rich," he said. "Pretty rotten for the poor. I hate to think of the drudges who had to deal with wood ranges and fireplaces and lug hot water up flights of drafty stairs in freezing weather so my antecedents could have a hot wash and shave on winter mornings."

He helped her off with her ranch mink coat, a souvenir of her early marriage years when she'd been able to nag Jacques into occasional generosity. "Is coffee okay—or would you prefer a drink?"

"Coffee sounds wonderful," she said.

She liked that Laird led her without ceremony into a huge modern kitchen where he deftly fixed coffee. Knowing she looked like an exotic bird among all the cream-colored ceramic tile and stainless steel, she settled herself at a work counter and rested her chin on her hands, watching him. She didn't offer to help; he obviously didn't need it.

"Does your household help live out?" she asked.

"I have a married couple. They live in a cottage in the back of the garden. It works out very well. They're on call if needed, and yet they have privacy, too. Mary does the cooking and supervises the live-out cleaning women, and Robert takes care of the grounds, does any necessary handyman work, and sometimes acts as my chauffeur. They've been with me for years."

"Do you entertain often?"

"When my social obligations pile up too high, I have an occasional dinner party and once a year I throw one big shebang," he said. "My profession demands I do a certain amount of business socializing, so my yearly bash solves that problem, too."

"Fascinating," Chanel murmured. "You do seem to cope very well with being a bachelor."

"I have a reputation of being a gadabout, but actually I lead a rather quiet life."

"You seemed to be enjoying yourself tonight."

"Oh, yes, I like being with people, but not in droves and not all the time. There's nothing I'd rather do than take off in my boat for a few days."

Her interest quickened. "So you're a sailor? Or is it a fisherman?"

"Both."

"Well, I envy you—Daddy taught me how to sail and fish, but I haven't had much chance to do either lately. Jacques loathed exercise—and just about everything else that was fun."

"Perhaps there was just too much difference in your ages," Laird observed. "After all, you're two separate generations."

Chanel hesitated. Did he think she was that much younger than Jacques, who was forty-four, or was he just being diplomatic? "Perhaps," she said. "It didn't seem all that important when I was twenty, but later on—well, I'm still too young to be buried alive in that mausoleum."

"And much too beautiful," Laird said. "You look particularly lovely in that pink dress."

"Misty rose—to quote the designer," she said. "I'm afraid this dinner suit is three years old. Jacques was . . ." She hesitated a few heartbeats, then smiled sadly. "Luckily, I do take good care of my clothes."

"And you obviously have great taste."

Again, Chanel smiled—and then changed the subject. Compliments were good for the ego, but the trick was to turn the conversation back to Laird and give *his* ego a few strokes.

"May I ask you something that puzzles me, Laird?"

"Fire away."

"Since you could sell your brokerage firm for an astronomical price—and you *are* the Fairmount and Kling heir—why do you keep on working? Obviously, you'd like more leisure time to pursue other interests—didn't you tell me once that you were a photography buff?"

"I enjoy my work. I can't take any personal credit for being born with a silver spoon in my mouth, but I do take pride in having succeeded on my own. I'd go crazy if I weren't doing something challenging. Balance—that's the key to contentment."

"But your life *is* a little unbalanced, isn't it? Having a family is part of a well-balanced life."

"Oh, I have plenty of time for that," he said, looking amused. "I'm only thirty-five."

"And so you play the field?"

"I'm honest about it. That way no one gets hurt. One of these days, I'll get married and start a family. When I'm ready for it. Meanwhile—"

"Meanwhile you play the field."

"Why not? I enjoy women." He grinned at her. "I particularly enjoyed tonight. You're great company, Chanel."

"And this is the best fun I've had in—oh, in ages. I hope—" She broke off, held her breath, and bit down on her tongue until warmth flooded her cheeks. Producing a blush on cue was a trick she'd learned while she was a teenager—and it always worked. Laird was smiling, obviously intrigued.

"You still blush—now, that's a novelty." His voice was teasing. "What was it you hope, anyway?"

"I hope my life will be better in the future," she said promptly. "I knew I'd made a mistake as soon as I married Jacques, but there were so many good reasons to keep trying to make a go of it, not the least to give Fern a stable home. Unfortunately, Jacques wasn't good with children. He was always complaining about Fern making noise. In the end, I was forced to send her away to boarding school. Even then, he was annoyed during the summer when she came home. It hasn't been easy for Fern—or for me. She's always blamed me for neglecting her, you see."

"I do see. I suspect you also hung on so long because you didn't want to admit failure."

"That was part of it. I kept hoping Jacques—that things would change." She made a small moue. "And now I'm on my own again. It's pretty difficult. Jacques is so vindictive—somehow he managed to bury his assets somewhere, which leaves me in a rotten position because I have absolutely no job skills."

"There's marriage. A beautiful woman can always take that route." It seemed to her Laird was watching her too closely.

Chanel shook her head. "That's not an option. I would never marry just for security. And I'll manage. I have some plans in mind. I've thought about opening a shopping service, for instance," she improvised. "You wouldn't believe how good I am at making money stretch. I know every specialty store in the city—and where all the bargains are." She forced a brave smile. "And let's not talk about my problems. Tell me about your boat—"

When Laird drove her home, Chanel was satisfied that he'd enjoyed the evening, even though he hadn't tried to make love to her as she'd expected. She had been prepared to let him go so far and no further, to gently point out that she hardly knew him. To her chagrin, he hadn't touched her while they were at his house or later, when they reached her apartment house. After he'd escorted her to the elevator, he told her he'd had a marvelous evening, that he'd call her soon, and left.

Since Laird was her entrée into the world she coveted, Chanel was in a foul mood as she took the elevator upstairs. Where had she gone wrong tonight? Despite Laird's compliments, which she was sure were sincere, he had treated her with a little too much respect. Maybe it was time to drop the brave little woman act and get down to the business of seducing him. But to do that, she had to be in his company—and he hadn't asked her for another date.

The next morning, her ill humor disappeared when Laird phoned to invite her to go boating with him the following weekend.

CHAPTER SEVENTEEN

THE ORAL COOKIE WAS LOCATED ON COLUMBUS, ONE OF NORTH Beach's busiest streets, with a head store on one side and a movie house on the other. The head store had a steady stream of customers, mostly male, which in North Beach meant it dealt in exotic things that couldn't be displayed in its dusty windows, but the movie house, which featured hard-core porn, had fallen upon hard times since the advent of videotapes, and there were rumors it would soon close.

The Oral Cookie was surprisingly posh for the district. It featured a red velvet carpet and upholstered chairs, rosy-hued lighting, and a long mahogany bar. Although the waitresses wore high heels, black hose, and showed a lot of skin, their uniforms were well made and not cheap, and Glory often thought that she could have done worse.

She had learned the requirements of the job quickly—a perpetual smile, a deaf ear, and a few quips to turn off the invitations and suggestive remarks and blue jokes, a good memory for taking orders, and a quick side step to avoid groping hands. The language she heard didn't bother her. She'd heard worse, had used most of the words herself at some time or other. And the tips were good for a waitress who was willing to work her buns off. Which she was.

In fact, now that she was used to working there, the only thing that really bothered her was the smoke. It floated in layers above the tables, too thick for the air-conditioning, which was at least a decade old, to draw off completely. Sometimes, as she fought her way through the gray haze, she felt as if she'd give anything for a breath of good clean air.

Tonight, which was a Friday, was no exception. The small tables were packed, and the decibel level was enough to make conversation impossible without shouting. As she deftly evaded a groping hand, Glory wondered if she'd make it through to her first break.

"Two Buds dark, two vodka gimlets, Jimbo," she told the bartender, who was large and rough-looking, and had a yen for her. She slipped onto a stool to rest her feet while she waited for her order.

"Let me guess," Jimbo said. "Two middle-aged couples; beers for the guys, gimlets for the ladies."

"Wrong. Two young couples. Slummers, from their clothes. Beers for the ladies, gimlets for the men."

"You gotta be kidding."

"Would I kid you?"

"Yeah, you would."

"Okay. Middle-aged man and woman with a young couple I figure as their daughter and son-in-law. But they're still slummers."

"It figures." Jimbo went to get the drinks, and she put her hands behind her waist, stretching her back muscles, her eyes closed.

"Rough night?" Jimbo was back with the beer.

"So far I've had one groper, one proposition—the cheap bastard only offered me fifty dollars—and one old gent who keeps staring down my front," she said. "Typical night at the Oral Cookie."

Jimbo's grin was sympathetic as he dumped a generous amount of ice in a vodka-and-lime-juice mixture and put it on the shaker. The hum of the machine drowned out the noise from the band as she watched, admiring his deftness. She liked Jimbo—he was an ex-fighter whose face showed evidence that he'd gone a few too many rounds in the ring. Although there was no chemistry there as far as she was concerned, his partisanship toward her was useful. No one was going to go too far with her, not with Jimbo glowering at them from the bar.

"Guy's been asking questions about you," he said as he set the gimlets on her tray.

"Oh? What did he look like?" she said, not really interested.

"Big, young, blond hair—good-looking dude, but he's got a pair of mean eyes."

Glory's indifference fled. "What did he say?"

"Asked when you got off work. I told him it was none of his business, like I always do." He gave her stiff face a long look. "Someone you been avoiding?"

"Like the plague," she said grimly. "It sounds like my ex. We didn't exactly part friends."

"You afraid of the guy?"

"I'm afraid of the guy. He's got a heavy hand."

Jimbo's face darkened. "He comes around again, I'll give him a bounce he'll remember for a long time."

Glory shook her head. "I don't want any more trouble."

"Maybe I'd better see you get home okay tonight," he said.

"It's out of your way and besides, the muni takes me half a block from my door. If he bugs me, I'll yell for help. Dammit! How did he find out where I work?"

"I seen him in here before. Maybe it was—y'know, a coincidence."

"Maybe. And I'd better get these drinks to those people before Russ fires me."

"He won't fire you. You're the best waitress he's got," Jimbo said.

"Thanks—you aren't so bad yourself behind that bar."

Although her tone was light, she felt as if a heavy weight had settled on her shoulders as she picked up the tray. For the rest of the evening, she was jumpy, looking toward the door every few minutes, scanning the men at the bar. To her relief, there was no sign of Buddy. Either it hadn't been him, after all, or he'd decided not to make trouble for her.

As it happened, it was anger at her own fear that made her careless. She could have asked Jimbo to walk her to the bus stop when her shift was over or waited for the other girls, but because she was determined not to give in to nerves, she was alone as she started down the alley that led to the street. Even so, she had looked it over carefully before she left the safety of the open door. That was why she was so startled when Buddy stepped out of the shadows and grabbed her elbow. She started to jerk away, then froze when he raised a threatening fist.

"You hit me and you'll find yourself in jail," she said, sounding much braver than she felt.

"You've got a big mouth. You'd better listen instead of popping off."

"You got nothing to say I want to hear, Buddy."

"You bitch—you think I'm going to let you get away with what you did? I'm going to—"

"What you're gonna do, fellow, is let go of the lady's arm, like right now. Then you're gonna apologize for being such a jerk."

It was Jimbo, looming up behind Buddy. Glory stared at him with a mixture of exasperation and relief. Relief because Buddy had dropped her arm, and exasperation because she didn't want trouble—and both men, it was obvious, were just itching for a fight.

"Both of you back off," she said. But Jimbo only edged closer to Buddy; his wide mouth was set in a grim line, and his eyes held an ominous shine. From the way Buddy glared back, she knew she had to defuse the situation—quickly.

"Buddy is just leaving," she said. "And I'm not feeling well, Jimbo. Would you please give me a lift home?"

Jimbo hesitated; he finally nodded and took her arm. "Yeah— but you'd better watch it, mister." He glowered at Buddy. "I don't like guys who manhandle chicks."

A little to Glory's surprise, Buddy turned and swaggered off down the alley. She knew that he wasn't a physical coward, and she wondered at his backing off. It was obvious he still bore her a grudge—but maybe not enough to do anything about it. Was it possible that she could finally put this particular fear out of her mind?

The ride home in Jimbo's car was uneventful although he looked in the mirror frequently as if expecting to be followed. Glory made no comment; she was having a hard time not crying, a weakness that shamed her. It wasn't because she felt any lingering affection for Buddy. He'd killed that a long time ago. It was just that she hated failure—and her marriage to Buddy had been the biggest mistake of her life.

To her relief, Jimbo didn't try to prolong the evening. His good night when they reached her street was subdued. But before he let her out in front of her door, he told her gruffly to be careful. "That guy's a hothead—you never know what that kind will do."

After Glory let herself in with her key, she was careful to put on the chain and double-check the dead bolt lock. It was only then that she felt safe. Her last act before she went to bed that night was to make sure the windows and door were locked.

The next morning, when she stepped on the scales she'd bought three weeks ago, she discovered she'd lost exactly ten pounds, the goal she'd been aiming for. When she called Chanel to give her the good news and to remind her about her promise, Chanel was agreeable to a shopping trip.

"Let's make it Monday," she said. "I'm in the market for something special in a nightie that I hope to be needing soon. We can kill two birds with one stone.'' And then she gave her tinkling laugh.

The following Monday, Glory met Chanel for breakfast at one of the trolley diners that had sprung up around the city. The weather was perfect, a typical October San Francisco day. The breeze that blew in from the Marin County headlands across the bay was so crisp, it seemed to sparkle in the sunlight, which was every bit as golden as the song said it was. God seemed to have laid his hand on the City (which the local newspapers always spelled with a capital *C*) for the exclusive benefit of the natives who were well aware that autumn, when they had San Francisco mainly to themselves, was the best time of the year.

Glory ordered the same breakfast that Chanel did—a strip of crisp bacon, a poached egg, half an English muffin, and half a broiled grapefruit that had a tangy, unfamiliar taste.

''Orange blossom honey,'' Chanel told Glory. ''I stumbled on this place by accident. I was looking for a seamstress I'd heard about who could duplicate anything you brought her, and I stopped in for coffee. Quite a discovery, wouldn't you say, considering the price?''

Glory nodded agreement although she was still a little hungry. ''This seamstress—why would you want to have something duplicated?''

''Sometimes I take home a gown on spec from one of the better dress shops. Then I have a seamstress who knows her business duplicate it before I take it back. So sorry, I tell the store, it just didn't suit. And I have a smashing new gown for a fraction the cost of the original.''

''But isn't that—'' Glory broke off.

Chanel looked amused. ''Dishonest? Why? Does it hurt anyone? I certainly wouldn't buy the original, not at those prices, so I didn't cheat some salesgirl out of a commission. As for getting caught—it's never happened yet. The store managers who okay the spec don't exactly move in my social circles.''

The unconscious arrogance in her words silenced Glory. In fact, she was aware of envy. To have that kind of guts—well, she did have guts, although she wasn't into cheating people. All she needed was to get her foot in the door. Not the same doors that were open to Chanel. No, she knew her limitations, and Chanel had been born to her world. But something better than what she'd had so far in her life—yes, she could hope for that much.

The shop Chanel took her to first was a revelation to Glory. Until now, she'd only had contempt for secondhand clothing stores, even though she'd shopped them most of her life. Not only did the Repeat After Me Shop look nothing like a thrift shop, it was actually elegant, with its thick carpets, mural wallpaper, and real wax models. One display case was filled with jewelry—and Glory was sure not a piece of it was fake. If it hadn't been for the shop's name, she would've thought Chanel was playing some kind of joke on her.

"So what do you think?" Chanel asked.

"I think the prices are way out of line," Glory told her bluntly. She pulled a dress out of a rack and pointed to the price tag. "They want more for this plain little dress than for a brand-new outfit from I. Magnin."

"That particular dress is a Jimmy Gamba original. It cost at least five times that much new—and it's only been worn a couple of times, if that. You can see it's never been dry-cleaned."

"But it's so plain."

"And perfectly cut. And beautifully tailored. Open your eyes, Glory! Take a look at those handmade buttonholes, the French seams. The sleeves were set in by hand—see how the curved seams fit together without a pucker? It's worth several times the asking price—and it'll give years of wear. Not only that, but the woman who runs this shop is French. She can be bargained with."

Glory put the dress back on the rack and took out another one. "I like this one better," she said.

Chanel snorted. "Shoddy workmanship, run-of-the-mill material, a poor copy of a Fiandaca original—which wasn't all that great to begin with." She gave Glory a severe look. "You have to be able to recognize real value, or you can make some expensive mistakes. This one isn't worth a tenth what they're asking for it."

Glory, who liked the dress, especially the bold pattern of the material, felt chastised. "I think I see what you mean," she said cautiously. "Where did you learn so much about clothes?"

"Observation. Study. All it takes is good common sense and the desire to learn. I can help you pick out something to wear today, but it won't do you much good in the long run. I can't shop with you all the time. You're going to have to learn on your own and then trust your own judgment."

She gave Glory a critical look. "The leopard-skin design on that tunic and pants outfit you're wearing is all wrong for you.

You're too flamboyant to wear anything so—so busy. You look like you just stepped out of a bordello."

"Bordello? What's that?"

"A cathouse. And before you do any serious buying, you should lose another ten pounds. As a size eight, you'd have the perfect figure for your frame. What do you wear now, a twelve?"

"A ten," Glory said testily. After all, she'd practically starved herself to death losing those ten pounds.

"If you say so. It's a matter of tightening up those flabby muscles. And also you should tone down your overall appearance. Simple, classic styles—but nothing tailored. That's not for you. Soft and feminine, simple and unadorned but not dowdy. And you can get away with whimsy as long as you don't overdo it. You can go dramatic—for evening wear—provided you're careful. I can just see you in a Diane Dickinson—"

"In a what?"

"Diane Dickinson. She's a designer and a good one. Perfect for you, but I doubt we'll find any of her originals at reduced prices. But there are others—we'll have to keep looking."

There was open relish in her voice. She's enjoying this, Glory thought. She herself hated to shop, hated being forced to hunt for bargains, hated always having to worry about the price. On the other hand, Chanel made no bones about never buying anything for its original price—and *she* was a real class act. . . .

"Did you get a good settlement from your husband—or is it none of my business?" she asked Chanel.

Chanel's face tightened briefly, but her tone was airy as she said, "Not as much as I wanted but I guess I'll have to live with it." She dismissed the subject with a shrug. "How about trying on this one? Just to see how you look in lapis lazuli blue."

For the rest of the afternoon, the two women went from store to store, some of them tucked away in places that Glory, although she had lived in the city all her life, had never heard of. As they walked, Chanel gave her a running account of where to buy accessories for the best price—an outlet store for a famous shoe manufacturer on Post Street; a small shop half a block from Macy's where seconds and odd lots from a European designer were sold; a thrift shop in the avenues that featured old theatrical costumes that, Chanel assured Glory, could be bought for a song provided she was prepared to do a lot of bargaining with the eccentric old man who owned the place.

Somewhere along the way, Glory discovered she was having a

good time. For one thing, Chanel, for all her classy appearance, was down-to-earth—and surprisingly candid. Before they parted— Glory to go to work and Chanel to keep a hair appointment—they made a tentative date to get together again when Glory had lost another five pounds.

"First I'll take you to Adolfo—he's my hairdresser—to see what he can do with your hair, and then we'll go shopping. I'm going to give you a crash course in style and fashion—real fashion, not the ersatz kind. After that, it's up to you," Chanel said, and to Glory's surprise, she found she didn't resent the other woman's patronizing tone.

That night Glory set her alarm for seven o'clock. In the morning, she would be starting the aerobics class Chanel had recommended. The sooner she lost those extra five pounds and got her body back in shape, the sooner she could begin her transformation.

Just call me Cinderella Browne, she thought.

CHAPTER EIGHTEEN

ARIEL WAS AWARE, EVER SINCE ALEX'S RETURN FROM HIS monthly trip to Washington, that she was on probation. For what, she had no idea. But there was repressed anger in every word he addressed to her, in every glance he sent in her direction. When he came to her for a conjugal visit, he was only interested in his own gratification, and she found it increasingly hard to cooperate because only when she herself was sexually aroused did she find these sessions even halfway tolerable.

At first, she endured his visits stoically, afraid of angering him further by telling him how she felt, and when the situation became unendurable, she discovered that wine or a glass of brandy, taken ahead of time and followed by breath mints, blurred the world around her during his visits. After he'd left her bed, she would have another couple of drinks so she could sleep. In the mornings, of course, she suffered—headaches, nausea, all the symptoms of a hangover. Since Alex only visited her twice a week now, on Mondays and Thursdays, even a hangover seemed preferable to the humiliation of servicing his needs. There was another humiliation, too. She herself no longer had any sexual release—and she needed it badly.

When it finally came to her that Alex had chosen this way of punishing her for whatever crime she'd committed, she rebelled. The next time he came to her room, she refused to talk to him, to touch him.

He didn't strike her although she half expected it, nor did he lacerate her with recriminations. Instead, he put his robe back on and stalked out of the room, shutting the door behind him. It wasn't until she heard a scraping sound that she realized he had locked her in.

Claustrophobia swept through her. She rushed to the door and began frantically twisting the knob. When the door didn't open, she backed away, staring at the delft blue flowers painted on the enamel knob. It was hard to breathe; there was a smothering sensation in her chest like the ones she sometimes got when she was in a crowded place.

Despair racked her. Alex would always win because he knew her fears, her weaknesses. For almost a year, week after week, she had poured out her secrets, told him what shamed her and made her feel guilty, what frightened her—such as her fear of being locked in a closed place.

With a mewling cry, she flew across the room and flung up a window. For a long time, she stood there, taking long breaths of night air into her lungs. If only she had something to drink in her bedroom—in the future, she would make sure she had an emergency bottle hidden away somewhere. But for now—surely, there was something in her medicine cabinet to help her.

Sitting next to the vitamins she took religiously, she found a bottle of sleeping pills that Alex had prescribed for her early in their marriage. She took two, not bothering to wash them down with water, then returned to bed. Although she expected to lie awake for a while, the pills worked almost immediately, and she sank into a deep, dreamless sleep.

When she awoke in the morning, the first thing she did was try the doorknob. It turned in her hand, and she leaned against the door, her eyes closed with relief. When had Alex unlocked the door—and why? To show that he could be reasonable—provided she didn't cross him?

Not wanting to encounter Alex, she tiptoed down the hall. The old house was so quiet that even through its thick walls, she could hear the traffic on Marina Boulevard. Because she hadn't eaten much at dinner (she never did on Mondays and Thursdays), she was ravenous. She got bread and cheese and a carton of milk from the kitchen, and was hurrying through the dining room, heading for the staircase, when she paused to stare at the old chinoiserie cabinet where an extra supply of liquor was kept. After a moment's hesitation, she opened the door, snatched up a bottle at random, and carried it upstairs to her bedroom.

She set the food down on a chest, then turned to lock the door behind her, wishing she could so easily lock out her own fears and confusion. As she hid the bottle in the depths of her closet, she discovered it was vodka instead of brandy. Well, she would save it for emergencies. Just knowing it was available would probably be enough.

She had finished off the food and was dozing on the bed when a sound awakened her. With fascinated eyes, she watched the doorknob's futile movement. A knock followed.

"Miz di Russy? You okay in there? The door won't open."

Ariel recognized the voice of their live-out housekeeper and released her breath in a long sigh. Of course—this was Friday, the day Maria gave the upstairs rooms a thorough cleaning. She slid off the bed and went to unlock the door, stepping aside so Maria could enter with her cleaning tools.

Maria was Chicano; she had come to California from Mexico when she was nineteen, already a married woman with three children. Two years later, she was a widow, raising four kids on a housekeeper's pay. It always seemed incredible to Ariel that they were the same age.

"You don't look so good, missus. You sick or somethin'?"

Ariel wondered what Maria would think if she told her that yes, she was sick, but that it was a sickness of the mind, not the body. "I didn't sleep very well last night," she said. "That's why I overslept this morning."

"Well, it's almost eleven, and Doctor, he say would I check on you. He's got a patient coming at eleven or he would check himself. That's what he say," she added, her voice noncommittal.

Ariel met Maria's brown eyes. They were veiled today, unreadable. Sometimes, Maria talked about her family, and Ariel knew that she had no relatives to help her raise her kids, that she was fiercely protective of them, that she lived in the Mission district in what she had once described as a rat hole.

She sensed that Maria was afraid of Alex, something she understood all too well. Her own relationship with Maria was very formal; from Maria's uncommunicative expression now, Ariel realized there wouldn't even be an exchange of idle talk today. Maria might not like Alex, but she knew on which side her bread was buttered, and she never invited confidences, making it very clear that she didn't want to get involved, not at the risk of her job.

"You want I should change the sheets in the guest room today?" Maria said.

"We haven't had any overnight guests since you changed them the last time," Ariel said, stating the obvious. After all, they never had overnight guests.

"So where you want I should start?"

"I'm going to take a shower now. I'll be out of my bathroom in a few minutes. Why don't you do his—Dr. di Russy's room first?"

"Okay, missus." Maria picked up her cleaning tools tray, but she lingered long enough to ask "You sure you feel okay? I can fix you some breakfast if you want."

"Thank you, but I've already had some cheese and crackers."

Maria nodded. "Doctor, he say do the blue guest room extra good 'cause you seen some cobwebs in there. I don't know how that could happen 'cause I run that rod thing over the ceilings just about every week. Maybe I need some glasses. A person can miss a lot of what's going on around them if they don't keep their eyes open."

Ariel stared at her. What was Maria trying to say? She discovered that she didn't want to know. Better to live with her head in the sand than to court more trouble. Sometimes it was better to be ignorant.

"Don't worry about it, Maria. I'm sure he was—was teasing you. I didn't complain about any cobwebs. Dr. di Russy knows what a thorough job you do," she said, surprising herself. She had sounded almost—well, diplomatic. "I'll be out of your way in a few minutes. I think I'll take a walk and see if that doesn't clear my head."

"You do that. But maybe you should wear a scarf or somethin'. The wind's real bad today, and you don't wanta catch no cold."

After Maria left, Ariel took a quick shower, then put on a warm sweater and a wool skirt. When she heard the wind whistling through the eaves above her bedroom window, she wished she had the nerve to wear jeans. Alex didn't like her in pants, even tailored ones. He preferred her in dresses, preferably very feminine. "The perpetual virgin," he called her, his tone mocking.

Ariel discovered she was breathing too hard; she wrenched her thoughts away from Alex and hurried down the hall. The familiar hum of the vacuum cleaner, coming from the master suite, was comforting. Why had Alex complained about cobwebs? He hadn't been teasing Maria—Alex never teased anyone. So he had probably done it to keep their housekeeper off balance because he knew how desperately Maria needed her job. It wasn't that she couldn't get work elsewhere, but the pay was better here, and of course, Alex always paid her in cash.

Alex, in an expansive mood, had once explained it to Ariel.

"The way you get the best work out of your help is to have something on them—and then pay them just a tad more than they'd get anywhere else. Keep them off balance by blowing hot and cold. One day you praise them and the next you jump on them for some minor shortcoming." And then he'd added, "That way you always stay in control."

Was that how he kept his wife under control, too, by blowing hot and cold and keeping her off balance?

Ariel was coming down the front staircase when the doorbell rang. Before she could retreat, Alex came out of the library and went to answer it. Although he employed a full-time secretary, she worked at home, transcribing his notes and typing his letters from tapes. He'd told Ariel that he wanted to create a more personal relationship with his patients by having their sessions in a homelike atmosphere, which precluded having a receptionist or nurse. That it also, in her opinion, violated medical ethics, she was careful not to point out.

As she watched, Alex welcomed his patient, a slender, very young woman who looked so troubled that Ariel wondered what her problems might be. Alex greeted her kindly, his voice unctuous, and a tiny smile lifted the corners of the woman's lips. He was ushering her in to his office when he glanced up and saw Ariel standing on the stair landing, watching him.

His eyes took on a frost whether as a continuation of the night before or because she had disobeyed his rule never to have any contact with his patients, she couldn't guess. He said something in a low voice to his patient, and they disappeared into the library.

Ariel had almost reached the hall when he reappeared unexpectedly, closing the door behind him.

"You finally got up, I see," he said.

"I overslept. I have a terrible headache, so I thought I'd take a
walk on the Green."

She avoided his eyes, afraid of the censure she would find there,
but his voice was normal when he spoke.

"Well, be careful. People don't curb their dogs the way they
should these days, you know." At her nod, he went on, "You
wouldn't be meeting anyone, would you?"

"Meeting someone?"

"Like that cousin of yours who's so concerned about you."

She flushed. "No, of course not. He's probably at work."

"Oh, yes, the big stockbroker. I'd forgotten he's into the pro-
ductive citizen thing."

His derisive tone angered Ariel, but she was careful not to show
it. "Why did you think I was meeting Laird?"

"You quote him so often, even though you know my opinion
of the man. He's a first-class snob—that's the trouble with your
old San Francisco families. The blood thins out, and they have
more neuroses than you can shake a stick at—which is why you're
such a psychiatric mess."

Ariel took a deep breath; strange how Alex could always find
the right words to hurt her. "You said I was cured."

"Cured? I gave up on you because you didn't really want to be
helped. That exhibition you put on last night, for instance. A
normal woman doesn't refuse her husband. You're sick, Ariel—I
think you should think seriously about having yourself committed
to a sanitarium."

He turned and went back into his office.

Ariel stood on the bottom step of the stairs, staring at the door,
wishing she could see through it. The woman had been so young,
so troubled. What was Alex doing right now? Was he drawing
her out, making her feel warm and comfortable and safe? Or had
they passed that stage? Maybe he was touching her, stroking her—
how many of his patients did he use his special therapy on? Once,
she would have said that she was the only one. Now, she wasn't
sure. One patient had fought with him bitterly in the hall just
before she dropped him. She had called him a satyr and then she'd
threatened to report him to the police.

Ariel had looked the word *satyr* up in the dictionary because
she wasn't sure she knew its correct meaning. *A lascivious man,*

it said. She looked up *lascivious*, and found it meant having wanton desires; being lustful and lewd. Did those things really describe Alex? Did he have unnatural desires? Was that why she was still a virgin?

Ariel turned slowly and went back up the stairs. She'd lost all interest in a walk. Right now, she wanted to be alone, and she hoped Maria had finished cleaning her room so she could get a drink from the bottle of vodka she'd hidden in her closet and then go back to bed.

Janice enjoyed giving parties. She had a deep interest in other people and what made them tick—which was the main reason she'd decided to become a sociologist. The old Victorian that was a white elephant in so many ways had one redeeming grace. It was made for entertaining large groups of people. There were so many downstairs rooms to spread out into, so many comfortable groupings of chairs and sofas, of nooks and crannies in abundance where two people could sit and talk undisturbed, letting the party flow around them.

This evening, for no reason she could pinpoint, she felt totally out of it. As she sat listening while Merv Scranton, her college roommate's husband, give a great imitation of a TM guru whose lecture Casey had coerced him into attending, she had to force herself to laugh. Which was strange because usually she found Casey's husband very amusing.

She wondered, as she had so many times, why Jake and Merv had never hit it off. Jake's favorite name for him was Ichabod. "Like in Crane," he said. "All he needs is a swaybacked horse and a pumpkin."

It was true that Merv had been shorted in the looks department. Everything about him was long and lanky and awkward. But it was also true that he was friendly, intelligent, and also amusing. Since Jake teased her sometimes about being too serious, he should be happy that she was one of those people who found Merv comical. His droll way of poking fun, never at the vulnerable but only at the stuffy, touched some chord of humor in her own nature.

Instead, Jake called him a bore. He was just as critical of Casey, whom he'd called "Icabod's hausfrau" until Janice had finally lost her temper and asked him to please stop.

Janice glanced across the room to where Casey was sitting, absorbed in a discussion with one of the older faculty wives. From the snatches of conversation she caught from time to time, they were talking about babies. Through the open door that led into the kitchen, she heard Jake's voice. He was telling someone about his experience with a surly mechanic, making it sound amusing when actually the whole incident had been embarrassing. But then—Jake was a born raconteur, a gift she certainly didn't have. When she tried to tell a joke, she always managed to mangle it thoroughly. Which was why she left such things to Jake.

She realized Merv had fallen silent. She met his quizzical smile and knew he'd noticed her inattention. "Your mind has gone a-wandering," he said. "What's eating you, Janice?"

"Nothing's eating me. I'm a bit tired is all. I had a rough day."

"Getting ready for this shindig? Or have you been stewing over your dissertation?"

"I see Casey's been talking," she said.

"Only to me. She's big on secrets."

"It isn't exactly a secret. Just something I'd rather keep to myself. The source of my research—well, it's a bit sensitive."

"Uh huh. Well, go for it. You deserve your chance. After all, Jake had his, didn't he?"

There was a note in Merv's voice that made her study him closely. Was it possible he knew that Jake disliked him? Or was he envious of Jake's success? No, she couldn't believe that. She'd swear Merv didn't have a jealous bone in his rangy body. So what was it with him and Jake? Why was she suddenly so sure that he returned her husband's dislike?

"How are things going in the English department?" she said when the silence began to be embarrassing.

"Going very well. Seems I may get my tenure soon, which is a real upper."

"Congratulations! I'm really happy for you," she said, her voice warm.

"Hey, not so quick. It isn't official yet. Just a maybe—"

"What's a maybe, husband mine? You two have had your heads together much too long and I'm getting jealous," Casey said as she came up behind Merv.

"Give me a break. Who can resist rapping with your gorgeous ex-roomie?" Merv said, moving over to make room for his wife on the sofa. Casey was six months pregnant with their third child; she had been wearing maternity clothes for three months now. In the past ten years she had picked up a lot of weight, but it was a mark of the affection between them that Merv didn't seem to notice—or care.

Casey had confided to Janice once when she'd had a bit too much to drink that their sex life had fallen into a rut in the past two years, but that when they tried to experiment with anything kinky, they both got to laughing so hard they couldn't make love. Janice thought of her own sex life and wondered if Casey would call some of her and Jake's more creative practices kinky. Probably so, she thought, but then—it was all good clean fun. She and Jake might have a few minor differences, but he could still ring her chimes in bed.

"So what were you rapping about?"

"Janice was just about to tell me all about her doctorate prospectus," Merv said slyly.

"Don't believe him, Casey. It shall remain a secret until I'm sure I want to go ahead with it. Jake isn't—well, he isn't too enthusiastic about it."

"Somehow I'm not surprised," Merv said.

"Why do you say that?"

Merv shrugged. "Because I'm sure that Jake wants the best for you. Naturally he doesn't want you to be disappointed again."

Janice relaxed, wondering what was wrong with her tonight. She seemed to be reading cracks where none were intended. "He *has* become a little doubtful about Dr. Yolanski lately. He thinks I should try to get another adviser."

"But Yolanski was Jake's adviser. I thought he was happy with him," Casey protested.

"He was—and actually, I prefer him to any other professor in the Sociology Department. He's tough, but he's fair. And he was right about my first two proposals. They certainly didn't have the potential for original research."

"And the new one does?"

"It does," Janice said firmly.

"What doesn't Jake like about it?"

"He thinks I can do better," she said evasively. Wanting to change a sore subject, she added, "How about some nibbles?"

"Do you have any more of those yummy crab popovers?" Casey said hungrily. She patted her ample stomach. "I know I shouldn't, but Baby needs refueling."

"I've got more in the kitchen," Janice said, glad for an excuse to escape.

When she went into the kitchen, Jake was holding court in the center of a crowd, most of them women. As she watched the animation and humor on his lean face, she wasn't surprised that they were hanging on his words. Why was it that even in a gathering packed with interesting and attractive men, he was the one who always drew the most feminine attention? Technically speaking, he wasn't handsome—was it because he radiated vitality, a vitality that seemed to be catching? Or was it his supreme confidence, his obvious enjoyment of people. There was no doubt he had charisma. If he ever went into politics, he would win all the female votes in his district, hands down. . . .

Jake finished his anecdote and in the midst of the laughter that followed, he spotted Janice. He beckoned to her and, when she came up, put an arm around her shoulder. "Honey, I don't think you've met Arlene Turner, have you? She's doing some work toward her doctorate."

Janice exchanged smiles with the woman. Arlene Turner was a decade older than Jake's usual students, which didn't surprise her since she was going for her doctorate. She was very striking-looking, with auburn hair and long, narrow eyes that studied Janice a little too closely. The Mexican blouse that bared her pale shoulders could have looked too young on her, but instead it looked just right. Sexy without being obvious. Casual without being tacky. Just right.

"Your husband is the most marvelous teacher," Arlene said in a husky voice. "I was just telling him that he should be teaching a TV course. My husband's in Public TV—he's program director at KQMB—and he's always looking for new talent for the morning credit courses. I'm trying to convince Jake to have a talk with him."

"It sounds interesting," Janice said politely. She smiled at Jake. "I'm on an errand of mercy. Casey is dying for some of those crab popovers."

She got a tray of the popovers from the freezer and put them in the microwave to heat. When the bell rang, she transferred them to a plate, carried them into the other room, and sat them down in front of Casey. "Enjoy, enjoy," she said, and earned Casey's laugh.

The din was rising; not for the first time, she was glad they didn't have any close neighbors. Everybody was having a good time, which wasn't surprising because Jake attracted bright, creative people of all ages, and invitations to their parties were highly coveted at the university. So why did she suddenly wish they would all go home?

No, that wasn't fair. It wasn't the people. They were as amusing as ever. It was she who was out of step tonight, in a mood she didn't understand, a mixture of uneasiness, of apprehension. Was she heading for a nervous breakdown or something?

Around her, the party went on. If she wasn't her most attentive, no one seemed to notice. A game of charades was in full swing now. When Jake's turn came, he did an imitation of a spouting whale so graphically that his partner, Arlene Turner, guessed it was Moby Dick in three seconds, winning the game. So the woman was clever, too, Janice thought. So why didn't she like her?

It was much later that night, after the last guest had departed and she was sitting with Jake at the kitchen table drinking coffee and having their usual after-the-party postmortem, that Jake told her he'd decided to talk to Arlene Turner's husband about a TV series.

"It means a lot of exposure, which is one of those good news/ bad news things. You have to be careful not to let ole debble jealousy raise its horny head. But on the other hand, we can use the money, now that you're not working. Arlene acts as her husband's assistant and she's promised to show me the ropes if he takes me on. The publicity could be helpful to my career. You have to stand out above the crowd to make it in education these days."

"Well, that's no problem for you. You never faded into a crowd in your life," she said, thinking how little he'd changed since the day they'd first met. How was it that the years could be so kind to a man and so hard on a woman? There were times lately when she felt—and suspected she looked—ready for Medicare.

". . . Then the poor slob made the mistake of saying that in his opinion some of the old teaching methods should be banned, and the old man about exploded." There was open relish in Jake's voice. "You'd think Walters would learn, wouldn't you? All those brains and he doesn't have one ounce of common sense in his head."

"He's really very nice," Janice said, although she knew Jake wouldn't appreciate her defending the professor he considered his main rival for the position that would be open when the present department head retired. "The students like him—or at least a girl who works in the college bookstore told me once that she was crazy about his class.''

Jake's face darkened. ''He's a loser,'' he said bluntly. ''He hasn't published one paper in the past five years.''

''Maybe he doesn't have a wife to type them up for him,'' she said teasingly.

Jake looked at her coldly. ''Is that a crack?''

''It was a joke. You know—like you're supposed to laugh?''

''Well, it sounded like you were trying to tell me something.''

''I enjoy typing your manuscripts, Jake. I don't even mind editing them. Like all geniuses, you're a little careless about mundane things such as punctuation and spelling.''

''I leave such things to the grubs. All us geniuses do.'' He grinned at her, his good humor restored. ''And you know what else I'm a genius at? If you can't guess, I'll demonstrate it in the bedroom in about five minutes.''

She groaned. ''Look at this mess—who's going to clear it away if we're upstairs doing what I think you mean?''

''So leave it. We can take care of it in the morning. Right now I want to ravish you—you lucky girl.''

She studied the shine in his eyes. ''People give you a high, don't they?'' she said.

''Right. So let's make out.''

''A good idea,'' she said, giving in. Why fight it? She wanted it as much as he did. ''In fact, that's the best offer I've had all evening.''

But later, after they had made love and Jake was asleep, Janice was awake, reliving the party in her mind. The food had been good and varied, the drinks plentiful, even though no one drank much these days with the new rigid California drunk-driving penalties, and from the din that had filled the house and the way everybody had lingered, it was obvious that the party had been a success. So what was bothering her? Was it Jake? He'd been so keyed up tonight. In fact, his lovemaking had been almost frenzied. Was it the possibility of teaching a TV class that had turned him on? Maybe he'd fallen into a rut lately and needed something new to stimulate his interest. Well, if that's what he wanted, who was she to point out how much time it would consume—time he didn't really have.

Janice was thinking about the next meeting of the club, wondering how on earth she was going to continue the farce that her marriage had failed, when she finally fell asleep.

CHAPTER NINETEEN

THE QUARREL WITH ALEX WOULDN'T HAVE BOTHERED ARIEL half so much if it hadn't erupted before a witness. Later, she would wonder if Alex hadn't done it on purpose. After all, when they'd eaten breakfast together that morning, although he'd been immersed in the morning paper as usual, he hadn't seemed upset about anything. His egg had been boiled exactly six minutes, the two link sausages he allowed himself were crisp, and his whole wheat toast was a delicate brown, just the way he liked it. He'd even complimented Maria on the excellence of her cooking. His verbal attack on Ariel came later—in front of Maria.

Usually, Ariel was careful to stay out of Maria's path, but today a restlessness, or maybe it was loneliness, sent her wandering into the kitchen where Maria was giving the cooking range its weekly cleaning. They were deep in conversation about Maria's oldest child, who was having trouble at school, when Alex stormed into the kitchen, holding an empty vodka bottle in his hand.

"What the hell is this?" he demanded.

Ariel felt the blood rush from her head. The last time she'd seen that bottle was the night before. After she'd had a nightcap, she'd returned it to its hiding place in her closet. It had been half full.

"I don't understand," she said, even though she knew it was hopeless. "It's a vodka bottle, isn't it?"

"Where do you think I found it? Hidden behind the shoe rack in your closet. I'm warning you—either your drinking comes to a halt or I'm taking away your tranquilizers. You know how dangerous mixing drugs and alcohol can be. I want your promise that the drinking will stop—and maybe you'd better turn over your sleeping pills to me for safekeeping, too. I don't approve of them for a healthy woman your age."

Ariel stared at him in bewilderment. "But I don't take tranquilizers. All I take is those vitamins you prescribed for me and an occasional sleeping pill—"

159

"Then, what happened to that last prescription of sleeping pills I had filled for you? There's only three pills left in the bottle."

"I don't know anything about that. The last time I took any, the bottle was almost full. And I haven't touched them since."

"Then, who did?"

To Ariel, it seemed that he was looking at Maria. Maria didn't seem to notice; she went on cleaning the range, her dark face expressionless.

"Why did you hide that bottle in your closet anyway?" Alex demanded. "There's a whole cabinet full of liquor downstairs."

"I didn't want—sometimes I have a drink just before I go to bed to make me relax. It's—uh, more convenient to keep a bottle in my room. I put it in the closet so it wouldn't get knocked over by accident. I wasn't hiding it—why would I do that?"

"Because the liquor in the bar has been disappearing at record rate? Because you didn't want me to know how much you've been drinking?"

"I only have a drink now and then—"

"Then, why the hell are our liquor bills so sky-high lately?"

He stared at her a moment longer as if expecting her to challenge him. When she was silent, he made an impatient gesture. "I think we'd better continue this conversation later—in private," he said, as if he'd just discovered that Maria was there. "I don't like lecturing you as if you're a child, but when you act like one— how does it look, a psychiatrist's wife behaving so stupidly?"

His gaze rested on Maria's stolid face. "And I don't want this business to go any further, Maria. You understand?"

Without waiting for an answer, he turned and was gone. Ariel was so humiliated, she couldn't look at Maria. Instead, she stared out the window at the gardener, who was planting Imperial bulbs, the great showy tulips that were always synonymous with spring to her.

"You like some tea, missus?" Maria said unexpectedly. "It make you feel better."

Her voice was matter-of-fact rather than sympathetic, but it released Ariel from her embarrassment. "I'm sorry you had to— that you heard that," she said.

Maria snorted. "Don't you worry none 'bout that, missus. At my house, somebody always fighting. Now it's the kids, yelling with each other. Used to be, it was my old man and me. When he got hurt, couldn't work, he used to carry on like crazy sometimes. Guess it runs in the family, 'cause my kids are the same. Always fussing about something.''

She busied herself with the kettle, putting loose tea in the old willowware pot that had belonged to Ariel's grandmother, setting out a cup and saucer. When the kettle began to whistle, she poured boiling water over the tea and set the pot in front of Ariel.

"What the doctor says 'bout mixing pills and liquor—he right 'bout that," she said then. "You be careful, Miz di Russy."

"But I don't take tranquilizers and I very seldom take sleeping pills," Ariel protested. "It was Alex's idea that I keep them around. I have no idea what happened to those pills. The last time I looked the bottle was almost full."

Maria's eyes turned oblique. "You be careful," she said darkly. "It ain't none of my business but—you be careful, you hear?"

She turned back to the range, her back so uncommunicative that Ariel knew the conversation was over.

To Ariel's surprise, Alex apologized for making a scene that afternoon at lunch. He also insisted that they go out to dinner, and although she would have preferred to stay home, she knew better than to say so.

They ate at The Blue Room as they usually did. It was a glossy restaurant with ultramodern decor and what their menu called California ranch cuisine. Ariel always was uncomfortable there. She would have preferred a smaller, more intimate place. As it was, she felt as if she were on exhibition in the brilliantly lighted dining room.

The food, too, was not something she would have chosen. She favored bland foods—cream soups, salads, pasta with vegetable sauce, fruit. Alex, however, preferred two-inch steaks—"Tell the chef not to butterfly that steak!" he told their waiter as he always did—baked potatoes, and the hearty baked beans that were the restaurant's specialty.

He ordered for both of them without consulting her, and when the food came, she looked at the red juice that dripped from the steak, her stomach lurching. If she could have continued to be a vegetarian, as she'd been before she married Alex, without causing a constant fuss, she would have done so. As it was, she ate meat as seldom as possible, and then only to keep the peace. Knowing that Alex was watching, she managed to force down a few bites she cut from the outside edge of the steak and finish off most of her potato.

As if to placate her for his accusations that morning, Alex kept urging wine upon her. She drank it willingly, hoping it would stimulate her appetite and make the steak more palatable. When Alex noticed that she was just playing with her food, he asked her if she was feeling okay.

The concern in his voice touched her. Mellowed by the wine, she smiled at him.

"I'm fine. I think I drank a little too much wine."

"You've barely touched your food," he said. "If you weren't hungry, why did you order a steak?"

Ariel discovered she didn't feel fine, after all. Didn't he remember that he'd ordered for her? She rubbed her temples with her fingertips, hoping the tight feeling would go away.

"Headache?" Alex said.

"A little," she admitted.

"Here—I have something that'll help." He reached in his pocket and took out a folded piece of cellophane. "One of the medical reps gave me this. Something new—potent but easier on the stomach than aspirin."

He dropped two white pills onto the palm of her hand. "Wash them down with wine."

Although the thought of putting anything else in her stomach was repellent, she swallowed the pills obediently. By the time the waiter came to clear the table and take their dessert order, she was convinced she did feel better, even though she found it hard to focus her eyes now.

"Well, Harry, that was a fine meal," Alex said, in the too-hearty voice he used with waiters and mechanics. "Unfortunately, my wife doesn't agree. She wasn't satisfied with her steak—as you can see."

"I'm sorry—do you want me to have the chef fix you another?" the waiter, a tall, cavernous man with too-perfect teeth, asked.

"Oh, no. It wasn't the steak—"

"I'm afraid my wife has overindulged again—she does like her wine," Alex interrupted. He winked at the man, who looked uncomfortable. "I've warned her about mixing tranquilizers with alcohol, but—well, she's pretty stubborn."

Ariel wanted to deny that she had taken any medicine except a couple of headache pills, to explain that it was Alex who had urged so much wine upon her. She opened her mouth to speak, but all that came out was a croaking sound.

"You look as if you're about to keel over," Alex said. "I think I'd better get you home. Bring me the bill, Harry."

Everything got a little hazy after that. Ariel knew people at nearby tables were staring at her, but her head felt so heavy that she had to use both hands to try to prop it up. Her chin dropped, as if her neck were too weak to support her head, and she slid forward until her face was resting on her folded arms. Alex must have paid the bill, because the next thing she knew he was pulling her to her feet. Half carrying her, he propelled her toward the parking lot. As he put her into the passenger's seat of his car, she tried to ask him why he had lied like that, but her throat was so dry, the words wouldn't come out.

She must have passed out—or fallen asleep—because the next thing she knew, she was undressed and in bed. At first she thought she was having a nightmare, until she realized there was no feeling in a dream. And she could feel hands—Alex's hands—on her body, feel his mouth at her breasts.

She heard his voice, too, talking, talking, talking. Later, she couldn't remember what he'd said, only that his words had frightened her. Then he was rearing above her, straddling her, and what he was doing now was so incredible that her mind went blank, blotting everything out.

The next morning when she awakened, she was alone in bed. Her down comforter was pulled over her nude body, and when she sat up, she discovered two large bruises, already turned dark purple, between her breasts. The flesh there was so tender that even touching them lightly with her fingertips made her wince with pain.

She felt very nauseated, but even worse, her old bugaboo, claustrophobia, was back, raging through her. She knew she had to do something to stop the hysteria rising in her throat, and she flung back the comforter, slid out of bed, and threw on a sweater and a skirt, then hurried down the stairs, through the kitchen, and out the back door.

Only when she was sitting on a stone bench in the garden did she regain some of her composure. What was wrong with her lately, anyway? Was she losing her mind? Had she imagined yesterday from beginning to end? First Alex's strange verbal attack, his accusation in front of Maria, then his lies to the waiter at the restaurant. . . .

And the thing that had happened later—no, she wouldn't think of that. It must have been some kind of hallucination, brought on by the wine. Maybe she was allergic to it. Hadn't she read somewhere that there was something in red wine that caused hallucinations?

She sat there for a long time, leaning her head against the back of the bench, her eyes closed. Although there was a November chill in the air, she was comfortably warm in her heavy sweater, and the tension slowly drained from her body. This particular bench had always been her favorite, mainly because it was out of sight of any window in the house. She'd hidden out here so often as a child, and even now, sitting here made her feel safe. . . .

And wasn't that a strange thought! Safe from what—or from whom? Maybe from herself? It was bad enough to have nightmares in the night, but when she started having them during the day, it was time to get help.

If she needed a psychiatrist again, as she suspected, Alex was the logical choice—and yet, how could she tell him the things that had been going on in her mind lately? How could she admit that for the past few months *he* was at the center of her worst nightmares?

Maybe she should talk to Laird. He'd always helped her before. The thing was—he was a man. It would be too embarrassing to tell him the sexual aspects of her dreams. Of course, there *was* her support group. Wasn't the purpose of the club supposed to be to provide help when one of them needed it? It would be impossible for her to discuss her problems with the whole group, but maybe she could confide in one of them. The question was— which one?

Glory was out of the question, even though she admired the redheaded girl for the way she'd taken control of her own life. But Glory's street wisdom would be no help to her. Her advice would be to—what? Tie Alex to a bedpost and beat him with his own belt?

But she did feel comfortable with Stephanie, maybe because they both had so little to say at the meetings. Of course, Stephanie was wrapped up in her own problems; it wouldn't be a kindness to involve her in someone else's. Janice, on the other hand, was so obviously willing to help. At the luncheons, she drew the others out with her tactful remarks, her casual and inoffensive questions. Yes, Janice was the logical one to approach. . . .

There was Chanel, too, who had been so friendly. Why had she left her until last? It was obvious that Laird approved of their friendship. When the three of them had lunched together at Greens, Chanel and Laird had really hit it off. They knew so many of the same people, and they'd laughed at the same jokes, just as if they were old friends.

Chanel was a different person around Laird—softer and more feminine. It was as if the two of them were communicating in a strange language that had no spoken words. Body language—hadn't she heard that phrase somewhere? The way Chanel leaned toward Laird and lowered her voice when she spoke to him—was it possible she was interested in Laird as a—well, as a man?

Ariel felt a deep ache in her chest, and she pressed her hands against her breasts, forgetting the bruises. As pain lanced through her, a realization came to her. She could pass off most of what had happened yesterday as hallucinations—but how could she possibly explain those oddly shaped bruises between her breasts?

That night, a nightmare awakened Ariel. She lay there, huddled under her comforter, her body covered with the cold, sour sweat of fear, her own harsh cry still ringing in her ears. She wanted desperately to turn on a light, but what if, when she reached out toward the beside lamp, something *touched* her? Something hot and dry or wet and clammy? A hand—or maybe tiny, pointed teeth?

She told herself to grow up, to stop thinking such fantasies, and forced herself to listen, but the only sound in the room was her own harsh breathing. Or was it *her* breathing? Wasn't there an echo that came just a beat behind her own inhaling and exhaling? There was also something else—a soft sliding-away sound. Like a snake slithering through dry grass, she decided, even though she'd never seen a snake outside of the San Francisco Zoo, much less heard one. And the odor—it was familiar and yet strange. Sweet and yet stale, like a ghost of her older nightmares.

No, she wouldn't think about *them* now. She would sit up—she would, she would!—and reach out to turn on the alabaster lamp beside her bed. And then she would search the room thoroughly, see for herself that all it contained was the tall chest-on-chest and low bureau with their creamy patinas of age and charming marble pulls and graceful, rococo lines, all so familiar and comforting. . . .

Then a floorboard squeaked near the door and she was plunged back into the nightmare. Or at least she was pretty sure the nightmare had something to do with squeaking floorboards and hard breathing and something touching her, something furtive and evil.

How strange that she could never remember her nightmares

clearly, only that they were so terrifying. When she awoke, it was always the same. She, awash in her own sweat, was filled with a terrible panic and paralyzed with fear. Only when Alex was lying beside her in bed could she be sure that the nightmares wouldn't plague her. Even the worst nightmare wouldn't dare share a bed with Alex. . . .

Other sounds intruded now. Traffic noises from the street; a woman's voice, plaintively calling her cat. "Here, kitty—here, kitty!" A plane passing high overhead. The neighbor's dog next door barking. . . .

The sounds were so normal, she relaxed against her pillows, hopeful that the nightmare was gone for the night. Only when she first awoke did she experience this terrible feeling of isolation, as if she were walled off from the real world. Maybe it was part of the nightmares, too. Maybe it simply took a while to dissolve.

Whatever the truth, she found it possible to move now, to reach out and turn on her light. The flood of light was so welcome, she smiled, but the smile froze on her face when a light tap came at the door. "Ariel? Are you all right in there?"

A few minutes later, she would have been abjectly grateful to hear Alex's voice. She would have begged him to come in and stay with her for the rest of the night. But now that the nightmare had been banished, she lay very still, hoping he would believe she was asleep and go away.

But the door swung inward and then footsteps were approaching the bed. Ariel kept her eyes closed, breathing shallowly, even though she knew she couldn't fool Alex. When had she ever been able to fool Alex?

"I know you're awake, Ariel. I was reading in bed when I heard you cry out. What was it? One of your nightmares?"

Sighing, she opened her eyes. Alex was wearing pajamas of thick, lustrous silk. It was a personality quirk, he'd told her once, but a harmless one, his liking the feel of silk against his skin when he slept. "Yes—but I'm fine now," she said.

He paid no attention. Throwing aside the quilt, he knelt on the bed beside her. His eyes had a feverish look as he bent over her. The material of his pajamas strained across his thighs, and she saw that he was already aroused. Was it her fear that had aroused him tonight? she wondered dully.

But she moved over to accommodate him and didn't protest when he pulled the top of her gown down to her waist, exposing the upper half of her body. For a moment, she thought he looked disconcerted as he stared at the purple bruises between her breasts, but he lowered his head without speaking, and as his mouth, hot and wet, moved over her flesh, a fear came to her that someday he would devour her entirely in his rush to sexual satisfaction.

Without speaking, he reached out and turned off the light. She heard the rustle of silk and knew he was undressing. In the dark, she felt his weight settling down next to her. He found her limp hand and pressed it against his body. "Touch me," he said, and she did as he asked, fondling him the way he'd taught her, knowing that in a little while, her own hot, dark lust would stir.

Tonight, she knew, he would see that she was satisfied after his own fires had been banked, so why did she feel as if she were mired in hot, fetid mud? And how could she ever tell anyone else—a psychiatrist, a minister, a friend, Laird—the whole truth? How could she confess that while she hated the things they did there in the dark because they made her feel dirty inside, still she couldn't refuse Alex because she needed sex so much, even the perverted kind they had together?

It was later, after Alex had returned to his own room, that she turned the lamp back on to look at the small ivory clock on the bedstand. It was only ten o'clock—surely Stephanie would still be up. From a hiding place in her desk, she got the list of phone numbers that Janice had given her and then, still naked, she picked up the phone and dialed Stephanie's number.

CHAPTER TWENTY

AFTER THE PERIOD IN HER LIFE THAT STEPHANIE ALWAYS thought of as the "bad time," during which she had been terrorized and her beloved kitten had died such a terrible death, she had never wanted another pet. The grief she'd suffered then had made her afraid of ever becoming fond of another animal, and even though the twins had been begging for a dog for years, she had resisted.

Even though she knew it was unlikely she'd develop an intense attachment to another pet, she couldn't face the twins' grief should something happen to one. It was impossible to tell Chuck and Ronnie the real reason for her refusal, so she talked about the mess dogs made around the house, about fleas in the rugs, chewed-up shoes, and veterinarian's bills, and they promised earnestly to feed it, walk it, clean up every hair it left on the carpets.

When they even offered to take a paper route to pay for dog food and vet bills, she lost her temper and told them she didn't want to hear one more word about a dog. The subject was dropped, but not the martyred looks, the sighs and pointed stories about their friends' awesome dogs.

Some of the reasons she'd given weren't totally lies. It wasn't that she was a compulsive housekeeper, but she wasn't really comfortable with a messy house. Even as a child, she'd been uneasy with untidiness. Which was strange because her mother had been an indifferent housekeeper, her excuse for allowing clutter to accumulate—when she bothered to give an excuse—being that she was much too busy to worry about a little dust. Once a neighbor had repeated a comment another neighbor had made about her housekeeping, and Stephanie's mother had told the women that other people's opinions didn't bother her.

But they bothered Stephanie, who had overheard. She always kept her own room neat and clean, her clothes hung up, her dolls and stuffed animals and toys lined up along a shelf, the old pine furniture in her bedroom dusted and polished. After the comment about her mother's housekeeping, she took on the rest of the house, too, for which she got small appreciation from her mother.

After she married, she kept her own home immaculate. Not that she was the demon housekeeper that David had called her once when she asked him to please put his dirty socks in the clothes hamper instead of dropping them on top. He'd apologized later, but she hadn't forgotten the remark, which she'd deeply resented.

And why was she thinking about David, today of all days, she wondered, when she should be worrying about that job interview in Noe Valley she was heading toward, planning what to say?

She steered the station wagon around a stalled car, then pressed her foot down on the gas pedal, increasing her speed slightly. She still had an hour until her appointment at Owens Public Relations, Inc., but she didn't want to take a chance that a traffic jam would make her late. Better to wait once she got there than to make a bad impression right off the bat.

Although nervous about the coming interview, she drove carefully, as always, so when a car suddenly swung out from the curb and into her traffic lane, she was able to put on her brakes in time to avoid a collision. The other car sped off, but Stephanie edged the station wagon into the curb because her nerves needed a few minutes to recover.

As she looked around to get her bearings, her eyes met those of a young man, standing nearby. He gave her a sympathetic smile and automatically, she smiled back—just as an older man came out of a florist shop and put a possessive arm around the young man's waist.

It was only then that she realized this was the Castro, the center of the city's homosexual population.

She pulled out of the parking place so fast that the car almost stalled. Staring straight ahead, she had to force herself to drive slowly when what she really wanted to do was to press the gas pedal all the way to the floor. The busy street, the men strolling in couples or standing in small groups, talking and laughing, made her stomach roll. Was this where David hung out these days? Did he make his contacts here in the Castro?

And where did he get the nerve to demand that he take Chuck and Ronnie fishing this weekend? The preceding Sunday, tired of always being the villain in the twins' eyes, she had weakened and allowed David to visit them at the condo. The boys had been in seventh heaven, but it had been an ordeal for her. Just watching the three of them together had been so painful, she hadn't been able to eat dinner afterward.

Not that she hadn't put on a good act. She'd served David coffee, listened silently while the three of them argued about the World Series. She even managed to hold her tongue when David talked about a fishing trip to Bolinas Bay he'd taken without them, earning her a few hard looks from the boys.

In his off-white Irish fisherman's sweater, the one she'd bought him for his fortieth birthday, he had looked so masculine that she felt sick. He knew it, too. Once, when he looked up and caught her watching him, a flush darkened his face, and when he looked away quickly, she felt a savage satisfaction. During his entire visit, she didn't speak more than a dozen words to him, although she never left him alone with the boys, and after he was gone, she'd ignored her sons' resentful looks and had gone to her room to lie down.

Well, at least David felt some degree of shame and guilt. So why didn't he stay out of the boys' lives entirely? The visit had been so traumatic that she'd told him no when he'd called later to ask if he could take them fishing next Sunday. He hadn't argued with her, but she had sensed his frustration, his anger.

A car honked at her, and she realized that in her preoccupation with her own thoughts, she had almost strayed into another lane. For the rest of the trip, she concentrated on her driving.

Half an hour later, she pulled into a parking lot. A sign admonished EMPLOYEES AND GUESTS OF OWENS PUBLIC RELATIONS ONLY! The brick office building it flanked was very old; it retained a rococo flavor that pleased her even though she had no illusions that she would be working there. How many times had she propped up her courage with good thoughts, only to be turned down for one reason or another? It wasn't that the personnel people who interviewed her were rude. It was just that the interviews all ended the same way, with a "Don't call us; we'll call you" brush-off. This one, she felt certain, would be more of the same.

She signed in with a guard in the lobby, who directed her to the personnel department. The halls had a fresh-paint smell, and the whole building had obviously been renovated recently, and she tried to be optimistic at this evidence that the company was prospering. Because she was a few minutes early, the receptionist in the personnel department told her to take a seat, Ms. Edwards would see her shortly.

The waiting room was bright and cheerful despite an overabundance of Formica surfaces and fake-leather upholstery. Stephanie sat quietly, as if she weren't shaking inside. Which was ridiculous. After all, what could Ms. Edwards do except show her to the door?

Ten minutes later, she discovered that Ms. Edwards was middle-aged, neatly dressed in a white blouse and gray flannel skirt, that she had a nice smile that seemed genuine. Not to Stephanie's surprise, the interview was a rerun of earlier ones. Ms. Edwards was just more discreet about her slowly diminishing interest as Stephanie answered her questions.

No, she was sorry, but she hadn't finished college—she had married at the end of her junior year. Yes, she had been going for a liberal arts degree. No, she didn't have any work experience, having elected to stay home with her twin boys. But now she was separated from her husband, was in the process of getting a divorce and needed a job. Thank you. I'm glad you think I look too young to have teenage children.

To her surprise, when the interview was over, the woman didn't dismiss her immediately.

"You really shouldn't apologize so much for your lack of experience. It's very off-putting," Ms. Edwards said, tapping the erasered end of her pencil on the desk. "Of course, you *are* rather mature for a low-level, entry job. The company prefers someone just out of school because they tend to be more flexible. Personally, I'm inclined to give you a chance, but I do have appointments with several other applicants, and of course my superior does have the final word."

She made a note on her desk pad, and Stephanie knew the interview was over. "I'll call you as soon as possible, one way or another."

In other words, don't call us; we'll call you.

By the time Stephanie reached home, she had steeled herself to expect another rejection—provided Ms. Edwards even bothered to call. Better to be prepared, she thought as she got out of her car, than to be disappointed.

One thing that Ms. Edwards had said did rankle—that she apologized too much for her lack of experience. It was true, of course—which was why it bothered her. In future interviews, she would try to act more self-assertive. Maybe she should take one of those est courses to build up her ego—only wasn't est out and something else in these days?

As soon as she put her key in the lock and opened the front door, she knew that David was in the house. Maybe a trace of his after-shave was sending a subliminal message to her brain—or was it simple instinct, like a hare sensing a fox hidden in the bushes? It wasn't his voice because the house was quiet, nor had he turned on the TV or put a cassette in the tape deck as he'd always done before their separation. Was this because he no longer felt as if this were his home? And why was she so sure he was here, anyway?

"David?" she called.

"In here, Steph," he said from the living room.

When she turned into the living room, he was sitting in the leather London club chair she'd bought him the first year of their marriage, their first "good" piece of furniture. Through the high, narrow windows behind him, sun streamed into the room. In the

strong light, David's face had a grayish cast, and there were deep
smudges under his eyes. Was it from late nights? Just where did
he spend his nights now? What kind of risks had he taken since
he'd left her? And how dare he bring those risks into the house
where his sons lived!

"What are you doing here?" she demanded. "And how did
you get in? I had the locks changed—"

"I still have the garage door opener in my car—you left the
inside door unlocked. As to what I'm doing here, I thought it was
time we had a serious talk."

"I don't want to talk to you, David. I want you to leave."

"This is my house, too. Have you forgotten that, Steph?"

"If I have to get a restraining order to keep you away, I will.
And don't think you can wait around until the boys come home
from school—"

"Shut up and listen to me. I want—no, by God, I *demand* to
see Chuck and Ronnie on a regular basis. I want to take them
fishing and to sports events and the zoo and out to dinner. You're
welcome to come along, but either way, I intend to have visitation
rights. Don't fight me on this, because you're going to lose."

Stephanie stared at him, unable to believe her ears. David was
different today. The hangdog look was gone, and he wasn't avoiding her eyes as he had the last time. He was also giving her orders—didn't he have any shame? Did he actually believe that he
could come here and make demands?

"We have an agreement. You can see the boys, but only here
at the house and only when it's convenient to me."

Despite her resolve to stay calm, her voice sounded shrewish.
David winced, and she remembered that he didn't like women
with shrill voices. Well, too damned bad. David's likes and dislikes, all-important for the past fifteen years, no longer mattered
to her.

"I never agreed to that," he said. "And let's not argue. We
have to come to an understanding, Steph."

He put out his hand as if to touch her. The gesture took her by
surprise; she flinched away and took a step backward. The muscles in David's jawline tensed, and she knew she had hurt him.

"I have nothing to say to you. Just looking at you makes me
sick," she said, deliberately cruel.

"That may be, but we still have to talk about Chuck and Ronnie. They don't understand any of this. Can't you see how torn
up they are? They need a father—"

"Not your kind of father. Not a flaming—"

"Don't say it, Stephie! I'm not gay or even bisexual, and I'm sick of trying to explain what happened. I did a stupid thing. Not only stupid but inexcusable and immoral, and I deserve your anger. But it has nothing to do with the boys. I'm a good father—can you deny that?"

Stephanie was silent. In all honesty, she had to admit that David had been a wonderful father. Which didn't change anything. What about subtle influence and role models and all those things? Besides, he didn't have any rights where the boys were concerned. He'd forfeited that when he'd let that man—

She swung around and went to hang up her coat in the hall closet. She didn't return to the living room until she was sure her face was under control again. David had a curious look on his face, and she felt defensive—of what, she wasn't sure.

"If the world caved in, if the big one, an eight-point-nine on the Richter scale, finally struck the Bay Area, you'd still hang up your wraps before you ran out the front door, wouldn't you?" he said.

"I don't know what you're talking about. But then, I often don't," she said bitterly. "You're the smart one. An expert on every subject under the sun, and I'm—I *was* the little wife without a brain in her head who picked up your clothes and ironed your shirts because you like cotton next to your skin and don't like permanent press. When we went out to dinner, we went to Mexican restaurants because you like Mexican food even though spicy food gives me heartburn."

"What has this got to do with—"

"And TV—I hate Monday Night Football. Hate it! And you turn it up so loud, I can't even sit in the same room and read a book. I don't enjoy football or baseball or hockey, either, because I don't understand them. And when I ask questions, you ask me if there's any more Coors in the fridge. I was willing to learn golf so we could share at least one outdoor activity, but you didn't want a beginner as a partner on Saturday mornings. Even after I took lessons from that—that jerk at the Peacock Gap Country Club, somehow you always had some excuse not to play with me."

"Why haven't you ever said any of this before, Stephie? If you felt so strongly—"

"Because I didn't want to spoil your fun. I thought you needed male companionshp—God help me, I didn't know how right I was! When I think how grateful I was that you married me—do you know that all our women friends envied me my handsome husband who didn't play around or gamble or drink too much at parties? God, how I loved being married to you. Making a home for you and the boys was all I ever wanted. I never apologized to other women for not wanting a career or a separate identity of my own. I was so proud of being Mrs. David Cornwall. I even felt guilty when I did volunteer work or went to an occasional concert or the ballet without you. When I asked you to come, too, it was 'Honey, that stuff bores the hell out of me.' And I never argued, never pointed out that maybe you'd enjoy 'that stuff' if you went with me a few times. I would have gone to sports events with you and the boys, too, but I was never invited to come along.''

"I thought a little time to yourself was something you needed. And why didn't you say you wanted to go along?''

"Because what I wanted was to be asked, to have an option. And because it wasn't really important as long as I thought you loved me.''

A muscle twitched in David's cheek. "I do love you. And I'm not a mind reader, Steph. I thought you were perfectly happy. And if none of it mattered, why are you telling me all this now?''

"You still don't understand, do you? I'm telling you this because now it *does* matter. I fell into the oldest trap in the world. I was a second-class citizen and didn't even care. When was the last time you asked my opinion about *anything*—even something as elementary as how we should invest our savings or where to go on our vacation? And all the time you were playing Mr. Wonderful at home, you were—what were you doing those nights I thought you were meeting with clients? Were you out cruising the Castro? Going to a bathhouse?''

"For God's sake, Steph—''

"Don't try to stop me from having my say. I don't feel inferior to you anymore. I don't have your background and my IQ is way down there somewhere in the one hundred fifteen range and my family uses paper towels for napkins sometimes, but I'm not a degenerate, which makes me better than you.''

"Don't say things like that, Stephie. I'm not any of the things you've called me. I swear it. I was drunk and Ted—no, I'm not going to blame it on him although I suspect he thought it quite a joke, getting me drunk and horsing around. I'm not used to that much liquor and I was horny as hell because you and I hadn't had sex for almost a month—''

"So you've finally gotten around to it, have you? I knew that eventually it would be my fault. You poor man! Your wife didn't take care of your sexual needs so you were a sitting duck for a pervert? That's your excuse?"

"I'm not making excuses. I'm only trying to explain that it had been a long time since we made love. You'd had that cold and then there were other things—"

"What does that mean?"

"Just what I said. I'm not blaming you, just trying to explain—"

"You bastard! You hadn't made love to me for over a month? Well, who's fault was that? My cold lasted less than a week. Was it because you knew Ted was coming for a visit and you were saving yourself for your lover?"

"I didn't make love to you because—well, the truth is that it seemed more trouble than it was worth."

"What do you mean by that little zinger?"

"For a long time, you've only seemed to tolerate sex. Okay, you seldom refused me, but—tell me something that I've wondered about lately: Have you ever had an orgasm? A real one, Steph? Or were you faking it all those years?" He stopped, looking startled. "God—I don't know why I said that. I didn't mean it—"

"But you did mean it," she said. "Now *you* tell me something. Why did you marry me, David? To have kids? As a cover-up for your sexual preferences? What is it they call people like you? AC-DC? I know you aren't totally gay or you couldn't have performed with me. But I wasn't even sexy enough to satisfy the AC side of you, was I?"

"I thought you were the sexiest woman in the world when I married you. But can you honestly say that you enjoy sex?"

"So we're back to that, are we? Have you ever considered the possibility, David, that you're simply a rotten lover?"

She saw his eyes narrow, saw his lips tighten, but she wasn't prepared when he stood up abruptly and took a step toward her, hand upraised. He stopped midway, looking like a man who'd just seen a ghost.

"God—I don't know why I did that. Yes, I do. You're deliberately trying to provoke me. There're some things you can't say to a man and not expect a strong reaction."

"But it's okay to tell a woman she's a failure in bed because she doesn't scratch and claw you? How interesting. The old double standard, huh?''

He ran his fingers through his hair, a gesture she'd once found so endearing. Suddenly, she couldn't stand the sight of him, and she turned away and went to stare down at the fireplace. How pristine white the marble still looked—they'd installed a gas insert when they'd moved in, but they seldom used it. The gas insert had been her idea, because she hadn't wanted to always be cleaning out ashes. Was that one of the things David held against her? That she didn't like dog hairs and ashes tracked on the rug?

"I'm sorry," David said behind her. "I had no right to make accusations.''

She turned to stare at him. He was so close, she could see a tiny broken vein in the side of his nose. He looked older, as if he'd aged overnight. And yet he was only a few years older than she. "And I apologize for—for what I said," she said tiredly.

"Okay, we've both apologized. Why don't we get back to the subject of the boys? You remember that before all this happened, I promised to take them white water rafting next summer? They've been bugging me about it—''

"Bugging you? I don't understand. They didn't say anything about it last Sunday—'' She stopped, staring at him. "You've been meeting them on the sly, haven't you?''

He didn't deny it. "I've brought them home from school a few times. And no, they haven't lied to you. I suspect they didn't mention seeing me because they didn't want to hurt you. It seems our boys are more sensitive than either of us.''

"What about the rafting trip? It's impossible, you know.''

"Why? I've already made the reservations and paid the fee. Those white water trips are very popular, and you have to make them months in advance—''

"No. The answer is no.''

"Aren't you carrying this thing too far? Do you think I'll corrupt them in four or five days?''

"I don't want them to depend upon you. They'll have to learn to get along without you.''

"I promised them, Stephie. They're going to be very disappointed if it doesn't come off.''

"And whose fault is that? I guess this makes me the villain again, but I'm not going to let you take the boys off somewhere alone.''

"Then, go along.''

"Forget it, David. I won't change my mind."

"What are you so afraid of? That I'll seduce my own boys? They're going to be disappointed, you know—"

"They won't be disappointed. I'll take them myself," she said. The words had popped out, too late to recall, but she was too proud to retreat.

"You're crazy. Raving mad. You hate the outdoors. How do you think you'd like a trip down the Rogue River on a raft?"

She studied him with reflective eyes. "Now, isn't that strange. I've gone camping with you and the boys for years. It was taken for granted that good old Mom would do the cooking and keep the camp fire burning while you three had a glorious time playing outdoorsmen. And all that time you must have known I didn't enjoy it."

"I knew you weren't as keen on it as the rest of us, and I admired you for being a good sport. Also, you always seemed to be having fun. Are you telling me now that you didn't?"

"I enjoyed part of it," she conceded. "The singing and storytelling around the camp fire, the being together. But I didn't like being left alone at camp while the three of you went off to do your woodsmen thing. I didn't like all the cooking and cleaning up—"

"But you didn't have to cook five-course meals. Didn't I try to get you to fix simple things like hamburgers and hot dogs? The well-balanced meals were your idea—I thought you loved cooking over a fire."

She didn't answer, and he went on, his voice dogged. "Look, Steph, rafting is pretty heavy stuff. Once you're on that raft, there's no turning back."

"That isn't any concern of yours, David. Since the boys are all excited about the trip, I'll take your chestnuts out of the fire for you. If you'll give me the phone number of that rafting company, I'll change the name on the reservation."

She thought he'd argue more, but instead he shrugged and wrote out the address for her. When he left soon afterward, she found it difficult even to say a polite "good-bye" and suspected he was having the same trouble.

But after he was gone, for some reason that was obscure to her, she got out the album that held their wedding pictures. It had been a simple wedding, but very traditional. In her wedding portrait, she was wearing white, which she technically hadn't been entitled to. Not only hadn't David been her first lover, but they'd been intimate for several months before the wedding. Standing beside her, David looked so—what was the word? Intense? And the expression on her own face could only be described as blissful.

She'd felt beautiful that day, a winner at last. In school, she'd never been the girl who dated the popular boys, the football players, or the class officers. She'd been so painfully shy that the few dates she'd had were with the brothers of friends or even, for a few months, the class clown, who was inches shorter than she. So she'd been full of pride on her wedding day, knowing her friends were finally envious of her. It had been an unworthy feeling but very human—how could she have guessed why David had singled her out for marriage?

Which was a big joke on her—really hilarious. So why was she sitting here crying like her heart would break?

She heard the boys coming in from school, and she wiped her eyes hastily. What they didn't need was a weepy mother—things were touchy enough these days. Sometimes she wondered what had happened to the sons she'd thought she knew so well. She would have said, a few weeks ago, that Chuck and Ronnie could take anything in stride and still behave reasonably well. But since David had left, they had been argumentive and sulky. For the first time, they reacted the same to every crisis. In fact, they had united into an exclusive group of two, shutting her out.

And to add to her troubles, David's mother had called several times, each call an endurance trial. The last time, she'd been so insulting that for the first time in her life, Stephanie had hung up on someone. The phone had rung off and on the next hour, but she hadn't answered—and her mother-in-law hadn't called since.

In a few weeks, when the divorce was final, Stella would no longer be her mother-in-law. Unfortunately, she would be the twins' grandmother for the rest of her life.

The boys burst into the room, then skidded to a stop when they saw her sitting idly on the sofa.

"You boys are a little late, aren't you?" she said.

"We walked home," Ronnie said. "Tony's mom didn't show up."

"You could have called. I would've picked you up."

"We didn't know if you'd be home yet," Chuck muttered. He fiddled with his book strap, his eyes so evasive that suspicion blossomed inside her.

"Tony's mom wasn't the reason why you're late, is it? It's because you were hoping your father would turn up to drive you home," she said with certainty.

"Ah, Mom. Okay, Dad's brought us home a few times. You won't let him come here so—" There was insolence in Chuck's shrug, and Stephanie had to fight not to show her anger—and hurt.

"In the future, I want you to be honest with me," she said evenly. "And the next time your father just happens to be passing when you get out of school, you tell him I've forbidden you to get into his car."

"You don't want us to have any fun these days, do you?" Chuck burst out, his face flushed.

"You know that isn't true. I want you to enjoy life. That's why I'm going to take you on that white water rafting trip in June. Your father and I talked it over, and it's all set."

The boys stared at her, obviously stunned; before they could speak, she added hurriedly, "And I have some more good news for you. Now that you're old enough to be responsible for taking care of a dog, there's no reason why you can't have one. Why don't we make the rounds of the kennels this weekend and pick out a puppy?"

After the house was quiet that night, the boys having gone off to bed without argument for a change, Stephanie settled herself on the sofa and picked up the book she'd been reading. But her mind was so busy that the glitzy novel about bed-hopping beautiful people couldn't hold her interest, and she finally got up and moved around the room, moving a figurine on the fireplace mantel an inch to the left and lining up the fronts of the books in the bookcase, too restless to settle down anywhere.

The phone rang just as she was snapping off the lights. Afraid the ringing might awaken the twins, she hurried to pick it up and say "Hello?" into the receiver.

"Stephanie?"

"Yes. Who is this, please?"

"It's Ariel—Ariel di Russy. I know it's really late, but—did I disturb you?"

"No. I'm still up. What is it, Ariel?"

"It's—you said that I could call you anytime I needed someone to talk to." There was a question in Ariel's light voice.

Stephanie groaned inwardly. It had been a long, traumatic day, and she wasn't ready to deal with anyone else's problems. But her voice was pleasant as she said, "And I meant it. What are friends for?"

"Are we really friends?" Ariel sounded so doubtful that Stephanie had to smile.

"We haven't known each other very long, but yes, I'd say we were friends. Is something wrong?"

"It's—it's very personal. Maybe I shouldn't bother you with it—"

"Honestly, it's okay. What is it?"

"It isn't something I can discuss on the phone. Do you think we could get together tomorrow?"

"Of course," Stephanie said, pumping enthusiasm into her voice. "Where? Over lunch?"

"Actually, I'd rather meet someplace where we'd be alone. I want to ask your opinion about something—sensitive."

"I have a job interview in the city tomorrow afternoon at two-thirty. Why don't we meet—say, on the Marina Green or maybe in front of the Palace of Fine Arts?"

"How about Sea Cliff? I like to go there to watch the sea otters."

"Great. What time is best for you?"

"Alex has patients until five. Anytime after one and before five would be fine."

"Then, let's make it one-thirty. Okay?"

"I'll be there—and Stephanie, I'm very grateful. I wouldn't bother you except there's no one else I can talk to."

After Ariel hung up Stephanie wondered how it was possible that she had no one to confide in except a woman she had only met three times. But wasn't that true in her own case, too? The couples they saw socially had all been David's friends first, most of whom he'd met through his profession. She couldn't think of one of those women that she felt free to tell her troubles to.

As for the boys, they were too young, and since David was the cause of all her heartache, he no longer qualified as a confidant and best friend. There were her parents—but they were near-strangers to her these days. In fact, she had yet to tell them that she and David were getting a divorce because she knew what their reaction would be.

"What did you do?" her mother would ask, instinctively ready to blame Stephanie.

"We don't get divorces in this family," her dad would say, his graying eyebrows knitted in a frown.

So the question she'd asked herself about Ariel was also true about her, wasn't it? At the moment, she couldn't think of one person she trusted enough to confide in totally. Which pointed out something about *her*, didn't it?

CHAPTER TWENTY-ONE

THE NEXT MORNING, AFTER STEPHANIE SAW THE BOYS OFF TO school, she did her housework and laundry, then made preliminary preparations for dinner that evening just in case something happened and she got hung up at her job interview. Wearing a gray-striped blouse over a gray skirt with a matching sweater, she got into her car and headed for the city.

A few minutes before one-thirty she pulled into a parking lot near the Cliff House, a venerable old restaurant that was something of a San Francisco landmark. To her surprise, since she was a little early, Ariel was already waiting for her. Her welcoming smile was so diffident, Stephanie wondered if she was going to have to coax Ariel's problems out of her.

For a while they strolled along the retaining wall at the edge of the crumbling cliff that gave the area its name. Despite the warning signs about rogue waves and falling rocks that were posted along the wall, two teenage boys were climbing over the rocks below, and as Stephanie watched them, she wondered how many dangerous things her own boys did despite warning signs or her admonitions.

It was too late in the year for the colony of the sea otters that usually occupied the rocks several hundred yards off the cliffs, but one lone warrior, his thick shoulders scarred, his muzzle gray with age, reigned in solitary glory and gave out an occasional bleat of defiance at the few spectators watching from shore.

"Do you suppose he was too old to follow the herd south?" Stephanie said idly.

Ariel stared at the old bull with somber eyes. "Maybe he was so overbearing and mean that his wives threw him out," she said.

They found a place to sit on the wall, and as if the words were all bottled up inside her, demanding to get out, Ariel began talking immediately.

"I know I shouldn't bother you with my personal troubles, but I don't know who else to turn to. I thought about Janice—she did ask us to call her if we need a shoulder to cry on—and Chanel is so sophisticated that I'm sure nothing would shock her, but I don't feel comfortable with them the way I do with you."

"Thank you for those kind words," Stephanie said, wishing Ariel would make eye contact with her instead of staring out at the ocean. "What was it you want to talk about?"

"It's—well, this is embarrassing, but something's really bothering me and I thought maybe you could give me some advice."

"If this is about sex—look, I'm probably not the one to help you. I'm a married woman, but I'm not any kind of expert on sex."

"I'm sure you know more about it than I do. I'm still a virgin."

If Ariel had said she was a werewolf, Stephanie couldn't have been more shocked. Briefly, she wondered if Ariel was putting her on, but the dead seriousness in the younger woman's voice denied that. Even so, it was a few moments before she asked, "Does your husband have some kind of impotency problem?"

"Oh, no. There's nothing wrong with Alex. It's just that he doesn't ever—you know, go all the way. At first, I thought he was being thoughtful, but—" She stopped, looking so miserable that Stephanie was tempted to pat her hand and tell her everything was going to be okay. She also wished she hadn't come.

"—Then when time passed and he still didn't—didn't complete the act, I knew something was wrong," Ariel was saying. Her face was flushed, and she still wouldn't look at Stephanie.

"You mean he doesn't approach you sexually? Have you thought that he might be—gay?"

Ariel gave her a glancing look. "No, he isn't gay. He does other things—and he has me do things to him. He—I guess you would say he had a thing about making out with virgins. That's why he wants me to stay—untouched. But anything else goes."

Again, Stephanie fought to hide her shock—and embarrassment. What did Ariel want from her? Reassurance that her husband's sexual habits were normal? How could she do that? What Ariel was describing was perversion—and the fact that the man was a psychiatrist made it even worse because he must know it was. If Ariel was asking for her advice, she'd come to the last person for that.

Her own sex life had been—well, not what she'd hoped for. Her two college lovers had been inexperienced, not much older than she, so it hadn't surprised her that she'd found sex with them disappointing. But she'd expected so much from David, who was older, more sophisticated. Oh, she liked the preliminaries, what the sex books called foreplay, loved having David's full attention, his kisses and caresses and soft words. But the act itself was something to be endured rather than enjoyed. She would reach a point—and then suddenly the tension, the excitement, would collapse and she could hardly wait for David to finish so she could go to sleep. So how could she give sexual advice? Who did Ariel think she was—Dr. Ruth?

"Have you considered talking to a marriage counselor?" was the only thing she could think to say.

Ariel shook her head. "Alex wouldn't go. He doesn't think there's anything wrong with what he—what we do."

"I don't have any other advice. It's obvious that the problem is your husband's, that he's—" But she couldn't say the word.

"Abnormal? I've read so many sex books, looking for answers, but nowhere does it say anything about a man who wants to—to do things with a virgin all the time."

Stephanie wanted desperately to help this troubled woman— no, Ariel *wasn't* a woman. Emotionally, she was still a child— and she'd come to the wrong person for help. During her own marriage, whenever she was faced with something she didn't understand, she turned to David for answers. In this case, she would have passed his opinions along to Ariel. But now that was impossible and yet—she really did want to help. There was something so vulnerable about Ariel, as if she had been born without any skin at all, not even a thin one. But how could she give advice on something about which she herself was so ignorant?

"I wish I could help you. I really do," she said. "I was married for fifteen years, but my own sex life is—was pretty conventional. I think you should talk to Janice. Didn't she say that she had a masters in sociology? She must know something about the subject, at least what's normal and what's not."

Ariel was silent; her eyes had a shuttered look, as if she'd withdrawn into herself, and Stephanie felt a surge of exasperation. After all, she had her own troubles, ones she was trying hard to handle alone. Ariel should be asking her own husband these questions. He was, after all, a psychiatrist.

"Ariel, have you ever talked to your husband about this?"

Ariel shrank back. "Oh, no. He'd be furious if he thought I was dissatisfied with—with our marriage."

"Then, I think you should go to a marriage counselor, even if you have to go alone."

Ariel's blue eyes considered her. "Did you and your husband go to one?"

Stephanie bit her lower lip. How could she explain the circumstances of her divorce to Ariel? To anyone? How would it help Ariel to know that she'd been happily married right up until the moment she'd discovered her husband having sex with his best friend? She shivered suddenly. How sordid those words sounded, and how difficult, even now, to connect David with homosexuality.

"When I caught David making love to someone else, I asked him to leave," she said cautiously, knowing Ariel was waiting for an answer. "No amount of counseling could have made me accept—what I'd seen. The thing that hurt the most was finding them doing it in the same bed David and I had shared since our wedding night."

"I'm sorry, Stephanie, so sorry. Will you ever get over it?"

"I will. In time. Right now, it's like a sore that won't heal. But I didn't come here to talk about my problems. I wish I could help you, but I'm so—so ignorant about such things. If you can't accept the situation, maybe you should have gone through with your divorce. Does it—are you repelled by what he wants from you?"

Ariel looked down at her hands. "Sometimes I think I'll die if he touches me again. . . ." Her voice faltered to a stop.

"You don't have to say any more," Stephanie said quickly. She got to her feet. "I have to go now—my appointment's at two-thirty." Her words sounded so abrupt that she added, "I know I haven't been much help, and I don't have any advice to give you, but anytime you need a friend, I'm available. I really do care, Ariel."

Since her words sounded so lame, she was surprised when Ariel's eyes filled with tears. "Thank you. Just talking to someone who's willing to listen makes a difference," she said.

They walked slowly toward the parking lot, each lost in her own thoughts. Stephanie couldn't help smiling when Ariel stopped beside a long, low-slung car she knew must be some kind of classic. It looked like Ariel—lovely, a little fey, and totally impractical.

Impulsively, she kissed Ariel's cheek before she returned to her own sensible station wagon, and as she drove off, she was aware that her mood had changed. She hadn't helped Ariel, not in a concrete way, but one thing had come out of their meeting: In the face of what she'd just heard, her own problems suddenly didn't seem quite so terrible.

She also felt a little flattered that Ariel had turned to her instead of Janice or one of the other women. After all, when was the last time anyone had solicited *her* advice?

Stephanie's mother called the next day. Since her parents regarded long-distance phone calls as something to use only for an emergency, her first thought when she heard her mother's voice was that something was wrong, her second that her parents had somehow learned that she and David were getting a divorce.

"I haven't heard from you for weeks," her mother started in. She had a thin, reedy voice that always made Stephanie want to clear her own throat.

"I'm sorry, Mom. I didn't realize it'd been so long. I've been so busy that—"

"What about Christmas? I can't make plans until I know if you folks will be coming here this year. Your brother's mighty busy now that he has his own business, but he's making time for us. We'll be a mite short on beds, of course, but I thought you and Aunt Mary could sleep on that convertible sofa we keep on the sun porch. The boys can bring their sleeping bags, and I'm sure David won't mind sharing a bed with your brother for a couple of nights."

A sound escaped Stephanie's throat. It started as a giggle, grew to a full-fledged guffaw. She knew she was having hysterics, and she pressed her hand over her mouth to choke back the sounds. When they didn't stop, she dropped the receiver back into its cradle and went to the kitchen sink to dash cold water on her face.

By the time the phone rang again, her hysterics were over, and she sounded almost normal when she picked it up and said something about being cut off. Before her mother could embark on another of her monologues, Stephanie told her she was sorry but they wouldn't be able to make it this year. An important client of David's would be in town over the holidays and David had invited him to spend Christmas with them.

"I'll write you soon," she promised, and then hung up with the excuse that someone was at the door, cutting through her mother's complaint about people who put other things before their own families.

As she made a mental resolution to bite the bullet and write her parents about the divorce soon, she thought how adept she was becoming at lying, at protecting herself from stress. Maybe she was finally catching up with the rest of the world—and if that was true, why should she let such things as job interviews throw her? What could possibly be worse than depending so totally on one man for happiness that you turned into a turnip?

The call from Ms. Edwards came that afternoon as Stephanie was preparing crust for the pizza she'd promised the boys for dinner. She had given herself a firm lecture against too much optimism, but evidently she hadn't taken her own advice because disappointment, painful and visceral, flooded her when Ms. Edwards informed her, with obvious regret, that Mr. Sommers, who headed the personnel department, had decided a younger woman would be more suitable for the job.

Although Stephanie's eyes filled with tears, she managed to thank her with only the slightest quiver in her voice, and was getting ready to hang up when Ms. Edwards spoke again.

"I really am sorry. I guess I shouldn't say this, but you were my first choice. However, I do have a tip for you. A friend of mine who's in personnel at Macy's tells me there'll be a job opening soon in better lingerie. It's partially sales but also there's some clerical work, too, assisting the buyer. They did want someone with sales experience, but you have such a nice appearance—well, if you're interested, I'll give you my friend's business phone number."

"That's very kind of you. And yes, I am interested, Ms. Edwards," Stephanie said. "And thank you—I really appreciate this."

"Well, I can't promise anything. You'll have to convince those people yourself. You just have to learn to present yourself in a more positive manner, Mrs. Cornwall."

After Stephanie wrote down the phone number Ms. Edwards gave her and hung up, she wiped away her tears and blew her nose. She discovered she felt surprisingly good. It was a pretty long chance—but it was the most hopeful thing that had happened to her in the past week. She returned to the pizza, but her mind was on Ms. Edwards's call, and she jumped nervously when the phone rang again.

This time, it was Janice's pleasant voice that asked, "Stephanie?"

"Hello, Janice."

"I just called to find out if you're coming to the next meeting," Janice said.

"I plan to come—unless I'm working. I just got a tip about a job opening. If I'm lucky enough to get it, it might mean I'll be working Saturdays from now on."

"Oh? What kind of job?"

"Well, it's at Macy's. . . ."

She went on to tell Janice about Ms. Edwards's call, and then, because Janice was so obviously interested, she added, "I'm afraid I don't come off very well during job interviews. Too nervous, I guess."

"You'll have to learn to relax. Look, when I worked as an office manager I did most of the hiring for the firm. Why don't you tell me about that interview? Maybe I can pinpoint some of your mistakes."

Stephanie spent the next few minutes describing her interview with Ms. Edwards. It wasn't difficult to reconstruct the conversation almost word for word because she'd spent the last couple of days thinking about it.

When she was finished, Janice was silent for a while before she asked, "Look, can I be perfectly honest?"

"Of course," Stephanie said, but she braced herself mentally.

"Why did you apply for that particular job?"

Stephanie blinked, taken off guard. "Why—because I thought I could do it," she said.

"If you believed that, why did you feel you had to apologize for wasting the interviewer's time?"

"But I didn't do that!"

"Not in so many words. But you apologized for not having a college degree instead of emphasizing that you did finish three years, that your grades were excellent—they were, weren't they?— that you took a liberal arts course, which is the best way to prepare yourself for the constantly changing job market these days and is especially advantageous for a career is merchandising."

"I see—but how should I have handled it? I *am* inexperienced, you know."

"When the interviewer—what's her name? Ms. Edwards?—

when she asked why you thought you could handle a trainee's job, you should have pointed these things out. As for work experience, you told her you didn't have any even before she asked. Then there's the other pertinent information she practically had to pry out of you—your volunteer work. Don't you realize how important to your personnel profile it is that you were involved in raising money for the building fund of your husband's professional society? In fact, you were vice-chairwoman of the committee, which probably meant you did most of the work—I know that from my own experience, raising money for the renovation of the University Club. From what you've told me, you wrote newsletters for the local chapter of your sorority for several years, were vice president of the PTA of two schools, and you still work as a Gray Lady at Letterman Hospital. Hasn't it occurred to you that these were jobs, albeit unpaid ones?''

''No,'' Stephanie said truthfully.

''Well, they are. You should have emphasized the responsibility they entailed. An entry level slot is the first step up the work ladder. For that, formal work experience isn't necessary. But the willingness to learn *is* a requirement. A flexible, well-rounded personality, someone who isn't afraid of hard work, plus the ability to accept change, move with the times, and have an open mind are also needed. Okay, you're a bit mature for an entry job, but your other qualifications balance that out. Just remember that when you go in for your next job interview.''

''I will,'' Stephanie said, ''and I'm very grateful. You really are a friend. I just wish I'd have you there to hold my hand the next time I go in for an interview.''

''You don't need anyone to hold your hold. You're going to be just fine.''

Stephanie's laugh was a little shaky. ''I hope you're right. The thing is—it's pretty scary, facing so many problems alone.''

There was a long silence. ''You aren't alone,'' Janice said, her voice low. ''That's something I hope you'll always remember, that I really do care about you—and the others, too.''

The intensity in her voice made Stephanie uncomfortable, as all strongly expressed emotions did, but she told Janice again that she was grateful before they hung up.

She was grating parmesan cheese for the pizza when a slamming door and a rush of sound told her the twins were home. A minute later, she was engulfed by the familiar odor of boys' heated bodies, by boys' voices, by too-wet kisses, one on each cheek. In tandem, they asked if she was feeling okay and if she needed any help fixing dinner.

So what am I, a creaky old lady? she thought. "You can set the table," she told Ronnie. "And Chuck, you'd better let Monster in before he breaks down the garage door."

Monster, a new family addition, was not the frisky puppy she had envisioned but a full-grown dog of doubtful ancestry, who had followed the boys home from school the day after she'd raised her moratorium on pets. Secretly, she thought the dog would be a shoo-in if they entered him in the annual Ugliest Dog of the Year contest in neighboring Sonoma County, but because he was so obviously a stray, she hadn't had the heart to refuse the boys' pleas to let him stay.

"And after dinner," she went on, "why don't the two of you take him for a run in the woods? He'll be howling in the garage all night if he doesn't get some exercise—and no, I am not going to allow him to sleep in either of your rooms."

"Aw, Mom—" Chuck stopped, swallowed whatever he'd been about to say. "Okay. We'll get him so zonked out he won't move a hair all night."

Stephanie studied him suspiciously. Was he sick? This just wasn't Chuck's style. Ronnie was the helpful one, always considerate and willing to run errands. Chuck usually could find an excuse to get out of anything that resembled work even though he was the first one in line when it came to any kind of sports.

She realized both boys were watching her. "What's the matter? Smudge on my nose?"

"You sick or something?" Chuck said.

"Yeah, Mom. Your eyes are all red—and so is your nose. You been crying?" Ronnie, always the most perceptive, chimed in.

Instinctively, Stephanie put her hand up to cover her nose. "I must be catching a cold," she said.

"It don't look like no cold," Chuck muttered.

"Doesn't look like any cold," she corrected automatically.

"Come on, Mom. You can tell us. Something bugging you?"

She hesitated, then gave in to the temptation to share her disappointment. "It's that job in Noe Valley I applied for. The woman called today. Seems they gave it to someone else."

"Hey, that's tough," Ronnie said. "How come they did that?"

"They thought your mom was too old for a trainee's job. Or maybe it was my interview. I tightened up—I guess I didn't make a very good impression."

Surprisingly, Ronnie added. "Yeah, that'll do it. I was reading this article in the Sunday *Chron* and it told how to get ready for a job interview. I meant to show it to you."

"Maybe you should've practiced ahead of time," Chuck said. "Remember how you rehearsed us when we had our tonsils out? Hey, we can help you—y' know, practice. What did you do with that article, Ronnie?"

A few minutes later, with dinner put on hold, Stephanie was laughing at the antics of the twins. True to character, they had thrown themselves into their roles and were improvising outrageously improbable scenarios—including one straight out of prime-time soap opera in which the interviewer was a lech who offered to hire Stephanie if she'd join him on the office couch.

"Well, after that last one," she said, wiping her eyes, "nothing can scare me. Bring on the interviewers!"

"We were really a help?" Ronnie asked.

"You were," she said, and gave him a hug.

"Wait until we tell Dad. He told us to—" Chuck broke off, looking chagrined.

"What did your dad tell you to do?" she said quietly.

"Ah, Mom—"

"You might as well tell me. You've already let the cat out of the bag."

Ronnie gave Chuck a hard look. "Big mouth. He's the one who told Dad how bitchy—how depressed you've been lately, Mom, and that it made us feel bad, too. Dad told us we weren't to blame you for—you know, the two of you splitting up. He said it was all his fault and that someday, when we were old enough to understand, he'd tell us the whole story. Then he said we should take good care of you and not make things tougher by fighting and all that. We've really been trying, Mom."

She gave both of them hugs this time. "Yes, you really have. I'm so proud of you."

"Just remember that the next time you get mad at us," Chuck said. "Like if maybe you should find out I left my down vest at school and someone stole it or something."

Stephanie giggled. Chuck stared at her with worried eyes, which made her laugh harder. Ronnie started to laugh, too, and then Chuck joined in.

"What's so funny? Chuck been telling you one of his dumb jokes?" David said from the doorway.

The laughter caught in Stephanie's throat; she tried to speak, but all that came out was a choking sound.

David's face lost its smile. "Sorry—I did ring the bell. When you didn't answer, I came in. The door was unlocked."

There was something—a restraint in David's voice—that made Stephanie aware how the sight of them laughing together must hurt. A responding ache started up inside her, but she wouldn't allow herself to feel pity. David had done it to himself. After all, she was the victim, not he. So why, suddenly, did she have to fight hard not to cry?

"Hi, Pop," Chuck said cheerfully. "We were laughing because—well, I'm not really sure. Mom started it."

"It was the way you dropped that business about losing your vest on Mom, you dope," Ronnie said. "Trust you to pick the right time." His eyes moved to Stephanie, and she found herself stiffening. "Mom's fixing pizza for supper. You wanta eat with us? We've got plenty, don't we, Mom?"

The last thing Stephanie wanted was to eat pizza—or anything else—with David. What she wanted was never to have to deal with him again. On the other hand, things were going so smoothly with the boys right now. It wouldn't hurt to include him in one meal . . . only what if it gave them the wrong impression? What if they thought there was hope they'd patch up their differences?

"I'm sorry, boys, but I've got a dinner date with a client," David said, and she knew he'd noticed her hesitation.

Unexpectedly, she was furious with him. David the long-suffering, the guy in the white hat, was it? Well, she was suffering, too, and none of it was her fault. All she'd done was be stupid and gullible, going through life with her eyes closed, always trying to please everybody. . . .

"How about a cup of coffee, Pop?" Chuck said.

David shook his head. "I've already had my caffeine quota for the day, son."

"But it's decaf. Mom uses it now because she can't sleep when she drinks the real stuff."

"I have to leave pretty soon. My client lives out this way so I thought I'd drop by and say hello." He produced a paper sack. "I picked up a new video game today—sounds like fun."

In the bustle of the boys taking off the cellophane and reading the directions aloud, Stephanie returned to grating cheese. The boys headed for the VCR in the living room, and she didn't realize David was still there until he spoke.

"Sorry about arriving here at dinnertime. I thought you would have eaten by now."

"It's okay. The boys were helping me rehearse for job interviews." She thought about Chuck's predatory interviewer role and despite herself, her mouth twitched.

"That's what you were laughing about?"

"That and Chuck's self-serving attempt to wriggle out of being punished for losing his new vest."

She didn't realize she was smiling until David's face tightened. "God, Stephanie, I miss you. I miss the boys, too. Can't you find it in your heart to forgive me?"

She shook her head and turned away, unable to face the pleading in his eyes. For all the bitterness between them, it hurt to see him humbled—David who was so sure of himself, of his own worth. But how could she possibly take him back? She couldn't be a real wife to him. Just the thought of him touching her made her feel sick. All those years—she'd lived in a fool's paradise for fifteen years. All of it, their whole marriage, had been a lie—except their mutual love for the boys. And even there—wasn't there something a little strange about David's devotion to Chuck and Ronnie?

"I love you, Stephanie. I know things haven't always been right with us, that I wanted more than you could give, but—"

She swung around, stung by his words. "What are you talking about? I did everything I could to be a good wife. When did I ever short you?"

"Hell. Look, I didn't mean—what I meant was that sometimes we didn't see eye to eye about things."

She stared at him in honest bewilderment. "What things?"

"Well, I'm into sports and you don't care for them. You go for classical music and I have a tin ear. Our priorities are different, but that isn't important—"

"It isn't even true. Okay, I loathe Monday Night Football and you fell asleep at the one concert you went to with me, but as for our priorities—what priorities?"

"I don't think we should talk about it now—"

"Oh, no. You aren't going to drop your little barb and then run. I want to know what the hell you meant about priorities!"

He winced, and she remembered that he didn't like to hear her swear. Well, the devil with that. What David liked or didn't like no longer mattered to her. In fact, she just might drop a few worse words on him.

"I meant things like—well, this house. I was perfectly satisfied with our place in the city—"

"It was too small, and the neighborhood was deteriorating, the schools were going downhill. And you weren't stuck there day after day, either."

"I know. And I agreed to move, didn't I?"

"Grudgingly. Too bad about all that commuting you were forced to do. A whole half hour each way, wasn't it? And what other things have been sticking in your craw—as we rubes from Oregon say?"

"You still remember that stupid argument, don't you?" he said with a twisted smile. "Honey, that was years ago—we were just getting used to each other."

"I remember you told me after a dinner party at your mother's house that you wished I'd go easy on the homespun Oregon expressions, that while you knew it was my idea of being funny, other people might take it seriously and think I was a—a displaced rube, I think you called it. It wasn't exactly a thrill to find out the way you talked grated against your husband's finer sensibilities."

"And all this time that stupid remark has been festering in your mind?"

"Are you asking if it hurt to be put down by my own husband? The answer is yes, it did. But I tried my best not to embarrass you in front of your relatives and friends. You never had cause to complain again, did you?"

"And you never forgot it, either, did you?"

"Is that another insult? If so, you can go to hell. I don't have to take your insults anymore—"

"What insults? God, Stephanie, I've never insulted you—or if I did, it was unintentional!"

"Or more like you were sure I wouldn't catch on? You don't think much of my intelligence, do you? All those lectures about how to deal with your friends or your business associates and clients or your mother. To not talk about politics in front of Rob Wilcox or to be sure to compliment Addie Moore on her dessert soufflé. But how sensitive were you to how I felt, David?"

David groaned. "What I don't understand is why you didn't jump all over me if it bothered you so much. Did you think I could read your mind?"

Stephanie shrugged; she began chopping green peppers for the pizza, wishing he could go away, wishing he had never come, wishing she could answer his question.

Why *hadn't* she told him how she felt years ago? Was it because she'd been afraid that he would stop loving her? Why had she always been so sure, deep in her heart, that eventually he would leave her? How ironic that in the end, she had been the one to file for a divorce. . . .

"You'd better go now," she said tonelessly.

"I promised to show the boys how to play the video game," he said.

"They can figure it out for themselves."

She thought he would argue with her, but instead he turned silently and left the kitchen. From the living room, she heard her sons' protests when David told them he had to leave. She waited for him to tell them their mother had asked him to go, but instead he reminded them about his appointment.

Again, his words angered rather than pleased her. Oh, yes, David made a big thing out of being reasonable and covering up for her bitchiness, so why didn't she feel guilty as he probably intended? In fact, she felt surprisingly good. Maybe it took a good argument—one she had won—to give her some backbone.

CHAPTER TWENTY-TWO

JANICE HAD ALWAYS HAD A SPECIAL AFFECTION FOR ARNOLD Waterford, even though her stepmother had complained so often that he was a rogue and entirely unsuitable as a godfather.

She'd never known what caused the rift between them, but since Arnold was a distant relative of her natural mother, and also the conservator of Janice's small inheritance, her stepparents were forced to at least be cordial when he came to visit her.

Janice had an entirely different opinion of him. Rogue he might be with his practice that catered to rich and near-rich women, flamboyant in his personal as well as his professional life, but he had taken his duties as a godfather seriously.

Never had a birthday or Christmas or any other milestone in Janice's life passed that a beautifully wrapped gift hadn't appeared, always appropriate both to the occasion and her age. And those milestones never passed when she hadn't received a personal visit or at least a long phone call from Arnold—and this had been far more important to her than the presents.

That he was sincerely interested in her welfare, she had never doubted, and so she never hesitated to pour out all her secrets, small and large, into his indulgent ear, knowing that they were safe, that she wouldn't be put down or made fun of. When she was sixteen, she had even gone through a brief spell of being infatuated with Arnold, but luckily he'd never shown any signs of noticing. Instead, he had become even more the favorite uncle, and the infatuation had quickly run its course.

Now, as she sat across the table from Arnold at Little Joe's, the small Italian restaurant where they were having lunch, she regarded him with fond eyes. Although she knew he was in his late fifties, he could have passed as a much younger man. Only his hair, still thick and full but now a snowy white, belied his youthful face and trim, well-knit body.

"Why the stare?" he said, and she realized that he'd been watching her in turn.

"Just wondering how you manage to stay so young," she said.

The wine steward came up, and Arnold ordered a bottle of gewürztraminer. The man accorded him unusual respect, whether because Arnold was a frequent patron or because of something more subtle, Janice wasn't sure.

"I *am* young," Arnold said after the wine steward left, as if there'd been no interruption to their conversation, and Janice reflected that this was one of the things that had always made her feel so special, that Arnold never brushed aside anything she said.

"I just can't understand why your four wives let you get away."

"That's easy. I'm a devil to live with. Too selfish by far." He looked at her over the top of his menu. "Like others I could mention."

"Are you including me in that category?"

"No, no. Not *you*," he said with a curious emphasis in his voice.

"Besides," she said, a bit belatedly, "you aren't selfish. Just eccentric."

"I've just been insulted or praised. Either way, I think I'm flattered."

"Great. Just keep on thinking that."

"And you, dear goddaughter, are a wiseass."

"Only with you. With the rest of the world I'm good ole reliable, predictable Janice."

Arnold tilted his head to one side. "Is that a tinge of bitterness I hear?"

"Bitterness? Why would I be bitter?"

"I have no idea. Life dealt you a full hand—with an exception or two. You've got class, brains, good looks—"

"And a wonderful husband," she said.

"Yes, that too—and how is the good prof these days?"

"Jake is fine. He's just been promoted, you know—or did I tell you?"

"To what? President of the Universe?"

"To department head."

"Do pass on my congratulations," he said.

"What's with you and Jake, anyway?" she said, asking the question she'd evaded for years.

Arnold raised his thick eyebrows. "I'm a great admirer of your husband. I've watched with awe his ascension up the academic ladder. I expect him to rise even further."

"But you don't like him, do you? The strange thing is that I just realized my best friend's husband doesn't like Jake, either. I can't ask Merv why, but I can ask you. What is there about Jake that bothers you?"

Arnold hesitated so long that she was sure he was going to evade her question. "It isn't that I don't like him," he said finally. "It's just that—hell, you're like my own daughter, Janice. And that means that in my eyes, Jesus Christ wouldn't be good enough for you."

"And that's all it is?"

"Of course. I'm delighted that he makes you happy. You deserve a perfect marriage."

"Nothing's perfect in this imperfect world," she said—and then wondered at her choice of words. "Jake and I do get along well together, and we're still lovers."

"I'm sure you are. There's a lot of passion under that cool exterior you show the world—and you were always a loving child. Not that those two cold fish who raised you ever seemed to notice. No wonder you fell for the first guy who came along."

"Is that what you think happened? You're wrong. I dated a lot of boys in high school, had the usual number of crushes. But it was love at first sight for me when I met Jake. There was a chemistry between us that—" She broke off, chagrined. She didn't believe in discussing the intimate details of her marriage, not even with Arnold.

"So that's how you do it," she said. "You get your clients to reveal all with an innocent question here, a compliment there."

"Is that what I was doing? Sorry," he said, but his smile was unrepentant.

Their waiter came and they ordered—spaghetti with pesto sauce for Stephanie, veal saltimbocca for Arnold. There were no pretensions about Little Joe's. An open cooking line revealed every detail of the food preparation, and the organized frenzy of the cooks provided entertainment as they waited for their order.

"Sorry to drag you here for lunch," Arnold told her. "I intended to take you to a posher restaurant, but I have to be at a meeting that can't be postponed. This is the closest place that has decent food—and a good wine list." He held his wineglass up to the light, admiring the golden color, then took a sip and nodded his approval. "Not bad. Domestic. Grapes from Simi Valley instead of a cooler climate like Mendocino or Sonoma, but—not bad."

She took a sip and agreed with a nod.

"I'm glad we finally made it for lunch," Arnold said. "I don't see much of you these days."

"I know. I thought I'd have more time once I quit work, but the extra classes I'm taking and the survey I'm doing for my dissertation, plus some other things, seem to fill up the space. I did promise Jake I'd finish my dissertation in a year."

"Why would you do that? Seems to me it took him almost three years to finish his. Something about writer's block, wasn't it?"

"He did have a spell when he couldn't seem to get it all together, yes. And why are we talking about Jake so much? Usually, you seem to avoid the subject."

"Temper, temper. We can talk about anything you like. Such as your dissertation. How is it coming along?"

"I've got good news and bad news," she said, using one of Jake's pet phrases.

"Such as?"

"The good news is that my survey is going well. Those names you gave me—the women all seem eager to answer my questions in depth. In fact, only one woman turned me down—which is an incredible response to a survey. It's obvious they want to talk about their divorces, to explain how they happened and tell me what they've been through. I have plenty of data on such things as getting back into the work force, learning to date again, adjusting to being a single parent, coping with ex-husbands and ex-in-laws. The women are widely varied, even though your clientele does lean toward the well-heeled—"

"Whoa, now. I gave you a cross section of my clients, with a fair percentage being the ones I charge a reduced fee."

"Your 'worthies'? I appreciate that. And I've noticed quite a difference in their priorities. The prosperous ones are mainly concerned about how their new marital status will change their social life. With the less affluent ones, their concerns are more basic—such as how to earn a living, find reliable baby-sitters, cope with loneliness and the loss of a sex life. Sometimes they can be devastatingly honest. I've learned more about sex problems than I can absorb."

"So that's your good news. What about the bad?"

"It's the support group. You know that I intend to make the four of them the core of my research, with a detailed accounting of the first year after divorce. The trouble is, I can't get them to discuss their problems. Instead, they talk about—you know, inconsequential things. I tried to steer them into more personal channels, but it ended up mostly with social chitchat."

"Give them time to get acquainted. People don't confide in strangers."

"I suppose you're right, only—well, it's possible the whole thing will collapse. I was a little surprised they all turned up at the second meeting."

"It's up to you to keep things going. And even if it did break up, you could continue with the survey—which you very well know. Is it possible that you've already formed some sort of attachment to these women? You do have a strong mothering instinct, you know. Which makes it so odd that you and Jake—" He broke off, looking uncomfortable.

"Finish the sentence, please," she said tartly.

"I was wondering why you and Jake never had kids. Which is none of my business, of course."

Janice hesitated. He had given her an out, that it wasn't any of his business. A light remark and he would drop it. So why did she suddenly want to answer his question honestly?

"We haven't started a family because I'm infertile," she said. "I found it out when I had tests done to see why I didn't get pregnant. Jake—well, he's been wonderful about it. Some men wouldn't be so understanding.''

''I see. Yes, I do see a lot of things.'' A busboy came up to remove their empty plates, and when he was gone, Arnold changed the subject. ''You'll just have to be patient with the support group. In their own good time, they'll start relating to one another and then you'll have all the material you need.''

''I'm sure you're right.''

''When's your next meeting?''

''Next Saturday.''

''At the University Club?''

She nodded. ''Maurice is reserving the Solarium Room for us the first Saturday of every month. It's really an ideal meeting place—very private. Also, the location is so central. Stephanie has a condo in Marin County. Chanel lives on Pacific Heights and Ariel at the Marina. I live in Palo Alto and Glory—God knows where she lives. In the Tenderloin somewhere, I would guess.''

''As a matter of fact, she has an unfurnished flat on Russian Hill. And I do mean unfurnished. She sleeps on a mattress on the floor.''

''She told you that?''

''She thinks I'm—what did she call me? A nice guy, I think it was. She didn't say nice *old* guy, but it was implied. After all, she just turned eighteen a few months ago. I must seem a thousand years old to her.''

''You like her,'' Janice said slowly. ''You like that street urchin, don't you?''

''She's got guts. She takes chances. And she plays by her own rules.''

''And you admire that?''

''Of course. How do you think I got where I am? When I couldn't break into the closed ranks of the legal profession in this town because I hadn't gone to the right law schools, I did it my own way. Most of my esteemed colleagues consider me bottom of the barrel, so how come I win so often when I come up against one of those elitists?''

''And that's why you concentrate on divorces?''

''Not on divorces. On women who are being exploited,'' he said, looking so righteous that she had to laugh.

''You're an old humbug,'' she told him.

''Right. At least, I'm old compared to you. Do you realize that I'll soon be sixty, goddaughter?''

"I know—in January. I'll send you a bouquet of yellow roses and baby's breath and make you feel young."

"Oh, I feel young. Which is part of my trouble."

"Too many women?"

"Plenty of women, not the right one. I did have my eye on one very delicious bird who could've made me forget my aversion to marriage, but I think I'm going to have to give up on her. Fact is, I've turned a new leaf. No more young things for me."

Janice started to make a teasing remark when a passing couple stopped to exchange greetings with Arnold. Then it was time for him to leave for his meeting.

They parted at the door of the restaurant, and as she watched him stroll off, a man other people instinctively moved aside for, she found herself reviewing their conversation—and wondering if the young thing he was interested in could possibly be Morning Glory Browne.

"I've been thinking we should get to know one another better," Janice said, looking around the table at the support group. It was raining outside, and the long, narrow room, with its overgrown plants and wicker furniture, its fusty odors of damp soil, of old plaster and old wood, seemed particularly cozy today. "It occurs to me that maybe we should choose a subject and each take a turn discussing it."

She paused, waiting for their reaction. Chanel looked amused— or at least she had a half smile on her face. Ariel was staring down at her spring salad, which she had barely touched, and Janice wondered if she'd even heard the question. Glory, on the other hand, was eyeing her with what could only be described as wariness.

"I'm willing to give it a try," Stephanie said. "I do think we should be careful about the subject matter. We wouldn't want to embarrass anyone."

And what subject are you afraid of, Stephanie? "You're right," Janice said. "Does everybody agree to give it a try?"

This time everybody nodded, although Glory hesitated a little longer than the rest. "What subject are you talking about?" she demanded.

"How about husbands?" Chanel said dryly. "They're the root of most of our problems, aren't they?"

"Anyone disagree?" Janice said, and when no one spoke, she added, "Who wants to go first?"

"Wait a minute," Glory said. "Are you talking about—you know, a physical description?"

"A description, background, how you met, why you broke up, whatever."

"Why don't *you* go first, Janice?" Chanel said, her voice silky. "It's your idea."

Despite herself, Janice hesitated. Until now, she had managed not to stretch the truth too much. But eventually she would have to out-and-out lie or else tell them that actually she had a very happy marriage. The trouble was—she wasn't good at lying or even at stretching the truth.

"Well, you already know that Jake is a professor at Stanford," she said finally. "Physically, he's of average height, just a couple of inches taller than me in heels. He has dark hair, dark eyes, and a great smile. I guess you'd describe him as attractive rather than handsome. He's good with people, and his charm isn't calculated. I'm sure it's unconscious—"

"And how charming was he after the crowds went home?" Chanel asked.

"The same. He likes to talk—there were no long silences between us."

"But did he listen?" Stephanie said. "David never did much of that, which may have been my fault. I was the listener in our family."

"Well, Jake does listen. At least when the subject is about—" Janice broke off, biting her lip.

"When the subject is about—what?" Glory asked.

"Things that interested him."

"What you're really saying is that he was a selfish bastard, interested only in himself." Chanel's tone was flat.

"No, that isn't true. It's just that he's so articulate and has a lot of strong opinions," Janice said, more sharply than she intended.

Again, Chanel fixed a dissecting look upon her. "Why are you defending the man?"

"I'm not. I just want to be fair."

"Well, my ex lives in his own world," Chanel said. "Jacques is interested in only one thing—his frigging collections. He's also a liar. When he proposed, he let me think that he had a lot of— that he was a lot of things he isn't." She brooded over her words a minute, then shrugged. "And how about your ex, Stephanie? What's he like?"

"I thought he was perfect. My whole life revolved around David and our boys."

"So you're divorcing him because he was unfaithful? He isn't unique, you know."

Stephanie flushed. "I can't forgive him because I found out in the cruelest way possible."

"How did it happen?"

"I came home early from a luncheon that had been canceled at the last minute. The boys were out—and David was in bed with a—a friend of ours."

"God, the old husband-and-best-friend thing," Chanel said.

"What did you do?" Janice asked.

"I called him a bastard and told him to pack his clothes and get out."

"And he did?"

"Oh, yes. He didn't want to go and maybe I would have forgiven him if I hadn't seen—what I saw." There was pain in her eyes, in her voice, and Janice wished she would stop, even though she knew that it was to her advantage if she didn't.

"I'm so sorry," Ariel said softly. Her long, slender fingers touched Stephanie's wrist briefly. "I've never actually caught Alex with another woman, but I'm sure . . ." Her voice faded out.

"You're sure what?"

"That he's intimate with some of his patients."

"My God, Ariel, do you realize what you're saying?" Chanel exclaimed. "You could hang him sky-high if you can prove that."

Ariel seemed to withdraw in stages, and Janice was glad when Glory said, "Well, I knew for sure that Buddy was screwing around. The other wives kept dropping hints, but I always pretended not to understand."

"Which means that all our husbands except Chanel's were unfaithful," Stephanie said, sighing.

"Not Jake," Janice said without thinking.

"So why are you divorcing such a paragon?"

Chanel's question brought Janice up short. How could she have forgotten, even for a few minutes, that she wasn't a spectator but supposedly a participant?

"As I told you, our personalities are totally incompatible," she said carefully. "It wasn't obvious at first, but after a while—well, the differences between us gradually eroded our marriage. But he was never unfaithful to me."

"How can you be so sure? Was the guy impotent?" Chanel's voice was skeptical.

Janice hesitated. "Something like that," she said reluctantly.

"Well, you're not alone. Poor Jacques couldn't get it up worth a damn. And when he did, it was over too quickly to do me any good." Chanel looked at Ariel. "What about you? Why did you change your mind about getting a divorce? It seems to me you have good grounds for one."

"Alex was the one who wanted it. I'm not sure why, but I think I did something to annoy him."

Chanel threw her head back in a laugh, and Glory jumped in. Even Janice felt a laugh bubble up in her throat. Only Stephanie didn't smile. In fact, she gave Chanel a hard look.

"I'm sorry, Ariel," Chanel said, dabbing her eyes with a tissue. "It was the way you said that. So—so understated."

Unexpectedly, Ariel smiled. "I guess it *was* pretty funny," she acknowledged. "The thing is—I really don't know why he got so upset with me. That's one reason I come to these meetings. I thought maybe if I understood things better, I wouldn't make so many mistakes."

Janice noticed that she seemed to be talking directly to Stephanie—who had sprung to her defense so quickly. Had the two of them formed a friendship outside the group? They seemed an unlikely pair—Stephanie, so conventional, and Ariel, who didn't seem to fit any mold.

"It's good, isn't it, to be able to talk about our problems," Janice said, feeling like a hypocrite. "Sometimes I feel so alone. My relatives live too far away to be any help, and I don't have any divorced friends. Wouldn't you know that all the couples Jake and I socialized with are still happily married?"

"It isn't that way with me. Most of my friends have been divorced at least once," Chanel said. "But I've learned not to spread my private business around. I tell anyone gauche enough to ask that Jacques and I grew away from each other." She gave a scornful laugh. "Grew away—that's a laugh. We never were close enough to grow away."

Glory sighed. "When I married Buddy I thought I'd died and gone to heaven—y'know? Buddy had just been signed by the San Jose Bees, and the future looked great. And I was really happy about the baby because—well, *my* guy was willing to marry me and all of my sisters' boyfriends had faded out of the picture as soon as they got them pregnant. I knew I'd have trouble with

Buddy's folks, of course. They didn't bother to come to the wedding, but they did turn up for the wedding brunch the next day. I figure they wanted to see how far along I was."

"They knew you were pregnant?"

"Oh, sure. I didn't show much yet, but they knew. His mother looked at me like I was something she'd stepped on in the gutter, and his father—well, he talked to me like I was a hooker or something. Okay, I wasn't a virgin when Buddy married me. So what? Hell, I wasn't even one when we started making out together. The first time was with this old guy who lived downstairs when we were living in the Mission. He caught me alone one day and about smothered me with a pillow while he did it to me. After that, I tried to keep out of his way, but sometimes I wasn't fast enough—"

"Why didn't you tell your mother?" Stephanie said.

Glory gave her a scornful look. "Tell Ma? She knew what was going down. She told me if I got him mad, she'd beat me to a pulp. The old guy gave her money all the time, see? Loans, she called them."

"So what happened?" Chanel said.

"He got arrested for child molesting," Glory said. "He did it to the wrong kid, and her parents went to the cops. Anyway, it really turned me off sex for a long time. When I began to develop and the guys in the neighborhood started coming on to me, I wouldn't have anything to do with them. I knew I'd have to get out of the projects or I'd end up like my sisters, so I worked real hard at school and that's how I made it into high school. I would've graduated, too, if I hadn't met Buddy. Not that I blame him. Man, I was really hung up on that guy."

"What about you, Ariel," Janice said. "How did you meet your husband?"

"He was my psychiatrist," Ariel said.

"You married your own psychiatrist?"

"Yes. I thought I'd be—" She broke off abruptly.

"Be what?"

"Safe."

"From what?"

"From—things."

"From life? Is that what you meant?"

"Yes. From life, I guess."

"And instead, life was right there, waiting for you," Janice said.

"My cousin Laird told me I was making a mistake, but Alex was the most important person in my life. I didn't want to lose him."

"It seems like a breach of ethics," Chanel said, frowning. "Naturally your own psychiatrist would know how to manipulate you. He must've really been crazy about you to risk his reputation and maybe even his license."

Ariel's luminous eyes moved to Chanel. "He doesn't even like me."

"That's hard to believe. You're a lovely young woman," Janice said automatically, and then discovered that what had been politeness was really true. Ariel *was* lovely—it was her lack of animation that made her fade into the background.

Ariel's face seemed to close up again. One minute she was a participating part of the group, revealing something of herself, and then she had retreated back into her shell. Janice was furious with herself. When was she going to learn to draw people out instead of rushing in with all flags waving?

"Well, I have some errands," Chanel said, glancing at the tiny bracelet watch on her wrist. "It's been fun and all that."

"Can everybody make it next time?" Janice asked.

"I'm pretty sure I can. How about you, Ariel?" Chanel said; she looked pleased when Ariel nodded.

"I'm not really sure," Stephanie said. "I'm starting a new job Monday."

"Hey, that's great," Glory said. "You shoulda told us earlier so we could drink a toast or something. What kind of job is it?"

"Actually, I'm just a gofer," Stephanie said. "I'll be clerking in the lingerie department at Macy's—and also helping the buyer. I'm scared to death. This is all so new to me."

"Piece of cake," Glory said airily.

"If you run into any problem, give me a ring," Janice said. "I'm your basic career woman type, you know."

Stephanie gave her a grateful smile. "I just might do that. Your advice about—you know, presenting myself the right way during the job interview was a real help."

"Will you be working Saturdays?"

"No—but unfortunately, I do have to work late two nights a week. I hate not being there when the boys get home from school."

"Why doesn't your ex-husband provide for you and your kids so you don't have to get a job?" Chanel demanded.

"I don't want his help." Stephanie's mouth took on an obstinate look. "Child support is all I'm asking for."

"If he doesn't have to pay you alimony, maybe he'll stay out of your life," Glory said. "Of course, it hasn't worked that way with Buddy. He was waiting for me last week when I got off work. If this friend of mine hadn't come along, it could've been pretty heavy. As it is, he left a few bruises on my arm where he grabbed me."

Chanel frowned at her. "Why didn't you have him arrested for assault?"

"I don't think you could call it assault, not really. He wanted to talk to me and I didn't want to talk to him. I started to walk away and he grabbed me by the arm."

"I hope you're being careful," Janice said. "He sounds dangerous to me."

"Yeah. I look both ways these days when I cross the street. This guy from work has been driving me home nights, making sure I get into the house okay. And I bought a second dead bolt lock, so it takes two keys to get into my apartment. The couple I rent from live upstairs. Their bedroom's right over my apartment, so I figure they'd hear any noise if he tries something dumb like trying to bust in my door."

Remembering what Arnold had told her, Janice had an image of Glory in her empty flat, sleeping on a mattress on the floor. Another image, of the big Victorian in Palo Alto with its empty bedrooms made her wince. Okay, life was unfair. She knew this intellectually, so why did she feel so guilty? Was it because, no matter how she rationalized it, she was still using these women for her own advantage? And what if they saw it the same way? What if they refused to give her permission to use their experiences in her dissertation? It could mean a whole year's work wasted. . . .

"Hey, it's okay, Janice," Glory said, and Janice realized that she had misinterpreted her silence. "I can take care of myself. I was dodging drunks by the time I was old enough to walk. Besides, Buddy don't hold a grudge for long. Right now, he's sore because I got the best of him, but he'll get over it."

Her words should have been reassuring, but Janice still felt uneasy. And what if he doesn't? she wanted to say. What if the next time he comes after you, your friend isn't around to rescue you?

"Take care," she said just as their waiter appeared with their bill, discreetly hidden under the tarnished dome of a silver tray. In the flurry of settling up, she wasn't sure if she'd said the words aloud or had just thought them.

CHAPTER TWENTY-THREE

THE LOCKER ROOM SMELLED OF SUCH EXOTIC THINGS AS JOY, Giorgio, and Coco perfumes, along with the odor of leather, canvas shoes, female bodies, and a pine disinfectant that was more an olfactory veneer than a genuine deodorizer. Although Glory seldom was thrown by new surroundings, she felt more than a little defensive as she sat on a bench near the junction of two rows of lockers, changing her shoes.

Her red high heels with their scuffed toes suddenly looked cheap and gaudy, although they were her favorite pair, and when she saw a dark-haired woman staring at them, she quickly tucked them away in the locker she'd been assigned. As for her exercise clothes—although she was wearing leotards and tights, as were most of the women in the room, there the resemblances ended.

Covertly, she eyed the woman who had stared at her shoes. The leotards and tights that covered her razor-thin but undoubtedly middle-aged body were made from suede-soft doeskin, the word Prince was prominently displayed at the rear of her athletic shoes, and from the rich colors of the rolled scarf tied another her forehead, it was obviously pure silk and probably bore a designer's label.

As Glory knotted her own scarf, purchased at K Mart, at the back of her head, she wondered why Chanel hadn't warned her how ritzy this place was.

"I'm a member of the Pacific Heights branch of the Golden Gate Health Club," she'd said as they were leaving the Mayflower Tearoom. "You're welcome to sign up for an aerobics class as my guest. There's a small fee, so if you want to pay me now, I'll have the club put it on my account when I make the arrangements for you."

The fee she quoted seemed a lot more than small to Glory, but she handed over the money without comment. After all, she would have to pay a charge, no matter where she took an aerobics class, and this Golden Gate Health Club must be good or Chanel wouldn't belong to it.

She was glad now she'd left off most of her usual makeup. Even so, her mascara, which she'd put on at the last moment because she'd felt naked without it, was sure to run when she started exerting herself. Her hair, too, was going to give her trouble. Already she could feel it frizzling in the humid air of the locker room.

If only those women would stop staring at her as if she had two heads. As it was, she was beginning to think she'd made a mistake, coming here. Was it a coincidence that Chanel hadn't offered to come with her this first time?

Suddenly annoyed by her own doubts, she gave her head a shake, again earning the attention of the matron at the next locker. Glory stared back and had the satisfaction of seeing the woman's eyes slide away.

"Okay, ladies, time to move your asses."

The voice was female, assertive, and slightly menacing. Glory was surprised at the ripple of nervous giggles that greeted the newcomer's words.

The speaker was tall, well built; despite a too-prominent chin and disconcertingly cold eyes, she was strikingly attractive. Her gaze fell on Glory, moved slowly over her K Mart workout clothes and athletic shoes. When she sighed and rolled her eyes, Glory felt a familiar burning sensation at the back of her neck.

"You're the new one, Ms. Devereau's guest?" the woman said as if she couldn't believe it, and when Glory nodded, she added, "I think you should know that this aerobics class isn't any picnic—right, Mrs. Tibbett?"

The woman standing near Glory blinked, then gave a jerky nod.

"First we do our warm-ups, then our calisthenics, followed by aerobics. And no flaking out. We stay up with the class or out we go—right, ladies?"

"Right, Ms. Claire," a chorus of voices said.

"No pain, no gain. That's the motto of the Golden Gate Health Club. And no excuses. If you can't hack it, you pack it."

She turned away and someone behind Glory let out a long breath and whispered, "The dragon lady is really in top form today."

"Shhh. . . . Don't let her hear you or we'll all suffer."

There was a round of uneasy tittering and then they were all trooping after the instructor, Glory trailing behind. She wondered why, for the exorbitant membership fee they paid, they put up with the instructor's rudeness. Most of these women looked as if they were used to giving orders, not taking them.

"Be careful around Claire." It was a short, thin woman, wearing light blue tights and a navy leotard. She stared at Glory's hair with fascinated eyes. "If she gets it in for you, she can really be a bitch."

"Why do you put up with it?"

The woman looked surprised. "She's good. You're lucky you got into her class."

Glory had her own opinion about that, but she held her tongue. "Is the routine hard?"

The woman groaned. "It's hell—but it does work. Look at my stomach—it used to look like a rubber tube." She patted her flat stomach. "I hope you've done some aerobics. This is an advanced class and she doesn't make allowances for beginners."

"Not aerobics, but I did gymnastics in school—"

"Okay, okay," the instructor's voice broke in. "Have you two ladies there in the back finished talking? Let's get with it—and I mean right now!"

For the next few minutes Glory concentrated on deciphering Claire's rapid-fire patter. Most of the jargon went over her head, but she followed the actions of the woman in front of her, half a beat behind. She felt pleased with herself for keeping up, especially when the pace quickened.

"Move it! Move it! Get those legs moving—raise those knees. You look like a bunch of fat clowns," Claire barked.

Glory had never before thought of the word *sneer* in conjunction with the smile of a real person, but the word popped into her mind now because it so perfectly described the contemptuous curl of Claire's upper lip. "Come on, you cows—show a little energy. No pain, no gain—bend those flabby knees! Up! Up! Up! Move ass or out you go!"

Glory had thought she was in excellent condition because of all the walking she did at work, but now she was finding out that she had muscles in places she hadn't dreamed existed. Although she kept on doggedly, she was sure she'd be so crippled the next day, she wouldn't be able to get up from her mattress.

The pounding of the music, pure acid rock that set her teeth on edge, was so irritating that she put all she had into the torturous jumping jacks, throwing her arms above her head and slapping her hands together so sharply that her palms stung, flinging her legs apart, then together in an abandon that was almost sexual. But later in the session, when she suddenly acquired her second wind, Glory discovered she was actually enjoying herself. There was still pain, but somehow it didn't seem to matter. Later, she knew, she would suffer, but for now, there was a high in moving in time with the music, moving quickly, rhythmically, smoothly—

"Stop! Stop!" Claire's harsh voice broke into her reverie. "What do you think you're doing back there? You're moving like an old woman—how the hell do you think you'll get rid of that gut if you don't give it all you've got?"

Glory blinked at the instructor. Surely, Claire couldn't mean her. Her hips might need an inch or so off, but her stomach was as flat as a board—and besides, she *had* been keeping up with the class, doing better than some of the others if the truth be known.

"I don't know what you're talking about, Ms. Claire," she said stiffly. She wiped the sweat from her forehead. "I'm keeping up with the other women."

"Oh, you are, are you? Tell me, ladies, is she keeping up with the rest of you?"

There was a scattering of "No, Ms. Claire," and even one "No way, Ms. Claire."

Claire pointed her finger at Glory. "Not only do you look like a cow, you move like a cow. Now, you keep your mind on what's going down in this here class. Watch me and give it all you've got instead of drifting off into some kind of trance—you understand?"

Glory just stared at her, and Claire's eyes narrowed ominously. The women beside Glory shifted uneasily. "Say yes," she said sotto voce.

"Yes," Glory said—unwillingly.

"Yes, *Ms. Claire*."

Glory gave her a long, cold stare. She knew what she was dealing with now. A bully—and there was only one way to treat a bully. "Yes, Ms. Asshole," she said softly.

For a moment, she thought the woman hadn't heard her, then Claire's face turned brick red, and Glory braced herself for a verbal attack. Claire met Glory's eyes, took in her unblinking stare, her tense stance, and obviously changed her mind. "Okay, back to work," she said loudly. "And this time, do it right."

Having made her point, Glory was content to let Claire pretend she hadn't heard the insult. Let the bitch save face. From now on, Claire would hate her guts, but she wouldn't push too hard. Verbal abuse, yes, but short of true insult. And that kind of talk rolled off her back like rainwater. She knew words that would curl Ms. Claire's hair, but she wouldn't use them. That would be overkill. When Claire had backed down in front of the class, she had lost the game, whether or not she realized it.

But wasn't it interesting that these women were willing to pay big bucks to be pushed around by someone like Ms. Asshole?

An hour later, she was coming out of the women's locker room, dressed for the street and carrying her exercise clothes in a canvas bag, when a large masculine body got between her and the door.

"That was pretty uncool, baiting Claire like that," the man said.

Glory looked up—and up. She felt a shock that made her mouth go dry. Except for his dark hair and eyes, the man could have been a double for Buddy. Instinctively, she threw up an arm to protect her face. The man's eyes narrowed, and then he was smiling.

"Hey, that was just my opinion. There are better ways to deal with people like Claire than antagonizing them."

"You do it your way and I'll do it my way," she said tartly, furious because she'd shown fear to a stranger. "I don't cave in to bullies."

"I can see you don't." His stare was making her uncomfortable. "I think—"

"You think you've got the right to give me advice? Listen, I don't know you, mister, and I don't want to."

He smiled again, still blocking her way. "Steve Golden's my name. I teach martial arts here. I'm also assistant manager of the club."

"So?"

"So I thought you might like to have a beer with me to cool off."

"I don't do alcohol," she said shortly. "And I don't waste my time on jocks."

"You don't like jocks?" he said as if he'd just made an important discovery.

"I don't like *you*," she snapped.

"Your loss," he said. "I'm not a bad fellow."

Glory looked at him closely. Was he for real? Or was this some kind of bait-the-new-girl game? "Well, I'll just take a chance and pass on it." She ducked under his arm and headed for the door.

His voice caught up with her just before she reached it. "I'll put that invitation on hold, just in case you change your mind."

In answer, Glory gave the door a hard push, but the door-closing mechanism thwarted her grand exit and she thought she heard a laugh before the door closed with a soft swish of air. Fuming, she stalked toward the bus stop, reflecting angrily that what she didn't need was another jock in her life. And she wasn't in the mood for any man-woman bullshit, either. No wonder she was edgy. She'd stopped eating everything except fruit, raw veggies, and low-fat yogurt, and her stomach was on a perpetual growl. Except for right now. The exercise seemed to have helped. Well, another few pounds and she would be ready for that shopping trip with Chanel.

The question was—would Chanel honor her promise?

The last thing on Chanel's mind these days was Glory Browne. She was in a constant state of frustration and uncertainty, a rare state for her. Her plans to ensnare Laird had succeeded to the degree that he had taken her out to dinner twice in the past two weeks, had invited her to the opening of an art gallery that he had a financial interest in, and had even called her twice just to talk, but so far, their relationship remained casual. After their dates, he took her straight home, gave her an expert kiss at the door, then refused her invitation to come in for a drink—and there had been no second invitation to stop by his place on the way home.

By now, she had changed her mind about a quick seduction and had decided to wait for the perfect occasion. Laird's nature was—well, austere, which could mean he'd be turned off by a too-easy conquest. On the other hand, she was great in bed. It would be to her advantage to give him a taste of what he could expect if he married her—but just one taste. If she read his attitude toward his cousin correctly, he admired women who didn't flaunt their sexuality and who had an aura of innocence about them. Which was why she was so careful to maintain her cool, tempered by a good dose of humor, and to do nothing that might give him the feeling of pressure. She had even turned down one dinner invitation from him with the excuse that she had a previous engagement.

Luckily, she had been discreet in her affairs while married to Jacques, and she doubted that Laird had heard any rumors about her. That she was playing a perilous game, putting all her eggs in one basket by concentrating exclusively on Laird, she was well aware. Despite their dates, he remained elusive. In fact, she knew very little about his personal life other than his obsession with boats and his interest in art. That he'd had affairs, mainly long-term ones, she had heard through the rumor mill. As one of the city's prime marital catches, everything Laird did was subject to gossip, but his affairs, mainly with divorcées, had been discreet, never sensational.

So she played a waiting game, which left her irritable and restless. For one thing, her financial situation was becoming increasingly worrisome. The settlement with Jacques had been disappointingly small, and after she'd paid Arnold Waterford's fee and settled her most pressing bills, what remained wasn't enough to cover her expenses for more than a few more weeks. She was doing her own housework now, something she wouldn't have admitted to her best friend—if she had one. And she was economizing on food, too, watching every penny, which was one reason she preferred that Fern stay at school over weekends.

Fern had exploded into one of her tantrums when her allowance had been cut to the bone and Chanel had sold her horse. Losing what little patience she had with her daughter, Chanel told her coldly to get a part-time job if she needed more money, then added that because she'd be very busy, she preferred that Fern curtailed her weekend visits until Christmas. In fact, if she got an invitation to stay with one of her friends over the holidays, she should take it.

One thing gave her encouragement—of a sort. Her own social status had improved dramatically since Laird had begun escorting her. She'd received several invitations that ordinarily wouldn't have come her way now that she was no longer connected with the Devereau family. That none of the invitations were from her old school chums was the only thing that marred her satisfaction.

Chanel's escort on the occasions when Laird wasn't available was Howie Brighton, as it had often been when she was still married to Jacques. One of the gay men who were socially acceptable to local society, he served a very useful function in that he could escort a married or otherwise attached woman to some affair without arousing gossip. Not only was he well connected to a socially prominent San Francisco family, but he was presentable and amusing, as well as being a talented architect. In other words, a perfect escort for Chanel.

That he also had a talent for being bitchy not only with his enemies but with his friends was a drawback she tolerated because of his usefulness.

"You'd better come up with something special if you want to marry Laird and all those Fairmount millions," Howie said as he was bringing Chanel home from a benefit banquet for the San Francisco Ballet. "He's been around the barn so many times that he knows all the tricks."

Chanel considered him coolly. "You've got it all wrong. I'm very fond of Laird, but I'm not out to marry him and his millions, as you so gallantly put it."

"You could have fooled me," Howie said, his smile sly.

"I'm sure that was meant to be funny, but I seem to have mislaid my sense of humor tonight," she said.

"I hope not. One of the things I find entertaining about you is your caustic wit. Just be careful how you flash it around Laird. He's never struck me as having much of a sense of humor."

Chanel changed the subject. She didn't want to antagonize Howie because he was so useful, but she also had no intention of giving him food for gossip. He might be fond of her—she was sure he was—but gossip was the lifeline of society, and she couldn't afford any about herself right now. Later, when she was Laird's wife, they could wag their tongues all they wanted. She would be above it all—and able to do what she damned well pleased.

When they reached her condo, she brushed Howie's cheek with her lips, told him sweetly that she'd had a marvelous time and do let's keep in touch, and then, feeling let down despite an amusing evening, took the elevator to her floor, looking forward to bed.

But when she let herself into her apartment, the lights were already on. Her lips tightened when she spotted Fern's denim jacket flung over a hall chair. She turned into the living room and found Fern huddled on a sofa, a sodden bundle of misery, her eyes red from crying.

"What the hell—what is it, Fern?" Chanel said sharply.

Fern rubbed her eyes with the back of her hand—a little too dramatically for belief, Chanel decided. She lifted a tragic face to her mother. "I've quit school," she wailed. "I never want to see any of them again!"

Fern's decision to leave school hadn't been an impulsive one. There had been hints, ever since Chanel's divorce from Jacques

Devereau, that she was no longer one of the "ins" at the academy. Oh, the snubbing hadn't been overt—not at first. For instance, she'd only found out by accident about a weekend party, given by a friend, that she hadn't been invited to. But the signs were there. Suddenly, she wasn't one of the most popular girls in school—in fact, not one of the boys who had been clamoring for dates had asked her to the all-important Christmas dance. And these days, when she joined the group she usually ate lunch with, she noted the studied coolness, the embarrassed silence, sure proof that they had been talking about her.

Fern found all this intolerable. Her first impulse was to fight back, to flay her former friends with caustic words. Only her knowledge that this would be futile and would probably make her persona non grata at school, stopped her. Instead, she pretended not to notice the subtle—and not so subtle—snubs, hoping it would blow over.

And then someone slipped a note under her door, and she discovered that Chanel's divorce had nothing to do with her sudden unpopularity. The note was from a friend—or so it was signed—and it seemed that a boy Fern had dated a few times had been the private property of another girl, the leader of the "in" pack, who had been conducting a whispering campaign against Fern.

Fern could have fought open antagonism, but fighting innuendos and ridicule was like fighting smoke. She also was deeply hurt by the desertion of her friends. Which was when she decided to retire from the field and leave school. The trouble was she knew she had to convince Chanel that this was a reasonable thing to do.

Which was why, when she heard Chanel's key at the door, she quickly arranged herself on a living room couch, rubbed her eyes with the heels of her hands until they stung, prepared to give the performance of her life.

Chanel's reaction to her dramatic declaration that she had quit school was to go to the liquor cabinet and pour herself a glass of cognac. "Would you like a drink?" she asked Fern. "You look like you could use one."

Fern shook her head. "I'd better not," she said. "I don't feel at all well."

"Well, if you're going to throw up, don't do it in here. That rug shows everything."

Chanel settled herself on a sofa, looking, Fern thought resentfully, like she'd just stepped out of a *Town and Country* ad. The room was white-on-white, the only relief from monotony being a wide variety of textures—the sheen of silk on the walls, the roughness of the merino wool carpet, the single, starkly modern painting—one dot of scarlet, like a drop of blood, in a sea of undulating white—and the hard, cold white marble of the fireplace. Even the brass-and-beveled glass tables, the brass lamps, and the collection of ivory figurines in a brass epergne were subordinate to the white purity of the room.

Fern, who had made a lifelong study of her mother and knew she never did anything without reason, knew there were no splashes of color in the room because Chanel wanted to make sure that she was always the focus of attention in the jewel-toned colors she favored. Only Chanel, she thought, would consider the effect she made more important than such a mundane thing as exorbitant cleaning bills.

"Don't worry. I won't mess up your precious rug," Fern said.

Chanel regarded her over the rim of her cognac glass. "I can see you're in one of your self-pitying moods. Well, get over it quickly because you *are* returning to school Monday. Your tuition cost a fortune."

"Jacques paid it, not you—and I'm not going back. I never want to see those snobs again!"

"Ignore them. You'll be out of it in a few more months."

"No way—I refuse to go back."

"Then, go find yourself a job—and while you're at it, find a place to live, too."

"That would really make you happy, wouldn't it?" The bitterness and resentment boiled over, and Fern's voice rose. "You're a rotten mother! You know that? A rotten mother!"

"Look, I've done my best for you. I could've had an abortion or I could've put you up for adoption or turned you over to your father's family to raise, but I didn't. You're old enough to take care of yourself now. You have two choices—finish school or get a job."

Caution and hatred warred inside Fern. Caution won, and she forced a conciliatory tone into her voice. "Why can't I stay here with you and go to public school?"

"Public school? You? You wouldn't last five minutes in a public high school. The kids would eat you alive."

"You think private school is all sweetness and light? Listen, it's dog-eat-dog at Burlingame Academy. In fact, it's rougher there because they're all such bloody hypocrites. They smile at you to your face and then rip you apart when you turn your back."

"Why are they so down on you? What did you do to them?"

"Why do you assume it's my fault?"

"It isn't? So convince me that you're an innocent little lamb."

She listened silently as Fern told her the bare facts of the truth, that she'd gone out with the boyfriend of one of her classmates, who was now conducting a vendetta against her.

"And that's all it is? A whispering campaign?"

Fern flushed. "You don't know what it's like, having everybody snubbing you and talking about you behind your back. I hate the whole bunch of them!"

"Come on. You're overreacting. And anyway, it was your fault. There are enough boys around that you don't have to steal some-one else's property."

"Trust you to blame me," Fern muttered.

"You have to admit you were a fool, making enemies out of the very people who could help you later on. There's such a thing as old school ties—and you'll need friends in the right places if you ever hope to make a successful marriage."

"Like you're planning to do? How is your little campaign to get Laird Fairmount to marry you coming along?"

Chanel took a sip of her cognac. "What makes you think I'm interested in marrying Laird?"

"Oh, come on, Chanel. It's obvious. You muffed it with Jacques and now you hope to recoup—" She broke off, uneasy because she'd used an expression she'd read in Chanel's diary.

Chanel moved so quickly that Fern didn't have time to duck before a stinging slap rocked her head back.

"You little beast!" Chanel hissed. "You've been reading my diary." Swiftly, she crossed the room to her writing desk and examined the lock. She straightened slowly, and turned to face Fern. "Where's my key?"

"I put it back in your jewel box," Fern said, knowing there was no use denying it now. "Okay, I read your diary and I know all your little secrets, including how you got Jacques to marry you. You outsmarted yourself that time, didn't you? He wasn't as rich as you thought. I know all about your lovers, too. You're really something, you know. You make judgments about other people, but what about you?" Chanel raised her hand, and Fern stared her straight in the eye. "If you slap me again, I'll hit you back, Chanel. I'm not afraid of you."

Chanel studied her; it was obvious her anger had been dispelled by the slap—or maybe by Fern's words. She went to get a cigarette out of an ivory box that sat on the cocktail table; she lit it and took a long draw before she spoke again.

"It's important that you return to school and brazen it out," she said, as if there had been no interruption. "After I had you, and Papa lost all his money, I went back to school and faced down the gossip, the put-downs, and you can do the same. After all, it's pretty much a tempest in a teapot, unless—good God, you aren't pregnant, are you?"

"No, Chanel, I'm not pregnant," Fern said tightly.

"Well, thank God for that. What I don't need right now is a pregnant daughter."

"Thanks for your concern."

"Look, let me point out the facts of life. If you want to be a winner, you need money—and power. And a woman has as little chance making it on her own as she ever did. Sure, a few do— but you can't count on it. If you had some kind of special talent— well, never mind that. My advice to you is to go back to school, make your peace with those kids, take a good look around, and choose someone who's really loaded, and go after him. Marry rich—and the whole world is open to you."

"You really believe that, don't you?"

"Yes, of course. Don't you?"

Fern considered her thoughtfully. Did she believe it? The answer was yes—with reservations. She intended to marry well— but it would have to be someone she found attractive, too. . . .

An idea came to her then, one so delicious, she couldn't help smiling.

"So your advice is to look around and find the most eligible man I can, and then get him to marry me, right?"

"Can you think of anything more sensible? If the marriage doesn't work out, a nice settlement can always ease the pain."

"You're right. And I'm going to take your advice, Mommie dearest. I even have a prospect." An image of Laird Fairmount filled her mind, and she laughed out loud. "You'll be proud of me when you see my catch. And you're right about that business at school. The whole thing is bound to blow over. I'll make sure of that."

CHAPTER TWENTY-FOUR

GROWING UP AS PART OF A FAMILY WHO MERELY TOLERATED her, Janice had learned to dread Christmas. Somehow the gift she wanted (she wasn't foolish enough to wish for more than one) never materialized under the family Christmas tree.

Katie, her youngest stepsister, would get a sleek, red sports car that her Barbie doll could actually sit in, and Stevie, the next oldest, would get a special birch baseball bat and leather catcher's mitt he had been teasing for, while Marleen, the oldest of the steps, would find the party dress with shoes dyed to match that she wanted under the Christmas tree. But the gayly wrapped package with Janice's name on it would invariably contain something practical—cotton pajamas or underwear, or, one memorable Christmas when she was a freshman in high school, a dozen pairs of white bobby socks that no California girl her age would have been caught dead in.

To Janice, Christmas had meant extra chores—wrapping presents for the smaller steps, cleaning away the debris of paper and twine and bows Christmas morning, helping in the kitchen, and making endless batches of cookies. It meant taking the younger steps to see Santa Claus because her stepmother was too busy, and getting down the ornaments from the attic and trying to decorate the tree with the other kids turning it into a disaster area that she inevitably got blamed for.

Once in a while, she got a verbal pat for being helpful, but usually she could have been the family maid for all the attention paid to her. Arnold Waterford's present, which inevitably appeared on Christmas Eve day, was the only bright spot of the season—and even then, she was made to feel guilty if it turned out to be something one of her stepsiblings coveted.

Janice had long ago become reconciled to her childhood, had come to understand that her stepparents had done the best they were capable of for the unwanted child in their midst. After all, they could have turned her over to the doubtful care of foster homes, and she'd never been physically mistreated.

She knew all this intellectually—but she still had moments of depression during the Christmas season, even after she'd met and married Jake.

Jake, on the other hand, was unashamedly sentimental about Christmas. There was the ritual of going to a tree farm to choose a tree every year, the fun of trimming it, with Jake acting crazy and excited. There was the exchange of presents Christmas morning right after Jake's favorite breakfast of fried ham and redeye gravy, scrambled eggs, and soda biscuits with strawberry preserves.

And there was their traditional Christmas Eve buffet for their friends, with everybody having a great time because Janice was such a good cook and Jake such a great host.

One of the reasons Jake had wanted to buy the house in Professorville was because it was perfect for the kind of Christmas he'd been cheated out of as a kid. With the front door decked with a huge holly wreath, with evergreen garlands wound around the staircase banisters, with a profusion of poinsettias and fat Santa Claus faces and a tree that must be tall enough to reach the living room's lofty ceiling, the house always looked like a page from a December issue of *Better Homes and Gardens*.

This year was no exception. In fact, the tree was especially fresh and aromatic. So why, Janice wondered as she put the finishing touches on the ham for the Christmas Eve buffet, did she feel the same sadness she'd felt as a child who was aware there'd be no special present for her under the tree?

She examined her depression but could find no cause for it. Jake was always generous with his gifts, and God knew it couldn't be because she was lonely. She *knew* lonely—and this year they had entertained or had been entertained just about every night for the past month.

In a couple of hours, the house would be jumping with their friends, all bent on having a good time. They would eat, drink, and be very merry. Inevitably, a group of diehard sentimentalists would sing carols in the second parlor where the piano was kept, and several especially close friends would sit around the fire until early in the morning, talking, talking, talking. Everybody would be on their best behavior because it was Christmas Eve and even the arguments, if any, that flared would be tolerant and mellow.

And Jake—Jake would be on a high because there were wall-to-wall people around him. He would lead the carols in his slightly askew tenor, be the perfect host, neglecting no one, putting the shy at ease and keeping the too-aggressive in line, talking and gesturing with the grace that was all his own. He would press food upon their guests, tease them in ways that never stung, making everybody feel important and clever and welcome, and they would all go home in a glow and tell their friends that the Christmas Eve party Jake and Janice Morehouse had thrown *this* year was the best ever.

And when the last guest had gone home, Jake, still on a high, would be ardent and loving and want to take her straight to bed. She would leave the dirty plates and soiled napkins and half-filled glasses of wine until morning, and go upstairs to their bedroom where he would make long, slow love to her and then they would fall asleep in each other's arms.

So what the hell was wrong with her? Why did she dread the evening ahead and wish she could crawl off in a hole somewhere? Okay, she'd been up late the night before—and most of the nights this week—but she wasn't all that tired. She'd slept until nine this morning, for God's sake. What was going on in her head? Was there such a thing as a twenty-year itch?

"I'm home, Janice," Jake said from the doorway. He was wearing his favorite Pendleton jacket, and the blue plaid was complementary to his olive skin and dark eyes. "I couldn't find that Dry Creek cabernet sauvignon Earl Wallis recommended, so I had to get another brand. Hope he doesn't notice."

"Not to worry." Janice put the last pineapple slice on the ham, brushed the top with brown sugar melted in orange juice, then slid it into the 225-degree oven to bake slowly until party time. "Bring it out late in the evening and he won't notice. He's usually halfway to the stars by ten o'clock."

"Hey, he isn't any worse than other people."

"No—just a little more vocal when he's tight."

"So? Aren't you being a bit intolerant, love?"

"Who, moi?" she said. Was she intolerant for mentioning what was obvious to everybody, that Earl Wallis was fast becoming an alcoholic? Wouldn't it be better to try to help him than to pretend not to notice? Or did Jake consider that kind of caring gauche?

"Hey, I didn't mean to criticize you." Jake sat the grocery sack down and came over to give her a hug. "I know how hard you've worked to get this party on the road. Why don't you go upstairs and take your shower and get dressed? I ran into Arlene Turner at the wine store, and I asked her and Clyde to come a little early—''

''You *what*? You know I still have a dozen things to do!'' Janice wailed. The thought of Arlene, with her cool smile and dissecting eyes, viewing her messy kitchen, dismayed her. Ever since Jake had started his TV class, Arlene and her husband had been part of their lives—a little too much a part, she often thought.

''Lighten up, honey. Just trust ole Jake, okay? You go upstairs and get ready, and I'll finish up here. And do that thing with your hair that makes you look so great. I want my wife to be the prettiest girl at the party.''

''I haven't been a girl for a long time,'' she reminded him.

''Well, we can pretend, can't we? You're only as old as you feel, you know.''

And right now I feel a hundred years old, Janice thought. But she pointed out the things that still needed to be done and went upstairs.

It took her longer than usual to dress. Most of the time, she was content to look well groomed, but tonight she applied make-up with extra care and wasn't satisfied until her skin had a perfect finish and her eyes were well defined with liner. When she slipped the Christmas-red cocktail dress she'd bought especially for the party over her head and looked in the mirror, she smiled with satisfaction. Not only could she pass for a ''girl''—in a dim light— but she could pass for a rather attractive one.

Maybe it was time she made some changes in her personal appearance. Twice in the past month, Jake had made jokes about matronly women. Had his remarks been aimed at her? Was he trying to tell her something? She *had* picked up a few pounds this past year—certainly it wouldn't hurt to go on a diet. That one Chanel recommended where you ate only yogurt and vegetables and fruit sounded easy, even though she'd probably have to stay on it for a while to get results. How ironic that Jake, who ate like a trencherman, never gained an ounce. It didn't seem quite fair somehow. . . .

When she came downstairs, she discovered that the party had already started. Either people had mistaken the time or Jake had invited more than Arlene and her husband to come early. After she'd made the rounds and greeted everybody, she slipped away to the kitchen and found the sink and the counters still full of pots and pans. She was clearing off the counter when Jake came into the room.

"You didn't clean up, you jerk," she said.

"I can't be everywhere at once," he said blithely. "I forgot I told the Wilsons and some of the others to come early, too. They got here just after you went upstairs. Then Arlene and Clyde came and—well, this was my first chance to get away." He examined her for a moment. "You look great, hon," he said, but she sensed a lack of enthusiasm in his voice.

"You like my sexy new dress?" she said, unashamedly fishing for a compliment.

"Sure—it's just that I thought you said once that red was too flashy for you."

"Flashy? This dress looks like a nun's robe next to that see-through outfit Arlene's wearing," she said tartly.

"She's a different type—sophisticated and all," he said.

"Thanks a bunch. You look great, too."

Jake looked hurt. Before he could respond, a tall brunette, the wife of one of his associates, came into the kitchen. "Can I help, Janice?" the brunette said, her eyes on Jake.

"Yes, indeed," Janice said briskly. "You can slice the ham for the buffet—watch out! I just took it out of the oven—and I could use some help setting out the food. Oh, and Jake—would you get the ice cubes for the punch?"

It was an hour later when she missed Jake. One minute he'd been deep in conversation with Dr. Yolanski, but when she looked up again, he was gone. She wanted to ask him to take over bar duties, and she was annoyed by his disappearance. He had promised to handle the bar and see that no one went overboard, but now Chris Barnes, who had a heavy hand with liquor, was acting as bartender. The vodka collins he'd just handed her, in fact, was so full of vodka that she'd almost gagged.

"Ah, Mrs. Morehouse—wonderful party," Dr. Yolanski said, beaming up at her. He was a birdlike man with iron-gray hair that gave him a distinguished look despite his diminutive size. He patted the sofa cushion next to him. "Sit down—I want to talk to you."

Janice glanced toward the bar, then shrugged mentally and dropped down beside the professor. "I'm so glad you and your wife could come," she said politely.

"Well, we don't go out much these days. Getting old, I guess. But we do enjoy your Christmas parties. And right now I want to ask about your dissertation prospectus. How's your research coming along?"

"Great," she said. "Really great."

"Oh? I got the impression from something Jake said that you had lost your enthusiasm for the project."

Janice frowned at him. "You must have misunderstood. Jake knows how hard I've been working. I had to slow down for the holidays, of course, but—"

"Then, I did misunderstand. I must confess I'm relieved. I'm looking forward to seeing the results—have you finished the main thrust of your survey?"

"Not yet. It isn't something I can hurry. It encompasses the first year after divorce in the lives of a random sampling of divorced women—well, you can see that I have a time span to consider."

"Yes, of course. Well, I wish you luck," he said, but she sensed a reserve in his voice that puzzled her.

Before she could question him, a friend of Dr. Yolanski's came up, and she relinquished her seat beside him. She was still looking for Jake when her old friend Casey hailed her. After they'd touched cheeks and exchanged greetings, Janice asked, "Have you seen Jake?"

Casey hesitated briefly. "Jake? Oh, he said something about needing some fresh air. I think he went out through the kitchen," she said, her tone a little flat.

"Fresh air? That's strange. I wonder if . . ." Janice paused, then added, "Excuse me, will you? I think I'd better find him and put him to work at the bar."

Several men were in the kitchen, their heads together, exchanging risqué jokes, but Jake wasn't among them. She slipped past them, into the service room. The outside door was standing slightly ajar, and when she went outside, the night air felt so cool and fresh against her flushed cheeks that she stood there, breathing deeply and wishing the party were over. Everybody was having a good time—why wasn't she? Was she, like Dr. Yolanski, getting too old for such things? Or maybe she was coming down with something. Yes, that had to be it. Tomorrow she'd indulge herself and sleep until noon. The hell with cleaning up the party mess.

She heard a crunching sound, footsteps on dried leaves, and she looked around, trying to see into the darkness. "Jake?" she said tentatively. "Is that you, Jake?"

Jake stepped into the rectangle of light that spilled out through the open door. "Hi, honey. I came out for some air. It's stuffy as hell in the house. Guess it's all that hot wind in there."

She laughed dutifully. "Maybe we should open a couple of windows. Look, will you take over for Chris at the bar? He's really loading down the drinks."

"So? It's Christmas Eve—let them have a good time."

"Not the ones who have to drive home. You know the police are out full force tonight. We don't want someone getting picked up for drunken driving."

"You're right—as usual." Jake brushed her cheek with a kiss and went past her into the house. Janice stood there for a while, looking up at the pale wisp of the moon. Lost in thought, she started nervously when a figure came around the corner of the house and almost bumped into her.

"Oh—Janice. I didn't see you," Arlene said. "I went for a walk. Had a tad too much to drink."

"You *are* brave," Janice said. "I wouldn't take a walk alone at night, not even in Professorville. Too many muggers running around the streets these days."

"I expect you're right. I didn't go far," Arlene said. "Guess I'd better go in now. I don't want to catch a cold."

It was only then that Janice realized Arlene wasn't wearing a coat. Something, a thin edge of suspicion, brushed her mind, but she put it aside as unworthy. Yes, it was possible Jake had gone for a walk with Arlene, but then that was his way. He was friendly with everyone, man, woman, or child—and wasn't that rare these days?

For the next few hours, Janice circulated among their guests, joining one group for a while then moving on to the next, keeping an eye on the buffet, heating more hors d'oeuvres and putting out fresh canapés when the supply got low.

It was past three when the final guest left. Janice slumped down into a chair, kicked off her shoes, and rested her aching feet on the coffee table. "God, I'm tired," she sighed.

"It was a great party, hon. Everybody had a good time," Jake told her. She watched him with amusement as he settled himself on the sofa. How could he look so fresh and alert, as if he'd just got out of bed?

"How about a drink—maybe some of that eggnog? I notice there's a lot of it left."

"Probably because it's nonalcoholic," she said.

"Well, people go to parties to drink. How about I add some rum to it and we'll sign off with a little nightcap?"

"Okay—but leave the rum out of mine. I've already had enough."

Jake gave an exaggerated leer, twirling the ends of a mustache he didn't have. "That sounds promising, me proud beauty."

Which translated, Janice thought, meant he wanted sex. What *she* really wanted was a good night's sleep, but she wouldn't refuse him. Not only would it hurt his feelings, but he would be sulky tomorrow—and she didn't want that, not on Christmas Day.

"What say we put away a few things that might spoil and go to bed?" she said.

Later, when they went upstairs and Jake made love to her, he didn't hurry. With the concentration he always gave to lovemaking, he took his time, moving through the rituals of sex as if they were still newlyweds. She responded as usual, despite her weariness, but after he had fallen asleep beside her, she couldn't help thinking about the chores awaiting her in the morning.

The party had gone well. But then, all their parties were successful—thanks to Jake. How did he do it anyway, make every woman there feel desirable without, at the same time, antagonizing the men? It was a gift, and she knew it was as natural and spontaneous to Jake as breathing was to other people. She had ended up having a good time, after all, so why did she suddenly wish that their social calendar was bare so they could stay home, just the two of them, for the rest of the week—including New Year's Eve?

Chanel had made the decision to let Laird seduce her Christmas Eve. My Christmas gift to the man who has everything, she thought dryly.

When he'd invited her to be his date at an important post-Cotillion party, she was elated. After all, these particular parties, given by the parents of Cotillion debutantes, were very special, a traditional part of the Christmas Cotillion mystique. By taking her instead of one of his other ladies, Laird was making a declaration. Or was he? There could be another explanation. Perhaps no one else was available or it was a simple act of kindness because she'd let him know that Fern had other plans so she'd be alone over Christmas.

Fern's "other plans" had been a relief. When she'd called to say she was spending Christmas Eve with a friend, that she'd try to make it home New Year weekend, she'd added, her voice honeyed, "So don't worry about me, Mommie dearest—and do have fun with that awesome Laird, you hear?"

Which Chanel fully intended to do. When Laird took her home, she would invite him upstairs for a drink—and after that, she would be innovative. One way or another, she would get him into bed.

The party, at the home of one of Laird's old Princeton friends, was everything she'd hoped for. She looked her best in a Beene black-and-silver evening suit with matching silver earrings. While several seasons old, only someone highly attuned to fashion would realize it because of the outfit's classic simplicity. Even so, she had wanted to buy something new and spectacular, but her finances just wouldn't permit it. She was confident, however, that she was as attractive as any other woman here—including her hostess's debutante daughter, so radiant and virginal in her Cotillion finery.

It was this knowledge that made it easy to smile when, an hour into the party, she came face-to-face with Laura Colton, one of the classmates who had snubbed her so royally her final years at Burlingame Academy. Laura looked her over; although her eyes were unfriendly, her smile was as wide—and as false—as Chanel's.

"You're looking good, Chanel," she said sweetly. "Who does your hair these days?"

"Adolfo, of course. He'd been my hairdresser for years," Chanel answered.

"Oh . . . Is he still around?"

"Obviously. However, it *is* a bit difficult to get an appointment with him. He's very particular and even has an unlisted phone number—it does keep away the *arrivistes*."

Laura's face stiffened. Although she belonged to the Hillsborough crowd—as Chanel always thought of them—her father, who was a self-made man, had come to social prominence via marriage and his father-in-law's patronage.

"I see your daughter's not doing the Cotillion this year. Isn't she eighteen?" Laura said, her tone arch.

Chanel had a hard time keeping her smile intact. Laura knew how exclusive—some said incestuously so—the Cotillion committee was. A few old families, most of them related by blood or marriage, controlled the list of debutantes. There was no way that Fern would ever be invited to make her debut at the Cotillion—

not unless Laird, as her stepfather, used his influence to get her an invitation.

"Fern is barely seventeen," Chanel said carelessly, stretching the truth a year. "And like so many of her friends at Burlingame Academy, she's indifferent to—you know, the Cotillion sort of thing. Says it's passé and—well, I won't tell you what else she says. Of course, she may change her mind by next year," she added prudently.

Before Laura could respond, Laird joined them; he linked his arm through Chanel's, a proprietary gesture it was evident Laura noted. The conversation drifted into a "Did you hear what happened to Barbra Gadsdon?" sort of exchange, all very civilized and polite.

So the evening had been very gratifying. Laird had given her a Christmas present when he picked her up, a jade hair brooch in the shape of a heart, and she'd presented him with gold cuff links, the price of which she couldn't really afford. She had been seen by the right people in the company of an attentive Laird Fairmount; tomorrow the rumor mill would be going full blast, and her social stock would rise. Although Laird was more talkative than usual, he hadn't asked if she'd heard from Ariel, for which she was heartily grateful. She was sick to death of doing the concerned-friend bit. In fact, if she never saw Ariel again, she would be delighted.

On the trip back to Pacific Heights, she told Laird what a marvelous time she'd had, how sorry she was to see the evening end.

Which made it very natural to invite him up to her apartment for a nightcap before he went home.

She thought he hesitated, but then he told her a nightcap sounded like a good idea. As they rose in the elevator, she was thankful that she hadn't tried to economize on where she lived. Of course, she'd spent far too much money furnishing her apartment in anticipation of a large divorce settlement from Jacques, but it had been worth it. Not that Laird would pay much attention to the custom-made furnishings. He was too used to luxury. But if she lived in a shabby, grubby place—yes, he would notice that.

When they went into the living room, whose only Christmas decoration was a cluster of potted pink poinsettias on the fireplace hearth, she didn't see the small figure lying on a sofa until Fern sat up, looking confused and dismayed.

"I must have fallen asleep," she said, rubbing her eyes. She was wearing a white lace-trimmed nightgown and robe, and she looked very young and virginal as she made a show of adjusting the robe, but not, Chanel noticed, before she gave Laird a good look at her long, slim legs.

Chanel seethed inside, but she was careful to hide her annoyance. "I thought you were staying with a friend tonight," she said, dropping her evening wrap on a chair.

"It turned into a riot. Carole invited these really tacky guys and it got too wild." She gave Chanel a demure smile. "I didn't realized you'd have a guest. I'd better toddle off to bed—"

"Don't leave on my account," Laird said, smiling at her. "I can't stay long anyway. It's pretty late."

"Well—I could use a drink if you two are going to have one. Something nonalcoholic."

"That sounds good to me, too," Laird said.

There was nothing for Chanel to do but leave them and go into the kitchen for soft drinks. As she hunted through a cabinet for a carton of Coke, she could hear their voices in the living room. They seemed to have a lot to say to each other. Later, she sat beside Laird, listening as Fern related the details of her "ghastly evening."

"I swear they looked like Hell's Angels, all leather pants and silver studs. I don't know what Carole was thinking about, inviting them. It was supposed to be an all-girl thing, chaperoned by her parents, but when I got there, I found out her parents were off on a Caribbean cruise. Then these guys came and—well, it got a little heavy. The other girls were having a great time, but I don't really go for that kind of thing. Then one of the guys—" She stopped, blinking her eyelids rapidly.

"You mean someone got fresh with you?" Laird said, frowning.

"This really tacky guy cornered me in the kitchen and said something that really bummed me out. When I tried to leave, he—well, I knew I had to get out of there. I told him I had to go to the powder room, and after I got away from him, I grabbed my coat and purse and split."

"That bastard," Laird said. "He needs to be taught a lesson."

Chanel bit down hard on her lower lip to keep back a retort. Was Laird so naive that he actually believed that Fern would go to a party that just included girls?

"You've had a rotten experience," she said smoothly. "Why don't you crawl into bed and get a good night's sleep?"

Fern rose in a flurry of bare legs; she seemed to lose her balance and staggered a little, wincing.

"Can you make it on your own?" Laird said.

"I think so." Fern gave Laird a tremulous look. "Thank you for your concern, Mr. Fairmount."

"Call me Laird," he said.

In a rush, as if she'd just had an uncontrollable impulse, Fern ran to Laird and gave him a kiss—squarely on the mouth. Laird looked embarrassed, but he was smiling as he watched her disappear through the door.

Chanel, determined to salvage what she could from the evening, offered him another drink, wine this time, but Laird refused. His kiss at the door, to be sure, was the most ardent he'd yet given her, and Chanel clung to him, letting her hip slip between his thighs. When he broke away, his face was flushed, and she knew he'd gotten the message. She was available—but only to someone she truly liked. She counted it a victory that he made a dinner date for the following week instead of phoning her in the morning as he usually did.

But her anger came surging back as she locked up for the night. That little bitch Fern—had she planned this on purpose? If so, for what reason? Revenge? To get her own back for the sale of her horse, her cut allowance—and for being forced to return to school? Well, she wasn't going to give Fern the satisfaction of letting her know that she'd succeeded in spoiling her plans for the evening. The best way to treat the whole business was to ignore it. Yes, that's what she'd do—simply ignore the whole thing.

Chanel's views about bargain hunting had rubbed off on Glory to the extent that she had bought a secondhand chest of drawers to store her underclothes in instead of piling them on a closet shelf. The chest was old, but it was well made and a far sturdier piece of furniture than anything she could afford new. Not that she had any special feeling for it. Maybe it took time to get oriented to the idea that quality often had nothing to do with price—or newness. To her, old was old—not quaint or a bargain or something to be handed down to your kids. She liked bright, shiny new things that had never been used by anyone else.

It was Christmas evening, and Glory was sitting cross-legged on her mattress, contemplating the old chest, while she finished off a half gallon of French vanilla ice cream. The ice cream was her Christmas present to herself, but now that she'd pigged out on it, she felt bloated and overloaded with sweets.

But she finished it off, anyway, pouring the last melted spoonful directly from the carton into her mouth. She had decided it would be stupid to do any Christmas decorating because she was the only one who would see it, but at the last moment, she'd weakened and bought a slightly faded poinsettia at the Payless at the corner for half its original price. Aside from her red hair, its scarlet blossoms were the only color in the room.

From her landlord's apartment overhead, she heard Christmas music and the shrill voices of overexcited children. Her landlord's grandchildren, all six of them, were spending Christmas with their grandparents, and the house was jumping—literally. To Glory's surprise, they had invited her to have buffet dinner with them, an invitation she'd refused with the excuse that she had a date.

It wasn't that she wanted to be alone on Christmas, but to be an outsider at a family celebration would have stirred up memories best left undisturbed. Somewhere in the city—at her mother's flat or maybe at one of her sister's—her own family were together right now. There would be lots of wine and beer, a spread of deli cold cuts and potato salad and cole slaw, and there would also be a lot of quarreling and backbiting that would end, as usual, in one big brawl—so wasn't she crazy to sit here, fighting the blue meanies?

Her lie to her landlady about a date forced her to stay very quiet so they wouldn't know she was at home. Once, when the phone rang, she let it ring seven times rather than pick it up right away and have them guess that she was home. It was a wrong number, which was what she'd expected, but she'd felt an impulse, instantly rejected, to keep the person on the line long enough to say "Merry Christmas."

Face it, she told herself, this is just another day in the life of Morning Glory Browne.

Last night, Christmas Eve at the Oral Cookie, had been a drag. Everybody had been boisterous and full of fake cheer—and mean. Why was it that the Christmas season brought out the meanness in some people? She'd made double her usual tips, and she'd earned every penny of it. If that old guy in the Hawaiian shirt had asked her once more what time she got off work, she would have decked him, so help her. . . .

It didn't help that she wouldn't have had to go straight home after the club closed. Not counting the come-ons from her customers, she'd had two legitimate invitations to go out for a late Christmas Eve dinner—or an early Christmas breakfast, take your choice. One invitation had been from Jimbo. The big bartender had asked her if she wanted to have a bite to eat at this key club he belonged to that stayed open until dawn, an invitation she'd refused as she always did.

Since Jimbo asked her out at least once a week, she hadn't been surprised at his invitation, but the second invitation—well, it had come out of the blue from an unexpected source.

She had been aware how often Steve Golden, the martial arts instructor at the Golden Gate Health Club, came to the exercise room's window to watch her aerobics class, but he'd kept his distance since that first day, and she hadn't really thought much about it. Then yesterday after she'd finished her class, he had been waiting for her. That's when he'd asked her to have Christmas Eve dinner with him.

Two invitations for the same night—wouldn't you know that both of them would be from jocks? Why was it that she seemed to attract the Mr. Machos of the world? Someone had told her once that she looked like a sexpot. Was that it? Did she look like the kind of woman that certain types of men fantasized about? If so, they were way off base. She wasn't about to get involved with another muscle man, even if he was nice like Jimbo. After all, she'd thought Buddy was nice at first, too.

For a moment, she felt an ache that was part physical, part emotional. The first date she'd had with Buddy had been a red-letter day in her life. He hadn't had much to say, but the way he'd looked at her, sort of heavy-lidded and sexy, had set up all sorts of vibrations inside her.

She hadn't made it hard for him. She'd been so damned flattered that he'd asked her out that after they'd had something to eat—at a Taco Belle, for God's sake!—she had gone to his place and let him make love to her without one thought of consequences. When he'd found out afterward that she wasn't on the pill, he'd really been pissed off, but then he'd kissed her and told her he'd take care of her if anything happened.

Well, something had, although this was a few months later, and Buddy had done the right thing by her. But even those first days of their marriage, when everything had been pretty good between them, he must have resented her, been ashamed of her. Looking back, she could see that now—all the times he'd gone to team parties without her, saying she wouldn't enjoy them because she didn't drink and besides, everybody was so much older, and then there were the excuses he'd made for leaving her at home when he went to see his folks.

When the baby came too early and was stillborn, he'd accused her of getting pregnant deliberately to trap him into marriage. Later, he'd apologized and blamed it on the shock of losing the baby, but she should have known then that it wasn't going to work.

It was humiliating now to remember how grateful she'd been that he hadn't left her then—like his folks had wanted him to. Bad blood, his mother'd said, right to her face, and his father had told Buddy to get rid of her before she got pregnant again. Buddy had never told her why he stayed, and she'd never asked him, because she'd wanted so much to believe that it was because he loved her.

And what a laugh *that* was! It hadn't been so bad his rookie year with the Bees. He'd been riding high with his "games won" average and the attention of the press. But the second year, after his accident, he'd used her as an excuse for every run he gave up, every game he'd lost. And then his contract had been dropped and the whole thing had come apart. . . .

Glory was putting on water for coffee when the phone rang. She hurried to pick it up this time because they were making so much noise upstairs—the kids must have drawn drums and skates from dear ole Santa Claus—that she was sure no one would notice. The blood drained from her head as Buddy's voice, like a continuation of her worst nightmares, spoke in her ear.

"Merry Christmas, bitch," he said.

Glory slammed down the receiver, the way she always did when she got an obscene phone call. A minute later, it rang again, and this time, she picked it up, depressed the button, then laid the receiver on its side on the floor.

As she drank her coffee, sitting at the folding card table in the kitchen, questions buzzed through her head. How come Buddy knew her phone number? She'd paid extra to get it unlisted for just this reason—and also because she slept late in the mornings and didn't want wrong numbers waking her up. Of course, Buddy's oldest brother *was* on the San Francisco police force. Is that how Buddy had located her? Well, it wouldn't do him any good. As soon as possible, she would have her number changed. Maybe she'd see if she couldn't be listed under a false name or something, too.

After she'd finished her coffee, she dropped the receiver back into its cradle. When it rang almost immediately, she wrapped it in several towels and then a pillow to smother the sound. Let him think she'd gone out again. Eventually, he'd get tired of his little game. The thing that really worried her was whether or not he knew where she lived.

A chill congealed the flesh on her upper arms. She checked the heat, but the needle was sitting on seventy degrees. Her stomach rumbled, and she pressed her fingers into her diaphragm, wincing. That ice cream had been a mistake, but then she'd been so good about skipping sweets lately. Chanel's fruit, veggies, and yogurt diet might be a real bust when it came to satisfying the appetite, but she'd lost eight pounds in three weeks, three pounds more than her goal.

She went into the bedroom to stare into the full-length mirror she'd installed inside the closet door. The mirror, bought secondhand from a Salvation Army store, was flawed, but that's why it had been dirt cheap. She hadn't bought it from vanity but because she'd wanted to watch herself when she did aerobics at home so she wouldn't fall into bad habits. It was surprising how quickly she'd learned even the most difficult moves.

Complacently, she ran her hand over her hips. By God, she'd done it—just like she'd done a lot of unpleasant but necessary things in her life.

So put that in your opium pipe and smoke it, Ms. Claire ole thing.

Her face darkened as she remembered her most recent encounter with Claire. The woman had been more than unpleasant; she'd been downright bitchy. She'd started out by making fun of one of the women who was heavyset, calling her One Ton, and the poor wimp had burst into tears and ran out of the exercise room. Never to return, Glory was sure. And when someone had had a coughing spell in the middle of calisthenics, Claire had stopped the class to tell her to get the hell out before she spread her lousy virus all over the place. The woman, her face red, had stomped away, and Glory was sure the club had lost another client.

There'd been signs of rebellion among the other women, too. While they were dressing, Glory had agitated things a little by saying, "I hope poor Mrs. Sims is okay. I bet we won't see her again."

One of the women nodded. "I think I'll change over to the Born in the U.S.A. Club," she said. "Who needs this kind of masochism?"

Glory laughed silently, noting the general nodding of heads.

Wouldn't it be a blast if Ms. Claire found herself in the center of a rebellion? Serve the bitch right.

She had run into Steve Golden as she was leaving the club. "All set for Christmas?" he asked cheerfully.

Glory studied him closely. She might have thought this was a casual encounter except that while he was wearing a sweat suit and carrying a towel, there was no sign that he'd just had a shower—or had been exercising. "I don't celebrate Christmas," she said.

"Are you Jewish?"

"No. I just don't celebrate Christmas," she said, and started on.

He put out his hand to stop her. "No folks, huh? But how about friends?"

"My friends will all be working," she said.

"Are you a working girl?" he said, grinning.

"You know something, asshole? You're so full of it, you make me sick."

"Hey, I'm sorry. I've got a big mouth—how about letting me make it up to you? What are you doing Christmas Eve?"

"What's it to you?" she said in honest surprise.

"I'd like to take you out to dinner. I'm at loose ends—and I'd really appreciate some company."

"Thank you but no thank you."

"Come on. Give me a break. I'll behave like a gentleman. Cross my heart."

"Look, I could be polite and make up some excuse, but the truth is that I don't want to go out with you. I don't like jocks."

Steve's eyes—they were that color that is more hazel than brown, she noted—darkened. "Okay. Your decision. We could've had fun together—but if that's how you feel, okay." He slapped the towel he was holding against his thigh. "I was going to compliment you on how quickly you've picked up Claire's routine, but I guess you'd consider that some kind of pass."

Glory had the grace to feel ashamed. Maybe she had been too rough on him. . . .

"It isn't personal. It's just that my divorce isn't final yet, and I'm not ready to get involved with anyone." She paused, then added reluctantly, "And thanks for the compliment. Claire isn't the easiest person to deal with."

"She's getting worse, which presents a problem because she's related to the club's manager by marriage. As far as I'm con-

cerned, she's bad news. We lost three clients this month because
of her power plays. At first, she did okay. The clients need a firm
hand or they take over. But Claire's gone too far now.''

"Well, I'm glad it's your problem, not mine. I just give her a
dirty look when she gets on my case.''

"Tough little bird, aren't you?''

She looked at him with jaundiced eyes. "Yeah, I'm tough. I
learned how to take care of myself early on. But I don't jump in
and out of beds—if that's what you're talking about.''

"I said the wrong thing again. Why do I keep doing that?''

She shrugged. "I have no idea. And if you'll get out of my
way, I'd like to go home.''

"Home being where?''

"Home being my own personal business,'' she retorted, and
marched off.

Thinking about that encounter now, two days later, Glory
shrugged and then dismissed it from her mind. She turned down
the thermostat, went back to bed, and when she found it hard to
sleep, tuned her radio to Larry King's talk show and finally fell
asleep with the voices of people, obviously as alone at Christmas
as she was, sounding in her ear.

It was midmorning when she awoke. Her eyes fell on the phone,
still wrapped in towels on the floor, and she had a sudden impulse
to call her mother.

Common sense stopped her. Ma would either have a hangover
and be belligerent, or, if she was still tight from Christmas celebrating, she'd get all teary about being neglected by her "girls.''
She'd talk about past Christmases, all fantasies of good times that
had never happened. Glory couldn't remember a Christmas celebration that hadn't ended in a blowup. Often, there had been no
Christmas at all. No tree, no presents, no socks hung up for dear
old St. Nick to fill.

Even so, as a child, she had looked forward to the season because there was always a party at school with candy and nuts and
cookies and fat red Santa Claus cutouts on the blackboard, happy
carols like "Jingle Bells,'' dime-store presents for those who had
one to exchange in return, a card and a small gift from the teacher.

Then there was the excitement of going to Union Square to see
the lighting of the tree, the wonderful window displays at Gump's
and City of Paris and other stores. Once in a while, when her
mother was in the early stages of a new romance, she would get

sentimental and drag in a tree. Sometimes it got decorated, some-times not.

One Christmas Day, faced with a bare tree still leaning against the living room wall, Glory had tied a few candles on the ends of the branches, but when she lit them, the tree went up in flames, smoking up their flat and getting them banished from public hous-ing for a year. Flora had never forgiven her. She still brought the incident up every Christmas—and was sure to do it again if Glory was stupid enough to call her.

Since it was very quiet upstairs, she knew her landlord and his wife were sleeping in, that it was safe to move around without being invited to join in on any post-Christmas cheer.

But while she was straightening the covers on her bed, the phone rang, making her jump. That lousy Buddy again—well, tomorrow she was going to have her number changed for sure. Or maybe she'd just have the phone taken out. She'd only had it installed because Janice had insisted they exchange telephone numbers, and she'd been ashamed to admit she didn't have a phone. So she'd said she was in the process of getting her number changed because of obscene calls, and then she'd gone right down and ordered one put in.

And now she'd have to tell them she'd had her phone taken out. Well, what did she care what they thought? None of them gave a damn about her. Stephanie was so—so buttoned down. Janice was pleasant enough, but she really liked to run things, while Ariel was a zero, just like she wasn't there. And Chanel—she hadn't even called to find out how the diet was going. Which was okay. Who needed her?

Glory's simmering anger exploded when the phone kept on ringing. She ripped out a curse and grabbed up the phone.

"Yeah? What do you want?" she snarled.

There was a long silence. "I—is this a bad time?" Ariel's light voice said.

Since she'd been expecting Buddy, it took Glory a couple of seconds to adjust. "No. I'm not busy, Ariel."

"I thought I'd call and wish you a Merry Christmas."

"You, too," Glory said, surprised into adding, "Did you have a nice Christmas?"

"Yes, thank you. We put up a tree—or rather Alex did. It was white-flocked—with all silver ornaments."

How like a polite child she sounds, Glory thought—but it was sort of nice that she'd bothered to call.

"That's great," she said.

"Well—I just thought I'd call. I'd better hang up now."

After Glory said good-bye, she fixed herself a hearty breakfast of pancakes and sausage and eggs, another Christmas present to herself. It occurred to her that she felt a lot more cheerful than she had the night before. Maybe, in a little while, she'd give Chanel a ring and wish her a Merry Christmas. She might even call Janice and Stephanie, too. What the hoo—it *was* the holidays, wasn't it, and who else did she have to call?

CHAPTER TWENTY-FIVE

CHANEL SAT ON A MAROON-STRIPED LOUIS XIV SOFA, NURSING a glass of wine that she'd snagged from a passing waiter a few minutes earlier. The sofa was an antique, not a reproduction, but it had been reupholstered, and the original padding had been replaced with down to make it as comfortable as any modern piece.

Not, Chanel told herself, that her hostess needed any extra padding for that fat derriere of hers. Nancy Dayton—no, Nancy Anderson now—had been one of the clique who had snubbed her unmercifully at Burlingame Academy. Chanel, who never forgot nor forgave an insult, watched with a bored smile on her face as her old enemy played the gracious hostess, circulating, circulating around the spacious ballroom now that most of her guests had finished eating their buffet dinner and were waiting for the musicale part of the evening to start.

"You well acquainted with our hostess?" the man sitting at the other end of the sofa asked. At Chanel's start, he gave a rumbling laugh and for the first time since he'd sat down next to her, she really looked at him.

He was a big one, all right—and it was hard muscle rather than fat. Middle-aged, probably in his mid-fifties. His hair was charcoal gray, very thick and coarse, and the deep squint lines beside his eyes emphasizing a rich tan hinting at years spent outdoors on open ranges and under scorching skies. He wasn't handsome, could never have been with that too-large nose and too-wide mouth, but there was a shrewdness in his light brown eyes, a vitality that radiated from his long, rangy body, that transcended good looks. Sexy, Chanel thought—and then wondered what this man, who looked as if he'd be more comfortable on a horse, was doing at a musicale.

Come to think of it, what was *she* doing here? She had a bona fide invitation, it was true, but in the years since graduation from Burlingame Academy, none of her former schoolmates had ever invited her into their homes before.

And Nancy was the ringleader of the Hillsborough bunch.

The question was—why the invitation? Was it because Nancy, who aspired to be San Francisco's leading society matron, was playing it safe? Being seen with Laird so often the past four months undoubtedly had everybody wondering if she might be the one to land him. Yes, that must be it. Nancy was just playing it safe. But why had she extended the invitation when Laird was out of town on business? It was a puzzle, all right. In fact, the only reason she was here without an escort—Howie had been unavailable— was curiosity. And prudence. She might hate Nancy's guts, but she didn't dare offend her by rejecting an invitation.

"You well acquainted with our hostess?" the man asked again, and this time she noted a drawl that could only be from Texas.

She gave him a polite smile. "We were schoolmates—at Burlingame Academy," she said.

"That's a pretty fancy snob factory, right?"

"Right," she said, suddenly amused. Rough-hewn he might be, but he didn't mince around with words. And Burlingame Academy *was* a snob factory of the most flagrant kind. Which was why Papa had sent her there—and why she'd sent Fern there in turn.

"You wondering how come I got invited here tonight?"

Chanel eyed him closely. Did he really want an honest answer, or was this some kind of conversational ploy? She decided to be honest. "You do stand out."

"So does my wife." He gestured toward a plump woman in a too-tight dress who was helping herself to a salmon mousse at the buffet. Chanel recognized the woman's dress as a Galanos; it was all wrong for her and fairly screeched that she'd bought it because some high-powered saleswoman had convinced her it did wonders for her imperfect figure. It was a very expensive dress; the alterations alone on a size fourteen, the largest size it came in, must have cost a small fortune.

"So why do *you* think you got invited?" she asked, suddenly curious.

"Big bucks. I struck it rich in the oil fields, and my missus decided she wants to get into high society. The thing is I'm afraid she's gonna get her heart broken."

The last was so unexpected that Chanel found herself smiling in sympathy. "My father made it in the oil fields," she said impulsively. "He was a diamond in the rough—but he was accepted by"—she gestured around the room—"these people because he bought his way in, and because he amused them. When he lost his money, he was out in the cold."

The man nodded. "Tincan O'Hara. Hit his first gusher in '54. He shoulda stuck to oil. When he went into the stock market and started playing with the big boys, he lost his shirt."

Chanel stiffened. "You seem to have done some research on my father. Now, why is that, Mr.—whoever you are?"

"I don't give a damn about your old man. It was you I was researching. For a very good reason. You wanna hear the rest of it or not?"

"Go on," she said.

"Well, it's Elsie. Like I say, she's got a yen to break into society, not Texas society where it'd be a whole lot easier, but here in San Francisco. She thinks all it takes is money, but I know different. She's been making a fool of herself, toadying up to the wrong people. My personal opinion is that it's a lot of hogwash, this idea she's got, but she did without all those years I was knocking around the oil fields, never complained or ran out on me, so if she wants to hobnob with these phonies, I'm willing to back her up."

"They aren't all phonies," Chanel protested.

"No. Some of them are okay, mostly them who was born to it. But Elsie's got about as much chance breaking in with *that* bunch as she has sprouting wings. She's going to have to settle for second-rate, but luckily, she won't know the difference."

"And all this has something to do with—what did you call it? Researching me? You must know that I have very little status now that I'm no longer married to a Devereau. I can't do anything for your wife."

"You can show Elsie how to dress, how to behave around these people, and how to make the right moves to get her in with this crowd—you know, opera and art and that stuff. Right now, her musical taste runs to Johnny Cash and Willie Nelson.''

"I still don't understand—"

"I want you to take her under your wing, teach her what she has to know, guide her. I'll pay the bills and see you get a bonus—"

Chanel stood up so quickly, she almost spilled her wine. "I've never been so insulted—"

"Sit down," he said.

Chanel sat back down. She told herself it was because she didn't want to make a scene, but she had an uneasy feeling it was because of the command in the man's voice.

"Remember, Mrs. Devereau, I had you researched. You're dead broke—or as near as you can get without selling your jewelry and other personal possessions. Your car will probably go next. It just might bring in enough to pay your rent and keep you afloat for another few months. You laid off your maid two months ago and are doing your own housework. You stopped getting a newspaper, are living on Top Ramon soup to save money. The next step is the pawnshops, only you don't want to give up your jewelry because you need it when you go places with Laird Fairmount."

He paused to take out a slim cigar; she was surprised that he asked her permission before he lit it.

"So let's talk turkey," he went on. "You're living on the shorts these days. You keep your kid in that ritzy school because your ex had already paid her tuition for the rest of the year. Your divorce settlement was so small, it just covered your past-due bills. That did save your credit, only the joker is that your husband canceled all his credit cards and charge accounts, and without an income you can't get them reinstated under your own name."

She started to speak, but he waved her to silence and went on. "Devereau refused to pay the expenses for your daughter's horse and you had to sell it. You tried to get a refund on her tuition, but the school authorities wouldn't even consider it. So you're pretty desperate these days. Since you've got something I want, I'm willing to pay for it, but not if there's going to be any more bullshit about you being insulted. You've got a lot of respect for the almighty buck, and you've got a good business head on you, too, but you made one mistake: You underestimated your former husband, and he screwed you. So what say we talk terms now?''

Chanel sat there frozen, staring at him. Funny—he reminded her of Papa even though they were so different in appearance.

Papa had been built like a bull; he'd radiated power, and his smile had been genial, engaging. This man looked as if he seldom smiled; his expensive suit hung on his rangy, loose-limbed body, and yet—yes, he did have presence. Too bad he didn't want her to groom *him* instead of his dumpy wife. . . .

"What kind of money are we talking about?" she said.

"Atta girl. That's the real you speaking. We're talking about all expenses paid with some pocket money to help finance your romance with that Fairmount fellow, and a sizable bonus if you pull it off and keep Elsie happy. Any extra you make, steering her to your hairdresser or to those fancy shops you've got a deal with is your own business. Just so she gets a fair shake."

Chanel felt the blood rising to her cheeks—and this time, she wasn't holding her breath to make it happen. His words had been nonjudgmental, and yet it was humiliating to realize that this stranger knew about her business arrangements with Adolfo and certain exclusive shops. "I don't know what you mean," she said stiffly.

"Listen to me and listen good. For this thing to work, you're gonna have to cut out the crap. You're after a rich husband, and the way you've been raised, to expect the best, I'm not surprised. Personally, I wouldn't buy a used car from anyone in this room, but that doesn't mean I won't do all I can to get Elsie what she wants. But if we close this deal, we're gonna have to be straight with each other. You agree?"

Chanel discovered she wasn't offended, after all. If she had enough money, she'd handle a similar situation the way he had—hire someone to find all she could about the people she intended to deal with. And it *would* be a relief to be honest with someone and not have to put up a front all the time.

"You're right," she said. "Laird's money is important to me. I got kicked in the teeth after that stock scandal broke and later, when Papa had his heart attack and died. My so-called friends treated me like dirt, and there was nothing I could do about it—then. So yes, I want money and power—the kind that opens doors for you. Laird has it. He was born with it. He can turn a dullish party into a social success just by dropping by for a few minutes. As his wife, I'd have the same power. He just might be my last chance. I'm not exactly a spring chicken, you know."

"You're a very classy lady—and that ain't bull."

"Thank you," Chanel murmured.

"Of course you're as mixed up in your own way as Elsie is in hers. But I ain't knocking it. It's natural you'd want to pay them back, the way they treated you after that stable hand knocked you up and you had to get married.''

"How the—where did you hear that?''

"Let me tell you something, lady. When you have as much money as I do, you can pay people to find out anything. And you can arrange just about anything, too. Don't make the mistake of making a deal with me and then reneging on it later.''

Chanel felt—not a chill, but something close to it. There was a ruthlessness in this man that didn't match his down-home Texas drawl. "Did you arrange for me to get invited to this party?'' she asked suddenly.

"No. I don't have any clout with your old schoolmate.'' He scratched the side of nose, looking quizzical. "Why don't you ask me how come the wife and me got invited?''

"How *did* you get invited? Money alone wouldn't do it. Nancy is a bloody snob. Always was and always will be. She's even worse since she married Lars Anderson.''

"I got invited for the same reason you did. I figure she'll start her pitch for that pet charity of hers any minute now. When she gets to you, it's going to be like getting blood out of a turnip, ain't it?''

The skin on the back of Chanel's neck chilled. Of course—she should have guessed it earlier. This wasn't a musical evening as the invitation had said. It was a money-raising affair—only why hadn't there been anything on her invitation about a charity drive? Was that why it had been handwritten? To get her here on a ruse?

"You've got the picture now, haven't you?'' the man said, watching her with shrewd eyes. "The lady invited you here to-night because everybody is expected to donate at least a thousand-dollar check to the cause. There's going to be a big to-do about signing the pledge and such. What did she do—send you a personal invitation? The one the missus and I got spelled it right out in print, what was expected. Anyone who doesn't chip in is gonna look like a cheapskate. By tomorrow morning, everybody is going to know that Chanel Devereau couldn't pony up a thousand bucks for a charity drive and yet she accepted an invitation to come to the party. How did she fix it so your friend Laird wouldn't escort you and pay your pledge for you?''

"He's out of town this week.'' Chanel stood up and smoothed down her skirt over her hips. "I seem to have suddenly developed a headache. I think I'll head for home.''

"And play into her hands? It'll be in that ass Dobby Robbins's column by tomorrow evening. I saw him lurking around the buffet table a while ago. Nothing libelous. Just a good laugh all around."

Chanel sat down again. "You're right. I could write it myself. 'Chanel Devereau, recently ex'ed by Jacques Devereau, developed an unexpected—and very convenient—headache at the Lars Andersons' swank musicale to raise money for the Endangered Species Society just before the pledge-signing ceremony.' My invitation was handwritten, you know. It said nothing about a charity drive. I thought—well, never mind what I thought."

"You thought your old school chum was sucking up to you because of your relationship with Laird Fairmount."

The man was impossible. He was also right. That was exactly what she'd thought when she'd received the invitation.

"Well, Nancy's filthy little plan worked," she conceded. "I'm going to look like a fool—or a tightwad—whether I leave now or stay and don't sign the pledge. I don't have a thousand dollars in the bank—which you already know. But I do wonder how Nancy found out. Through that banker father of hers?" She smiled painfully. "I'm transferring my checking account to another bank in the morning."

The man laughed. "Still got your sense of humor, I see. Well, I admire that. And I'll be glad to bail you out. In return, I expect you to make a society woman out of my wife. She's got a grasshopper mind, my Elsie. Once she gets invited to a few more of these affairs, which you have to admit can be pretty dull, I figure she'll be satisfied and lose interest. Then I can take her back to Houston where she belongs."

Chanel felt a pang of envy. That dumpy woman with her dyed hair and her too-ingratiating smile had something she herself would love to have—a man, a rich one, who really gave a damn about her. Since she was always honest with herself, if not with other people, she knew very well that she'd never have that kind of relationship with Laird. If she married him, he would treat her with respect, even with passion at first, but he would never let her inside his mind—or his heart.

Well, that was okay. She was willing to settle for something far more important. Money and social status—and power.

"When do I start—what *is* your name, anyway?"

"William Stetson. My friends call me Stet. You can call me that if you've a mind to," he said, extending a large, muscular hand.

* * *

Chanel had forgotten her promise to go shopping with Glory, so when her call came, a couple of weeks after her encounter with William Stetson, she was taken off guard.

"I've lost twelve more pounds," Glory stated without preamble. "When can we start shopping for my new wardrobe?"

Chanel made a face. Dammit—she'd been so involved with trying to make a silk purse out of Elsie Stetson that she hadn't had time for anything else lately. To her surprise, since she'd sized the woman up as a total wimp, Stet's wife had turned out to be surprisingly hard to deal with.

When Chanel advised her to tone down her jet-black hair and go on a diet, she took offense and went whining to Stet. He had been diplomatic, and had finally coaxed her back into a good humor, but he had also backed Chanel, which hadn't endeared her to his wife. Their relationship had gone steadily downhill after that.

With Elsie on her high horse, Chanel knew she had some fence-mending to do. She did need that bonus Stet had promised. Already, he had been surprisingly generous. Not only had he paid her contribution to Nancy Anderson's charity, but he'd quietly slipped her a check that was enough to pay her back rent and other pending bills. There was even a modest surplus for her checking account.

So she didn't really have time to go shopping with Glory. On the other hand, she *had* made a promise. Well, maybe she could squeeze it in, after all. She rather enjoyed Glory's company, which was strange because they had nothing in common. Was it because Glory stroked her ego, the way she asked her advice?

"Look, I'm all tied up the next three days, but how about Friday?"

"That's great. I'll switch nights off with one of the other girls, and that way I won't be dragging my tail at work. When should we meet—and where?"

"Let's get an early start. I'll make an appointment for you with my hairdresser at ten. We can meet there—it's Adolfo's on Maiden Lane. Once that's out of the way, we can go shopping. How much money can you spend?"

"I've got about five hundred saved, but I want to hold some back in case—"

"Well, we'll see what we can do with five hundred," Chanel said.

There was a brief silence on the other end of the line. "Okay. I'm real grateful," Glory said.

"Glad to do it—even though I have been very busy lately," Chanel said cautiously. "I'm not even sure I can have lunch with the support group Saturday."

Chanel wasn't sure why she didn't just drop out of the group. It wasn't Ariel that stopped her. That relationship had served its purpose, although she still called Ariel once in a while so she could tell Laird that she'd just talked to his cousin.

As for her relationship with Laird, they still weren't lovers. True, they had come very close to it a couple of times, but he had never gone beyond a few intimate caresses—and a lot of hard breathing. She knew she turned him on, so what was the problem? Well, he'd get around to it eventually, and then, with the right kind of pressure from her, the next step was a proposal. Because he did have one weak point—he was a thoroughly decent man.

She realized Glory had asked her a question. "I'm sorry— there's some kind of interference on the line. What was it you said?"

"I asked how much your hairdresser charges," Glory said.

"Adolfo doesn't come cheap, but he's worth his fee because it always pays to get the best, you know."

"And how much does the best cost?" Glory persisted.

Chanel felt a grudging respect for Glory. She might be a product of the ghetto, but she knew what was important, and she didn't let herself get sidetracked. Maybe she'd make an exception this time and see that Glory got the discount she usually collected from Adolfo when she brought him a new customer he deemed worthy of his attention.

"In the neighborhood of a hundred dollars," she said, "but I'll see you get a discount. I was one of Adolfo's first customers when he opened his shop, and I've sent a lot of my friends there. Actually, that's quite reasonable for the kind of job he does."

Later, as Chanel dressed for her date with Laird, who was taking her to a reception at the Asian Art Museum to see an exhibit of fourteenth-century ink-on-paper drawings and then to dinner at L'Etoile with a group of his friends, she thought about her conversation with Glory. It was strange how much she was looking forward to their shopping trip. The little waif amused her with her down-to-earth ways—or was that her down-to-*street* ways?

Not that she'd ever dream of introducing her to Laird—or anyone else she knew.

* * *

Chanel was a few minutes late arriving at Adolfo's Salon. She paused briefly to study Glory, who was already there, talking to the receptionist. Glory was wearing the same dress she'd worn to the second luncheon at the University Club, but now it hung loosely on her body because she'd lost so much weight. With the right kind of clothes, a becoming hairdo, a change of makeup, she would be stunning-looking—and wasn't that a hoot?

Adolfo was short, wide, and very Italian, with an accent to prove it; he was also inclined to be arrogant, which had cost him a lot of customers in the past. He took one look at Glory and a gleam showed in his black eyes. Chanel recognized that gleam with relief. It meant Adolfo was intrigued, certainly challenged by Glory, which meant she would get his personal attention and wouldn't be passed along to a subordinate.

"Those ugly little screws of hair will have to go. Soft curls— that pussycat face just screams for soft curls." Adolfo wasn't speaking to Glory, who was unimportant to him as a person, but to Chanel, who was. "The color is impossible—so out, out, out with it. A light brown rinse to tone it down—"

"No way," Glory interrupted. "I fought too many battles over this red hair to change the color now. If people don't like it, they can stuff it, Mr. Adolf."

"Adolfo! Adolfo!" he barked, and turned an incredulous stare onto Chanel. "What is this you've brought me? Some kind of smart mouth?"

Glory didn't give Chanel time to answer. "You can knock off talking to Chanel like I'm not here. I'm the one who's paying the bill. From now on, I'll thank you to address your comments to me."

"Such a spitfire," Adolfo muttered, but Chanel, who knew him so well, was aware that he wasn't really offended. "Very well, Ms. Smart Mouth, I'm going to fix you up so you can pass as a classy act—until you open your mouth. And I'm going to start by layering your hair so it frames your face instead of hiding it. You'll look like a gamine—you know what means that word?"

"What do you think I am—stupid?"

"Stupid you're not. Ignorant you are. Which is not my worry. How you look when people see you walk out of Adolfo's salon— that's my worry."

Chanel, who had yet to say one word, watched with interest as Adolfo snapped his scissors together in what could only be called a ferocious manner, his eyes glinting with malice, before he made the first cut. Adolfo, although one of the best hairdressers in San Francisco, had a wide streak of perversity in his nature. He liked very few women, and if he took a dislike to a customer, no matter how important she might be, that person got short shrift. Glory had just put him on his mettle, which meant her cut would be his very best and creative work.

Chanel went to get a shampoo and set from one of Adolfo's assistants. Now that she had money again, she had renewed her twice-a-week appointments. Usually Adolfo did the honors, but today she'd given up her appointment to Glory.

An hour later, she was staring at a transformed Glory. Her face, which had been overwhelmed by her mop of hair, was revealed to be a near-perfect oval with high cheekbones and a soft, rounded chin. Although Glory's eyes still dominated her face, they no longer overwhelmed it. Adolfo, always capricious, had thrown in a gratuitous facial and makeup job, and the eye shadow that tinted Glory's lids so subtly pointed up the violet in her eyes. Her hairstyle, a riot of soft curls, wasn't in fashion at present, but it suited Glory to a tee. In fact, Chanel couldn't imagine her with any other style—which was a mark of Adolfo's genius.

"Well?" Adolfo asked; the smugness in his voice showed what answer he expected.

"You're fantastic, Adolfo," Chanel said, meaning it.

Glory said nothing; she was staring into the mirror, her eyes wide. "I should've had this done a lot sooner," she said finally.

Adolfo snorted. "You couldn't've got your foot in the door without Mrs. Devereau to recommend you," he huffed.

"Right. It's that way at the Golden Gate Health Club, too. They play that snob stuff to the hilt."

"Watch your mouth," he said. "I just might charge you for the makeup job and empty your bank account." But he was smiling again. "I hope you were paying attention when I made up your face, 'cause I'm not going to do it again, not for free."

"No problem. I guess you're going to charge me an arm and a leg for doing my hair?"

"For you, I charge cost. It's worth it for the entertainment value," he said, surprising Chanel. Adolfo wasn't noted for his altruism. In fact, he could pinch a penny even tighter than she could. She turned a speculative stare upon Glory. How had she gotten to him? It couldn't be sex. Adolfo leaned a different way.

"You need a manicure," Adolfo said. "Those nails look like claws."

"I keep my nails real nice," Glory said indignantly.

"Too long. Color—wrong, wrong, wrong. I tell you what: You came back next week, and I'll have Mario show you how to do your nails." Glory opened her mouth and he put up his hand, stopping her. "Half price—provided you keep your mouth shut."

Glory grinned at him. "It's a deal," she said.

When they were outside, Chanel said, "You two seem to have formed a mutual admiration society."

"Oh, we understand each other. Adolfo comes from my old neighborhood in the Tenderloin. It's like we're related or something."

Chanel whistled softly under her breath. "It's a small world," she muttered.

"He puts on that accent, you know. Says it's good for business." Glory was quiet for a moment, her eyes reflective. "I figure if he could make it out of the Tenderloin, so can I. Of course, I have a fucking lot to learn."

"What exactly do you want out of life?" Chanel asked curiously. "A rich husband?"

"Well, I wouldn't turn one down—not if he was right for me. But I don't want some old geezer with hot hands and nasty ideas, either. I want nice clothes, plenty of food in my belly, and a place to live that I own myself and can't be turned out of. I ain't never going back to the projects, no matter what. And when I get old, I don't want to end up dead broke, living on the streets or in some ratty hotel in the Tenderloin, eating dog food to stay alive. If some guy comes along who'll treat me decent, that's just pure gravy, because we all need love—y'know?"

Chanel couldn't think of anything to say to that. They were both silent as they walked down Maiden Lane toward her car, which she'd parked on Kearny, thereby saving herself a fat parking fee.

"Well, the next thing on the agenda is finding you a new wardrobe," Chanel said finally. "First we hit a shop on Gough that's the outlet for Anne Klein seconds, and if we find something suitable there, we can shop for a pair of shoes that doesn't make you look as if you're walking on stilettos."

CHAPTER TWENTY-SIX

"YOU LOOK WONDERFUL, GLORY," JANICE SAID WITH AN EN-
thusiasm that stemmed almost as much from the knowledge that
now she had something to add to Glory's dossier as it did from
her approval of Glory's surprising metamorphosis.

"Thank you," Glory said, flushing, and Janice made a mental
note that while Glory could handle with aplomb such things as
working in a North Beach nightclub and growing up in the grim
halls of public housing, she wasn't as easy with compliments.
"Chanel was—well, she recommended her hairdresser and took
me shopping a couple of times."

"The makings were already there," Chanel said. "Adolfo just
had to peel off a few layers of makeup."

Since there was a sting in her words, Janice expected Glory's
trigger temper to flare. Instead, Glory laughed. "Go to hell, Chanel," she said good-naturedly.

"I was beginning to think we weren't all that much a support
to one another—but I see I was wrong," Janice observed, not
trying to hide her satisfaction. They had just finished lunch and
were working on dessert—or rather Stephanie and Ariel were. The
other three had vetoed sweets. "You two seem to have become
good friends."

"Oh, we're two of a kind," Chanel drawled.

Janice felt a moment's uncertainty. Was Chanel poking fun at
Glory? Or was she just trying to sound clever? Maybe it was best
to take her words at face value. . . .

"I had a rather good idea this past month," she said. "You
know how we're always being asked to fill out bios? Where we
were born, our likes and dislikes, personal background, and such?
Why don't we do the same thing and then pass them around? It
would be a good way to find out what our common interests are."
She waited for a response; when no one spoke, she added, "What
do the rest of you think of my idea?"

"Not too much," Chanel said.

"I got a bellyful of that kind of thing in high school," Glory said. "The universities were always doing some kind of survey at Lowell High. Who needs it?"

"*You* went to Lowell?" Stephanie said.

"For two years. Why do you sound so surprised?" Glory said.

"Oh, I didn't mean—it was just that I'm impressed. It's a very difficult school to get into. They only take the best, I understand."

"That's what they say. I've got my doubts, though. After all, Buddy graduated from Lowell."

Ariel giggled. When everybody looked at her, color flooded her pale skin. "Sorry," she murmured.

"That's okay," Glory said. "I meant it as a joke."

"What do you think about doing bios, Stephanie?" Janice said, determined not to let the conversation get away from her this time.

"Well, the truth is I got pretty sick of filling out forms when I was job hunting," Stephanie confessed.

Chanel smiled at Janice. "Good try, Janice, but—majority rules. What say we order more coffee?"

Janice pressed the service bell, hiding her disappointment. The conversation, as always, seemed to have a mind of its own. It was surprising how seldom she managed to steer it onto subjects that would fill the gaps in her research. She had no idea, for instance, if any of the women had resumed dating, and if so, what difficulties they were encountering. Stephanie and Glory had reentered the job market, of course—the trick was to get them to talk about any problem areas. So far, no one seemed willing to confide her troubles, if any, at least not at these luncheons.

As she listened to Glory describe her encounter with Chanel's irascible hairdresser, she wondered why she didn't just give it up and rely totally upon her interviews with the other divorcées Arnold had steered her to. Unfortunately, these four women were the in-depth group of her survey. Without them, without a detailed month-by-month account of the changes that were occurring in their lives, her dissertation would be flat, incomplete, and like a dozen others about divorce she'd read. Dr. Yolanski had warned her of this, that she had to use detailed and original material in her dissertation—where else, at this late date, could she find a group of interacting divorcées that she could follow on a monthly basis? And she *had* promised Jake that she would only take a year—

"Janice?" Stephanie interrupted her train of thought.

"Sorry—did you say something to me?"

"I said I've been thinking and—well, if you think it would help us get better acquainted, I'd be glad to do a bio." She gave Chanel an apologetic smile. "We didn't actually vote on it, you know."

"It's okay with me, too, even though filling out forms is the pits." Glory shook her head, looking rueful. "I applied for a credit card at Macy's but when I came to the part where they asked my occupation and where I worked, I gave the whole idea up. Can't you just see their reaction if I told them I worked as a cocktail waitress in a joint called The Oral Cookie?"

There was a charged silence. Chanel's laugh broke out first. Then the others, including Glory, were laughing, too.

"God, you're something else, Morning Glory Browne," Chanel said, wiping her eyes.

Oscar, their waiter, arrived with their coffee, and as they drank it, they talked about Glory's transformation and Stephanie's new job. When Janice brought up the bios again, they all agreed to write one and bring it to the next luncheon. Janice wanted to suggest that they do it before they broke up that day, but she hid her impatience. As she listened to the lively conversation, it came to her that for the first time they were a cohesive group, however thin their support for each other really was. Trying to be optimistic, she decided that there was a good chance it would all come together finally and she could get the information she needed for her dissertation.

As Glory strolled along Taylor Street, heading for the nearest bus stop, she was aware of admiring glances following her, which was heady stuff for someone who'd attracted a different type of attention most of her life. The winter sun, although its heat was filtered somewhat by a northwestern breeze, held a welcome warmth, and she decided to walk home, even though she knew she'd be sorry by the time she got off work that night.

Part of her feeling of well-being stemmed from the reception her new look had received from the support group. When she'd arrived at the University Club, she'd been in a defensive mood, prepared for anything from indifference to outright cattiness. What she hadn't expected was the genuine approval of the other women. Not one insult or put-down. Not that she was kidding herself. Changing her hairdo and wearing different clothes didn't make all that much difference. She still didn't fit in with those upper-class types. But they did like her—although sometimes she wondered if Chanel's friendliness didn't stem from—what had Adolfo called it? Her entertainment value?

At least, they never snubbed her openly, like when she'd first enrolled at Lowell High. The kids there, most of them, had treated her like a freak, laughing at her tacky clothes and the traces of Arkansas twang she'd picked up from Ma. Too proud to show her hurt, she'd dressed even more outrageously, made jokes about living in roach city, about being an Arkie, even about never having any lunch money.

By the end of the year, the other girls were bleaching their jeans until the seams turned white, and fraying the hems and knees with a file so they would look like her. They copied the outsize denim work shirts that she bought at St. Vincent de Paul for a quarter apiece, and wore beat-up tennies without socks. And they'd laughed like crazy at her clowning and self-insults, telling her she was really b-a-d. She hadn't liked being popular that way, but it was better than being an object of pity. . . .

Glory almost crashed into a woman pushing a shopping cart, and only then realized that she hadn't been paying attention to where she was going. She gave herself a sharp scolding. Not only was daydreaming dangerous out here on the streets, but brooding about the past at *any* time was downright stupid. Okay, she'd enjoyed herself today, but those women weren't really important in her life. Maybe it was time she dropped out of the club. The only reason she'd stayed this long was because she'd wanted to pick Chanel's brain. Since she could still see Chanel anyhow, why waste her time with the rest of them?

That evening, she was a little nervous about going to work with her new hairdo and her new makeup job, even though she was dressed as usual in jeans and a windbreaker. Her boss, a short, pudgy man with droopy eyelids and a face like a bullterrier, looked her over, then asked if she had some rich guy on the string. Most of the other waitresses didn't comment on the change, although there were a couple of oblique comments behind her back that she chose to ignore. Only Susan, the fellow worker she liked the least because she was lazy and had round heels, asked if she had a new body perm.

As for the customers, most of whom she recognized by sight now, there was no reaction at all, and she realized to them, the waitresses at the Oral Cookie, in their skimpy costumes, were just warm bodies, part of the scenery. Well, all cats look alike in the dark—wasn't that an old saying? And the club *was* dark. No getting around that.

Her only real surprise was Jimbo. When she gave her first order, four draft beers, he looked her over silently, then turned away and went to draw the beers. For the rest of the evening, he ignored her, and she realized he'd overheard Russ's remark and believed she had a new lover. She couldn't very well march up and tell him she hadn't, so she did her best not to let it bother her. But she couldn't help feeling a little hurt, too.

When her shift was over, she headed for the bus stop. Jimbo's car was nowhere to be seen, although his hours coincided with hers on Saturday nights. Which meant he was really sore. Well, so be it. Like Ms. Claire said, no pain, no gain, and at least she didn't have to worry about him asking her out in the future.

After she got off her bus, she walked assertively, defensively, toward her apartment, which was located halfway up a steeply inclined hill. The narrow street seemed too empty, especially for a Saturday night, and she found herself staring into the dark doorways she passed and making a wide detour out into the street when she came to an alley. It wasn't that she was afraid, just that she was careful. Having been raised in a jungle, she knew the best protection was to never let down your guard, never take chances.

But she breathed a sigh of relief when she reached the Santorinis' house. Her landlord's lights were off upstairs, but as always, they had left a small bulb burning outside the entrance of her apartment. Her key ready in her hand, she looked around carefully before she inserted it in the lock. As she turned the key, she felt a tingling in the back of her neck, but when she whirled to look behind her, the street was empty, very quiet. Come to think of it, there wasn't even any wind—maybe that's why she was so jumpy tonight.

Once inside her apartment, she shut and locked the door before she switched on the lights. The tiny apartment, although almost bare of furniture, looked cozy and welcoming in the flood of light. Thank God she was home—and maybe it was time to start thinking about changing jobs. She was sick of working nights. It was like living in a twilight world with everything turned upside down. More and more, she found it impossible to relate to people who were coming home just as she was going to work.

Still wearing her windbreaker, she turned the thermostat up before she went into her bedroom. She skirted the mattress on

the floor and, humming under her breath, pushed open the closet
door. It was good to be home, to know that the world, with all its
problems and—yes, all its terrors—was shut out for the night.

She slipped off her windbreaker and reached in the closet for
one of the wood hangers Chanel had talked her into buying.

"Wire hangers are brutal on clothes," Chanel had said. "Invest in good padded or wooden hangers—and always air the things
you take off for a while before you put them away. Brush your
clothes—soft bristles, please!—after every wearing and send them
to the cleaners only when it's absolutely necessary, because chem-
ical cleaners are murder on natural fabrics. As soon as you can
afford it, invest in muslin garment bags for your out-of-season
clothes. If you buy the best fabrics you can afford and choose
timeless styles, you can wear your garments for years, even decades."

Glory smiled, remembering the lecture—and the shopping excursion with Chanel. What would the support group say if they
knew that the navy blue dress she'd worn to the luncheon today
had come from a secondhand store? It wasn't a color she particularly liked, but Chanel had convinced her that it toned down her
appearance, was becoming to her fair coloring.

The price Adolfo had charged her, which Chanel had declared
a steal and which she thought exorbitant, hadn't prepared her for
the bargains Chanel had found for her later. In fact, she had three
new outfits, including a cocktail dress she wondered if she'd ever
have an occasion to wear, and there was still enough left in her
savings fund to either buy a secondhand easy chair or a small TV
set.

Glory slid the jacket into the closet, then slipped her sweater
over her head. She reached in for another hanger, but the one
she'd used that morning wasn't where she expected it to be. She
hunted for it, finally found it lying on the floor of the closet. She
bent to pick it up, started to straighten—and then her whole body
froze as she stared at the boots—men's boots—that protruded
from beneath the row of clothing. She raised her eyes slowly and
found herself looking straight into Buddy's grim smile.

"Hello, bitch," he said, stepping out of the closet.

Later, Glory would live those few seconds over and realize
where she'd made her first mistake. If she had shoved the hanger
she was holding into Buddy's face, then turned and run, if she
had yelled as loud as she could as she was running—maybe things

would have been different. But at the moment, all she could do was stare at Buddy, paralyzed by the knowledge that not only had he found out where she lived but he'd broken into her apartment.

Fear, like a jolt of electricity, released her from her paralysis. She started to run, but it was already too late. Buddy's arm clamped under her chin, forcing her head back, and when she started to struggle, when she tried to scream, he tightened his hold, cutting off her air.

"Where's your ugly bodyguard now?" he gloated. "We're all alone, just you and me—and it's pay-up time. Go ahead and squirm, why don't you? That just makes it better."

Glory knew he was right. Her struggles were exciting him; she could feel his erection against her buttocks. She stopped struggling and went limp, sickened by the sharp odor of liquor, by the musty smell of his body, by his harsh breathing in her ear.

"That's better," he said. "I'm going to loosen my hold so you can breathe, but if you try anything stupid, I'll hurt you—bad. If you behave yourself, maybe—just maybe—I won't break your bones or do too much damage to your face. You know what I want—any trouble and you're going to end up looking like something out of The Texas Chainsaw Massacre."

The pressure against her windpipe eased, and she took a long breath, then another. When the grayness receded, and she could see again, she said, as calmly as she could, "This is really dumb, Buddy. Why don't we talk this over before you do anything you'll regret? After all, we're even now. You hit me a few times and I hit you back. So what's the big deal?"

"The big deal is you made me look like a jerk. One of the cops who cut me loose trained with my brother at the police academy, and he recognized me. The bastard spread it all over the department, and everybody got a big laugh out of it. Now I've got Bob on my back, too. So it's pay-up time for you. I'm really going to enjoy this. I've been thinking about it for a long time, planning how I'd take you out. I can make it easy on you, or it can get real nasty. It depends on how you cooperate for the next hour or so."

With a quick twist of his wrist, he brought her down to her knees. The pain in her arm was excruciating. When she moaned aloud, he slapped her hard across the mouth, rocking her head back; from the flat, metallic taste in her mouth, she knew he'd split her lip.

Everything got a little hazy after that. She knew that he was tearing off her clothes, knew that he'd knocked her down when she felt the softness of the mattress under her naked body. She gave a moan of despair when he fell on top of her.

There were other things—Buddy's frenzied movements above her, then inside her, the foul words he used as he violated her, then afterward, the flat, dull sound that could only be his fists, hitting her breasts, her face, her abdomen. She no longer felt any pain; that would come later. He stopped hitting her finally, but only to force her over on her stomach and mount her again.

He was so confident that he'd knocked the fight out of her that he hadn't bothered to gag her. From some inward source of strength—and pride—she found it possible to open her mouth and scream at the top of her lungs.

Buddy cursed and struck the back of her head with the flat of his hand, so hard that her senses began to slip away. In one last act of defiance, she turned her head and sank her teeth into his hand, biting down with all the strength remaining to her.

The last thing she heard was the pounding of footsteps on the stairs flanking her bedroom. Someone—her landlady or landlord—had heard her scream and was coming to investigate.

CHAPTER TWENTY-SEVEN

SOMEWHERE NEARBY THERE WAS MOVEMENT AND SOUND, BUT A silver-gray veil surrounded Glory, blinding her when she opened her eyes. Pain drove her back into the darkness again; images passed through her mind, so swiftly that they didn't have time to register. For this, she was thankful because she knew that the images were graphic, terrifying, ugly. Another sensation intruded, penetrating the gray darkness—a medicinal odor, alcohol or ether. The gray veil began to dissolve at the edges, and suddenly she was staring into the calm face of a middle-aged woman.

"So you're back with us again," the stranger said.

Glory noticed several things simultaneously: She was lying on a hospital bed. The woman was wearing a white uniform. She hurt all over.

She must have groaned, because the woman bent over her, her smile changing to a look of concern.

"There now; you're safe. You're in Memorial Hospital. You've been badly beaten, but mostly it's bruises. There are no broken bones or cuts except for a split lip. And as soon as I give you the medicine the doctor left, the pain will go away."

Glory nodded; she couldn't speak. The memories came pouring in, blocking out everything else: Buddy's rage-engorged face . . . his hot, angry eyes . . . his huge fists, pounding, pounding, pounding on her . . . the weight of his body as he—

A ragged cry left her throat and she tried to struggle up to a sitting position. The nurse's hand against her shoulder held her down. "No—you can't sit up. Now, you be a good girl and lie still. You're perfectly safe now—the police have your husband in custody, I understand—"

"Ex-husband," Glory managed. "We're divorced."

"The worse for him. He won't get out of this with some stupid technicality that a man can't rape his own wife. I hope he gets twenty years."

Her words were so surprising that Gloria lost her voice again. The woman patted her hand. "You were lucky your landlord heard you scream. He beat the stuffings out of your hus—your ex-husband before the cops got there."

"Mr. Santorini did that to Buddy? But he's in his sixties, and Buddy is a professional athlete."

"And your landlord was an ex-Marine—or so the cops who brought you here said. I guess Buddy didn't put up much of a fight. A nurse is supposed to be objective, but I have to confess I'm glad they took that bastard to San Francisco General for treatment instead of bringing him here."

Glory laughed, then winced at a sting of pain from her cracked lip. At the nurse's appraising look, she said, "I'm not freaking out. It's just that you surprised me."

"Well, nurses are human—more or less. And nothing bugs me more than seeing a woman come in, beaten up by some freaking man. By the way, is there someone you want to call? Your family or maybe a friend? If so, I'll see to it personally."

Glory thought about it. Her mother and sisters were the logical ones to contact, but did she really want them to know what had happened? They would blame her, not Buddy. In fact, her mother would probably start nagging her not to prosecute him. But she *would* have to notify her boss, or she wouldn't have a job when she was able to work again. Which brought up another question. How long would she be off work—and how bad did she look?

"Could you bring me a mirror?" she asked.

"A mirror—oh, I see. Well, of course. I'll be right back—but first the pills."

Meekly Glory swallowed the small white pills. After the nurse bustled out of the room, she tried to judge the extent of her injuries. She hurt everywhere, it seemed, but the nurse had assured her that there were no broken bones to heal. If she didn't look too bad, maybe she could go back to work in a few days. Unexpectedly, her eyes watered. She'd been so proud of the way she looked today. Well, didn't they say that pride goeth before a fall?

A few minutes later, when the nurse brought her a small pocket mirror, she discovered that a large purple bruise covered her left cheekbone, that her mouth, under a small bandage, was swollen out of shape, and there were red welts on her throat. She swallowed hard and let the mirror drop to the bed.

"You'll be surprised how fast the bruises will fade," the nurse said. "They look worse than they really are because of your fair complexion. Just be thankful that the skin wasn't broken except for that split lip. And you were going to tell me who to notify. Your landlord didn't seem to know much about your personal life."

"Maybe you should call my boss. His name is Russ Hogan . . ." She gave the number at the Oral Cookie, and then, maybe because of the pity she saw in the nurse's eyes, she gave her another name. "Oh, would you call Janice Morehouse? Her number's listed in the phone book—she lives in Palo Alto. She'll notify the rest of my friends."

The basket of flowers came later that morning. It was a spring assortment—tulips and daisies and daffodils. Since it was the first time in Glory's life that anyone had sent her flowers, she had the nurse put them on the table next to her bed so she could gloat over them. The card was signed with the names of all of the support group, but since they were in the same handwriting, she was sure that Janice had sent them on her own. But no matter. They brightened the room, and they held back the demons a little.

And there *were* demons. Lots of them. One was fear. She'd never been hurt so badly before although she'd been slapped around by Buddy that time, and before that, by her mother and

by bigger neighborhood kids, and even by a couple of her mother's
live-ins.

There was also shame and self-disgust because she'd handled
the whole thing so badly. To begin with, she never should've tied
Buddy to that bed and whipped him with his own belt. She knew
his macho pride. But having made that first mistake, she should've
been more careful. If she hadn't let him surprise her, maybe she
could've escaped before he grabbed her—or at least have screamed
for help sooner.

Then there was another demon. Always, even when things were
at their worst, she'd had a good feeling about herself. Now she'd
been brought down, and she resented it, hated the feeling of helplessness, of weakness.

There was a sound at the door. When she opened her eyes, the
room seemed full of women. She sorted them out—Ariel, Chanel,
Stephanie, Janice. The whole bunch—the whole fucking bunch
had turned out.

Their faces blurred and she realized she was crying. She wiped
her eyes furiously, and when she could see again, she discovered
that she wasn't the only one. Even Chanel's eyes were suspiciously
bright. And wasn't *that* something she'd never thought to
see. . . .

"For God's sake," she said, rubbing her nose on the sleeve of
her hospital gown. "You want to drown me on top of everything
else? Who needs it?"

Everybody started talking at once, giving her a chance to get a
tissue from the bedstand and blow her nose. Briefly, she explained
what had happened, making a big story out of her ex-Marine
landlord, who was built like an ox, and who had taken on Buddy
single-handedly.

"I'm sorry I didn't see it happen," she added. "I was out of it
by then."

"And there's no permanent damage?" Janice looked so concerned that for the first time Glory really warmed to her.

"Only to my pride," Glory said; she wondered if they knew
about the rape, too. "I'll be out of here in a day or two. And I'll
be slinging gin fizzes in a week. I guess I look pretty awful,
right?"

It wasn't a question—she knew how she looked—but they must
have taken it for one because Ariel averted her eyes and Janice
looked embarrassed and murmured, "Don't worry about it now.
Just get well."

"You have some bruises on your face, but they'll be gone in a few days," Stephanie said. Glory eyed her curiously; Stephanie's voice sounded strange, and her face was very pale.

But it was Chanel who said what they all were thinking. "You look like hell. You won't be back to work in a few days, Glory. Rotten luck."

Glory agreed. Not only did she have a hospital bill to worry about—she had no insurance—but she'd lose a couple of weeks' wages, too. Rotten luck was right.

"It was good of you all to come," she said. "And the flowers are super."

"They came fast," Janice said, giving the bouquet an appraising look.

The conversation turned to other things—the kind of light, polite conversation with which Glory usually had no patience. But it occurred to her now that there was something to be said about casual chitchat. It was a lot less painful than having to give a blow-by-blow account of Buddy's attack, something her family would have expected.

In fact, she felt surprisingly comfortable with these women, considering what a disadvantage she was at with her messed-up face. Was it because they cared enough to come to see her? It wasn't because of the small gifts they produced now, although she'd always been a sucker for wrapped presents.

Each of the gifts was useful, and each was wrapped in fancy paper, tied with ribbons—almost, Glory thought, as if they knew that opening presents really turned her on. There was a box of cologne and matching talcum powder from Ariel. It was a little flowery for her taste, but she knew she'd use it all up. Stephanie's gift was a box of Godiva chocolates, which Glory promptly opened and passed around. She didn't offer it a second time; instead, she put the box away in the stand beside her bed to dole out to herself, a couple at a time, until they were gone.

Chanel's gift was very practical; shampoo and soap, toothbrush and paste, as was Janice's box of note cards with an Oriental design, plus a ballpoint pen and a supply of stamps.

By the time she'd opened the presents, drawing it out as long as she could to prolong the pleasure, visiting hours were over. Ariel, who'd had little to say, gave her light kiss on the cheek, and then the others were doing the same. She felt embarrassed as hell, but—well, good, too.

But when they were gone, common sense stirred, telling her

not to make too much of their visit because someone, probably Janice, had organized things, got them together to do the decent thing. But even so, it was nice they'd bothered to come.

She examined her presents, one by one, and then had another chocolate. It was better than Christmas, she reflected, even if it was one helluva way to get a few presents.

Later, another bouquet, this time white carnations, arrived from the Santorinis. An accompanying note told her not to worry, that they would look after her apartment, that they'd be in to see her in the morning. She had the nurse put the flowers next to the first bouquet.

That evening, she got another visitor. She was taking a nap when someone coughed near the bed. Her eyes flew open, and when she saw it was Steve Golden, she released her breath in a long relieved sigh.

"Sorry I scared you," he said.

"You didn't scare me. Just surprised me is all."

"Okay, you're tough, and getting mauled by that Neanderthal ex-husband of yours was a piece of cake. But you were scared just now when you saw a man standing by your bed. Why don't you admit it?"

"I don't have to admit anything to you—and don't judge me by those Barbie dolls you go for."

"What makes you think I like Barbie dolls?"

"Who's lying now? I've seen them hanging all over you at the club. It's enough to make me puke."

"Uh-huh. So you've been watching me. Very interesting."

She tossed her head, then wished she hadn't when a sharp pain shot up the back of her head. The smile slipped off Steve's face and he stepped closer to the bed. To her relief, he didn't mention what must have been obvious. Instead, he whipped his arm out from behind his back and presented her with a bouquet of roses. They were pink, wrapped in tissue paper, and to her chagrin, she felt a flush warming her face. To hide it, she buried her face in the roses.

"Thank you," she said, her voice muffled. "You didn't have to—and how did you know I was in the hospital anyway?"

"You didn't turn up for your aerobics class this morning, so I called the phone number on your registration card. Your landlady answered, and she told me what happened." He laid his hand on hers, squeezed it gently. "I'm sorry as hell, Glory. I knew something was bugging you, but it never occurred to me that you were having husband trouble.''

"Ex-husband trouble. My landlord beat him up." She didn't try to hide her satisfaction. "He's over at San Francisco General now—or so I've heard."

"Are you going to file charges?"

The question brought her up short. "I don't know. I'm mad as hell, but still—I guess I asked for it. I hurt his pride real bad, so maybe some of it's my fault. Not that it excuses him for what he done." She looked him square in the eye. "He raped me, you know. It was a total bummer."

"God—if you don't file charges, that animal will be back on the street again. You need protection—"

"I can take care of myself."

"Like you did last night? Be sensible. Don't take the blame. There's nothing you could've done to him to justify this."

"Not even tying him to the bed while he was drunk and whacking him where the sun don't shine with his own belt?" she said dryly.

He winced, but all he said was, "Not even for that." He pulled a chair up close to the bed and sat down. He surveyed the room, his eyes lingering on the flowers, on the gifts piled at the end of the bed. "You're lucky to have a room to yourself," he observed, nodding toward the empty bed against the wall.

"I'd be luckier if I could pay for it." She smoothed down the sheet that had bunched up under her chin. "They probably would've turned me away and sent me to San Francisco General, only I still have an insurance card in my wallet made out to Mrs. Buddy Prichett from back when Buddy was pitching for the Bees. When they find out it's expired, I'll probably have to leave my right arm before they'll release me."

Steve whistled softly. "Buddy Prichett—he was some kind of local high school baseball star a few years back, wasn't he?"

"Yeah—but he bombed when he went professional."

"And then took it out on you?"

Glory felt uncomfortable. Was that really true? "I didn't help. I was all mixed up because—because of some personal problems. Which is why I'm not going to file charges—provided he pays my hospital bills," she said, making up her mind.

"And that's it? You think you can just walk away from this as if it never happened? It isn't that easy. There's always trauma after a rape. The Rape Center can help you—all you have to do is ask."

"I don't need them. If I want to talk to someone, I have plenty of friends."

"Male or female?" he said.

"That's my business, isn't it? I'm not about to pay out good money to a shrink. As far as Buddy bothering me again is concerned—well, maybe you can help me with that."

"Like what?"

"Like teaching me some martial art stuff so I can protect myself."

She was sure he would refuse. It was in the cards that he would. So she wasn't surprised when he was silent.

"I thought so," she said in disgust. "Lots of advice but no help. Isn't that just like a man."

"You're jumping the gun, tiger. I'm trying to decide if learning martial arts would help you. It might give you the wrong kind of confidence. Also, martial arts is synonymous with discipline— and you have about as much discipline as a two-year-old. It isn't Bruce Lee doing flashy kicks and twirls with all his opponents politely waiting their turn. It entails months, even years, of practice, the willingness to follow directions, to control your temper and take a few hard knocks—which are inevitable. I know you have guts. But do you have what it takes to accept discipline?"

"Try me," she said. It was hard not to show her elation. He was going to give in. This lecture was just window dressing.

"Okay—but the first time you start complaining, that's the end of it. Also, you stay for the full course or it's no go."

"Don't worry. I'll pay you for your time. You'll hafta wait for your money until I'm back on my feet financially, but I always pay my debts—"

"Shut up and listen. That's one of your troubles. You jump in, your fur all ruffled, before you hear what other people have to say."

"Listen, if I hadn't learned to be quick on my feet, I'd be walking the streets for a living right now—or be dead. So don't knock it."

There was a subtle change on his face; she couldn't tell if he was trying to hide a smile or a frown. She glared back because neither was acceptable.

"Okay, you've made your point," Steve said. "Someday I hope you trust me enough to tell me just what the hell goes on in that head of yours. I'm not worried about you paying me. I have a proposition to make you—"

"That does it! Out—get the hell out of here!"

"There you go again. I don't want your body—at the moment, you look about as sexy as a rag doll."

She stared at him, at the anger on his face. Unexpectedly, a quiver started up in her swollen lips. She put her hand up to cover her mouth, and Steve moved so quickly that she didn't have time to put out her hands and hold him off. One minute he was lounging in his chair and the next he had his arms around her. She didn't struggle. She didn't do anything except close her eyes and lean against him a little.

"Okay, I'm sorry. That was a rotten thing to say. You do look like hell, but I didn't have to say so. And I lied. I do want your body. But that has nothing to do with the proposition I have for you."

She pulled away so she could look at him. "So what were you talking about?"

He returned to his chair. "Let me start at the beginning. You know how Claire has been acting up lately? I tried talking to her, and she promised to behave, but yesterday I came in and heard her calling one of the women a spoiled bitch. We've lost seven women out of her classes in the past month, and some of the others formed a committee to tell me that if she stays, they go."

"I don't understand. Why would they come to you?"

"Because I'm managing the club now. Didn't you know that?"

"How would I know? And why are you telling me all this, anyway? What does Claire have to do with me?"

"I'm getting to that now. I had to fire Claire, and now I need a replacement. Virginia and Marsha are doubling up and taking Claire's classes for now, but they can't do it indefinitely. I want you to take over her beginner's classes."

"That doesn't make sense. Why would you want me? If this is some trick to soften me up so you can get into my—"

"Shut up and listen. I want you because you're a natural. I've never seen anyone pick up aerobics the way you have. Also, you're tough. Our clientele isn't used to taking orders. Give them half a chance and they'll walk all over an instructor. Which is why Claire got her job in the first place. Unfortunately, our former manager misjudged the reason she was tough. He didn't realize she has this compulsion to dominate other women."

He hesitated, then went on. "There's another bonus you should consider. As an employee of the club, you're entitled to things like health benefits—and also all the free martial art lessons you want. It's one of the perks of the job, a serendipity thing.''

"You sure use big words for a jock," she muttered.

"Oh, there're all kinds of jocks. I picked up a few big words at Yale."

"Don't try to con me. What would someone who went to a fancy college like that be doing teaching martial arts?"

"What indeed. And let's get back to my job offer. How about it, Glory? Want to give it a try?"

"But all I know about aerobics or calisthenics is Claire's routines," she protested. "Don't you have to have a phys ed degree to be an instructor?"

"It helps, but you'll get all the training you need to handle beginners, and after a while, you'll develop your own style, your own routines. As I said, I'm banking on one thing—that you're a natural. It's obvious you love it. The way you throw yourself into aerobics is bound to rub off on the clients. At first, you'd be on probation, of course, but I'm sure you'll catch on quickly."

Glory considered his words. She'd run out of arguments—except one. "What does it pay?" she asked.

"I thought we'd get around to that eventually."

"Why not? How do you think I pay my rent and buy food?"

"I did it again, didn't I? Put my foot in my mouth."

"Yes, you did. And I'm sick of it. I don't know if I want to work for you."

"I'll top the wages you're making now by twenty percent—including tips. If it doesn't pan out, you can always quit. Meanwhile, you'll get your martial arts instructions for free. You may even have a little fun in the process. What do you say?"

Glory sighed deeply. "I have a feeling I'm making one big mistake, but okay—I'll try it. It's better than dodging drunks at the Oral Cookie."

CHAPTER TWENTY-EIGHT

EVEN BEFORE THE DEATH OF HER KITTEN, STEPHANIE HAD HAR-bored an aversion to violence of any kind. On the fall day every year when her father slaughtered hogs, she always managed to hide until it was all over, and no amount of punishment could make her help her mother wring a chicken's neck, then scald and clean it for Sunday dinner.

She'd avoided the violence in movies, too, even though it was only acting. On the occasions when her parents allowed her to drive into Milton, the county seat, with the kids of a neighboring farm family to see the Saturday afternoon movie, she was always prepared to hide her face in case the movie got scary or turned violent. Once, when her friend's family took her to see a rerun of *Bambi*, she was caught by surprise when Bambi's mother was killed by hunters, and had a fit of hysterics.

Her kitten's death by hanging exacerbated this aversion. Which was why she monitored the twins' TV viewing even after they were teenagers. What they saw at the movies or on their friends' TV sets, she couldn't very well control, but she made sure that the only violence in her own home was Monday Night Football.

So it was inevitable that Glory's beating would hit her harder than it did the other women. Only because of her strict sense of duty did she consent to go with Janice and the other women to see Glory at the hospital.

"We *are* her support group, after all," Janice said when she called to tell Stephanie about Glory. "After all, if it were any of us, we'd expect the same support, wouldn't you?"

Stephanie thought she was prepared, but when she saw Glory's battered face, everything inside her shrank away. She also felt a rush of anger that Glory, who had already seen so much trouble in her short life, would be subjected to such treatment from a man. Not that she said anything like this to Glory, who was so nonchalant about the whole thing. If it hadn't been for her misshapen mouth and the bruises that stood out like a stigmata against her fair skin, it would've been hard to believe that she was the victim of a beating.

Once, when Glory raised her arm to push back her hair, the side of her breast was exposed through the gaping armhole of her hospital gown. A large purple bruise gave evidence that the beating had been more than the "few bashes" that Glory called it, and Stephanie found it hard to speak normally the way the others did.

Oddly, it was Ariel who sensed Stephanie's reaction. As they were following the others down the hall toward the elevators, she slipped her hand into Stephanie's. "Are you okay, Stephanie?" she asked.

"I'm fine," Stephanie said, then changed it to, "No, I'm not! I want to—to scream! Why are men so full of violence and deceit?"

Ariel was silent for a moment. "Some men aren't. My cousin Laird, for instance. He's a very gentle man—he wouldn't lift his hand to a woman no matter what the provocation."

"You're right. David wouldn't either," Stephanie said slowly. "But men can hurt you in ways other than physical violence."

"Yes. . . ." It seemed more like a sigh than a word. "I guess that's what our support group is all about, isn't it? Women helping other women during the bad times?"

Stephanie found herself nodding, even though she had some serious doubts about the effectiveness of the group. "I'm sure Glory was grateful for our visit."

"Janice was right to ask us to come together. Now we all know that if things get really bad, we can count on one another."

There was a question in her voice, and Stephanie squeezed her hand in answer. They were both silent as they joined Chanel and Janice, who were waiting by the elevators.

"Well, I'll see you all in March," Chanel said, glancing down at her watch.

"I was hoping we could have coffee together," Janice said.

Stephanie studied her curiously. Why did Janice work so hard to get the group together when she seemed the one most able to cope with her divorce? Or at least she didn't talk much about her marriage or her ex-husband. Was it all a facade, a mask she wore to hide her loneliness and fear of the future? If so—maybe it wasn't just Glory who needed a little company today.

"I'm free," she said. "How about you, Ariel?"

"I could use a cup of tea," Ariel said in her fadeaway voice.

"Sure you can't make it, Chanel?" Janice asked.

Chanel shook her head. "I'm sorry, but I have a hair appointment. I talked Adolfo into fitting me into his schedule, and if I don't turn up—well, he'll be in a snit. And I do have an important date tonight."

"With Laird?" Ariel asked.

Chanel gave her a quick look. "As a matter of fact, it *is* with Laird. He's taking me to a showing of French antiques at the Waterson Gallery."

"Laird has always been interested in antiques," Ariel said. "He believes it's important to preserve old things because of their link to the past." She sighed, looking restive. "Alex hates anything old. He's always talking about replacing the furnishings of our house with something more modern."

"What kind of antiques do you have?" Chanel said, looking interested.

"Actually, they aren't quite antiques, not technically, although some of them are quite valuable. Alex calls them 'art decadent,' but they're mostly art nouveau from the turn of the century and art deco that my grandparents bought in the twenties. I'm glad they belong to the estate and can't be sold because I feel comfortable with familiar things around me. Of course, they could go into storage, I guess." She seemed depressed by the thought.

"Laird's house is furnished in early Victorian. He must like it that way, or he would have replaced it by now," Chanel said.

"I've never been there," Ariel said. "Because of the family feud, you see."

Stephanie started to ask about the feud, then changed her mind. Chanel was looking at her watch again, and besides, Stephanie had developed a headache and there was a grainy feeling under her eyelids. She realized she desperately needed that coffee, and was glad when the elevator arrived, ending the conversation.

Later, as she sat with Ariel and Janice in a small café near the hospital, sipping her second cup of coffee, she finally began to relax. It was at times like this, when the conversation was about inconsequential things, that she enjoyed the group the most. But when the conversation turned to more personal things she always stiffened up. Because what if someone started asking *her* personal questions—such as whether David had married the friend she'd caught him in bed with?

"How are you getting along on your job, Stephanie?" Janice asked her.

"Well, I was pretty nervous at first, but then it came to me that the work I was doing wasn't nearly as demanding as taking care of twin babies. I'm even learning to cope with situations that would have floored me a few months ago."

"Such as?" Janice said.

"Would you believe I fended off a pass from my boss last week? A few times he's said—you know, suggestive things, but I've always pretended I didn't understand him. Then he had me stay late to help him inventory some old stock. We were alone in the stockroom when he asked me if I had a boyfriend to take care of me in bed now that I'm divorced. I started to pretend I didn't hear him, but all of a sudden I got really mad. So I told him to knock it off or I'd report him for sexual harassment. I sounded just like Glory. I guess some of her spunk rubbed off on me."

"So what did he do?" Janice said.

"He went back to inventorying French teddies."

Janice laughed. "Good for you! I wish some of Chanel's grooming would rub off on me. Never a ruffled hair or a crease in her skirt. I don't know how she does it."

"She works very hard at it," Ariel said.

Janice looked thoughtful. "I'm sure you're right. Well, she must have a closet as big as our whole house—" She broke off, looking embarrassed for no reason Stephanie could see.

"She's been helping Glory change her image. I wonder if she would give me some advice on how to dress," Ariel said. "I feel so out of step sometimes."

Stephanie smiled at her. "You don't need advice, Ariel. You have your own individual style. But sometimes I fantasize about going to one of those spas and getting a whole new look."

"They cost a mint, you know," Janice said.

"It might be worth it—provided I had the money," Stephanie said dreamily. "Just think—a new look, a new wardrobe, and who knows what could happen. I might even—"

She broke off, flushing.

"Find a new man?"

"Something like that. But he would have to be totally different from David." Her curiosity stirred. "How about you, Janice? Now that you're divorced, are you in the market for a new man?"

Janice drained her coffee cup before she answered. "What on

earth would I do with a new man? My life is already too busy these days.''

"What do you do? I know you used to work as an office manager but—''

"Oh, I got my old job back. I work for a group of engineers who are in business together.''

"Lucky for you that you didn't have to start out fresh after your divorce,'' Stephanie said.

"Yes, I'm very lucky.'' Janice beckoned to their waitress for the check. "Let's keep in touch between meetings,'' she said. "Maybe the three of us could have lunch together next month.''

"It sounds like fun,'' Stephanie said politely, thinking of her own overcrowded schedule. She was glad when the conversation shifted back to Glory.

An hour later, when Stephanie reached home, she heard music blaring from both of the boys' bedrooms simultaneously. As usual, it was total chaos because Ronnie preferred a sound he called "cool jazz'' while Chuck was addicted to new wave music.

Stephanie made a face, but she didn't call upstairs to tell them to cut down the volume as she once would have. The boys had been unnaturally cooperative lately, and although she was sure it wouldn't last, she didn't want to instigate another rebellion.

Besides, her headache was really giving her trouble. Which wasn't surprising because the day had been so depressing. Remembering Glory as she'd been at the luncheon yesterday, then seeing her at the hospital with her face swollen and bruised, had been a real shock. What a brute that man was. David, for all his faults, had never been violent . . . and why did she keep thinking about him? Just because he wasn't the sort to use violence didn't excuse what else he was.

Chuck's footsteps clattered on the stairs, and she turned with relief to greet her son because now she'd be too busy to brood about David—or anything else.

A few days after Janice had organized the trip to see Glory at the hospital, she had a conference with Dr. Yolanski. She had already turned in her prospectus for his opinion and/or advice, and although she was careful to appear untroubled, inside she was tense with suspense.

She needn't have worried. Not only did he compliment her on her meticulous research and her restraint in not rushing to any conclusions prematurely, but he also approved of the organization of her material.

He had asked her to come to his office, and after his student typist had served them coffee and returned to her typing, he got down to business.

"I see that you've learned something about structure from Jake," he said. "Well, that kind of outside help is legitimate, as long as it's limited and has nothing to do with the actual writing of your dissertation."

Janice looked at him with surprise. "Jake? He hasn't seen any of this. He's been too busy with his TV class lately."

There was a peculiar look on Dr. Yolanski's face. She would have said he didn't believe her if his next words hadn't been a conciliatory "Well, I see I've made a wrong assumption."

"I am quite good at organization," she said, disappointed that Dr. Yolanski held such chauvinistic ideas about women. "I've worked all my married life until recently, so I know how to use the limited time available to me."

"You've quit your job?"

"I'm taking a leave of absence. The job will be waiting for me when—if I return."

"Then, what's your problem with time?"

"I'm overseeing the restoration of our house. Jake thought— we decided that since I would be home most of the time, this would be a good time to have it done."

Dr. Yolanski began stacking her papers into a neat pile. "Well, I don't think we need have any more discussion about this. You seem to have everything under control. I'm looking forward to seeing the finished paper."

Although his words were cordial, Janice felt uneasy as she left his office. Why was she so sure that despite his complimentary words, Yolanski had reservations about her dissertation?

She didn't get a chance to voice her doubts to Jake when she got home. As soon as she came through the front door, the phone in his den rang. In her hurry to answer it, she barked her shin against a chair that had been left sitting out in the middle of the floor, and her voice was sharp as she said, "Yes?" into the mouthpiece.

"Hey, what gives?" It was Casey's voice. "Someone leave your cake out in the rain last night?"

"Oh, it's you, Casey." Janice's eyes roamed over the clutter on Jake's desk, the welter of newspapers on the floor, and the empty glass sitting on the small serving table near the door. Had Jake had company—no, there was only one glass. So why were there so many cigarette butts in Jake's ashtray when he swore he'd cut down to six a day?

"I've been ringing you all morning, but no one answered. Explain yourself, gal."

"I had an appointment with Dr. Yolanski, but Jake should have answered the phone. Maybe he went out—or he could be down in the basement, sorting through his old sports equipment for Goodwill. He promised to get to it this weekend."

Casey gave a shrill laugh. "That'll be the day!"

"Okay, okay. Your paragon of a husband never hoards old tennis rackets and old golf clubs, right?"

"Wrong. Our garage is packed full of his junk—but he's still nice to have around."

"So what was the urgency of this call?"

"Just wanted to make sure dinner is still on for Sunday. I have to arrange for a baby-sitter. Out here in population-explosion land, that isn't always easy to do."

"It's on. Sunday evening, eight o'clock, casual. We're just having you two and the Turners."

There was a long silence. When Casey spoke, her voice had a flat sound. "Oh? I didn't realize they'd be coming."

"Didn't I mention it—no, I guess it was a last-minute decision. Jake invited them—you don't mind, do you?"

"Not if you don't."

"That's a strange remark."

"What I meant was—the guests you invite to your own house are your business—okay?"

"Okay. Look, I just got home and I'm still wearing my coat. I'll see you Sunday. . . ."

After she hung up, Janice went into the kitchen. To her surprise, Jake was home, after all. He was sitting at the kitchen table, a glass of amber-colored liquid between his elbows. From his flushed face and red-rimmed eyes, he had been drinking heavily—and in the middle of the day, too.

"Want some Scotch?" he said. Before she could answer him, he lurched to his feet and got a highball glass out of the cupboard. His hand was shaking so hard that she took the glass out of his hand. "I'll get it," she said.

"Pour me another one, will you?" he said, his words slurred.

"What's this all about?" she said. "You usually don't drink before six—"

"This is my own home. I'll have a drink when I want it," he said belligerently. His face crumbled suddenly. "Dammit, Janice, I've had a rotten day and I don't need your lecturing."

"Very well." She put the bottle of Scotch down in front of him. "Drink all you want. Just don't complain about hangovers in the morning."

He stared up at her with bleary eyes. "You're mad at me," he said. "You think I'm a weak sister, don't you?"

"I know things get sticky at work sometimes," she said soothingly. "How about coffee instead of Scotch? I can use a cup myself."

"Okay—but put a little brandy in it, will you?"

"Okay," she said agreeably, but as she went to set out cups and heat water, she made a mental note to forget the brandy. "What happened today?"

"Your friend's husband and his dirty politicking is what happened."

"Are you talking about Merv Scranton? I just talked to Casey on the phone and she didn't say anything about—"

"She wouldn't. That mealymouthed, sanctimonious hypocrite. Going behind my back—I don't want him in my house again, you hear? From now on, he's on my shit list."

"Tell me what happened."

"He got himself appointed to that vacant slot on the Arts Council Committee is what happened. Went sucking up to the chairman, and today at the Faculty Club that old mossback Chaney dropped it on me. 'Oh, by the way, we've appointed Scranton to the Arts Council. I know we halfway promised it to you, Morehouse, but—well, your TV project does seem to keep you busy these days.' I almost hit the bastard."

"You didn't say anything, did you?"

"No, I didn't say anything. I was real cool, but I got away from there fast. I came home to tell you about it, but you weren't home—"

"You knew I had an appointment with Dr. Yolanski this morning."

"I forgot." Jake's voice was sulky. "I wondered why the house was so messy. My den looks like a pigsty—"

"I cleaned your den before I left," Janice said, her tone unargumentive because she knew how much Jake had wanted a slot on the prestigious Arts Council.

"Okay, kick a guy when he's down. I don't have to stay here and listen to your shit."

Jake started to get up. A startled look crossed his face as his legs went out from under him. He started to bend at the waist, and a second later, he was stretched out on the floor. As Janice got him back on his feet, helped him upstairs, got him undressed and into bed, she suspended everything, including anger. She was pulling a quilt up over him, when he opened his eyes and gave her a weak smile.

"You're so good to me, Janice," he said.

She didn't answer him, but she bent to kiss his cheek before she drew the blinds against the late afternoon sun and left the room, shutting the door quietly behind her. A thought came to her as she started downstairs. After all these years, she was still cleaning up other people's messes, still playing the good little stepchild.

I never really left home, she thought as she began picking up scattered newspapers from the floor of Jake's den.

CHAPTER TWENTY-NINE

CHANEL WASN'T CERTAIN LATER WHEN HER ATTITUDE TOWARD the job for which William Stetson had hired her became as much a personal challenge as something she was doing for profit.

It wasn't that she'd developed any rapport with his wife; it was just that she'd always had a stubborn streak. Set an obstacle in her path and she was bound and determined to overcome it. And getting the woman from Texas into even the fringes of San Francisco society had swiftly become a challenge of the first order, not because of any particular resistance from the level of society into which she hoped to launch Elsie but because of the woman herself.

No matter what she advised, Stet's wife seemed determined to

thwart her. Since part of the deal was that Elsie not be told Chanel
was in Stet's pay, it seemed incredibly stupid of her to be so
obstructive to someone who she must believe was trying to do her
a favor.

Sometimes, as Chanel tried to talk Elsie out of an unfortunate
choice of clothes, such as wearing a short cocktail dress to a
formal evening affair, or diplomatically tried to teach her some of
the niceties of local behavior such as never, never calling San
Francisco "Frisco," she felt as if she were trying to break through
an impenetrable wall.

If she suggested that Elsie wear the long slenderizing silk shift
that she'd coerced her into buying to the opening of the opera
season, Elsie was sure to turn up in a flashy, too-tight dress that
showed all the flaws of her dumpy figure and made her look like
a pouter pigeon. When an invitation to a totally unacceptable
dinner party came from a social-climbing matron who wasn't
even on the outer fringes of society, Elsie was as delighted as a
child and insisted on going against Chanel's advice. And when
Chanel suggested that Elsie spend a couple of weeks at La Costa
to lose a few pounds and firm up her body, Elsie inexplicably
burst into tears and lumbered out of the room, leaving Chanel
thoroughly nonplussed.

She was finally forced to call Stet at his office to ask for an
appointment although it hurt her pride to have to admit she was
having trouble.

Stet's office, in the financial district, was a surprise. He had
given Chanel the impression that he was semiretired, so she expected something small, not a suite that encompassed a quarter
of the tenth floor of a New Montgomery high-rise. She also hadn't
expected an elegant decor with modern custom-made furniture
and chestnut-paneled walls enlivened with splashes of contemporary paintings.

One particularly vivid painting, showing a desert sunset, framed
Stet's head as he rose from behind a massive teakwood desk and
came forward to shake her head.

"So what's this all about, Chanel?" he said. "My wife giving
you trouble?"

"Either you convince Elsie that I know what I'm doing or it's
all off," she said shortly, out of temper both with his wife and his
amused look. "She is so damned obstinate and scatterbrained.
She forgets hair appointments—and you have no idea what it took
to get Adolfo to take her on as a client! She also refuses to take

my advice on clothes or anything else. She turned up at Madge Blender's luncheon in that tacky—in a summer dress that was totally inappropriate, then told me that since the weather had turned so warm, she didn't want to bother with anything heavier.''

"That makes sense—"

"It isn't *weather* that determines what you wear! This isn't southern California, for God's sake. During the winter season in San Francisco, you wear winter clothes. Period. As it was, she stood out like a sore thumb. Everybody was staring at us—and then she asked Madge Blender how much of her donation would actually buy food for those Native Americans and how much it cost to throw a fancy luncheon like this. You should have seen Madge's face!''

"I'm sorry I missed it." Although Stet's voice was smooth, his eyes were cool and Chanel tempered her next words.

"It isn't that I don't agree with her. I've often thought if they didn't spend so much money on parties for the volunteers, they would have a lot more for charity. But you just don't say that to the chairwoman of the drive, not if you want to be accepted.''

"So what did you do?''

"I covered up for her, of course. I convinced Mrs. Blender that Elsie had a droll sense of humor. But it can't go on. It isn't so bad when you're along, but at these women-only affairs, it's murder.''

"Elsie isn't used to the company of women. Out in the oil fields, she was surrounded by men. That's why she seems so blunt. The important thing is—is she satisfied with her progress so far?''

"Well, as it happens, she is. I'm sure she doesn't realize—'' Chanel broke off. How could she tell Stet that his wife obviously didn't realize she was being patronized most of the time, that she was only acceptable because her husband was a generous contributor to her hostesses' pet charities?

"Elsie doesn't realize that she's only welcome when she brings along her checkbook? No, she wouldn't understand that. She doesn't think that way. Just keep on doing what you're doing— how are your finances these days, Chanel?''

Chanel held her breath. Was he suggesting that he'd be amenable to another advance? Despite her problems with Elsie, she was doing very well financially on the deal.

"There have been a few expenses I hadn't planned on,'' she said with studied casualness.

"Make out a bill and give it to my secretary. I'll see that you get a check—and a preliminary bonus." Stet regarded her closely. "You look a little pale. Getting enough rest?"

"I was out late last night," she admitted. "I didn't get to bed until three."

He whistled through his teeth. "Would you believe that I used to get up at four when I was stockman on a ranch? Elsie always had a hot breakfast waiting for me, too. To this day, I still wake up early. Can't seem to get out of the habit."

A vision of Stet, wearing washed-out Levi's and a cotton flannel shirt, sitting down to eat a huge breakfast of pancakes and eggs and bacon, made Chanel smile.

"Were you out with that Fairmount fellow?" Stet asked.

"As it happens—yes. He took me to a dinner party at the Lloyd Hamiltons."

"That the couple who talk about horses all the time? Must have been pretty boring to a city gal like you."

She started to say no, then didn't because she *had* found the Hamiltons and the other guests boring—and the end of the evening disappointing. By now, she and Laird should have become lovers, but the sum of their lovemaking last night had been a few deep kisses and again, a lot of hard breathing on Laird's part. What was the problem? Respect for her? Or was Laird low on hormones? He certainly wasn't gay, although that was always a possibility in San Francisco.

She realized Stet was watching her, waiting for an answer to his question—and she didn't like the smile on his face. "As a matter of fact, I had a wonderful time," she said loftily.

"You wouldn't josh me, would you? This Laird Fairmount—he always reminds me of one of those overbred racehorses. Great lines, but only good for sprinting. Wouldn't last a week out on the range, doing hard work at a steady pace. Now you—you're built for the long run. Good sturdy stock, the Irish."

Chanel would've loved the luxury of reminding Stet that *he* was the one who was trying to buy his wife's way into the world of the Hamiltons. Instead, she smiled and murmured something about having to dash because she had an appointment.

But after she'd left Stet's office building and was walking toward the underground garage where she'd left her car, her heels clicking angrily on the sidewalk, she had a few thoughts about inconsistency and hypocrisy. What was the reason for Stet's less than flattering comments about Laird? Was it possible that he had designs on her himself? If so, he was in for a surprise. She wasn't some sex-starved divorcée. At present, her sexual needs were being taken care of quite satisfactorily—and discreetly.

Johnny Lister was a tennis pro, twenty-four years old, presentable enough that he sometimes filled in as an extra man at the parties of the members of the Burlingame Country Club, where he worked. He was also great in bed, which was the extent of her interest in him.

So she wasn't about to have an affair with Stet—if that's what he had in mind. It was the quickest way to start the gossip mills grinding—and also to lose his respect. And on second thought, it didn't seem likely that he was interested in her that way. He was very much married, and even if he wanted to play around, he would surely choose someone like his flashy secretary, who had looked her over so thoroughly when she'd ushered her into Stet's office.

Well, if Stet *was* cheating on his wife, it was none of her business. This project had been a godsend. Her bills were paid up; she had a breathing spell as far as her day-to-day expenses were concerned, and if that bonus he'd promised was substantial, she'd end up with a tidy nest egg. Stet's generosity was making it possible for her to keep up her own social life, such as it was. Squiring Elsie around certainly hadn't improved her image, but all that would change once Laird proposed. The important thing was that she was solvent again and Laird was still dating her regularly. So why was he holding back? And what could she do about it?

Chanel finally succeeded in getting Laird into bed in March, six months after they first began dating. She planned it carefully, and for a change, nothing went wrong. They were returning from a quiet dinner at a hilltop restaurant in Sausalito, and when she invited him up for a nightcap, he accepted with what she was sure was eagerness.

With only one lamp burning, the corners of the living room were appropriately shadowed, the music she put on the stereo was romantic but not too obviously so, and the drink she brought Laird was more than generous. As she slipped off her pumps and curled up on the sofa beside him, she let one foot slide under his thigh. For a while, they sipped their drinks, talking amicably about the excellence of their dinner and then about a minor scandal that was brewing in city politics. When Chanel yawned, Laird started to get up, but she put her hand on his arm and told him softly to stay, that she really wasn't sleepy.

He sat back down; casually, he dropped his arm around her shoulders and she let her head drop against his chest.

"It was a wonderful evening," she murmured. "I always have such a good time with you, Laird."

He kissed her then, and she moved closer, pressing her breasts against his chest. He stroked her hair, then let his hand drop to the nape of her neck. She relaxed her full weight against him, giving him silent permission to continue.

His touch as he gently rubbed the skin under her chignon was more exciting then she'd expected, and any suspicions she might've had about his sexual preferences dissolved as he stroked her breast, then ran his hand along her hip, adroitly gathering up the soft material so he could touch the bare flesh of her thigh.

Although she was normally easily aroused and brought to climax without much foreplay, the quickness of her response tonight took her by surprise, and a heady feeling of triumph and sexual tension made her sigh as he kissed her breast through her clothes, which was surprisingly erotic. It was obvious, a few minutes later, when he stood up, facing her, that he was ready for the next step.

"Where should we go?" he asked.

She led the way to the master bedroom that she'd decorated in blue-and-gold to complement her coloring. Her own perfume still lingered in the air as she sank down in the middle of the white fur spread that covered her bed. She knew she was in the hands of an expert when Laird undressed her without awkwardness, the sure sign of an accomplished lover. From his expression, it was obvious that the voluptuousness of her naked body surprised him. Dressed, she gave the appearance of extreme slenderness because of her small bones and finely tuned body. Naked, she was all woman—something she'd exploited all her adult life.

Laird, too, she soon discovered, was a contradiction. In his perfectly tailored clothing, he looked elegant, even a little effete. Naked, his lean body was taut, virile, masculine. It was a bonus she hadn't expected, just as she hadn't expected that he would be such a skillful lover. As he led her through the preliminaries of foreplay, she was so aroused that she had to hold back so as not to get too caught up in their lovemaking. After all, the idea was to fully satisfy Laird's needs, which was why she forced herself to think of mundane things as Laird caressed her, as she fondled him in turn, doing the things she knew no man could resist.

But the strength of her own response defeated her. She reached a point, in fact, when Laird's leisurely stroking was too slow, and despite herself, her back arched and she clawed his back in a spasm of frustration. Laird entered her fully, then pressed her thighs together, adding a new dimension of sensation to the friction of his strokes, and sending her completely over the edge.

She climaxed, her whole body pulsating, but still he moved against her, inside her, and another climax shook her, surprising her with its strength. When he stiffened, when she felt his own spasmodic release, she pulled him closer, still greedy for more. He laughed softly and stroked her with his hand, extending her pleasure in a series of small explosions that gradually diminished.

Finally satisfied, she curled up against him. "Hmmm . . ." she murmured, too debilitated to speak.

"Hmmm is right," he said, his mouth against her breast. "That was wonderful. *You* are wonderful."

"Then, why haven't you made love to me before?" she asked, stroking his chest hair, which was very soft, very thick. Like tambourine mink, she thought and then smiled because the simile was so appropriate for Laird Fairmount.

"Because I had another commitment," Laird said. "I don't go in for multiple lovers."

"Had?" she said, snatching at the word.

"Had. It's over now—as much to her relief as mine, I'm sure."

"I don't believe that. No woman would give you up willingly."

He gave her a final kiss and then sat up. "Thank you for those kind words. But I'm not a Don Juan. In fact, a lot of women find me a pretty dull fellow."

"They're fools," she said, her voice flat. "You're—let's say that right now, I feel so good I could purr like a kitten."

"Then, stay right where you are so I can remember you curled up in the middle of your big white bed, all pouty lips and sleepy eyes."

"Do you have to go?"

"I do. I'll call you in the morning—late morning—and if you're free tomorrow night, how about having dinner with me at my place? Just the two of us—no parties or gallery openings or charity bashes."

She smiled up at him. God, it was working out even better than she'd planned. . . . "I'll be expecting that call—and I'd love to have dinner with you at your place."

"It's Mary and Robert's night off, so I'll do the cooking honors this time. I'm quite an accomplished chef, you know." He bent and kissed her and then was gone.

Chanel rolled over on her back and flung her arms out in an exultant gesture. She had done it, landed the biggest catch around—well, *almost* landed him. All that remained was an official proposal—which was just a formality now. Laird was smitten with her. He'd had a taste of what he could expect if he married her. One more night of lovemaking and he would be eating out of her hand.

Chanel raised her left hand and contemplated the pearl ring on her third finger. Soon there would be a diamond—a really spectacular one—on that finger. Tomorrow evening she would hold her own needs in check and initiate some moves that would make Laird believe that he had died and gone to Valhalla. And in a short while she would be Mrs. Laird Fairmount. She might even insist on a June wedding, like all the little virgin brides did.

And wait until those bitches out in Hillsborough heard the news. It would knock them right out of their three-hundred-dollar Delman pumps. It was going to be a blast, being forgiving and gracious to their faces—and cutting them down to size behind their backs whenever she got the chance. Well, they deserved it. They had put her through hell at the first and last time in her life when she'd been truly vulnerable. Now it was her turn—and she was going to enjoy every last moment of it.

Chanel fell asleep with a smile on her face, and the next evening, after a long, leisurely bout of lovemaking that tested all her skill and expertise, an exhausted Laird proposed. It was, Chanel thought later, a peculiarly cold-blooded proposal, considering what had just gone on between them, but she had no complaints. A proposal was a proposal was a proposal—but because she never took chances if she could help it, she changed her mind about a June wedding and opted for late May instead.

It never was wise to give a man too much time to think.

CHAPTER THIRTY

FERN LAID HER PLANS CAREFULLY. IT PLEASED SOME MACHIA-vellian turn of her mind to picture herself as a spider, weaving a web to catch a particularly juicy fly. Not that Laird Fairmount was a helpless fly. Like so many of the very rich people she'd known, he had the superb confidence of a winner. Apart from his inherited wealth, he was also a very successful businessman in his own right, which meant he wouldn't be all that easy to fool. On the other hand, she'd learned a lot about psyching out males in her short life—and she'd also done her homework on Laird.

Not only was he loaded, but he had a social conscience, an inconvenient trait for someone in his position. Once she, the seventeen-year-old daughter of his lover, lured him into bed, she was sure she could bring the rest of it off. After all, she'd been turning boys on since she was thirteen—why would Laird Fairmount be any harder to handle, just because he was older?

And what an awesome catch for someone who intended to live in total luxury for the rest of her life! Even without the revenge angle—and how good it was going to be, paying Chanel back for her neglect, her indifference!—she would have gone all out to snare him.

Part of her plan depended upon getting back into Chanel's good graces, of course, so she'd be welcome to come home weekends. Knowing she had years of hostility to overcome, she moved carefully to court her mother's favor.

It wasn't easy. "Never try to kid a kidder" was one of her mother's favorite homilies, and it certainly applied to Chanel. She was a first-class manipulator who recognized the same tactics in others. At first, she merely tolerated Fern when she came home for weekends, but gradually, when Fern jumped in to help with the cooking, the cleaning, the other domestic chores that Chanel detested, her weekend presence was not only accepted but expected.

On the nights when Laird came to take Chanel out, Fern was very careful to treat him in a friendly but nonprovocative manner. She was also careful how she dressed. Nothing obviously sexy, but her jeans were always skintight, her sweaters, which looked so casual, she wore without a bra—and she didn't bother with panties, either. Her makeup was a masterpiece. Before Laird came to collect Chanel, Fern locked herself in her room and made herself up to look all pink cheeks and lips, a schoolgirl on the verge of womanhood that Chanel had once told her was such a turn-on to men of a certain age.

That Laird liked her was obvious. He teased her about her boyfriends, paid her extravagant compliments, and it was all so casual that she knew he really didn't see her as a woman—not yet.

It did surprise her a little, now that the hostility between she and her mother was no longer overt, what good company Chanel could be. She had a sly, ironic sense of humor that made Fern laugh, could talk for hours about "woman things" without being bored—and she never made the mistake of trying to regress to her daughter's age level or use the current teenager buzzwords, something Fern detested in older people.

To her surprise, Chanel seemed really interested when Fern related a censored account of her treatment from the snobs at Burlingame Academy. She even loosened up and told how she'd been an "out" among a whole schoolful of "ins" at the same place. For a few moments, Fern actually felt empathy with her mother.

But when she found herself thinking of Chanel as an ally instead of an enemy, she drew back. Chanel was clever with people. She knew how to manipulate them, but that pet phrase of hers about not trying to kid a kidder worked both ways. For all her sins, her mother deserved to lose Laird to a more clever woman—to her own daughter, in fact. How delicious to do it following Chanel's advice about marrying rich!

Then, just when Fern was ready to make the next move, Chanel threw her a curve and announced that Laird had proposed. The engagement would be formally announced at the annual party that Laird gave every April for his friends. They would marry a month later, and then go off on their honeymoon.

"I don't have any idea where we'll go," Chanel added. "Laird is a closet romantic. He insists on surprising me. I'm hoping for the best—such as Paris during the spring showings. I just hope he isn't planning on taking a romantic cruise on that smelly old boat of his.''

Fern found it hard to conceal her dismay. An engagement was far different from a casual affair. Was she too late? If she decided to go on with her plan, she would have to move fast. Of course, the fact that the engagement was still secret might help—or maybe not. Since Laird had committed himself to Chanel, it wouldn't be easy, winning him away. For one thing, he considered himself an honorable man—whatever the hell that meant.

On the other hand, Laird was vulnerable for the very reason that he did have pretensions of honor. How many times had Chanel said that Laird was a gentleman, all the way from his toes to his capped teeth?

Which was how she'd trap him. His sense of duty would work against him. Once he had compromised her, a seventeen-year-old high school girl, he would have to deal with his own conscience. If she played her cards right, gave him a sexual encounter like nothing he'd ever experienced before, she was sure he would fall right into line.

And that part shouldn't be too difficult. Chanel had been around, of course, and undoubtedly knew all the tricks, but what kind of competition, at thirty-four, could she be to a seventeen-year-old? So all it took was careful planning—and timing. And when she had Laird where she wanted him, she wouldn't be stupid like Chanel. She'd get him to Reno or Vegas as quickly as possible. No short engagement or society weddings for her.

The next weekend, Fern put her plan into motion. The first problem was place. To have her plan work, she had to get Laird alone. And that wouldn't be easy, because he lived in one of those houses on Marina Boulevard, probably with all kinds of live-in domestic help.

As it turned out, this was a minor problem. It wasn't too hard to find out from Chanel that Laird's domestic couple lived in their own cottage in the rear. Which simplified things greatly.

She chose a Monday, reasoning that most people stayed home that evening. To make sure that Laird was home, she dialed his number and when he answered the phone, she hung up, having learned a crucial fact. The second crucial fact, that he would be alone, she would have to take on faith.

The senior dorm hummed around her. She locked herself in her room so she wouldn't be disturbed. Not that she got many visitors these days, but there was always the occasional dorm mate who wanted to borrow something—or relay a bit of gossip. She had already decided what she would wear—a white silk blouse, ripped down the side to reveal a tantalizing peek of her breast, a skirt with an artfully split seam that showed a lot of thigh. Over this, she put on a full-length all-weather coat for concealment. The coat was a little too warm for Burlingame, with its valley climate, but just right for San Francisco's night winds and winter fogs. After long thought, she used pale beige makeup to give her skin a pallor and lined her eyes skillfully in black, but she left off blush and lipstick. When she was finished, she was well satisfied that she looked like a girl who'd just been through a very bad experience.

It was almost ten when she reached the marina district. She parked her compact on a side street and hurried along Marina Boulevard so she'd be out of breath when she arrived at Laird's doorstep. To her satisfaction only one light was burning in a downstairs window as she ran up the stone front steps. What if his housekeeper opened the door? What if he was entertaining someone? Well, she'd just have to play that part by ear.

She rang the bell, rang it again. A couple of minutes later, when the door swung open, she was slumped against the doorjamb, trying to look completely beat.

"What the hell . . . What are *you* doing here, Fern?" Laird said, and he didn't sound particularly friendly.

"I—I'm in a jam and I didn't know who else to turn to." Fern didn't have to pretend the break in her voice. For all her bravado, she was really nervous. "I went out with this guy from school on his father's boat"—she gestured toward the marina—"and he tried to—he tried to—"

She let her coat fall open so he could see her torn shirt and ripped skirt. "I pretended to be seasick, hoping he'd leave me alone, but he kept coming on to me. I finally told him that I was willing to—to do it, only it would have to be on solid ground. So he turned the boat around, and as soon as we reached the dock, I jumped off and—well, I just ran as fast as I could. But I had to leave my purse behind and I don't have any money and—it was really terrible! He was always so cool at school. I never heard any gossip about him—" She stopped to take a long, shuddering breath.

"Why didn't you call the police?"

"Oh, I couldn't! Chanel would kill me. You know how she is—

she'd cover up a murder rather than cause gossip. And besides, I didn't have any money for a phone.''

"You could have called from the harbormaster's office.''

"I didn't know that—and besides I don't want anyone to see me looking like this. I'm not supposed to date on school nights. Chanel will cut off my allowance if she finds out. So when I remembered that you live here on Marina, I thought surely you'd help me—''

She dug her fist into her eyes, then let her hands drop away so he could see her tears. She expected him to put his arms around her to comfort her, but instead, he asked, "What is this, Fern? Some kind of joke?''

She hadn't expected that. In fact, nothing was working out the way she'd expected. Here she was, her clothes all torn and obviously in distress, and he was asking if it was a joke. The bastard—well, she had a few more tricks up her sleeve.

She managed a realistic sob. "I don't know what you mean,'' she said. "Surely you don't think I led him on. It wasn't that way at all. I—I thought he was nice. I never dreamed he'd come on so strong—''

She shuddered violently and edged closer, so close that she knew he could smell her perfume. When he didn't move away, she closed her eyes, swaying, then fell against him as if she'd lost control of her legs. With a gasp, she locked her hands behind his neck and clung to him tightly. His body began to tremble, and she felt a rush of triumph. It was working—God, how easy it was to fool men because of their filthy penises. . . .

And then, incredibly, Laird was pushing her away. She opened her eyes and saw that what she'd thought was passion was amusement. He was laughing—the bastard was laughing at her. . . .

Thoroughly humiliated, she whirled to leave, but the door was shut and she couldn't seem to get it open. Laird swung her around to face him, and she saw that he had stopped laughing.

"Listen, Fern, I'm sorry. I wasn't laughing at you. I was laughing at myself. When I was about your age, this really sexy English teacher had my glands going full blast. If I told you some of the schemes I concocted to get into her bed—well, you'd understand why I couldn't help laughing. Look, why don't you go upstairs and wash that artistic makeup job off your face, and then I'll walk you to your car and we'll forget the whole thing. You're going to be living here with your mother and me in a few weeks, so let's make it easy on each other by pretending this never happened. Is it a deal?''

The kindness in his voice made her want to throw up. She had never hated anyone so much before—and she'd hated a lot of people in her life. She wanted to claw his eyes out, rake his face with her fingernails, but despite her anger, she knew that would be a mistake.

''You're a bastard, just like I suspected all along,'' she said, hitting him with words instead of her fists. ''You think you're so smart, do you? Well, wait until Chanel gets her claws in you. You won't know what hit you. You're just another poor fish who landed in her net. You don't believe me? Then, wait until after you're married—and I hope she swallows you whole, you—you self-righteous geek!''

She didn't wait for his response. When he reached out to touch her, she slapped his hand away and twirled around. This time she got the door open, rushed through, leaving it open behind her. Her last glimpse of Laird before she went storming down the street was the look of pity on his face.

The drive from the Marina to Pacific Heights took only fifteen minutes, but it was long enough for Fern to plot her revenge. It was too late, of course, to salvage her original plan because she'd misjudged Laird completely. He had seen through her act—how had she given herself away? It had been such a good plan. It should have worked. Well, she was going to fix Laird's wagon, but good. No one laughed at her and got away with it. And while she was at it, she would settle her old score with Chanel, too.

Chanel was still up, curled up on a living room sofa with a copy of *Profile* magazine when Fern came flying through the door. She was shaking with rage, and this time, she didn't have to fake her tears.

''What on earth happened to you? My God—you haven't been mugged, have you?'' Chanel demanded.

''It's that animal you're engaged to,'' Fern said, her voice shrill. She let her coat slip to the floor so Chanel could see the rip in her blouse. ''Look what he did—he tried to tear my clothes off!''

''Who are you talking about? Surely, you don't mean—''

''I'm talking about Laird! I cut my afternoon classes so I could shop for a dress to wear to your engagement party. I wanted you to be proud of me.'' She began to cry again, almost believing her own story. ''I was coming out of that boutique in the lobby of the

Mark Hopkins when I ran into Laird and he asked me to have dinner with him. To get acquainted, he said. It sounded like fun—how could I know what kind of man he is? So we had dinner at this really cool place on Bush, and then he invited me to see his house because, he said, I must be curious about where I'd be living soon. We had some wine and then some brandy. I only drank a little, but he was really pouring it down. Then—then he was all over me. It was all I could do to get away from him.''

It seemed the appropriate time for more tears, so she covered her face with her hands. ''He said it would be good, that I'd enjoy it, that he'd make sure my allowance was more than generous after you two were married. It would be our little secret, he said.''

She started to sob, so it was a while before she realized that Chanel hadn't said a word. When she peeked out between her fingers, she saw that Chanel was staring at her, her face a mixture of emotions.

Fern gave a shuddering sigh and let her hands drop away from her face. ''The worst part was when he stuffed some money in my purse and told me that there was more where that came from,'' she wailed. ''I hate him! You can't marry him—you just can't! I'd be afraid to be in the same house with him.''

Chanel moved then. She sat down beside Fern and took her hand. It was so rare for Chanel to touch her, that Fern jumped nervously.

''Listen to me, Fern. I don't know why you've concocted this—this fantasy, but I do know it's a pack of lies. There're a dozen holes in your story. The thing that puzzles me is why you'd want to cut your own throat. When I marry Laird, you'll benefit enormously. His connections are impeccable—you'll get your Cotillion debut next year, if you like, and you can go to any college in the country, regardless of the cost. You'll associate with kids from the best families, and you can marry well, have the life you want. But if you try anything like this again, the gravy train will stop for you. Do you understand me? It will all *stop*. So no more of these stupid lies. Either you behave or you can clear out right now. I won't have you messing up my life just because you want to play games.''

Fern met her mother's eyes. How cold they were—how penetrating, as if Chanel could see deep into her brain. She had failed—that was obvious—and the desire to hurt Chanel, hurt her the way she'd been hurt so many times in her life, was so overwhelming that she lost all control.

She jerked her hand away and jumped to her feet. "You hate me," she stormed. "You've always hated me. How do you think I feel, knowing my own mother would have aborted me if it hadn't been for her father, that she's resented me all my life?"

Chanel sighed deeply; briefly, she looked years older than her thirty-four years. "I don't hate you. For God's sake, use your head! Okay, your father was a liar, a con artist, but you're *my* daughter, too. You're also Tincan O'Hara's granddaughter, something you should be proud of. I've done my best for you, but I'm not going to let you rain on my parade. So back off, Fern. Go to your room, take off those ridiculous clothes, go to bed, and sleep it off. I don't know what your problem is, and I don't really care. From now on, you're going to behave yourself or so help me, I'll toss you out in the street."

Fern had never hated her mother as much as she did at that moment, but she felt something else, too, something that surprised her. Chanel had seen through her, just as Laird had—and she couldn't help feeling a grudging respect for both of them.

"Very well," she said with as much dignity as she could dredge up. "You've won—for now."

She paused briefly, half expecting Chanel to say something more, but her mother only looked at her, silent now. She started for the door, and just before she left the room, she glanced back. If it hadn't been ridiculous, she would have been sure she saw tears in Chanel's eyes.

CHAPTER THIRTY-ONE

GLORY WAS MOVING IN TIME WITH THE MUSIC, A SOFT ROCK PIECE that had become a standard for her Queens aerobics class. The women facing her, who came in all ages with shapes that varied from heavyset to grossly obese, were emulating her, more or less accurately, and certainly with unflagging enthusiasm.

The room was humid despite the hardworking air conditioner, and as she watched them groaning and suffering, their faces glistening with sweat, but all of them still managing to maintain their good humor, a wave of affection made her smile. The affection wasn't for anyone in particular, but for the group as a whole. They were her "Queens," her special charges, a class composed entirely of the vastly overweight, an innovation she herself had initiated.

The idea had come to her when she'd taken a phone call at the switchboard two weeks after she'd started working at the club. She had still been in training and was filling in at the switchboard while the regular operator had lunch. The woman on the line identified herself as Mrs. Robert Morrison, then asked a question about fees. Glory caught the desperation in her voice, and a careful probing elicited the information that Mrs. Morrison, who described herself as being "a real blimp," wanted to take an aerobics class but was intimidated by all the trim women she'd seen at the Golden Gate Health Club during a visit there with a friend.

Glory took the woman's phone number and then told her that she would be in touch with her about a new program that was in consideration at the club. During the conversation, it had occurred to her that there'd been a pattern in Claire's class of very large women signing up and then, after one or two sessions, dropping out, even though the enrollment fee for club membership was nonrefundable. She'd chalked it up to loss of interest or, more likely, Claire's bullying and snide remarks, but maybe it had been something else—the intimidation a very heavy woman must feel, exercising beside women with already trim bodies.

That afternoon, she sought out Steve Golden in his office.

"I think you're missing a bet here," she said. She'd maintained a businesslike attitude toward Steve since she'd come to work at the club. Part of it was her belief that it was always wise to stay on impersonal terms with one's boss, but there was also another reason for her coolness. It would be so easy to drift into a relationship with Steve—and a jock was a jock, even if he wasn't working at it now that he was managing the club.

So her voice was brisk as she told Steve, "There're a lot of women who would join up in a minute if they didn't have to exercise with a bunch of skinny women."

"Thin—or slender," he said, grinning. "We never call our clients skinny, Ms. Browne."

"So suppose we start a class for really big ladies?" she said, ignoring the interruption. "No skinnies or even near-skinnies allowed. We could even set some kind of standard, such as being fifty percent heavier than their ideal weight. The pace would be slower, the exercises and dancing less strenuous, and a medical exam beforehand would be a requirement. It would be held at a time when the club was closed to everybody else, so no one could gawk at them. Early in the morning, say—or better still, after the club closes. No gawkers allowed—not even other instructors. Just me and my ladies. I even have a name for it—the Queens Class. What do you think?''

"I think you're wonderful," Steve said softly.

She bristled immediately. "Are you or are you not going to take this seriously?''

Steve's face became suspiciously grave. "Okay, I'm listening—and you should know, going in, that I think your idea is a winner.''

The next day, she called Mrs. Morrison and told her the club was beginning a class for queen-size women. It would be held three times a week, starting fifteen minutes after the club closed to other customers, and there would be no audience, no spectators, not even other employees of the club, just the instructor and the ladies of the class. The pace would be realistic, and those who joined would be expected to be supportive toward one another.

"No fang and claw stuff," she said. "Who needs it?''

Mrs. Morrison signed up on the dot, not even waiting to find out what the fees would be. What's more, she recommended several friends for the class, and three days later, it started with seven women. Now, three weeks and nine sessions later, the class consisted of seventeen women, and the calls were still coming in from others eager to join. Like an underground movement, it was reaching its audience—and this despite the fact that Steve had agreed there would be no promotions or publicity of any kind except word of mouth.

Because it was her baby, Glory loved the class. She used gentle persuasion instead of bullying or ridicule to keep the women on course. She reasoned that since she was dealing with the walking wounded, her choice of music should be as unorthodox as the class itself—all upbeat soft rock with a few bouncy pop songs thrown in during the warming-up period.

The only competition between the women was in weight loss, and from the way some of them were dropping pounds, even after only a few sessions, she knew that they would eventually become ineligible for the class. Maybe there should be some sort of ceremony when one reached her ideal weight? And maybe the club could start another class for graduates of the Queens Class. She'd talk it over with Steve.

As she stepped up the pace and began the aerobics phase of the session, keeping her patter light, and clowning a little to make them laugh, she reflected how drastically her own feelings had changed this past month. She had expected the class to be a success, of course. It was a natural, one of those ideas that had the fine scent of success from the beginning.

So originally the class for queen-size women had simply been a calculated effort on her part to further her own ambitions. What she *hadn't* expected was to become a sort of surrogate mother hen to a group of older women—and to enjoy it immensely. In fact, their gratitude, the way they hung on her every word, touched a part of herself that had always remained aloof from other women.

The suspicion that a few months earlier she probably wouldn't have been able to handle this puzzled her. When had she, after a lifetime of being wary of other females, begun to not only trust them—to a limited degree—but to enjoy their company? Had it happened in the hospital while she was opening those gifts the support group had brought her? Or had the change come earlier? Maybe just belonging to a support group had turned her around without her realizing it.

Which brought up another question: Wasn't it dangerous to let down her guard, even a little?

After class, when she came out of the women's shower room, Steve Golden was waiting for her in the hall. "I was tempted to join you in there—but I didn't want to shock the pony brigade," he said.

"Don't call my ladies that!" she said sharply.

Steve looked amused. "Sorry. I wasn't thinking. You're pretty fond of them, aren't you?"

"They're okay."

"Maybe they aren't as sensitive as you think. I heard one of them joke about the floor caving in while they were doing jumping jacks a few minutes ago. And everybody laughed."

"They can laugh about themselves to one another. Not to outsiders. What they don't need is some smart ass male making fun of them."

"I said I was sorry—how does it happen that you're always so defensive about those women, Glory? I'll bet you've never weighed more than a hundred and ten pounds in your life—if that."

"Look, I don't have to explain anything to you. If I did, I'd tell you that having bright red hair that frizzles if it even gets near a water faucet is a lot like being too fat. And having a name like Morn—" She broke off, chagrined at her own loose tongue. "And I'm tired. I'm going home, fix myself a cup of cocoa, and then I'm going to bed. I'll be seeing you."

"So how about having that cup of cocoa with me? I want to talk to you. Strictly business."

Although she could have pointed out that they could talk business right there in the hall or in his office, she was too tired to argue. The coolness between them, all of it on her part, was beginning to get her down. Maybe it was time to loosen up with Steve. By now, he should realize that there wasn't a chance that things between them would develop into a relationship.

A little to her surprise, Steve did have something to discuss. As they sipped hot chocolate in the small café across the street from the club, he got right to the point.

"When do you want to start your martial art lessons?"

"Right away," she said without hesitation.

"Like tonight?"

"Of course not. Tomorrow will be soon enough."

"Okay. Come to work an hour early. We'll use the judo room. No one will bother us there. But first, I have this speech I always make. You want it now or in the morning?"

"Speech?"

"About martial arts. And street smarts. They go together."

She gave him a scornful look. "What could you possibly teach *me* about street smarts? I grew up in the Tenderloin. Hell, I could write a book about it. Where were *you* raised? It wasn't in the slums, that's for sure."

"I wasn't raised in an inner city, no. But I worked at a shelter in the Bronx during college vacations for three years while I was going through my social conscience phase. I kept my eyes and ears open—I know the problems."

"Inner city—that's just a fancy name for garbage heap. And working there isn't like living there. At the end of the day, you could walk away and go back to your nice safe suburb—or whatever. You couldn't possibly know what it's like to live in a condemned building with no utilities, no garbage collection, no locks on the doors. I learned how to survive the hard way. Never play in the halls alone. Never walk near the mouth of an alley. Stay away from friendly strangers who ask you directions or want to give you gum. And never, never get careless. So what can you teach me about street smarts?''

"How to defend yourself from a mugger. How to recognize trouble before it starts. To never trust a rapist who says he won't hurt you if you cooperate. It isn't sex that motivates a rapist. It's hatred—of women, of the world, of themselves. And a helpless and submissive woman brings out the sadist in this kind of creep.''

"I know all that," she said scornfully. "I don't need your lecture. What I want from you is the right moves. How to throw a guy to the ground. How to take him out with a kick in the balls—''

"How to get yourself killed.''

"Are you telling me not to fight back?'' she demanded.

"I'm saying that it's mainly a matter of attitude, of prevention. Victims radiate their vulnerability—''

"Oh, come on! Can you see *me* looking vulnerable?''

"No," he admitted, grinning. "Any sensible mugger would run like hell if he saw you taking a stroll alone through Golden Gate Park late at night.''

"Look, I'm tired. If you're going to sit there making cracks, I'm going home.''

His smile vanished. "I was trying to get a point across. You've already been a victim once. Since you refused to press charges against that gorilla, he's still out there on the streets. And if he comes at you again, it's unlikely you could fight him off, even if you had a black belt in karate. One on one, a man who is twice your size is going to take you down. What you *can* learn is how not to be caught by surprise, how to escape if you do get cornered. That kind of knowledge could save your life someday.''

Glory nodded grudgingly. "Okay, I'll buy that. So teach me those things. Starting tomorrow.''

When they left the warmth of the café and went outside, the night air made Glory shiver. She took a deep breath, enjoying the saline taste of the wind. Both of them were silent as they walked toward the club's parking lot. Rather than start another argument, she had agreed to let Steve drive her home with a mental note that she wasn't about to invite him inside once they got there.

"Your first lesson starts right now," he said. "Eventually, you are going to buy a car, right?''

"When I can afford it.''

"If you already had one, where would you park it?''

"In the club lot, of course.''

"Where in the lot?"

"Wherever there's an empty space. What do you think I am—stupid?"

"Not stupid. Just not thinking clearly."

"So? Where should I park it?"

"You come to work during the day, but on nights when you have your Queens class you go home after dark. So park it as close to a light post as you can, one near the entrance of the club if possible. Muggers like the dark and hate the light. And try to stay with other people when you leave the club—or any other place, such as the supermarket. Have your key ready in your hand, and be alert as you approach the car. Stand back and check under it, too. Sometimes muggers spot you when you get out of the car alone and then they hide beneath and grab your feet when you return with your arms full of groceries. If you are attacked, drop your packages immediately and run—and never linger around the car. After you've checked under the car and in the backseat, get in quickly and lock the door behind you."

"Look, all that is just common sense—"

"That's what self-defense is all about. Calculated common sense. Not taking chances."

She shook her head. "I don't intend to go around being afraid all the time. What kind of life is that?"

"Learning the rules until they're second nature isn't being afraid. It's being smart."

"Okay, so I learn all the rules. None of this would've helped when Buddy attacked me. But if I'd known some defensive tactics, I could've got away."

"Maybe. The trick is to always be alert, to expect a few surprises. Then you have time to put yourself in a better position. From what you told me, he got a stranglehold on your throat from behind. If you had turned your head as soon as he started choking you, he wouldn't have cut off your air and you could have screamed."

"What else could I have done?"

"Stomped down as hard as you could on his foot. Not his toes—on his instep. It takes very little weight to crush an instep. Used your teeth. Bit his arm or any part of him you could reach."

"I did. I almost bit a piece out of his hand, but it was too late by then," she said.

"Lucky for you that you managed to scream, too. A scream is a great weapon, but don't rely on it alone. People don't investigate

screams these days—and with good reason. So if you're attacked—say, in the parking lot at the supermarket—try to hurt
him enough to make him let you go, then swing around so you're
facing him and use your car keys to slash his eyes. Remember,
you should have them ready in your hand when you approach your
car. And really go for his eyes—no squeamishness. Remember
what he'd do to you if he got the chance. If you can manage it, a
knee to his groin will paralyze him briefly—long enough so you
can get away. Don't try to *kick* him in the groin. It's too easy for
him to grab your foot and throw you to the ground. And remember—always run if you get the chance. Don't stay around to fight
him if you can get away. Run and scream—yell 'Fire' instead of
'Help.' People are much more apt to come running if you yell
'Fire.' And it might scare him enough so he'll take off in the
opposite direction.''

Glory digested this a moment. ''Where did you learn all this?''

''I took lessons from the Guardian Angels while I was in New
York. The shelter where I worked was for battered women. Since
I sometimes had to deal with violent husbands, I figured I should
learn how to survive.''

''And you really did go to—where was it? Harvard?''

''Yale.''

''You aren't rich or something, are you?''

''I live on my salary, just like any other working stiff.''

She regarded him thoughtfully. ''Okay,'' she said finally. ''All
you've said makes sense. So teach me what I need to know. I
don't ever want to be a victim again.''

They had reached his car, a dark blue Porsche. As he opened
the door for her, she noted that it was parked directly under a
light post. Briefly, she gave him directions and then leaned back
against the seat, enjoying the feel and smell of real leather. Despite herself, she was impressed. She wouldn't have guessed that
the salary he made at the club, even though he was manager now,
was enough to cover a Porsche. And this was a new one. Maybe
she was missing a bet here—no, that was stupid! Okay, he'd been
real nice, coming to see her at the hospital twice, and bringing
her flowers both times, then giving her a job. Even though she
liked him—no, to be honest, it was a lot more than that—anything
personal was out. She'd learned her lesson. After all, she'd had
great sex with Buddy, at least at first, and look what had happened.

So when Steve offered to check out her apartment for her, she said, "No, thank you. See you in the morning," and was out of the car before he could get his own door open.

When she turned on the lights, she made her own quick search. Her bedroom was no longer bare because she'd bought a bookcase at the Goodwill, and already there was a whole row of paperbacks, mostly mystery and suspense, and even a few hardcover books that she'd bought at the same thrift shop.

She'd also found a lamp she liked. It was brass, and after she'd rubbed the tarnish off, very handsome. Because she didn't have a lamp table, it was sitting on the stacked set of luggage she'd taken when she left Buddy.

As she looked in the closet, it came to her that Steve would find the apartment pretty grubby. He probably lived in one of those jazzy singles places that had a Jacuzzi and a hot tub. Not that she cared what he thought. She'd get around to buying more furniture when she had the money—and not before. The next item on her list was a comfortable easy chair, a place where she could read or listen to the radio instead of piling up on the mattress all the time.

When she'd come home from the hospital, the Santorinis had made a big fuss over her. Mrs. Santorini had offered to lend her a few pieces of furniture until she got her own, even though the flat rented unfurnished. Glory had turned the offer down because she was already so indebted to Mr. Santorini for rescuing her from Buddy. To be further obligated would have made her even more uncomfortable. In fact, she found it difficult to talk to Mr. Santorini at all. Not that he invited her gratitude. "Put it out of your mind," he'd said when she'd tried to thank him.

The phone rang as she was hanging up her coat.

"Glory?" a familiar voice said when she put the receiver to her ear.

It was a few seconds before she answered. "I don't want to talk to you, Buddy."

"Look, don't hang up on me. I called to tell you that—well, I'm moving to Detroit tomorrow. I'm going to stay with my uncle—you know, the one who's a cop? He's going to try to get me on the police force there. Sort of a new start—you know what I mean? I'm sorry as hell about what happened. I was crazy drunk that night or I never would've done that to you. I still love you, Glory, even though things went sour between us. I don't expect you to forgive me, but I want you to know how sorry I am. I borrowed money from my dad to settle up your hospital bills like I promised. You'll get the paperwork in a couple days. I wanted you to know that, even if it doesn't make up for what I did to you.''

He paused, as if expecting an answer. When Glory was silent, he went on, speaking quickly as if he were afraid she'd hang up before he had finished. ''It was decent of you not to file charges against me. With a felony on my record, it would've killed my chances to get on the Detroit PD. God knows I deserved to go to jail, beating up on you like that—''

Glory finally found her voice. ''I agree,'' she said tartly, ''but I'm willing to put it out of my mind. Good luck on your move to Detroit.''

She got rid of him as soon as possible. How strange that she was no longer afraid of him. Maybe that was because her worst fears had come true—and she'd survived. If Mr. Santorini hadn't intervened, would Buddy have killed her that night? That was something she would never know. And was she a fool to take him at his word, to believe that he was moving away, that he had changed? Probably—she could always call his folks and find out if it was true. . . .

No, crazy as it seemed after what he'd done to her, she believed him. There had been a ring of truth in his voice—and Buddy had never been any good at lying. Better to put the whole business out of her mind—and get on with her life.

Glory started her martial arts training, what Steve called self-defense techniques, the next morning. Despite the necessary body contact when he was demonstrating the elementary moves of self-defense, he was impersonal, totally professional, and while Glory welcomed this intellectually, she found herself missing his former warmth and even his amusement at her expense. Once, she started to tell him to loosen up a little, but stopped in time. After all, she didn't want to encourage him, did she?

It was after their fifth lesson that he asked her out to dinner again. She was tempted—after all, she had that cool cocktail dress she hadn't yet had an occasion to wear—but in the end, she said no.

He didn't ask her again.

When Steve Golden first decided to settle in San Francisco, it was directly after a blowup to end all blowups with his father, who owned, along with a dozen other business operations, the Golden Gate Health Club franchise chain. Most of his life, being a person who didn't seek out controversy for its own sake, Steve had gone along with his father's high expectations for him—and also his high-handedness. But this time, Earl Golden had gone too far.

Not only had he tossed the same old recriminations at Steve, but he'd practically dared him to make something out of himself on his own. It wasn't a matter of money. Steve's maternal grandmother, who had doted on her only grandchild, had left Steve enough stocks and bonds and treasury notes that he could have retired at twenty-one if he'd so desired, and lived like a prince on the income from his inheritance, something that rankled his father no end.

Earl Golden would have loved, Steve knew, to have held all the cards, to be able to hold the threat of disinheritance as a sword over his son's head. When, following his graduation from Yale, Steve had decided to spend a year bumming around Europe instead of going directly to work in his father's New York offices, the old man's temper had really exploded. One of the lesser things he'd thrown at Steve was the accusation that his grandmother's legacy had ruined him, that his indolence stemmed from the knowledge that he didn't have to work and could be a lazy bum all his life if he wanted.

Steve, his usually even temper flaring, had pointed out that being a workaholic and devoting your life to piling up more and more money to the detriment of a good family life was far worse than wanting a little slack time before you joined the rat race—and the family business.

And when his father's threats and arguments and cold rage failed to move Steve, when he went off to Europe anyway—and had one hell of a good time—Earl Golden had disowned him on his return, declaring that he no longer had a son.

Steve had taken it harder than he would've thought possible. All his life, he had lived in the shadow of his father, who had ambitions for him that Steve was well aware he was never going to fulfill. To succeed in the world of big business took tunnel vision and a special kind of ruthlessness, and he knew he didn't have those particular qualifications, even if he was the son of the man the newspapers called The Franchise King.

Had his rebellion, his year-long sojourn in Europe, been a subconscious desire to drive a permanent wedge between himself and his old man? To be disowned? To not have any choice about working or not working for Golden, Inc? Whatever the truth, he had decided, following that monumental quarrel, to put as much distance between him and his father as possible.

San Francisco had fit the bill admirably, and his first apartment there had been on Russian Hill on the top floor of a converted firehouse. It was a neighborhood of steep hills, hidden cul-de-sacs, and views of the bay that seemed to never end. Within walking distance of downtown and the financial district, it was a place of contrasts. Every social class from white-collar—and a few blue-collar—workers, aging hippies, struggling artists and writers, to the city's chic professional singles and even the wealthy lived in its motley collection of aging semidetached houses (which could have become slums but which perversely managed to retain the charm that is San Francisco's alone) as well as modern apartment buildings and condominiums that looked out of place among all that charm.

It was also, increasingly, a very expensive place in which to live. Which was why Steve had wondered, when he'd first learned that Glory Browne lived there, how she could afford even the smallest flat in Russian Hill on her wages as a cocktail waitress and later, as an aerobics instructor.

It had been this, plus her outrageous appearance, her street language, and, yes, her feistiness, that had given him the wrong impression at first. By the time she'd set him straight, he was in love with her as well as just lusting after her. Both conditions were becoming increasingly hard to live with. She never gave an inch with him, not for a minute, because she had this crazy aversion to jocks—which God knew he had never been.

Okay, he'd started his career at the Golden Gate Health Club as a martial arts instructor. He'd taken a few karate and judo trophies in college, made the Yale rowing team, and been active in other sports such as fencing, but he didn't have the jock mentality, the killer instinct that motivates a champion. To be classified with her ex-husband really stung. Which was why he'd put the whole thing on hold and stopped trying to get a date with her.

So what the hell, he asked himself, was he doing here today, driving around Russian Hill, trying to find a parking spot? It would be simplistic to say it was because Glory had sounded like hell when she'd called in sick this morning. After all, how else would she sound with a bad cold? No, the truth was, he was here because he was worried about her, because he couldn't stand by and do nothing when she could very well be flat on her back without anyone to fix her a cup of herbal tea with lemon or heat a can of soup for her. Stupid and not very cool to worry about someone who made it plain she couldn't stand the sight of you, but there it was.

He finally found a parking place on Larkin, a good four blocks from Glory's apartment. He was passing Fettuccine Bros., a take-out pasta place, when, on impulse, he turned in to buy a supply of fresh pasta and sauce. Just to make sure, he also stopped at a small Mom-and-Pop grocery and bought several cans of chicken soup, adding a box of herbal tea bags, six lemons, and a quart of French vanilla ice cream as afterthoughts.

When he rang Glory's doorbell, it was a while before he heard feet shuffling toward the door. "Yeah? Who is it?" she said, her voice so hoarse that for a minute he didn't recognize it.

"It's your Jewish mother. I've brought you some chicken soup," he said.

There was a long silence on the other side of the door. "Wait until I get something on," she said.

When Glory opened the door, a few minutes later, he had to fight hard not to laugh. She was wearing a man's denim work shirt that hung down to her knees over what looked to be gray sweat-pants. Her hair stood on end, looking like curly red wires, and her eyes were glazed with fever above a swollen nose with nostrils that looked as if they had been outlined in red ink.

"If you say anything, so help me, I'm going to knee you in the balls," she warned hoarsely, and he knew she'd caught his strug-gle not to laugh.

Steve shifted the position of the sacks he was carrying and raised his free hand, palm out. "I promise," he said solemnly, and she let him in.

He looked around the tiny kitchen as he set his offering on the drain board of an ancient zinc sink. The room was bare except for the sink, a dwarf-sized refrigerator, an even smaller two-burner range, a rickety-looking card table, and a rusty chair. So where did she sit when she wanted to relax? he wondered. He glanced through an open door into what looked to be a bedroom. All it contained was an old chest of drawers, a bookcase, a mattress on the floor and a lamp, sitting on top of a stack of luggage.

"Where's the soup?" she croaked.

"In the bag. I'll warm it for you," he offered. "You go back to bed."

To his surprise, she turned silently and disappeared into the bedroom. He found a pan, a can opener, opened the soup, and dumped it into the pan to heat. Surprisingly, there was a decent supply of pots and pans and dishes, even four crystal glasses in the cupboard under the sink. The room was also very clean despite an unwashed cup and saucer in the sink.

When the soup was hot, he poured it into a bowl and carried it into the bedroom. Glory was asleep, lying on her back, her mouth slightly open. For a while he stood beside the mattress, staring down at her. What was it that got to him, that made him, at this very moment, want to crawl under that sheet and make sweet love to her?

Not her looks. Oh, she had a certain piquancy. But he'd known a hundred girls who put her in the shade in the looks department. And it certainly wasn't her sweet disposition. She didn't have an ounce of give in her whole makeup. No softness, no vulnerability, just prickles and contrariness—and bullheaded stubbornness. So why did he want her so badly, right at this moment, that his loins ached?

"You can stop staring at me," Glory said, and he realized her eyes were open. She struggled up to a sitting position. "Okay, I look lousy, but I wasn't exactly expecting company. Uninvited guests have to take what they get."

"Well, this unexpected guest just heated you some soup. How about eating it?"

She took the bowl from him. As she spooned the soup into her mouth, she made little slurping sounds.

"I brought some pasta and sauce, too—and a quart of ice cream," he said. "French vanilla."

Her eyes gleamed. "You can put the pasta in the fridge, but we'd better eat the ice cream before it melts. The freezing part of the fridge doesn't get cold enough to keep ice cream hard."

She finished her soup while he put away the pasta and sauce. He noticed that the metal utility cabinet—there were no cupboards except for the small one under the sink—held junk foods like potato and corn chips, pretzels, a package of iced cupcakes, candy bars, pickles, and, in the refrigerator, two forlorn hot dogs and several bottles of condiments.

To go with the hot dogs? he wondered disapprovingly.

No fruit, no fresh vegetables, or salad greens. True, one shelf in the utility cabinet was packed with what he thought of as survivalist foods—dried beans, rice, canned meat, sardines, and tuna. Preparations for an earthquake? Or for another type of disaster, like losing her job?

Steve spooned the ice cream into two bowls and took them into the bedroom. He sat on the edge of the mattress while he ate, watching Glory dig into the ice cream.

"Do you live on junk food?" he asked her finally.

She bristled immediately. "So what if I do? What business is it of yours?"

"It's my business because I want you in to work every day," he said bluntly. "You can't sustain hard physical work on the kind of junk food you eat."

To his surprise, Glory regarded him silently, as if mulling over his words. "So what are we talking about here? Rabbit food? I gave all that up when I got into shape. Now I eat stuff for quick energy to keep me going."

"That's where you're wrong. Your body needs vegetables. Fruit. Whole grains. Carbohydrates—but not empty ones like pretzels and potato chips and candy bars. A steady diet of that kind of stuff will kill you. Knock off the sweets and hot dogs and other quick foods. And take it easy with the ice cream. You don't need all that sugar."

"So how come you just scarfed down a whole bowlful of it?"

"To keep you from eating the whole quart."

"Well, you brought it here. How do you explain that?"

"I thought your throat might be too sore to eat anything solid."

Unexpectedly, she gave him a tiny smile. "My fever's going down. I should be back to work in a couple days." She was quiet for a moment. "You think it would help—you know, my staying power, if I ate health foods?"

It took him a moment to recover from his surprise. "I *know* it would help. I saw a health food store about a block down the street. To get you started, why don't I pick you up a supply of the right kind of foods? And while I'm gone, get some more rest. I'll be back shortly."

She didn't tell him to butt out, that her diet was none of his business; she didn't say anything at all. She settled back on her pillows with a sigh and closed her eyes. A few minutes later, when he'd finished rinsing out their dishes, he looked in on her and discovered she was asleep again.

He was turning away when his eyes fell on a collection of photographs, lined up on top of the bookcase. Most of them were in old wood frames, but a couple were framed in silver or pewter. At first, as he studied the old-fashioned clothes, the dated hairstyles, he thought these must be Glory's parents and grandparents, but then he recognized one smiling couple as character actors who specialized in homey sitcom roles. As for the older photographs, there was too much of a conglomeration of nationalities in those faded faces. Whatever nationality Glory might come from, one thing he was sure—she wasn't Oriental, and yet one family group was Chinese. So what the devil were they doing in her bedroom?

His jaw tensed as the answer came to him. Hell, she'd raided the Salvation Army stores and bought herself some instant ancestors. Which brought up an interesting question: What was wrong with the ones she'd been born with?

Figuring that he'd worn out his welcome, he intended to leave the food in the kitchen, write her a note and go, but by the time he'd put the supply of food away, Glory was awake again.

He brought her a cup of herbal tea, and although she made a face at the first taste, she finished it off. But being Glory, she had to grouse about it.

"Is this the kind of sh—stuff you want me to live on?" she asked.

"You'll get used to it. You'll feel so good in a few weeks that you won't want to go back to your old eating habits."

"I'll give it a couple of months, and if it doesn't do what you say, I'm starting back on hot dogs and tacos."

Prudently, Steve was silent, and she gave him a long cool stare. "How come you came here to see me? You wouldn't be checking up to make sure I'm really sick, would you?"

"I wasn't checking up on you—well, I was, but only to find out if you needed anything."

"What if I'd had a boyfriend staying here? I could have, you know. Lots of guys come on to me."

"That's hard to believe. You look like a mongrel pup someone tossed out of a car in the middle of the night."

He had intended it as a joke. To his dismay, Glory slid under the sheet and pulled it up over her face. "You'd better go now. I think I'll take another nap," she said, her voice muffled by the sheet. "Thanks for the stuff. Leave the cash register receipt, will you, so we can settle up later."

He stood there, thinking hard, and suddenly he understood what had happened. It was that misguided word—mongrel. Was that how she thought of herself? Was her background that bad? If so, it would explain so many things—her wariness, her prickly nature, her unwillingness to believe in anybody or anything.

He could have pretended he hadn't noticed her hurt. He could have said any number of things and bowed out gracefully. But he didn't. He knelt on the mattress, gathered her up in his arms, sheet and all, and gave her a hug. She didn't fight him or try to get away. She lay in his arms, eyes squeezed tightly together, not hugging him back, not doing anything.

It only lasted a few seconds because he was too conscious that he was probably making a fool out of himself, a fact he was sure she'd point out any minute now. But when he laid her back on her pillows, she didn't come up with the sharp words he expected. Instead, she closed her eyes, rolled to her side, and went back to sleep.

That afternoon, Steve sent Glory two dozen scarlet roses and a vase to put them in, and a week later, when he asked her out to dinner, she accepted.

He took her to a small Basque restaurant in the Sunset district, where the food was served on long common tables, boarding-house-style. They stuffed themselves on bean soup, roast lamb, and hot bread served in the same iron skillet it had been baked in, and finished off the meal with bowls of flan.

Afterward, they went to Steve's apartment on Nob Hill, where he took her to bed and found out that she really was a natural redhead. He also discovered that, pound for pound, inch by inch, she had more energy and sex drive than any woman he'd ever made love to—and that he was one hell of a lucky man.

CHAPTER THIRTY-TWO

IT OFTEN SEEMED TO ARIEL THAT SHE SHARED THE OLD HOUSE on Marina Boulevard not only with Alex but with the ghosts of the grandparents she'd never known, her parents, whom she'd lived with and never understood, and an assortment of great-aunts and -uncles who had lived and died there, most of them long before she was born.

During the day, she never had these fantasies. The house, in the heart of vigorous, bustling San Francisco, was too obviously a part of the present. But at night when she lay alone on her bed with the sound of street traffic muted by the night fog, and the gray light from the windows casting murky shadows on the walls of her room, there were whispers and rustlings outside her bedroom door, and it was easy then to believe that the shades of long-dead people moved along the hall or browsed through the books in the library or had tea with others of their kind in the room that had once been the company parlor.

Tonight, a fog, unusually heavy for May, lay over the city, so thick that it seemed to have weight and substance as it pressed against the windowpanes. The foghorns on Alcatraz boomed out across the bay, a haunting, hurting sound, while the muffling fog swallowed up lesser sounds, isolating the old house and casting it adrift from the city.

Ariel wasn't afraid of the restless spirits of the past—if they truly existed. They were a part of the house, just as she was. The house was an extension of her own being—or maybe it would be more accurate to say that she was an extension of the old house.

She pulled a down comforter around her shoulders, fighting off a sudden chill. She'd had a glass of wine just before she turned off the lights, and now she wished she'd had a second one. Although the wine had blunted her senses, one glass hadn't been enough to make her sleepy—and she did so want to sleep until morning.

It was Wednesday, and Alex had just left after one of his conjugal visits. But tonight she had refused to service him, and his face could have been set in granite when he'd left the room. His step measured, he'd gone downstairs, taking each step with such force that she knew he was furious with her. Still huddled under her comforter, she tensed when she heard his footsteps returning.

He came into the room and set an uncorked bottle of zinfandel and a wineglass on the nightstand. "Here, drink up," he said. "*This* is what really turns you on these days."

For a while after he left, she resisted temptation, but then she gave in and poured herself a brimming glass of wine. It was bloodred, a domestic zinfandel, still young and not one of her father's treasured estate wines, and it tasted bitter, as if the grape skins had fermented too long in the vats, but it warmed her insides and blunted the edges of her consciousness. However, she was soon aware that drinking the wine had been a mistake because now, as if she'd opened the gates to temptation, she had a raging thirst for more.

She fought the temptation, even while the insidious rationalization came to her that if she finished off the whole bottle, what would it matter? It was only wine, not vodka or brandy. Of course, *he* would know. In the morning, when he saw the empty bottle, he would pick, pick, pick away at her, his beautifully modulated voice slowly stripping away her pride. He would comment upon her pallor, her lack of appetite, parade her faults before her until she felt as worthless and unsubstantial as the shades that haunted the house.

Of course, even if she didn't drink the rest of the wine, he would still do this. So why not guarantee herself a night without nightmares? Since she'd stopped taking the vitamins he'd prescribed for her, she had suffered from insomnia, and when she did sleep, the nightmares came raging back, leaving her feeling drained and listless in the morning.

Just thinking of the nightmare raised the hairs on her upper arms, and to break the spiral of fear, she sat up and swung her feet over the edge of the bed. As if a door were open somewhere, cold air curled around her ankles, and although she knew it was only a window draft, she shivered convulsively and fought the desire to crawl back in bed and pull the comforter over her head.

Which would be stupid. Even if it were a ghost—which she didn't really believe for a minute—why would it harm *her*? She was one of them, a Fairmount, and this was her home. She had been born in the room where Alex slept; her old nursery was just down the hall. If anyone had something to fear from the house, it was Alex, the intruder. . . .

The thought was comforting. It gave her the courage to carry the bottle of zinfandel into the bathroom and pour it down the sink. She dropped the empty bottle in the wastepaper basket, and after she'd returned to bed, she made herself think of things pleasant, like planning a trip to Scotland, where she'd always wanted to go. She fell asleep, and this time, she dreamed that she was sitting on the shores of a small highlands lake, watching a stag drink its fill at dawn. . . .

It was later that same night that the nightmare returned. This time she dreamed she was a little girl again, lying in bed with her eyes closed but very much aware, with every shrinking inch of her body, that the bedroom door was slowly opening, that someone—or something—had come into the room, bringing a bone-deep chill with it. In the dream, her eyes were open, but there was nothing to see. It was much too dark—and anyway, the rustling sound could be a draft, or even a mouse, scurrying across the rug.

Then she heard another sound, this one unmistakable. It was the sound of heavy breathing, of air rasping through someone's tight throat, and she was aware of movement, a furtive, rubbing sound—familiar, threatening, ugly. The sound went on for what seemed hours, and then there was a low groan, like someone in pain.

A creaking started up, and she heard footsteps—coming closer to the bed. She lay very still, afraid to move, even to breathe. And then, something—a cold hand—touched her face, and she knew that it wasn't a nightmare, after all, that it was very real.

She screamed, a high-pitched sound that hurt her ears and released her from her paralysis. Frantically, she scrambled backward, away from the hand, until the cold headboard was pressed against her back and she could retreat no farther. When the footsteps moved, this time toward the door, she flung herself across the bed and switched on the lamp, her desire to put a face on her tormentor stronger than her fear.

It was Alex—or at least the flash of blue she saw before the door closed was the hem of the silk Sulka robe she'd bought him for their first Christmas together. She wasn't really surprised. Who else would come into her room in the middle of the night to act out old childhood fears that only Alex knew? As for why he would do such a cruel thing, she couldn't even guess his motive. But one thing she was sure of: Alex had come there to frighten her, to make her believe that she was having another nightmare.

The fear that he might return spurred her next action. She darted across the room, and when she found the key was gone, she pushed a straight chair under the doorknob. She returned to bed and fell asleep with her bedside lamp still on, and this time if she dreamed, she didn't remember it later.

In the morning, when she took the chair away, she discovered that the door was locked. This time, she didn't go to pieces and run to throw open a window. Instead, she picked up the phone, and even when she realized the line was dead, she didn't panic. Alex had to unlock the door eventually because this was the day Maria gave the bedrooms their weekly cleaning. And when he did—then she would escape.

But Maria didn't come that day, and the door remained locked. Late that evening, Alex brought her a tray of food, set it down on the bed, and turned to leave again.

"Where's Maria?" she asked.

"I fired her. She was incompetent," he said. He left the room without once having looked in her direction.

Although she quivered inside when she heard the key turn in the lock, Ariel didn't call him back. That would have been a defeat, a step backward. During the night, she'd made an important discovery. She was still desperately afraid of being alone, afraid of the nightmares—but not so much that she was willing to sink back into her former apathy. By resisting the lure of the vitamins, which she was now convinced had been tranquilizers, by rejecting Alex's sexual games, by pouring out the wine he'd left, she had discovered a strength that she hadn't known she possessed. She was getting stronger—did Alex sense this? Was this why he was so angry with her?

She examined the sandwich and soup he'd brought. The soup, when she tasted it gingerly, was very salty. Was that to cover up the taste of something he'd added to it? Was he trying to sedate her—or was her imagination working overtime?

If only she could talk to Stephanie—or anyone else in the support group. Surely, they would help her—or would they think she had gone over the edge, that her suspicions were fantasies, sprung from her own disturbed mind?

She didn't dare tell them everything about her marriage—and her sex life. Stephanie, for all her sympathy, had been shocked at the little she'd already revealed. So all she would dare to say was that Alex had locked her in her room, that she'd just discovered he'd been coming to her room at night, acting out the childhood incidents that were the source of her nightmares. And even to her own ears, that sounded pretty paranoid.

In other words, she was on her own. She didn't even have Maria's doubtful help now. And if she wanted to get away, she must convince Alex that she was completely cowed, that her rebellion was over and she was willing to return to her old submissive role as his wife. Could she pull it off? She was no good at lying or playacting—but that might work in her favor. Alex had such a poor opinion of her intelligence that he surely was expecting her to cave in and beg his forgiveness. He wouldn't be looking for deceit.

It wasn't until the next morning that Alex returned with another tray of food. Ariel had been waiting in the bathroom for almost an hour, huddled on a rattan stool, and because she was wearing only a towel, she was shivering as she came through the bathroom door.

She stopped dead, as if startled to see Alex there. His eyes moved over her half-naked body and she wanted to turn and run, to lock herself in the bathroom because how could she possibly bear for him to touch her, knowing what she did? But instead, she let the towel slip, as planned, then made an ineffectual grab at it as it dropped to her ankles. She didn't have to fake her embarrassment. Alex's scorching look seemed to burn through her skin and penetrate her bones.

The rest was inevitable. Without a word, Alex took her to bed, and during the next half hour, she tried to block out what he was doing, what she was doing, by pretending that she was one of the ghosts that did or did not haunt the old house.

Later, she was properly apologetic for being "difficult." She blamed it on nerves, on her drinking, and swore that she had learned her lesson. And all the time, her inner self stood back and marveled at how easy it was to lie. When had she learned such duplicity? Had she finally caught up with the rest of the world? Whatever the reason, part of her mourned her lost innocence. She didn't want to live in the real world. What she really wanted was never to have been born.

When Alex finally left her bed for his first morning appointment, he didn't bother to lock the door behind him. Ariel waited until she heard the doorbell and knew he was greeting a patient before she dressed quickly, throwing on the first thing she found in her closet. It wasn't until later, when she caught the stares of people she passed as she was hurrying along Marina Boulevard, that she realized she was wearing a sweater with frayed sleeves and the mud-spattered jeans that she wore on the rare occasions when she dared Alex's disapproval and helped José trim the rosebushes.

Had she unconsciously chosen her oldest clothes because she felt so worthless, so adrift? Was it pure coincidence that she had left home looking like a homeless street person?

It started to rain while she was still looking for a pay phone. She could have used the ones in the kiosks outside the Marina Safeway, but they were too exposed to passing cars. By now, it was possible that Alex had discovered she was gone—and she had so little faith in her own spurious courage that she didn't dare face him.

Already, she was beginning to wonder if she had done the right thing, running away. Where would she go now—how would she live? All she had was the few dollars in her wallet. Alex had complete control of her money as well as possession of the house. She hadn't even dared take her car out of the garage because she was afraid he'd hear it start up. It wouldn't be long before he missed her and realized that she had faked her surrender. If she went back now, she might never get another chance to leave again.

After all, he was a doctor. He had access to all sorts of drugs. It would be so easy for him to force-feed her something to make her so dependent upon him that she'd lose all desire to leave.

She turned up Bay Street, eager to get away from the marina area, and a few minutes later, she was dialing Stephanie from a drugstore pay phone. It wasn't until the phone had rung several times that she remembered it was Friday, that Stephanie wouldn't be home from work until late afternoon. She hung up the phone and tried to think what to do next. She could phone one of the other women in the support group—but would they understand the significance of what she'd just found out and realize the urgency of her problem? She wasn't even sure Stephanie would understand. How could she take a chance on someone else?

In the end, she decided to take a bus to Mill Valley and wait on Stephanie's doorstep until she came home from work. Surely, if she remained calm and spoke quietly, Stephanie would listen to her, believe her, help her. Maybe the other women would rally around, too, like they had for Glory. Of course, Glory had earned their respect by her lack of self-pity, her courage. What would they think about someone who had so easily allowed herself to be victimized, who had waited so long to take the first step toward independence, and who even now, wanted desperately to return to the familiar comfort of her own house?

Although the rain was coming down hard, Stephanie spotted Ariel as soon as she drove into the courtyard. Ariel was sitting with her back braced against the front door of Stephanie's condo, her face buried in her folded arms, and she looked so forlorn that Stephanie's first instinctive dismay was quickly replaced by pity. Something must be very wrong or Ariel, who had such exquisite manners, would never have come here uninvited. Since Ariel was her friend, albeit a recent one, it behooved her to dispense some comfort—and also a cup of tea.

She parked the car in front of her unit. When she touched Ariel's damp shoulders, Ariel lifted her head and tried to speak, but her teeth were chattering so hard, she could only stammer a few incoherent words. Murmuring reassurances, Stephanie helped her to her feet, unlocked the door, and guided her inside. A vagrant thought, that it was lucky the boys were spending the night at a friend's house, crossed her mind as she closed the door behind them.

She didn't ask any questions. Instead, she got Ariel settled on the living room sofa, tucked an afghan around her, then went into the kitchen to put water on to boil and to get out cups and saucers and tea bags, to slice a lemon. While the water heated, she poured whiskey into a glass and carried it into the living room. Ariel was still sitting on the sofa. Since she was very wet, Stephanie had a fleeting thought about her sofa, which luckily was Scotch-guarded.

"Drink this down," she said.

As obedient as a child, Ariel sipped the whiskey, and gradually color seeped back into her cheeks. "I feel better now," she volunteered. "But I'm still so cold."

"No wonder—you're wet to the skin. I'll get you a robe to wear while you take off those wet clothes—and not to worry, the boys are staying with a friend tonight."

She went upstairs to get an old plush robe that David had left behind. It was well worn, with patches on the elbows, but it was also much warmer than her more decorative ones. When she returned to the living room, Ariel had already undressed and was huddled in one corner of the sofa, the afghan draped around her shoulders. As she rose to take the robe, the afghan fell away and Stephanie felt a small shock of surprise. Because Ariel was so slender she'd assumed that she was flat-breasted. Instead, although she had very little body fat, her breasts were fully developed and her hips were rounded below a narrow waist. It was the loose clothing she always wore, Stephanie realized now, that gave her such a boyish look.

Realizing she was staring, she turned away and picked up the clothing Ariel had discarded. "I'll pop these into the dryer," she said briskly.

After she'd tossed Ariel's wet clothes into the dryer and turned it on, she went into the kitchen to pour boiling water over the tea bags in the cups. As she got out a package of cookies, she found herself dreading the next hour. Ariel was sure to talk about her marital troubles—was she ready to be a confidante when she had so many of her own problems to worry about?

What if she told Ariel about her fear of being on her own, about the new job that was so much more difficult that she'd let on to the group? And what if she admitted that for all the brave face she put on, she was sometimes so desperately lonely that she was almost willing to take David back, just for the companionship of another adult?

But when she returned to the living room, Ariel seemed in no hurry to talk about personal matters. Shyly, she admired the bronze statue of a dancer she said could have stepped out of one of her grandfather's Degas paintings. When Stephanie questioned her, relieved that the conversation was impersonal, she confided that her father had added two Monets and several Picassos to the collection, which would someday go into a museum.

Next, Ariel commented on the clear, basic colors of a primitive that hung above the fireplace, and when Stephanie handed her a cup of tea, she took a sip and asked if it was English or Indian. Just when Stephanie was relaxing, sure it wasn't going to be bad after all, Ariel set down her cup and told her that she had just left her husband.

As Ariel's voice went on, Stephanie had a hard time concealing her dismay. What Ariel was telling her was bizarre, grotesque, like something out of an old gothic novel. That a man, a psychiatrist at that, would deliberately provoke his own wife's fears by drugging her, then stealing into her bedroom to enact a traumatic experience from her childhood, just wasn't believable. She found it easier to believe Ariel when she explained where she'd found the courage to defy her husband.

"It was Glory, the way she was in the hospital," Ariel said. "She looked so terrible with that split lip and all those bruises, but she kept on making jokes—you remember the funny things she said? She must have been hurting, even with pain pills, and yet she didn't complain once. I was so ashamed of myself for being such a—a jellyfish that I decided I wasn't going to be exploited anymore. That's when I stopped taking the vitamins Alex gave me, because I always felt so weak and sleepy and dragged out after I took them. I think they were tranquilizers."

"Didn't your husband say anything when you stopped taking them?"

"He didn't know. I've been flushing them down the sink so he wouldn't catch on."

"If you suspected he was up to no good, why didn't you leave him before this?"

"I wasn't sure until last night when he came into my room and started acting out my nightmare. I think he got careless because he thought I'd had a lot to drink. Oh, I've known something was wrong for a long time, but my mind was so fuzzy most of the time that I wasn't thinking straight. I'm sure those pills were messing up my brain."

"Why would he do such a terrible thing?"

"I don't know. It doesn't make sense—unless he's insane."

"Is there a practical reason why he might want you to be—uh, more dependent upon him?" Stephanie said. "Something to do with money?"

Ariel stared at her, her eyes bleak. "I don't have any life insurance, if that's what you mean. There's the trust Papa set up for me, of course, but I only draw the interest from it. If anything should happen to me, the principal goes to the de Young Museum. I didn't realize this until Mr. Waterford called Papa's lawyer that time I filed for a divorce. Mr. Nelson must've explained how the trust works at the reading of the will, but—well, I was in such a state that day that all I could think about was getting home, so I signed the papers he gave me without bothering to read them. The interest goes into a checking account—Alex took that over when we first got married because I couldn't keep my checkbook balanced."

She paused, her eyes brooding. "I always wondered the real reason why he changed his mind about the divorce. It must have been because he found out about the trust and realized for the first time that he'd have no control over it if we got a divorce."

"What about your house? In that location, it must be worth millions."

"It's part of the bequest to the museum. I can stay there as long as I live, but when I die it becomes a museum. My father wanted a permanent home for his paintings and other collections. He was sure his art nouveau and even some of his art deco—he always called them moderne, not art deco—collections would be very valuable someday."

"Then, your husband hasn't any monetary reason to do you harm, has he? In fact, it's to his advantage that you two stay married. Is it possible that you misinterpreted what happened? Maybe he was just concerned for you—"

Ariel's eyes filled with tears. "You don't believe me. You think I'm neurotic. I didn't imagine any of this—I swear it, Stephanie. Maria warned me to be careful. Looking back, I think she realized the vitamins were—something else. But I didn't understand her warning, you see."

"Maria?"

"Our housekeeper. Alex fired her yesterday. He must have realized that she was on to him."

"Well, don't think about it now. Why don't you take a hot shower while I fix us something to eat?" Stephanie said. "You're staying here tonight—and no arguments about that. We can talk some more in the morning. I don't work on Saturdays—and the boys won't be home before noon."

"It must be comforting, having children," Ariel said. "Alex never wanted any—and I didn't really mind. I've never been around children, not even while I was growing up. I don't know the first thing about taking care of babies."

"Raising kids is strictly a learn-as-you-go thing with most women," Stephanie said. "And I'd better start dinner. How does a cheese omelet sound? I know you don't eat meat."

"An omelet is fine—please don't go to any trouble."

"Oh, I won't. But I just might show off my culinary skills by putting a pan of soda biscuits in the oven."

She was relieved when Ariel smiled. Although she suspected that some of Ariel's troubles stemmed from a too-vivid imagination, she also knew her friend was hurting. And her own protective instincts were going full blast now.

Later, they sat down to a cheese-and-green-pepper omelet, spinach salad, buttermilk biscuits, and hot tea. Stephanie was gratified by Ariel's appetite. Maybe it would all blow over now. After Ariel was asleep, it might be a good idea to phone Alex di Russy and tell him Ariel was all right—no, better not. Ariel was sure to consider it a betrayal of her confidences. Better to just pretend Ariel was an ordinary overnight guest.

Ariel was very quiet as they watched the ten o'clock news on Channel 2. When her eyelids began to droop, Stephanie took her up to Ronnie's room. She changed the sheets quickly and then closed the minishades at the windows. "Sleep as late as you like in the morning. You'll be comfortable here. Even my mother-in-law couldn't find fault with that mattress when she stayed overnight with us once." She hesitated, then asked, "Does Alex have any relatives?"

"His parents live in the East. I've never met them. I think Alex is ashamed of them because they have thick Italian accents. Once he told me that it had taken him forty-two years to overcome his background. He never goes to see them. I didn't know they were still alive until his mother called to tell Alex that his father'd had a minor stroke. As it happens, Alex wasn't here and I answered the phone. We talked for a long time—Alex was furious when he found out she'd called. I thought surely he'd go to see his father, but he said he was too busy."

Stephanie felt uncomfortable suddenly. She seldom went home to visit her own folks. In fact, the boys had only seen them a few times—and she had never invited her parents to come visit her in San Francisco. She'd told David that their place in the city was too small for overnight guests, but had that been the real reason? Was she ashamed of her parents, of the farm in Oregon that had barely supported them until they'd leased out the fields to a commercial grower, of their country ways, even their fundamentalist religion? David never ran them down, of course, but she couldn't help comparing them to his mother with her Baccarat crystal and Gorham silver and ancestors she could trace all the way back to the Norman Invasion of England. . . .

After she said good night to Ariel, Stephanie took a shower and went to bed. Tomorrow she would try to help Ariel with her problems. For now—she was too exhausted to do anything but sleep.

Something—a sound that shouldn't have been there—awakened her. Was it one of the boys, crying out in his sleep? No—no, the twins were staying over with their friend Kevin. So what was that sound, like someone crying?

Ariel, she thought as she came fully awake. It had to be Ariel, having one of her nightmares.

Half-exasperated and half-concerned, she slid out of bed quickly and, not waiting to put on a robe, hurried down the hall to Ronnie's room. She rapped on the door, and when there was no answer, she pushed it open and went in. Ariel, her face buried in a pillow, was huddled under Ronnie's red-and-white Star Wars comforter. She didn't move, even when Stephanie called her name. But when Stephanie went to the bed and lifted her to a sitting position, Ariel began to cry. Stephanie put her arms around her, making soothing sounds, and Ariel clung to her, her body shaking with the force of her sobs.

"Let it all out, Ariel," Stephanie said, as if she were comforting one of her own sons. "Let it all come out. . . ."

Ariel buried her face in the hollow between Stephanie's breasts, still crying. Stephanie murmured reassurances, stroking her hair. How silky Ariel's hair felt—and how oddly it clung to the fingers, as if it were full of static electricity. Ariel smelled of the floral soap that Stephanie had put out for her, and her body felt soft, as if it were boneless. And how fresh her breath was, like a child's, so hot against the valley between her breasts. It had been so long since she'd held a crying child.

But of course, Ariel *wasn't* a child. She was a fully mature adult woman. . . .

Stephanie felt a sudden warmth—much too warm for the cool room. A flush rose to her cheeks, as if she'd suddenly contracted a fever, and a tingling, an ache started up between her thighs. Her arms must have tightened because Ariel snuggled closer, her own cone-shaped breasts tightly pressed against Stephanie's fuller ones. The ache deepened; Stephanie found herself stroking Ariel's soft hair, her hand drifting down to stroke Ariel's shoulder, her upper arm. . . .

Ariel was very still now, almost as if she'd stopped breathing. And then she was nuzzling Stephanie's breast, her mouth moist against Stephanie's hardening nipple, her hands clutching at Stephanie.

For a long moment, during which time seemed to be suspended, Stephanie yielded to the tingling, the fever. Later, she would try to convince herself that she'd been half-asleep, confused, that she'd been taken by surprise and had overreacted to what was a very natural desire to comfort a friend. She would even reason that her long abstinence had weakened her normal defenses.

But she couldn't rationalize away the fact that for one moment in time she'd felt something she should only feel for a man, that she'd wanted to stroke Ariel's soft breasts, wanted to touch Ariel in the most intimate way possible, wanted Ariel to touch her back. . . .

Reality came rushing back. She gave a cry and stood so abruptly that her movement spilled Ariel backward on the bed. She met Ariel's startled eyes, and revulsion prompted her next words.

"Oh, God, Ariel—are you gay?" she said, her voice hoarse with disgust.

She didn't wait for an answer. She turned and fled from the room, feeling dirty and soiled, as if she'd just stepped into a pool of mud. A few minutes later, as she huddled on her bed, she heard Ariel's footsteps approaching her room. She held her breath, wishing she had locked the door, and only started breathing again when Ariel's footsteps passed her room and went on down the hall, toward the stairs.

Stephanie knew she should call Ariel back, tell her to wait until morning to leave, but because it was impossible to come to terms with what had just happened, she kept quiet.

It was later, when false dawn turned the bedroom windows gray, that worry for Ariel replaced her self-disgust. It was dangerous out there on the streets for a woman alone at night, even in Mill Valley—she never should have allowed Ariel to leave. Where had Ariel gone—had she found an all-night café, or a local cab to take her back to the city so late at night? Or was she walking the streets and lanes of Mill Valley, waiting for morning when the Golden Gate Transit buses would start running again? Did she have enough money for busfare—for breakfast?

Stephanie's first instinct was to call Janice—like the others, she had come to accept Janice as their leader—but she forced herself to wait until seven o'clock before she picked up the phone. To her relief, Janice answered on the second ring. She listened silently as Stephanie gave her a censored version of what had happened— that Ariel had come to her for help, had spent part of the night there but had left before morning. Not to Stephanie's surprise, because she'd come to respect common sense, Janice had a good suggestion.

"Maybe she changed her mind about leaving her husband and was too embarrassed to face you after making such a fuss. Why don't you try to reach her at home? If she hasn't returned, then it's time to start worrying."

Although Stephanie was doubtful—after all, she'd caught the fear in Ariel's voice when she'd talked about her husband—she thanked Janice, promised to contact her as soon as she knew something more, and hung up.

She dialed Ariel's number, noting that her hands weren't quite steady. If anything had happened to Ariel, she would never forgive herself. Just when she'd been needed, she had failed a friend. Ariel had turned to her for comfort—and nothing more. And after she'd asked that devastating question, she should have explained that she really didn't mean it, and then told Ariel why she had blurted it out, no matter how much it violated her own sense of privacy.

A man's voice, smooth as velvet, came on the line. "Yes?"

"May I speak to Ariel?"

"Ariel—you want to talk to *Ariel*? Who is this please?"

"It's a friend of hers—Stephanie Cornwall."

There was a brief silence. "I'm afraid I've never heard my wife mention you," he said, and somehow it sounded like an accusation.

"We haven't known each other long. Can you tell me when she'll be back?"

"Back? Oh, I see what you mean. Well, I'm afraid she isn't available just now. I'll tell her you called, of course." Again there was a silence. "Do you mind telling me how you met Ariel? I thought I knew all her friends."

"We met through—through a mutual friend. We occasionally have lunch together, but actually we're more like acquaintances," she said cautiously.

"I see." He said the words as if he didn't really see at all. "I'm afraid secrecy is one of Ariel's traits. I don't know if she told you but she's been under psychiatric treatment for a long time. If she should call you again, I'd appreciate it if you'd contact me immediately because she's in a rather confused state of mind. As it happens, I'm a doctor—or has she told you that?"

"We seldom talk about personal things. Our common interest is—uh, art."

After Stephanie had hung up, she sat there for a while, thinking. It was obvious that Ariel hadn't gone home—so where was she? And why had she lied to Alex di Russy when he'd asked about her connection with Ariel? Because it was obvious that Ariel hadn't told him about the support group? Everything he'd said was so reasonable—why didn't she believe a word of it? Was it because that smooth, controlled voice, which should have been reassuring, had instead aroused her distrust?

And what had happened to Ariel after she'd rushed out into the night? Had she found a refuge with someone else? Had she gone to a hotel?

Or had something terrible happened to her?

"Oh, Lord. What have I done?" Stephanie said aloud.

She called Janice, and told her she'd talked to Ariel's husband

and instinct told her not to trust him, that now she was ready to believe that everything Ariel had told her was true.

"Ariel's story sounds pretty wild, but I believe her. It's weird, I know, but—"

"No, it isn't. I don't believe Ariel is capable of telling a lie. The important thing is to find her—fast. It's possible that she—she isn't thinking straight. As soon as we hang up, I'll start calling hotels and hospitals. Meanwhile, why don't you contact Chanel and Glory? It's possible that she went to one of them for help."

But when Stephanie dialed Chanel's number, she got a recording, and after she'd left a message for Chanel to call her immediately, she dialed Glory's number. Glory heard her out to the end without interrupting. When Stephanie finished, she was blunt.

"She's been living on her nerves too long. No telling what she did after she left your place. Sounds to me like she went over the edge."

"Janice is phoning hospitals and hotels," Stephanie said, and despite herself, her voice sounded defensive.

"Oh, shit—look, don't start feeling guilty. We have to try to think where she could've gone. Did she ever mention any special place that might seem like a—you know, a refuge?"

Stephanie thought for a moment. "We did meet once at Sea Cliff. She told me that when things got too much for her she liked to sit on the wall with her back to the city and pretend she was on an island somewhere."

"The edge of a cliff is not the greatest place for someone who's feeling rocky mentally," Glory said. "I think we should look for her there. If we find her, maybe we can straighten her out. I remember how cool it was when the rest of you came to the hospital."

"Good thinking. I'll call Janice again—and maybe I can reach Chanel this time."

"And I'll head for Sea Cliff. See you there."

The phone rang a few seconds after Glory had hung up. It was Chanel. Stephanie plunged into an account of Ariel's visit and disappearance, and a little to her surprise, Chanel told her, "I can leave here in five minutes. I'm closer to Sea Cliff than the rest of you, so I'll probably get there first. If Ariel is there—well, I'll play it by ear."

Stephanie found herself smiling at the mental picture of Chanel—undoubtedly without a hair out of place—racing to the rescue. Since it wasn't really funny, she knew how close to tears she was, and she paused a few seconds to down a cup of leftover—bitter and very cold—coffee before she left the house.

Usually, the trip to Golden Gate Bridge took fifteen to twenty minutes, depending on traffic, while the drive from the bridge to Sea Cliff should have taken another ten to fifteen minutes. But it was less than a half an hour later that Stephanie pulled into the parking lot of Cliff House, and why she hadn't been stopped for speeding or for weaving in and out of traffic, she didn't know.

As she slid out of her car, she saw Chanel walking toward her. That Glory was with her was a surprise. Had Chanel picked her up—or had Glory taken a taxi all the way from Russian Hill? If so, it must have made a dent in her wallet—and Glory was always so careful about spending money.

They didn't waste time talking. Single-file, Glory in the lead, they hurried toward the lookout point where Stephanie had met Ariel before. She let out an explosive sigh of relief when she saw Ariel sitting on the wall, staring out at the turbulent waves of San Francisco Bay. The wind, always so strong here, was whipping her pale hair into a frenzy, but she sat with her hands in her lap, making no effort to brush it away from her face. Did she welcome the veil of hair that hid her from the rest of the world? Stephanie wondered.

Then Ariel leaned forward over the wall. Stephanie stopped in the middle of the path, her hands clasped at her breast like the heroine from an old melodrama, and it was Glory who moved swiftly forward, who sat down on the wall beside Ariel and put her arm around her shoulders.

"Hey, you nut," she said. "You wanna get yourself killed? This is one hell of a place to do your daily meditations."

Ariel brushed her hair back so she could look at Glory. She started to rise, and Stephanie cried out a warning, sure that Ariel meant to throw herself over the cliff. A strangled sound came from Ariel's throat, and when Stephanie realized she was laughing, her mood changed and suddenly she was furious, so furious that she had to turn away from the others for fear they would sense her anger.

It was a while before it was safe to turn around again. She found the two women still sitting on the wall, Chanel standing a few feet away, downwind of Ariel, smoking a cigarette. Ariel was talking rapidly to Glory, the words spilling out so rapidly, it was hard to understand her. As she listened, Stephanie realized that Ariel had only told her a small part of her marital problems. She felt hurt that it was Glory she was confiding in, but there was also relief in the knowledge that now Glory and Chanel could take over. She'd already messed things up royally.

When Ariel's voice faltered to a stop, Glory took over. Her words weren't particularly sympathetic. In fact, they were downright cross.

"It was stupid, coming here. What were you thinking of, anyway? Jumping off the cliff? If you hurt yourself, do you think that bastard would care? He wants you to do something crazy so he can put you away in a nuthouse and get control of that—what did you call it?"

"A trust fund," Ariel said.

"Yeah, a trust fund. Once he has you tucked away, he can spend your money any way he wants. And who would stop him, him being a shrink? But if you stand up to him, he can't do a thing. You've already shown some backbone—but you gotta do more. You've already got a good lawyer. Mr. Waterford'll see you get possession of your house again. Meanwhile, you have to stay somewhere—don't you have any relatives to take you in?"

Ariel shook her head. "There's only Laird, and I can't ask him for help. That's why I went to. . ." She paused; for the first time, she seemed to see Stephanie. A dark flush covered her face; she looked as if she were going to start crying.

"Well, you can stay with me if you like," Glory said. "I don't have much furniture, so I crash on a mattress on the floor, but you can share it with me. At least, it'd keep you dry." She stared up at the dark clouds rolling in from the ocean. "Looks like we're in for more rain."

Stephanie wanted to say that Ariel was welcome to return with her to Mill Valley, but the truth was, she didn't want Ariel under her roof again, a reminder of her own inexplicable behavior, of the cruel words she'd flung at her. So she looked away and didn't say anything.

Chanel dropped her cigarette and ground it underfoot. She picked up the butt and put it in a trash can. "You can stay with me, Ariel," she said. "I have an extra bedroom."

Ariel hugged her chest with her arms. "I can't involve any of you in my problems. Don't worry about me—I'll go to a hotel. But thank you for your offers."

"What are friends for?" Chanel said, dismissing the subject with a shrug. Her eyes moved over Ariel. "You look as if you could use some food. What say we have breakfast at Cliff House?

I haven't had my morning jolt of caffeine, and I'm ready to chew nails.''

"Shouldn't we wait for Janice?" Glory said.

Stephanie stared at her in dismay. "Would you believe I forgot to call her back?" she said.

"Well, don't sweat it. It's all for the best. She would've had to come all the way from Palo Alto." Glory shivered in the morning air. "Let's get out of this wind. It's cold enough to freeze an Eskimo's balls.''

No one spoke as they started back toward Cliff House. The old restaurant, a relic of the days when the area had been something of a resort, was almost empty, and they were able to sit by the windows that provided a sweeping view of the bay. Their conversation over breakfast was anticlimactic. Chanel held the floor now and her advice, although different from Glory's, was just as practical.

"It's possible that by leaving your husband, you've put yourself in an unfavorable legal position. Desertion and all that," she told Ariel. "You don't want to play into his hands by acting in an erratic way.''

"But I can't go back to Alex as if nothing's happened," Ariel protested.

"Not as if nothing's happened, no. But it's your house. He's the one who should leave.''

"It's all so complicated," Ariel sighed. "Alex loves that house—sometimes I think he married me because of it.''

"Then, you'll have to get a court order to evict him. Why don't you take Glory's advice and call Arnold Waterford? He'll know what your rights are. As for going back, why not? Once your husband knows you've consulted a lawyer, he'll be afraid to try any more of his tricks." Chanel paused, then gave a tiny shrug. "I'll go with you if you like. You probably should have a witness to testify that you asked him to leave. Let him try to wriggle out of that. From what you tell us, he has no claims to the house under community property laws.''

"You'd actually go with me?"

It was Glory who answered. "I will, too." There was a light of battle in her eyes. "If he even looks cross-eyed at you, I'll give him something he won't forget.''

"No need to get physical," Chanel said dryly. "We know you can lick your weight in wildcats now that you're into judo.''

"Karate." Glory made a jabbing motion with her hands, looking very pleased with herself.

"Well, it won't come to that. When he realizes Ariel has friends to back her up, he'll back down fast enough. He might even move out without you having to get a court order."

Ariel shook her head. "I doubt that—and I don't want to involve you in this mess. Alex can be very vindictive. Besides, I have to start solving my own problems. And about time, wouldn't you say?"

"Don't get too cocky," Glory warned. "Your old man sounds like a real jerk."

"I'll be fine." Ariel looked at Chanel. "Would it be too much trouble to drop me off at my house?"

"You're going back there alone? Do you think that's wise?" Chanel said, frowning.

"Don't worry. Everything's going to be all right. I'll keep in touch."

"Is that a promise?" Glory said, looking gloomy.

Stephanie wanted to protest Ariel's decision, only what would she say? She couldn't offer Ariel shelter—how could she after what had happened? But she could offer her money.

"Ariel, are you all right financially? You said something about your husband controlling your money—"

"Please don't worry about it. It's no problem." Ariel's tone held a finality, and Stephanie had to be content with that.

For the rest of the meal, everybody tried to be cheerful—and amusing.

Chanel told them an anecdote about her daughter, who had tried to seduce an older man she'd taken a fancy to, and how Fern's plan had backfired when she'd gone to his house, playing the damsel in distress, only to have him laugh at her.

Then Glory told them in her nonchalant way that she was "seeing" her boss, the infamous Steve Golden, who wasn't really so bad—for a jock.

When it came Stephanie's turn, she couldn't think of anything funny or witty, so she talked about the twins—and their latest passion, the video game their father had bought them, based on a science fiction trilogy by the juvenile writer, Zilpha Keatley Snyder, which she herself heartily approved of because, unlike so many video games, it didn't glorify violence.

Ariel listened quietly; several times she smiled and once, at Glory's description of how Steve had descended upon her apartment with chicken soup, announcing himself as a Jewish mother, she laughed out loud. But to Stephanie, who was so aware of Ariel's every expression, she seemed to be listening a little absently now, as if she were thrashing out a problem in her mind.

After they'd settled their bill, they went outside to discover that it had started to rain again. As Chanel and Glory made a dash for Chanel's car, Ariel touched Stephanie's arm, holding her back.

"Stephanie, I want you to know that I didn't mean anything when I—you know, last night. It was just that—well, I'd had a nightmare and I was confused and scared, but I wasn't making a pass at you. Honestly, I wasn't. I just needed so badly to be close to someone."

"You don't have to tell me that," Stephanie said. She knew what she had to say next—but the words came hard, and it was a few seconds before she added, "I was lashing out at David, I think. The friend I caught him in bed with was a man, you see, and—" She stopped because she couldn't think of how to explain in simple words something that was so complicated.

"You were transferring your anger at your husband onto me?" Ariel finished for her. "I'm so sorry. The whole incident must have stirred up a lot of painful memories."

Stephanie nodded with relief. It had been easy, after all. In fact, she suddenly wished she hadn't been so frank. As Ariel hurried to Chanel's car and she ran for her own station wagon, she was glad she hadn't told Ariel the whole truth—that it had been her disgust at a weakness in her own nature that had made her lash out so cruelly at someone even more vulnerable than herself.

CHAPTER THIRTY-THREE

LAIRD FAIRMOUNT, DESPITE HIS REPUTATION IN SOME QUARTERS as a womanizer, was really a very fastidious man when it came to choosing his sexual partners. As a rule, he dated a woman for a while, sizing her up, before he either did or did not become sexually involved with her. Invariably, he chose women who were not only attractive and charming, but who were also sophisticated enough to accept the limitations inherent in a relationship with him.

All this had changed recently, making him wonder if men had their own biological bomb. He had been spending a weekend at the Carmel Valley estate of an old friend who had recently turned his back on bachelorhood and, with all the enthusiasm of a convert, had embraced domestic life wholeheartedly. Laird had been amused when he first saw the trappings of his friend's new lifestyle—swimming pool, toys on the terrace, even a station wagon—until it occurred to him that his friend was several years younger than he. Which meant that if he ever intended to get married and have a family while he was still reasonably young, it was time to get cracking.

He had come home from his weekend in Carmel Valley a thoughtful, if not yet totally convinced, man. At the time, there hadn't been anyone in the offing who came remotely close to his idea of a woman with whom he was willing to spend the rest of his life. Most of the women he dated, although sexually desirable and socially adept, just didn't fit into the category of wife. When he married, he wanted it to be permanent. What he didn't want was to fall into the maelstrom of divorce and remarriage that seemed de rigueur among his friends. As far as Laird was concerned, his friend had the right idea. Once he married, he meant to drop out of the social rat race, however diverting that rat race had been, and settle down for good.

The problem was—it took two to make a marriage.

It was at this point in his life that he'd started dating Chanel. Even before that, he had admired Chanel—in an academic way. Because she was married at the time, his admiration hadn't gone any further. Then, now in the process of getting a divorce, she'd befriended Ariel and had not only won his gratitude but, as he got to know her better, his affection. She was attractive, sophisticated—but there was also something very earthy about her, and her unexpected flashes of candor always managed to take him by surprise. Like the time she'd made the comment that his taste in cars matched his personality.

"You mean I remind you of a navy blue Mercedes—or a gray Rolls?" he'd said, amused.

"They both suit you. Underplayed and almost decadently well bred. Personally, it's my belief that if you've got it, flaunt it—but within limits. You don't want to go overboard on the conspicuous consumption thing, of course.''

''So if *you* had it, what kind of car would you drive?'' he asked.

She thought a moment. ''A flaming red Maserati—with mink upholstery.''

He'd thrown back his head in a laugh, sure she was joking— until he caught her half smile and knew she was being honest about her penchant for flaming red Maseratis—with or without the mink upholstery.

Most of all, he admired her insouciance in the face of what must have been a crushing disappointment when her divorce settlement turned out to be a pittance. The front she put up although she couldn't have many resources left these days was downright amazing. It was lucky she had that sharp-edged wit to deal with the people who chose to snub her—like those ex-classmates of hers, the ones she called the Hillsborough crowd.

There was some kind of story there, but since it wasn't any of his business, he'd never probed. In fact, he liked the fact that Chanel never put down her detractors. Not that she couldn't hold her own. She could—in spades. And he liked that, too. Yes, she was some kind of woman, all right.

That she'd turned out to be surprisingly good in bed was a bonus. That cool exterior had been misleading. And good sex was important to a marriage. Sex, after all, was an integral part of life—and he was sure a marriage bed shared with Chanel would never be boring.

As for the rest—yes, she would fit into his world because she knew all the right moves—such as how to dress. She was shrewd about money, too, and how to manage it. Which was very important to him. After all, never dipping into one's principal had been bred into his bones by his parents, both of whom were financially conservative. Which was why he could never put up with a too-extravagant wife.

Even though Chanel hadn't come from old money, she'd been educated as if she did. Burlingame Academy was one of the better prep schools in the country, in league with Burke's School or Groton, certainly the highest rated on the West Coast. Moreover, she shared the same interests that he did in music, art, even in sailing, although he'd sensed during their one and only excursion on the bay that she was less enthusiastic than he.

But that was okay. He didn't expect perfection because he was imperfect himself. He had no doubts that Chanel would be tolerant of his limitations—of which, he was well aware, he had more than his share. He was a little self-centered and used to getting his own way, so life with him wouldn't be easy. Luckily, since Chanel had put up with the peccadilloes of that ass Jacques Devereau for years, surely she would allow him a few faults, too.

He wasn't kidding himself, of course. Marriage to Chanel would be pleasant, satisfying, but it wouldn't be the great love match of the century. Theirs would be a mutually rewarding but basically unromantic relationship. Which was fine with him. He was too old, at thirty-five, to believe in romance anymore. It was his observation that marriages that began in the clouds too often came down to earth with a bang. Better to go into it as if it were a business deal, something to be negotiated, all the limits clearly defined. No starry-eyed stuff for him—and he was sure Chanel felt the same.

There *was* one thing. Chanel had been married twice before. Once wouldn't matter, but *two* failures? Of course, her first marriage had been one of those unfortunate adolescent mistakes that could happen to anyone, including him. He'd been a pretty naive teenager, and there'd been at least once when he'd almost run off to Reno with the wrong woman. Luckily, he'd come to his senses in time and realized she was more interested in the Fairmount money than in his charms, but it had been a near miss.

As for Chanel's second marriage—it was hard to think of Chanel being married to that stick, Jacques Devereau. He didn't doubt for a moment that she'd married Devereau to give her kid a good home—and who could fault her for that? In a way, it made his decision easier. There would be no illusions on either side.

So his proposal had been well considered in advance, even a little cold-blooded. He'd been perfectly honest with Chanel. He wanted children, wanted a mutually pleasant marriage and a wife to share his interests as well as his life. Chanel had agreed on every point; she wanted the same, she assured him—and he had no reason to doubt her.

So the deal had been made. She had accepted his emerald-and-diamond ring, which she would wear for the first time the night they announced their engagement. This would be at the party he gave every April to discharge his social obligations. They had kept their engagement secret, deciding it would be best to spring it on everybody at the same time. Chanel would act as his hostess and, as usual, the party would be at his house. Knowing Chanel, it would be one of the best-run social affairs of the spring season.

Yes, everything was smooth sailing—so why did he feel so—
so flat about the whole thing? Was it the realization that in a little
while, he'd no longer be a free man, able to do what he wanted
when he wanted?

Laird was lingering over an after-dinner cognac-and-coffee,
trying to come to a decision about where Chanel and he should
spend their honeymoon, when the doorbell gave out a hoarse ring.
It was the original doorbell, which had been cast in bronze in the
late nineties, and Mary, the feminine half of his domestic couple,
kept it polished to a fare-thee-well because, she'd told him once,
it represents what the Fairmounts meant to San Francisco. Laird
never bothered to point out that the house had originally belonged
to his grandmother's family, the Klings, not his grandfather's, the
Fairmounts.

Leisurely, he took another sip of his cognac. It was a little too
cool, so he held it in his mouth for a few seconds to warm before
swallowing it. The doorbell rang again, and it was only then that
he remembered that Mary wasn't in the kitchen tonight, cleaning
up the dinner dishes, because she and Robert had gone to visit an
ailing relative in Oakland, leaving him alone in the house.

"Hell," he muttered, wondering irritably who would be calling
on such a lousy evening. It had been raining off and on for the
past twenty-four hours, and right now, gusts of wind were sending
sheets of water against the windowpanes. It must be murder out
there—whoever was calling had chosen a lousy evening to go
visiting.

Briefly, he was tempted not to answer the doorbell, but then he
shrugged and changed his mind. He was very glad he had when
he opened the door and found Ariel standing there.

She was wearing an old raincoat, which drooped around her
ankles and showed dark patches where the rain had penetrated the
canvas material. His first thought was that she looked like a
drowned cat; his second was that she could be an undine, with
her face so pale, her hair soaking, and her eyelashes stuck together
in peaks by the rain—or was it by tears?

"Hello there," he said inanely, trying to hide his shock.

She tried to say something but failed. Then she was in his arms,
clinging to him as if she needed help to stand. Her whole body
shook with sobs, and as he put his arm around her shoulders to
hold her up, he was deeply concerned, not so surprising because
he'd always been fond of his cousin, ever since he'd helped her fly
her kites on the Marina Green.

It wasn't until he'd half carried her inside and was unbuttoning he soggy raincoat that he realized she was stark naked under it.

"My God, Ariel," he said, totally shocked.

She didn't answer. It was as if she hadn't heard him—or wasn't ready to discuss her reason for coming naked to his house in the middle of a rainstorm. Instead, she looked around the living room, her gaze settling on the pastel-tinted painting of a ballerina that hung above the fireplace.

"You have a Degas, too," she said.

He looked at her closely. Surely, she must know that the family feud had started over the disposition of this particular Degas.

"Didn't your parents ever tell you what started the great Fair-mount family feud?" he asked, willing to give her time since that obviously was what she wanted.

"They never talked about it," she said. "I thought our grand-parents quarreled over their parents' estate."

"Oh, that was part of it. Your grandfather was a very shrewd man. He got our mutual great-grandfather to appoint him executor of his estate. After Great-grandfather Fairmount died, your grand-father tied up the estate and eventually ended up with most of it, including all of the family art collections except for this one De-gas. It was probably all for the best, because my grandfather didn't have much of a business head. Luckily, the old boy married into the Kling family, so he ended up with his own house on the marina and enough money that he never had to work a day of his life."

He steered her into the library, got her settled on a sofa, then poured her a glass of cognac and put it between her cold hands. "Okay, it's time for straight talk. Why were you out in the rain with no clothes on to speak of? Why did you come here tonight? I've invited you here so many times, but you never would cross the threshold before."

Ariel bent her head to stare into the amber depths of her cognac as if unable to meet his eyes. He found it interesting that she answered his last question first. "I never felt right about coming here. It seemed as if I'd be betraying my parents if I accepted your invitation."

"I can understand that," he said, although he didn't. "So why are you here tonight?"

"Because I need help, and you live so close. I don't want to involve you in my problems, but I don't have any money, not even enough for a phone call. I should have listened to my friends today—they told me not to go back to the house, but I wanted to prove that I wasn't weak, that I could handle things myself—''

"By handling things do you mean your husband, Ariel?"

She lifted her head now, and the bleakness in her eyes made him flinch. "I thought if I talked to him and told him I wanted him to leave, I could make him see reason, but I was wrong. He—he locked me in my room and took away all my clothes. If I hadn't found this old raincoat the gardener keeps in the potting shed, I don't know what I would have done."

"How did you manage to get out of your bedroom?"

"I—I climbed out the window and went down the tile drainpipe."

A muscle tightened in Laird's jaw. "Has that bastard been abusing you, Ariel? Is that what this is all about?"

Ariel shook her head. "Not physically. He's never hit me but—oh, I don't want to talk about it!"

"How can I help you if you don't tell me what's wrong?"

"It's—too painful. I feel so ashamed—"

"Look, this is your old buddy Laird you're talking to. You can tell me anything. It will do you good to get it off your chest."

She sighed deeply. "It doesn't matter now. I've left Alex. I'm going to get a divorce," she said, so unemotionally that he was fooled—until he saw her hands twisting in her lap.

He took her hands between his. They were so cold that he began to massage them, trying to restore circulation. "How can I help you?" he said.

"Just—just be my friend," she said, her voice so low, he could hardly hear her.

"I've always been your friend. And since you're soaking wet, you need a shower, some dry clothes—and a hot cup of tea." He broke off when she began to laugh. "Did I say something funny?"

She shook her head, and then suddenly the laughter turned to sobs. Although he didn't consider himself an expert on crying women, Laird knew enough to get a tissue from a desk drawer and put it in her hand, to sit there silently while the sobs became hiccups and finally stopped.

"Sorry," Ariel said finally, blowing her nose. "It was what you said about getting out of my wet clothes and taking a hot shower and drinking a hot cup of tea. That's exactly what my friend Stephanie said yesterday when I went to her for help." She gave a hiccuping laugh. "It—it struck me as being funny."

"Well, there's a bit of déjà vu about this business to me, too," he said dryly, thinking about Fern's visit. "And I'm glad that's out of your system. Why don't you go upstairs and—"

"I've changed my mind about telling you what happened. I might not have the courage if I wait," she said.

Laird didn't protest. Even though he was worried that she'd catch a chill, he settled back on the sofa, and for the next few minutes, as Ariel told him about her marriage, he listened in total silence. She seemed to expect his skepticism, but she couldn't have been more wrong. He believed every word she said—and even suspected she was leaving out the worst parts. When he'd first heard that she planned to marry Alex, he had made it his business to find out something about the man, and what he'd learned had made him afraid for her. When she'd ignored his carefully worded warnings and married Alex anyway, he had wondered if he hadn't been too careful. But when she never complained, his suspicions had been somewhat lulled—the more fool he.

When Ariel was finished, she stared at him with expectant eyes, almost, he thought, as if she expected him to produce a miracle and make all her troubles go away. Since he wanted to help her, he did his best.

"First, I want you to take that hot shower, put on something warm, then come back downstairs to drink the tea and sandwiches I'll have ready for you. And when you've finished, I want you to call that bastard and tell him you're okay."

Ariel started to speak, but he shook his head, stopping her. "Wait. Let me finish. I don't mean you should tell him where you are. Only that you're staying with a friend, that you'll be filing for a divorce as soon as you can talk to your lawyer, and that you want him out of your house. And tell him that witnesses are listening in on the conversation just in case he has some idea about calling the police to report you missing and that you were in a dangerous mood when you left the house—or whatever words a psychiatrist would use."

"Probably that I'm psychotic and suicidal," she said, shivering.

"After that, I'm going to call my lawyer—"

"I have my own lawyer—remember? You recommended Mr. Waterford to me."

"So I did. Okay, I want you to tell Waterford everything—and I do mean everything, no matter how embarrassing. I'll let you have all the privacy you want for your call, but be completely candid. You do understand why, don't you?''

"Because a lawyer needs to know if you've done something illegal before he can do his best job of protecting your rights?''

Laird felt a small shock of surprise. He couldn't put it better himself. "Right," he said. "He'll want to dissolve your marriage as quickly as possible. Starting with a court order to evict Alex from your house. And possibly a restraining order to keep him away from you. Alex is very vulnerable to public opinion because of his profession. He can't afford any scandal.''

"No, he'd hate that. He specializes in treating young women—did you know that?''

"I'd heard something along those lines," he said cautiously.

"Did you know that he—he exploits them? Is that common knowledge, too?''

"There've been a few rumors. Why don't you put it out of your mind for now? He's past history—or will be soon.''

"I hope I never see him again as long as I live," Ariel said in a low voice.

Her hair had dried to wisps of pale gold around her face, and Laird was suddenly remembering the child she'd been. Sensitive and shy and achingly lovely—how often he'd wished, when he was eighteen and she was six, that there was no family feud so he could treat her like the little sister he'd never had. But that particular boat had sailed. She wasn't a child any longer, hadn't been for a long time—why did he still find it so hard to think of her as a woman, one who was involved in a sordid and dangerous situation?

Ariel shivered suddenly; he stood up and pulled her to her feet. "Use my bathroom—my bedroom is the second door to the right at the top of the stairs. Put on anything you find in my closet. One of my jogging outfits should do if you push up the legs and arms. Come down when you're ready. I'll be in the kitchen, making tea. That was my mother's cure for everything from a hangnail to a broken heart, you know.''

She stared at him fixedly; briefly, something moved in the depths of her eyes, some emotion he couldn't put a name to. Before he could ask what she was thinking about, she turned without a word and left the room.

Half an hour later, Ariel's phone call to Arnold Waterford was obviously satisfactory because she was smiling when she came into the kitchen, wearing one of his jogging suits, to say that Mr.

Waterford was going to get a restraining order against Alex immediately.

Laird noted the color in her cheeks with relief. What she'd needed was the dispassionate advice of an outsider, someone not involved with her personally. He wanted to ask how her call to her husband had gone, but he checked himself in time.

"After you drink this and have a bite to eat, you'd better get some sleep," he told Ariel. "You look tired—and no wonder, after what you've been through."

"I didn't get much sleep last night," Ariel admitted, and again he caught something elusive in her expression. "I—I went to a friend's house after I left Alex yesterday afternoon. She put me up for the night, but I didn't sleep well at all. I had a nightmare and—well, it wasn't very pleasant. This morning, I had breakfast with the support group I belong to. A couple of them—Chanel was one—offered to put me up until I could make permanent arrangements but—"

"But you went back to Alex."

"It wasn't because I wanted to resume our marriage. It was the house. Except for last night, I've never spent a night away from it. I thought if I sat down and talked to Alex, we could come to some agreement—but I might have known that he would never let me go that easily."

"And this time when you ran away, you came to me," he said, smiling. "Blood *is* thicker than water, isn't it? I want you to stay here as long as you like."

"But won't people talk?"

"Who's to know? My friends—and even my enemies—don't drop in on me unannounced. You could be a thousand miles away from San Francisco as far as Alex knows. If you feel you need a chaperon, my housekeeper and her husband will be back tomorrow." He frowned at her as a thought hit him. "You didn't call anyone else, did you? It might be best if no one knows you're staying here. Wagging tongues and all that. This is a small town in many ways, you know."

"I didn't tell anyone. You don't have to worry—Chanel won't find out unless you tell her."

"Why do you single her out?"

"I thought—well, you *have* been seeing Chanel socially."

So Chanel hadn't told her support group about their engagement. Which proved she was that rare thing, a closemouthed woman—or was that a sexist statement?

"Maybe I should go to a hotel," Ariel said, and he knew she'd misinterpreted his silence. "Actually, I came here to ask if you could lend me some money. I'll need it for the hotel and meals and to buy some clothes. My credit cards are in my purse, back at the house—"

"Nonsense. You're going to stay here. It's best you drop out of sight until the restraining order is in effect. Besides"—he smiled at her—"I wouldn't send a dog out on a night like this."

Her laugh was so high-pitched, he knew she was running on pure nerve now. He took the cup from her hand and lifted her to her feet. Her body felt boneless, so fragile that again he was reminded of the child she'd been. He'd always been bemused by the way she seemed to float as she followed her kite across the Green, her sober little face totally absorbed in what she was doing. He'd also been touched by her capacity for joy over small things—like the caramel corn he'd bought for her from the peddlers. It pained him that she'd had so little joy in her life.

He'd give a lot to change all that.

Laird awakened with a woman's scream echoing in his ears, a sound so alien to the sedate old house that for a moment, he thought he was dreaming. Then the scream came again, and he realized it was Ariel. He didn't bother with slippers and robe; a few seconds after his feet hit the floor, he was running down the hall toward the bedroom where Ariel slept, his bare feet thumping on the hall boards.

He flung open the door and then stood there, staring into the dark room, trying to get his bearings. When he heard a moan, he headed toward it. His hand touched the nightstand beside the bed where Ariel slept; he groped until he found the lamp switch.

In the flood of light, he saw that Ariel was crouching in the middle of the bed, her eyes so wild that he knew she was in the throes of a nightmare.

"It's all right, Ariel," he said soothingly. "You've had a nightmare."

At the sound of his voice, she scooted backward until she came up against a bedpost. When he kept talking quietly and didn't come any closer, awareness finally filtered back into her eyes.

"I—I had a nightmare. It was—" She shuddered violently, and he sat down beside her, careful not to touch her. She was close to collapse—what else had that bastard done to her? And why? To keep her under his thumb so she wouldn't leave him? What had gone on in that house down the street that she hadn't told him?

"I'm sorry I bothered you. You must wish I'd never come here," she whispered.

"None of this is your fault. Blame it on that bastard you married."

"When I told you I was marrying Alex, you tried to warn me but I—I wouldn't listen."

"Put it out of your mind. Do you think you can sleep now?"

She lifted haunted eyes to his face. "I'm afraid it will come back."

She began to cry, and although he usually had little patience with crying women, he did the instinctive thing and put his arms around her shoulders. She pressed her face against his chest; it was surprising how familiar she felt in his arms, as if this weren't the first time he'd held her like this.

A warning flashed in his mind, and he started to pull away. But she wouldn't let him go. "Please—stay with me for a while," she said. "Just hold me until I fall asleep."

The warning was going full blast now, but he pushed it away. This was Ariel; although she wasn't a child any longer, she would always be one to him. And she needed him. He liked that, being needed. So he pulled back the comforter and sheet, got Ariel settled on her pillow, then slid in beside her and threw the covers over both of them. She snuggled up against him, her arms around his waist; a few minutes later, she was asleep.

Afraid to move for fear of awakening her, he decided to stay there a while longer just in case she awoke again. But he must have fallen asleep because suddenly he came awake with a start. There was a pressure on his thigh, and a stirring of warm air against his face. He realized that it was Ariel's breath, that he was still holding her. When he opened his eyes, the room was gray with early dawn light and he saw that Ariel's eyes were open, too, that she was staring at him.

He started to speak, but Ariel spoke first.

"Make love to me," she said, her voice so low he had to strain his ears to hear her. "I want you to make love to me, Laird."

He knew he should pretend he hadn't heard—or that he hadn't understood what she wanted. But some force that was stronger, more elementary, than prudence seemed to have taken over his will. The feeling of pressure increased, and he knew now what it was. He was fully aroused, God help him. He wanted her—he wanted desperately to make love to Ariel. . . .

He fought against temptation. Later, he would marvel at how hard he fought. But he'd been taken by surprise when he was at his weakest, and the battle was already lost even before he kissed her, kissed that incredibly soft mouth, invaded its moist depths with his tongue, and knew that he'd been wanting to do this for a long, long time, that the only reason he hadn't was because he hadn't been willing to admit that he had a carnal desire for someone he'd thought of as his little sister for so many years.

There was none of his usual finesse to the lovemaking that followed. The desire to possess Ariel was urgent, overwhelming, immediate. He took her without any of the niceties of seduction, the skillful foreplay that one of his lovers had called state-of-the-art sex. He caressed her, but he did it fiercely, for his own facile pleasure, and so he was surprised to find that her intimate tissues were already moist and ready for love. Out of control now, he plunged into her softness with a half groan, half growl. Her readiness to receive him so quickly he could accept. She was, after all, a woman who'd been married for almost three years. But what his feverish mind rejected was the resistance he encountered. In his drive for satisfaction, he couldn't stop. He plunged into her again—and this time, her cry told him that the barrier had been broken.

The next few minutes were a kaleidoscope of sensation. He was aware that Ariel's fingernails were raking his shoulders, but he was under the grip of a passion too strong to control. He'd always taken pride in being a considerate lover. Now he only had time for one stark thought—that he didn't really know the man whose frenzied movements were shaking the bed—before all thought faded and there was only sensation, as if every cell in his body had imploded at the same time.

He came back to earth, to reality, with a sickening thud. Ariel lay under him, silent and still, and now it was time for regret, for guilt—and for disbelief. How could she possibly have been a virgin? His mind must have dreamed up that part from some lingering image of her as a child. She'd been married to Alex di Russy for three years—and hadn't she told him, just a few hours ago, that Alex had forced her to have sex with him today when she'd returned to her house?

As for his own behavior—he was as monstrous as her husband. Ariel had come to him for help, and he'd betrayed her trust. He had gone at her like an animal—the ramifications of his actions were horrendous. What had he done in his lust for her?

He groaned and tried to roll away, only to find that Ariel wouldn't let him go. Her arms tightened around his neck, holding him there. He forced himself to look at her and was stupefied to find, not fear or censure, but sensuous satisfaction, a sexual blush that covered what he could see of her body.

"I love you," she said. "I think I've loved you all my life."

Her words sank in, and suddenly everything came together in his mind. There must be a dozen reasons why this was wrong, but he couldn't think of a single one right now.

"Why didn't I realize I loved you before this?" he said. "Was it because you were married and I knew it was too late?"

"But it isn't too late. I'm divorcing Alex—remember? Make love to me again, Laird. I want to feel you inside me."

Her words stirred up a memory. "You were a virgin," he said. "How is that possible?"

Her expression changed. Her arms fell away, leaving him feeling bereft. "Alex never made love to me like this. He did other things—he called them therapeutic scenarios. I thought that it was impossible for me to—to enjoy sex the normal way. I even thought—" She broke off, blinking hard.

"You thought—what?"

"I can't tell you. I'm too ashamed. Something happened that made me wonder if I was—but I was wrong. What I feel for you is normal and wonderful and a miracle. But let's not talk now. Make love to me again."

Laird knew it was too soon. He wasn't, after all, a sixteen-year-old boy in his sexual prime—but that didn't stop him. He kissed her, then went on to other things, and she responded so quickly that he knew she was a highly sexed woman. No wonder Alex's "therapeutic scenarios" had been effective. A clever, experienced man could make a sensual woman respond even against her will—was that what she'd meant by being afraid she was abnormal?

Rage consumed him at the thought of Alex touching her, trying to pervert her. It was only when Ariel gave a small cry of pain that he realized he was holding her too tightly, his fingers biting into her arms. He loosened his grip and began a slow procession of kisses down her pliant body. She moved beneath him, mutely telling him that she was ready anytime he wanted to take her.

Again the miracle happened, and in the afterglow of what would have tasked a horny teenager, he marveled at his own prowess. He'd heard men brag about multiple intercourse, but he'd never quite believed them because once a night had always been enough for him. But then he'd never made love to Ariel before. He loved her, not just wanted her—and obviously that made all the difference.

And now that he knew the truth, how could he give her up? How could he live without her? And yet—there was Chanel. In another few days, they were planning to announce their engagement at his annual spring party.

What the *hell* was he going to do about that?

CHAPTER THIRTY-FOUR

JANICE HAD FINISHED CLEANING THE UPSTAIRS BATHROOMS AND was downstairs in the kitchen, putting the finishing touches on a luncheon salad, when the phone rang. She put down the stalk of celery she'd been chopping, then paused to wipe her wet hands on a towel before she went to answer it, only to find that Jake had already picked up the extension in his den.

She listened, intending to cut in if it was for her, and heard his voice say, "She's upstairs doing her hausfrau thing. And you know you shouldn't call here, sweetcakes. Most of the time, she gets to the phone first."

A female voice, young and self-consciously sultry, said, "But I missed you today. I thought you'd wait for me, but you'd split by the time I got to your classroom."

"Yeah, well, I had an appointment. You know how busy I am these days."

"I know, I know." There was a pout in the voice now. A picture formed in Janice's mind—of a tall, leggy girl with long blond hair, beating eggs for an omelet in their kitchen. What the devil was her name? Peggy—no, Teri Something-or-other. . . . "I haven't seen much of you lately."

"I've been up to my eyeballs in work. That TV class takes up all my extra time."

"Not all of it. I saw you at The Chimes last week with a red-haired woman. She was hanging all over you."

"Business—strictly business. That was Arlene—her husband's the producer of my TV show." There was a jovial note in Jake's voice that sounded false. "Don't tell me you're jealous? Hey, she's a married woman."

"You're a married man. You know what the kids at school call you? Jake the Make."

There was a long silence. "I see you're in a bitchin' mood. Why don't we just call it quits? It was fun while it lasted—"

The phone slipped from Janice's hand, but she snatched it out of the air before it could hit the counter. When she put it to her ear again, there was only a hum. She replaced the receiver in its cradle, handling it carefully, as if it might explode.

She returned to the salad, finished it off, and slid the bowl into the refrigerator. She got a glass from the cupboard, filled it with ice water from the refrigerator dispenser, but instead of drinking it, she held it to her hot cheeks, then to her throat. She'd had several of these hot spells lately, but this was the first time it had occurred to her that she might be starting an early menopause.

And wouldn't that be great timing? Menopause at forty and a husband the students called Jake the Make. The bastard—the horny bastard. . . .

Her own reflection, in the metal sides of the toaster, mocked her. In her blue knit shirt and jeans, with her brown hair neat, her face bare of makeup, she looked—nice. Unexciting but nice. A hausfrau, Jake had called her. Was that how he saw her these days? As a rather nice but unexciting housewife who cooked his meals, kept his house clean, serviced him when he was feeling horny?

She jumped nervously when the phone at her elbow buzzed like an angry fly. She was tempted to let Jake answer it again, but habit was too strong and she picked it up on the second ring.

"Janice? This is Ariel."

"Ariel?" Janice turned the name over in her mind as if it were strange to her. She felt light-headed, a little dizzy; her voice seemed to be coming from a deep wall as she said, "How are you, Ariel?"

"I guess you know that I left Alex?"

Janice fumbled with the meaning of Ariel's words, finally got them in focus. "Oh, yes. Stephanie called me yesterday morning. She was worried because you'd left her house without telling her where you were going. She called again later, said she'd talked to you and that you'd decided to go back to have a talk with your husband. Where are you calling from?"

There was a brief silence. "I don't think I should tell you. That way if Alex tries to find out where I am, none of you will have to lie. I left your phone numbers behind in my desk. It's possible he might find the list and call you."

"I'm sure you're right." Janice's head throbbed, keeping time with her pulse. She felt so weak that she wondered dully if she was about to pass out. "I hope things work out for you," she said, knowing how lame and inadequate that must sound.

"Yes—yes, everything is great now. I'm staying with a friend, and I've already made an appointment to see Mr. Waterford. He's going to handle my divorce."

Janice's curiosity stirred sluggishly. Ariel sounded as if she were on a high—had she been drinking or was she simply relieved to be out of a bad marriage?

"I guess that's best," Janice said. "What happened when you went to see your husband?"

"I'd—I'd rather not talk about it. But everything is great now."

To Janice, whose world was collapsing around her, the lilt in Ariel's voice seemed a mockery of her own misery, but she forced herself to speak pleasantly.

"I'm really sorry I wasn't there yesterday when the rest of you had breakfast together at Cliff House. I was on the phone for ages, calling hospitals and hotels." She forced a laugh. "Do you have any idea how many hotels there are in the city?"

"Oh, I'm sorry! I caused so much trouble—"

"To use one of Chanel's favorite phrases—'What are friends for?' " Janice said, although she wanted to tell Ariel that she had her own troubles, that she'd just found out her husband was having an affair with one of his students. How many others of his lame ducks had he seduced through the years? Some of them? All of them?

"You will keep in touch, won't you?" she went on, determinedly cheerful. "Did Chanel tell you about her party—well, actually it isn't her party. Your cousin Laird is throwing it, and she's going to act as his hostess. And it seems we're all invited. You *are* coming, aren't you?"

"I—I'm not much for socializing," Ariel said.

"Well, gear yourself up for this one. Chanel says she has an important announcement to make that night, but she wouldn't say any more. She's being very mysterious. What do you suppose it is?"

Ariel hesitated so long Janice wondered if they'd been cut off. "I'm sure I don't know." The animation had left her voice now. "And I doubt if I can make the party. My—my friend thinks I should get away from the city for a while."

"Well, I hope you change your mind," Janice said politely, although she didn't care if Ariel came to the party or not—or even if the sun rose tomorrow. She was glad when Ariel said she had to go, that her friend was waiting to take her shopping.

The phone felt heavy in Janice's hand as she hung up—or maybe it was the weight of her own thoughts. She was still slumped on the utility stool when Jake came breezing into the kitchen.

"I'm going out for a while, so don't bother to fix me any lunch," he said.

"Sit down, Jake. I want to talk to you."

"Can't it wait? You know I always have a dozen things to do on my free afternoon."

"Such as rolling in the hay with Little Miss Sweetcakes?"

Jake's face changed color, but he tried to bluff it out. He even managed to sound aggrieved. "I see you've taken up eavesdropping. That's pretty gross, isn't it?"

"And you still use the same old buzzwords you used at Berkeley. I don't have to explain myself to you, but as it happens, I picked up the kitchen phone just after you did and I listened in to see if the call was for me. That's when I heard that scintillating conversation between you and—what's her name? Teri Something-or-Other?"

"Look, there's nothing going on between me and Teri. Oh, she's got this giant-sized crush on me, but it's strictly one-sided. I've been kidding her along so she won't get hurt—she's just a kid, you know. What do you think I am? A cradle-snatcher?"

"I don't know what you are, Jake. Jake the Make or the husband I've been living with for twenty years and thought I knew." Janice stopped to take a deep breath because there was a sharp pain just behind her ribs.

"I swear to you it's totally innocent. Okay, Teri and I had a little flirtation going, but that's all it was. We met a couple of times for drinks, but even that's over—"

"Why? Because you started something with Arlene? I've really been stupid, haven't I? All the signs were there—including the hints my friends dropped and which I didn't pick up on. I remember how the two of you disappeared at our Christmas party. What were you doing, groping each other in the backyard? Dumb me. Isn't one of the first signs supposed to be when the wife notices a drop in the husband's libido? But that hasn't changed—you're always ready to jump into bed at the drop of a hat. How on earth do you manage to keep two—or is it three?—women satisfied at the same time?''

"You're talking crazy, Janice. Sure, I like women, but I've never cheated on you—"

"How many people know about it? Just our friends or the whole damned university?''

"Look, this conversation is going nowhere. You're way off base about Teri. What's really bothering you? That damned dissertation? You're bogged down, aren't you, but you just won't admit it. So why don't you give it up—or at least shelve it for a while. I'll make a bargain with you. You're always saying that the TV class takes up too much of my time, so why don't I drop it? I'm tired of it, anyway. Besides, the publicity I've been getting is causing too much envy in the department.''

He'd managed to confound her. ''You're offering to give up your TV class?'' she asked.

"Hell, honey, if it will make things better between us, I'd give up breathing. Our marriage is what keeps me going—you know that, don't you? You're my rock. I don't know what I'd do if you got some crazy idea to leave me.''

He put his arms around her. She breathed in the familiar citrus scent of his after-shave lotion, the odor of wool from the Pendleton shirts he favored in cool weather, the muskiness of healthy, virile male flesh, and her certainty began to fray at the edges.

Jake kissed her, and suddenly the phone call she'd overheard seemed open to another interpretation. Was Jake right? Maybe it was the dissertation, the frustrations and doubts and uncertainties connected with it, that had colored her suspicions. After all, what exactly had she heard during that phone conversation? A very young, very jealous eighteen-year-old making something out of nothing. . . .

Maybe she *was* starting into an early menopause. Some women went absolutely bonkers then, didn't they?

Jake's hand slid down her back. As he stroked her, then insinuated his hand between her thighs, she came to a decision. She would put the phone call out of her mind, banish it for good. If the support group had taught her anything these past few months, it was the knowledge that there were few, if any, perfect marriages. Why would she expect hers to be the exception?

For the past week, Chanel had been so deeply involved with preparations for Laird's party that she scarcely had time for sleep, much less worrying about anything except the party at the St. Francis Hotel.

She had known at once that Laird's house, large as it was, wouldn't accommodate the number of guests on their combined lists. Not that some of the ones she'd added to the list knew that *she* had invited them. Oh, no, it wouldn't do to reveal her hand too soon. It was too important that they accept the invitation— and it wasn't likely anyone would turn down one from Laird Fairmount.

As to why she'd made sure the Hillsborough bunch were invited, it was central to her own plans that they be there on her night of triumph. And why not? She had dreamed of this day ever since the debacle of her first marriage. The announcement of her engagement to Laird would make up for so many things—such as the humiliation she'd suffered after her divorce from Jacques that had made her persona non grata to so many people.

Oh, yes, she would get her own back in spades Saturday night— and how she was going to enjoy it! Not that she intended to show, not by the flicker of an eyelash, how she felt. The idea was to be accepted by the women who'd made her life miserable those last two years at the Academy. Her revenge would come later, bit by bit, incident by incident. An open feud would never accomplish that, no matter how satisfying it might be to rub their noses in her new status.

The only dark spot in the whole thing had been the difficulty of finding an acceptable place for the party. The best spots, such as the Huntington and Stanford Court, were already booked up for May, but she'd finally managed to get one of the ballrooms at the St. Francis. Not her first choice, but acceptable. And it was a central location on Union Square—that was a plus.

It was a symbol of Laird's social position that there had been only four regrets and two no-replies, which was a very high ratio for a guest list of that size. Of course, it was being held on a socially quiet weekend when, as far as she knew, there were no other important parties or charity affairs or openings. She had no doubts that Laird's party was going to be the social event of the month, outshining by a country mile the Black & White Ball, which was strictly a media event everybody she knew avoided like the plague because anyone with the price of a ticket could attend.

Of course, Ariel's domestic problems had intruded briefly on her busy schedule, but now that Ariel was staying with a friend and had started divorce proceedings, she could put that whole business out of her mind. She wasn't even going to mention it to Laird. Of all the women in the club, Ariel was the one she related to the least, even though, being Laird's cousin, Ariel was also the reason why she'd joined the group. Privately, she considered her a bore, someone Fern would probably call a wimp.

Chanel frowned suddenly. Fern . . . that business she'd concocted about Laird trying to rape her was a mystery. What was behind that? It was patently a lie made up from whole cloth. Laird was too much of a gentleman for anything so—so physical. True, he was quite good in bed, but he was still the last thing from a libertine. Stet had compared him to a Thoroughbred racehorse, but actually he reminded *her* of a Russian wolfhound—well bred, sensitive, and also much tougher than his decorative exterior revealed.

They hadn't seen each other for more than a week, not since he'd called to say that he was fighting a virus and was staying home until he got over it. Since his voice sounded perfectly normal, she suspected he was just giving her space so she could do the thousand-and-one things a party of this magnitude demanded.

Chanel approved of his tact. She hadn't asked for his help with the party, and he hadn't offered it. "I'll leave the details to you," he'd told her. "You have carte blanche—on additional guests, arrangements, expense. Just send the bills to my office. I trust your judgment."

She felt a little guilty about that. Carte blanche was one thing, but she'd gone overboard on such things as ordering the top-of-the-line buffet from John Glover, Caterer, who charged outrageous prices even for their rock-bottom economy spread. In fact, there had been no stinting on anything—for a very good reason. Even the smallest sign of economizing would be apparent to the guests, who patronized the same caterers, the same florists, hired the same dance bands. She wanted them to get the message loud and clear that she, Chanel O'Hara Devereau, was now in control. Oh, they would find fault and talk about her behind her back, pick, pick, pick, but their gossip would be built on cobwebs, not from any real flaws in the party.

A sound at the door interrupted her musings. Fern came into the room, bringing the odor of apples with her, and flopped down on the small chaise longue Chanel kept there for an occasional nap. Ignoring Chanel, she bit into the apple she was holding, chewed it noisily. Chanel held her tongue, even though Fern looked so grubby, she itched to tell her to go take a shower and change her clothes.

Ever since the incident of Laird's supposed rape attempt, Fern had been baiting her. No open insults or arguments, just those cold, venomous stares and long brooding silences. Well, this, too, would pass. Fern was a realist; she knew on which side her bread was buttered. For one thing, as soon as the wedding was over, there'd be money to send her to whatever Ivy League School she could qualify for this fall. . . .

"Have you decided on a school yet?" she asked, breaking the silence.

Fern shrugged. "I'm not sure what I want to do."

"Oh? Well, you're a big girl now. If you don't want to go to college, you can always get a job."

Fern flung the apple core into a crystal ashtray. "You'd like that, wouldn't you? It would save your precious Laird the price of my tuition and expenses. What would you say if I told you I'd decided to enroll at Radcliffe—or Harvard?"

"I'd say bully for you—provided your profile can get you accepted," Chanel said, her tone dry.

"Oh, I'll get in. And I don't intend to scrimp, either. I'll need a new car—do you think Laird will buy me a Porsche? I've always fancied one."

"Laird is generous, but he isn't a fool."

"He's a wimp—a sexless wimp. I give you a month before you start cruising again, looking for some young dude to warm your bed."

Chanel fought back the hot words that rose to her lips. "Why are you so vitriolic about Laird?" she asked. "That story you concocted—did you throw yourself at him and get rejected?" With satisfaction, she eyed the hot flush that rose to Fern's cheeks. "That's it, isn't it? You never learn, Fern. You have a very bad habit of biting the hand that feeds you. As for Laird being sexless—take my word for it, there's nothing wrong with his sex drive *or* his technique."

Fern jumped to her feet and stormed out of the room. Chanel stared after her, a crease forming between her eyebrows. Absently, she smoothed it away with her fingertips. Fern was going to be a problem, but then—when hadn't she been? True, there for a while they'd seemed to be getting along pretty well. Not friends but close to it. Well, Fern would come around—but wouldn't it be nice if they could live together without all this hostility between them?

Chanel returned to the guest list. She smiled with satisfaction as she checked off Lars and Nancy Anderson's names, denoting their acceptance. How sweet—how very sweet—it was going to be.

She came to the names of the support group, which were listed together. Except for Ariel, they had all accepted her invitation. Janice, who moved in Stanford circles, would fit in without any trouble, while Stephanie, who was Mrs. Suburbia personified, would look a little out of place—but not conspicuously so. Ariel, if she had accepted the invitation, would have fit in best of all—and wasn't that odd? On the other hand, Glory would stand out like an exclamation mark, even though her appearance had changed for the better in the past months.

Thanks to me, Chanel thought complacently.

She'd told the women that they could come with or without an escort, and she rather hoped Glory would bring this Steve Golden she'd been dating so steadily. He claimed to be a Yalie—well, time would tell. And certainly *she* could tell as soon as he opened his mouth. If he was a phony, she would warn Glory off, because that's the way Glory would want it. In her own way, Glory had the right stuff, despite her street language and her sometimes disconcerting frankness.

Would any of them guess that this was her last hurrah with them? With the active social life she'd be leading as Laird's wife, she wouldn't have time for those once-a-month luncheons. After she and Laird came back from their honeymoon, she would have to keep in touch with Ariel for a while. Laird was very fond of his cousin—he'd told her once that Ariel was the closest thing he'd ever had to a sister—but she'd make sure that the invitations grew further and further apart, and after a while, Ariel would fade out of their lives.

Even if she did want to stay on with the club, which she didn't, it would be inappropriate. As a happy bride, she would be out of place among a group of divorcées, even though they seldom talked about their marital problems these days. Mostly it was chitchat with few serious overtones, a lot of banter and a surprising number of laughs. Janice, it was true, was always trying to get them back on serious subjects, such as when they'd first realized their marriages were in trouble, but—"Who wants to dwell on the past?" Stephanie had once said, and the rest, all but Janice, had agreed.

Chanel's newly hired housekeeper, a stolid Italian woman named Sophia, came to the door of the den. "Someone to see you, Mrs. Devereau—claims he's the caterer for your party."

Chanel laid her pen down and rose. "Show him into the living room. I'll be there shortly. And do get the names of visitors in the future, Sophia."

"Yes, ma'am," Sophia said.

Chanel went to smooth down her hair and add a touch of lipstick. Just one more day until the party—and wasn't that going to be a night to remember?

Ariel was lying on her stomach on the teakwood deck of Laird's skiff, *Sea Lark*. She was stark naked. A three-sided wooden enclosure protected her from the unwelcome attention of any passing boat. It had been installed for just that purpose in mind because Laird, too, liked to sun in the buff. The railing also served to protect her from the worst ravages of the sun although, Laird reflected now, it was surprising how much sun that fair skin could take without burning or even tanning.

As Laird watched, Ariel yawned and stretched luxuriously, extending her long, slender legs and arms as far as they would go. Her body was lithe, her muscles tight, her pubic hair the color of ripe wheat. Despite her slenderness, she was all woman, and even though they'd made love less than an hour ago, Laird felt a familiar ache start up in his loins again.

He had always thought of sexual intercourse as "having sex"; now, the words didn't seem to fit the explosive coming together, the melding he felt with Ariel when they made love. And to think that he'd believed he was too old for romance—or was that word as inaccurate for what he felt for Ariel as "having sex" was? Whatever it was, he was torn with indecision, unable to come to any conclusions about what to do about Chanel.

One thing was for sure—no way could he allow Ariel to find out about his engagement from someone else. This was the reason why, late this morning, he had taken her out for a run in his boat even though he was slated to pick up Chanel and her daughter at seven.

It was late afternoon now and they'd have to turn back soon. So why hadn't he told Ariel that he was engaged to another woman? What was holding him back? There was no question of jilting Chanel. First off, he had made a commitment to her. How could he, at this late date and after she had worked so hard on their engagement party, change his mind? He wasn't even sure if he wanted to.

Yes, Ariel enchanted him, excited him in a way no other woman ever had, and he felt protective toward her to a degree that bordered on obsession, but how long would that be enough? How long before the fire that flamed every time he touched her burned out?

As for what Ariel felt for him—it was obvious that she was happy. Every time they made love she told him how much she loved him. But wasn't her judgment suspect? She was, despite her marriage to Alex di Russy, totally unworldly. Might she not be mistaking longtime affection for him, and the passion that flared so quickly between them, for love?

So how did he go about telling her that it would all have to end between them? Did he just sit down beside her and say that this past week had been a blast but it was all over because he was going to marry Chanel? What would it do to her? To him?

"What are you thinking about?" Ariel asked, and he realized that she'd rolled over on her back, and was watching him. Strange that she wasn't a bit shy about stripping in front of him. In fact, she seemed to revel in it. And there was no doubt she was well aware how her nakedness was affecting him. From the way she was stretching again, arching her body so provocatively without taking her eyes off him, she was trying to entice him into another session of lovemaking.

And he was ready. God, he'd had no idea that he, man-about-San Francisco Laird Fairmount, could be as randy as a sixteen-year-old.

They made love again on the sun-speckled deck. It had surprised him, after that first time, how uninhibited Ariel was. In fact, making love to her was so natural, so much a mutual thing, so free of worry about satisfying her that for the first time in his life, he realized how much time he'd spent stewing about technique.

Chanel was a skillful, innovative, and lusty lover, but he'd never lost himself in her—or in any other woman. It was different with Ariel. When their bodies merged, their minds went into a state of total sync, and he knew instinctively what she was feeling, knew where to touch her, when to vary the rhythm of their lovemaking so that they always reached the peak of ecstasy at the same moment. It was humbling to realize how unknowing he'd been about the act of love before Ariel. It wasn't a contest, a source of masculine pride. It was a giving, a taking, a communication above all—and he'd never felt this way with anyone else.

So what was this thing that had been missing in his life until now?

Was it—love?

Was it as simple as that?

CHAPTER THIRTY-FIVE

As soon as she'd made one final call to the banquet manager of the venerable old St. Francis Hotel to make sure there would be no last-minute problems, Chanel disappeared into her bedroom to get ready for the party, but first she took the phone off the hook, not wanting to be distracted during this important part of the evening.

It was necessary that she look her best tonight—and it had nothing to do with vanity but with image. To that end, she'd spent more time then she could spare shopping for a gown, finally deciding on a stunning new Bill Blass design that was so unusual that she knew she'd only be able to wear it once to any local affair—a minor consideration under the circumstances.

Even though the gown would eventually cost Laird an arm and a leg when the bill came through, it was necessary to make a statement that she wasn't some Cinderella, marrying the city's most eligible bachelor. And wasn't it lucky that she wouldn't be paying for it herself? She was almost broke, the last of the money she'd received for launching Elsie Stetson into San Francisco society going for such mundane things as food, overdue bills, utilities, and rent.

After giving it a lot of thought, she'd invited the Stetsons to the party. They weren't the type of people she would be cultivating as Laird's wife, but decency demanded that she give Elsie this chance to rub elbows with the elite of local society. She couldn't abide the woman, but she did have a soft spot for Stet, who reminded her so much of her father.

Although he wasn't flamboyant the way Tincan O'Hara had been, he had the kind of innate self-confidence that springs from inner strength of character rather than from money or breeding. Yes, Stet would fit in with the other guests, but that socially inept wife of his might be a problem.

Not that it really mattered. Even if Elsie turned up looking like a dance hall girl, it was doubtful if anyone would notice. They'd be too busy absorbing the news that Laird Fairmount was marrying Chanel Devereau.

As Chanel applied a light dusting of eye shadow to her eyelids, she reflected that it was too bad she didn't have a male relative to make the engagement announcement. As it was, Laird would have to do the honors. She had meant to ask Laird what he planned to say, but she hadn't been able to reach him for the past two days. When she called his house, no one answered, which was rather strange because even if he was out, he did have live-in domestic help. Well, it didn't matter. She could trust Laird to say the right thing. In his entire adult life, he'd probably never done anything unconventional or off the wall. Which was fine with her. Sometimes, he came across as a little too conservative, but after they were married, she intended to coax him into using his wealth to its fullest. Not that she meant to be so extravagant that it would cause friction between them, of course.

She finished applying her makeup, then examined herself in the mirror above the dressing table. She was gratified to find that she looked every bit as good as she felt, which was saying something. Funny how important appearance was to a woman—well, to some women. It didn't seem to matter to others. Janice Morehouse, for instance. Those wool tweed jackets and pleated skirts and that wash-and-wear hairstyle—all very suitable for her life-style, no doubt, but it was obvious she spent very little time worrying about her appearance.

Glory, on the other hand, was really becoming a stunner. At the April luncheon, she had looked marvelous in a blue silk chambray dress, her narrow waist belted by several strands of chalk-white shells that, she'd told Chanel, she'd bought from a street peddler on Market Street. These days, she had a mind of her own. At first, she'd copied Chanel slavishly, but now she was blossoming out with her own ideas. How strange that she still hadn't finished furnishing her apartment. "First things first," she'd said when Chanel asked if she was still sleeping on the floor.

Chanel felt a laugh bubble up in her throat. She'd miss Glory, who could always make her laugh. But there'd be no place in her life for the Glorys—or the Stephanies or the Janices and certainly not the Ariels—of the world after she became Mrs. Laird Fairmount.

She slipped her narrow feet into silver opera pumps, then gave herself a final inspection as she always did before leaving the house.

Make up—perfect. A subtle shading of blush to highlight her cheekbones, lipstick a discreet rose, because Laird preferred the natural look in his women. That would change once they were married, but for now, she was still catering to his tastes. Later, she would reeducate him—but subtly, subtly.

Jewelry—a narrow strand of emeralds, set in silver, one of the few things of value Jacques had ever given her. How lucky that silver settings were back in fashion again. No rings because she wanted her fingers to be bare when Laird slipped the emerald-and-diamond engagement ring on her finger tonight. She would give it to him at the party; at present, it was safely tucked away in her evening bag.

Then there was her gown, a dramatic silver lamé with a black silk backing that was a perfect match to her silver-blond hair; it fell from one shoulder, just barely brushed her breasts and hips, then ended in billowing fullness at her feet. It was one of Bill Blass's best concoctions—very striking, very becoming, very expensive.

Hair—smooth, with a braided chignon that Adolfo had slaved over half the afternoon, alternately bitching and paying her extravagant compliments.

Other women might wear the flyaway hairstyles that were so popular lately, but not she. "Regal lady," Adolfo had called her when he was finished. Regal—yes, that was the word for Chanel Devereau, once Chanel O'Hara, Tincan O'Hara's daughter, soon to be Chanel Fairmount, Laird Fairmount's wife. . . .

And look who landed on top of the heap, Nancy Anderson with

your antiques and your short, portly husband, and your butt that's wide enough to knead dough on. . . .

There was a tap at the door, and Fern came into the room. Chanel looked her over with judicious eyes. Fern's slim, long-legged body was striking in a champagne-colored mid-calf gown she'd chosen herself. It was surprising how attractive she could be when she wasn't wearing those horrid punk outfits.

"You look like a princess," Chanel said aloud. "Champagne is a perfect color with your dark hair and eyes."

"What's this? A compliment? You usually have something snide to say about the way I dress," Fern said.

Chanel's lips tightened, but because she was determined that nothing would spoil her evening, her voice was light and unargumentative as she said, "But think how much it means when I do compliment you. You know it isn't just flattery."

She picked up her silver evening bag. "Well, I'm ready. Laird should be along any minute now."

"Right. It wouldn't do to keep the lucky—and oh, so rich—bridegroom waiting."

Chanel frowned at her. "Fern, you will be careful what you say tonight, won't you? Remember, you have a stake in this, too. These people—well, their good opinion will matter to you someday."

Fern shrugged. "I doubt that. But okay, I'll be good. When they tell me—and they will—that I don't resemble my gorgeous mother, I'll blush demurely and won't tell them to go to hell."

"You're a lovely young woman—and don't you forget it," Chanel said sharply.

Fern gave her a surprised look. "I do believe you mean that, Chanel," she said.

"Of course, I do. I may not be your average doting mother, but I am proud of you. And I want you to be happy. I don't want you to end up living some kind of scruffy life."

"Well, we agree on that. Rich is better than poor. If I have a choice—I'll take rich."

"That's my girl. Just don't—don't fight me at every turn. I really do want the best for you."

Sophia appeared in the doorway. "Your car's waiting downstairs, Miz Devereau."

"Tell Mr. Fairmount we'll be there shortly."

"He ain't here. It's his driver. He says he's parked double, so you'd better get going, ma'am."

"Not here? I don't understand—well, no matter. Tell the man we'll be along as soon as we put on our wraps."

A few minutes later, they were seated in Laird's gray Rolls, heading downtown toward Union Square—and the St. Francis.

"What do you suppose happened to Laird?" Fern said.

"I have no idea. Something important must have come up."

She leaned forward and slid open the glass panel that separated them from Laird's driver, the middle-aged man who doubled as his gardener and handyman. "Do you know what delayed Mr. Fairmount, Robert?" she asked.

Robert glanced at her over his shoulder, then turned his eyes back to the traffic ahead. "No, ma'am," he said. "This morning, Mr. Laird, he told me to get the Rolls out of the garage and service it, to pick you ladies up at seven, but I ain't seen him since. The missus thinks he went out for a run in his boat around noon, but he's still not back. I wouldn't worry about him none, Mrs. Devereau. He's got one of those ship-to-shore contraptions on his boat. He'll be along shortly, I suspect."

"Thank you," Chanel said. As she slid the glass back in place, she decided to take his advice and not worry about Laird. Of all the people she'd ever known, he was the most reliable. If he'd been delayed because of engine trouble, he'd simply call for help. Meanwhile, she would handle things until he got there.

When they reached the St. Francis, Robert parked at the main entrance and then hurried around the limo to open the rear door before the doorman could reach them.

"You know what time to pick us up, don't you?" Chanel asked.

"Yes, ma'am. Mr. Laird says I should go back home and wait until he calls. That okay, ma'am?"

There was a deference in his voice that Chanel contributed to his awareness of what her status would shortly be. Trust the servants to know first, she thought with amusement.

"That's fine—you might ask Mary to chill some champagne for us before she goes to bed," she said, reveling in this first direct order to Laird's staff.

As she followed Fern into the faded elegance of the old hotel, she couldn't resist a complacent smile. How good it was—and tonight was only the beginning.

The ballroom was old and gracious and immense, the relic of an earlier era. Tonight, it had been decorated according to Chanel's specifications. Giant potted palms and tree ferns softened the corners of the long, rectangular room and created pockets of semiprivacy for the small groupings of gilded ballroom chairs and tables. Sprays of creamy orchids adorned each table, and urns of long-stemmed white roses and carnations, interspersed with greenery, complemented the elaborate Victorian trappings of the hotel. Above, the crystal chandeliers that dated from early in the century cast a frosty light over all.

On a raised platform at one end of the long room, the members of a seven-piece band were tuning their instruments, preparing for the evening's entertainment. Chanel had tried to import an Eastern band, first Peter Duchin and then other groups that catered strictly to society affairs, but in the end she'd been forced to settle for one of the better local orchestras. Well, they looked dignified enough in their tuxedoes—and all they were really required to do was to play the old standards that were perfect for dancing but never intrusive to conversation.

As she crossed the gleaming floor of the ballroom, she regarded with satisfaction the ivory-colored silk tent at the far end of the ballroom. She had decided against a sit-down dinner because of the size of the guest list, and then had gone all out to come up with something different in the way of a buffet. The tent, vaguely Oriental and certainly innovative, which had cost a mint, had been an inspiration. Not only did it discreetly conceal the serving tables from the rest of the ballroom, but it also would provide refreshments continuously throughout the evening.

She found the head caterer inside the tent, overseeing the crew of workers who were busily setting up the buffet. Knowing he was watching her, she gave the service tables a leisurely inspection, her face impassive. The flower displays—dozens of sprays of creamy orchids—were perfect, as was the crystal, the silver chafing and serving dishes, the immaculate Spode service, but to keep the caterer on his toes, she changed the position of a spray of orchids and smoothed out a tiny wrinkle in a snow-white linen tablecloth.

The caterer cleared his throat. "Is everything okay, Mrs. Devereau?"

Chanel didn't answer his question directly. "Do ask the servers to put out fresh food as soon as platters and chafing dishes become three-fourths empty—oh, and would you check their uniforms? I noticed that one of your men looked—well, rather slovenly at the Blacks' dinner party last month," she said. "Also, tell the waiters to stay on their toes. I don't want any guest to be forced to carry his own plate back to his table after he's made his selection—and make sure the tables are cleared off quietly and as discreetly as possible after the guests have eaten. Also, Mr. Fairmount has an important announcement to make midway through the evening. When you hear a drumroll from the bandstand, make sure the waiters are prepared to serve the guests the special champagne I ordered. It must be done quickly, because a toast will be made at that time. Do you understand?''

''Yes, Mrs. Devereau,'' the man said, looking so flustered that she knew he'd jack up his help as soon as she was gone.

She dismissed the man with a nod and was leaving the tent when a masculine voice spoke at her elbow. ''You do that very well, Chanel. You should have been a general.''

She turned, already smiling because she expected to see Laird. But it was William Stetson who stood behind her, looking amused.

''Oh—I thought you were Laird,'' she said.

''I didn't realize Fairmount had a Texas drawl,'' Stet said, his tone dry.

Chanel's smile was cool; she was in no mood for an exchange of banter with Stet. Pointedly, she glanced down at the tiny jeweled watch on her wrist. ''Aren't you a bit early? The invitation said eight o'clock—''

''I am, and I apologize. I realized I was much too early when I reached the hotel, so I stopped at the lobby bar for a drink. I saw you and your young daughter passing through, so I followed you here to say hello.''

''How nice. Will your wife be coming along later?''

His smiled faded. ''I had to put Elsie in a nursing home. She tried to burn the house down—the doctors say there's been a sudden deterioration in her condition and she has to be kept under constant guard now. I would keep her at home, but she's developed this—this antagonism toward me.''

''Her condition?'' Chanel asked. ''Is she ill?''

''Alzheimer's disease.''

Chanel suddenly felt cold. So many things about Elsie Stetson's bizarre behavior were clear now—but why hadn't he told her earlier? Fear that if she knew about Elsie's condition, she wouldn't have taken on the job of grooming her? She started to say how sorry she was, but he was already going on.

''I had nurses staying with her around the clock, but she still managed to light a second fire.'' For a moment, his eyes belied his casual tone. ''Her doctor is sure she'll be happier in a controlled environment. This place he recommended is supposed to be tops, so I'm giving it a try—and you don't want to hear my troubles. You must have a dozen last-minute things to do.''

"Everything is running smoothly, and besides, most of our guests will arrive fashionably late." Chanel laid her hand on his arm. "I'm so sorry about Elsie. How does she feel about being in the nursing home? Does she resent it?''

"She seems content enough. It's located in one of those old Victorians on Nob Hill, just a few blocks from our place—very homey and not at all institutionalized. She's developed this delusion that she's a houseguest there, that one of the day nurses is her hostess—luckily she's taken a fancy to the woman. She even tolerates me as long as I don't stay too long. The—the paranoia she's suffering from is something new." Stet looked so haggard that she knew it was even worse than his dry, matter-of-fact words indicated. "The latest twist is her belief that she's being poisoned, but she thinks she's safe as long as she only takes food from the day nurse. It's working out pretty well, at least for the present.''

"I'm sorry—I'm really sorry," Chanel murmured.

"It's been hell. Why don't they find a cure for that rotten disease?''

"They will—in time."

"But too late to help Elsie. It's the slow progress of the disease that's so hard to accept. The doctors tell me that her faculties will deteriorate one by one through the next decade or so. Right now, she looks younger than she has in years, as if all stress has been wiped off the slate for her. All that remains is this obsession that I want her dead. It isn't true. I don't want her dead. I want her the way she was when we were first married.''

His eyes had a sheen now, as if tears were gathering under his eyelids. Chanel pitied him—but it was also embarrassing to see him, this strong-willed man, reduced to tears.

"I never thought I'd see you indulging in self-pity," she said crisply. "This isn't the William Stetson I know."

He gave her a thin smile. "Hard as nails, aren't you? And you know instinctively the right thing to say, too, don't you? Which is my roundabout way of saying I admire you, Chanel Devereau. I'm not sure I like you, but I do admire you. And to change the subject—what is this fancy shindig all about, anyway? Are you and Laird about to make the big announcement?''

Chanel was chagrined. Was it so obvious? Well, it was foolish to deny it when everybody would know in a couple of hours, anyway.

"You guessed right. But please—we'd like to keep it a secret until Laird makes the announcement. You do understand, don't you?"

"Of course. He's going to make an honest woman out of you in front of all his friends at the same time. Well, good luck. I still think you're making a mistake, but of course marrying Fairmount is one way of getting what you want."

The hotel's banquet manager, an unctuous man in his late forties, came up with a question, and when Chanel turned back to Stet, he was gone. A few minutes later, the first guests arrived. Not to her surprise, the women from the support group were unfashionably on time.

She looked them over silently as they came toward her. It was obvious that Glory had gone all out for the party. Her hair was a riot of burnished curls around her piquant face, and she wore a flaming red gown that clashed with her hair and should have been all wrong, but managed instead to look striking and innovative. The tall, husky man she had in tow was wearing a perfectly tailored tuxedo that obviously wasn't rented. His blue eyes were quizzical as he studied the still-empty ballroom, then Chanel. He looked so familiar that she realized she must have seen him around the Golden Gate Health Club. So this was Steve Golden. How interesting—and how like a woman, even a smart one like Glory, to jump from the bed of one jock into another. . . .

"Has anyone heard from Ariel lately?" she said with perfunctory interest after the first flurry of greetings and exchanges of compliments.

"She called a few days ago to say that she would keep in touch." Janice's voice dragged a little, and she looked tired, unusually pale. She was wearing a long black silk shift; although its classic lines were slenderizing, it obviously wasn't new, and Chanel wondered absently how many faculty parties it had graced before her divorce.

"I'm sorry she isn't coming," Chanèl murmured—untruthfully, because now Laird wouldn't be distracted by concern that his cousin was having a good time. "I want you three to be the first to know. Laird and I will be announcing our engagement tonight. The wedding is planned for late May."

Everybody spoke at once, and because she would have sworn their congratulations were genuine, Chanel felt a warm glow that dispersed quickly when Fern came up, her eyes lingering on Stephanie's white satin blouse and long black skirt, so obviously bought off the rack, then moved to Glory's flaming hair. A cynical smile quivered in the corner of her mouth. She turned her attention to Glory's escort, and her smile became provocative.

"This is my daughter, Fern," Chanel said, surprised how she resented Fern's barely concealed amusement at the expense of the support group. To her satisfaction, Glory's escort gave Fern a polite nod, then turned back to Glory with a remark about a boyhood visit to the St. Francis with his parents.

A covey of guests arrived, and Chanel was soon so busy that she lost track of her friends. Although Laird's absence was inconvenient and involved constant explanations, she handled it effectively by saying that he'd been tied up by an urgent business problem. She consoled herself with the knowledge that because she was acting as hostess in Laird's absence, it was apparent how important she was in his life. Several of the guests obviously suspected the reason for the party, but Chanel only smiled mysteriously when they dropped hints.

It was almost nine o'clock when she was approached by the hotel's assistant manager. He was sweating profusely, and even before he spoke, a feeling of foreboding sent an unpleasant chill through her body.

"Mr. Fairmount's chauffeur brought this for you, Mrs. Devereau," he said, and dropped an envelope into her hand. "There was some kind of mix-up and it went to the wrong person—you should've received it a couple of hours ago. The hotel is dreadfully sorry—"

He was walking away, moving a little too quickly, before she could question him. She excused herself from the guests she'd been talking to and turned aside while she opened the unsealed envelope and took out a folded piece of paper. As she read the first few words of the message inside, a random thought came to her—relief that no one could see her face.

"I'm sorry, Chanel. I owe you my deepest and most abject apologies for the pain this letter will cause you. I never intended this to happen," the message said; she noted, all emotion suspended, that the handwriting was crabbed, obviously not Laird's, that two of the words—*abject* and *apologies*—were misspelled. "I realize now that our engagement was a mistake. Ariel has been staying with me for the past week, and I've tried to fight my feelings for her, aware how this will hurt you. But I love Ariel. I think I've loved her most of my life.

"I'm sending this from the *Sea Lark*. Although I've tried to call you several times, I kept getting a busy signal, so I've been forced to dictate this to my housekeeper. You don't have to worry—she is very discreet. Robert will relay it to you in time for you to cancel the party, which I realize is cutting it pretty short, but I have no other choice. When we started out this morning, it was just to be a short trip around the bay, a sort of farewell outing. Then I knew that I couldn't give Ariel up and—well, we're heading for Mexico. I hate leaving you in such a position, but I didn't make up my mind until just now. I know you can never forgive me, because what I've done is unforgivable. My only excuse is that sometimes love is stronger than promises or commitments to other people.

"I know nothing can really compensate you, but I've wired my accountant to place substantial funds in your checking account Monday morning. If you ever need a favor, please call on me first. Ariel, incidentally, has no idea that you and I were anything more than just good friends. I hope she'll never find out differently. As soon as her divorce is final, we'll be married.

"When you cancel the party, you can tell the guests that I was taken ill, that I apologize deeply. I know you can manage things so you won't be embarrassed. When I return, I'll back up anything you say. Even the truth, if you decide that's best.

"If not, no one, including Ariel, need ever know that we intended to announce our engagement tonight. She's a complete innocent, Chanel. She would grieve if she thought she'd caused you—caused *anyone*—pain. The guilty party is me. Someday, I'll make this all up to you.

"Meanwhile, my deepest regret and affection.

"Laird."

CHAPTER THIRTY-SIX

LATER, WHEN THE SHOCK, THE SICKENING DISAPPOINTMENT, THE raw fury, had had time to disperse a little, Chanel would be proud of the fact that only a few seconds after she'd finished reading Laird's letter, she had turned back to Fern and the two women she'd been talking to with a smile. If she looked a little sick, it was something no one commented on.

"Oh, what a bore," she said. "Poor Laird!"

"What's happened to Laird?" It was the middle-aged wife of one of Laird's business partners. She'd made it very plain earlier that she regarded Chanel's playing hostess for Laird a personal affront; her voice held speculation now, and Chanel's defenses went up immediately.

"It seems Laird took his boat out for a run this afternoon—you know he just can't resist good boating weather—but unfortunately, he slipped on deck and hit his head against the railing," she said smoothly. "His doctor insists that he stay in the hospital overnight for observation—wouldn't you just know it would happen today?"

"How lucky you were here tonight to take over for him," the other woman said. "Or *is* it luck?"

"What do you mean?"

"Now don't be coy, Chanel. There've been a few rumors about you two. This wasn't to be an announcement party, was it?"

"Of what? Surely you don't suspect—oh, dear, you really are off base. Laird and I are the very best of friends, but that's all there is to it." Chanel lips felt numb from smiling. "In fact, he's very much in love with another woman, who happens to be a dear friend of mine."

The words were like gall in Chanel's mouth. From the corner of her eye, she caught the shock on Fern's face and braced herself for disaster. But to her surprise, Fern backed up her lie.

"Mother's been playing matchmaker again," she said.

"I see," the woman said, but there was skepticism in the way she drew out the two words.

"I suppose I should make an announcement to the other guests," Chanel said. If she didn't get away from this woman soon, she was going to scream and bang her head on the floor—or maybe throw up. She felt ravished, as if rage and hate were clawing at her insides. Somehow, she managed to keep a smile plastered on her face as she turned and walked at a deliberately slow pace toward the bandstand. She waited until the band had finished an elegant rendition of an old Hoagy Carmichael standard before she asked the bandleader for a drumroll to get the attention of the guests.

"I have an announcement to make," she said when the noise in the ballroom subsided. She raised the pitch of her voice so it would be heard. "I'll be substituting for your host for the remainder of the evening. Laird had a boating accident this afternoon, and while it isn't serious, his doctor thinks he should spend the night in the hospital for observation. Seems this is the proper thing when one has a slight concussion." She waited for the waves of whispers to subside before she added, "Meanwhile, Laird insists that the party must go on. Why don't we all toast Laird's quick recovery with champagne?"

She nodded to the assistant headwaiter, who was in charge of serving drinks. "Please see that Mr. Fairmount's guests all have champagne."

After the toast, she answered a dozen concerned questions, even managed a couple of quips. She must have brought it off, because no one seemed to guess that she was lying with every word.

Then finally, most of the guests had wandered off toward the buffet tent or back to their tables or had returned to their dancing. A large hand scooped up Chanel's elbow and led her out onto the dance floor, but she didn't realize it was Stet until his deep voice said, "You've got guts, little lady. Don't look now, but everybody is having a good time. Maybe their host should stay away more often."

To her surprise, Chanel heard her own laugh.

"What happened? Laird get cold feet?"

She drew away a little so she could look up at him. "Whatever do you mean?"

"Come on. The bastard left you to face the music—I'll bet my first oil well that he didn't have any boating accident. Why would he go out on his boat on the day he's throwing a big party like this?''

To her dismay, Chanel's sight blurred. She blinked hard, but her eyes continued to fill with tears. "You're right. He is a bastard," she said thickly. "He sent the message to his housekeeper by ship-to-shore, and she relayed it to me here at the hotel in an unsealed envelope, which means it's all over the hotel by now that I got jilted royally. How long do you think it will take the guests to find out that Laird has run off with that whey-faced cousin of his? Well, they deserve each other. A bore and a wimp. May they rot in hell.''

"Atta girl. Call them names. It'll make you feel better.''

"Son of a bitch, lowlife, jerk, bitch!" Chanel said—and discovered she did feel better. "You know the thing that really burns me? That I knocked myself out, putting this wretched party together.''

"So send him a bill. A very large one. Your services come high, as I know so well—and they're worth every penny of it.''

Chanel ignored the compliment. "I just might do that. Laird's note said he was going to transfer 'substantial funds' to my checking account—which could mean anything since he isn't exactly free with his money.''

"Are you going to send it back?''

She gave him a surprised look. "Not on your life. He can spare it—and I need it. He's in my debt now—he may be a weak-kneed bastard, but he has a conscience, and he's going to pay—and I'm not talking about money.''

"Uh-huh. I almost feel sorry for him.''

"You'd better. Any important party I give from now on, he'll be there. That you can bank on. Socially, the Fairmount name is like negotiable bonds. And now I must get back to the guests—I see some late arrivals coming in." She nodded stiffly, turned, and threaded her way through the dancing couples. It wasn't until much later that it occurred to her what a surprisingly good dancer Stet had been—for an ex-wildcatter.

When she reached the edge of the dance floor, Fern was waiting for her.

"Who was that man you were dancing with, Chanel?" she asked curiously.

"A business acquaintance . . ."—Chanel paused briefly—". . . who has recently become a friend.''

"He's really neat-looking. Why don't you set your cap for *him*—provided he's loaded."

"He owns half of Texas, but unfortunately, he also has a wife he's very devoted to," Chanel said.

Fern studied her. "You're pretty good, you know. If I didn't know better, I would've believed that speech you made. What's the real story?"

Chanel started to brush off the question, then decided to be honest, because Fern would eventually find out the truth anyway. "While I was busy planning this party for Laird, a friend of mine was moving in on him. Now he wants to marry her—and that means it's back to pinching pennies for us. You want to desert the sinking ship? I wouldn't blame you, you know."

Fern's expression was thoughtful. "I think I'll stick around for a while—for the laughs." She hesitated briefly then added, "You're okay, Chanel. I was—well, I was proud of you out there. You didn't give an inch."

Chanel had held onto her composure through the ordeal so far, but when the son of one of Laird's friends came up to claim Fern for a dance, she found herself fighting tears again. There was also a hollow feeling in her stomach, and her hands were sweaty, unsteady.

Oh, God, don't let me get sick—not now. Just let me get through the next few hours, and then I can collapse.

"Can we do anything, Chanel?"

It was the support group—all three of them. Chanel stared into Janice's concerned face; she wanted to cry on her sensible shoulder, which was odd because she really wasn't all that fond of Janice. "How did you find out about Ariel and Laird?"

Stephanie gasped, and Janice looked shocked. Only Glory didn't seem surprised. "We didn't," she said. "We asked if we could help because Fern said you needed our support."

"That doesn't sound like my daughter. And I'm okay—but thank you for asking."

"What are friends for?" Janice said, and Chanel found herself smiling at the familiar phrase.

"Yeah, Chanel. You really did a number on them. I don't think anyone caught on." Glory looked around the room. "What a turnout. I'll bet if the jewels in this room were laid end to end, they'd reach to LA."

Stephanie touched Chanel's arm. "How can we help?"

"I just have to tough it out," Chanel said, her voice tight. "God, I'd like to kill Laird."

"And Ariel?"

"And Ariel—the little beast."

Stephanie looked troubled. "I'm sure Ariel doesn't have any idea you and Laird were seriously involved with each other. She wouldn't do anything to hurt you, you know."

"No, I don't know. I could hang her up by her heels. Going behind my back to—" Chanel stopped; she gave an exasperated sigh. "That's a lie. I know Ariel isn't to blame for this—Laird said so in his note, and I believe him. Wouldn't you just know that I don't even have the solace of hating her?"

"What will you do now?" Janice asked.

"Get through the rest of this evening—and then go home and lick my wounds."

"And after you finish licking your wounds, what then?"

"Oh, then I may start selling pencils on the street. Get a job slinging hash in some greasy spoon. Have a nervous break-down."

"You can always find another rich man—if that's what you want," Glory said.

"There's that, too," Chanel said, nodding. "But right now, I don't have any prospects."

"How about that gray-haired guy you were dancing with ear-lier?"

"Stet? He's just a friend—and he's also very married." Chanel decided it was time to change the subject. "Your Steve looks interesting. I can believe that he's a Yalie—for one thing, he's got those cool, don't-mess-with-me Yalie eyes."

"Is that so? And I thought he was born with those eyes." But Glory looked pleased, Chanel noted. "Oh, oh, here comes trou-ble—that woman in the blue dress has been staring holes in you for the past ten minutes. If she had a feather in her mouth, you could call her puss—do you know her?"

Chanel glanced around and recognized Nancy Anderson. "An old schoolmate."

"She looks ten years older than you. I thought rich women all looked young."

"Not the horsey set. Too much sun and too much wind—and too much horse manure."

The four women were laughing when Nancy came up. "Well, I see you're all enjoying yourself. I must say—Laird is full of surprises. Too bad about his fall. He looked so well last week when I saw him at L'Etoile. He was there with his cousin—such a lovely young woman. I have to admit I was surprised—I thought Laird was the last of the Fairmounts.''

"Are you talking about Ariel?" Janice spoke up. "She's Laird's only living relative, I understand."

The woman gave her the hard stare. "I don't believe we've met."

Chanel introduced her friends quickly. Nancy seemed fascinated by Glory. "Your name is Brown?"

"With an ''e''—and here comes my escort, Steve Golden," Glory said, her eyes full of fight.

Steve Golden acknowledged the introduction with a nod and a polite smile. Nancy Anderson looked him over with obvious interest. "Haven't we met somewhere—you wouldn't be related to the Earl Goldens, would you?"

Steve hesitated briefly. "As a matter of fact, they're my parents," he said.

"Why, of course—you're a friend of my niece Sylvia."

"How is Sylvia?"

"She's still living in New York. You know what a clever artist she is? Well, she's earning quite a name for herself as an illustrator of children's books. . . . ''

As she went on talking about her niece, Nancy didn't seem to realize that Steve was deftly moving her away from the others. Glory stared after them, her face like a cloudburst.

"Don't worry. He'll be back," Chanel said.

"I'm not worried about *that*. He can go jump off the Bay Bridge for all I care. He never told me he was Earl Golden's son. That's the guy who owns the chain of health clubs I work for."

"So give him credit for wanting to make it on his own and not riding his father's coattails."

"He could've told *me*."

"And what would you have done?"

"Dropped him like a hot potato," Glory said promptly. "Dating a jock is bad enough but a rich jock—that's suicide."

"Why don't you let it ride, Glory?" Stephanie said. "If you have a good relationship with Steve—well, you must've realized he didn't come from poor people, didn't you?"

"I didn't think about it, one way or another. What do I know about rich people? And it does make a difference. For one thing, I feel like a fool."

"Join the club," Chanel said, sighing.

Glory's face softened. "Yeah, you've been through hell tonight."

"And it still isn't over. The rumors will be really flying tomorrow."

"You'll be okay," Glory said. "You're one tough lady. Look, we're all going to stick around until this shindig is over, just in case you need us."

Chanel produced a smile. "Thank you. I appreciate that."

"What are—" Janice started.

" . . . friends for?" Glory finished, grinning.

Everybody laughed, including Chanel. She discovered that she did feel better—which didn't make sense with her whole life in a shambles. For one thing, she was broke. The money Laird had said he would transfer to her bank account—however much it was—would help, but when it ran out, she'd be right back on square one. Unmarried and with no prospects in sight. What did she do then?

She put the question aside to think about later and began moving among the guests, all of whom seemed to be enjoying themselves—probably because they had a juicy bit of gossip to speculate about. She made herself a vow. Next time—and there would be a next time—she would come up winners, and she didn't give a damn what she had to do to pull it off. From now on, it was gloves on and all bets off.

CHAPTER THIRTY-SEVEN

IT WAS THREE DAYS LATER THAT CHANEL HAD A VISITOR. SHE'D spent the three days with the phone off the hook, licking her wounds—and trying to decide what to do next. All her life, she'd been decisive, pragmatic, seldom brooding over past failures. Usually, she had contingency plans for just about everything that could happen. But this time, she'd made the mistake of being too complacent. She'd been too sure of herself—and of Laird. In other words, she had put all her eggs in one basket, a mistake she intended never to make again.

As soon as the banks had opened Monday morning, she'd called to find out how much money Laird had deposited in her checking account. Because she'd never noticed any spendthrift tendencies in Laird except when he'd given her carte blanche on the party, she was surprised to learn that the amount was twenty thousand dollars, a princely payoff, even for a broken engagement. It didn't make her feel any kinder toward Laird, but it did help to ease the pain.

And then there was the ring. How lucky that Laird had given it to her for safekeeping before the party! It had been a bona fide gift, and she didn't hesitate to put it out for consignment at one of the better jewelry stores. Better her than Ariel, was her reasoning. And wasn't it a hoot that the old saw about money gravitating to money was true, after all? Between the two of them, Laird and Ariel probably had enough to pay the national debt for a month. What's more, given their natures, they'd still have it fifty years from now.

Sunday morning, in a fit of economizing, she had given notice to her housekeeper, who had promptly left in a huff, which was why, when the doorbell rang Tuesday afternoon, she answered it herself and found William Stetson standing there. Although embarrassed that he'd caught her still wearing a robe this late in the day, she was careful not to show it.

"Well, this is a surprise," she said airily. "You caught me just as I was getting ready to take a shower."

She ushered him into the living room, excused herself, and went to put on one of the jewel-toned caftans she wore for lounging. She didn't hurry. Let him cool his heels. Whatever he'd come for, she doubted it was something she wanted to hear. With the run of bad luck she'd had lately, why expect things to change?

When she returned to the living room, Stet seemed in no hurry to state his business. He had been examining her collection of ivory figurines and boxes, and now he looked her over with a frank interest she'd once found flattering and which, in her present mood, was irritating as hell.

"Would you like a drink?" she asked—a little too politely.

"Bourbon—no water, no ice," he said, and settled himself on a sofa as if he belonged there, looking impossibly long-legged and self-possessed. Chanel poured a shot of bourbon into a Manhattan glass, and handed it to him without comment.

"You seldom drink, do you?" he said.

"Only when I need it."

"You look like you could use a good stiff drink right now."

"Did you come here to tell me I look like hell?"

"I came to make you a proposition."

"More lessons on social climbing?" she said snidely.

His face closed up. "That wasn't something I wanted. I only went along with Elsie—and I'm glad I did. It made her happy—for a little while."

"I realize that," Chanel said, relenting. "How is she?"

"About the same. The progress of the disease is unpredictable. She's still in good physical health—the doctors say she can live for another twenty years. And it's all a big waste. Half the time she doesn't recognize me, and the other half, she wants to kill me. The disease is like that—no rhyme or reason or logic."

"I'm sorry," Chanel said, meaning it. She *was* sorry, not so much for Elsie as for Stet, who must live in a half world between being married and being a widower.

"And that's enough about me. What are you going to do now? Have you made any plans?"

Chanel, not willing to admit that she hadn't, only shrugged.

"If you're at loose ends, perhaps we could come to an understanding. Are you willing to listen?"

"Why not? What's on your mind?"

"I may have a solution to your problems. I am—well, to put it neatly, I am a normal man, and still not over the hill, and I find you extremely attractive. I know you don't dislike me—is it possible that you would consider a relationship with me? I'd pay your bills, of course, and it could be a very discreet arrangement."

Surprise had kept Chanel silent; now her ire erupted into angry words. She jumped to her feet and pointed her finger toward the door. "Get out!" she stormed. "I'm not reduced to being a kept woman yet."

"Now, wait a minute. I'm not suggesting a fly-by-night affair. This would be a long-term deal. In fact, I'm quite willing to back you financially if you still want to crash into society. Frankly, I think you're wasting your time. This local bunch—most of them are only a couple of generations away from railroad workers or miners or lumberjacks. They'd be laughed out of town by the Eastern crowd, the real aristocrats of this country—whatever that means. But if this is what you want, I'll finance you. That party you hosted was a success—it could start the ball going. All I ask in return is that you be my woman."

Chanel's anger dissipated as quickly as it had appeared. What he proposed made sense. With unlimited money to back her, with shrewd volunteer work and by cultivating those few people who were already inclined to accept her at face value, she could probably find acceptance—to a limited degree. So why was she hesitating? She liked Stet, found him sexually attractive, and God knows, she wasn't above having an affair. She'd had a dozen or more in the past few years, most of them with men who only had good looks or sexual prowess to recommend them.

No, the affair part was no problem. She would enjoy having sex with Stet—and what he offered in return was more than generous. So why did she feel—uninterested? The fiasco with Laird must have taken more out of her than she'd suspected. It seemed she had lost her drive, her starch. . . .

"Sorry, but no, thank you," she said, and then wondered again why she was turning him down. It wasn't because of scruples. She was much too sensible to consider it wrong to have sex with a married man whose wife was totally out of it. After all, who could possibly be hurt?

Stet was silent. He whirled the bourbon in his glass, his expression brooding. When she found herself wanting to apologize for turning him down, she got up and went to add bourbon to his glass and, this time, to pour herself a drink.

When he spoke, his voice was brusque. "I halfway expected you to turn me down. Why would you take on an old goat like me?"

Chanel eyed him suspiciously. "If that's intended to stir my sympathy—"

"Didn't work, huh? Well, I had to try. As it happens, I have an alternative proposal for you, and this one is pure business."

"Business? What kind of business?"

"I think I told you that I sold out my oil interests a few years back—and just in time, too. But then I got bored. Elsie and me did the travel thing, then took that stab at San Francisco society, and now that she's in a nursing home, I have too much time on my hands. Oh, I keep my hand in the market. I manage my own stock portfolio and have an interest in several businesses, but it isn't enough to keep me really busy. I had hoped that you would take care of that. Since you turned me down—" He shrugged. "One of the businesses I'm involved in is a health spa that opened up in Napa Valley about three years ago. Just recently the manager absconded with most of the funds—you may have heard about it?''

Chanel, who remembered reading about the scandal in the newspapers, nodded.

''I can buy up the outstanding shares at rock-bottom prices, but I need a working partner, someone to run the spa for me. Most of the requirements for the job can be picked up by any reasonably smart person, but one qualification is essential— knowing how to deal with the kind of customers the spa is aimed at—rich, upper-crust women.''

''What exactly are you proposing?''

''That you run the spa for me. You have the qualities I'm look- ing for—intelligence and charm and, above all, class. Anyone who charges an arm and a leg for a week of dieting and exercise has got to be a living advertisement for the business. They also have to talk the same language as their clients.''

''And you want me to—what? Invest in the spa? How much capital would it take?''

''None. You'd be managing it for me for a good salary and a cut of the profits. And you'd have to give the business one hundred percent of your time. I'm talking about a place so exclusive that only the rich and the near-rich can afford it. How does that grab you?''

''It would be almost impossible to pull off,'' Chanel said, her tone flat. ''It would take perfect timing, perfect planning, and a lot of just plain luck.''

''Don't be so negative—and don't sell yourself short. If anyone could do it, it's you.''

''I could handle the business part, yes. But I don't have the name to pull in the initial clients. The most successful of the spas start with—well, a titled person who is willing to put her name on the letterhead, or someone who has already made it big in some other line of work or even the wife of a famous man. I can't qualify for any of those.''

''Horseshit. A few complimentary big-name guests at the be- ginning, word of mouth—''

''And plenty of turndowns. First, you have to ask those big- name guests to be patrons, and after they turn you down, they're going to make jokes about those upstarts who want to cash in on their fame, and then your name is poison and other women wouldn't be caught dead in your spa. Of course, if you could make it so hard to get in that everybody would be groveling for an invitation . . .''

Chanel paused, considering her own words; she shook her head as other problems occurred to her. "It would probably be a losing proposition for a long time even if it did click with the rich and/or the famous. They'll pay large fees, yes, but they expect enormous coddling. The ratio of employees to clients should be two to one—at the least. The overhead would be horrendous.''

"So? I can use the losses to counter my gains elsewhere for a while. You'd have a time limit, a reasonable one, to make it start paying off, but you'd also have a say on refurbishing the spa—up to a point. I've already accepted a bid from a San Francisco contractor to build a new gymnasium and to reconstruct a bathhouse over the spa's natural hot spring.''

Chanel studied him curiously. "No strings attached? No cozy little get-togethers at your place or mine?''

Stet grinned at her. "Would I do that?''

"I think you'd do anything, short of murder, to get your own way,'' she said with total conviction.

"You've wounded me.'' Stet put his hand over his heart. It was a very large, very utilitarian hand, a cowboy's hand, despite well-groomed nails and the ruby signet ring it sported.

"Sorry if I've insulted you,'' she said, letting her skepticism show. "I'd want a contract—drawn up by my lawyer.''

"How about having both our lawyers draw it up?''

"That's satisfactory.''

"So your answer is yes?''

"Tentatively. We'll have to work out details.''

"You've got it, little lady.'' His Texas drawl, she noticed, was back again. Funny how it came and went, just like his indifferent grammar. "I think we're gonna work together without any problems 'cause we see things the same way. When can you start?''

"First you'd better get possession of those shares—''

"Oh, that's already been taken care of. I made an offer they couldn't refuse.''

"You were pretty confident, weren't you?'' she said, a little disconcerted. "How did you know I would accept your offer?''

"I didn't. If you'd turned me down, I would've found someone else. And I'm still chasing you. Be prepared for that. But I won't get too pushy. I'll just be hanging around in case you change your mind.'' His face lost its grin suddenly. "One thing you should know. I'll never divorce Elsie. I love her—or at least, I love the

Elsie I married. I meant those marriage vows, and I'll stick to them until death do us part. Do you understand what I'm saying?''

"I do," she said tartly. "And that's fine with me because I have no intention of jumping into bed with you. Just so there'll be no misunderstandings, maybe this should be included in the contract."

"That won't be necessary." For the first time, Stet seemed out of sorts. "My word is as good as any contract. It's never been broken."

"Sorry," she said. "Right now, I don't have a very good opinion of men—or their promises."

"Well, don't confuse me with Laird Fairmount. He really blew it when he ditched you for that conniving cousin of his."

"You do have a way with words," she murmured. "I hate Ariel's guts right now, but in all fairness—well, let's say she doesn't have enough brains to cut in on purpose. I'm sure she has no idea that Laird was engaged to me."

"And do you intend to tell her?"

"The first chance I get," she said grimly. "It's about time Laird paid the piper. Ariel should know before she marries him what a weak vessel she's getting."

"Maybe he really got blown away by her. It happens, you know."

"Oh, he's crazy about her, all right. I realize that now. I should have remembered that they were *second* cousins. But he did a job on me, and no one gets away with that. Which is something you should know about me."

"Okay, I'm warned. Remind me not to cross you. And I doubt she'll pay any attention to your warning. Love has a way of putting blinders on folks. She'll just think that you did the running after him. Besides, I never could see you as Fairmount's wife."

"Jealous?" she said mockingly.

"You bet."

"Well, remember our bargain. No personal involvements. This is strictly a business proposition."

"Right. Shall we shake on that?" They shook hands solemnly, and suddenly Chanel was remembering what she'd said to Fern in the taxi during the long way home from Laird's party.

"Something will turn up," she'd said. "And when it does, don't think I won't use it to get my own back."

CHAPTER THIRTY-EIGHT

SEVERAL TIMES DURING THE SPRING, STEPHANIE HAD TRIED TO make definite plans for the Rogue River rafting trip she'd promised the twins, but she never really came to terms with it. It was so much easier to simply push it to the back of her mind to think about later, when the time came. And then, suddenly, it was late May and the trip was looming directly ahead, no longer just a circled date on the kitchen calendar.

Chuck and Ronnie had talked of little else for the past month. They read aloud the brochure that had come in the mail until she thought she'd scream, in particular the overblown descriptions of the joys of tackling the wild waters of the Rogue River. They discussed ad nauseam such things as Duluth packs and flotation bags and the virtues of aluminum over wood paddles, so knowingly that an outsider would have thought they'd been born on a raft or kayak. As the date drew closer, they took to nagging her about outfitting them for the trip, citing such experts as Schwind and the Arighis, whose books on rafting they'd borrowed from the library, and the greatest expert of all in their eyes, their father.

"Pop says we should outfit ourselves right," Chuck told her importantly. "He says if you don't want to bother, he'll see to it." He looked her over, taking in the neat suit she'd worn to work that day. "You don't have no clothes that's suitable, he says."

"Don't have any clothes," Stephanie said automatically, hiding her pique. What right had David to discuss her with the twins? Okay, he'd been surprisingly cooperative about visiting rights, staying within the perimeters she'd set up for his Sunday visits— movies, sports events, the zoo, Marine World U.S.A. But he still was like a thorn in her flesh. If only he would move away or lose interest in the boys so she wouldn't have to see him every weekend.

"So what does the rafting expert think I should buy?" she said, her voice testy.

"He made out a list, Mom." Ronnie pulled a sheet of notebook paper from his pocket. "Here—he says to charge it to him. His treat."

"I can afford to pay for it," she said stiffly. She stalked into the kitchen and began fixing dinner, Chuck and Ronnie following in her wake.

"Hey, Mom, you aren't going to change your mind, are you?" Chuck said anxiously.

"Did your father tell you I would?"

"Naw—but he did say he'd take us if something came up and you couldn't make it. Look, it's okay with me and Ronnie if Pop takes us. Honest, it is."

"I'll just bet," Stephanie muttered under her breath. Aloud, she said, "I have no intention of changing my mind."

"That's what I told him. Mom's a real good sport, I said. And Ronnie told him how you took us to see the Raiders train in Santa Rosa and about going to the Russian River and renting those canoes last week."

"And how did your father take that?"

"Well, he seemed kinda surprised. He said miracles would never cease."

Stephanie felt a twinge of guilt. Okay, she wasn't into the great outdoors, and she hadn't complained when David and the boys went to sports events without her, but then a man should be alone with his boys occasionally, shouldn't he? Bonding and all that stuff? Or so she'd told herself. The truth was she didn't enjoy sitting in grandstands. So shoot me. . . .

"Dad offered to go shopping with us for our rafting stuff, Mom," Chuck went on. "I told him I'd ask you."

He looked so expectant that she started to say yes, then changed her mind. An *en famille* shopping trip was not her idea of a fun excursion, and right now, she didn't need any more stress in her life.

Sometimes, she was sure that if she had to face one more crisis or problem or aggravation, she would go out of her mind. The winter had been one thing after another—budget worries, problems at work, transportation foul-ups. The car had broken down twice, and the boys had both come down with bad colds—and then she'd caught it, too. Because she couldn't afford to lose any wages, she'd gone to work, sniffles and all, which hadn't gone down well with her boss or her fellow workers.

What with her job, housework, shopping, laundry, and cooking, with trying to be both father and mother to the twins, while all the time she had to budget like mad in order to stay financially afloat on entry-level wages and the modest child support check she got from David, she just wasn't getting the sleep and rest she needed. And now this rafting trip, looming up like a dark shadow ahead . . .

Well, she would charge the things they needed on her credit cards and pay them off when she could. Or maybe she'd take David up on his offer, after all. It was his fault she had volunteered for the trip. He hadn't paid any of the boys' expenses lately except for the child care specified in the divorce agreement, and she wished now, too late, that she'd taken Mr. Waterford's advice. He had warned her to get what she could before any papers were signed, but at the time, she'd only wanted it to be over with.

She'd even had a few naive—and self-righteous, she saw now—illusions about not being greedy. Which had been another mistake. The payments on the condo were eating up her resources, and there seldom was anything left in her checking account at the end of the month. Eventually, although it put her in a bad light with the boys, she would have to go back into court and ask for more money from David, even though it would be admitting that she couldn't make it on her own.

And just whose fault was that? True, she hadn't argued when David asked her to stay home, even before she got pregnant. She had believed in the old myth that marriage was forever after; if anyone had suggested that hers might fail, she would have told them off. If she ever had a daughter, she would give her this advice: Learn a trade; keep your skills current so that if the worst happens, you can support yourself and your kids properly.

Or, as Chanel had put it at one of the luncheons, repeating the advice she'd given her daughter, Fern: "Never believe a man when he says he'll always take care of you. If it happens that way, great. But if, when you're past your prime, he starts sniffing around after younger women, he won't give a damn about you or how you survive. He'll invent a thousand reasons why it's all your fault and why he shouldn't be burdened with an old wife."

Chanel had paused briefly, her eyes reflective. "And then I told Fern that she should always know where the family money is located and be prepared to fight to get her share. The bastards start burying their assets right after the wedding—and a good lawyer is a girl's best friend, right?"

Remembering now how the others had nodded, even Janice

who seldom had anything derogatory to say about her ex-husband, Stephanie sighed deeply, earning a curious look from Chuck.

"How about feeding Monster?" she said to forestall any questions, pointing toward the cupboard where the dog food was stored.

That evening, Stephanie took the boys shopping. She followed David's list religiously because she was afraid that if she didn't, something vital would be left out. This whole rafting trip business was a nightmare—it had already caused her trouble at work. Her vacation, which would be unpaid because she had so recently been hired, had caused a problem. At the last minute, she'd been bumped by someone with more seniority who wanted the time slot she'd signed up for. When her boss, Mr. Spengler, shrugged off her complaints, she went over his head and made an appointment with the director of personnel to explain why it was so important that the original date stand. To her surprise, the man had taken her side.

"Fair is fair, Mrs. Cornwall," he told her. "Since you've already paid for that rafting trip, and your boys would be disappointed if you have to cancel out, you go ahead and take the first week in June off. I'll square things with your boss."

What he'd said to Mr. Spengler, she never knew, but the vacation schedule was changed back to the original one without comment—or a lecture—from her supervisor. She had mixed feelings about how she'd handled the whole situation. It felt good to come out on top for once—but if she hadn't protested the change, she would have a good, face-saving excuse to get out of the rafting trip.

On the other hand, David would offer to go in her place. If she refused, the boys would sulk for the rest of the summer—and she didn't need that. As it was, she sometimes felt as if she were in a war, under constant fire. It wasn't that the boys were acting up again. Although she was pretty sure their present good behavior stemmed from their fear that she'd cancel the rafting trip if they misbehaved, she did appreciate the peace. Even so, she dreaded the coming trip and was secretly convinced it would be a disaster.

Then, inevitably, the day of departure arrived. The teenage son of a neighbor had offered to keep Monster, and another neighbor, a retired widower who lived in the next unit, was going to keep an eye on the condo and water her houseplants, but she was still feeling apprehensive as they packed the car and drove off, heading for Interstate 101—and Oregon.

But her mood soon lightened, not the least reason being that the boys were in such good humor. Maybe it wouldn't be so bad, after all. It wasn't as if she were a complete novice at camping out. True, she hadn't done any camp chores such as putting up tents or chopping wood, but she had handled the cooking and cleaning up. So she'd just have to assume that the rafting trip guides would take care of anything heavy, and no matter what came up, she'd try hard to be a good sport—and keep remembering that this, too, would eventually pass.

Stephanie's resolve to be a good sport faltered a little at the first assembly of the rafting group. Her fellow rafters—they ranged from a seventy-year-old grandmother to a family of eight—all seemed to be some kind of experts on white water rafting. She realized this couldn't be true, but still—why was it they all were so knowledgeable that none of them asked, as she wanted to do, what was meant by such terms as souse holes and chutes and standing waves, which the head guide kept dropping into his orientation speech?

Even Ronnie and Chuck nodded wisely when the man, who had introduced himself as Clay O'Connors, explained the hazarads of something called hydraulic pools. It was then she realized that David must have briefed them thoroughly on what to expect. Instead of feeling grateful, she was annoyed. Another example of pointing out her incompetence and setting himself up as an expert?

Clay O'Connors finished what was obviously a set speech on safety tactics and was now explaining the various equipment that made the inflatable river rafts they would be using superior. Words like bow dodgers, d-rings, brass oarlocks, made little sense to someone who had only been in a boat once in her life—and that the steamer she and David had taken to Catalina on their honeymoon. When he started demonstrating the life preservers, a ribbed vest with a waistband and short skirt, and told them the preservers would not only save their lives but protect them from sharp rocks in case of a spill, she rashly raised her hand and asked if a spill was likely.

Clay O'Connors studied Stephanie as if wondering what rock she'd crawled out from under. He was a lean, athletic-looking man with short-cropped hair, the kind she secretly thought of as the Rambo type, and from his clipped speech, she suspected he preferred solitude to rafting a bunch of amateurs down the Rogue River.

"Anything is possible, which is why we prepare for every contingency," he said. "However, we don't usually expect spills. If it happens—well, that's part of the game. If you expect to stay dry, I suggest you remain in the truck with the portage crew."

Stephanie's frayed temper, which she usually held in check, exploded. "I asked a sensible question and all I want is a sensible answer. If you expect me to not ask questions, then *you* stay with the—the portage crew."

She could see that she'd embarrassed the boys. Ronnie's face turned dark pink and Chuck muttered, "Ah, Mom."

Surprisingly, the man smiled. "Sorry. I read something into your question that wasn't there. You must be a good sport to take your boys on a trip like this when you're obviously a city girl."

"As it happens, I was raised on a farm," she said stiffly.

"Then, I'm wrong again, aren't I?" he said and went on with his orientation.

That evening, as they ate barbecued ribs and beans, prepared on a stone outdoor fireplace by the staff, Chuck made friends with the boy at the next campsite, and after dinner, he went off with his new friend to help the guides get the rafts ready for the launch in the morning. Ronnie, as usual, had held back, taking his time about making friends. If he didn't find anyone compatible, Stephanie knew, he would be perfectly happy to go it alone. Like David, she thought.

She was trying to untangle the guide ropes of the tent that had been issued to them when Clay O'Connors came up. "Here. I'll show you how it's done. It's something you'll have to do during the trip. We don't have enough hands to set up tents for the guests."

As he explained the intricacies of anchoring the support lines properly, she couldn't help comparing him with David. David would have taken the task away from her and done it himself—and it wouldn't have occurred to her that she should be pulling her own weight. How strange that she had never wondered if she was imposing upon him, letting him take over any difficult mechanical chore.

"This your first raft trip?" Technically, it was a question, but it sounded more like a statement of fact.

"My twins coerced me into it—I don't know a thing about rafting."

Clay's grin held sympathy. Stephanie had always been partial to men with white, white teeth, and she found herself smiling back. "You'll be okay. We even take handicapped people if they aren't too physically impaired. Just listen to the guides, and if you have any questions, ask. You'll quickly learn the ropes." He held out a tanned hand. "I'm Clay O'Connors, head rafter and leader of the pack."

"I'm Stephanie Cornwall."

"I know. You've got a couple of fine boys there."

"You can tell that just by looking at them?"

"This job teaches you to make snap judgments about people. Your kids are curious, quick, and bright, and entirely different in nature, right?"

"You're pretty close," she admitted.

"As for you—recently divorced and on your own again, a working mother who's trying to keep in tune with her boys."

She looked at him suspiciously. "How could you possibly guess that from just looking at me?"

"Oh, did I say that?"

His grin was so infectious that she couldn't take offense. "I see I'll have to have a talk with my boys," she said darkly.

"Don't blame them. I pumped them very skillfully. I spotted you when you signed in."

"Is this part of your job? To be charming to unaccompanied women on trips?"

"Touchy, touchy. The truth is I seldom mix business with pleasure. In your case, I could make an exception. And speaking of business—did you bring the things listed in the brochure we sent you?"

For the next few minutes, he examined her gear, and although it was David who had provided the list she'd followed, she was pleased by Clay's "You did a good job. You'd be surprised at the number of people who arrive here without such elementary things as a change of socks or mosquito repellent. A bit of advice—leave off the cologne and use unscented soap to wash up with and you probably won't have too many problems with mosquitoes. Oh, and line your Duluth pack with a plastic trash bag to make doubly sure it stays waterproof. The canteen carries a supply—and other essentials, too."

"Is there anything else we need?"

" 'Bring along a little joy of living and you'll take home good memories of your white water trip,' " he said, quoting the words

with which he'd ended his orientation speech earlier. He nodded
to her and strolled off. Probably to charm some other female, she
decided.

The following morning, even before the sun was up, the camp
was aroused by the clatter of a Klaxon. Since each person was
responsible for getting his or her own gear to the service vans in
the mornings, Stephanie was soon too busy to worry about what
came next.

Breakfast consisted of the hot oats, scrambled eggs, ham, and
hot biscuits provided by the camp crew. There was plenty of
coffee, rich and strong, but Stephanie only drank one cup because
she was uneasy about sanitary accommodations on the rafts.

An hour after dawn, she and the boys climbed aboard the giant
rubber raft they'd been assigned, along with a few others, and got
settled near the helm. It pleased her that their own particular rafter
was Clay O'Connors, and she wondered if he had arranged things
that way—and if she was going to have any trouble discouraging
his personal attention during the trip.

Three nights later, as she tossed restlessly in her sleeping bag,
trying to find a comfortable spot, she remembered that particular
worry with chagrin. Not once during the past three days—and
three evenings—had Clay O'Connors said anything more personal than an occasional "How're things going, Mrs. Cornwall?"
or, once, "You're doing just fine. By the end of the trip, you'll
be an old white water hand."

It wasn't, she thought, that she wanted him to make a pass at
her. It was just that it was so—so insulting that he hadn't. He
teased the seventy-year-old grandmother to a fare-thee-well, calling her "Tiger" and kissing her cheek and getting her all flustered. He flirted openly with two teenage girls, both of whom
obviously had a crush on him, and he chatted amicably with the
married women in the group. But he still addressed Stephanie by
her last name, and in fact, treated her as if she were a hundred
instead of thirty-six. She'd tried to figure out Clay's age, but since
the white squint lines beside his eyes could come either from the
passage of time or hours in the sun or both, she finally gave it up.

The first two nights, she had slept as if she were dead, but for
some reason she couldn't get comfortable tonight. For one thing,
it seemed so warm in the tent. Even after she'd unzipped her
sleeping bag, it didn't much help. For yet another time, she shifted
positions, and when that didn't work, she finally sat up and groped

for her clothes. Rather than toss and turn half the night, she would go outside and look at the stars for a while. Anything to make her sleepy.

She dressed as quietly as she could in the dark. The boys were sleeping in the same tent, and from their regular breathing, they were sound asleep. Her face softened as she thought of the past three days. Although she wouldn't have believed it, she had enjoyed herself. That she had also succeeded in remaining a good sport no matter what happened was something she was proud of. Ronnie's and Chuck's praise, that she was really neat, was worth every heart-stopping encounter with human-eating rapids and raging torrents of water.

By the end of the first day, she was so wrung out both physically and emotionally that she found it almost impossible to join in with the camp fire fun, but the realization that if David were in her place, he would rise above his natural reserve and participate wholeheartedly for the sake of the boys, kept her from collapsing in her sleeping bag.

So she laughed at the horseplay and the good-natured banter, and sang "You Are My Sunshine" at the top of her lungs during the sing-along. She made friends with the grandmother, carried her own load when it came to camp chores, and her reward, the knowledge that she had indeed acted like a good sport, made up for her aching muscles and creaking joints.

The second day was easier, even though it entailed some horrendous rapids, because the strangeness was gone, and she was as thrilled as the boys when they caught sight of a black bear foraging the banks of the Rogue, and later, when a majestic eagle maneuvered the air currents above the gray cliffs of the gorge.

Tonight, she felt exhilarated rather than tired. "It's adrenaline, pumping through your veins," Clay had told one of the guests who commented on feeling keyed up as they sat around the camp fire, eating broiled steaks and potatoes roasted in hot coals. "There's nothing like a Rogue River high—unless it's sex."

Stephanie smiled at the memory now and moved forward, away from the cluster of tents. The night wind caught up the ends of her hair and tossed them in the air as she headed for a path she'd seen earlier. It wandered through a growth of knee-high scrub pines that formed a crescent around the small beach where they had camped for the night, and because there was a nearly full moon, she wasn't afraid of getting lost.

A few minutes later, when the path became shadowed by a

thicker, taller growth of pines, she knew it was time to go back, but as she started to turn, a hand touched her arm. She gave a gasp, but before she could scream, Clay O'Connors's amused voice came out of the dark.

"Sorry—didn't mean to scare you. What's the matter, can't you sleep?"

"No—and I can't understand it. I'm really tired."

"Nerves. The strangeness of it all. Nostalgia because tomorrow is our last full day. And maybe a little fear, too. Remember the old legends about spontaneous terror in the wild? The old Greeks had an explanation for it—the god Pan. Seems Pan had the power to arouse fear in the hearts of mortals when he encountered them in the forest."

She tried to see the expression on his face, but the shadows under the trees were too dark. "You're a strange sort for this kind of job."

"Why do you say that?"

"I don't know—the way you talk, I guess."

"You expected a redneck with a beer can in each pocket?"

"Something like that."

"Well, I fit the steriotype to one extent. I love being outdoors, love the excitement of battling the white water. As for the way I talk—I took my degrees in business, worked for five years in a bank in Seattle, got three promotions, and hated every minute of it. One day, I decided that I'd given up too much for security, so the rest of my life I'd live the way I wanted. My wife, unfortunately, didn't agree, so we went our separate ways. I got this job, which is something of a compromise, because I still have to deal with people, but a person does have to eat. And I've never looked back."

"You're a lucky person, being able to do what you want and make a living at it."

"It hasn't been all that easy. I've had problems—which I won't bore you with. So that's my story. Tell me, Mrs. Cornwall, what is it *you* want out of life?"

It wasn't a question that was easily answered, certainly not off the top of one's head. "I'm not sure I can answer that," Stephanie finally said.

"No copping out. But I'll give you—oh, a few seconds to think it over."

Stephanie tried to think of a clever answer, but she found it hard to concentrate. What a strange question—and why was she so aware of the man, as if he were twice as large as he really was? Larger than life—that was the expression for someone who seemed to intrude upon one's territory, wasn't it?

"Time's up. Okay, what is it you want out of life?"

"To be without any responsibilities for a while—which probably sounds pretty selfish to you."

"Not at all. The whole world would be a lot happier if people didn't live their lives to please others. When you say responsibilities, do you mean your boys? Are they getting to be too much for you? Why don't you send them to live with their father for a while—or isn't he a responsible person?"

"Oh, he's responsible, all right. He's a very successful lawyer in San Francisco. He pays his bills on time, invests wisely, plays handball twice a week, eats the right foods, and takes his vitamins every day."

"Pretty predictable, huh? Is that why you two split up?"

"I loved my husband and had no complaints until—well, it's a personal matter."

"Right. But for all that he was so responsible, you're the one who has custody of your boys. Why is that?"

Even though the light under the pines was too dim to reveal her expression, Stephanie looked away. She wasn't about to tell this stranger why David hadn't fought for custody of the twins. She'd only told one person, Ariel, and she still regretted that.

"Which also comes under the heading of personal business, right?" Clay said. "Well, that's okay. There's a log over there. Why don't we sit down on it and talk until you get sleepy?"

It occurred to Stephanie that he hadn't said what he was doing out and about in the middle of the night, but she dropped down on the log and stared up at the few stars that hadn't been overpowered by the moon. How close they looked—was that because the air was so clear here or just her imagination? A night-flying bird made a whirring sound nearby, and she started, instinctively covering her hair with both hands.

"It's not a bat. Just an owl," Clay said. "Are you cold?"

"No, I'm fine," she said, and then shivered as the owl gave a haunting cry.

"The Indians believed the owl was the soul of the dead," Clay said. His breath fanned the side of her face and again, she was very much aware of him, of his body heat, his sheer presence.

His hand found her forearm; he pulled her toward him. When he kissed her, finding her mouth with unerring aim, she didn't try to get away. She knew, from her own lack of surprise, that she'd been expecting it—and that she would have been disappointed if he hadn't tried. The kiss lengthened, and a stirring, a sensation she'd almost forgotten, started up inside her. The feeling intensified, and she realized she was sexually aroused, far more so than she should be from a simple kiss—and why did she feel relief because she was so easily stirred by the kiss of a man she barely knew?

Then Clay was touching her breast—not delicately and gently as David always had, but with a firmness that bordered on roughness. His breath rasped in her ear as he pulled her into the circle of his legs. She felt his erection pressing against her hip, and again she was pleased by her own response.

Even when he slid his hands under her sweater, finding her bra and unfastening it, she didn't pull away. Instead, she leaned against him, deliberately pressing her hip against the telltale hardness between his thighs. He groaned and pulled her around until she half sat, half lay across his knees. He fumbled with her belt; finally got it unfastened. When he unzipped her jeans and stripped them down over her shoes, taking her panties with them, the night wind chilled the warm flesh of her abdomen and stirred her pubic hairs.

"Here, lie on this," Clay whispered, and slid his down-filled jacket under her body. She heard a rustling, and when he lowered himself beside her a few seconds later, he was naked. He slipped her sweater over her head and pulled away her bra, and then his body, hot and heavy and blatantly male, was covering hers, keeping her warm.

He kissed her, his tongue invading her mouth for the first time. There was little finesse about his lovemaking, but it didn't matter because she was already on fire, her body straining toward fulfillment, anticipating and wanting his invasion.

He suckled her breasts, covering them with his open mouth until she was sure she would melt into the jacket beneath her. Then he was stroking the triangle between her thighs, so roughly that she gasped with surprise.

She was used to David's careful foreplay, a solicitous progression in their lovemaking, always the same, always predictable. This man ignored such niceties. He fondled her for a while, and when he took her, it was with a lusty enthusiasm that assumed she would be as ready as he.

And she *was* ready. Her skin tingled from the heat within, and she was wild with need as she matched him stroke for stroke, thrust for thrust, holding nothing back, digging her fingernails into his shoulders because she was afraid he would leave her behind. She had had orgasms before, although rarely, but she wasn't prepared for what happened next. When release came in a great wave of sensation, her whole body, inside and out, vibrated with an intensity that bordered on pain. She returned to reality in slow stages, and now she was aware of bewilderment— and shame. What must Clay think of her, clawing at him like that, behaving like a crazy woman?

"You're wonderful," Clay said, nuzzling her throat with his lips. "Give me a few minutes, and we'll have an encore."

Stephanie didn't answer. She lay there, stiff with embarrassment. What had happened to her? She wasn't even sure she liked this man, and yet she'd fallen into his arms, acted like a nymphomaniac.

Carefully, she pulled away and began groping around for her clothes. The cold wind that hadn't bothered her earlier bit into her flesh now, making her shiver. Some of the chill she felt wasn't physical, and she felt like crying. How could she face this man, this near-stranger, in the light of day when she'd acted like a whore tonight in the dark?

"Is something wrong, Stephanie? If you're worried that this is something I do with every good-looking woman who takes the trip, forget it. I'm usually all business. I mean that, Stephanie. Do you believe me?"

And strangely she did. She sat back on her heels, hugging her warm sweater to her breasts. "Nothing's wrong. I'm just cold," she said.

"We'll take care of that." He pulled her to her feet, and draped his jacket around her shoulders. "That better?"

"It feels good, but I'd better put my clothes back on—if I can find them."

"Wait there a minute while I get them together." He bent, began picking up things from the ground as if he could see in the dark. And maybe he could, she thought. Maybe that came after years in the outdoors.

Not giving her time to dress, he steered her along the path, away from camp, his hand on her shoulder, and she was too numb with cold and embarrassment to protest.

When he stopped, she caught a glimpse of something pale on

the path ahead. "I always pitch my tent away from the others. I like to be alone."

He separated the flaps of the tent so she could enter. She slid through the opening, not sure why she didn't simply tell him she wanted to get back to her own tent.

He pulled her down upon something soft and very warm. "Here—I keep this for emergencies." He put a tin cup in her hand, and when she took a sip, she discovered it was rum. She handed it back to him, and as they shared the rum, she discovered her embarrassment was gone.

Later, they made love again. Having dropped the barriers once, it seemed silly to protest when he began kissing her—and besides, she wanted it just as much as he did.

The second time was even better than the first. When both of them were fully aroused, he lifted her until she sat astride him and lowered her onto his body, penetrating her. All inhibitions left Stephanie, perhaps because he was so matter-of-fact, so natural, about his lust for her. In a frenzy, she rode him selfishly, using him and taking her own pleasure without regard for his, not worrying about the ridiculous picture they must make as she rose and fell above him, as he bucked beneath her like a young stallion. When she finally collapsed on his chest, they were both covered with sweat.

"That was wonderful," she said, her voice high and breathless.

"Tomorrow night, our last night, we'll be camping on a beach that stretches for almost half a mile along the river," he said. "The sand there is as soft as pumice. We'll take blankets and lie under the stars and make love until morning—how does that sound?"

An uneasiness filled her. "But what about the boys? What if they hear us—or someone else does?"

"They won't. The place I have in mind is very private. I promise you'll be crazy about it. Each time will be better than the last, Stephanie. God, I'm so glad you came on the trip. It makes me sick to think how easily we could have missed each other."

She snuggled up close, feeling drowsy and content. In a little while, she'd dress and go back to her tent, but for now, how good to feel a man against her naked body again—and to know that the secret fear that had been bothering her ever since her encounter with Ariel had been dispelled. No matter that she, at a very vulnerable time in her life, had briefly responded sexually to another woman. It had been a fluke, a freak—and it would never happen again.

And why did those words seem so familiar?

CHAPTER THIRTY-NINE

STEPHANIE EXPECTED HER RELATIONSHIP WITH CLAY O'CONnors to end the day the rafting trip was over. She had no illusions about that. Clay was strictly a temporary lover; she accepted this even though she couldn't help wondering what a long-term relationship with him would be like. Would he wear well—or was the only thing they had in common their lust for each other?

So she was totally unprepared when he turned up on her doorstep ten days after she and the boys returned to Mill Valley. From his wide grin, she knew he expected an open-arm welcome, but her feelings were so mixed that she could only stammer, "You didn't say anything about coming to California."

"I wasn't sure when I could get away. During the season, we need a full crew—and we've had a rash of summer flu lately. We've been so shorthanded that this is the first time I've had a chance to take a couple of days off. Luckily, the whole gang turned up yesterday, so I made the orientation speech, declared a holiday for myself, and cut out. I didn't want to take the chance that you'd forget me."

Stephanie had never liked surprises, because most of the ones she'd encountered in her life had been unpleasant, but this surprise was more than pleasant, even though she knew instinctively that it would complicate her already complicated life.

"Not much chance of that," she said, and she was smiling as she opened the door wider so he could enter.

She ushered Clay into the living room, where the twins were sprawled out on the sofa, watching TV. "Look who's come to see us, boys," she said brightly.

The twins' greeting must have warmed Clay's heart. From the way they took him over, it was obvious they assumed he'd come to see them. During the past ten days, they'd only seen their father once and that for only an hour the preceding weekend. According to David, he was snowed under with work, something Stephanie doubted because David seldom let his work intrude upon his private life. Deprived of their father's company, it was natural that the boys would welcome Clay enthusiastically—and what the devil was David up to now? Did he have a new boyfriend who was taking up his time?

The suspicion hurt. With an effort, she put David out of her mind and went to put on a pot of coffee. When she joined Clay and the twins, they had coaxed him into a new movie trivia game that was their current passion and were deeply involved in such things as the name of Hopalong Cassidy's horse and who had starred in the original version of *A Star Is Born*.

Stephanie kibitzed for a while, then went to fix dinner, deciding upon spaghetti with clam sauce even though Clay was a self-proclaimed meat-and-potato man.

As she put a kettle of water on to boil for spaghetti and got out the ingredients for the sauce, she listened to the lively conversation in the living room. No matter what happened to her relationship with Clay, surely she wouldn't have to worry about how the boys would react. At the campsites, they had followed Clay around like twin shadows, listening to his stories, jumping when he gave them an order. No, there'd be no problem about getting them to accept Clay if he became a regular visitor—and what was she thinking of, jumping the gun like that? She wasn't even sure she *wanted* to continue her affair with Clay, for God's sake. . . .

But after the boys had gone off to bed, she forgot her doubts. Clay made love to her in the flickering light of the fireplace gas jets, and she responded to his lovemaking as if it had been years since she'd left Oregon instead of just ten days.

Maybe she'd been afraid it wouldn't be the same, that it had been the novelty of being cut off from everything familiar that had made it so special before. Now she discovered it was just as exciting—and a lot more comfortable—making love on a rug.

When Clay kissed her, her pulse rate was so rapid that she was afraid her heart would jump out of her chest. They undressed with indecent haste, and even before he touched her intimately, the sweet juices of her body were already flowing, prepared for him. As he rose above her, teasing her by withholding what she wanted so desperately, she urged him on with her wet mouth, her frantic fingers, and afterward, when they lay exhausted on the rug, she stroked him back to turgescence and then mounted him to make love again.

Later, they drank coffee in the kitchen, and that's when he told her he was crazy about her, that he couldn't stand the thought of her getting away from him.

"I know it's too soon to talk about anything permanent, but I want you to know that there's nothing casual about the way I feel. I'm really crazy about you, Stephanie. I want to see you every chance I can. Do you feel the same way about me?"

"I—I think I do," she said, dazed by his declaration—and because it was happening so fast.

"That's all I'm asking for now. Give me—and this thing we've got going—a chance. Is it a promise?"

"It's a promise," she said, and leaned across the breakfast counter to kiss him.

July, always so capricious in San Francisco, chose to come on strong this year. The morning fogs and sea breezes that had earned it the title of the "air-conditioned city" faltered, and there were record temperatures day after day, goading the local TV meteorologists into extravagant statements about broken records and changing weather patterns. People sunbathed on the grass of the city parks or took chances with the dangerous tidal undertows off the beaches of The Great Highway, and there were daily warnings from PG&E about overuse of air conditioners.

Stephanie, who had been raised in cool Oregon, had never really appreciated the thick walls of the University Club until today, the first Saturday of July, when she left the blistering pavements of Sutter Street for the delicious coolness of the club's old-fashioned lobby.

She was early on purpose because she wanted to talk in private to Janice, who was usually the first to arrive, about how to handle the delicate problem of Ariel and Chanel—provided both of them turned up.

The June meeting had been canceled. Ariel had called Janice from the *Sea Lark* to say that she'd be gone most of June, and Chanel had begged off because of "personal business," while Stephanie herself had been on the rafting trip that weekend. When she'd made a dutiful call to Chanel, she'd been careful not to mention Ariel's name because she didn't want to be in the position of taking sides.

As Glory had said when she phoned to ask how the rafting trip had gone, there were no sides. In her opinion, both Chanel and Ariel had made the mistake of trusting the same man. That Ariel, according to the postcards she'd sent the support group women, was blissfully happy, didn't really change one thing: Laird had placed Chanel in a rotten position when he hadn't showed up at his own party, leaving her to make excuses to his friends.

"Chanel has guts. She didn't turn a hair," Glory said. "But it musta really hurt. And Ariel's not to blame, either. Chanel's so closemouthed that how could Ariel know she was getting it on with Laird, that they were going to announce their engagement at that party?"

So it looked to be a very uncomfortable luncheon. In fact, Stephanie had seriously considered making an excuse and staying home, just to avoid the whole thing. God knew, she had enough trouble in her own life these days. . . .

The thought of her recent—and totally unexpected—problems with the twins made her steps lag as she moved along the musty-smelling hall toward the solarium. With Clay coming down from Oregon every chance he got, the last thing she needed was the boys' turnaround in their attitude toward him. But they did object—obstinately and unreasonably—and for this, she blamed David, even though she wasn't sure what he had done to aggravate the situation.

When it became obvious to Clay that the boys resented him in the same proportion that they once had looked up to him, he only laughed and told her to give them time.

"They've had your complete attention since your divorce, and they're spoiled," he said. "Naturally, they resent me. They still hope you and your ex will get back together. They'll accept the situation when they realize that nothing's going to mend things between you and their father. So just ignore it."

But she couldn't ignore it. For one thing, it was so uncomfortable, the way her sons always found an excuse to go to their rooms when Clay came to take her out to dinner. When Chuck, always the spokesman for the twins, told her they never saw her these days, a blatant exaggeration because Clay came down from Oregon only between scheduled rafting trips, she finally lost her temper.

"You two have made it so awkward for me to entertain Clay here that now we're forced to go out to dinner. When you're ready to be sensible, let me know, and I'll invite Clay to have dinner with us. Until then, I don't want to hear any more nonsense about being neglected.''

"Ah, Mom, we just don't like him. He takes over and orders us around like he's our dad. Besides''—Chuck gave her a veiled look—''we know you want to be alone with him. We can't even come downstairs for fear we'll catch you two making out in front of the fireplace.''

Stephanie knew her face had changed color, but she gave him a long, hard look. "I don't like that kind of talk. So junk it, you hear?''

"You even talk like him, Mom," Ronnie, who had been silent until now, complained. " 'Junk it'—that's something he says all the time. Dad said—'' He broke off, looking uncomfortable.

"Your father said what?''

"I can't remember now.''

"I'll just bet you can't. I'd like to listen in on some of the conversations you three have about me.''

"That isn't fair! You talk about him a lot more than he talks about you,'' Chuck burst out. "All he ever says is 'How's your mother?' and things like that.''

"So how does it happen he knows about Clay?''

"It just came up. I said something about this guy who'd been hanging around, so Dad asked who he was, and—well, we told him how you met Clay on the rafting trip. Dad looked kind of funny, and then he said we should trust your judgment and give this guy a chance.''

"Oh, he did, did he? Well, you tell him—no, don't bother. It isn't important,'' she said.

But it was important. She didn't need David's defense, which undoubtedly had been meant to reach her ears. David knew his boys, knew they'd eventually repeat what he said—was it going to be this way from now on? Tension and stress every time the boys saw their father?

Maybe it was time for a change. What if she sold the condo and moved away—say, to Oregon? David's contact with the boys would, by necessity, be limited then. If he wanted to see them, he would have to make the trip himself. After all, there was nothing in their divorce agreement about allowing the boys to stay with him during holidays and summer vacations—maybe because it had never occurred to David that she might take the boys and leave California someday.

And why had Oregon popped into her mind? Because she'd

spent her own childhood on an Oregon farm? Or because Clay lived there? Which was really premature. True, they were lovers, but Clay had never mentioned marriage. Of course, they'd only known each other a few weeks.

Still deep in thought, Stephanie turned into the solarium where Chanel's smooth voice brought her back to the present.

"You look as if you're lost in another world—and where did you get that tan?"

"On the rafting trip—but it's already fading fast," Stephanie said. Chanel, as always, looked soigné in a white, raw silk summer suit set off by ebony-black earrings and bracelet. As they settled themselves in the wicker chairs, Chanel's scrutiny seemed a little too intent.

"You look marvelous, Stephanie, and I don't think it's just the tan. Either you have a new man or you've just hit the state lottery."

"As it happens, it's a man," Stephanie confessed. "I met him on the rafting trip."

"So you have a lover now, huh? Well, bully for you."

Stephanie felt a stab of resentment. "Why do you assume that we're lovers?"

"Oh, come now. Once you get used to regular sex, you don't turn it off just because you got a divorce. Like I say, bully for you. But be careful. When you're on the rebound from a bad marriage, you're particularly vulnerable. You can read a lot of things into a new relationship that aren't really there."

"Oh, I think I'll be able to recognize the real thing when it comes along," Stephanie said stiffly.

"Oh, lord—I forgot about your thin skin. And I'm getting as bad as Glory, blurting out whatever comes to mind. I don't know if that's good or bad."

Stephanie relented and smiled at her. "It's good. I've been trying to be more outgoing myself."

"Well, you could be right. I have to admit that Glory is unique—"

"Did I hear my name?" It was Glory; she was wearing white slacks, a white silk blouse, with a hot pink scarf knotted around her waist for a belt. She plopped down in a chair and crossed her long legs, grinning at them.

"Yes, we were talking about you, Morning Glory Browne," Chanel said, sounding amused. "We agreed that part of your charm is your—uh, insouciance. And of course there's not a phony bone in your newly svelte body.''

Unexpectedly, Glory's eyes clouded. "Oh, I can lie when I want to. My old lady used to slap me alongside the face when she thought I was hiding something. Since I'm a fast study, I learned real quick to say what she wanted to hear, even if I had to lie. Of course, she was full of stories herself, most of them wishful thinking.''

She paused for a laugh, but the expression in her eyes made Stephanie wince. "The garbage she gave out about how rich her folks used to be. 'My granddaddy was wiped out in twenty-nine,' she'd say, putting on airs. And all the time, her current live-in would be laughing at her and swilling down the beer she bought out of her welfare checks instead of food. It's a good thing I was quick on my feet and could rip off the supermarket, or I would've starved to death.''

"You really had an interesting childhood, all that subculture shit," Chanel said, her eyes bland.

"Right. You, too. Eating caviar off a gold plate with a platinum spoon and drinking champagne from the bottle instead of milk.''

"You just know it. What did you nurse on? Rat urine?''

Stephanie sat frozen, waiting for the explosion. She was non-plussed when both of them started laughing. They sounded like—well, like two people who understood each other perfectly and were very comfortable about it. She wanted to join in and say something witty or funny, but the truth was she wasn't good at that sort of thing. The only people who ever laughed at her jokes were the boys—and David.

As she listened to Glory and Chanel's exchange of banter, she felt left out. Although she had come to like, in varying degrees, the other women in the club, she hadn't formed any real friendships. True, for a while she and Ariel had been drifting toward it, but after what had happened—well, it was too painful to think about *that* now.

"Just before you came, Stephanie was telling me that she has a new beau," Chanel told Glory, widening her eyes in a way Stephanie had become familiar with and which always made her feel uncomfortable.

Glory gave Stephanie an appraising look. "It's about time. You can't live like a nun the rest of your life.''

"So tell us about him—he must be the outdoor type if you met him on a rafting trip,'' Chanel said.

Stephanie found herself describing Clay and explaining how they'd met and even talking about the problems with the twins that had come up lately.

"All of a sudden, Ronnie's started wetting the bed again." She paused, remembering the look on her son's face when she'd confronted him after realizing why he was changing his sheets so often and why he'd taken over the job of doing his own laundry. He'd begged her, with tears in his eyes, to please not tell Chuck, and then she'd cried, too, feeling his humiliation, his shame. "I'm sure it has something to do with my seeing Clay. I don't know what the boys have against him. They adored him on the rafting trip."

"Has his attitude toward them changed?" Chanel said.

"Not really. He's—well, he isn't like David, of course. David treats them like adults, which means they feel they can question everything that comes up. Clay doesn't take any back talk. They resent that, I'm sure, but I have to admit it's a relief, not having to explain every last thing you tell them to do."

"You can't have it both ways," Glory pointed out. "Either they're independent and have their own opinions about things or they're so polite and well behaved you wanna smack them. Besides, getting used to a new man around the house has gotta be hard on them. My mom's live-ins came and went so fast that sometimes I got mixed up and called them by the wrong name."

Stephanie didn't know what to say to that. Until she'd gone away to school at San Francisco State, she'd never encountered a promiscuous man, much less a promiscuous woman—at least not to her knowledge. Her own father and mother were a unit—inflexible, straitlaced, and conservative. To them, divorce was unthinkable. In fact, she was still getting letters from her mother, bemoaning her divorce from David, and revealing in every line her assumption that it was due to some failing on Stephanie's part.

"I didn't have that kind of problem with Fern," Chanel said. "Of course, she never knew her own father, but I think she was rather fond of Jacques. They still have lunch together once in a while."

Stephanie, who hadn't much cared for Chanel's daughter on their one and only meeting at Laird's party, was trying to think of something to say when Ariel appeared in the doorway. The change in her was so marked that Stephanie could only gape. When she'd last seen Ariel at the Sea Cliff restaurant, she'd looked like a pale wraith. This woman was vibrant; her skin glowed, her eyes sparkled. Only her smile, still shy and childlike, was the same. She was wearing a summer dress, a pale blue georgette, and her hair, fine and long and simply dressed, swirled around her shoulders as she came toward them.

Stephanie caught Chanel's catlike smile and braced herself. Here it comes, she thought. She's going to say something devastating. She wished again that she had stayed home.

As Chanel took in Ariel's smile, the hairs on the nape of her neck stirred. How innocent she looked—the little bitch. Like a puppy exposing its soft belly to an older dog to prove how harmless it is. But it wasn't going to work. In a few seconds, she was going to reduce Ariel to mincemeat by pointing out a few home truths that would wipe that smile off her face for good. . . .

"Hello, everybody," Ariel said. She put her hand on Chanel's shoulder, and incredibly, her eyes were swimming in tears. "I'm so happy, Chanel, thanks to you. You were right all along. Laird and I really do belong together."

Chanel opened her mouth, closed it again. She *had* said something like that—but in a different context. She'd been talking about their physical resemblance—those long, elegant bones, the fair hair and thin noses and those intensely blue eyes, so shrewd in Laird's face and so ingenuous in Ariel's. But of course Ariel was absolutely right about them belonging together. They were two parts of a whole in a way that was rare in the practical eighties. . . .

"Congratulations," she said, and, with the word, knew she couldn't be a spoiler. Hell, she might even go to their wedding, wearing a new Bill Blass original—and a big fake smile. . . .

Ariel perched on the edge of a chair. Oscar, their aging waiter, trotted in to take their luncheon orders, as always, starting with Ariel, and Glory took advantage of the distraction to lean toward Chanel and whisper "You're okay, Chanel."

"Just good business," Chanel said. "Laird owes me—I'll collect when the time comes." She ordered her usual salad, vinaigrette dressing on the side, then asked Ariel, "And how was the trip? Catch any fish?"

Color rose in Ariel's slender throat. "We just got back yesterday morning. We took our time, stopping whenever we felt like going ashore—it was wonderful. I'd never been on a long boat trip before, but Laird says I'm a natural sailor. We plan to spend a lot of time on the *Sea Lark* after we're married."

Chanel bared her teeth in a smile, and Stephanie said quickly, "Have you started divorce proceedings? I hope you won't have any trouble with your husband."

"Mr. Waterford arranged for a court order to evict Alex. He moved out a few days ago." The pupils of her eyes darkened. "He took several of my grandfather's paintings with him. I would just let it go, but they're part of the estate, and besides, one of them is a Degas, half of a pair that my great-grandfather bought in Paris in the twenties. Laird has the other one and—well, he thinks they should hang side by side to symbolize the end of the family feud. Besides, I wouldn't want Alex to think he got away with anything."

The expression in her eyes made Chanel wonder if she hadn't underestimated Ariel. In fact, it might be wise to stay in her good graces in the future. Just being seen with Ariel in public would give the lie to the rumors going around that Laird had ditched her for his cousin.

Despite her decision not to blame Ariel for the destruction of her plans, the desire to vent her outrage on Laird hadn't changed. Well, there were ways and then there were ways of coming out on top. Right now, Laird must be sweating blood, wondering if she'd tell Ariel about their engagement—and the real purpose of the party he'd skipped out on. When he found out she'd held her tongue, he was bound to be grateful. As to how to use that gratitude—she had an idea about that, too.

Janice arrived, looking pale and out of sorts, but she congratulated Ariel with obvious sincerity, telling her she'd give her a hug except she was just getting over a miserable cold.

During the luncheon, the conversation was lively, and no one seemed to notice how quiet Chanel was. She listened as Stephanie related the highlights of her rafting trip, and then with more interest when Glory confided that she'd "dumped" Steve Golden after she'd found out he was Earl Golden's son, that she was now looking for another job.

Ariel, with not too much coaxing, described her trip to Mexico, and every time she said Laird's name, her eyes glowed, lending animation to her face. Despite her resentment toward Laird, Chanel found that she really did wish the little mouse the best. Which was strange because Laird's betrayal still rankled. Was she getting soft? If so, that would never do. Soft people were vulnerable people—and she intended to be in the driver's seat from now on.

She waited until the others were discussing a new TV miniseries to tell Glory that she might be calling her soon to discuss "something of interest to both of us."

Glory looked curious, but she didn't ask any questions, much to Chanel's relief. It would be premature to discuss the idea that had come to her. First, she had to talk it over with Stet. Although she was feeling so mellow right now after a third glass of French Colombard that she was actually toying with the idea of telling the group about the spa, she rejected the temptation. Time to talk about it when everything was set—including the date of the grand opening.

She looked around the table at the other women, and it occurred to her that everyone here would be genuinely glad if the spa turned out to be a success. The five of them, during the past year, had finally bonded—and wasn't that a hoot? It was something new to her, having friends who didn't carve her up every time her back was turned. Wasn't it a shame that none of them except Ariel was really socially important?

Well, she just might invite them to the opening anyway. After all, she owed them something for the way they'd rallied around her during that fiasco at the St. Francis. . . .

Chanel and Stet had fallen into the habit of conducting their planning sessions over lunch or dinner. Chanel welcomed this, not only because it meant a few free meals at the city's prime restaurants but because being seen in Stet's company was salve to her wounded ego and made it clear to anyone who might have heard the gossip that she wasn't sitting at home, nursing a broken heart over Laird.

When Stet called to say that he'd made a luncheon reservation for them at Compton Court, she was more than pleased by his choice. The restaurant—its official name was simply The Restaurant—at the Compton Court Hotel was the current "in" restaurant in the city. To get a luncheon reservation there meant you either had political clout, big money, or social position. Was Stet making some kind of statement, or was he simply ignorant of the significance of being seen with her at Compton Court? She wasn't surprised that he'd been able to get a reservation, of course. He was very rich and, as she was finding out, he also knew a lot of important people.

The restaurant was beautifully appointed with Wedgwood china, Swiss linen, walls covered with peach-colored cloth, and perfect acoustics that reduced noise, even raised voices, to a low hum. The service was refined, unobtrusive, the wine list impeccable, and the food eclectic—and superb. Even if the food and service didn't come up to snuff, Chanel reflected, it would be worth coming here just to look at the clientele.

After the host, whose English accent was clipped and possibly Oxford-bred, ushered them to a table by one of the double glazed windows that rose from floor to ceiling, she looked around with interest. Her eyes rested on Will Hearst, publisher of the *San Francisco Examiner*, who was sitting at the table next to Cyril Magnin, the man called "Mr. San Francisco." Bemused, she turned her attention to Her Honor, the mayor, who was with a party of eight in the rear of the long rectangular room.

Ann, the female half of the Gettys, was here today, and so was Herb Caen, who had written a column for the *Chronicle* for as long as Chanel could remember. What kind of tidbits for his column had he picked up today? Some juicy political morsel from Willie Brown, the State Assembly Speaker, who had stopped to exchange a few words with him? Or maybe something from a different power source like Denise Hale, who was the current A-list social arbitrator in San Francisco?

"Impressed?" Stet murmured in her ear.

She gave him a cool look. "Should I be?"

"It all depends on what impresses you," he said, which she thought a little ambiguous.

Before she could answer him, a man stopped by their table.

"Well, hello, Stet," he said easily, his eyes on Chanel. Although they'd never met, she recognized Senator Brach, the junior senator from California. When Stet introduced them, she gave him her best smile.

"Chanel and I are celebrating a business deal," Stet said. "She's a partner—and will also manage—one of my enterprises, a health spa in Napa Valley. The grand opening will be in early December, in time for anyone who needs a week or two of rejuvenation before the holidays to sign up. By invitation only, of course."

The large onyx-and-diamond ring on his left hand glittered as he lifted his wineglass to his lips for a sip. His good-ole-Texas-boy accent fairly crackled as he added, "Chanel will see that you and your wife get one soon. I'm sure Mrs. Brach would find the opening interesting—and rewarding. We're going to have a wine tasting. Napa wines, so the wine crowd will be there, of course—good constituents and supporters of yours, I believe?"

Senator Brach's shrewd eyes surveyed Stet, then moved to Chanel. He included both of them in the genial smile he was famous for, murmured something about calling Stet soon, and then moved away.

"I think I got my point across, don't you?" Stet said, looking amused.

"With a trowel," she said dryly. "He'd have to be stupid not to understand you."

"He isn't stupid. He's a fox who has raided a lot of hen houses in his time. His wife will not only accept the invitation for the opening, but she'll also sign for a week at the spa. Elsie would've liked that, having a senator's wife as a guest," he added, and didn't seem to notice that he'd used the past tense. "And we'd better get the fine details of the opening worked out soon. We have less than four months. The renovations won't be a problem. I've promised the contractor and the decorator a hefty bonus if they meet their deadlines. But you've still got to hire a staff and get them trained. Have you given any more thought to how you want to handle the clients?"

"As pampered guests, of course. Most women go to a spa to lose weight—and they want to do it the easy way. They expect an exercise-and-diet program, but at three thousand plus a week, it had better be sugarcoated. That's why I'm going to try to convince Jean-Pierre Auirre—he's the chef at La Belle France—to take over our kitchen. I hear he isn't happy with the present management at La Belle France—some kind of personality clash. He doesn't come cheap, but he's worth every cent of it because he specializes in diet cuisine. He can turn out a sumptuous meal, and you'd never guess the food was all low-calorie. More importantly, he loves a challenge. I think we can get him under contract if we move fast."

Stet nodded agreement. "How important is it that the clients actually lose weight? After all, they'll only be at the spa one or two weeks."

"It's very important that they come away a few pounds lighter. And they believe what they see on the scales," Chanel said. "There are tricks all the spas use. An eight-ounce glass of water weighs a pound, so dehydration is a big factor in weight loss. No salt, no alcohol, and limited liquids will drain it off in a hurry. It's not a real weight loss, but the guests seldom seem to realize that. I've been doing some research—as you know. One woman I interviewed for a job used to do publicity for a famous New York fat farm. She let her hair down for a bit and told me the place where she'd worked actually changed the scales so the clients would believe they'd lost more weight than they had.''

"A little tacky, don't you think?''

Chanel shrugged. "True—and it could backfire, too. We won't juggle the scales, but a water weight loss is certainly legitimate. As for the beauty salon—it's even more important. We need a top person to run it. It should be equipped to give the guest a complete overhaul while she's at the spa—haircuts, coloring, makeup application, honey waxings, body wraps, collagen and elastin treatments, and even electrolysis. Our clients will come out looking years younger and feeling good about themselves. Of course, most of them will fall back into their old bad habits, but when they first go home, their friends will accuse them of having had a face-lift—or a new lover.''

She assumed a haughty expression. " 'You're looking just marvelous, don't you know. Have you found the fountain of youth by any chance?' " she said, mimicking Nancy Anderson's carefully cultivated drawl so accurately that Stet's hearty laugh rang out, drawing a few curious stares.

Chanel decided she liked his laugh—there was nothing phony about it. Despite his business acumen, Stet was earthy, unpretentious, easy to talk to. Too bad he was permanently tied to that wife of his, or she'd set her cap for him. But it would be a tactical mistake to settle for anything less than marriage. Affairs were fine as long as they were discreet and casual and could be quickly terminated when they became tiresome. But as Stet's mistress, she would have no social clout, no power, none of the things that an advantageous marriage gave an ambitious woman. How ironic that Ariel, who cared nothing for those things, had hooked herself such a big fish.

"What are you thinking about?" Stet asked. "You look like someone just punctured your balloon.''

"You do know how to turn a neat phrase, Stet.''

"And you know how to turn the knife, don't you? Why are you evading my question?''

"I was thinking how difficult it's been, trying to find the right assistant, someone hardworking and competent and reliable,'' Chanel lied.

"Raid the other spas for good help. Dangle a big salary jump in front of their noses. Ambitious people go where the money is.''

"And they leave just as quickly for more salary elsewhere.''

''Not if you establish personal loyalty. There's an art to that, you know—it has to work both ways. If you want loyalty, you have to give it back.''

''Is that how you handled your crew during your wildcatter days?''

''I also paid them more than they could get anywhere else—but not all that much more.''

Chanel was silent. Did she have the knack for instilling loyalty in the people who worked for her? She felt a little uncomfortable suddenly, remembering that she'd never given a thought to the problems of her domestic help. She'd hired and fired with equal indifference. . . .

''There *is* someone,'' she said. ''Unfortunately, she uses gutter language on occasion, and I'm not sure how she'd fit in with the kind of clientele we're courting.''

For the next few minutes, she filled Stet in on Glory's background. Stet listened intently as she described some of Glory's more outrageous stories about her past—including how she'd handled an abusive husband.

''She actually tied him to the bed and whacked him with his own belt?''

''She did. One across his tender parts, too.''

''And you say she works for the Golden Gate Health Club? That Pacific Heights branch has a pretty fancy clientele, doesn't it?''

''Mostly upper–middle-class housewives and professional career women—not the class we're trying for. But I do happen to know that Glory is looking for another job right now.''

''She's not a job-hopper, is she?''

''She's happy enough where she is, but she just broke off a relationship with the manager. Which makes it pretty uncomfortable for her.''

''Why did they break up—or do you know?''

''She has this thing about jocks. Seems her ex-husband was a professional baseball player. Which was one strike against Steve. Then she found out he was Earl Golden's son—and she claims he lied to her, let her think he was just a—what she calls a working stiff. Which is pretty stupid. It's obvious he's crazy about her. She could do a lot worse than latching onto a multimillionaire's son.''

''According to your lights. Has it ever occurred to you that you have the instincts of a predator?''

She gave him a cold look. "What's wrong with marrying money?"

"Nothing—for you. For your friend, it obviously isn't something she wants. I think I'd like to meet this Glory Browne. She wouldn't do as your assistant—that calls for good administrative skills—but she could be just what you need as honcho for the aerobics program. Why don't we drop by the place where she works and—no, better yet. She'll have to deal with a class of women who are used to the best—and that can be pretty intimidating. Let's see how impressed she is by a swanky place like this. Why don't you invite her here for lunch tomorrow? I'll reserve table twelve—it has the best view of the room—and we'll get here early so we can watch her reaction when she realizes she'll be eating lunch practically in the lap of Her Honor, the mayor."

Stet had suggested inviting Glory Browne to lunch not only because he was curious about her, but also because it gave him an excuse to see Chanel again. He'd been attracted to her from their very first meeting, but he also had a healthy sense of self-preservation, and he had his doubts about the way she thought, the ambition about which she made no bones. Not that he wouldn't set her up as his mistress in a minute. Originally, this plan to get her involved in the spa had partially been because he wanted a legitimate excuse to see her often. He had every intention of eventually changing her mind about becoming his mistress. He had also thought, however, that she would make a good hostess for the spa. What he hadn't expected was for her to take hold and make cool, calculated and surprisingly astute decisions about everything from refurbishing the spa to hiring and training a staff to drawing up a first-rate brochure for the printers.

Stet wasn't sure he totally approved of this side of Chanel. Chanel as an independent and successful businesswoman was not as likely to fall into bed with him as Chanel, slowly going broke and getting a little desperate. But—it was early times, as the limeys said.

As he sat across from her at Compton Court for the second time in two days, he discovered that he was impatient for the arrival of their guest. Chanel had described her as a street waif who was the quickest study she'd ever encountered. He'd always considered himself an old country boy who learned fast, so he was very curious about Glory.

Even though Chanel's description of the woman wasn't totally flattering, it was obvious she was fond of this Glory Browne. Which was a surprise. Chanel, for all her social savvy, was a loner—which made it all the more curious that she'd invest time in someone totally unimportant socially. So he kept his eyes on the door as he listened to Chanel's chatter, not sure what to expect.

At first, he didn't connect the woman who followed in the wake of the host with Glory Browne. For one thing, she was much younger than he'd expected. Her hair, a shade of red that was totally new to his experience, was skillfully layered so the curls formed what looked to be petals over her head, and she was wearing a yellow tunic over matching pants, her narrow waist tightly clinched by several strands of gold links. From the stares she was collecting, especially from men, the other patrons were as fascinated as he was by her long-legged stride and the way her hair seemed to light up the air around her.

More important to Stet was the coolness with which she looked around, her eyes lingering on the table where Herb Caen and the mayor were sitting, deep in conversation. That she recognized them both was obvious. That she wasn't particularly impressed was also apparent, as she took in the mayor's neat blouse, the bow at the neck that had become her trademark as much as her meticulous grooming, then moved her attention to Herb Caen, the consummate columnist, in his rumpled suit and askew tie.

Caen looked up, and his eyes sharpened. For a moment, Stet thought he would speak to Glory, but she was already past, moving with the ease of a model. She spotted Chanel and waved. She saw Stet then, and he thought she looked a little wary. When he rose quickly, she acknowledged his politeness with a brief smile.

"What is this place, anyway? Where the elite meet to eat? That *is* the mayor over there, isn't it?"

"Impressed?" Chanel asked.

"No. I didn't vote for her," Glory said, dismissing Her Honor with a shrug.

The host seated her, then hurried away. "What does impress you?" Chanel asked Glory.

"Not much."

"That's Cyril Magnin, sitting by the window, you know."

"The one they named the street after? I thought they only did that after you was dead."

Stet hid a smile. "This is a pretty fancy place, little lady. Sort of San Francisco's version of Elaine's in New York."

"But is the food good?" Glory said, and Stet would have sworn it was a genuine question and not a quip.

When both of them laughed, Glory looked surprised. She studied Stet for a long moment. "I've seen you somewhere before. At Chanel's party, wasn't it?"

"This is Stet—William Stetson," Chanel said as their waiter came up. "What say we order and talk later?"

Over a lunch of rib-eye steak and sweet potato fries for Stet, a lobster salad for Chanel, and a watercress-and-tomato salad for Glory, Stet set about drawing Glory out. She seemed very willing to talk about her job at the Golden Gate Health Club, and was especially sympathetic to the queen-sized women for whom she'd started a class. She was also, she let him know, a dedicated health nut. She had even given up ice cream, she told him, in the interest of lowering her cholesterol.

"When I was a kid, I spent every cent I got my hands on for ice cream and pretzels—you know, those big fat ones you eat with mustard? Now I'm into veggies and salads, but sometimes, when I get the blue meanies, I still pig out on French vanilla ice cream."

"What turned you around?"

"It was this guy I know. He convinced me I was going to end up with clogged arteries if I didn't stop eating junk foods. I used to live on Big Macs and french fries—and ice cream."

"Are you talking about Steve Golden?" Chanel asked.

"Yeah. I guess I owe him something for that."

"It must be uncomfortable, working for him now."

"You know it. Which is why I'm going to change jobs as soon as I can find one that pays as much as I make at the health club."

"I still can't believe you'd break up with the man just because you found out he has a rich father."

"It wasn't just that. The thing is—he lied to me. He was real careful not to let me know that his old man was Earl Golden. Steve was raised like some kinda prince, and yet he put on this act that he was just a working stiff. I guess that's how he gets it off, making fools out of other people."

Chanel raised one eyebrow at Stet as if to say "See, I told you so."

Stet discovered he liked the way Chanel seemed more human around this girl. Was it because she felt noncompetitive with Glory? Whatever it was, Chanel's guard seemed relaxed, which was just what he wanted, wasn't it? To catch her with her guard down?

By the time they ate dessert—Grand Marnier soufflé for Stet, fresh fruit compote for Chanel and Glory—he had made up his mind. When a lull came in the conversation, he nodded at Chanel, then listened while she told Glory about the spa and offered her the job of setting up and supervising the aerobics classes. Glory accepted—but not before she was satisfied about wages and benefits.

Maybe, he thought, thoroughly enjoying himself, Chanel and Glory weren't that different, after all.

CHAPTER FORTY

THE LIVING ROOM WAS STUFFY WITH LATE SEPTEMBER HEAT, and perspiration beaded on Stephanie's upper lip as she dropped her purse on a chair, kicked off her pumps, and went to turn on the air conditioner. Usually the boys were there when she got home from work, and she returned to a cool house. Today, they were off on a two-day field trip to Yosemite, and while she was glad for them, she also missed their chatter. God help her, she even missed their wrangling.

And what was she going to do, just three years from now, when they went off to college and the house was *always* empty when she came home? The empty nest syndrome was going to be doubly hard for her—no husband, and no boys to coddle, although she did as little of that as possible these days, aware that smother love was not what fifteen-year-old boys needed.

What they needed was both a mother and a father—and ever since they had returned from the rafting trip, David had been conspicuous by his absence. According to the boys, he was dating again. He and his woman friend had taken the twins to the zoo, a cozy little family group, and when they returned home, the boys declared that "Dad's friend" was a real pill, that all she did was act silly.

Stephanie had wanted to ask if she was young and pretty, but she held her tongue. That David was dating a woman knocked a hole in her supposition that he had finally come out of the closet—was this woman simply a ruse to turn off any suspicions the boys might have?

She decided it was too hot to think about anything heavy and went into the kitchen to pour herself a glass of iced tea. Although the air-conditioner was working full-time and the temperature was slowly dropping, the house was still stuffy, and she decided to change into something cool and comfortable—and loose. The air conditioner had been making strange wheezing sounds lately, and she fervently hoped it would last out the summer, because she couldn't possibly afford a big repair bill now.

These days, anything that wasn't absolutely necessary was too much for her budget. With two teenagers, both with voracious appetites, to feed, her food bills were sky-high even though she shopped carefully, utilizing every discount coupon she could get her hands on. Even with her first raise and the child support David paid her, she was living on the edge of financial disaster. It wouldn't hurt David to take over some of the boys' expenses, the extra things that child support didn't cover, but that never seemed to occur to him. Not that she would *ask* for his help at this late date. She'd eat beans five times a week before she'd do that.

Stephanie took off her work clothes, in this case a four-year-old summer suit, hung it in the closet, and stripped off her underwear and hose. She took a shower, letting the water run over her for a long time, her thoughts muzzy and disjointed. The play of water on her skin was erotic, bringing back memories of Clay's last visit. They had gone to a hotel—and she hadn't returned until very late, a piece of information she was sure had already been relayed to David, no matter how the boys denied that they talked about her to their father.

She still wasn't used to her new sensuality, but there was no doubt that it existed. What a shame that Clay wouldn't be here for another two days. Tonight, they would've had the house to themselves, could have made love in her own bed instead of going to a hotel or coupling quickly on the fireplace rug. . . .

Would it bother her to have sex with Clay in the bed she'd shared with David for fifteen years? It probably would—but not enough to stop her. Something had happened to some of the sensitivity that had once made life so complicated for her. Having to face up to the hard realities of life had desensitized her toward things that once had seemed so important. Was that good or bad?

Well, at least she was learning to stand up for her own rights. In fact, she'd won a couple of battles lately at work, including demanding and getting her own desk. For the first few months on the job, she'd been assigned a worktable in the stockroom, which meant that not only didn't she have any drawer space but she had to lock away every pen and paper clip and personal item in her locker before she went home nights.

She'd finally had enough and had marched into Mr. Spengler's office and demanded a desk of her own. He had huffed and puffed awhile and then, to her surprise, had arranged to have one set up in his outer office, across the room from his secretary's desk. Of course, this hadn't gone over well with the secretary, who considered herself several steps above a lowly clerk. Which meant there had been another war of wills that, miracles of miracles, she had won.

And wasn't that a kick—as Chanel would say?

Stephanie had almost finished blow-drying her hair when the doorbell rang. She muttered a "damn," but it didn't occur to her to ignore it. When she opened the door, a slender, fair-haired woman, a stranger, stood there. There was something unnerving about the way she stared at Stephanie, as if she couldn't decide whether to speak or just walk away.

"Yes?" Stephanie said.

"Are you Stephanie Cornwall?" the woman asked.

"Yes, I am."

"I—I'm Jocelyn O'Connors, Clay's wife."

The woman burst into tears.

Afterward, Stephanie was surprised that she'd had enough presence of mind to steer the sobbing woman inside and lead her to a chair, to wet a washcloth and put it in her hand, then excuse herself on the pretext of getting a glass of water from the kitchen so the woman could have privacy while she regained her composure.

When Stephanie came back into the living room with the water, Jocelyn O'Connors had stopped crying, but she hadn't made any attempt to repair her makeup. In fact, she looked dazed, as if she weren't quite sure where she was. Was there something—well, mental about her?

Stephanie studied her doubtfully. Blond—natural, she would

guess. Blue eyes—and, she suspected, very pretty although it was hard to tell because of her tear-ravaged face.

Jocelyn looked up, met her stare; her mouth began to work, as if she would start crying again, and Stephanie hastened to hand her the glass of water. As if they were following some mutually agreed-upon terms, both women were silent while Jocelyn drank the water.

"Why don't you tell me what this is all about?" Stephanie said finally, although she dreaded the woman's answer.

Jocelyn's hand trembled as she set the glass down on the nearest table. "I know you've been seeing my husband. I found one of your letters in his jacket pocket. I knew there was someone else, but I thought—I hoped it was just a casual relationship. Women just won't leave Clay alone, but always before it wasn't serious. This time—"

Her eyes filled with tears again. She dabbed at them furiously and gave a shaky laugh.

"I know I'm making a fool out of myself, coming here, but I didn't know what else to do. When I showed Clay the letter, he told me he wanted a divorce so he could marry you. I—I just couldn't let him go without talking to you. The girls and I need him so much, you see."

Stephanie felt as if someone had struck her a hard blow on the back of the head, but she managed to ask "Girls?"

"Linda and Susie. Didn't he tell you about them? They're eleven and ten. How can he do this to us? He's had everything his own way. I stay home and take care of the house and the girls, and I never nag him or—" She broke off and made a helpless gesture with her hands. "I'm just making things worse, aren't I? When Clay finds out I came here, he'll be furious with me."

"I won't tell him."

Jocelyn met her eyes. "You love him, don't you? I was afraid of that. Well, I can't fight you. You have all the weapons. All I have is a marriage license—and it isn't enough to hold a man like Clay. I hope you can make him happy because I never could. He's—he's restless and moody and he hates routine. I made the mistake of having kids, of not being able to go off with him anytime he wanted me to. I thought it was enough just to stay home and take care of the girls and do all the things he hates about domestic life. I thought if he had his freedom, he'd always come back to me, but I was wrong, wasn't I?"

She studied Stephanie for a while, her eyes puzzled. "Clay said you were sexy and so much fun, that you were ready for anything at any time. I'm sure you're all those things, but it just never occurred to me that you would be so much like me, too."

She rose and picked up her shoulder bag. "I'm going now. It's a long drive back to Oregon. Don't worry—I won't bother you again. If you love Clay and can make him happy, I won't stand in your way."

She was gone before Stephanie could speak. Stephanie sat there, stunned and confused, Jocelyn's words still ringing in her ears.

"It just never occurred to me that you would be so much like me," she had said.

But they weren't alike, not at all! Jocelyn was blond with pale skin and light blue eyes, while she was shorter, with chestnut hair and brown eyes. So what had the woman meant?

And Clay—how could he have lied to her like that? No, he hadn't really lied. He'd said that after he'd quit his bank job, he and his wife had gone their own separate ways, not that they were divorced. But it couldn't be a coincidence that he'd never once mentioned that he was still living with his wife, that he had children. . . .

And why had he told Jocelyn that he was going to marry her when he hadn't proposed? Had he taken it for granted that she'd marry him? Maybe Jocelyn had been lying—had she come here to try to make her rival feel sorry for her?

Well, she did feel sorry for Jocelyn, but there were always losers in any relationship. Ex-wives and ex-husbands, ex-lovers, children. And she had been so lonely until she'd met Clay. Not that he was just someone to fill that loneliness, a stop-gap while she recovered from the destruction of her marriage. She would have been attracted to him even if she were still married to David. But of course she wouldn't have done anything about it.

Unlike David.

She heated a can of tomato soup, ate a few spoonfuls of it, put the rest away in the refrigerator. Although it was still early, she got ready for bed. But after she turned the lights off she couldn't sleep, not with her brain seething with questions. When she finally dropped off, she dreamed of Jocelyn, and in her dream, the two of them were one, sometimes dark-haired and brown-eyed, sometimes pale blond with blue eyes.

Two nights later, Clay came to see her. The moment she saw him, she knew that Jocelyn had told him about her visit. When he put his arms around her, she leaned against him, listening to the beat of his heart. His pine after-shave lotion suited him; it made her think of evergreen forests, fresh-washed with rain, of wildflowers and the dark-brown humus odor under the tree where they'd first made love.

"I'm sorry, Stephanie," he said. "I meant to tell you, but it never seemed to be the right time. My marriage fell apart a long time back. I stayed with Jocelyn because of the girls, but we haven't slept together for over a year. I asked her for a divorce last week. I was never happy with Jocelyn—oh, maybe right at first, but even then, I knew I'd made a mistake. We married too young, too fast, before we really got to know each other. Then the girls came and—well, that was enough reason to just keep drifting along. I would have split eventually even if I hadn't met you. I don't want you to think that you broke up my marriage, because you didn't."

"I believe you," she said, but when he kissed her, she found it hard to respond. She felt detached, as if a heavy weight were hanging over her, ready to fall—or as if something were nagging at her, just out of reach, getting in the way of her pleasure. When Clay made love to her, something seemed to be missing, and when it was over, even though her sexual tension had been relieved, she felt frustrated and dissatisfied.

"What is it, Stephanie?" Clay said. "You aren't still thinking about Jocelyn, are you?"

"I don't know what's wrong. Maybe I'm overtired—or maybe it's guilt because I've just had sex with another woman's husband."

"Put it out of your mind," he said impatiently. "Jocelyn has nothing to do with us. Okay, I should have told you about her—I made a mistake there. But it's too late for regrets. Let's talk about the future. There's no reason why you can't pack up and move to Oregon so we can be together while I get my divorce. These long trips back and forth are murder. Besides, I want more time with you."

"And the boys? Do you want them, too?"

"What do you think? Of course, I want the boys. They'll love Oregon. When they get a little older, they can make themselves useful and help out on the spring and fall weekend rafting trips. During the summer, when they're off visiting their father, I can schedule some free time so we can do some traveling. We'll have a great life, Stephanie. I make a good living—you'll never be bored."

She started to tell him that it sounded wonderful, but the words wouldn't come because it was then that it hit her—what Jocelyn had meant when she'd said they were alike. She hadn't been talking about appearance. She had sensed that they were alike in being ordinary women who had been perfectly content to build their lives around a husband and children and a home.

From Clay's description, Jocelyn had expected someone different, a female version of Clay. Instead, she'd found a near-clone of herself. How had Clay read her so wrong? Had he been deceived by her determination to be a good sport on the trip—and maybe by her sensuality, which had even surprised her? Whatever the cause, he had built up a false image of her as a sexy, adventure-loving woman, a feminine duplicate of himself. No wonder he'd assumed that she would ship the boys off to their father every summer so she could have freedom to do whatever he wanted her to do.

And what about his own girls? Strange that he hadn't said a word about his own duties as a father.

She raised up her elbow to stare down at Clay. During her long silence he had drifted off to sleep. She studied his long upper lip, his blunt, well-shaped nose, his thick dark hair, still damp from lovemaking. Did she have the good sense to give him up? If she were out of the way, maybe he would go back to his wife and girls. Or maybe not. Either way, it had nothing to do with her. Because she couldn't, mustn't, make another mistake and marry a man under false pretenses. From now on, she was going to be what she was and not try to conform to other people's expectations. It was a scary thought but it felt right, too.

CHAPTER FORTY-ONE

CHANEL, DURING THE SUMMER FOLLOWING HER BROKEN ENgagement to Laird, made a discovery about herself. She had always believed that she had an indolent nature, a low tolerance for boredom. What she hadn't suspected was that she also had an infinite capacity for work, a gift for organization, for detail, for defining and then solving problems, large or small.

From her first sight of the villa in Napa Valley, she had fallen in love with it, even though she realized that there was something a little vulgar about its opulence. But then, she told herself, wasn't there a touch of vulgarity about Chanel Devereau, Tincan O'Hara's daughter, too?

Originally built in the thirties by a Hollywood mogul as a retreat, the great sprawling structure with its red-tile roof, its forty bedrooms and thirty bathrooms, was the mogul's idea of a Spanish villa, complete with a tiled courtyard, a spacious movie-viewing room, a full-fledged library with leather-bound books that Chanel suspected had been bought by the pound rather than by content. It even had a bowling alley, fully operative, in the basement.

To give it maximum privacy, it was located in the center of a large tract of land, some one-hundred-and-twenty acres, most of which had been leased out to a neighboring vintner for grape cultivation; the tract lay across the tip of a narrow valley that was an offshoot of lush, still-rural Napa Valley. Despite its pretensions, the villa was surprisingly well constructed. It had been allowed to run down over the years when it had served as an inn, a country club, and lately as a spa, and had suffered from some unfortunate renovations by former owners, but nothing could diminish its thick, sturdy walls, its excellent architectural design, and the spaciousness of its rooms.

The estate also included a small natural hot spring that bubbled up inside a separate building a few hundred yards away from the villa itself. Stet had ordered the old springhouse with its musty showers and rusty plumbing to be torn down and had contracted for a new building, all brown-tile roof and arched doorways, with luxurious shower rooms, mud baths and private massage rooms, plus a warm-water pool, complete with pillars that, in Chanel's private opinion, looked more Romanesque than Spanish.

To Chanel, the villa's air of opulence bordering on decadence was a plus. Anything that set the spa apart from dozens of health farms that had sprung up around the country was all to the good because the competition was horrendous. Everybody, it seemed, was in the spa business these days—and a surprisingly large number of prominent people were lending their names to the enterprises.

Knowing the spa needed something unique, Chanel had decided it had to be more than merely exclusive. Reservations would be unobtainable to arrivistes and the nouveaux riches unless they had some redeeming quality such as fame—or even a certain kind of notoriety to add a bit of variety to the guest list. As Stet had so shrewdly advised, reservations would be by invitation only. The rich—the very rich—who loved their own company to the exclusion of all others, were mainly, if not totally, interested in impressing their own kind. Because they were also the very ones who could afford to pay the fat fees, it behooved the spa to provide privacy and exclusiveness and a not-so-discreet snobbery.

There would be other perks. The male attendants she was presently hiring were young, virile, and attractive, with orders to smile a lot but never, never to touch. The female attendants, whom she had yet to interview, would also be attractive, prime advertisements for the spa, but not so much as to overshadow the clients. And there would be take-aways aplenty, because no one loved freebies more than the very rich, who went through life convinced, often with good reason, that everybody was out to gouge or cheat or somehow take advantage of them.

To this end, Chanel had ordered large quantities of brand-name makeup kits, lotions, hard-milled soap, and specially designed model's robes and exercise suits that the guests would wear during their exercise routines, their massage and makeup and hair sessions, then take home as souvenirs. There would be fresh flowers in their rooms every day, the most current movies would be shown every afternoon and evening in the villa's spacious viewing room, and she'd already arranged for a different entertainment every evening— concerts, Monte Carlo nights, bridge and other card tournaments for avid gamblers, and dances with the male attendants present to provide dance partners and to add a little spice to the brew.

"*By Invitation Only* is a gimmick, but it's going to pull them in," Chanel told Glory with as much confidence as she could muster.

They were drinking orange juice—Chanel's laced with vodka— on the small fieldstone patio behind the manager's cottage that Stet had redecorated to suit her taste, and which blended in perfectly with the Spanish motif of the villa and the newly built guest cottages.

Chanel was feeling comfortable and relaxed in one of her hostess caftans, and Glory, who had been working out in the new gym, was wearing a bright blue exercise suit and sporting a matching sweatband under her short bangs. She wore no makeup, and Chanel envied her flawless skin and the natural color in her cheeks, and wondered how anyone who'd been raised on hot dogs, Twinkies, and orange soda could have such a perfect complexion.

Not to Chanel's surprise, Glory had plunged into her new job with her usual aplomb, and Chanel congratulated herself every day for her foresight in hiring her. Glory's uncanny knack for fitting in wherever she was and still retaining her own individuality was either instinctive or she'd learned it on the mean streets of the Tenderloin and even meaner halls of the Pink Palace. Either way, she was going to be one of the spa's best assets. And to think, Chanel thought complacently, she was getting Glory at bargain wages, too.

"How are the invitations going?" Glory asked, swirling the orange juice and ice in her glass.

Chanel's complacency fled. "Not as well as I'd hoped. Most of the acceptances so far have come from Stet's business contacts, all perfectly acceptable, of course, or they wouldn't have been invited. But we haven't grabbed any of the movers and shakers that really matter except Senator Brach and his wife."

"You ever think of opening the spa to just anyone who has the bread to pay the fees?"

Chanel shook her head. "There're too many spas around that do just that—and most of them are failing. We'd just be another Johnny-come-lately. No, the plan is sound. The trick is to get the ball rolling."

"But you know so many prominent people."

"Know them, yes. Influence them, no. It's going to take a miracle to pull it off. And enough of that. How is your aerobics program coming along?"

"I'm still working on it. Like I told Mr. Stetson, it can't be too tough and yet it has to tighten a few muscles. Most of all, it has to be fun, something the ladies will really enjoy, and yet hard enough to make them feel righteous. Would you believe I'm using part of the program I set up for my queen-size ladies?" She gave Chanel an oblique look. "Who knows? I may decide to tape it for video and make myself a million bucks. If Jane Fonda can do it, why can't I?"

"Jane Fonda was a star before she put together her exercise program. She has a slight advantage on you."

"For now—but watch my steam."

"Well, go for it. But let's make the spa a success first, please," Chanel said indulgently.

Glory grinned at her, and it came to Chanel that they could be mother and daughter, having a friendly chat on a warm October afternoon. She felt depressed suddenly. She had done her best to interest Fern in the spa, offering her a job on weekends and during school holidays, but Fern, who was enrolled at Berkeley, told her, "I've got plans for my weekends—and for the Christmas holidays."

And then she went on to say that Jacques was treating her to a trip to Europe. Chanel lost her temper, and they had a shouting match, which ended with Fern slamming out of the cottage, declaring it would be a cold day in hell before she returned. . . .

Glory left to catch her bus back to the city, and Chanel went to her office in the villa, closing the door behind her to shut out the sounds of construction. The former manager of the spa had indulged his instinct for overkill with oak-paneled walls, a massive oak desk, and built-in oak bookcases that reached from floor to ceiling. Since he'd taken his books, if any, with him, the room had a stripped bare look, which Chanel resolved to remedy as soon as possible.

She settled herself at the desk and picked up the phone. For weeks, she'd been postponing this call—and for a very good reason. Although the events of the past few months had eased her anger toward Laird, she'd decided to wait until she was sure she could talk to him without blowing up, an indulgence she knew she couldn't afford since she'd be asking for a favor.

She punched out Laird's office number, and to her surprise, she reached him reasonably fast, having to beard only one switchboard operator, one secretary, and Laird's male administrative assistant first.

"Chanel, how great to hear from you." The warmth in Laird's voice, since she suspected its sincerity, set Chanel's teeth on edge. "I've been intending to call you, but I've been up to my neck in work since we got back from Mexico. That latest churning scandal hit the market hard, you know. There've been all sorts of repercussions—"

"I've been busy, too. Would you believe that I'm now in partnership with William Stetson? In the spa business, no less."

"Congratulations." Laird paused to clear his throat. "I wish you all the success in the world."

"I need more than your good wishes, Laird." Chanel's eyes smarted from her effort to keep her voice light. "You owe me for pulling your fat out of the fire. Remember?"

"I remember. What I did was unforgivable. I know this isn't much of an excuse but—the truth is, I fell in love for the first time in my life, and it took me by surprise. I did try to make amends, but I know money is an inadequate way of saying I'm sorry. It was incredibly generous of you not to tell Ariel about the engagement. I'm very grateful—what more can I say?''

"Look, let's cut through the garbage, shall we? When I got the message that you were jilting me and going off with Ariel, I almost had a heart attack. If my own friends hadn't backed me up, I don't know if I could have carried it off.''

"That never should have happened. I tried to reach you earlier, but your phone was busy—and there was some kind of mix-up at the hotel about the delivery of the message. You should have received it long before the party started—''

"That isn't important now. I lied for you and saved Ariel and you from some ugly gossip. Jilting your fiancée in front of half of San Francisco is a no-no, even for Laird Fairmount. Everybody seems to know that Ariel's living with you now, but they didn't find out from me. So you owe me, and I'm calling in the marker.''

"I agree. How much do you need?''

His words sparked off her anger again. The smug bastard—did he really think he could get off that easily, with money, the one thing he was loaded with? How dare he assume that she had come to him with hat in hand, asking for charity!

But her voice was cool as she told him, "I don't need your money. I accepted the twenty thousand you put in my account as payment for the hours of hard work I put in on your party. Stet is financing the spa. What I need is your name—and influence. The spa's grand opening is the first Sunday in December. We're throwing a gala party—a wine tasting, an open-air concert in the oak grove, balloon rides over Napa Valley, dancing in the courtyard, the whole bit. I want you to convince your friends to accept my invitation and to sign up for a week or two at the spa, and I want them to do it willingly. They'll come out feeling and looking better than they have in years, but if they're coerced into signing up, they'll bad-mouth the spa, too.''

The silence on the other end of the line was unnerving. When Laird finally spoke, his first words were such a relief that Chanel let out a long, soundless sigh.

"Yes, I think I can deliver.'' His voice was cool and businesslike, but she sensed that he was relieved, too. And why not? She wasn't asking for the moon—or for his backing in a new business venture. Once he'd delivered, his conscience would be clear, and Laird Fairmount would have had it all his own way, unencumbered by guilt.

"What would you say if I became a minor partner in the spa?''

Laird went on. "Anything that William Stetson has a hand in has to be a good investment. That way, you can use my name on the letterhead as a partner. And how would you like a member of British royalty as a client? The Duke and Duchess of Chunings-way are coming to the city at the end of November. They'll be staying until after the holidays. I'm sure if I tell Lolly about this marvelous spa in Napa Valley that will do wonders for her figure, she'll sign up for a week or two—and also attend the grand opening. Would that help?"

Chanel's breath caught. Would that help? Talk about an understatement. . . . Laird's name on the letterhead, as well as the Duchess of Chuningsway as a charter guest, would be a double whammy for the spa. Entertaining the Chuningsways—or even getting an invitation to any social event they attended—had become the favorite indoor sport for local society matrons ever since it got out that they would be spending December in San Francisco. To have Lolly Chuningsway not only at the opening, but as a charter guest at the spa—what a coup! The woman was not only married to a duke, she had strong ties to the royal family. . . .

"That would be fine," she said, almost succeeding in sounding unimpressed. "But can you guarantee she'll accept?"

"Oh, I think so," Laird said. "Archie was my roommate at Coates—he has an American mother, you know. We hit it off and have been good friends ever since. I'm sure his wife will do a small favor for me when I tell her I'm a partner in the spa, especially since it won't cost her a dime. You do intend to make it complimentary, don't you?"

"Of course," Chanel said smoothly. Complimentary? Hell, she'd *pay* the duchess to come. . . . "In return for the right to discreetly use her name, of course. Nothing blatant—just a little word of mouth in the right places."

"I'm sure that would be acceptable. When the news gets out, every socialite on the West Coast, including that Hollywood bunch, will be flocking to sign up. But you do realize how fickle people are, don't you? You'll have to keep on satisfying them or they'll flock somewhere else."

"I'll worry about that when the time comes," she retorted. "Get me the Duchess of Chuningsway and I'll take care of the rest. And if you're wondering—yes, that wipes out your debt as far as I'm concerned."

"Thank you." There was a long pause, and then Laird said,

"By the way, there's something Ariel and I would like your advice on. It's about our wedding plans . . ."

Four days later, a thick cream-colored envelope came in the mail. The postmark was London, there was a discreet coat of arms on the flap, and the note inside graciously accepted the invitation, relayed through "our good friend, Laird," to be a guest of the Napa Hot Springs Spa for the first week of December. The duchess also acknowledged the grand opening. Her husband and she would be pleased to attend. It was signed "Lolly."

It only took a few days for the news to get around. The first sign that Chanel's discreet "plants" were bearing fruit was the sudden influx of letters and notes and phone calls, some accepting invitations Chanel had issued earlier and others inquiring if the spa was filled up and if not, how could they make a reservation? Interestingly, most of the former were from women who had already declined their original invitations, asking if it was too late to change their minds.

To those women, she sent courteous letters, saying that she would be delighted to reinstate their invitations. Two weeks later, the spa was fully booked for December and January, with February filling up fast as more acceptances came in. To those who hadn't received an invitation but who still made inquiries, she wrote, a little less graciously, to say how sorry she was that she couldn't accommodate them. Perhaps sometime in the future. . . .

Chanel was gloating over the booking log when her daughter came to see her. Fern was wearing her usual faded jeans, so tight they looked as if they'd been sprayed on, and a tattered top that sported the name of a Berkeley café, famous for its steam beer and its MADE ON THE PREMISES logo. Although she kissed Chanel's cheek before she flopped down on a chair and flung her legs over the arm, Chanel knew she hadn't come out of any daughterly affection. Fern wanted something. The question was, what did she want—and how much would it cost?

"Look at all these beautiful acceptances for the opening," Chanel said, picking up a stack of envelopes and letting them slide through her fingers. "And the spa is full up until March."

"All *right*! Did you hire enough people to handle a full house? Or could you use a little extra help?" Fern said.

"Are you asking for a *job*? I thought you were off to Europe over the holidays. Didn't you tell me Jacques was paying the freight?''

Fern's mouth turned down at the corners. "There was one small catch. He wanted to come along—as my roommate. I told him to shove it.''

"Sorry," Chanel murmured.

"Are you? Why don't you say what you're thinking, that you told me so?''

"I really am sorry—and I have no intention of saying I told you so. Let's talk about that job. It could involve hard physical work, you know. Are you sure you want to take it on?''

"I'm not lazy, whatever you think. I want to start pulling my own weight. It's time I stopped being a burden to you financially.''

Chanel's silence seemed to embarrass Fern, because she looked uncomfortable. "Okay, that isn't the whole story. The truth is Berkeley's a total bore. I want to knock off for the rest of the year. Working in a spa sounds like something I'd like to do.''

"Scrubbing floors and making beds? You're unskilled labor—even giving mud baths takes training.''

"I want to work in the kitchen. I love to cook—but then, you wouldn't know that, would you?''

Chanel eyed her closely. What was Fern up to now?

"I can't remember you ever mentioning it, but I'll take your word for it," she said cautiously. "You did cook up some pretty good meals for us those weekends you came home this spring. We could use an apprentice sous-chef. You'll start at the bottom, you know, and I think I should warn you that Jean-Pierre is a real tartar, a kitchen bully.''

"He's also sexy," Fern said, rolling her eyes.

"Sexy? Are we talking about the same man? Jean-Pierre looks like an ex-wrestler gone to seed, and he's a grandfather four times over, for God's sake.''

Fern cocked her index finger at Chanel. "Gotcha! I already knew that. But he's one of the best chefs around. I can learn a lot from him. Ever since I took that home ec course at the Academy, I've been interested in the culinary arts.''

"And all the time I thought you took it because it was an easy credit," Chanel murmured.

Fern groaned. "Easy! It was pure slavery. But I really dug it, too. Seems I have great taste buds and a knack for being innovative—to quote my home ec teacher. So why not give it a whirl, say I.

If I'm still of the same mind six months from now, maybe I can
talk you into staking me to a year of Cordon Bleu training in Paris.''

"You'd better learn to speak French if you plan to go to school
in Paris. They take a dim view of people who mangle their language," Chanel said.

Fern grinned at her. "*Je parle un meilleur français que
quelques unes de mes amies qui parlent anglais.*"

Which translated, Chanel thought in some surprise, meant that
Fern spoke French better than some of her friends spoke English.
"You're full of surprises," she said.

"And so are you, Mommie dearest. So are you."

Fern stayed for lunch, and before she left, she bent and gave
her mother another light kiss on the cheek, surprising Chanel so
much that she didn't go back to work immediately. Instead, she
sat staring out the window at the rolling vineyards surrounding
the château, at the vines that showed the yellow and red and dark
maroon foliage of October.

She finally came to a conclusion of sorts—and subject to change.
Fern's hostility toward her had taken a turn for the better, something
she wouldn't have bet on a year ago. It had started at that ill-fated
party at the St. Francis—and was still evolving. It even seemed
possible that in time they could become friends, even closer.

The thing was—it was easier to deal with Fern as a problem
than as a daughter. Was she ready for motherhood and all the
emotional responsibility that entailed? True, she sometimes felt
downright maternal toward Glory—why not toward Fern, who
really was her daughter? It wasn't something that could be forced,
but maybe it could happen—in time. And wouldn't that be a kick?

She returned to her correspondence. The next letter was from
Nancy Anderson. Oozing graciousness, the letter said that she'd
just discovered that she could accept her invitation to attend the
grand opening of the Napa Hot Springs Spa and also to enroll for
a week's stay, after all. Would it be possible to get a booking for
the first week in December?

Chanel was smiling as she stabbed out Nancy's phone number
with the end of her pen.

"Yes? Who is this, please?" Nancy's careful drawl said a moment later.

"This is Chanel Devereau. How are you, Nancy?"

"Just fine—but terribly busy. With the season just a month or so
away, it's unbelievable how crowded my calendar is becoming.''

"I'm so glad to hear you say that because it makes things easier for me," Chanel said sweetly.

"I beg your pardon?"

"I'm afraid I have bad news. The Napa Hot Springs Spa is all booked up for December—in fact, through February. The next opening is . . . let's see . . . oh, yes, in March. I'll be glad to sign you up for then, but I should warn you—we're getting quite a rash of bookings. We expect to be filled up through summer very shortly."

For a long moment, there was only the sound of breathing on the other end of the line. "Why, yes, I believe I can make it in March. I see that the first week is open on my calendar."

Chanel felt like purring. Now for the kill. . . .

"Oh, I *am* sorry! I should have told you that we'll be closed that week. Laird and Ariel's wedding is scheduled for the first Sunday in March. Since neither have any living relatives, they've asked to have the wedding here at the villa, and of course I agreed since they are my dearest and closest friends. I also agreed to handle the wedding details for them. The Chuningsways—Laird and Archie were roommates at Coates, did you know?—are coming over from England for the wedding. They'll be my house-guests that week. You *have* met the Chuningsways, haven't you? Such a charming couple—you'd never guess that Lolly is a royal, would you? I'm really sorry but—what can you do? Friends come before business, don't they? However, I'll be glad to book you for the *second* week in March."

The strain in Nancy's voice was apparent as she said, "I'll have to cancel a couple of things but—yes, do put me down for March."

"One or two weeks?" Chanel said.

"One—no, make it two. I'll need a rest before we go east to our place in Far Hills for the summer."

"Two weeks it is—and I'll let you know well in advance if there are any changes."

"Thank you, Chanel," Nancy said.

Chanel hung up. As she added Nancy's name to her log, it came to her that she'd been waiting for this moment ever since she was seventeen. The strange thing was that it didn't seem to matter all that much anymore.

CHAPTER FORTY-TWO

JANICE'S COLD LINGERED ON THROUGH OCTOBER—IF IT REALLY was a cold. Sometimes, when she dragged herself out of bed in the morning, coughing and sneezing, she wondered if something psychological wasn't going on inside her. If so, she had no idea what the origin could be. Things were going well in her personal life. She and Jake hadn't had a quarrel in a month, and she was finally putting the finishing touches on her dissertation.

The latter should have given her great satisfaction but, in truth, she was dragging her heels, finding frequent excuses not to work on the manuscript. It wasn't that she didn't have all the research and survey material she needed. It was just that something—her objectivity, perhaps—had changed.

When she wrote succinct, telling sentences about Subject A, who should have been a breeze to analyze and dissect and to fit into her thesis—*Subject A is a twenty-year-old female, raised in the gray world of public projects; mother an alcoholic, father unknown; pregnant, married, and a high school dropout by sixteen; divorced at eighteen; worked as a cocktail waitress, then an aerobics instructor*—the image of a prickly, hot-tempered redhead who was also irreverent, gutsy, pragmatic, and totally upfront, kept getting in the way of her objectivity.

And when she wrote about Subject B, who could be described as your all-around predatory female, the spider lady herself, she kept seeing Chanel making them all laugh and giving out commonsense advice like an urban earth mother to Glory and even, on occasion, to Stephanie.

But never to me, Janice thought, and suddenly felt depressed again. Which was downright unreasonable. She hadn't gone into this project to make friends. She was doing it to get a doctoral degree.

She sneezed violently, and groped in the pocket of her smock for a tissue. In the guest room down the hall, she could hear Jake

424

moving around. He had been very subdued lately. "In a mood," her stepmother would have called it.

Janice suspected part of it was her cold. Jake was always so resentful of her rare illnesses—which was strange because he went into shock if he even stubbed his toe. But something else was bothering him, too, something he wasn't talking about. It had started around the time he'd stopped teaching that course on TV. Did he resent her because she was the cause of his decision to quit? Or was something wrong at work? If so, he was keeping it to himself.

Maybe it was time for a good heart-to-heart talk with him. But not until her cold had cleared up. Jake had a pathological fear of infection; in fact, they hadn't been intimate since he'd moved into the guest room, saying she'd sleep better alone. Maybe that was his problem. Maybe he was feeling horny and she wasn't available.

She went back to work. Her notes, so neat and orderly, should have absorbed her attention totally, but she found it difficult to concentrate. What on earth was wrong with her lately?

Was it possible that she was having a case of the guilts?

Janice's fingers tightened around her pencil. Of course. *Guilt* was the reason for her ennui. Which was stupid, stupid, stupid. But there it was, and it did no good to tell herself that no one in the support group would get hurt, that only Dr. Yolanski and the doctoral program committee would ever read the dissertation. Oh, maybe an occasional student, researching his or her own thesis or dissertation on a related subject, would sign it out at the Stanford library and give it a cursory reading, but even then, who could possibly connect Subject C with Ariel—or Subject D with Stephanie?

So it was ludicrous to worry about it, to feel as if she were betraying her friends. The truth was they weren't her friends—not really. The others had formed warm personal relationships, but she always seemed to be odd woman out. Which had been her own doing. It had been her own choice to keep a certain distance between herself and the others so she could remain objective.

The phone at Janice's elbow buzzed. She picked it up immediately, a habit she'd formed this past year because it would be so difficult to explain to the support group why a man answered her phone.

Sure enough, it was Stephanie's husky voice that came over the line. "Janice?"

"Hi, Stephanie," she said.

"I was wondering—do you have a minute? There's something I'd like to ask your advice about."

"I'm not busy. Fire away," Janice said, feeling pleased.

But Stephanie seemed reluctant to begin, and when she finally made an abortive attempt, she tripped over her own tongue and stopped.

"Why don't you start at the beginning?" Janice suggested.

"It's this man I met on my rafting trip . . ."

For the next few minutes, Janice listened to Stephanie's impassioned outpouring of words. Despite herself, she couldn't help smiling when Stephanie described her lover as a stud, a word she probably wouldn't have used a year ago.

Glory's rubbing off on all of us, she thought. Or maybe it would be more accurate to say that they were rubbing off on one another. Odd, when they weren't all that close. Was that the key to the influence they had on one another? Maybe she should make that point in her dissertation, that a support group could be effective even if the members never really became close friends. It might even be an advantage. . . .

After all, who wanted to deal on a social and personal level with a person who knew all your darkest secrets?

Janice put the idea aside to think about later. She concentrated on listening to Stephanie, noting the desperation that underlaid her monologue. Stephanie was really upset or she wouldn't be telling such intimate details of her new romance—did she really want advice or just a sounding board?

"I'm so mixed up I don't know what to do," Stephanie was saying now. "I still—the physical attraction between Clay and me is still so strong, but I have to make a decision and stick to it. One day I'm sure I can't live without him and the hell with his wife and girls. The next, I know I can't live with him, either, not and end up with another failed relationship. There just doesn't seem to be any solution."

"Why does his wife bother you so? Both of them told you their marriage was on the skids before you came along. What's that old saying—that you can't break up a happy marriage?"

"I know. I tell myself that. But the truth is—well, I don't know what the truth is. You know what's so strange? I keep seeing myself in Jocelyn. A year ago, I was just like her—a homebody totally wrapped up in my husband and family. The thing that haunts me is that I'm not all that different now. If Clay and I started living together, he'd soon realize that I'm not really this fun girl he visits every couple of weeks and takes to bed. And I'd end up like Jocelyn, waiting for him to find someone else more exciting."

"He must have seen something very special in you, Stephanie." The words didn't sound quite right, and Janice added diplomatically, "You're a very special person."

"He saw me under unusual circumstances. The woman on that raft trip wasn't the real me at all. And then there's this—this chemistry between us. I never realized before that I'm a very sexual woman. David didn't bring out that part of me, but then, I could also be myself with him because he liked me the way I am. If I marry Clay, I don't think I can keep putting on an act—"

"Maybe it isn't an act. Maybe the real you was there all along, camouflaged as a domestic being."

"I love being a housewife. I'm not cut out for a career. I realize this more every day. Oh, I do my job and I get by, but I don't really have the—the drive for that kind of success. I loved keeping house and cooking and being there when David and the boys came home nights. That's the real me. When I was a kid, I dreamed about having my own home someday. I planned how I'd decorate it and how I'd take courses in gourmet cooking and sewing and upholstering. I know that sounds dull to most women these days, but that's how I am. But all that domesticity would turn Clay off. He's a mobile person—and he wants a woman who can keep up with him."

"In other words, you're like Robert Frost's lightning bug. You just can't sustain the light," Janice said, nodding. Who would have guessed that Stephanie could be so articulate—and see her own predicament so clearly?

"Exactly. Oh, it would work for a while. We'd have an exciting life at first, but eventually he'd find me out and then he'd be sorry he'd exchanged one housewife for another just as dull."

"Not dull," Janice said sharply. "And you're not in a minority. During my survey, half the divorcées I interviewed didn't want a career. They wanted—"

She broke off, biting her lip. Stephanie was silent a moment, and then she asked, "Survey? What kind of survey?"

There was no suspicion in her voice. Janice could have evaded the question. She could have said she'd become involved in a survey for the sociology department at Stanford. She could have made any number of explanations or evasions, but instead she heard her own voice blurting, "I'm doing a survey on divorced women for my doctoral dissertation."

"Really? I didn't know you were going after a Ph.D. Did the support group give you the idea?"

"No. I had the idea first. I got it the day we first met in Arnold Waterford's office—which is why I was so eager for all of us to have lunch together. And I might as well tell you—I wasn't there to get a divorce. I had a luncheon date with Arnold. He's my godfather. I've been using the four of you to get material for my dissertation, along with conducting a more generalized survey of other divorced women."

"You've lost me. Are you saying—"

"I'm still married to Jake. We aren't getting a divorce. I organized the support group for my own selfish purposes, and it has nothing to do with my marriage."

It was a great relief to say the words out loud. She waited for Stephanie's shock, her condemnation. Instead, Stephanie's troubled voice said, "I hope you intend to use false names. I wouldn't want my affair with Clay to become general knowledge."

Janice laughed. She couldn't help it. "You're unbelievable, Stephanie," she said. "Doesn't it bother you that what I did is unethical as hell? No matter how carefully I'm prepared to guard your identities, it's still unethical."

"Well, I don't see it that way. If it can help other women cope with divorce—besides, people are involved in surveys all the time and they spill the most intimate details of their lives, too."

"But they do it voluntarily. That's the difference."

"Well, I think you're worried about nothing. Why don't you ask the other women what they think next week at the November meeting? You are coming, aren't you? Chanel is making a big thing out of something she wants to tell us. As usual, she's being very mysterious."

"I'll be there. But I'm not sure I'm ready to tell them about the dissertation."

"I'll keep your secret. It *is* your business, after all."

At this astonishing statement, Janice was speechless. "I have a great idea," Stephanie went on. "Why don't you come for lunch sometime soon? I'd like you to meet my boys."

After Janice had hung up, she went downstairs to fix herself a hot toddy while she mulled over her conversation with Stephanie. That Stephanie, the most straitlaced of the support group, was having a torrid affair, she could accept. That Stephanie hadn't turned a hair when she'd learned that one of the support group had misled the others from the start—that was harder to believe.

Finally deciding that she'd never understand how Stephanie's mind worked, she mixed a hot toddy and took it back upstairs. As she sipped the tangy brew, her thoughts returned to Stephanie.

Where—*where* had she ever gotten the idea that Stephanie led a staid and dull life? From Stephanie's burst of confidences, her sex life could rival an X-rated movie. Sex under the stars with a rafter—it was enough to blow a sociologist's mind.

A week later, as Janice was having lunch with the support group, she was still undecided whether or not to tell them about the dissertation. So far, there'd been little chance, even if she'd wanted to. Chanel was dominating the conversation with the news that she was now in the spa business and that Glory was creating an exercise program for her. To Janice's eyes, Chanel seemed different today—more approachable, less astringent. To say she was acting like a career woman seemed simplistic. Maybe it was just that Chanel was committed to the new project to the exclusion of everything else.

"Stet has given me a free hand, but of course he's a businessman through and through," Chanel said. "If the spa doesn't show a profit within a year, I'll be out on my derriere. I did buy in, but it's just a tiny percentage, and he holds all the real power. And Stet is a bottom-line man. He expects the business to be a success. Which is why we're charging rates that would land a money-lender in jail for usury. Luckily, the customers have been signing up in droves."

"What she isn't telling you is she's using snob value, this duke guy's wife, to pull them in," Glory said.

"Don't knock it, guttersnipe," Chanel said. "It's going to put money in your pocket."

"But not enough. Which is something I want to talk to you about soon."

Chanel gave her a wary look. "You just can't win," she complained. "You do a friend a favor—"

"A favor? You're getting a bargain. I'm pretty damned good at my job—and don't you forget it."

"Pretty pushy for someone who had trouble eating with a fork when we first met," Chanel retorted.

"So my mom never cooked. The only meat we ever ate was hamburger and hot dogs and bologna—and then it was inside a bun. And look who's talking! The first time this bunch met, your nose was so high in the air you woulda drowned if it had started raining."

Everybody laughed, including Chanel. "Well, times have

changed. I'm in trade now. If I could just find myself a good administrative assistant, my worries would be over.''

Ariel, who was looking radiant—a word they all used to describe her lately—asked a question about the spa's grand opening, and the conversation shifted to other things. Toward the end of the luncheon, after they'd moved to the wicker chairs to drink their coffee, Janice finally got her chance to speak. She had planned what she would say, how she would lead up to her confession gradually, but when there was a lull in the conversation and her chance came, she simply stated the words baldly.

''Something's been bothering my conscience, and I think it's time I made a confession. . . . ''

When she was finished, no one spoke. No one looked angry or shocked or surprised, either. Chanel finally said, ''I guessed it was something like that.''

Strangely, Janice felt a prick of anger. ''You guessed that I was writing a dissertation?''

''How could I know that? But I did sense that you had some motive other than needing support for organizing the group. For one thing, you never really talked about your private life.''

''Who did until lately?'' Glory said, shrugging. ''We're just beginning to—y'know, trust one another. I thought you were reserved is all, Janice. And all the time, you were writing about us.'' She sounded more intrigued than annoyed. ''And since it's confession time—I have to admit I don't really go for the networking thing. Who needs it, I figure. The reason I joined and then kept coming back was because I wanted to brush elbows with all you upper-class types. I thought maybe some of it might rub off on me . . .'' She paused, looking rueful. ''I don't think it did. I'm still the same person.''

''Thank God for that,'' Stephanie said. Glory's stare seemed to embarrass her, because she flushed. ''What I mean is—you're great, just the way you are.''

''Thank you—I think.''

Chanel set her cup down on the wicker coffee table. ''I might as well confess that the idea of a support group never appealed to me, either. Like Glory said, who needs it? I hung in there for a reason I'm not about to tell you—but it had nothing to do with needing support.''

''You were cultivating Ariel,'' Glory said.

All expression left Chanel's face. ''Well, she did seem to need a friend at the time,'' she said finally.

Ariel gave her a shy smile. "You've been a wonderful friend. If it hadn't been for you, I probably wouldn't be with Laird now. And I've never forgotten how all of you helped me when I left Alex."

Everybody was silent. Janice knew they were all thinking that any help Chanel had given Ariel to further her romance with Laird Fairmount hadn't been intentional.

Stephanie was the first to rush into speech. "I guess I'm the only one who joined because I did need support. I don't make friends easily, so I thought sharing my experiences and problems with other women in the same boat would help. And it did."

She smiled at Janice, a wan smile that made Janice wonder what she had decided to do about the new man in her life. Maybe she'd find out next week when she had lunch with Stephanie and her sons.

"About my dissertation," Janice said. "I know this is no excuse, but you *were* all strangers to me a year ago. If you think I should forget your part in the survey, just say so. I can base my conclusions on the secondary survey I took."

"Why do that? But give me a phony name, okay?" Glory said. "And be sure to change Buddy's name, too, will you?"

The rest nodded agreement or, in Chanel's case, said, "I'd like to have a talk with you later, but in general—sure, why not?"

Janice didn't know what to say. A simple thank-you seemed inadequate. She compromised finally with a heartfelt "You're a great bunch—you know?"

"Yeah. Great bunch. We know." Glory stretched like a lithe young cat. "I hope we don't bust up, because I get a real kick out of you all—y'know what I mean?"

Janice, who knew exactly what she meant, nodded. "Let's talk about it at the next meeting. Can everybody make it in December?"

"Glory and I will be up to our necks in work that Saturday," Chanel said. "The opening's scheduled for the next day, the first Sunday in December. Look, I've got a great idea—why don't we cancel the December meeting and you all come to the opening as my guests?"

Not to Janice's surprise, everybody, including herself, accepted the invitation on the spot.

When Ariel came in from the luncheon, Laird was in his home office, working over a stack of tax reports. As soon as he looked up and saw her standing in the door, he laid his work aside and went to put his arms around her.

"Hmmm . . ." he murmured. "You smell like roses. I thought maybe you might come back from that luncheon smelling like lilies." At her questioning look, he laughed. "Never mind. A private joke. How did it go?"

"It was fun. Everybody seemed to be in a good humor today— we talked mostly about pleasant things."

"And Chanel? What's she been up to lately?"

"She finally told the others about the spa, but she didn't say anything about making the arrangements for our wedding. She did say you were a partner." There was a question in her voice.

"A very minuscule one."

"I see—so your name can be on the letterhead?"

Laird reflected that sometimes Ariel surprised him—that other worldly air of hers could be deceiving. "Something like that. I owe her—as she reminded me sweetly—for bringing the two of us together."

"And for not making a fuss when you jilted her?"

It took Laird a moment to recover from his shock. "So she told you," he said slowly.

"She didn't say a word—and neither did the other women. I figured it out for myself."

"Look, Ariel, I didn't tell you because I was afraid you'd think you ruined a good relationship between Chanel and me. And you didn't. We just drifted into that engagement. It seemed the right time in my life to get married and start a family, and Chanel was available. Both of us knew it wasn't love, only convenience. I'm sure now that we never would have gone through with the wedding, even if you and I hadn't fallen in love."

"I know you never loved her because you loved *me*." There was a fierceness in her voice that surprised him. "I know that you—that most people think I'm pretty naive, and of course, I am. But I'm not stupid—"

"I don't think you are stupid," he protested.

Her eyes softened. "I know. You love me. But my mind doesn't work quickly, and sometimes it takes me a while to figure something out. However, I do notice things. When Chanel invited all of us to your party, I guessed that you two were going to announce your engagement. I couldn't let it happen. I just couldn't. That's why—"

"That's why you came to my house the night you ran away from your husband instead of going to one of the women in your support group for help. You conniving little devil—you set me up." He began to laugh. "That nightmare in the middle of the night and you in my pajama top—you seduced me, and I didn't guess a thing."

"I had to. I couldn't let you marry Chanel. She's all wrong for you."

He pulled her down on his lap and nuzzled her throat. "And you're right for me. I'd be miserable, married to anyone but you. I guess I've loved you for a long time, only I wouldn't admit it because there was something a little kinky about wanting to make love to someone you thought of as your kid sister. Thank God you had the sense to do something about it."

For some reason Ariel flushed. "Actually it wasn't an original idea," she confessed. "When we had breakfast at Cliff House that morning, Chanel told us about something her daughter did when she had a crush on an older man. She went to his house at night with her clothes ripped half off and told him someone tried to rape her. Chanel called it the damsel-in-distress ploy. It didn't work for Fern because the man saw right through her, but I thought it might work for me because I knew you loved me, even if you didn't. And you're right about the nightmare, too. You were being such a gentleman that I realized I had to do something drastic to get you into bed with me."

Laird whistled softly through his teeth. "I see I'm going to have to watch you. You're two steps ahead of me all the time, aren't you?"

He tried to kiss her, but she had something else to say. "I guess I may as well tell you the whole story and get it off my chest. After Chanel drove me home from Sea Cliff that day, I didn't go inside. I hid in the potting shed and waited until it got dark, then I took off my clothes and put on the gardener's old raincoat. By the time I got here, the rain was coming down really hard and I didn't have to pretend to be cold."

"I thought you looked like a half-drowned kitten—or an undine."

"Are you mad at me?"

"Mad at you? Never!" This time he succeeded in getting his arms around her. "Do you have any idea what I've been going through, afraid you'd find out about Chanel and me? I was sure she'd drop it on you at the luncheon after we got back from Mexico."

"She intended to. But I turned her off."

"How did you manage that?"

"I thanked her with tears in my eyes for getting us together.

Then I reminded her that she'd once said we belonged together, and I thanked her for that, too.''

"And what did she say to that?"

"She congratulated me.''

He flung his head back, laughing, and she watched him for a while, then kissed him, which led to other, even more exciting things. Later, over one of Mary's excellent dinners, he told her about a new debenture bond fund his company was launching. She asked him questions, made him explain in detail the complications of setting up such a fund, and he knew she was really interested, that anything he was involved in would always interest her.

God hope I never fail her, he thought. And thank you, thank you, Chanel.

CHAPTER FORTY-THREE

As GLORY PACKED HER OUT-OF-SEASON CLOTHES INTO CARD-board cartons, preparing for her move to Napa Valley, nostalgia dogged her every movement. She may have changed since she'd moved here, but the apartment still looked much the same—bare, colorless, and a little dreary. Even so, it had been her home for almost a year, a place where she still felt safe despite her dark memories of Buddy's violent attack.

She was almost sorry that Chanel had convinced her to move into one of the guest rooms at the spa. Although she suspected Chanel's generosity was motivated by the desire to have her read-ily available any hour of the day or night, it was the sensible thing to do. Not only would she save on rent, a major consideration, but she wouldn't have to make those long bus trips back and forth to the city every day.

It was also a good way to avoid Steve. He had called so many times, she'd finally taken the phone off the hook. He'd even come to her door once, but luckily, she'd been late getting home that night and she wouldn't have known he'd been there if he hadn't left flowers and a note.

She was ashamed now that she'd quit her job over the phone without giving notice. She should have marched right into Steve's office and told him she was leaving. There was nothing he could've done except argue with her—and when had she ever been swayed by other people's arguments?

But she did feel guilty—which didn't make sense. After all, Steve was the one at fault, not the other way around. Okay, she could understand why he'd kept quiet around the health club about being the big boss's son. He'd wanted to make it on his own. But after they'd started seeing each other, he should've told her the truth. Who knows? She might have gone on seeing him. Instead he had lied, let her think he was an ordinary Joe, scratching around for a living like everybody else.

And that she couldn't forgive. It hurt like hell that she'd been taken in by the only man she'd allowed herself to trust since she'd broken up with Buddy. God knew, she'd been honest with Steve. He knew what her background was, where she came from, her whole history, even parts she wasn't exactly proud of.

Well, she wasn't going to make the same mistake again. Twice a fool was enough yet. It shouldn't be too hard to get over Steve. After all, she could hardly remember what Buddy looked like and yet she'd been crazy about him once. It would be the same with Steve. This time next year she wouldn't remember if his eyes were blue or brown.

The phone rang as she was packing her bed linens into a soap carton she'd got from Safeway. She picked it up without thinking, then made a face, realizing her mistake. She was tempted to compress the button and then leave the phone off the hook, but that seemed so cowardly.

"Hello?" she said into the mouthpiece.

There was a brief silence as if the caller were surprised to hear her voice. "This is Steve. I have to talk to you."

"I'm real busy, Steve. I don't have time to—"

"I'm calling from the Payless at the corner. This won't take long."

There was a click in Glory's ear. She slammed down the phone, steaming mad at Steve for forcing a confrontation, at herself for answering the phone. A few minutes later when the doorbell rang, she flung the door open before he could push the button again.

"I told you I was busy, Steve," she said hotly.

"I have something to say to you. It won't take long, and then

I'll get out of your life for good." He looked past her at the cartons on the floor. 'You're moving? You hate me that much?"

"I don't hate you. But you're bad news to me, Steve. I don't want anything more to do with you."

"Because of my dad? What does he have to do with us?"

"Everything. The last thing I need is a boyfriend who thinks he's out slumming when he's with me."

"You're wrong. You're the best thing that ever happened to me. Why can't you see that?"

"I see that you lied to me. Sure, I'm okay to sleep with. We really got it on in bed. But that's all it was. We both know that after you've had your fling with this tootsie from the projects, you'll take up with some blue-blood type you can take home to meet your mother and father—or do you call them mater and pater?"

"I call them Mom and Dad." Steve's tone was short. "And I haven't taken you home to meet them because they live in New York. I haven't seen them myself for four years. My father and I didn't exactly part company amicably. In fact, he tossed me out on my ear. He thinks I'm a bum—his word—because I bummed around Europe for a year after college. He's a hardheaded businessman, and he never took a vacation in his life. He sent me to Yale Business College so I could step into his shoes someday and run his holding company. That was before I cut out and went to Europe. When I came home, he kicked me out, said he no longer had a son."

"So how come he gave you a job?"

"He didn't. I came to San Francisco on my own. I was looking for work when I heard there was an opening for a martial arts instructor at the Golden Gate Club. I got the job. It was my way of thumbing my nose at my old man, I guess. He has no idea that I'm working at one of his health clubs. The chain has four hundred branches, most of them under franchise. Besides, he has other business interests that take up his time."

She gave him a skeptical look. "The whole thing sounds pretty weird to me. And you'd better leave now. I have to finish packing."

"Where are you going?"

"Why should I tell you that?"

A muscle in his jawline tensed, a sure sign that he was angry. "Before I go, answer one question for me. It's obvious you never gave a damn about me or you wouldn't be looking for excuses to drop me. So why did you go to bed with me?"

Glory fought the sudden thickness in her throat. *Because I thought I was in love with you, you bastard!* "Why not?" she said. "You aren't too bad in bed—for a rich jock."

His mouth tightened. "I see. Well, you don't have to move away because of me—"

"I'm not. I have a job, a damned good one, out of town. That's why I'm moving."

"Doing what—or am I being nosy?"

She shrugged, suddenly tired of baiting him. "I'm going to work for a new health spa."

"The one in Napa Valley that's been getting all the publicity? Doing what?"

"Setting up their exercise program. I'll be supervising the other instructors when the spa opens."

"How did you happen to get the job?"

"I know the new owner."

"William Stetson? He's a friend of yours? How good a friend?"

Glory bristled immediately. "I only met Mr. Stetson once. It was his partner who hired me—Chanel Devereau."

"The woman who had the party at the St. Francis? Pretty strange friend for someone who hates rich people."

"She isn't rich. And I don't hate rich people. What I hate is rich dudes who think their money gives them the right to play games with other people's lives. And I want you to leave, like right now. I'm too busy to talk anymore."

After Steve left, his face set in grim lines that made him look years older than the twenty-six she knew him to be, Glory didn't go back to work immediately. There'd been something so final about the way he'd said "Good-bye, Glory—and good luck." She felt depressed, a little weepy, as if she'd just been to a funeral.

Maybe she should reconsider—no, she was right! She'd get over this—whatever it was. She'd made a mistake, dropping her guard with Steve and letting him get close to her. The sooner she put the whole thing behind her and got involved with her new job, the better.

Hell, this time next year, she wouldn't remember what color Steve Golden's eyes were.

Steve waited a week before he made his move. It wasn't because he was unsure of his feelings for Glory. No matter how he cut it, he was going to be miserable until they were back together again. Whether their relationship continued as it had been, or whether he managed to persuade her to move in with him—or to

get married, although that would take some heavy thinking first—
he was going to fight for her.

But he waited, more or less patiently, a full week, giving her
time to cool off, to reconsider, maybe even to have a change of
heart, before he went to see Chanel Devereau.

When he'd met Chanel at the St. Francis, he'd sized her up as
the kind of woman he'd met so many times in his life—superficial,
brittle, a snob. He'd wondered then why she bothered with Glory,
who was so totally different. But what kind of person she was didn't
concern him now. The amusement in her voice when he'd called to
ask for an appointment—and what it might denote—was the important thing. Because he needed her help—if his plan was to work.

Chanel had given him directions to the spa, and she was waiting
for him when he arrived, a few minutes late because he'd taken a
wrong turn somewhere. At first, they talked politely about the
renovations that were still going on, and then about the party at
the St. Francis. With deliberate effort, he set about disarming
Chanel, and knew he'd succeeded, at least a little, when she offered him a glass of Gray Riesling.

"From a Napa Valley winery, of course," she said, smiling.

It was over the wine that Steve told her he'd come to apply for
a job.

If he'd managed to surprise her, it didn't show on her smoothly
planed face. "I thought you had a good job," she said. "I understood from Glory that you're a branch manager of the Golden
Gate Health Club now. Surely your opportunities for advancement are much better in a large chain like that?"

"I want to make a change."

"You're tired of big-city life?" Her tone was faintly mocking.
"Or does Glory Browne have something to do with this?"

Steve didn't make the mistake of lying. "She does. She has the
wrong idea about me. I want the chance to change her mind."

"And if you don't? Then you pack it in here and go back to
work for your father?"

"I'm not a quitter. I'll stay on here, whether or not she changes
her mind about me. As I said, I'm ready for a change."

"Even if it means taking a few steps backward? For instance,
how would you like taking orders from Glory?"

"I'm perfectly willing to start in any capacity, including aerobics instructor. I didn't come here to try to get Glory's job."

"I'm glad to hear that." Chanel laced her fingers together on the polished top of her desk, watching him. She nodded finally, as if making up her mind about something.

"I have a better offer for you, something that would be advantageous to us both," she said. "How would you like to be my administrative assistant? I need someone reliable to do the paperwork, run the office, handle personnel problems, and take some of the day-to-day hassle off my hands. Just being the social director of this place is going to be a full-time job."

Steve concealed his elation. "It sounds great to me."

"Very well, you have the job. But you'd better work out your differences with Glory—and quickly. The business comes first. There'll be no love spats in front of the guests."

"Don't worry. I intend to bring Glory around—but I won't push."

"That's up to you. As long as there's no trouble. And don't expect me to intervene on your behalf. I'm not in the matchmaking business."

"Glory would resent any interference, even from you. She's too stiff-necked and proud for her own good."

"So why do you bother with her?"

"I'm crazy about her."

"Well, that's a good reason. But a word of advice: Glory's been pushed around most of her life. She just might enjoy doing a little pushing back these days."

CHAPTER FORTY-FOUR

THE SPA'S NEWLY REMODELED GYMNASIUM, A LARGE, WELL-designed building that was separated from the main house by an arbor-covered walkway, featured bleached oak floors and wall panels; several exercise rooms, each with a mirrored wall, a full-length barre, and a wide assortment of exercise equipment; two Finnish steam rooms, complete with Nile green tile and white birch benches; individual dressing and massage rooms; plus a large, tiled indoor swimming pool; everything very state-of-the-art quality and blatantly expensive.

The main exercise room, which would be Glory's domain, was located on the east side of the building. It caught the morning sun through amber-tinted ceiling-to-floor windows that looked out over the villa's spacious grounds, where gardeners were hard at work, preparing for the grand opening, which was just a few days away.

Glory loved the gymnasium. The windows of her own small office, in the northwestern corner of the building, overlooked beautiful Napa Valley. She already had a proprietary feeling for it, as much as she permitted herself for anything that could be transitory. She had no illusions. At present, she was useful to Chanel—and she came cheap, something she intended to change in the not-so-distant future. But if she couldn't do the work, such as satisfying the guests and keeping the instructors in line, and do it more than adequately, her friendship with Chanel wouldn't make a bit of difference. She would be out on her ass. Not that she was worried. She knew her strengths, and meeting new challenges was one of them.

As she did her warm-ups, as she stretched and bent and rocked her hips, she watched her own mobile image in the mirrored wall. Every one of those sleek, taut muscles had been earned by hours upon hours of exhausting exercise, but the guests who took her classes wouldn't realize that, nor did she want them to. What they *would* believe was what they wanted to believe—that a few hours of exercise a week would give them the same trim body. Actually, there was little she could do for them in one or two or even three weeks. It took long sustained effort to attain a perfectly coordinated body. Whether or not they went on with their exercise program after they left the spa—well, that was up to them.

The thing she *could* do was to make the aerobic classes fun, to give the guests such a high that they would go home feeling on top of the world—which was what her new program was aimed toward. Hopefully, they would continue on their own. To this end, she had drawn up a small booklet that spelled out the program in detail for the guests to take home. The writing style was flip, funny, and casual, and the booklet, which was now at the printers, had been illustrated by her own irreverent drawings. If the program it outlined was followed, it would work.

Glory sincerely hoped it would be followed.

The sun was midway up the sky as she neared the end of her routine, a series of jumping jacks. Sweat soaked her blue leotards and plastered the thin material of her tights to her skin. She was making her last move, a slow scissor split, when the door to the exercise room opened. Annoyed because she'd put a DO NOT DISTURB sign on the door, she looked up—into Steve's eyes.

"What the hell are *you* doing here?" she demanded, jumping to her feet. He raised his eyebrows as if wondering why she was angry, which irritated her further. "I asked you a question. Why are you here? If you think—"

"I work here," he said.

"What are you talking about?"

"I'm Chanel's new administrative assistant. Any objections?"

"You'd better believe I object. Wait until I get done telling her what a prick you are!"

"Do you also plan to tell her that I'm not qualified for the job? That I didn't run—and very successfully, too—a branch of the Golden Gate Health Clubs? As for the administrative side of the job—have you forgotten that I have a business degree from Yale?"

"I'm going to tell Chanel I refuse to work with you because you're a bastard."

"You do that. Paint yourself into a corner. And what are you going to do if she tells you to go fly a kite?"

That stopped her. He was right. Chanel wouldn't appreciate having her judgment questioned. The arrogant bastard—he'd done this on purpose to embarrass her—no, to make her quit. That's what he wanted. Well, the hell with him. If she didn't get out of here quick, she was going to sock him—which was probably what he wanted, because it would put her in the wrong. She turned and started to stalk away, only to have him stop her.

"No, you aren't going to walk away this time, Glory. We're going to have it out, and by God, you're going to listen to me. This paranoia of yours has got to stop. It's crazy—and you know it. Why don't you admit that you're using my background as an excuse to end our relationship because you're scared to death?"

Glory stared at the face so close to hers. Wouldn't you know he'd look like he just stepped out of a shower stall while she was all sweaty and hot? As for being scared—that was stupid. Was this some kind of joke? Steve was always saying things she didn't understand, smarting off, she called it, but he did look—well, serious. Did he really think she was scared of him?

"That's nuts. I'm not scared of anyone. Don't you know that by now?"

"You're afraid that if you get in too deep, I'll walk away.

Doesn't it mean anything to you that I just gave up a high-paying job with a big future so I could be near you? Does that sound like the money-crazed son of a rich man?''

"It sounds like someone trying to—to—" She couldn't think of an end to the sentence.

"Someone who's willing to go all the way for his girl?"

"I'm not your girl—"

"Sorry. I meant woman. Me, man. You, woman."

Her lips twitched. She put up her hand to cover her mouth because she didn't want him to know she was smiling. Not that she was amused. She still wanted to lay him out with one punch.

Unexpectedly, he caught her hand and jerked her closer. Before he could kiss her, she bent sideways from the waist, lashed the back of his knee with her foot, flipping him onto a floor mat. She expected retaliation and prepared for it by going into a half crouch, her hands posed in the classic karate gesture, but instead he lay there, looking very comfortable, staring up at her. She circled him, itching for a fight, and he began laughing and couldn't seem to stop.

When he rolled over on his stomach, pounding the floor mat and still laughing, she was furious. She wanted to kick him in the ribs, but because he wasn't resisting or fighting back, her martial arts training, which involved a lot of junk about custom and fair play, restrained her. She delivered a curse that would have made even her mother blanch, and started for the door again, but when she reached Steve's prone body, she didn't detour around him. Instead, she stepped on his leg and walked the full length of his body, stomping a little, ignoring his groans and his "Have a heart!"

He caught up with her before she reached the door. "Sorry about breaking up like that, but you have to admit you looked as funny as hell, doing the Bruce Lee thing."

She tried to get past him, but again he stopped her.

"If you don't take your filthy hands off me, I'm going to scream," she said through tightly clenched teeth. "And a few seconds after I yell, half a dozen construction types will be in here, taking you apart. You wouldn't believe what they'd do to someone who tried to rape a nice girl like me."

"Nice girl! You're a witch—and let's stop this wrangling. I'm crazy about you and I'm not giving up. From now on, you're going to stumble over me every time you breathe. Eventually, you're going to give in and admit you're crazy about me, too. So why waste all this time when we could be together, loving each other."

"Okay," she said.

He blinked. "What did you say?"

"I said okay, I'll marry you."

He stared at her; his mouth opened, but no words came out.

Glory planted her fists on her hips, glaring at him. "I knew it. All that stuff about being crazy about me was garbage. So you can go to hell. You hear me? Go to *hell*, Steve Golden!"

"Is tomorrow morning okay with you?"

"Tomorrow morning—what are you talking about now?"

"To get the marriage license."

"I don't believe this. This is some kind of trick—"

"No trick. When do we get the license?"

"I don't want to marry you!"

"The hell you don't. You proposed, didn't you? And I asked if tomorrow morning is okay for getting the license." His grin faded suddenly. "Look, Glory, I need you the worst way. I want to make love to you—and when it's over, I don't want to get up and go home. I think we can make a go of it—no guarantees, because there aren't any in life. But this thing between us is prime stuff. I'm willing to take a chance—why the hell aren't you?"

Glory's answer was a long time coming. Why *wasn't* she willing to take a chance? Was he right? Was she scared? At the worst, she'd end up getting her heart bent again. But at the best—wasn't she the best worth gambling on?

"I've been taking chances all my life," she said aloud, talking more to herself than to Steve. "Maybe—maybe it's time to do it again." Steve made a move toward her, but she pushed him away. "No promises. There's a lot of things we have to iron out, but—okay, it's on again. Only forget about the marriage part—and don't push me too hard, you hear?"

Steve nodded. He went to lock the door and drop the vertical blinds at the windows. In a minute, they were naked and making love on the exercise mat.

The opening of the Napa Hot Springs Spa was spectacular—which was the word that not only the *Napa Register* but the *San Francisco Chronicle* and the *Oakland Tribune* used later. It was not only elegant but it also had a carnival air, a combination only Chanel could pull off, Stet decided as he stood on the lush front lawn of the villa, staring around at the activity, bemused.

And there was a lot of activity. The guests could elect to dance to the music of a band imported from the city in the large, enclosed courtyard, now bright with potted poinsettias, or take a ride over

Napa Valley in one of the gaily striped balloons the spa had rented for the day, or taste a hundred varieties of Napa Valley wines, supervised by wine experts, in the rebuilt springhouse. And for those with a taste for whimsy, a genuine Gypsy fortune-teller was giving tarot card readings in a purple-and-gold tent in the gardens.

The food, prepared by chef Jean-Pierre, was superb, miles above the usual fare for such occasions. He had outdone himself with the fennel-flavored poached sea bass, the herbed chicken and red chard, the sweetbreads with sea urchin sauce, and asparagus with Jean-Pierre's own version of sauce Maltaise. The serving was informal, continuous, with the guests helping themselves at the buffet laid out on serving tables in a huge red-and-white tent, located in the meadow behind the villa, then eating alfresco at glass-topped tables set among a row of grapevine bowers or, if they chose, at picnic tables in the grove of giant oaks that bordered the meadow.

When Chanel, with her usual impeccable timing, waited until well into the festivities to announce that every entrée on the buffet was fewer than three hundred calories a serving, there was an involuntary ripple of applause. Stet, who had been keeping as low a profile as possible for a man six-foot-four wearing a dove-gray Stetson and Western clothes, caught the speculative stares toward the buffet tent and wasn't surprised when there was a renewed rush for the food.

Knowing from personal experience how the affluent love anything free, he hadn't complained when Chanel told him that she was adding gifts to the already sky-high price of the party. He *had* thought that Gucci makeup kits and Hermès scarves and bottles of Coco perfume were an unnecessary extravagance, but now, watching how greedily the wives of men he knew to be in upper one-percent income brackets tucked their gifts away in their handbags, he had to concede Chanel's shrewdness.

Yes, Chanel was smart, surprisingly business-oriented. All great qualities for a business partner, it was true. But the thing that concerned him at present was when she was going to give in and have sex with him.

That she eventually would, he didn't doubt. He suspected she was playing it cool, enhancing the product to increase the price, but he was willing to play her game—for a while. Eventually, he would collect on his investment—as he always did—and she would benefit from being his lover. He was a rich man, far more so than anyone suspected, which was the thing that would lure her into his bed. He was also one hell of a good lover—and that's how he meant to keep her there.

But wouldn't it be great if he *wasn't* forced to bring out the big guns—a spectacular diamond bracelet or maybe a Maserati sports car, which he happened to know she had a yen for? How much more it would mean if she did it for the simple reason that she wanted to go to bed with him?

He must have sighed unconsciously, because Chanel, who was standing beside him, asked, "What's with the sigh? Something wrong?"

He tucked her hand into the crook of his elbow, smiling down at her. She was wearing a wool hand-knitted suit with clean, lean lines that was casual, strikingly becoming, and he decided that he liked her in blue, which she seldom wore, because it made her look softer, more approachable. "Everything's right. You've got them eating out of your hand."

"Let's hope. I'm sure most of them accepted their invitation because they knew the Chuningsways—thanks to Laird—and Senator and Mrs. Brach—thanks to you—would be here. Did you notice that the covey of witches from Hillsborough all came?"

"You never told me how you managed to pull that off. I thought that bunch had it in for you."

"Oh, I have my ways," she said airily. She laughed suddenly. "What goes around comes around, doesn't it? I booked Nancy Anderson for two weeks in March—she practically begged me to find a slot for her. How sweet it is."

"How sweet, indeed," he said, studying her. "I hope you never turn on me. I'd hate to have you as an enemy. You remind me of this little ole mare I had once. Sweetest horse flesh you'd ever want to ride until she got a chance to dump you into a cactus or down a ravine. Had to get shed of her—sold her to a neighbor who uses her as a breeding mare. Kicks the hell out of the stallions, but she drops some mighty fine colts, too."

"Is that your subtle Texas way of telling me to watch it?" Chanel asked.

"Would I do that?"

"I think you're a very complex and dangerous man. And I don't buy that on-again, off-again horseshit accent. Where'd you really come from? Back east somewhere is my guess—like Ohio maybe?"

"Watch it," he said with mock anger. "You could be dumped,

you know. I've had some offers—all of a sudden, it's in to run a spa.''

"No chance of that," she said coolly. "You're too much of a businessman to dump someone who's making money for you."

"What money? Have you taken a look at the deficit column in the books yet?''

"It'll come rolling in. And I do mean rolling," she said with superb confidence.

"Well, we'll see. I'd like to sit in on the next staff meeting—if it's okay with you."

"Why ask my permission? You're the boss."

He shook his head. "No, you're the head honcho around here. I'm turning it over to you.''

Her eyes widened. "You're giving me my head?"

"You've got the picture."

Her face relaxed into a smile. "You won't be sorry," she said. She hesitated, then said, "I scheduled a staff meeting for tomorrow morning. Why don't you stay over tonight and save yourself that long trip back to the city?"

"Good idea. It'll give me a chance to see how comfortable those fancy brass beds you ordered for the guest cottages are."

"Oh? You mean you prefer a guest cottage when you could sleep in the manager's bed?''

Stet stared at her; all of a sudden, his throat was as dry as dust. "Are you saying what I think you are?" he asked cautiously.

She pressed his hand, which was still resting on her arm, against the side of her breast. It was a very soft, surprisingly full breast, he noted. "Why don't you stick around and find out?"

A guest came up, gushing about the fabulous food, and Chanel told her smoothly that, as a guest of the spa, not only would she dine like a queen on low-calorie food, but if she liked, her cook could take a course in preparing those same foods from Jean-Pierre himself—for a nominal fee.

Stet listened with only half an ear to Chanel's practiced spiel, which he'd heard before. He felt as excited as a kid again—and also like a hunter closing in for the kill. Would sex with Chanel be as good as he anticipated? He had sized her up as a sensual woman, but what if he was wrong? What if she was as cool and calculated in bed as she was out of it?

On the other hand, she did have that touch of—call it earthiness. When she was with her friends, that support group bunch, she was more giving, less wary. She also was one to pay her debts, good or bad. Had she invited him to bed purely out of gratitude? Did he really want to know the answer to that? He wasn't even sure it would make a difference.

You're an old lech, Stet, he thought. But what the hell—he'd paid his dues, and no matter how this business with Chanel turned out, it was going to be damned good fun.

CHAPTER FORTY-FIVE

STEPHANIE WASN'T ENJOYING THE PARTY. IN FACT, SHE WISHED she hadn't come. For the past hour, she'd been sitting in a small covered arbor in the rear garden of the villa, hiding out. She'd realized at once that the brown wool suit she was wearing was much too townish. To people from the city, Napa Valley was "country," and although the other women guests were expensively dressed, they all looked very casual in their natural fabrics clothes, their tweed jackets and cashmere sweaters and Italian leather boots, the throwaway casualness that Stephanie knew she could never achieve in a million years.

She wondered miserably why it was that she never seemed to dress to suit the occasion. No matter how much she paid for her clothes—and lately, that indulgence had gone out the window—she always looked as if they came right off the racks of Macy's or the Emporium, something she wouldn't even have been aware of a year ago.

But Ariel, in her middy-collared jacket and pleated skirt, which Stephanie would have passed by in a store, with her fine pale hair casually pinned back by a small tortoiseshell brooch, looked just right. Maybe it was a matter of breeding. For all Ariel's unworldliness, she did belong among these people by birth.

It wasn't, Stephanie told herself, that she had the slightest desire to move in high society. She was perfectly happy as a middle-class woman from the suburbs. It was just that this past year, being exposed to Chanel, she sometimes felt like a country girl, straight off the farm.

How odd that she'd never felt inferior around David, even though he certainly was several cuts above her socially. His parents had not only been very comfortably off, but both of them had been lawyers, and that really meant something in Morgan, Oregon, even if it didn't in San Francisco or Marin County with their large professional populations. One of the reasons why her parents were so upset about the divorce was because they considered her lucky to have married a lawyer. On the few occasions when they'd had the chance to show David off around Morgan, her dad had managed to bring David's profession into the conversation every chance he got.

And why was she dwelling on the past today? David had made it very plain that he had given up on her. In fact, he seemed to be avoiding her lately. When he picked up the boys, he waited for them in his car, and once, when she'd gone out to ask him for the key to their bank deposit box, he'd been so formal that she'd retreated back into the house. From the bits of information the twins dropped from time to time, David was living with his girlfriend now—or at least, she was always there when they went for a visit. Although they still professed to dislike her, her name seemed to creep into the conversation a lot lately. . . .

"Hey, I've been looking for you!" It was Glory, who was looking stunning in a copper-colored sweater with a matching wool skirt. Although she looked as flamboyant as ever among the other guests in their studied country look, somehow she managed to carry it off with aplomb.

And doesn't give a damn, one way or the other, Stephanie thought. Was *that* why she herself felt so out of place? She did care, maybe too much, about how she looked to other people.

"I've been hiding out," she confessed. "I feel like the maid among all this elegance."

Glory looked surprised. "They've got big bucks, sure, but some of them aren't worth shit as people."

Stephanie was startled into a laugh. "You've got an attitude problem, Glory. If you feel that way, why are you working here?"

"Because it's a challenge—and besides, the pay's not bad. Of course, you have to be careful with rich people or they'll walk all over you."

"No danger of that with you," Stephanie said.

"Yeah, I can handle it. You aren't letting them get you down, are you? Look, the way you've been raising your boys on your own, that's the kind of thing that impresses *me*."

Stephanie was silent. Was she overly impressed by outward

appearance? A year ago, she'd been embarrassed to be seen in Glory's company. Now, she was proud to be Glory's friend—and yet Glory hadn't changed, not essentially. She was still flamboyant, still too frank at times and impatient with the defenses that other people put up to hide their vulnerability, and, it had to be admitted, her language still needed to be cleaned up. So the changes must have been within herself.

Stephanie felt a sudden worry. "I hope the group stays together, even if we meet less often," she said. "Not that the rest of you need support these days. You've all worked out your problems. I guess I'm the only one who still hasn't adjusted to being single again."

"Uh-huh. Got the blue meanies, have you? Anything I can do? I'm willing to listen even if I'm not much for giving advice."

Stephanie hesitated. Did she really want to tell Glory her problems? Would Glory understand the special terror of being responsible for the welfare of two teenage sons? Would she have any sympathy for someone who found it hard to take life as it came, to roll with the punches? How could Glory possibly understand the fear that came in the night and clutched at her chest so she could hardly breathe, of the dread she felt every morning when she went to work—that she'd do something wrong and lose her job, that somehow she wouldn't measure up and would have to go to David or to her parents for financial help?

"I'm just tired," she said evasively, and was relieved when Glory nodded and asked if she'd tasted any of that wine they were making such a fuss about.

"This wine expert guy pressured me to take a taste. Said I could spit it into one of these little paper cups if I didn't want to swallow it. God, how gross! Well, I did take a sip and—ugh, it was sour as hell. You can bet I spit it out, and I musta made a face, because he began lecturing me about its bouquet and dryness and a lot of other junk. I told him I'd rather have some grape juice, and I thought he'd have a stroke. He said my ignorance was criminal, and I said, 'So sue me,' and—"

"Did you say someone was suing you?" It was Laird. He was holding hands with Ariel, and he looked very handsome in a navy blue blazer and open-necked shirt. Stephanie took in the high color in Ariel's cheeks, and was aware of envy. It wasn't that she was interested in Laird. The truth was, he made her uncomfortable. What she envied was the rapport between these two. She'd had it with David once—or had it all been in her mind? Something

450   THE CLUB

she'd dreamed up because it fit in with her own image of a happy marriage?

The thought was troubling; she murmured something about getting herself a glass of wine and slipped away. But she didn't go to the springhouse. Instead, she went to the parking lot, got into her station wagon, and started for home without saying good-bye to her friends or even to her hostess.

Chanel wouldn't miss her. When she'd first arrived, Chanel had greeted her warmly, had even introduced her to several of the guests, but since then, she'd been totally involved with her role as hostess. In fact, there was something about her that even Stephanie, who had no illusions about her own perception, recognized as being odd. She had seemed jumpy, distracted, as if she had a lot on her mind. And when Mr. Stetson had come up behind her unexpectedly, her face had turned bright pink. Was Chanel worried about the party? That didn't seem likely. She must know that it was an unqualified success. . . .

The trip back to the city seemed interminable. For one thing, the car was acting up again. She'd just spent a small fortune on the transmission, and now the motor had developed a knock that promised future expenditures she could ill afford. She brooded over her rapidly diminishing savings account, remembering how Arnold Waterford had warned her not to close the door on future support from David.

"Right now, all you want is to be free of him," he had said. "But pride doesn't pay the bills. And you should let me arrange that all your sons' medical or dental expenses be sent to your husband. That should be in the divorce agreement."

"I'd rather manage on my own," she'd said. "If I can't, I'm sure David will offer to pay that kind of expense. After all—" She had stopped, not willing to tell this man, even though he was her lawyer, that after all, the divorce was David's fault, that he was the one who had been unfaithful.

"If you were about to say that the boys are his, too—I think I should tell you that some men have very short memories. At first, they may be conscientious about their obligations, but after a while, especially if they remarry, their attitude changes, and they find excuses to shift that responsibility onto their ex-wives. This is the time, at this point in the divorce proceedings, to get these things pinned down, Mrs. Cornwall."

But of course she'd wanted only to put the whole mess behind her. And Mr. Waterford had been right. David had stopped putting money into her checking account as soon as the divorce papers had been signed, and he hadn't offered to pay any of the boys' medical or dental bills, either. Another mistake in the long list of mistakes she'd made. How many more crises must she cope with before she finally got the boys raised?

As if to answer her question, the car gave a final cough and then stopped dead in the middle of the freeway.

By the time Stephanie reached home—after a long wait for a tow truck, an even longer wait while a mechanic at an all-night garage in San Rafael evaluated the broken-down car and gave her an estimate—she was totally exhausted. The repair bill would take most of her remaining cash reserve, but she'd had no choice but to okay it.

And that wasn't the worst of it. The garage couldn't promise how long it would be before the car was serviceable again, which meant daily commuting via Golden Gate Transit and muni-buses for the next few days. One break—a mechanic who lived in Mill Valley was just getting off work for the night, and he gave her a lift home. It was the only break she'd had all day.

The living room lights were still on when the mechanic, a cheerful young man who'd told her the story of his life on the ride home, dropped her off. She'd tried to call the boys from the garage three times, but the line had been busy. Probably with toll calls, she thought drearily.

After she got out her house key, she paused briefly to fix a smile on her lips, but when she went inside and called out a cheery "Hello! I'm home!" there was no answer. Well, that was par for the course. The boys must be upstairs, sulking. They had been so obnoxious this morning during breakfast that she'd finally lost her temper and confined them to the house until her return.

She'd been sorry as soon as she was a block away from the house. They hadn't been all that bad, and the punishment, to be restricted on a Sunday, didn't fit the crime. And wasn't it time to do something about her own attitude problem these days? It was all very well to tell other people that she was coping, but the truth was she was barely functioning. She lived on her nerves from one day to the next, always worrying about the next crisis, the next expense. Where was the strength that was supposed to come from being independent and on your own? This mood she was in, what Glory called the blue meanies, had started when she'd finally broken up with Clay and told him she didn't want to see him again, and it was getting worse by the day. She had to get hold of herself before she totally alienated the twins. What if they got so disgusted with her that they went to stay with their father? What would she have left to live for then?

The quiet in the house was unnerving as she stopped to put away her suit jacket in the hall closet. It was too early for the boys to be in bed, yet there were no TV sounds, no stereo blast from their rooms, no sound at all—had they gone to bed early?

She was passing the living room door, on her way to the kitchen, when she saw David. He was sitting in his leather English club chair, and it was obvious that he was waiting for her.

For a brief moment, her mind skipped a cog, and she forgot that he had no right to be here. During their marriage, on the rare occasions when she'd gone to a concert or to the opera with a friend, he'd always waited up for her, saying he couldn't sleep until he knew she was safe at home again.

They would have a drink together while she told him about her evening, and he was always willing to listen even though he had no interest in music. Once, when she'd commented on this, he'd told her that he liked the way her face lit up when she talked about music, and then he'd remarked that it was only fair since she always listened to him when he wanted to talk just before a hearing, even though he knew she had no interest in law.

Tit for tat, he'd added, making it sound suggestive.

She smiled at the memory, but the smile died when David rose, his face tight. "Where the hell have you been?" he said roughly.

Anger, caused as much by the whole frustrating day as by his question, surfaced. "What right have you to question me? You're not my husband anymore."

"I'm the boys' father. They had no idea where you were. You been hitting the singles bars?"

"No—have you? Is that where you picked up that—that woman?"

"If you're talking about Sylvia, I met her at—at a friend's house."

"Oh? I suppose all our friends have been rallying around, trying to fix up poor David with a new woman? Isn't it strange that they haven't done the same for me? Why is that, you suppose?"

David's face darkened. "Don't try to change the subject. The boys called me a couple of hours ago. They heard someone prowling in the bushes under the living room windows, and they were scared to death."

"They could have phoned our next door-neighbor, who happens to be a retired police captain. The boys have standing orders to call Mr. Coogan if anything comes up while I'm gone, and in return, I feed his cats when he's off visiting his daughter in San Diego. I made it a point to tell him I would be gone most of the day, and Mr. Coogan assured me he would be home. I think that should be sufficient protection for two fifteen-year-old boys, don't you? Or maybe I should have dropped them off at your place. I'm sure your woman friend would be delighted to wash their clothes and cook their meals and pick up after them, even if you aren't.''

"That's unfair, and you know it."

"Oh? It's obvious that you don't have any time for your sons lately."

"Think what you like. You will anyway."

"You're damned right I will. I'm not your house mouse anymore. I'm my own person, and it feels good. You hear? It feels *wonderful*!''

"You've made that plain. Which makes me wonder if you weren't looking for an excuse to ditch me all along. Maybe you wanted to be on your own, to be a career woman."

Unbidden, an image of a typical workday came to Stephanie. The dull, repetitive chores that took up so much of her time . . . the strain of relaying the department head's orders to women half her age who were technically her superiors . . . the humiliation of having to deal with a man who treated her with contempt—and to not be in a position to tell him off. . . .

A career woman? *Her?*

A laugh bubbled up in Stephanie's throat and escaped. The expression on David's face was almost comical, but suddenly she stopped laughing and was crying instead.

She felt David's body warmth even before his hands gripped her shoulder. He pulled her close, and although she knew it was a mistake, she buried her face in his shoulder. The familiar odor of citrus after-shave, of soap and leather and something intangibly male that she always associated with David, were so comforting that she didn't pull away—not until he told her to get it out of her system, even if it took her all night.

She snuffled, hiccuped, and stopped crying.

"Storm over?" he asked, and the anger came rolling back.

"Why don't you leave?" she snapped. "You came here uninvited, and you think you have the right to criticize me. Well, let me tell you something—I'm a better mother than you are a father. If it hasn't occurred to you yet that the boys were playing games tonight to get you over here, you're pretty damned gullible.

They're upstairs now, straining their ears to hear what we're saying, thinking they're pretty clever, and I'm not going to call them on it because their motives were understandable. Totally wrong, but understandable. They want a father as well as a mother, and you've been making yourself pretty scarce lately.''

"That's unfair. I thought—okay, I thought it best if I stayed out of your life and gave this guy you've been seeing a chance. I even started dating Sylvia to prove that divorced people need—'' He stopped and gave her a quick look.

"If you're inferring that you took up with this woman in order to make Clay more acceptable to Chuck and Ronnie, I don't believe it.''

"The word is implying—you always did get those two words mixed up.''

"And you always did correct my grammar.''

He looked at her steadily. "You asked me to, Steph. Don't you remember?''

"Don't call me Steph. It makes me feel like a virus.''

"Sorry. Anything else you don't like?''

She bit her lip. It was unfair to expect David to know what annoyed her when she'd never pointed it out. Instead, she had held her resentment inside her—and what outlet had it taken, all that hidden resentment? Had she tried to punish him in bed?

"I'm sorry, too," she said reluctantly. "I can't expect you to read my mind.''

He frowned at her. "You've changed. Is it your job, being out there on your own, or is it this new fellow you've been seeing?'' His voice roughened as he added, "If he's brought you out of your shell, he must be good for you. I tried, but I never could reach you.''

Stephanie wished he would shut up, that he'd go away. They'd been over this before, and nothing had been resolved. Why had he chosen tonight, when she was so tired, to bring it up again?

"I *have* changed. I'm not as narrow-minded and intolerant as I used to be.''

The words came welling up from her subconscious, and it was a moment before she realized she'd spoken them out loud. What did they mean? That she was finally willing to believe David? Dear God, she did want to believe that his—his aberration had been an isolated incident, signifying only that he was human, as she herself was human.

How could she, in all fairness, condemn David for a momentary lapse when she'd experienced the same thing herself? Oh, yes, she did understand now how it could happen—but knowing something intellectually was not the same as feeling it emotionally. *Could* she forgive him? After all, she hadn't given in to that moment of temptation—why had he?

But if she, like David, had been drinking heavily—would she have pushed Ariel away? Only if she could accept her own fallibility, could she forget the past and put the bitterness, the sense of betrayal, behind her.

One thing—no, *another* thing she'd learned this summer was the strength of the sex drive. How frustrated David must have been those nights when she'd lain, unresponsive and emotionally detached, in his arms while he worked so hard to make it good for her. And yet he'd never reproached her. Why hadn't he? Why hadn't he raised hell with her and accused her of being frigid?

"Why didn't you ever throw it up to me for not being as interested in sex as you?" she asked.

David looked startled. "Because—well, because of that business with your brother and his friend. I was sure it was the reason you were—cool about sex. I thought that eventually you would learn to trust me, but I never did get through to you, did I? This fellow from Oregon—has he succeeded where I failed? Is he better in bed than me?"

Stephanie didn't answer for a moment. It was time for honesty, but even honesty had different faces—and could hurt. And she still was uncomfortable talking about sex. She probably would never change in that respect.

"Not better," she said carefully. "Different. More aggressive and not so—so concerned about how I felt. You're a much better lover."

"Well, my ego is still intact." But David's smile was strained. "And what you're really saying is that even so, he turns you on and I didn't. At first, you put on a pretty good act, you know. Tell me—did you fake it all those times I thought I had satisfied you?"

"Not every time. Just when I was tired or worried or my mind was wandering. You would keep trying and trying and yet I'd know that it wasn't going to happen and it seemed easier just to let you think—I know now that was wrong. I thought you should do it all. It never occurred to me that I had the responsibility of making it work, too, of telling you how I felt."

They stared at each other for a long time. "Does this mean you've forgiven me, Steph—Stephanie?"

"Oh, call me Steph. I was just being bitchy."

"You *have* changed." He was smiling, a real smile this time. "And you didn't answer my question. Have you forgiven me?"

"Yes. I want to cross this last year out as if it had never happened."

He didn't say anything for a long moment. "You're willing to try again?"

"If you are." She held her breath; what if he told her that he was perfectly happy without her these days?

"What about the man you've been seeing?"

"I broke it off. He—it didn't work out."

"Are you doing this for the boys?" he said; his face was strained, very pale.

"I'm doing it for me. For us. I'll never be happy with anyone else. You accept me, faults and all, and don't have any illusions about me."

David's tense face relaxed into a smile. "Faults? What illusions? The first time I saw you, I knew you were for me. Do you remember? It was in the library at San Francisco State. I was researching something in the law book section, and you were doing a report. You dropped a book, and I picked it up and—"

"—and when the librarian made a shushing sound and glared at us, you apologized for dropping *your* book. Oh, yes, I remember. I think that's why I married you, and maybe that was a bad reason. I went right on expecting you to protect me from anything unpleasant."

"I thought it was what you wanted, and God knows, I'd had my fill of assertive women. You were so different from my mother—but I won't make that mistake again. From now on, you can be a red-hot women's libber for all I care."

"Uh-huh. I might take you up on that," she said, knowing she never would—and that David was well aware of it. She knew she should feel ashamed for letting her own sex down, but the truth was, she didn't function well without a man. Was that why, except for that one time with Janice, she'd never really opened up to any of the women in the support group? And yet—hadn't she learned a lot about being a woman from them?

"Can we make it this time?" she said, suddenly afraid. There were so many things for both of them to forget—and forgive. "We've both hurt each other. Can we forget what's happened and go on from there?"

"We'll make it. We know all the pitfalls now."

She smiled at him, reassured by the certainty in his voice. "It's going to seem strange, going through a marriage ceremony again. What are the rules for a second wedding to the same man? Do we invite our parents? Should we elope or have another formal ceremony? Does the bride wear white? Do we take the boys with us on our second honeymoon?"

He took her hand. "I want to make love to you, Steph."

"I know. Let's go upstairs."

Holding hands, they climbed the stairs. Once she stumbled, almost falling. She felt an almost uncontrollable desire to giggle when David lifted her into his arms and whispered in her ear, "Thank God you've lost weight or I couldn't manage this."

When they reached their bedroom, he let her slip to the floor. She felt shy, as if this were their first time. She also discovered that there was something very erotic about undressing in front of David. Her sexual needs had changed drastically in the past few months—which was something she had Clay to thank for—but would David accept the change?

David's first caresses were tentative, but when she touched him back, stroked him intimately, his whole body trembled, and she gloried in his loss of control because it made her feel incredibly sexy. When he groaned, "I can't wait much longer, Steph. I'm going crazy," she pushed him backward on the bed, then settled down on top of him and opened her thighs to receive his first thrust. As he entered her, she cried out and flung back her head, matching him, movement for movement.

We'll make it work this time, she thought fiercely, and then the thought slipped away as sweetness exploded within her.

CHAPTER FORTY-SIX

JANICE FINISHED HER DOCTORAL DISSERTATION THE FIRST WEEK in January, which, as she told her friend Casey a few days later, hadn't been a minute too soon. They had met by accident in the

Stanford Shopping Center and were sitting in the doughnut shop, visiting over croissants and coffee.

"I'm sick to death of it," Janice went on. "I must have cross-checked my survey figures a dozen times."

"I'm sure it's top-drawer stuff," Casey said. She was looking very matronly in a loose-fitting jacket and slacks; there were deep circles under her eyes as if she'd been ill. "Yolanski should be pleased. I understand he's a stickler for accuracy."

"*And* integrity. *And* the orderly progression of logic. Tell me about it," Janice said ruefully. "It isn't the charts or the survey results that worry me. It's the writing. He has a reputation for turning papers back just because of what he calls pedestrian writing. And I already have one strike against me. Jake's dissertation was so brilliant that I'm sure Yolanski will be comparing our work. He wouldn't be human if he didn't."

"You'll pass with flying colors. After all, you did most of the work on Jake's dissertation for him, didn't you?"

Janice stared at her friend, appalled. "Where did you get that idea? Certainly not from me."

"I'm not stupid, Janice." Casey's smile was a little sour. The front of her blouse gaped open as she reached for another croissant. "How many times did I come to see you and find you up to your ears in Jake's notes? Besides, I read part of the manuscript when it was finished—remember? I know your writing style. It was unmistakable."

"You haven't said anything about this to Merv, have you? Jake would be furious if he thought—"

"Your secret is safe with me. I wouldn't have mentioned it today except I was trying to get the point across that your writing style has *already* passed muster with Yolanski."

"That's only a small part of a dissertation," Janice protested. "The original concept was Jake's, and it was brilliant. I did some of the research and editing, but—"

"Okay, okay. I'm sorry I said anything. Don't stew about it, okay? Yolanski will be crazy about your dissertation. Trust me."

"He's already had it a week," Janice said, sighing. "I haven't been sleeping well lately, waiting for his verdict. If he likes it, and the committee agrees and I pass the orals—"

"You'll be fine. And we'd better change the subject before you have an anxiety attack. What about that new assistant prof in the art department? He's a real hunk, isn't he?"

For a while they discussed the physical assets of the new assistant professor, then reminisced about their Berkeley days. Casey finished off her croissant, drained her coffee cup, and glanced at her watch. She made a face, said she had to pick up the baby at the sitter's before her oldest two got home from school, so she'd better get cracking.

After she was gone, Janice exchanged a Christmas gift from Jake, a sweater that didn't fit, at the Emporium, did some grocery shopping, and then went home. As she put her groceries away, her thoughts drifted to Casey. It was always good to talk to her old friend. Too bad they'd drifted so far apart this past year. Not because she'd wanted that. It was just that Casey always seemed to be so busy whenever she called her. Meeting her today had been a lucky break although—well, they did seem to talk a lot more about the past than they did the present.

It didn't help that Jake refused to socialize with the Scrantons any longer. She'd known for a long time, of course, that Casey didn't like Jake any more than he liked her. Not that Casey ever said anything against him. It was just that she avoided talking about him altogether. Was it because Jake was never at his best around Casey, who seemed to irritate him? It was obvious that Jake resented Merv's advancement, too. He called him "that egghead Scranton" most of the time. Someday, he was going to slip and call him that in front of other people. . . .

The phone rang, making her start. It was Professor Yolanski. "I'd like to talk to you, Mrs. Morehouse," he said. "Do you have any free time this afternoon?"

Professor Yolanski lived on a quiet street in one of the older sections of Palo Alto. The turn-of-the-century cottage, fully shingled, dripping with gingerbread trim and overshadowed by giant cypress trees, reminded Janice of the witch's cottage in *Hansel and Gretel*. But it suited Professor Yolanski and his plump wife to a tee. In fact, Janice couldn't imagine them living anywhere else, certainly not in a modern apartment building.

As she went up the front steps, she almost tripped over a large ginger cat. The cat growled at her and then stalked away, twitching its fat tail. She resisted the impulse to say "Scat!" just to ruffle its fur, then wondered why it was that she had such an aversion to cats. Jake had once told her it was because she had an inferiority complex, but she suspected the real reason was because, while she was growing up, the steps had paid more attention to the family cat than they had to her—and wasn't that a crazy reason for disliking the whole feline species?

Professor Yolanski answered the doorbell himself. Although he greeted her with his usual courtesy, his face was grave as he ushered her into a large room off the central hall. She felt a little intimidated as she stared around at the walls of books, the sturdy, well-worn oak and leather furniture, and the family photographs filling several bookcase shelves. She'd always wanted a room like this, but it wasn't something you planned ahead of time, she decided. It had to grow over a lifetime—as this room obviously had.

"Sit down, Mrs. Morehouse," Professor Yolanski said. He waited until she was seated in a spindle-backed rocker before he settled himself behind a desk so large, it overshadowed his diminutive figure.

"I've read your dissertation," he said. She expected him to say more, but he only stared at her, as if marshaling his next words.

"Have you come to any conclusion?" she asked finally.

"Yes—a very disturbing one."

Disturbing? What did that mean? "I don't understand," she said.

"Don't you have something you'd like to tell me, Mrs. Morehouse?"

"Tell you?" she said, completely bewildered now.

"You do understand that a doctoral dissertation must be completely original, based upon original research, and that it must totally be the work of the candidate?"

"Are you questioning its originality?"

"You haven't accepted any outside help?"

"Of course not. Oh, I used a student typist for some of my notes—but you're not talking about that, are you? What is it you suspect? That I copied someone else's paper?"

"You do remember that I was your husband's adviser when he got his degree, don't you? He has a very individual writing style."

"Surely you don't think—Jake hasn't even read my dissertation. He's been too busy this year with his TV class."

"Yes, yes. I was sorry when they terminated his contract."

"He resigned. The station didn't terminate—"

"If Jake had nothing to do with your dissertation, how do you explain the similarities in writing style?"

Janice was too stunned to speak. It was just the reverse of his suspicions. She had helped Jake with his dissertation, not the other way around. But how could she say that to Professor Yolanski, of all people?

She felt a little dizzy as she gathered up her purse and rose. "You're quite wrong, but since you obviously don't believe me, I think it best we forget the whole thing."

She turned to go, but Professor Yolanski's voice caught her before she could reach the door. "Come back. It's possible that I've made a mistake." Janice hesitated, her hand on the doorknob, and he added, "If so, I apologize. And the dissertation, at least on first reading, is excellent. Yes, excellent. If it stands up on a second reading—well, let's say that I am very impressed."

Reluctantly, Janice returned to her chair. "Are you saying—just what *are* you saying?"

He seemed to be avoiding her eyes as he fussed with a piece of paper on his blotter. "That I think I've made a mistake. For which I apologize. As for the dissertation, it was very well executed. Your premise, your conclusions, although a bit unorthodox, are intriguing, logical, and well thought-out. The subject matter is timely and relevant to today's world, which is something so many candidates forget to consider when they choose their subject. This business of support and mutuality among unrelated women is not new, of course—I'm thinking of the old sewing circles and quilting parties—but your conclusions are presented in such a logical way, especially your theory that maintaining a certain distance between individuals in a support group such as you researched may actually be helpful. Since your ideas are so provocative—and, mind you, I'm not sure I agree with all of them—they might well be publishable by a university press, or even by a commercial publisher. . . ."

He went on talking. Janice wanted to tell him that publication of her dissertation was impossible, not for the least of the reasons being that Jake wouldn't approve. As if to make up for his earlier suspicions, Professor Yolanski was so extravagant in his praise that she was sure he would regret it later. She broke in finally, citing a dental appointment as an excuse to leave, and with his usual old-world courtesy, he saw her out.

But at the door, he said, "Oh—by the way, you might tell Jake that he was wrong about the—the importance of your research and the subject matter of your dissertation." There was an element in his dry, rustling voice that Janice found disturbing. "He made such a case for you, asking that I not judge the work too harshly, that I got the wrong impression. I can see now that it was just husbandly concern. I was wrong to even suggest that he—well, that your work was not your own. I'm sorry that I—what's the expression? That I went off half corked?''

"Half cocked."

"Yes, yes. I'll be in touch shortly."

"Thank you," she said, eager to get away.

She wouldn't allow herself to think about Professor Yolanski on the way home. There was a leaden feeling in her chest, and she wondered if her virus had returned or if it was one of those post-flu depressions she'd heard about. Or maybe it was the sickening suspicion that wouldn't go away. . . .

Jake's yellow Corvette was parked in the center of the driveway when she drove up. When she went into the house, he was in the small room off the kitchen where they kept their TV set, watching a sports program. He didn't notice her until she walked in front of him and switched off the TV.

"Hey, what did you do that for?"

"I want to talk to you. I've just been to see Yolanski."

Jake took a long draw from the bottle of beer in his hand. "And what did the good professor have to say?"

"That my dissertation is excellent," she said, her voice deliberately flat. "He thinks it would make the basis for a commercial book."

Jake's eyebrows moved upward in surprise. "One of those pop sociology things? He has to be joking."

"No. He wasn't joking. And why are you so negative? Wasn't publication what you hoped for when you were sending your dissertation around to all those publishers?"

"I wanted to get it published, yes. But mine was a—well, it was on a very serious subject."

"Because it concerned men and their problems? If the subject is women, then it's not serious?"

"What is this? Why are you so hostile?"

"I'm not hostile. I'm hurt, bewildered. You deliberately tried to give Professor Yolanski the impression that you did most of the work on my dissertation, didn't you? Why? Were you afraid he'd recognize my writing style and guess that I'd helped you with yours? Didn't you realize that Yolanski isn't the kind of person to just give the dissertation a cool reception and then let it go? He doesn't think that way. He confronted me in person."

Jake sat up straighter in his chair. "What the hell did you say to him?" he demanded.

"I told him that you'd been much too busy with your TV classes this past year to even read my manuscript. And that's when he told me he was sorry the station had canceled your show."

Jake rubbed his nose, a sure sign he was embarrassed. "I was going to tell you about that, but—well, I didn't want you making a big thing about something that was just a stupid mistake."

"Whose mistake? Yours for getting caught slipping around with your producer's wife? That's what happened, isn't it? The funny thing is that all the signs were there. Casey tried to warn me at our Christmas party, but I was too stupid to see—"

"Casey? What did that jealous bitch say? She was just sore because I dropped her for—" He stopped, looking appalled at his slip of tongue.

The leaden weight was back, making it hard for Janice to breathe. She wondered if she was having a heart attack—or did your heart break just because you'd learned that not only had your husband betrayed you, but so had your best friend? No wonder Casey had been avoiding her. She, at least, had a conscience.

"Why did you do it, Jake?" she said, her voice deceptively mild. "Couldn't you resist coming on to Casey because she was my best friend—or was her dislike of you a challenge to your ego? Or was it because Merv's career was going so well, even though he wasn't playing the game, that you had to bed his wife to prove you were the better man? Well, you aren't. You're a spoiler—a cheat and a liar—"

Jake's face was dark red; he gave his nose a hard pull. "Knock it off or I'll—"

"You'll what?"

He glared at her for a long moment. When he looked away with a shrug, she wasn't surprised. How long had she known Jake was a coward, both physically and morally? And what a fool she'd been, looking the other way all these years. Had she needed the security of a husband and a home so badly that she'd deliberately blinded herself to his faults, to his promiscuity? Or had she simply been unwilling to admit that she'd made a mistake, marrying Jake?

"I want a divorce," she said.

"A divorce? You must be crazy."

"No, not crazy. I'm finally sane. I should have done it years ago."

He met the contempt in her eyes, and his lips twisted into an ugly smile. "So pack your things and get out. Who needs you? I'm sick of you and have been for a long time. The only way I

can get it up these days is by pretending you're someone younger—
and prettier."

His words, deliberately cruel, hurt. Even though she knew she
should be glad that he was finally showing his true colors, it still
hurt. But not enough that she didn't realize his attack was self-
serving. If he got her mad enough to storm out of here, it would
leave him in possession of the house that meant so much to his
own self-esteem. How clever he was—and yet how much he underestimated her, too.

"I have no intention of leaving," she told him. "A year ago, I
would have gone to a hotel. But I've learned something about the
mechanics of divorce this past year. Before I do anything, I'm
going to have a long talk with Arnold Waterford. Since I'm his
goddaughter, I'm sure he'll have some good advice for me." She
stared at him fixedly. "I just realized why Arnold doesn't like
you, never has. He must have seen through you all along."

"Oh, but he likes *you*, doesn't he? When did he first crawl into
your pants? When you were twelve? Fourteen? Or did he wait
until you came of age? How is the old lech in bed? Is he any
good?"

"You're really disgusting. Just because you sleep around, don't
try to put the same onus on me. With all the diseases going around,
I just hope you've been careful who you've slept with lately."

She turned and walked out of the room. Jake yelled something
after her, but there was such a roaring in her ears that the only
word that registered was "bitch." For which she was grateful.
She'd taken all she could for one day, and yet—there was relief
under the pain, too. How long, in the deep recesses of her mind,
had she known about Jake? And what did it say about *her* that
she'd stuck it out so long?

It was an hour later she heard Jake's car pull out of the driveway.
She checked his closet and saw that he'd taken most of his clothes,
those cashmere sports coats and hand-knitted sweaters, the Pendleton shirts he favored in winter and the Banana Republic khaki
shorts and camp shirts that were his summer uniform. Where
would he go? To one of his women? Would he try to fight a
divorce? Thank God for California's community property laws
and no-fault divorces. There was no telling what lies he would
spew forth in court if it was to his advantage.

And what did she do next? Should she call Arnold and find out
what her rights were? She didn't really want the house. On the
other hand, she didn't want Jake to have it, either. Did that make

her the bitch he'd called her—or did it just prove that she was human enough to want to get some of her own back?

Grief, piercing and painful, caught her by surprise. She clasped her arms around her chest and rocked back and forth. She felt so—so empty and depleted. For so long, Jake had been her—what? The person her world revolved around? The child she'd never had? She had really loved him—no use trying to fool herself about that. Even after she'd come to realize what he was—shallow, self-indulgent, selfish—she had buried her head in the sand, told herself that she wasn't all that perfect herself, which God knew was true. . . .

The crazy thing was that even now some part of her wanted desperately for Jake to walk back through the door, that cocky smile on his face, asking her if there was any Coors in the fridge.

But of course that would solve nothing, only prolong the agony. Jake would never change—and so she could never trust him again. And she couldn't live without trust, couldn't live in a perpetual state of suspicion. And yet, how was she going to face life without him? Eventually, she would tear him out of her mind, her heart—but what about tonight? Tomorrow? Next week?

Financially, she would be okay. If she got her doctoral degree, she could teach, maybe at college level, something she had always wanted. Until then, she could go back to her old job—or get another just as good. Eventually, she would make a new life for herself, make new friends, develop new interests. But that was off in the future somewhere. How was she going to make it through the night, much less through the next few weeks?

Nausea struck her. She hurried to the bathroom, but she didn't get sick, after all. For a long time, she sat on the edge of the tub, too filled with despair to move, to think, to make any plans. When she finally rose, her legs had gone to sleep, and she staggered like an old woman.

Restlessly she wandered through the house, unable to settle down in any one place. The familiar rooms looked so—so empty and alien, as if she'd never really lived there at all. Life stretched out ahead of her—dark, full of unknowns with no ready answers. And lonely. How had the women in her support group survived the initial pain, those days, nights, weeks, after their marriages broke up?

Tomorrow she would call Arnold and get him started on divorce proceedings. But for now, she needed to talk to someone who would understand how she felt, someone who would listen to her, give her advice, stand by.

Mentally, she ran down a list of her friends; she winced when she came to Casey's name. Of all the things Jake had done to her, this was the worst, that she no longer could call Casey her friend.

But there *was* one person who filled the bill, that she could talk to, confide in, someone whose down-to-earth attitude would jack her up, put everything in perspective. . . .

She dropped on the edge of the bed, the same bed she'd shared with Jake for twenty years and where she would sleep alone that night. Her hands shook slightly as she picked up the phone and tapped out a number.

The phone rang three times before a voice said "Hello?"

"This is Janice. I just broke up with Jake—and I'm really hurting." She took a shaky breath before she could add "I need help."

"It'll take me a while to get there. Do you want me to bring the others?"

"Just bring yourself. And thank you—"

"What are friends for?" Chanel said.

EPILOGUE

IT WAS APRIL AGAIN, AND THEY WERE WAITING FOR JANICE, which was a surprise because she was never late, and for Ariel, which wasn't a surprise because she was usually the last to arrive.

Chanel had ordered wine, a white zinfandel, and at the moment, she was holding the floor, describing her encounter with a local TV celebrity who not only had been impossible to please, but who had paid the spa with a bad check. When they had stopped laughing at her description of the celebrity's peccadilloes, Stephanie lowered her voice slightly and asked Chanel, "How is Janice taking—you know, the divorce?"

Chanel shook her head. "It's not good. All the rotten things that man pulled, and the way he keeps trying to cheat her out of her share of the house, and yet I think there're times when she still wants him back.''

"Oh, God," Glory said. "Women can be such fools." She was drinking New York seltzer water instead of wine, and she had never looked better, Chanel decided. Even so, it was too bad her own Pygmalion efforts hadn't taken. Glory was still Glory, flaming red hair and outrageous clothes and colorful—to put it mildly—language. Still, she did have a certain unconventional charm. No one ever overlooked her, that was certain, and no one crossed her or slighted her, either, not for long. Which wasn't bad. . . .

She must have been smiling because Glory gave her a questioning look. "Something funny going on in that blond head of yours?''

"Just thinking of Janice—and women in general. Sooner or later, even after we know better, we all go soft over some man."

"Not me."

"Oh, come on, Glory. What about your jock—oops, wrong word. We don't call Steve a jock these days, do we? Are you trying to tell us that you aren't crazy about the guy? Why don't you marry him and put him out of his misery? If you let him run around loose too long, some little twit is going to snatch him up."

"That's my business. You may be my boss, but butt out of my personal life.'' Glory's hair seemed to give off sparks as she glared at Chanel. "And besides, look who's giving me advice about men—a two-time loser."

Chanel regarded her coldly. "I may have to fire you, after all," she said.

"You just do that—"

"Hi, everybody," Janice said. She was smiling as she came into the solarium and dropped into the vacant chair next to Stephanie. "Sorry I'm late but a rear-ender in the north lane tied up the freeway for half an hour."

"No problem. We're all a little early," Stephanie said, and from the relief on her face, she was glad for the interruption. Chanel, too, was glad. Glory's anger had been real, not one of the teasing exchanges they both enjoyed. What had caused it? Did Glory have a problem at work—or with Steve?

"I wonder what's keeping Ariel?" Glory said.

"She probably so busy dusting those dreary objets d'art deco and objets d'art nouveau and early Victorian that his and her houses are packed with that she's lost track of time," Chanel said, a little tartly. "I wonder which house they'll end up in? Frankly, it's hard to find a difference. They both look like museums."

"Oh, so we're in one of our snide moods, are we?" Glory said. "Why don't you admit that Ariel did you a favor? Which is more fun—running a multimillion-dollar business or being a social butterfly? Now be honest, Chanel."

"I'm always honest," Chanel said; she smiled suddenly. "As it happens, I'd like to have both."

"Maybe you can," Stephanie said. "Mr. Stetson—well, he's really crazy about you, isn't he?"

"Yeah. The two of them brighten whatever corner of the spa they happen to be in," Glory said. "I wouldn't be surprised if the manager's cottage didn't burn down some night."

Everybody laughed—except Chanel. "What's going to happen, Chanel?" Stephanie asked curiously. "Do you think he'll divorce his wife and marry you?"

"No. He'll never divorce Elsie. Stet and I are—just friends."

"Friends? I should have a friend like that." Janice sighed.

"Are you dating anyone yet?"

"Not really. Oh, I went out with one of the engineers from work, but he was just looking for some free sex. I was telling Arnold about it over lunch last week, and he said I'd have to get used to the new permissiveness. The thing is—permissiveness is already out-of-date, what with herpes and AIDS. I missed the parade all around."

Chanel regarded her thoughtfully. "You see Arnold pretty often, don't you?"

"Oh, sure. We go a long way back. He *is* my godfather, you know."

"He must have been a pretty young godfather. How old is he, anyway?"

"Sixty."

"And you're—how old? Forty-three?"

"Forty. I just look older these days."

"Sorry," Chanel murmured. "Anyway, there isn't any insurmountable gap in your ages, is there? You ever consider him as a possible—you know, beau?"

"No," Janice said—a little too sharply. "I'm sure Arnold only thinks of me as a friend."

"Don't be all that sure," Glory said. "Why don't you set your cap for him? He's a nice old guy. You could do worse."

Janice gave her a cool look. "I'm not looking for a man. Right now, I like living alone. For the first time in my life, I'm not cleaning up someone else's messes. Things are just great the way they are.''

"Arnold has never even hinted that he wants a closer relationship?" Chanel persisted.

Janice looked away. "He may have said something along those lines. But he was just teasing me."

Chanel settled back in her chair. "Well, well. This is interesting," she murmured. "You're either very naive or very cautious or—"

"And this conversation is at an end," Janice said sharply. "I'm sick and tired of your amateur psychology."

"Look who's talking! Dr. Janice, the great sociologist herself, always ready with a quick opinion on what makes the rest of us tick!"

The two glared at each other; unexpectedly, a trickle of amusement invaded Chanel's anger, and suddenly she was smiling. After a moment's hesitation, Janice smiled back. "We just had our first quarrel," she said, making a joke out of it.

"And about time," Glory said. She popped an ice cube in her mouth and crunched it between her strong teeth. "I was getting pretty bored with all the sweetness and light."

"Well, you were raised in the middle of a battlefield," Chanel said, pleased with the way things were going. Because this was their last meeting, why not go out on a light note?

"Hello," Ariel said from the doorway. "Did I miss a joke?"

She was wearing yellow organdy—on an unseasonably cold April day, of all things—but on her it looked good. Chanel had to give Ariel that much.

"Oh, we're all a bunch of comedians today," Chanel said. "Do sit down. You look like a butterfly, ready to flit away any minute."

Obediently, Ariel sank into a chair. A ray of spring sunshine, falling through the skylight, turned her pale hair to shimmering gold. If it had been anyone except Ariel, Chanel would have suspected she'd chosen that particular chair on purpose.

"You look lovely," Stephanie said. "What is that shade of yellow? Daffodil?"

"Yes—Laird chose the dress for me. It's strange how he seems to know just what I like, isn't it?"

Their elderly waiter came to take their orders, and as always, his back was a little straighter and his manner more gallant when he reached Ariel. Chanel wondered why he bothered to go through the motions since Ariel always chose the same thing—a spring salad, iced tea, and a piece of whatever melon was in season for dessert.

Remembering Laird's similar eating habits, Chanel said, with a tinge of acid in her voice, "Laird and you should have been twins, Ariel."

Ariel took her words as a compliment. "Oh, yes," she said eagerly. "We have the same taste in just about everything. I love old black-and-white movies—you know, from the twenties and thirties?—and so does Laird. And we're both vegetarians—"

"But how is your sex life?" Chanel asked. "You do have one, don't you?"

Color rose under Ariel's fair skin. How strange that with all the boating she did these days, that pale ivory skin never seemed to tan.

"We're very much in love, you know," Ariel said quietly. "I don't think that will ever change."

"Oh, you *are* naive," Chanel said, but she suddenly felt tolerant toward Ariel. Who knew—maybe she and Laird *would* have that rare thing: a lifelong romance. She hoped so.

She started to make a conciliatory remark, but Stephanie, who had been staring into space, obviously only half listening to the conversation, spoke first. "I know we decided to break up the group since we're all—well, have such busy lives these days, but I've been thinking that I'll really miss these luncheons. Everything is great now that David and I are back together, but sometimes I want to talk things over with other women who—who understand. Maybe we're being too hasty. What do the rest of you think?"

Chanel gave her a hard look. After all, it had been her idea to end the luncheons. "I think we should remain friends, of course, and keep in touch, but these monthly meetings do interfere with my schedule—and Saturday is the busiest day of the week for Glory and me."

"We can always make it another day," Stephanie said. She gave Glory a pleading look. "What do you say, Glory?"

Glory shrugged. "I'll go along with the majority."

"Ariel?"

Ariel hesitated briefly, then said, "I'd miss them, too. I know I don't contribute much, but—"

"I still need you," Janice said abruptly. She flushed at Chanel's appraising stare. "I know. I've given the impression that I've adjusted to—to things, but the truth is there're a lot of unresolved problems in my life. I'm still putting in applications for teaching jobs, and it looks to be a long search. And there are times when I feel so—so bitter and lonely. I hate having to admit that, but—''

"What she really means is that having made us her own personal project, she doesn't want to let go," Glory said.

Janice laughed with the rest of them, but Chanel noted that she didn't deny it.

"What about you, Chanel? You're the only holdout."

Chanel shrugged. "Okay, I'll go for it. But I think we should make a point of sharing our personal news, good or bad," she said, because it had just occurred to her that it might be fun to share some of her triumphs and even her setbacks with the group. Besides, it was such a relief to let her hair down and not have to put on an act all the time.

"You want some personal news, Chanel? I'll give you some," Glory said. "Steve and I are about to take the plunge."

"You're getting married?" Stephanie said. "Oh, that's lovely. Another wedding—"

"Hell, no! Not a wedding. The jury's still out on that. We're going to New York to see Steve's folks. They invited him to their fortieth anniversary party next month. Steve says that means his old man wants to make up."

"You sound nervous about it. Going to see Steve's parents can't be all that traumatic," Chanel said.

"You think not? A Jewish mother who isn't really Jewish, and a Jewish father who's part computer, part tyrant?"

Chanel shook her head. "I see what you mean. They do sound pretty formidable. If Steve was describing his mother as a certain type of Jewish mother, that doesn't bode well for you. Maybe you should stay home and let him go alone."

"I'm not afraid of them," Glory said quickly. "They're just people, after all. And no way am I going to let Steve go alone."

Chanel hid a smile. It was her belief that Steve's parents wouldn't know what hit them. Glory would have them eating out of her hand by the time she left New York. Which was evidently something Steve was counting on.

"Well, lots of luck. As for my news—the spa is doing even better than we expected—well, better than Stet expected. Personally, I never had any doubts about the outcome."

"You mean you didn't lose any sleep over it?" Janice said.

"A little maybe," Chanel admitted. She hesitated, then said, her tone offhand, "Stet's building a place up on the hill behind the spa. We're going to live there." She gave Glory a sidelong glance. "The manager's cottage will be vacant. I guess someone else could use it—it's plenty big enough for a couple."

Glory looked thoughtful. She didn't say anything.

"How about you, Ariel? Any problems these days?" Chanel asked.

Ariel gave her a serene smile. "I'm deliriously happy," she said.

And she's probably telling the truth, Chanel thought. "And you, Stephanie? Anything new going on in your life?" she asked.

Stephanie thought a moment. "Well, Ronnie has stopped wetting his bed," she said, and then looked surprised when everybody laughed. "It was really very serious—he was so humiliated. But he hasn't done it since David came back."

"So everything is working out fine for you, right?" Glory said.

"Yes—oh, we still have problems, but we talk them out now. For one thing, I've taken Chanel's advice, and now I know where we stand financially and where the family money is. David is very careful with money, which isn't bad in itself, but I didn't much appreciate that quality in him while I was struggling to keep afloat on my wages and child support. So now everything is in both our names. I think he's still in shock over that and—and other things." There was something in her smile now that Chanel decided was smugness.

"Anything else you want to share?" Janice asked, sounding like the old Janice.

Stephanie glanced at Ariel and then away. "I never told you the whole story, and it's too complicated to go into at this late date, but I realize now that I was much too rigid and narrow in my—my outlook on life. I expected David to know how I felt—and of course that was unrealistic. Now we talk things over openly and get into each other's heads. David believes that I need some outside interests, and I agree. That's why I'm going back to school to get my B.A. I should have done it years ago. I let myself fall into a rut—and didn't even know it was happening. As for our marriage—there's still some resentment there. On both sides. But we're a pair again—or maybe I should say that we're finally a pair."

There was silence, broken only by the faint sound of street noise filtering in through the windows. Chanel turned Stephanie's words over in her mind. Some mystery here—but it wasn't really any of her business. Not for her, Stephanie's life-style, but then she didn't have to live it, did she? At Ariel and Laird's wedding, they had finally met David, and to her astonishment, he was not only very personable, but surprisingly handsome. Strange that Stephanie had never mentioned this. It still was hard to see Stephanie, pretty though she was, married to a man who looked like a movie star. Well, it must be chemistry—or maybe he saw things in Stephanie that another woman wouldn't see.

The waiter brought their order, moving around the table at a slow pace, as if his bones ached today. Why on earth was the poor man still working as a waiter? Chanel wondered—and then wondered at herself. A year ago, she wouldn't have given Oscar or his aching bones a thought. Was she getting soft? No, not Chanel Devereau . . .

"Well, let's all gather at the table," Janice said, rising. She had picked up a few unbecoming pounds since the breakup of her marriage, and Chanel made a sudden decision. Her contribution to Janice's well-being, in payment for the support she herself had received from the group in the past year and a half, would be two free weeks at the spa. There was nothing like being coddled and pampered to give a woman a new lease on life.

In fact, she just might make Janice her own personal project and see if she couldn't talk her into doing something about that outdated hairstyle. Yes, that's what she'd do. She'd call Janice tomorrow and give her the news. But maybe she'd only make that one week at the spa. No use overdoing it.

Feeling righteous and pleased with herself, she picked up her wineglass and followed the others to the table. Strange how they always sat in the same chairs—she with Glory on her right and Janice on her left, Ariel and Stephanie across the table. It had been their original seating—and how prophetic since she and Glory had become such good friends. As for the others—yes, she was fond of them, too. A little less so with Ariel, but what the hell—she wished the little birdbrain well. Come to think of it, she wished them all well.

"Here's to us—and whatever comes next," she said, raising her wineglass.

About the Author

Ruth Walker was born in Cincinnati, Ohio. After she married her childhood sweetheart, George St. Clair Walker, an Air Force careerman, they lived in fourteen states, including Hawaii, and traveled extensively in the Far East. Their only child, Sharon, was born in the Philippines.

Ruth Walker was first published in 1964. Her books to date range from mysteries and romantic suspense to contemporary novels. Now a widow, she lives in Petaluma, near her married daughter and grandson.